THE AEGIS OF MERLIN OMNIBUS

VOL. 1

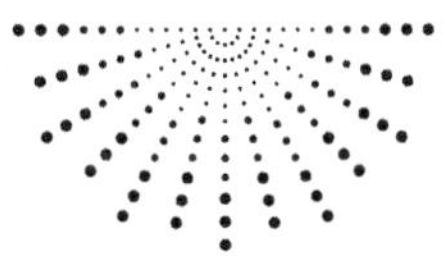

JAMES E. WISHER

SAND HILL PUBLISHING

Copyright © 2018 by James E Wisher
All rights reserved.
No part of this book may be reproduced in any form or by any electronic or mechanical means, including information storage and retrieval systems, without written permission from the author, except for the use of brief quotations in a book review.
ISBN: 978-1-945763-31-1
Edited by: Janie Linn Dullard
Cover Art by: Paganus

031520181.0

THE IMPOSSIBLE WIZARD

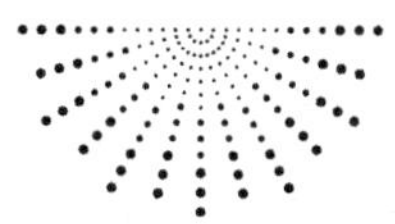

THE AEGIS OF MERLIN BOOK 1

1
TESTS

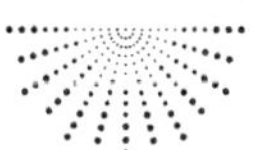

"Love you, Mom. Gotta go."

The apartment door slammed behind Conryu, cutting off his mother in mid harangue. It wasn't like he didn't know he'd gotten up late. The hall outside was empty, all the residents having gone to work hours ago. Mom had only stayed home because she had some research to do for the Science Department and could do it as well at their apartment, saving herself the commute. It was just Conryu's luck that the one morning this week he overslept she decided to work from home.

He sighed and sprinted down the drab beige hall toward the stairwell. The elevator took too long for just four floors. He found the stairwell as empty as the hall so he had no trouble rushing up to the penthouse three steps at a time. If anybody had seen him right then they'd have thought the building had caught fire.

Conryu skidded to a halt on the top landing and paused to catch his breath. Four flights of steps wasn't so many, but at three to a stride his legs were swearing at him a little. He straightened his t-shirt and gave a little sniff to make sure he hadn't overwhelmed his deodorant. All good.

Bad enough he arrived late, if he showed up at Maria's door

stinking too she'd really let him have it. Satisfied that he was as put together as he could manage, Conryu yanked the steel fire door open and stepped into the hall that led to the Kane family's penthouse apartment.

Burnished oak paneling covered the walls and soft tan carpet silenced the tread of his leather biker boots. A jade vase filled with fresh-cut roses sat on a small table and filled the air with their fragrant perfume. At the end of the hall a tall set of double doors carved with symbols and a pair of pentagrams marked the entrance to the Kanes' apartment.

Maria's mom oversaw the wards protecting the building from magical and mundane threats and the doors served as a sort of anchor. She'd tried to explain the process to him once, but it went right over his head. All Conryu knew for sure was that in exchange for her magical protections the Kanes got the best apartment in the building rent free. Pretty sweet deal.

He strode past the elevator and paused before the doors. Every time he touched one of the creepy things he feared it would burn his hand off. It hadn't happened yet and he doubted today would be the day. He rapped twice and clasped his hands behind his back.

Half a minute later the door opened and he looked down into the jade eyes of Maria's mother, Shizuku. The short, slender woman's eyes crinkled when she smiled at Conryu. She wore a red silk kimono embroidered with storks that looked like it cost more than all the clothes Conryu owned. Midnight-blue slippers peeked out from the bottom of the robe. Shizuku Kane was one of the most talented wizards in the city, but he'd always thought of her like a second mother.

"You're late, Conryu."

"Yeah. How mad is she?"

"This is your lucky day. Maria's still getting ready."

Conryu's eyebrows shot up. Maria was never late. Ever. "Really?"

"Don't look so shocked. This is a big day for her. For all the girls. It's no surprise she wants to look her best for Testing Day."

Conryu sighed. Testing Day. A big deal for the girls and a waste of time for the boys. They would all take the test of course; couldn't have anyone feeling left out. What did it matter if boys couldn't become wizards? Fair's fair after all.

The truth was, most of the girls wouldn't pass either. When they tested the seniors last year, only two out of the whole class of three hundred and sixty-seven had passed and gotten a full ride at the North American Alliance's Arcane Academy. All Conryu and the other boys would get was hours of standing in line and a sneer of disdain from the woman administering the test.

The patter of shoes on hardwood reached him a moment before the whirlwind that was Maria Kane appeared behind her mother. She rushed to the door in a swirl of black skirts, her purse over one shoulder, and paused to kiss her mother on the cheek. She grabbed his hand and dragged him towards the elevator.

"Nice seeing you, Mrs. Kane," Conryu called over his shoulder.

Maria jabbed her finger into the call button. When the door didn't open at once she stabbed it again and again.

Finally Conryu grabbed her free hand and held it. "Relax. We'll make it in plenty of time."

Maria looked up at him with her liquid brown eyes. She was only three inches taller than her mother and had the same long black hair. "Relax? How can I relax? Today will make or break my whole life. If I don't pass the test and get into the academy..."

"I know, I know. You've talked about nothing else for the past month."

The elevator bell chimed and the doors slid open. Conryu let go of her hand, stepped inside, and punched the button for the parking garage.

When the doors slid shut he continued, "Even if you don't pass—"

She made a choking sound and stared at him, aghast.

Conryu grimaced. Maybe he wasn't helping. "What I'm trying to say is with your grades you can get a full ride at any college you want to attend. You can do anything you put your mind to. I know you'll be disappointed, but it really won't be the end of the world."

She groaned and hugged him. A muffled "thanks" barely reached his ears. She stepped back and stared at him. "I'm going to pass."

He smiled and nodded. If sheer willpower affected the test, she'd have no problems. "Of course."

The elevator chimed and the doors slid open revealing the almost-empty garage. Conryu led the way to his bike. When he saw her he smiled. She had a sleek black tank and fenders, fully rebuilt flat-head motor, and the coolest skull-and-chain license plate holder.

Maria walked past him, pulling him along as she went. "Stop drooling. I swear every time you see that bike you act like it's the first time."

Conryu let her drag him across the garage. Their helmets dangled from the handlebars and he handed Maria hers before buckling his on. He settled into his seat and she swung up behind him. The soft leather creaked under him as Conryu got comfortable. He touched the starter button and the flat-head roared to life, sending a vibration through his whole body.

God, he loved that sound.

Maria swatted him on the side of his helmet, her less-than-subtle signal that it was time to go. He twisted the throttle and roared up the ramp and into the bright sunlight. The shining steel-and-glass skyline of Sentinel City spread out before them. Beyond the city, little more than a shimmer, was the Atlantic Ocean.

Conryu shot down a side street then merged with the endless traffic running along the main thoroughfare that would take them to school. It was only ten miles, but their late start would make it a near thing. Maria's grip tightened around his middle when he opened the throttle. He loved the highway; no speed limit.

About halfway to school they rode through a shadow spreading across the street. Conryu glanced up. The floating island made its patient way through the sky, as indifferent to them as the earth itself. Which reminded him.

"We're still on for the Shadow Carnival this weekend, right?" He had to shout to be sure she heard him over the roar of the bike.

"Of course, it's our last one as juveniles. Next year we'll have to pay full price."

Conryu snorted. For someone from such a rich family, Maria worried a lot about money. Full price at the carnival only cost ten bucks.

They reached the ugly, tan stone school in five minutes, giving them a whole three to spare. Conryu pulled into the first open parking space he came to, put the kickstand down, and swung his leg off. Plenty of cars in the lot, but no people. The seniors must have started lining up already.

Maria hopped down, handed him her helmet, and started fussing with her hair. Conryu shook his head and hung their helmets from the handlebars. Maria was the most beautiful girl in school and the windblown hair only added to her looks.

"Maria!" A slightly pudgy blond girl in too-tight jeans, her cleavage threatening to spill out of a low-cut blouse, ran toward them waving her hand.

Maria looked up and smiled. "Rin."

"Come on, the government wizard is here already and the girls are lining up. If we don't hurry we'll be last."

Conryu watched Maria and Rin run ahead to find places in line. So enthusiastic, you'd think your place in line had some bearing on the results. He gave his bike one last affectionate pat and ambled toward the main entrance.

They didn't have classes today. Everyone had taken their finals already. Only the seniors actually needed to show up to take the wizard's test. They'd also get their final report cards and find out if they'd qualified for their chosen college.

He ran up a short flight of steps, waved to some underclassmen he recognized from shop, and pushed the heavy glass doors open. Why anyone would come to school if they didn't have to was beyond him. At least two of the juniors were dating seniors. They'd probably tagged along to provide moral support.

The day should only last a few hours, but since a government wizard was in charge they'd probably be here until mid-afternoon. Dad liked to say the one thing you could count on was the slowness of the government. His father actually meant it as a compliment since it usually took the council years to screw something up.

He had barely stepped through the doors when a familiar voice said, "You're late, bro."

Conryu turned to find Jonny Salazar, his best friend after Maria, strolling toward him, hands thrust into the pockets of his torn jeans.

"Not my fault. Maria was late getting ready."

Jonny raised a fist and Conryu bumped it. "I call bullshit on that one."

Conryu made a little X over his heart. "Swear to god. She was still primping for the test. Like the shoes she wore would make any difference to the wizard."

"Girls. I tell you man, they're all loco."

Conryu grinned.

"But we love them anyway," the boys said in unison.

When the laughter subsided Conryu asked, "Where did she set up?"

"Nurse's office." Jonny started down the deserted hall. "We're going to be last in line."

"So what? They always take the boys last anyway and each test takes, what, two minutes? At least they're not going to give us any homework."

"Amen, bro."

The test line snaked down the hall and around the bend, ending in front of the library. Two girls sat at one of the tables pretending to read, but really checking out a couple of guys in varsity athletics jackets four ahead of Jonny.

They took a step forward as the line advanced. "You still going to waste your time going to that rinky-dink vocational school?"

"You bet. Two years and I get my mechanic's license. Mr. McShane has a place for me the day after I graduate and his shop is only two blocks from Dad's dojo. Two of the things I love most in the world, bikes and kung fu, within walking distance of each other. How could that not be perfect?"

Jonny shook his head. They'd had this argument at least ten times in the last three months, but it seemed his friend wanted to have one more go around. "I'm telling you, man, you should go to the military academy with me. You love to fight and you've got the brains for it if you just put in more than a half-assed effort."

Conryu yawned, stretched, and took another step. "Fighting in a tournament is different than fighting in the army."

"Different how?" Jonny demanded, hands on hips.

"For one thing, no one at the tournaments actually wants to kill me. Not to mention there are no guns."

"Details, man. Just imagine, after graduation we're posted to patrol a beach in Florida, protecting bikini girls from the zombies that occasionally wash up on shore. You just know how grateful they'd be." Jonny hugged himself and made kissing noises, fully immersed in his delusion.

Conryu smiled at his friend's overactive imagination. Only the sons of generals and others with connections got soft postings like that. "Picture this, Jonny. We graduate and get sent to the northern border where it drops to sixty below at night and the girls don't wear bikinis. We'd spend every day dressed in seven layers of clothes, hunting white drakes and ice wolves if we were lucky and frost giants if we weren't."

"Why do you have to shit on my dreams, dude?"

"Or how about this?" Conryu went on without mercy. "We get posted instead to the southern garrison where it's 120 in the shade and we fight insane, half-human demon worshipers who'd like nothing so much as to cut your heart out as an offering to some monster whose name you can't even pronounce. Sorry, bro. It's bikes and kung fu for me."

"Wuss." Jonny offered him a good-natured grin then turned to watch as a quartet of girls walked by, their heads hanging. Looked like they failed the test.

"Wuss, huh? How about we head over to the dojo when we're finished and spar for a few rounds?"

Jonny waved his hands. "No, man, I'll pass."

"Come on. I heard you made brown belt last month at your dojo."

"Yeah, and I heard you got a fifth band on your black belt and your dad made you assistant instructor. If I want to get my ass kicked I'd prefer it was by a stranger."

Conryu raised an eyebrow. "Wuss."

Jonny shook his head. "Cold, dude, stone cold."

An hour later they'd made it around the bend and the entrance to the nurse's office came into view. Conryu could just make out the back of Maria's head. She wasn't the last girl in line, but she was close. If she failed he just knew she'd blame him.

* * *

A bead of sweat ran down the back of Maria's neck before her already damp blouse absorbed it. Six people to go and it would be her turn. Her hands trembled and she had to pee so bad she feared she'd burst. She just had to pass.

Another girl came out of the nurse's office, head hanging,

slumped and trudging. The wizard administering the test hadn't passed a single girl and only ten of them remained standing in line. Last year had been a bad year, with only two passing. At the rate they were going, this year would end up worse yet. She took a deep breath and let it out slowly, trying to picture her stress rushing out with the air like Conryu had taught her.

Maria smiled when she thought about Conryu. He was the closest thing she had to a brother or boyfriend, depending how she felt on a particular day. Her mom and his dad had grown up in the same village in the Empire of the Rising Sun. She and Conryu had been born within a week of each other and actually came home from the hospital on the same day. It seemed like since that day they hadn't been apart for more than a week at a time. How would she manage a whole school year away from him?

Another somber girl emerged and Maria took a step forward. Five to go. Rin's hands touched the back of her blouse prompting her to turn around. Her best friend looked down at her with wide blue eyes.

"Do you think they'll fail everyone?" Rin spoke Maria's thoughts out loud.

"No, I'm going to pass." Maria spoke with a great deal more conviction than she felt.

A high-pitched squeal was followed by a brown-haired girl in a short plaid skirt and white blouse dancing out of the office. It was Kimmy Morrow. Maria didn't know the girl well, but she had the third-highest GPA in their class. If anyone else had a chance of getting picked it didn't surprise Maria that Kimmy would be chosen.

"That's one," Rin muttered.

"Kimmy, what'd you pull?" Maria asked. Most people considered it rude to ask a wizard's power level, but Maria couldn't resist.

Kimmy stopped dancing and grinned. "Nine fifty."

Maria nodded. A respectable result, almost exactly at the fiftieth percentile. "Congratulations."

"Thanks, and good luck." Kimmy continued her spinning dance down the hall, drawing the boys' gazes to the occasional glimpse of her underwear.

Maria couldn't blame her for getting excited. Kimmy had just joined an elite group. When Maria passed she'd be equally excited, but she certainly would not be dancing down the hall flashing her panties for the whole school to see.

The rest of the girls ahead of her went quickly in and out with no more passing. Then Maria's turn arrived. She took one last steadying breath then stepped into the nurse's office. A folding table had been set up in the front room beside a white cabinet marked with a red cross. A drawn curtain hid the four cots in the back section of the office. A pale woman in gray robes, her face lined with deep wrinkles, sat on the far side of the table.

In front of the government wizard rested the simple device that would determine Maria's future. It consisted of nothing more than a wooden rectangle with a gauge in the center that ran from 0 to 10,000. An extension with a vertical grip jutted out from the base toward the empty chair.

Maria tried to swallow, but found her throat too dry. She clenched her fists to stop the shaking of her hands.

The wizard looked up at her with a bland expression. "Sometime today would be good."

"Sorry." Maria dried her hands on her skirt, sat across from the wizard, and nodded.

"Grasp the handle," the wizard said.

"Right or left hand?"

The older woman groaned. "One of the women in your family is a wizard, isn't she?"

"Yes, ma'am. My mother. How did you know?"

"All the girls from families with wizards are the same. They all want to make sure they do everything perfectly, afraid if they make a single mistake they won't pass."

Maria winced at the flawless description of her emotions. Had the wizard used a spell on her?

"Let me tell you something, kid." She gestured at the device on the table between them. "All this thing does is give a rough measure of how much magical energy your body can process. That's it. Anything over a hundred means you can cast at least simple spells and you need to go to the academy to be trained. Now grab the damn thing and let's get this show on the road."

Maria found the woman's indifferent attitude exactly what she needed to alleviate her nerves. The wizard had done this thousands of times and found the process ordinary to the point of tedium. This might be the most important day of Maria's life, but to the wizard it was just another day at work. Somehow that took all the pressure off.

She grasped the handle with her right hand and stared at the gauge.

Nothing happened.

The seconds ticked by like hours as the little red needle sat frozen at zero.

Maria's heart raced.

This couldn't be happening. She squeezed until her knuckles turned white.

Move!

Damn it, move!

"Sorry, miss," the wizard began.

The needle twitched.

"Did you see it?" Maria asked, the relief palpable in her voice.

"Yeah. Let's give it a couple more seconds."

The needle twitched again then climbed. 100. 200. Steadily on past 1,000.

When it passed 1,500 Maria's head spun and it took all her

focus not to let out a hysterical laugh. That put her in the ninetieth percentile.

It continued on before finally stopping at 1,950. She'd finished fifty points higher than her mother.

"Congratulations, kid. You're going to the academy."

Maria peeled her aching hand off the grip. A red, curved impression ran the length of her palm. She rubbed the mark and smiled. "What happens now?"

"You get out of here so I can test the next girl. The Department of Magic will send you something in the mail before the end of the summer that'll explain the rest of the process. Now scoot."

Maria hopped out of the chair. She had to tell Conryu.

* * *

"I pulled nineteen fifty." Maria quivered with excitement. Conryu couldn't remember ever seeing her this worked up.

"Congratulations."

Jonny gave her a thumbs up. "Awesome."

"Thanks. I need to call Mom." She spun to go then turned back. "You guys want to go to Giovanni's for pizza after to celebrate? My treat."

The test must have damaged her brain. Maria never offered to pick up the check. "I'm in."

"Me too." Jonny never passed up a free meal, let alone free pizza.

"Great. I'll meet you by the bike." Maria walked off, digging through her purse.

When she'd gone Jonny asked, "Is nineteen fifty good?"

"If she volunteered to buy lunch it must be fantastic. Savor this pizza, Jonny. She may never offer again." They shared a laugh.

The last four girls took their turns, but none of them passed. The boys came next. Each one was in and out in about thirty seconds. An hour later Jonny came out and shrugged. "Hurry up. I'm starving."

Conryu entered the office. Instead of Nurse Abrams with her long legs and ridiculous heels he found a withered old woman in gray robes sitting behind a cheap folding table holding some contraption. Would it have killed them to send a nice-looking wizard to administer the test?

"You the last one?" she asked.

"Yeah."

"Sit down and grab the handle."

Conryu plopped into the plastic chair and grabbed the dowel. The little needle on the gauge snapped over to 10,000.

"Oh, come on." The wizard rapped the device twice with a gold ring just above the swollen knuckle of her right middle finger. The needle didn't move. "Cheap piece of junk. Let go."

Conryu did as she said, not at all certain what was going on. "Can I go?"

"No. Sit still and keep quiet."

Her tone didn't invite argument so Conryu folded his hands in his lap and watched as she muttered in a language he didn't recognize while waving her hands over the device. A minute later she stopped and touched the grip with one finger. The needle went to 300. She removed her finger and it sank back to 0.

"Grab it again."

Conryu gripped the dowel and the needle immediately snapped back to 10,000. He looked up at the wizard. Her face had twisted into a vicious snarl.

"Sorry."

She snatched the device off the table, muttering about cheap bureaucrats, faulty equipment, and how could she do her job if the junk they gave her didn't work right. Conryu wouldn't have dared speak even if he had some idea what was happening. She dragged a tan satchel out from under the table and started rummaging through it.

"Ma'am—"

"Quiet. We're going to have to do this the old-fashioned way." She pulled out an eighteen-inch length of slim, tapered black wood. A second later the tip glowed with a faint light.

"Is that a magic wand?" Conryu asked.

"Not in the way you mean. It's a first-generation tester. If it glows you can do magic and the brighter it lights up the stronger you are. Same as the first one you tried, but without the gauge so it's less precise. Hopefully it's also less apt to break. Take it."

He took the wand and it immediately burst into a blinding glow. He clamped his eyes shut.

"Drop it!"

The wand clattered to the hard tabletop and the light went out at once. The wizard stared at him with a curious little frown that made him more uncomfortable than the earlier snarl.

"What's going on?" he asked in honest confusion. "Everyone knows boys can't do magic."

"Young man, that's an excellent question. Either there's something wrong with all my equipment or we have a serious situation. Whichever it is, I can't resolve it here. You and the young ladies are going to have to come with me to the Department of Magic. They have a much more precise unit they'll run you through. Can you do me a favor and collect Miss Kane and Miss Morrow? I'll call my superiors and meet you out front. You'll see a panel van with the government seal on the side."

"Yes, ma'am." Conryu stood up and left the office in a daze.

No way could he do magic. There were no male wizards and never had been. Something must be wrong with her equipment, nothing else made sense.

Jonny jogged up to him. "Pizza time."

Conryu looked up, noticing his friend for the first time. "What?"

"Dude, you okay? You look like you seen a ghost."

"I'm fine, I think. Pizza's going to have to wait. The wizard wants to take me, Kimmy, and Maria to the Department of Magic for retesting. She thinks there's something wrong with her equipment. Want to help me find Kimmy?"

"Sure."

They walked down the all-but-empty hall. It looked like everyone had gone home already. Conryu hoped Kimmy hadn't left yet. He didn't have her cell number and it would be a bitch to have to track her down.

They continued on past the empty library and Jonny stopped. "Why would they need to test you again?"

Conryu sighed. "Because the machine reacted to me. The little needle went all the way to 10,000 when I touched it. It's got to be broken, but she says they can only straighten it out at the Department."

"That's nuts."

"Tell me about it. Why don't we have the office page Kimmy? We could wander the halls for hours and never find her."

"Good call. What about Maria?"

Conryu shook his head. "She's waiting out front, remember? Shit! What about my bike?"

Jonny laughed. "With everything that's happened, that's what you're worried about?"

* * *

"What do you mean 'retest'?" Maria asked.

"Yeah!" Kimmy added.

They stood beside a blue van with a picture of bronze scales of justice on the side. The plates on the front simply read, GOV. The wizard hadn't joined them yet and the girls were getting antsy. Not that Conryu blamed them. He wasn't exactly thrilled about things either.

It was an hour after noon on what Conryu had hoped would be a short day of school and a long afternoon of tweaking the carbs on his bike. He gazed longingly at the sleek black machine twenty spaces to their right. Maybe the wizard would let him follow along behind her. It wasn't like he planned to run away. He wanted this sorted out as much as anyone.

"I don't know what to tell you. The wizard asked me to find you and bring you here, so I did."

"But why? There had to be some reason she wanted us to take the test over again." Maria eyed him. "You're hiding something."

"What are you doing here at all?" Kimmy asked. "Testing us again makes a little sense, but why you?"

He wracked his brain, but saw no way around telling them. "The machine reacted to me. She didn't know why, but just to be safe she wanted me to be tested again at the office. The wizard seemed to think there was something wrong with her equipment."

The wizard emerged from the main entrance, her satchel slung over one shoulder. She raised her hand and the lights flashed on the van. "Everybody in."

Conryu pulled open the sliding door so Maria and Kimmy could climb up. When the wizard reached them he asked, "Can I follow on my bike? I don't want to leave it here."

"No. My boss doesn't want you out of my sight. She almost took my head off for sending you to find the girls. We've kicked a hornet's nest with this and I'm afraid things will be tricky for a little while."

Conryu shook his head, gave one last look at his bike, and climbed in. She'd be okay. He had the key and the parking lot was covered by video cameras. Besides, how long could a retest take?

"Did you speak to my dad?" Maria asked.

In all the excitement Conryu had forgotten Mr. Kane was the number three man in the Division of Magic and the city chief. They had always gotten along well. Maybe he'd be able to get Conryu out of this mess.

"Not directly." The wizard started the van and pulled out of her space. "But I'm sure word will reach him soon enough."

"I should call my mom." Conryu fished his cellphone out of his pocket.

"No calls until after the retest." The wizard pulled out onto the highway and turned toward the city center. "Just be patient. This shouldn't take any time at all."

Maria took his hand, whether to comfort him or herself he couldn't say and didn't care. He felt better at once.

"Don't worry. Dad will let your mom know what's happening. She's only one building over after all."

"Mom was working from home today, but I'm sure you're right. He'll let her know." Conryu shook his head and laughed. "And I thought the only excitement we had to look forward to was the carnival this weekend."

"Hey," Kimmy said. "What about me? My parents don't work for the government or have anyone to contact them."

"Everybody relax," the wizard said. "My boss will take care of everything and have you guys home in time for supper."

They spent the rest of the trip to the city center sitting quietly, each lost in their own thoughts. The van finally stopped in front of a stone-and-steel building with a giant iron pentagram hanging three stories up. They all piled out and gathered in front of the van.

The Department of Magic was one of four buildings all connected by enclosed walkways. To the left was the Science Department, where Conryu's mother worked. To the right was the sector seat that housed courts, the DMV, and a variety of other small bureaucracies, far more than Conryu cared to keep track of. The final building held the security force headquarters. The only difference between the four buildings from the outside was the symbol hanging from the facades.

"Come on, come on, everyone's waiting." The wizard hustled them toward a bank of doors.

Conryu did a quickstep and held the door for the ladies. When everyone had passed by he followed, letting the door close behind him. A tingle ran through him as he stepped past the wards. The magic wouldn't allow anyone to enter if they carried weapons. The spell was much more efficient than metal detectors.

The lobby consisted of an open area with polished stone floors, bland artwork on the walls, and three secretaries behind a bank of windows. Four halls branched left and right leading deeper into the building. Their guide showed no hesitation, taking the second on the left.

"Where are we going?" Kimmy asked.

The wizard glanced back, but didn't break stride. "To the primary testing machine. It's enchanted with permanent runes and tied to the building's defensive wards. There's no way it'll give a false reading."

"What does it mean if we get the same results here?" Conryu asked.

She shook her head. "That problem's above my pay grade. Soon as I deliver you, you're someone else's problem."

Conryu appreciated her honesty if not her compassion. The wizard finally stopped in front of a door labeled Testing Department. She knocked once and pushed the door open.

Four people waited inside, three standing, one pacing. The only one Conryu recognized was Mr. Kane. He had a salt-and-pepper goatee and sharp brown eyes. They had all gathered around a steel-and-ceramic cylinder. Two handles protruded from the rune-covered device below a digital readout. It looked way more impressive than the flimsy wooden thing they'd given the wizard.

"Dad!" Maria ran over and hugged her father. She barely came to his shoulder. "What's going on?"

"I'm not certain yet, sweetheart. Conryu."

Conryu went over and shook his hand. "Mr. Kane. Did you call my mom? What's going to happen?"

"Take it easy, son. Connie's on her way and she said she'd fill your father in." Mr. Kane turned his gaze on Kimmy. "I contacted your parents as well, Miss Morrow. They'll be here as soon as they can."

"Thank you, sir." Kimmy's whole body visibly relaxed.

"We may as well start the retest. Thank you for bringing the kids in, Mercia," said one of the other occupants of the room, an older woman whose bright blue eyes were surrounded by fine wrinkles. Her graying blond hair seemed to meld with her matching gray government-issue robe.

The wizard began touching a series of runes on the device, causing them to light up. When she finished she grasped both handles and the digital readout said 1,376. She nodded once, seeming satisfied.

"Excellent idea, Terra, thank you," Mr. Kane said. "Would you like to go first, Maria?"

"I'll just get out of your hair," Mercia said.

"No one's going anywhere until this matter is settled." A hard-eyed man in a red-and-gray security service uniform moved to block the door.

"It'll be okay." Mr. Kane patted Mercia on the shoulder and guided the wizard to an empty chair in the corner of the room. He turned back to Maria. "Go ahead, sweetheart."

Maria walked over and grasped the handles. A few seconds later 1,943 appeared on the readout.

Terra consulted a notebook she'd removed from her robe. "Your original result was 1,950 so this is well within the margin of error for the portable device. Miss Morrow, if you please."

Kimmy switched places with Maria and touched the machine. Her result was 953.

Terra nodded. "Good, also well within the margin of error. Mr. Koda, your turn."

Conryu took a breath, said a silent prayer for zero, and grasped the handles. Three seconds later the readout read 12,756. Stunned silence filled the room. Conryu couldn't take his eyes off the display. How could this be happening to him?

Finally Mr. Kane said, "I thought you only pulled 10,000 on the portable device?"

"The portable tester only goes to 10,000," Terra said before Conryu could gather his thoughts. The blond wizard looked at him, her eyes shining. "I'm looking forward to determining how you can exist, Mr. Koda."

Good thing someone was looking forward to it, because he sure as hell wasn't.

* * *

The Department wizards and Mr. Kane huddled up in a little conference as far from Conryu and the girls as possible given the size of the room. For five minutes they talked in low voices, totally ignoring the subject of their deliberations, that is to say, him.

Finally the last member of the gathering said, "He can't be human."

She was an attractive woman in her late thirties with pixie-cut brown hair and eyes so dark they almost looked black. The wizard dressed in the familiar gray robe of a government wizard though unlike the others hers had a small badge with a scale on it.

Conryu moved away from the machine and stared at her. "Say what?"

The door to the little room burst open, nearly flattening the man in red as Conryu's mother came running in. She rushed over, hugged him, then patted him all over looking for injuries. Just what did she think these people had done to him?

"Mom, relax, I'm fine. Where's Dad?"

"At the dojo, where else? He says he's sure you'll be okay and he'll see you at supper." She turned to Mr. Kane. "What's going on, Orin?"

"That's exactly what we're trying to figure out. It appears

Conryu has wizard potential and we're trying to determine how that can be."

Conryu's mother stared at him as if seeing him for the first time. "He's a boy. Boys can't be wizards."

The wizard that had been speaking before his mother burst into the room cleared her throat. "As I was saying, Mr. Koda must have some non-human blood in him, probably demon, probably from long ago. Like a recessive gene, it's come to the surface after many dormant generations."

"Conryu doesn't have any demon blood." They all turned to find Mrs. Kane standing in the doorway. She'd traded her kimono for a sharp black pantsuit. "If he did he wouldn't be able to live in a building protected by my wards. He's as human as you or I."

"Shizuku." The government wizard's lip curled in an ugly sneer when she spoke. Definitely some history there. "If it was thin enough I'm sure he could slip past your wards."

"No, Clair, not even a drop of demon blood could get past."

The two women stared at each other like angry cats. Conryu's head spun and he couldn't stop thinking that if anyone else showed up they'd need a bigger room.

"Clair, Shizuku, please." Mr. Kane raised his hands in a placating gesture. "The test is simple enough, assuming Conryu is willing to let us take a little blood."

Everyone stared at him. "Yeah, sure, help yourself."

"You don't have to do this, Conryu," his mother said. With her pale and drawn face she looked as worried as he felt.

"Yeah, I do. At this point, I'm a little curious to see if I'm human or not. I'm not sure what's worse, that I have demon blood or I'm a wizard. Either one makes me a freak."

Maria ran over and hugged him. "You're not a freak and we all love you no matter how the test turns out."

"Thanks," he whispered in her ear.

Terra raised a narrow strip of yellow paper and a needle. "Ready?"

Conryu gently moved Maria aside and held out his trembling right hand.

Terra poked his finger and caught a drop of blood on the paper. "If it turns black you have demon blood, white angel blood, and blue elf blood."

They all stared as the seconds ticked by. Nothing happened. After a full minute Terra flipped the paper into a trash bin. "He's human, Chief."

"That's a relief," Conryu said.

"Actually it isn't." Mr. Kane scrubbed his face with one hand.

"It isn't?" Conryu asked.

"No. If you were a human with demon blood and some powerful if limited magical powers, that would fall well within our range of experience. Unusual, but nothing to get worked up about. On the other hand an ordinary, fully human male, with the most powerful magical potential ever recorded..." Mr. Kane shook his head. "Not only is that something the entire world would say was impossible, it totally rewrites everything we thought we knew about wizardry. You, my young friend, are about to cause me a giant headache. When word of this gets out..."

"Aren't we overlooking an obvious explanation?" Clair said. "Maybe our testing device is also malfunctioning."

Mrs. Kane sighed and walked over to the machine. She grabbed the handles and 1,926 appeared on the screen. "If you check your records you'll see the power level is the same as my last test. Clair?"

Clair glared at Mrs. Kane then took her place in front of the machine. 1,754. "Mine is the same as well."

"As was mine," Terra said. "The machine is functioning properly. We simply need to accept the reality that Conryu Koda has the potential to be a wizard and that we may never know why."

The wizards and non-wizards began muttering amongst

themselves. Conryu didn't know what to think, but it seemed pretty clear his fate was being quietly decided for him.

He raised a tentative hand. "Excuse me. The thing is, I'm not interested in being a wizard. Can't we just forget this ever happened?"

"I'm sorry, Conryu." Mr. Kane laid a hand on his shoulder. "But the law is very clear. Anyone with the potential to be a wizard must be trained at the academy. The penalties for failing to do so are quite severe for you and anyone that helps you avoid going."

"Why?"

Mr. Kane sighed. "Let's take a walk, Conryu."

"Orin!" his mother said.

"Sir, I'm not sure that's a good idea," the security man added.

"Adam, Connie, calm down. I think our young friend needs some fresh air. God knows I do."

Mr. Kane guided him out of the stuffy lab and into the cool hall. Conryu gulped huge lungfuls of the fresh air. "Thanks. If I didn't get out of there soon I was going to lose it."

"I had a hunch. I'm sorry this has all fallen on you so suddenly. I know you had plans."

"I still have plans."

Mr. Kane shook his head. "Whatever they were, your plans are gone. In the fall you'll be on the train to the academy with the other young wizards. The sooner you accept that the better off you'll be."

Conryu couldn't believe what he was hearing. "I've known what I wanted to do since I was twelve and first entered Mr. McShane's bike shop. Now you're telling me I have to give up my dreams?"

"You don't have to give them up, but you do need to delay them by four years. Once you've completed your training there's nothing that says you have to work as a wizard." Mr. Kane scratched his bald head. "I've never heard of a wizard that did some other type of work since wizards can make fantastic money, the strong ones anyway. My point is you need to accept that for the next four years your plans are on hold. You've got all summer to make peace with it."

Conryu clenched his jaw and badly wanted to hit something. "What's the big deal anyway? It's not like I can even use magic as I am now. Why not just leave me like this?"

"How do you like your truth, ugly or gentle?"

"Ugly. Nothing about this day has been attractive since I touched that woman's toy back at school."

"Okay, here it is. The state regards wizards as indispensable assets. In a time of crisis the more wizards we have to call on the better our nation's chance of survival. Even one wizard, especially one as powerful as you will become, might be the difference between winning and losing a war."

"So I'm just a weapon in the government's arsenal?"

Mr. Kane shrugged. "You said you wanted it ugly."

* * *

Orin had sent the kids and their parents home and led Adam and Terra from the cramped testing lab to a more spacious conference room. Clair had remained behind to check the testing equipment one more time. He doubted she'd find anything, but better safe than sorry. The door had barely closed when Adam and Terra started going back and forth about the best way to handle the revelation about Conryu.

He felt bad for the kid. Conryu was a good boy, and he hated to yank the rug out from under him all of a sudden, but the law was clear. Not to mention if he achieved even half his potential he'd end up as the most powerful wizard in recorded history. Orin couldn't simply throw away that sort of resource.

As the argument continued Orin only listened with half an ear. He leaned on the windowsill and stared out over the city. Everything looked exactly the same as it did yesterday. Same skyline, same floating island, same everything. Nothing to indicate that the whole world had changed.

"We can't let word of this escape." Adam slammed his fist on the conference room table, drawing him back to current debate. "We'll institute a total intelligence blackout. Keep it totally quiet, send him to the academy by special flight."

"That's exactly the wrong thing to do," Terra said. "At some point the media will find out about Conryu's existence. When they do we'll be accused of a cover up which will make everything worse. We need to have a press conference and announce that a male wizard has been discovered. We don't need to provide details, but we do need to get out in front of the situation."

"Chief?" He turned to find Adam looking at him, hands on hips. "It's your decision. What are we going to do?"

"If there's one thing I've learned after fifteen years in government it's this: a cover up is always a bad idea, except for national security issues. We'll schedule a press conference for tomorrow afternoon. No questions, just a brief announcement."

"The boy will have to be there," Terra said.

Orin nodded. Conryu wouldn't be thrilled, but she was right, he had to be there. Orin seldom had to ruin someone's life and the fact that it was a young man he thought of like his own son made it even worse. He needed an antacid from the bottle in his desk.

The conference room door flew open and an old man with wild white hair wearing a tan cardigan and black pants rushed in. "Where is he? Where's the boy wizard?"

Orin groaned. Just when he thought the day couldn't get any worse. Leave it to Professor Angus McDoogle to make a liar out of him. "I sent him home, Angus. Conryu's had a long, exhausting day."

"You sent him home without introducing me? That boy is the key to proving my theory."

"Your theory is garbage, Angus," Terra said. "Conryu isn't going to change that."

"It is not garbage." The old professor's face turned bright red. "Despite what those narrow-minded fools at the Glasgow Institute might say. The Aegis of Merlin is a perfectly reasonable hypothesis."

Terra shook her head. "You think the idea that Merlin was not only real, but that his spirit is watching over and protecting humanity is a reasonable theory?"

"I do and it is. When everyone said my theory was impossible what did they claim as the primary reason? That men couldn't be wizards. Well, this boy puts the lie to that argument. If one young man has the potential to be a wizard then there's no reason another one couldn't have become a wizard fifteen hundred years ago."

"Even if I grant you that another male wizard existed and served as the basis for the Merlin legend, that in no way proves his spirit somehow lingered beyond death to watch over the world."

"Stay a skeptic if you wish." Angus tried to smooth his white hair to no effect. "Now that I've got evidence to support the first half of my theory, it's only a matter of time before I prove the rest of it."

Terra drew a breath to launch into another argument, but Orin cut in. "You two can continue this argument on your own time. What we need to focus on now is Conryu. It's up to us to make this transition as smooth and painless for him as possible. I'll send word to some reporters I know and set it up for three tomorrow. Adam, see about security for the press conference. We'll have it outside in front of headquarters so we can retreat directly back inside when we're finished."

Adam nodded and left the room to begin.

"What about me?" Terra asked.

"Try to think up some reasonable ideas for why a male wizard might have turned up after all this time. We can't just drop a fact like that on the world without offering some sort of explanation."

"I'll get Clair to help."

"Are you sure? She has certain political leanings that may make this difficult for her."

Terra stood up. "Just because Clair was a member of the Le Fay Sorority at the academy when she was young doesn't make her sympathetic now. She's a professional. I'm sure she can set any personal feelings aside and do her job."

"Fine, but keep an eye on her."

Terra took her leave and Orin found himself alone with Angus. The bright-eyed Scotsman closed the distance between them. "When can I meet him?"

"I'll introduce you tomorrow, before the press conference." Angus grinned, prompting Orin to raise a threatening finger. "But only if you promise to stay on your best behavior. I won't have you harassing that boy or turning him into the poster child for your pet theory."

"But—"

"No buts. You put so much as a toe out of line and I'll see you transferred to the most remote outpost I can find. Clear?"

"Of course." Angus spun on his heel and stalked out.

Orin watched Angus until the door closed behind him. Why did the crazy professor have to end up at his department? Orin's lips curled in a bitter smile and he rubbed his throbbing temples. Was it bad luck or the spirit of Merlin?

2

THE PRESS CONFERENCE

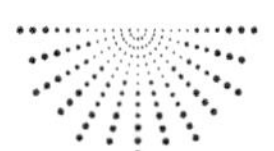

Lady Raven quietly digested the news that a male wizard had been found. She sat on the edge of her soft couch in the richly appointed apartment she used when she needed privacy. Illusion magic blocked out the last annoying shafts of sunlight, leaving her with nothing but the dim, red glow from a pair of drift lights. Though the magic blocked the light she could still look through the window at her city. The Hierarchs had assigned Sentinel City to her because they trusted her to oversee the great task.

A light floral incense burned in an infuser, filling the room with a pleasant scent. Both the light and the smell served to settle her nerves and enhance her focus. If ever Lady Raven needed to focus, it was now.

The impossible thing the Le Fay Society feared most had come to pass. To think she'd live to see a male wizard born. It was impossible, yet she'd seen the test results with her own eyes. She could scream, rail at the gods, or deny to her heart's content, but it wouldn't change the essential truth.

The boy existed, and in her city no less. That made it Lady Raven's responsibility to deal with him. Such an abomination couldn't be allowed to survive. It wasn't natural. In fact he was an insult to the natural order.

No man had the wit or grace to wield magic safely. All they were good for was brute labor and producing the next generation. If not for the latter necessity she would have wiped them all off the face of the earth without a second thought. Lady Raven pitied the poor women forced to endure their crude touch. She would happily cut her own throat before she let any man lay a hand on her bare flesh.

She stood up and paced, unable to focus despite her efforts. Plans needed to be made and Conryu Koda needed to die. Luckily Lady Raven had made allies for just such an eventuality. Not that she ever imagined needing to kill a male wizard, but the zealots would be happy to kill any wizard, including her, if they learned who she really was.

Lady Raven laughed and went to her casting chamber. The witless males would never guess the truth. She'd never even met them except on an encrypted online forum. It sickened her to think how many of the psychopaths wandered her city, but a good craftsman used the tools at her disposal.

The casting chamber held even less decoration than the almost-empty living room. No windows to offer distraction, no comfortable seats that might lessen her focus. All she had was a simple wooden desk and hard-backed chair. On the far wall a full-length mirror hung in a black, rune-scribed frame.

Lady Raven frowned at her reflection. When had she gotten so old? It seemed only months ago she'd been young and beautiful. She snorted at her useless thoughts. Who wouldn't trade youth and beauty for knowledge and power? Besides, looks were easy enough to fix.

She chanted, weaving words of water and light to shape an illusion around her wrinkled body. Her face smoothed and lifted, lips plumped, and teeth cast off their yellow stain. When the spell concluded, the youthful face of her favorite persona stared back. Once she changed into an appropriate outfit, men would stare as she walked past, drooling like the dogs they were. Though she cared nothing for their opinions, Lady Raven enjoyed the power her new look gave her over the weak-willed fools.

Ten minutes later Lady Raven stood in front of her apartment building dressed in a short skirt, torn stockings, and half-buttoned blouse. With her magically enhanced figure and revealing outfit it didn't take long to flag down a taxi to take her to this persona's so-called job.

When they arrived at the internet cafe Lady Raven paid the cabbie and climbed out. The cafe occupied an old, run-down building that drew so much electricity through its under-maintained electrical box it was a wonder the place hadn't burned down long before now. Not that she had any intention of letting anything happen to the place until she'd finished with it.

"You're late, Lacy!" a fat thug said, playing his part as her obnoxious boss to perfection.

She'd told the man when she hired him to shout at her and run her down at regular intervals and he seemed to take a certain joy in the task. Once he'd dared to lay a hand on her and that offense had earned him a lesson in pain he'd never forget. It certainly hadn't happened again.

"Sorry, boss," she said.

Lady Raven rushed down between two rows of tables, each supporting four computers. They had a good crowd tonight, only three empty stations. Most of the men—it was always men in the cafe—were staring at cavorting nude figures and touching themselves under the tables. It disgusted her, but she expected no better from them.

She slipped into the back room where the routers and servers sat in their racks and shut the door behind her. Her laptop rested, closed, on her tiny station. It whirred to life when she opened the lid. When it finished booting up she activated a program that would disguise her current location and logged in to a private chat room where her dupes liked to hang out and talk tough.

As usual, the vitriol directed at women in general and wizards in particular on the site was truly horrific. If they didn't have a part to play in her plans, Lady Raven would have been thrilled to murder them all.

It took a bit of searching, but she finally found one of her pet zealots. She struck up a conversation, playing the part of a wizard-hating true believer. After a bit of back and forth using particular phrases that established they were who they claimed Lady Raven tossed out the bait, mentioning a rumor of a male wizard.

Disbelief greeted her pronouncement. No surprise there. She insisted it was true and the idiot argued that it was impossible. They went back and forth some more before Lady Raven said there was going to be a press conference at the Department and if he wasn't a gutless coward he'd be there to kill the abomination.

She logged out and smiled a self-satisfied smile. Nothing motivated the idiots like questioning their courage. Her tool would show up tomorrow, no doubt about it.

* * *

Conryu's fist hammered into the quarter-inch rope wrapped around the wooden training dummy. Like a machine gun his palms and forearms smacked the wooden dowels that jutted from it at odd angles. His shin slammed into the fake leg with enough force to crack it. Sweat dripped off his nose and soaked his hair.

He'd come to the dojo early, both to help Dad with the morning class and to take his mind off the press conference Mr. Kane had set up for this afternoon. So far neither correcting the basic poses of the beginners or pounding out his frustrations on the dummy had done the least bit of good.

Mr. Kane had stopped by late the night before to tell them what he'd decided, just like Conryu had no say in the matter. At least they didn't expect him to speak. All they wanted him to do was stand there while the reporters snapped some pictures, like he was some new sort of animal being delivered to the zoo.

He hit the center of the dummy with a double palm strike, rattling it in its frame.

"Your form is a mess."

Conryu turned toward his father's deep voice. The master of the dojo knelt before a small shrine that held a katana and wakizashi set that family legend claimed one of Conryu's ancestors had wielded during the Elf War. He didn't know if that was true, but the swords certainly looked old enough with their scuffed black scabbards and frayed ray-skin hilts. They were the oldest weapons in a room lined with just about every type of hand weapon imaginable, from simple staves to swords.

"Just trying to work off some stress."

"Violence won't help your anger, they feed on each other. Take deep breaths, move slowly. Let your chi flow from your core to your limbs, carrying the negative emotions away."

Dad hopped to his feet and began the familiar kata. Like a man moving in water his father shifted from one pose to the next, each movement accompanied by deep breathing. Conryu joined in, falling into the rhythm of movements he'd first learned as a four-year-old.

As usual Dad was right. With each shift a little more anger left him until they stopped and Conryu felt at ease once more. They faced each other and he looked into the warm, gentle eyes of his father. Deep and brown, framed by fine wrinkles, those eyes held depths Conryu doubted he'd ever plumb.

"Better?"

"Yeah. Thanks, Dad."

They bowed to each other and his father finally smiled. "May as well enjoy your five minutes of fame, Conryu. In a week they'll have forgotten all about you."

"I hope you're right."

"Of course I'm right. With age comes wisdom."

"And humility."

"Smart ass. When are you supposed to head over?"

Conryu yawned. "Mr. Kane's supposed to pick me and Mom up at two."

"You'd better take a shower and head home. Can't have you smelling like a dojo on your big day." Dad sniffed and pulled a face. "Though it might convince the reporters to keep their distance."

"Thanks. You coming to the show?"

"Sorry, I have an afternoon class. I'm sure you'll do fine."

Conryu nodded, not at all surprised that his father didn't plan to join them. Outside the dojo Dad didn't like dealing with people. Conryu didn't know why, but Dad seldom went anywhere besides home and to the dojo.

He headed to the locker room while his father returned to meditating in front of the shrine. Conryu took a shower and swapped his sweaty black gi for jeans and a t-shirt. He checked his phone. Only twelve thirty; he had time to stop by the garage on his way home. He had to tell Mr. McShane that he wouldn't be coming to work for him as soon as he'd first hoped. It seemed only right to tell him in person rather than letting him hear it on the news tonight.

Conryu paused to dry a drop of water from his forehead with the bottom of his shirt then slipped out the side door into the alley between the dojo and the pawn shop next door. A car whizzed by as he walked to the end of the alley and turned up the street to the shop. He stopped to look in one of the pawn shop's windows. He'd found some valuable parts over the years, but alas not today. A shiny red electric guitar in the display caught his eye.

He'd never learned to play—too busy with martial arts—but

he'd always wanted to. It seemed a funny thing for someone that hated attention to be interested in, but there you go.

It only took five minutes to walk from the dojo to the garage. Conryu centered himself as he approached the familiar two-bay structure. The right-hand door stood open and a huge gut covered in bib overalls stuck out from under a lift holding a sleek, green racing bike imported from the Empire. The rapid-fire click of a ratchet mingled with the acrid stink of spilled gas. Conryu sighed. What a great place.

"Mr. McShane?"

The ratchet fell silent and the gut jiggled as the master mechanic worked himself out from under the lift. A kind, grease-smeared face gradually appeared. The handlebar mustache twitched twice followed by an explosive sneeze.

"Conryu, my boy. Come to give this old man a hand?"

"Don't I wish. Unfortunately, I have bad news."

Mr. McShane heaved himself to his feet. "Your folks are okay, aren't they?"

"They're fine, it's nothing like that. It's just I won't be able to come work for you as soon as I was hoping." Conryu quickly filled him in on the gist of the situation. Mr. McShane listened in silence, his only reaction a slight widening of his eyes. It was nice to find someone besides Dad that didn't freak out the moment they heard. "Anyway, I have to graduate from the academy before I can move on to get my mechanic's license. There's going to be an announcement today, but I wanted to tell you myself."

"I appreciate that. Don't worry. Sooner or later there'll be a place for you here whenever you want it."

"Thanks." They shook hands and a weight lifted from Conryu's chest. He really didn't have to give up on his plans. If he was patient he could still do everything he wanted to. That thought buoyed him all the way to the press conference.

* * *

Conryu tugged at the itchy collar of the stiff shirt his mother had presented him with upon his return home. She must have gone shopping since he knew for a fact he didn't have anything in his closet this uncomfortable. At least she'd let him wear jeans, a brand new, stiff pair, but he'd take what he could get at this point.

The two of them stood together in the entry hall of the Department of Magic. The secretaries were gone and the building silent. No one had even bothered to turn the lights on. All they had to see by was the diffused sunlight from the ceiling windows and what came in through the doors.

Across the road four panel trucks with satellite dishes on their roofs had gathered along with a collection of reporters and cameramen. A hasty platform had been erected just outside the main entrance. Since it was a Saturday the traffic was minimal, nonetheless eight men in security service uniforms had gathered at either end of the driveway to keep confused visitors from entering the area. It was quite a circus, and all for him. Who'd have thought?

"I wish Maria was here."

"I know." His mother patted him on the back. "Orin didn't want to confuse things by having a second student on the platform. Don't worry, in another hour we'll be back home and this will be nothing but a memory."

"Connie, Conryu, there's someone I'd like you to meet."

They turned to find Mr. Kane approaching along with an old man who looked like a mad scientist from a horror movie. He had a bright, not quite sane gleam in his eye. He stared at Conryu with an intensity that Conryu usually reserved for the latest model of motorcycle, the ones with bikini models lying across them. Sweat beaded up on Conryu's back and he forced himself to relax. If Mr. Kane knew the man he couldn't be dangerous.

Mr. Kane gestured to the stranger. "This is Professor Angus

McDoogle. He's a visiting scholar from Scotland. He has a hypothesis that you might not be the first male wizard."

The professor rushed over and grasped Conryu's hand in his clammy fingers. "An absolute pleasure to meet you, my boy. Your appearance will be a boon to my work. I hope the two of us can be friends."

Conryu reclaimed his hand and wiped it on his pant leg. "Yeah. So if I'm not the first male wizard, who was?"

"Merlin."

Conryu raised an eyebrow. "Like from the movies? King Arthur's advisor?"

"Not exactly. The Merlin you're familiar with is based on old legends which in turn are potentially based on a real person. I'm still searching for definitive evidence, but you at least prove that a male wizard is more than just a fantasy. I also believe the great wizard's spirit has lingered after his death to influence our world. I will be forever in your debt for proving part of my theory."

What a nut job.

"Um, you're welcome?"

"Okay, Professor." Mr. Kane grabbed the crazy man by the shoulders and turned back toward the interior of the building. "Why don't you head back to your office? We need to begin the press conference."

Angus shrugged off Mr. Kane's grip. "Surely you'll want to have the world's leading expert on male wizards out there with you to answer any questions the reporters might throw your way."

Leading expert? This guy thought a make-believe character was a real person. Conryu didn't know which part of Scotland the professor came from, but they ought to send him back. Preferably in a straight jacket.

"Angus, we talked about this." Mr. Kane spoke in the tone he used to use when Conryu and Maria got into something they shouldn't have. "Now get back to your office while you still have one."

The professor shuffled off, grumbling.

When he'd gone Conryu asked, "Where'd you dig him up?"

"Conryu!" His mother scowled at him.

"It's okay, Connie. Angus takes a little getting used to. He's been overexcited ever since he learned about Conryu. You essentially validate half his thesis. Try not to take it personally."

"Whatever you say. Can we get this over with? This collar's driving me nuts."

Mr. Kane laughed and guided them towards the front doors. The little group climbed up on the makeshift platform. Ten reporters and cameramen milled around in front of them. One lonely photographer snapped pictures. The blond wizard from yesterday joined them from another direction. She carried a folder tucked under her arm.

"I trust you came up with something, Terra," Mr. Kane said.

"Yes, though it's mostly nonsense and jargon. Nothing that would convince an actual scholar."

Mr. Kane smiled. "Never underestimate the power of nonsense and jargon. It's the grease that keeps the wheels of government turning."

"I thought money did that," Conryu muttered.

His mother slapped him on the shoulder, but she had a faint smile.

Mr. Kane stepped up to the podium and raised his hands. The assembled reporters fell silent. "Ladies and gentlemen, thank you for coming out today. I'll keep my remarks brief and please remember, no questions. The Department of Magic, in the course of our duties, has discovered the world's first confirmed male wizard."

Silent stares of disbelief greeted this announcement followed by a blizzard of questions. Everyone was shouting at once and Conryu couldn't make out a single word other than "impossible." Every question seemed to have that word as an essential component.

Mr. Kane raised his hands again, this time to considerably less effect. After several minutes of being completely ignored the reporters fell silent once more.

"Thank you," Mr. Kane continued. "As I was saying, we're not taking questions, but when I finish my remarks our leading researcher will have more information for you. Now, this remarkable young man beside me..."

He paused as all eyes and cameras turned to focus on Conryu who offered a feeble wave.

"This young man is Conryu Koda. Over the course of our standard annual testing the portable device indicated he possessed wizardly potential."

Mr. Kane droned on, telling the press everything that happened yesterday. Conryu's attention went to the photographer. The man had put his camera away and was staring at Conryu with an intensity that made him uncomfortable.

Conryu started to point him out to his mother, but the photographer broke eye contact and reached for his gear bag. Conryu blew out a breath. Just his imagination.

The photographer came up with a saw-backed bowie knife and charged the platform.

"For the True Face of God!" he screamed as he reached the edge of the platform.

Reporters shouted.

Cameramen rushed to adjust their target.

The lunatic with the knife leapt onto the platform.

Conryu stepped in front of his mother.

"Die, abomination!" The photographer charged, the knife raised above his head.

Conryu stepped in, grabbed his wrist as the knife descended, twisted and yanked him off balance. The man's wrist locked and he doubled over. Conryu plucked the knife from his opponent's disabled hand and tossed it over beside the podium.

Fists hardened by years of training lashed out, pummeling the attacker in the jaw and temple. Conryu hit him eight times in two seconds. When he finished, the unconscious man slumped to the stage, just as the security men arrived to claim him.

Fat lot of help they were.

Once again Conryu found himself the center of attention. Questions were shouted his way. He shot Mr. Kane a desperate look.

"Ladies and gentlemen," Mr. Kane shouted over the questions, "that concludes our press conference. We'll email you copies of our researcher's notes. Good afternoon."

Everyone retreated to the Department building. As soon as they were inside Mom rounded on Mr. Kane. "I thought you said there'd be good security? Conryu might have been killed."

"No way," Conryu said. "That guy had no idea how to properly use a knife."

"What if he'd had a gun?"

Conryu couldn't argue with that.

"I know you're upset, Connie, but please try to keep calm."

"Calm! What if it had been Maria out there? Would you be able to keep calm?"

"I take your point. However, the assailant has been subdued and we're all safe now."

"This assailant. What about the next one? I never should have let you talk me into this. You've made my son a target."

"Mom, relax. We read about these True Face of God guys in school. They want to kill all wizards. The girls are in just as much danger as I am. Besides, they aren't very good at their job. As of six months ago they'd only managed to murder three wizards, and they've been around for like twenty years."

"Am I just supposed to accept the fact that lunatics with knives are hunting you?"

Conryu cocked his head. "Is there some other option?"

* * *

Detective Lin Chang pulled into the parking lot of the Department of Magic. One of the security officers raised her hand to stop him until he flashed his badge. The woman moved aside and waved him toward a mixed group of police and security officers. They were all gathered around a beat-up, rusted-out, once tan pickup. That had to be the assailant's vehicle.

When Lin had gotten word that Conryu had been attacked by a knife-wielding maniac on national tv he'd jumped to get the case. It didn't surprise him to learn Conryu had subdued the attacker. He attended the Koda dojo and had seen the young man fight. He might be seventeen, but Lin would have put him up against just about any two men he knew and be confident of Conryu coming out the winner. Lin simply couldn't let someone get away with attacking a brother warrior, it was a matter of honor.

He clambered out of his green sedan, attempted to straighten his perpetually wrinkled suit, gave up and ambled over to the gathering. "Someone want to tell me what happened?"

One of the red-shirted security officers stepped away from the group. "The assailant drew a weapon in the middle of a Department press conference and attempted to stab the victim, Conryu Koda. He was subdued and taken into custody."

One of the cops laughed. "Subdued? The medic said that kid fractured the nut's skull. Be a wonder if he ever wakes up."

Lin turned his gaze on the cop. "And where is the assailant now?"

"Ambulance took him to Sentinel Central Hospital. Don't worry, Sarge, we told them to put the guy in a secure room and sent two of the boys along to make sure they did it."

Lin smiled when the officer used his nickname. He'd served six years in the Alliance military before being discharged with the rank of sergeant. "And the victim?"

"We took his statement and got an address, then sent him home."

Lin clapped him on the shoulder. "Good man. We get an ID on the attacker?"

The same security man handed Lin a shoulder bag. "This was all he had on him."

Lin took the bag. "Who are you again?"

"Adam Warren, head of security for the Department."

The truck had no tailgate so Lin set the bag in the bed. He dug a pair of rubber gloves out of his pocket, slipped them on, and pulled the bag open. Nothing too exciting inside. Photography accessories, film, lenses, and, hello, a business card. He took the card out and held it by the edges.

Smith's Freelance Photography. There was a picture of a black guy in his mid-thirties, a phone number, and an address. "This the attacker?" Lin asked.

Adam shook his head. "Naw, the perp was a white guy."

"Well, well, the plot thickens." Lin dialed the number on his cell, but it went straight to voicemail. He tapped his chin for a moment. "O'Shea!"

One of the officers, a twenty-five-year-old kid with hair so red it almost glowed moved closer. "Sir?"

"Go over to the hospital. I want the assailant fingerprinted as soon as he's secured."

"It's Saturday, sir."

"So it is. We'll make a detective out of you yet."

"I mean the lab's closed on the weekend, sir."

Lin ground his teeth then took several calming breaths, trying to remember what Sensei said about clarity of thought. "They don't turn the computers off, do they? Scan the prints and run them through the database. Maybe this clown has a record."

"The techs don't like us messing with their computers, sir."

"If I have to tell you to get those prints just once more you're going to be riding a desk for the rest of your exceedingly short career."

"Yes, sir." Officer O'Shea hurried away to a squad car without further debate.

Lin shook his head. What was the world coming to? Was it too much to expect a little initiative? Christ, they had an attempted murder and he was supposed to wait until Monday to start his investigation rather than annoy the techs.

"Anything else I can help you with, Detective?" Adam asked.

"Can't think of anything. What's your cell number? If I think of more questions I'll call." Lin entered the security man's number into his contact list. "Thanks."

"My pleasure. I'd appreciate it if you contacted me about any threat to the Department."

Lin nodded. "Will do."

He memorized the address on the attacker's card and returned it to the bag for the crime scene guys to process. The photographer's shop was across town and Lin needed to check on the man. If the attacker stole his gear there might be a body waiting for him. He really hoped not. He hated dealing with bodies.

* * *

Orin massaged the bridge of his nose. What a fiasco. He couldn't blame Connie for being furious with him. Who would have imagined one of those cultists showing up at the press conference?

After seeing Conryu and his mother to their car Orin had retreated to the conference room they'd used the night before to think. He stared out the window and watched the floating island drift across the city, one of six that constantly circled the globe and had for as long as anyone could remember.

He'd often wondered what let the massive things stay in the air. It obviously involved magic of some sort, but he'd read several reports by wizards that had made it their life's work to figure the islands out and after centuries of study they had no more idea how the magic worked than he did. No one could even land on the things. Some sort of impenetrable force field surrounded them.

Orin turned away from the window. He was trying to distract himself rather than face the problem in front of him. It all boiled down to this: How had the cultist learned Conryu would even be at the press conference this morning? Only a handful of people had known ahead of time and before today he had full faith in them, most of them anyway.

The door opened and Adam entered. He looked as worn out as Orin felt. Not that the security chief would find much sympathy after this afternoon.

"Well?" Orin asked.

"The cops searched his car and bag. Not much there. Turns out his press credentials were fake. The camera he had was a cheap knockoff. I turned the investigation over to the city police."

Orin nodded. "This was not our finest hour, Adam. If anything had happened to that boy..."

Adam snorted. "That boy didn't look like he needed our protection. He handled that guy better than I could have. Do you know where he trained?"

"You're kidding, right? Conryu is Sho Koda's son. As in Grandmaster Sho Koda, of Koda style kung fu."

Adam rubbed the back of his neck. "Well, that explains it. I assume you realize we have a leak."

"Yes. It shouldn't take us long to figure out who did it. There were only five people who knew Conryu would be there."

"My money's on the professor. That old man's out of his mind."

"Not a chance. Conryu represents his best hope for getting his precious theory acknowledged. Angus would cut his own throat before he let any harm come to Conryu. He's the only one I have complete faith had nothing to do with it."

"What about me?"

The door opened admitting Terra. She looked around. "Where's Clair?"

"I didn't call her in," Orin said.

Terra frowned. "You still don't trust her. What does the poor woman have to do to convince you of her loyalty?"

"Funny you should ask." Orin held up his right hand displaying the silver rune-etched ring on his middle finger. He'd grabbed it from the secure room on his way up. "I had nothing to do with the attack on Conryu Koda."

He pulled the ring off and flipped it to Adam.

"A ring of compulsion?" Terra asked in a horrified tone.

"That's right. There's no other way to be sure." Orin never took his eyes off Adam.

The security chief put the ring on. "I had nothing to do with the attack on Conryu Koda."

Orin nodded and looked at Terra. "Your turn."

"I have no obligation to put that thing on. Only suspected criminals are required to testify with one of those."

"You're right," Orin said. "You have no obligation, nor do I have any obligation to work with a wizard I don't fully trust. I can have your transfer ready on Monday."

"You wouldn't."

"Try me. I'm going to sort this out one way or another. Even if it means a whole new staff."

Terra held out her hand. "Give it to me."

Adam passed the ring over and she slipped it on. "I had nothing to do with the attack on Conryu Koda."

Orin caught the ring when she threw it at him.

"Satisfied, Chief?"

"Yes, thank you. It's not personal, Terra. I had to be sure. Angus is in his office. I'll test him and then Clair on Monday."

"What if neither of them is responsible?" Terra asked.

"Then we have an even bigger problem than I thought."

* * *

Despite the Saturday traffic Lin made it across town in under half an hour. He parked in front of a rundown, six-story brick apartment building. The fire escape didn't look like it would hold a toddler, much less a grown man. Lin would have to mention it to code enforcement on Monday.

The ground floor didn't have a storefront so Mr. Smith must work out of his home. Technically another violation, but not one that could get somebody killed and therefore none of his business.

Lin got out and walked around the rear of his car to the main entrance. A call box with fifteen names beside buzzers hung on the wall near a locked door with a steel-mesh-reinforced window. Lin ran a finger down the list until he reached Smith, Damon. Since there were no other Smiths on the list that had to be his photographer. The buzzer actually worked when Lin pressed it, but no one replied.

Frowning, Lin pressed the buzzer labeled "Superintendent."

"What?" a metallic voice asked.

"Sentinel City Police, open up."

A minute of silence passed before a skinny, shirtless white guy sauntered up to the door. "Badge?"

Lin showed him. "Let me in, please."

"Got a warrant?"

"I don't want to arrest anyone, I'm just curious if there's a body in apartment 3B. Supposed to be pretty hot this week. I can just wait until you call me if you prefer."

The super punched a button and a buzzer sounded followed by the clunk of the lock opening. "Central air's already busted. Last thing we need is a body stinking up the place. Which apartment did you say?"

"3B, Damon Smith."

"Oh, the shutterbug." The super went back to fetch his keys and Lin followed. "Jesus, he's the only guy living here that ain't into drugs or worse. You didn't hear that from me."

"Of course not, Mr?"

"Marco."

"Do you know Mr. Smith, Marco?"

"Not well." The super opened his door, reached in, and came out with a ring of carefully labeled keys. Lin caught the sour smell of spilled beer. "Gonna have to take the stairs, elevator's busted too."

"Does anything work in this building?"

Marco grinned. "Just me and a couple hos up on six. Ugly and Uglier I call 'em. Come on."

Lin followed his guide to a flight of steps so decrepit he feared his foot would crash right through them. The skinny little man didn't pay them any mind, stomping up without a care in the world. Lin tiptoed along behind him, sweating from more than the heat, a silent prayer on his lips that the body removed from the building wouldn't be his.

They reached the third floor in one piece and Marco went straight to the door marked with a tarnished bronze B. When the super reached for the door Lin stopped him. It was already two inches ajar.

Marco looked at him and started to speak. Lin held a finger to his lips, pulled his automatic, and motioned him aside. The little man obliged without complaint.

Lin nudged the door open and winced at the rusty screech. He peeked into the main room. A recliner and tv tray sat in front of a flat screen hung on the wall, with a ragged mattress off to one side. No body.

Pistol leading, Lin lunged through the door. A kitchenette was separated from the main room by a waist-high wall. No joy in there either. The only door in the place had to lead to the bathroom. If he planned to store a body that's where Lin would put it.

Two deep breaths to steady his nerves then he toed the door open. A body slumped in the tiny shower. Black male in his early thirties. Nasty head wound. Naked except for a soiled pair of boxers. His chest rose and fell, slow and steady. Not dead, thank god for small favors.

Lin holstered his pistol, took out his phone, and dialed dispatch. "I need an ambulance at 6678 Greenway. Black male, unconscious with a head wound. Send the crime scene boys over too."

He listened for a moment. "No, he's not bleeding, just unconscious."

Smith groaned.

"Look, I need to go. Just send them here as quick as you can." Lin hung up and shook his head. The weekend crew was nowhere near as efficient as the regular dispatch team.

Smith groaned again and his eyes fluttered.

"Mr. Smith? Can you hear me? I'm with the police. You're safe now."

Smith tried to stand up before slumping back down. "What happened?"

"I was hoping you could tell me. We found your gear and photography equipment at the site of an attempted murder."

"That son of a bitch hit me with something."

"Yes. You're lucky, he had a knife on him as well. He might just as well have gutted you. Did you know the man that did this?"

"Yeah, Mort Call from 2C. I passed him on my way out from time to time. When he knocked I didn't think much of it. My phone rang and when I turned to answer it, he hit me. Next thing I know I've got a cop in my bathroom."

"Better than a mortician. You say the man that attacked you lived in this building. Did you know him well?"

"No. Like I said, I passed him on my way out sometimes.

Seemed like a nice guy, friendly, polite, the kind of person you wouldn't look at twice if you saw him in the street."

Lin nodded. "Sounds like our boy. Thanks, Mr. Smith. The ambulance is on its way. Try not to move around too much in case you have more injuries."

Lin left Smith lying in his bathroom and returned to the waiting super. "You heard?"

"Yeah. I suppose you want to go poke around in 2C now."

"Not just yet. For this I will need a warrant. Excuse me while I make a call."

Fortunately, Lin knew the judge on duty this weekend so it wouldn't be a problem getting him to sign a warrant and email it to Lin's phone. Fifteen minutes later a *bing* announced the email's arrival. Lin pulled it up on the little screen, glanced through it, and turned to the super. "Now I want to look through 2C. Here's my warrant."

Marco didn't even glance at it, he just headed back to the stairwell. Another death-defying trip down the rickety steps and they stood in front of a locked door. "You want me to unlock it or would you prefer to kick it in?"

"If I wanted to kick it in do you think I'd have brought you along? You're certainly not here because of your charm."

"Alright, alright, no need to be a dick about it. Just a second." The super flipped through his key ring, finally settling on the correct one. He opened the door and motioned Lin through with a theatrical flourish. "Have at it. I'm heading back to my office. Unless you want to pester any of the other tenants?"

"If I do, I know where to find you."

The super marched off muttering about cops and not in a good way. Lin put the man out of his mind, drew his pistol, and slipped into the room. He didn't expect trouble seeing as how the resident of the unit was in the hospital shackled to a bed, assuming the guys did their jobs right. Still, better safe than sorry.

Unlike Smith's efficiency, Mort's apartment had a proper

bedroom. It didn't take a detective to deduce there wasn't a woman in Mr. Call's life. Takeout food containers littered the small kitchen; it seemed he had a taste for tacos. The apartment's sole bookcase was filled from top to bottom with porn: dvds, magazines, comics, you name it. If there was a naked woman on the cover Mort had a sample. Not exactly what you'd expect from a religious zealot. Maybe the True Face of God cult had a lower bar for membership than the official church.

On a cheap desk in the bedroom Lin found an equally cheap laptop. He opened the monitor and the hard drive spun to life. The screensaver appeared and, fingers crossed, Lin tapped the spacebar. The home screen appeared, no password required. It appeared Mr. Call wasn't terribly security conscious. Good for Lin, bad for Mort.

After an hour of browsing through an obscenely large porn collection, Lin finally found something interesting. Last night Mort had visited a website chatroom where he discussed wizards and what an affront to God they represented. He found nothing overt about the attack, but Mort and his mystery partner did discuss the press conference and how wrong it was for the networks to give so much coverage to such blasphemy. It ended with Mort promising to give them something more important to cover.

As far as Lin could tell Mort had acted on his own with just a little prodding from the other party. The tech guys would trace the forum, but most of the chatrooms where the nuts, kooks, and other weirdoes hung out were set up to be anonymous. At the very least it didn't appear to be an ongoing conspiracy. He'd have to go over and speak to the Kodas in the morning.

3

SHADOW CARNIVAL

Lady Raven switched off the tv and considered blasting it to pieces. No, that wouldn't do any good. Besides, the company that owned her apartment building didn't know she was a wizard and she wanted to keep it that way. She hopped off the couch, tossed the remote behind her, and started pacing.

They'd actually broken into regular programing to show the news conference live. That demonstrated just how big a deal Conryu Koda's existence was. She'd realized it as soon as the main testing unit at the Department confirmed his results. Lady Raven would see to it that his death became every bit as big a deal.

Not that her zealot had helped much. What had the world come to when you couldn't trust a grown fanatic to kill a teenager? On the other hand, considering how easily this particular teenager handled a man with a knife, maybe she hadn't chosen the best method to eliminate him. Lucky for her she had plenty of other options.

She went to the back wall of her casting chamber and muttered a spell. The wall shimmered and she reached through it to remove a sealed coffer. The moment it was clear the wall solidified. Lady Raven ran her finger over the smooth ebony and whispered another spell.

The lid popped open, revealing the flat black gem inside. It looked like a black diamond the size of her thumb knuckle, but in reality it was a magical construct that, under the appropriate circumstances, would open a gate to the netherworld. For someone as skilled in dark magic as Lady Raven it was a simple matter to alter the requirements of the spell.

Simple, but not quick. When she'd finished prepping the spell night had fallen. That actually worked to her advantage. What she needed done was best completed after sunset and by others. The zealots would have nothing to do with her new plan, but her personal enforcers could handle it easily enough.

Lady Raven closed the box and slipped it into the folds of her black robe. The Skulls lived on the far side of town, well away from anything and anyone that might potentially lead back to her.

She left the casting chamber and crossed the living room to the sliding glass door that led to her balcony. The apartment was on the thirtieth floor so the odds of anyone even noticing her were minimal, but she cast an invisibility spell before she stepped outside just to be safe. The breeze whipped her robe around her.

Perfect. The wind spirits were active tonight. That would make the flying spell easier to cast. A minute later Lady Raven was flying across the brightly lit city like her namesake bird. Instead of flying straight to the Skull's hideout she swung out wide toward the floating island.

Even without a spell to perceive magical auras, the power radiating off the mass of earth and stone overwhelmed her. The islands had fascinated wizards forever, but no one, not even the founder of the Le Fay Society herself, the great Morgana, had ever penetrated the wards protecting the islands from trespassers. What secrets did the islands hold? Lady Raven doubted anyone would ever know.

Enough wasting time. She had work to do. At her mental

command the wind carried her west over the city towards the dull, ragged edge where the dregs went to kill each other or fry their brains with the drug of the month.

She landed in front of a particularly dismal example of local housing, a rotting, almost ready to collapse two-story shack. Lady Raven sent the wind away before an errant gust flattened the place and killed her thugs before she'd finished with them.

The invisibility spell faded away as she walked up the cracked, weed-filled path to the front door. She rapped on it and waited. A few seconds later a belligerent, leather-clad man opened the door. The grip of a pistol jutted out from his belt and a red bandana covered his face. Whether to disguise his appearance or to ward off the smell of urine and worse that wafted out of the open door Lady Raven couldn't guess.

"Good evening, Bloody. Where's your master?"

"Mistress Raven. Iron Skull's in the kitchen with the guys. Numb shot a bunch of rats and we're frying them up. There's plenty if you want some."

Lady Raven swallowed the gorge that rose in the back of her throat. "I have already dined. Take me to him. I have a job."

"Yes, Mistress."

Bloody led her through the filth and past bare studs to what served as their kitchen. A barrel with a fire burning in it covered with a grate served as the stove. A cast iron pot filled with oil snapped and bubbled. She didn't move close enough to see the contents.

Iron Skull leapt to his feet when he spotted her, prompting the others to follow suit or make their leader look bad. His black mohawk stood straight up and stiff today. It looked like he'd used some sort of automotive grease on it. His broad-shouldered chest strained his leather jacket to its limits.

"Mistress Raven. What brings you here?"

"I have a task. A simple one, but it will require a bit of finesse."

Iron Skull scratched his head and belched. "Finesse ain't my bag. Bone, you're up."

Where Iron Skull was broad and thick, Bone Skull was thin, almost skeletal, thus his gang name, with slicked back black hair and only a single tattoo. Lady Raven and the slender biker shared a look of mutual distaste. Bone didn't like her and worse, didn't trust her. She had Iron Skull wrapped around her finger, but Bone was far too intelligent for her liking. Lady Raven preferred her tools dull.

She removed the box from her hidden pocket. Sometimes you just dealt with a less than ideal situation.

"That the same as the other ones you had us hide?" Iron Skull asked.

"Similar. I need this hidden on the grounds of the Shadow Carnival tonight."

"Where?" Bone eyed the black box, his lip curled in distaste.

"It doesn't matter as long as it's out of the way." She held out the box to him.

Bone nodded toward the only other small man in the room. "Give it to Numb. The two of us will get the job done."

He definitely didn't trust her. Lady Raven smiled. He also feared her, though he'd never admit such a thing.

She gave the box to a scowling Numb Skull. The moment it settled in his hands she spoke a spell. "There, now you're the only one that can open it. Your instructions are simple. Find a hidden place, kill someone, doesn't matter who, and drag their body into it. Inside the box you'll find a black gem. Touch the gem to the body and the magic will activate. Leave the box next to the body and go. Nothing to it."

Numb looked from her to Iron Skull. "What about dinner? I shot the rats. Don't seem like I ought to miss out on eating them."

"We'll save you some leftovers. You two get a move on."

Bone grabbed Numb by the shoulder and dragged him toward the door. "Come on."

Lady Raven nodded to Iron Skull and followed the other two out. Assuming her tools did their job the boy would die tomorrow.

* * *

Bone and Numb left their bikes two blocks from the park where the carnival had set up. Despite the clear night the thin crescent moon offered little in the way of light. It was perfect for sneaking around, especially since the island blocked most of the moonlight above the carnival. The shops that lined the street had closed for the night so they had no trouble finding a spot to pull in. The roar of their choppers would alert the carnies if they drove the whole way and the bitch queen said she wanted the job done quiet.

Bone didn't especially give a shit what she wanted, but if they fucked up Iron Skull would have a fit that might end with one or both of them dead. The leader of their club wasn't known for his even temper and gentle disposition. Not exactly shocking for someone in their line of work, but no less dangerous for all that.

They dismounted and Numb headed for the park.

"Hold up," Bone said.

"What? I want to get this done and get back before the guys eat all the leftovers."

"Will you forget about the fuckin' rats? That shithole we're livin' in is full of them. You can shoot some more tomorrow. Now open that box."

Numb pulled the black box out of the satchel of tools he'd brought. "Why do you want to open it now? She said we're supposed to leave it with the body."

"Fuck her. Open it."

Numb shrugged and pulled the lid open. Inside was a matte black gem that didn't reflect the meager light. "What now?"

"Take the gem and put the box in my saddlebag."

"That's not what she said to do, Bone."

Bone grabbed Numb by the front of his jacket and yanked him close so their noses almost touched. Bone might have been skinny, but he was stronger than he looked. "She ain't here. Now do what I tell you. And make sure you wrap it in my spare bandana. Last thing I need is to get a curse off the fuckin' thing."

Numb's eyes went wide, as if the idea of a curse never crossed his mind. Since he was an idiot it probably hadn't. Numb did as Bone told him and when he finished asked, "What now?"

"Now we do the bitch's job and split."

They walked down the sidewalk toward the park, side by side, just like they owned the street. Nothing made people suspicious like a person sneaking around.

When they reached the edge of the parking lot Numb stopped. "What are you going to do with the box, Bone?"

"Nothing, right now. But sooner or later that witch is going to fuck us over and when she does I want some leverage. If I threaten to show the cops her box it might make her think twice."

"Iron Skull's not going to like that."

He certainly wasn't. That's why Bone didn't plan on telling him. "The boss has a soft spot for her. I'm trying to save him from himself. Now shut up and focus."

They swung out wide around the parking lot then moved in closer to the fence surrounding the carnival. In the dim light they couldn't make out much beyond the closest stalls. They circled around until they reached a spot behind a large tent.

Numb sniffed and sighed. "Too bad we couldn't come back during the day. I smell hotdogs."

Bone shook his head. Fuckin' moron. "Gimme the cutters."

Numb pulled a pair of short-handled bolt cutters from the satchel and in less than a minute Bone had an opening big enough for them to slip through.

The carnival grounds were quiet; no one was out and about at this time of night. That should make it easy to find a place to hide the stone, but would they find someone to kill?

The bikers darted from tent to display to shed. They'd have to risk going out into the main part of the carnival if they wanted to find someone. Bone inched along the side of a food trailer.

"Hey, Bone, look at that." Numb pointed at what looked like an artificial mini-mountain.

"Will you shut up?" Bone looked closer. There was a faint light coming from the mountain. If someone was there they could kill two birds with one stone.

He grabbed Numb's sleeve and tugged him along across the open space separating the trailer from the mountain. They stopped beside a dart game. There was an opening in the front of the mountain, that's where the light was coming from.

Numb started to move closer, but Bone stopped him. If there was a light someone had to be inside. The hunters had to stay patient.

Soon enough a shadow moved in the feeble light and a moment later a pudgy woman in a polka dot dress emerged from the cave. She had a clipboard and no visible weapon.

She would do nicely.

"Go get her," Bone said.

"Thanks, Bone." Numb drew his knife and jogged toward the woman.

She never knew what hit her. Numb came up behind her, clamped a hand across her mouth and swung around, driving his blade into her chest. She twitched a couple times and went still. He might be an idiot, but Numb was a fine killer.

Bone took a quick look around to make sure no one had noticed the ambush. It looked clear. He ran over to Numb. "Let's move her out of sight. There must be a place in there we can hide her body."

Numb grabbed her under the armpits and Bone got her ankles.

They lugged her back toward the cave. Too bad they couldn't have found someone skinnier. The bitch weighed a ton.

Once they moved inside, out of sight, Bone dropped her legs and sighed. "No sense lugging her around until we have somewhere to take her. Let's check this dump out."

They walked deeper into the mountain, following a set of narrow train tracks. The mountain was a ride. Pretty elaborate for a piddling operation like this.

"Hey, Bone, a light."

A thin glowing line in the wall beside the tracks drew the two bikers closer. Bone worked his fingers into the gap and yanked. A door opened revealing a small room filled with machinery.

"For maintenance, you think?" Numb asked.

"Probably. This should do nicely. We'll dump her body here and seal it back up."

They retraced their steps, grabbed the corpse, and hauled it to the maintenance room. Bone dropped his end in a clear area at the rear of the room.

"Fuck!"

"What?" Numb stared at him, a worried frown on his face.

"We left her clipboard outside. If anyone notices that they might come looking. I'll grab it. You fire up the magic."

Numb's eyes went wide. "You want me to do it?"

"She gave you the gem. Hurry up. I want to get out of here."

Bone left Numb to his task and retreated toward where Numb knifed the woman. He'd never admit it, but magic made Bone nervous. He supposed it made everyone nervous, but it really gave him the shakes.

After a minute of searching he found the dead woman's clipboard. He bent to pick it up and froze. Voices were coming from the opposite way. In the night with his black jacket and jeans Bone should have been all but invisible.

The voices faded and Bone risked looking up. He caught a glimpse of movement heading into the mountain.

"Fuck." Bone switched the clipboard to his left hand and pulled his dagger with the other. It was a wicked, eighteen-inch, double-bladed beast, with a deep blood groove running down the center. The beast would take care of any problems he ran into.

* * *

Numb wanted to argue when Bone left him alone with the dead woman, which didn't bother him, and the magic stone, which did, but he'd gone before Numb could work up the nerve. He knew he shouldn't be such a coward, especially in this job. On the other hand a little fear had kept him alive more than once when the other guys got in a killing mood. Those days when the wrong word or even a funny look might get you gutted.

Fuck it. Best to just do the job and go before someone showed up. He fumbled around in his bag and finally came up with the black stone. It chilled his hand to the marrow. Was there somewhere in particular he should put it? Mistress Raven hadn't said.

He shivered when he thought of the wizard. If ever there was a person to fear it was her. Numb didn't know how Bone found the guts to risk going against her. He'd do just what she said, when she said it. Way safer than plotting against the terrifying woman.

"Hey!"

Numb fumbled the stone and it bounced into the corner of the room. He spun and found two men that looked like twins with matching brown hair and eyes. They wore grease-covered overalls with tools jutting out of the pockets.

"You ain't supposed to be here," the left-hand man said.

"Is that Gerty?" the other brother asked. "What'd you do to her?"

Numb groped for the hilt of his knife and finally dragged it free of the sheath on his belt. Bone would be back soon. He could hold off a pair of mechanics for a minute or two.

The brothers pulled out their heaviest tools, a monkey wrench and a long screwdriver. Not the most wicked weapons, but either one of them could do you in if it hit you in the head.

"We'll bash you good for what you done," the guy with the wrench said.

He lunged at Numb who dodged the clumsy blow and opened a long slash in the mechanic's forearm, not deep, but bloody.

Numb grinned. These chumps didn't know how to fight. They were just stupid carnies who walked into the wrong place at the wrong time. He could take them. No problem.

"Jobe!"

The brother with the screwdriver leapt at Numb with no thought for defense. Numb's knife drove deep into the man's chest, but his weight bore the biker to the floor.

Numb struggled to throw the body off.

"You bastard! You killed my brother."

The second guy fell on him. The heavy wrench crashed into Numb's head and set the room spinning. A second blow turned out the lights for a moment.

When his vision returned Bone was standing behind the wrench guy, his big dagger poking out the front of the carnie's chest. Bone tossed the body aside and knelt beside Numb. He reached down and Numb flinched when he touched the side of his head.

"Don't look good, Numb."

Numb tried to say he'd be okay, but only garbled nonsense came out. That, combined with the way Bone was looking at him said he wouldn't be okay. That look said he was about to die.

Bone cleaned his dagger on the dead mechanic's overalls and returned to Numb. He held the ugly blade and shook his head. "You can't ride, brother."

Numb tried to argue, but more nonsense emerged. His thoughts were so jumbled he couldn't even form an argument in his own mind.

Bone reached for him with the dagger. The razor edge touched his throat and the lights went out again.

* * *

Bone grimaced as he watched the last of Numb's blood spill out across the floor. It was a shame when you had to kill a brother, but he couldn't ride, and that mushy spot on the side of his skull wasn't something they could just sew up. Maybe a hospital could have done something for him, but Bone doubted it. Numb's brain was as pulped as his skull.

The black gem sat on the floor in the corner of the mechanical room. Bone had no intention of touching it. A quick search of the bodies turned up a pair of pliers in one of the brothers' pockets. It opened just wide enough for Bone to pick up the gem and drop it on the woman's chest.

It seemed to melt into her, a black stain that covered her from breasts to hips. Dark sparks shot out and formed lines and squiggly figures. Bone had seen enough.

"So long, brother."

He left the bodies where they lay and fled the room, pausing only long enough to push the door to the hidden room shut. A catch clicked, securing the door so that not even a glimmer of light leaked out. That should satisfy the bitch.

Bone paused at the mouth of the cave. No one was waiting and nothing moved in the unlit carnival. At least the fight hadn't drawn any attention.

He ran back the way they'd come, following the outer fence until he reached the opening. Once he was clear of the carnival grounds Bone slowed to a walk and took his time getting back to the bike. He'd have to call Iron Skull and tell him what happened. He needed one of the guys to come pick up Numb's bike.

Bone had been preparing for this moment for months. He knew exactly where he'd hide the box. Maybe he was wrong and the wizard wouldn't betray them. He hoped so, but if she did he'd make damn sure the witch suffered the consequences.

When he finally reached his bike Bone sat down and pulled out his phone. Now the tricky part: breaking the news to Iron Skull in such a way that their unpredictable leader didn't blow up.

"Boss," he said when Iron Skull answered. "Job's done. Yeah, there was a problem. Numb bought it."

Bone held the phone away from his ear while Iron Skull shouted. When his leader fell silent Bone said, "It was just bad luck. A couple carnies showed up while I was out cleaning the kill sight. Numb killed one of them, but the other bashed his head in before he could free his knife. Yeah, I gutted him. The magic stone did its thing. Can you send a couple of the guys over to ride Numb's bike to the dump site?"

Bone gave Iron Skull the address and hung up. It would take at least twenty minutes for the others to arrive, plenty of time to set things up.

Half an hour later when Bloody and Tough showed up he had everything transferred over to Numb's saddlebags. Numb getting himself killed made his plan much simpler to put into motion. Bone had no idea how he would have explained his missing bike to the guys, but having to hide Numb's made a perfect excuse.

Tough climbed down from behind Bloody who roared off back to the house without a word.

"So what happened?" Tough asked.

Bone gave him the condensed version, leaving out the bit about cutting Numb's throat himself. "We'll drop his bike at the storage site down by the docks."

Tough nodded, not offering so much as a word of argument. Unless fighting and killing were involved Tough generally didn't have many opinions. That's what made him so valuable, especially at times like this.

The two bikers roared off to the east. A small part of Bone

almost wished the wizard would betray them just so she'd see what it felt like to have someone beat her.

* * *

Mom stood in front of the apartment door with her arms crossed. "You can't go."

"Why not?" Conryu had thrown on his comfortable, frayed jeans, shapeless t-shirt, and boots with the intention of heading out to the Shadow Carnival. A few hours without having to think about wizards and politics was way up on his to-do list.

Ten had just come and gone. It was the last day of the carnival and he needed to go if he didn't want to miss it. He was supposed to grab Maria and then they were going to meet up with Jonny and Rin.

"Why not? You were almost murdered yesterday!"

"Come on. I can't stay in the apartment for the rest of my life. There'll be hundreds of people there. No one would be dumb enough to try something with that many people around."

"Did that man yesterday strike you as the rational sort? Sho, say something."

Dad was sitting in his robe at the kitchen table reading the paper. Conryu's face covered half the front page. He gave it a shake and looked back over his shoulder toward them. "Connie, he has a point. Conryu can't hide in here forever. If he wants to go, let him go."

Conryu grinned, but his mother didn't budge.

When the doorbell rang she jumped a foot off the floor. "Who could that be?"

"It's probably Maria, wondering where I am."

Mom looked out the peephole. "I don't know him."

"Let me see." Conryu stepped up to the hole and looked out. "It's Detective Chang."

Conryu opened the door. Lin Chang stood in the hall wearing

his usual rumpled blue suit and scuffed shoes. Thick, black eyebrows went up when he saw Conryu.

"What brings you here, Sarge?"

"Business. Can I come in?"

Conryu stepped aside so the detective could come in out of the hall. He spotted Dad in the kitchen and bowed. "Sensei, Mrs. Kane. I've been assigned to investigate the man that attacked Conryu yesterday. I can't share many details, but I wanted you to know, from our preliminary efforts, he appears to have acted alone, egged on by others in his online community. We see no ongoing threat to your son. Conryu just had the misfortune to draw the attention of a disturbed individual."

"See, Mom? No ongoing threat."

She sighed. "Fine, you can go. But for heaven's sake be careful. And bring me back a bag of caramel corn."

"Will do." Never one to question his good fortune, Conryu reached for the door before she changed her mind.

He took the elevator upstairs and found Maria waiting out in the hall for him. She had on a cute black dress with a scoop neck, silver necklace and bracelets, and white sneakers. Conryu gave her a wolf whistle. "You're going to cause a wreck on the highway."

She swatted him on the shoulder. "What took so long?"

"Mom didn't want to let me go."

Maria winced and they stepped back into the elevator. He hit the button for the garage.

"I guess I can't blame her. I saw what happened on the news last night. It was kind of funny. It looked like the cameras terrified you, but the guy with the knife was no big deal."

"I know how to deal with a guy with a knife, I've trained for it. Cameras and reporters?" He shook his head. "Way out of my comfort zone."

The elevator chimed and the doors slid open. Unlike last time, today the garage was almost full. They wove their way through the cars toward his bike.

"Conryu! Conryu Koda!" A slim, nice-looking brunette in a pale blue suit with a cameraman behind her was running his way. He didn't recognize her or which station she worked for, nor did he care. They were all of a piece to him.

He shouldn't have been surprised, especially since Mr. Kane had warned him the press would come calling, but he was. He had hoped maybe they'd take Sunday off, like normal people.

"Shit!"

"Did Dad tell you what to say to them?"

"He said, nothing."

"He didn't offer you any advice?"

"No, his advice was to say nothing. Which was excellent as that's what I planned to do anyway."

They ignored the shouting woman and hurried on to his parking spot. By the time they got their helmets on and mounted the bike the reporter was five feet away and right in their path.

"Kat Gabel, Channel 7 news. Just a few questions." She showed no sign of moving. "How does it feel to be the first male wizard?"

Conryu touched the ignition and twisted the throttle. Without a helmet the roar from the big engine reached an almost deafening volume in the enclosed garage. The woman frowned and covered her ears. When the engine had died back down to an idle she took a breath to try again.

She was determined, he had to give her that. He twisted the throttle again, farther this time. The volume forced the reporter back a step. Conryu cupped his hand beside his head and shrugged.

The reporter shook her head and moved aside, motioning her cameraman to join her. Conryu tapped the side of his helmet with his index finger and roared up the ramp, grinning beneath his helmet.

It was a ten-minute ride to the carnival grounds. The company that ran it set up in one of the city parks not far from the government offices. You could see the Ferris wheel from a mile away. They parked in a field just outside the shadow and headed toward the grounds. A temporary fence surrounded the carnival with a single opening, a slanted shack sitting beside the gate. He hoped the carnival company didn't pay whoever built it too much.

They stepped into the shadow and entered another world. The bright morning sun changed to twilight. Conryu glanced up, but the bottom of the floating island lay in shadow so deep he couldn't make out any details.

Sunday was always the darker of the two carnival days since the island hung directly over the grounds from dawn to dusk. The Ferris wheel looked like it almost brushed the bottom of the island, but that had to be a trick of the light. The island flew over skyscrapers, certainly a Ferris wheel would be in no danger of hitting it.

"Does it look lower than usual this year?" Maria asked.

"I thought it was my imagination. It can't be though, can it? I mean the island flew over dozens of buildings to get here. It must be a trick of the shadows."

Maria cast a worried look up at the island and shook her head. "You must be right. Where are we meeting Jonny and Rin?"

"By the snack stands, where else? By the way, you still owe us a pizza."

Maria stopped and dug through her purse. She finally came up holding a thick silver ring covered in runes. "Mom would have killed me if I forgot to give this to you."

Conryu accepted the band and looked it over. It was simple enough, smooth and cool to his touch. "Thanks, but what's it for?"

"It's magic. Mom enchanted it herself. The ring creates a barrier around whoever wears it powerful enough to stop anything short of a point-blank shot with a large caliber bullet. It's useless against knives or clubs, something about velocity and deflection. I didn't really follow her whole explanation."

If Maria couldn't follow the explanation Conryu didn't even want to try. He slipped the ring on and it seemed to shrink a little for a better fit. At least it wasn't gaudy. And if it worked as well as Maria said, it would be worth wearing. "I'll be sure to thank your mom, but don't think you're getting out of buying lunch."

"I just gave you a potentially life-saving magical artifact."

"Yeah, thanks again. I like pepperoni and sausage on my pizza."

"You're horrible."

They resumed walking through the twilight toward the carnival gate. It was definitely darker than last year and it would only get worse the closer they came to the center. Conryu fished a ten out of his wallet and when they reached the little shack handed it to a woman in a clown suit. She stamped their hands with little smiley faces and they went onto the grounds.

"Thanks." Maria got a nostalgic smile when she looked at the stamp.

"Sure. Does your bling do anything?"

"My necklace does the same thing as the ring I gave you and I just thought the bracelets looked pretty."

They walked down a path lined with rip-off games featuring cheap stuffed animals and plastic jewelry. Six people sat in a row, trying to hit a clown's nose with water guns so they could pop a balloon. Conryu grinned when they passed a ring toss game that used glass milk bottles for targets.

"Remember the year you made me spend thirty bucks trying to win you a stuffed cow at the ring toss?"

"Sixth grade. I was in my 'barnyard animals are cute' phase. I thought you were going to strangle that carnie when he tried to talk you into taking the giraffe instead of the cow."

"I could have bought you an actual calf for what I spent on that game. I wasn't going anywhere with a stupid giraffe."

"You were really sweet." They linked arms and continued on.

A little past the bumper cars Conryu caught a whiff of frying food. Not far now.

"Five bucks says Jonny has funnel cake in one hand and a giant soda in the other."

"Double or nothing Rin's trying to steal some."

"You're on."

* * *

Conryu spotted Jonny trying in vain to keep Rin from tearing a chunk out of his funnel cake. The pair of them were standing beside a picnic table ten feet from the concession stands. They both had on jeans, though Jonny's were torn and Rin's a size too small.

Rin reached for another piece and Jonny tried to stop her without spilling a half-gallon soda. Conryu glanced at Maria and they both started laughing.

When he caught his breath Conryu said, "Do we know our friends or what?"

Maria managed to nod between giggles.

"Hey!" Jonny waved them over and in the process moved his snack out of Rin's reach.

They all sat around the table. Conryu snatched a chunk of funnel cake and ate it before Jonny could complain. "What's wrong, Jonny, didn't they have full gallon cups?"

"Give me a break, I'm splurging. Saw you on the news last night. You really laid that dude out."

Conryu shrugged. "He almost kept me from coming today. Mom was pretty freaked out. Detective Chang stopped by this morning, he pulled the case. Looks like I'm in the clear for now."

"So what's the plan?" Maria asked. "The usual? Too much food, ride the rides, waste some money on games, head home and sleep it off?"

"Works for me." Jonny took a huge bite of cake and almost choked.

"They have a new ride this year," Rin said. "It's called the

Haunted Cavern. Sort of a mixture of haunted house and roller coaster. Looks like fun."

"It must be popular," Jonny said when he'd caught his breath. "Damn thing takes up a quarter of the grounds. Bet it took a week to set up and they did it right in the center of the park."

"That's not far from here," Maria said. "Let's check it out."

"I thought it was going to be food then rides," Jonny said.

"You're always hungry." Conryu grinned. "A pound of funnel cake ought to hold you for one ride. It probably only takes five minutes."

"You always take Maria's side."

"That's because I'm always right." Maria flipped her hair over her shoulder.

"She's got you there, Jonny," Rin said.

"Okay, okay, I know when I'm beat." Jonny inhaled his food and stood up. "Let's do this."

The four of them walked toward the center of the carnival, Jonny and Rin in the front, Conryu and Maria bringing up the rear. The darkness increased with every step.

Conryu shivered. He knew he wasn't imagining it, the grounds had never gotten this dark before.

Maria grabbed his hand and held it in a death grip. "Do you feel it? Something's wrong."

"You mean the chill? I think it's just because so much sun is being blocked."

"It's not a physical chill. It feels like someone walked over my grave."

"What does that mean?" Conryu's gaze darted around, trying to spot whatever was making Maria nervous. In the shadow he couldn't see more than fifteen feet in any direction. The only real light came from the flashing bulbs above a concession stand selling hotdogs and all they did was make the shadows dance.

They'd slowed to a crawl, letting Jonny and Rin pull well ahead.

Jonny glanced back. "What's the matter, you two chickening out?"

"Come on, Maria. This ride looks really cool." Rin waved at them to hurry up.

Maria huddled against Conryu's chest, her whole body trembling. "We need to go, now."

"Alright." Conryu motioned Jonny and Rin to go on ahead. "Maria's not feeling well. I think I'd better take her home."

Rin rushed back. "What's wrong? You haven't eaten anything yet so it can't be the food."

A deep snarl filled the air and red spots of light appeared behind Jonny and Rin.

"It's too late," Maria murmured.

The shadows swirled around the crimson lights, getting darker and more solid by the second. Half a minute later two hounds as black as a moonless night stood in the middle of the carnival grounds, their eyes glowing like molten lava.

"Cool special effects," Jonny said.

"They aren't special effects." Maria tugged Conryu back the way they'd come. "Those are shadow hounds. Run!"

Conryu and Maria ran back toward the gate, Rin and Jonny right on their tails. They dodged annoyed visitors when they could and shoved them aside when they couldn't.

Shouts turned to screams when the shadow hounds let out a roar that was half bark and half snarl.

"They've fully entered our plane of existence," Maria said.

"Plain English for those of us whose mother isn't a wizard," Conryu said between gasps.

He glanced over his shoulder. The hounds were pounding after them, ignoring all the other patrons. Rin had fallen three paces behind Jonny.

The hounds were only ten feet from her.

"Can I hurt them?" Conryu asked.

"No. They have no substance. They kill by draining the life from you. Only magic can destroy them."

The hounds leapt over Rin and kept on coming.

Just as he feared. They were after him.

"Jonny, break right, circle around, and help Rin. Get her out of here."

"What about those things?"

"They want me. I'll draw them off. Help Rin and get out of here."

"No way, bro. I'm not letting you face those things on your own."

"I'm not going to face them, I'm going to run like hell for my bike. Now go."

Jonny scowled, nodded and broke off. The hounds ignored him the same way they did Rin. If Conryu had had any doubts about his theory, that settled it. He turned to Maria.

"Don't even say it." She glared at him.

He grinned despite the danger. That was exactly the reaction he'd expected. "I was going to say, is there any way we can stop them?"

"Not without magic."

Conryu snagged a ketchup bottle off the counter of a food stand, spun, and flung it at the hound behind them. It passed through the monster without slowing it.

Wait, weren't there two hounds?

He turned back just as the second hound emerged from the shadow of a dart game and leapt at them.

Conryu tugged Maria aside. The hound missed them by inches. The chill of its passing froze Conryu to the bone.

He staggered as suddenly cold muscles started to cramp. "How much further?"

"I can see the fence. We're almost there. What are those people doing?"

Conryu looked up. Hundreds of people were milling around in front of the fence.

"Shit!" Maria said.

"What?" Maria never swore. Whatever she saw must be bad.

"There's a barrier. No way we can escape that way."

They couldn't lead the hounds to all those people. It would be a slaughter.

"What do we do?"

"I don't know." Maria sounded on the verge of tears.

Conryu knew. He just hoped Maria didn't hate him, assuming he somehow survived.

He worked his hand free of her grip and lunged left between a pair of stalls. If he could draw the hounds away she'd have a chance of escaping.

"Conryu!" Maria screamed after him.

He ignored her pained shout. Conryu needed an open space, somewhere they couldn't sneak up on him He had to keep the things busy long enough for everyone to escape.

Straight ahead was the petting zoo. The panicked animals had smashed the fence and fled, leaving a round opening. He doubted he'd find anything better.

A chill on his back was the only warning he got. Conryu leapt to the right, rolled, and sprang back to his feet.

The two shadow hounds stood facing him, wisps of darkness rising off them like steam, jagged black fangs filling their mouths.

They circled right and Conryu went left, trying to keep the monsters in front of him. He wished he knew more about them. Unlike Maria, this was all new to him.

The hounds rushed him.

One leapt high for his throat and the other lunged low for his legs. Conryu jumped and twisted, going over one and under the other. Passing so close between them left him shaking with cold.

All at once it grew brighter. The hounds whined and some of the warmth returned to Conryu's shaking body.

The whines turned to snarls as the hounds gathered themselves to leap again.

Lances of white light shot out, piercing their sides and driving the monsters to the ground. More beams, these orange as flames, came from another direction, engulfing the hounds and burning them to nothing.

"Conryu!" Mrs. Kane waved at him, her hands still crackling with white light.

Conryu slumped to his knees. It was over, for now anyway. He'd survived, though he doubted his mother would ever let him out of the apartment again.

* * *

Maria hit him with a flying tackle, wrapping her arms around his neck and crying at the same time. "You scared me to death! I ought to slug you for ditching me like that. What were you thinking?"

"Let him breathe, dear." Mrs. Kane placed her hand on his back and warmth and energy flowed into him.

Conryu had never been healed by a wizard before, but if it felt like this he wouldn't mind doing it again. Maria shifted, settling onto his lap. "Thanks, Mrs. Kane. If you hadn't gotten here when you did I'm not sure I could have dodged those things again."

"It's a wonder you dodged them once," another voice said.

Conryu moved Maria a bit to the side so he could see who was speaking. It was the blond wizard from the Department, Terra. She must have shot the fire blast.

"Thanks for the help. Where'd those things come from?"

"That's what we're here to determine," Terra said.

"We?" Maria looked at her mother.

Mrs. Kane nodded. "Your father asked me to lend a hand. Since it's a weekend I didn't have any client meetings so I agreed.

We would have been here sooner, but we didn't expect the barrier."

Maria frowned. "How did you know we needed your help in the first place?"

"Conryu's ring. It does more than provide protection. I can also monitor his surroundings through it. I sensed the dark energy the moment you entered the grounds. We rushed here as fast as we could."

"Shizuku," Terra said.

The tone in her voice grabbed Conryu's attention. He craned his neck and looked around Maria's head. Three bodies were shambling toward them in bloodstained clothes. Their eyes were nothing but black pits and faint, echoing moans filled the air around them. He and Maria scrambled to their feet.

"First shadow hounds and now zombies." Mrs. Kane raised her hands and chanted a spell. A stream of fire shot out toward the undead. The fire struck a barrier of darkness and sputtered to nothing.

The zombies kept coming.

The Department wizard cast a fire spell of her own, stronger than the one Maria's mother used judging by the amount of heat coming off it. After just a second a sheen of sweat covered Conryu's chest.

Despite the extra heat the zombies kept coming. The Department wizard jogged over to them and the group backed away, putting more space between them and the undead.

"Magic's not going to do it, Terra," Mrs. Kane said. "Their darkness aura's too strong."

"We could bury them with earth magic," Terra said.

"They'd just dig themselves out. We need to force our magic through their barrier."

"Force it through how?" Maria asked.

"Direct physical contact." Terra ground her teeth as the zombies continued to advance.

"I can do it," Conryu said.

"That's crazy." Maria grabbed his arm. "You'll get yourself killed."

"She's right." Mrs. Kane shook her head. "I can't let you take that kind of a risk."

"What risk? Those things are so slow I could run circles around them. They're getting closer and we're running out of time."

"He's got a point, Shizuku," Terra said. "One spell per fist ought to do it."

"There are three of them," Maria said.

"Put one on my right foot." Conryu clenched his fists and held them out.

The two wizards exchanged looks, raised their hands, and began to cast.

"Mom, no!"

Mrs. Kane ignored Maria and kept chanting. It felt like his hands were in an open oven, hot, but not painful. Terra finished first and began again, this time pointing her hands at his right foot.

When both wizards had finished their spells Terra said, "Make solid contact to the head or chest. The spell will detonate with a one-second delay so in and out fast. Got it?"

"No sweat."

Conryu rushed the leftmost zombie. It had on greasy overalls and tools dangled half in and half out of its pockets. It moaned louder and shambled toward Conryu.

He darted in, punched it right between the eyes, and leapt back. The zombie exploded into flames. The others ignored their burning comrade and shuffled toward him.

Conryu leapt between them, punching one in the head and kicking the second in the chest as he flew by. They both burst into flames.

He rolled to his feet and spun, ready for another round. He

needn't have bothered. The first zombie was nothing but ash and the others weren't far behind.

Maria ran over and hugged him. Jonny and Rin had caught up at some point and they joined the group.

"We need some marshmallows," Jonny said.

"Or chestnuts," Rin added.

"Chestnuts roasting on an open zombie." Conryu grinned. "Got a nice ring to it."

"Are you all crazy?" Maria looked up at him. "You could have been killed. Twice."

"But I wasn't. So what now?"

"Now you kids go home and let us handle the rest," Terra said. Sirens wailed in the distance. "The cavalry will arrive soon. If there are any more zombies the police can shoot them for us."

* * *

Conryu worked himself free of Maria after a minute or two. It wasn't that he didn't like having her wrapped around him, but it made it hard to breathe when she squeezed him so tight. Out near the fence the police had set up a cordon and were getting the people out in a semi-orderly fashion. There really didn't seem to be much for them to do at the moment.

"We need to find the source of that spell," Terra said.

Mrs. Kane turned to him and Maria. "I trust you two can make your way back to the apartment on your own? I've strengthened the wards so you'll have nothing to fear there."

"Sure, Mom, no problem," Maria said.

"We have a great deal to discuss," Mrs. Kane said. "Perhaps we should all have dinner together tonight. I'm sure your parents would appreciate an explanation, Conryu."

"I expect they would, and they aren't the only ones."

Mrs. Kane nodded. "Our apartment then, as long as Sho and Connie don't mind."

"I'll tell them. Thanks again." Conryu led Maria off toward the parking lot with Jonny and Rin tagging along behind. "Think we can get out of here before the press arrives?"

"I don't think so." Maria pointed at a pair of satellite dishes rising in the distance.

"Damn them all! Am I going to have to dodge those vultures for the rest of my life?"

"Nope. No press allowed at the academy. Only teachers and students."

Conryu grinned. "Finally something to look forward to. How did you know what those things were? Your mom teach you?"

"About the shadow hounds, yes. A lot of what I know comes from The Basics of Wizardry. All the girls have to take it junior year. It's a national requirement. Thanks to you, I bet the boys have to take it starting next year."

"They're not going to let you come back to the carnival next year, dude," Jonny said.

Conryu barked a humorless laugh. "I ought to sue. I've heard about the danger of carnival rides, but this is ridiculous."

When the little group reached the exit a mob of reporters had gathered behind a line of yellow tape. A dozen cops attempted to keep them under control. Detective Chang was talking with the woman in the clown outfit and jotting down notes. He noticed Conryu, ended his interview, and headed their way.

"You okay, Conryu?"

"Sure. No ongoing threat, huh?"

Detective Chang looked away then back. "What I should have said was, no ongoing threat from the True Face of God cult. This was clearly something else."

"How can you be sure?" Conryu asked.

"Because they used magic," Maria answered for the detective. "The cultists hate all magic and would never have anything to do with it."

"What she said. I'm still investigating the guy from yesterday. Since you were attacked again I got the call in case it was related."

"Is it related?" Conryu asked.

"Way too soon to say, but if I was you I'd lie low. You guys want an escort home?"

Conryu shook his head. Regular cops wouldn't be much use against magical attacks. "I'll take an escort through the reporters."

"No problem." Detective Chang whistled to draw his men's attention. "Let's make these kids a path."

Six officers made a circle around Conryu and his friends then proceeded to push their way through the gathered throng. All manner of questions were shouted, most of which he didn't know the answer to and wouldn't have answered if he did.

When they reached the edge of the throng the officers made a gap for Conryu and the others then shifted to block the reporters from following.

"Later, bro." Jonny broke off to head for his bike, a piece of crap import that Conryu had helped him fix up.

"I'll be going too." Rin hugged Maria and trotted off to her little car.

"Just you and me," Conryu said.

Maria took his hand and the pair continued on to where he'd parked his bike. They arrived to find Kat Gabel dressed pretty as you please in black slacks and a crisp white blouse leaning on his handlebars. Conryu frowned, both because she was there in the first place and had the nerve to touch his bike without permission.

"You can't take a hint, can you?" Conryu asked.

Kat shrugged. "I wouldn't be much good at my job if I took no for an answer. What happened in there?"

"How should I know?" He grabbed Maria's helmet and handed it to her. When he reached for his the reporter snatched it first and held it above her head. "Are you kidding me?"

She danced away. "Answer my questions and I'll give it back."

A deep spring of anger welled up in Conryu. After everything that had happened over the last three days he didn't have the patience to deal with this. It was a game to her, nothing but another story. She didn't care what happened to him, she just wanted a scoop.

He darted forward, leapt, and kicked the helmet out of her hands and straight up into the air. When he landed Conryu immediately gathered himself and jumped again, snatching the helmet out of the air. He turned a flip and landed behind her.

The reporter stared at him, mouth hanging partway open.

"Here's all I have to say. If you'd pass it along to your colleagues I'd appreciate it. No. Fucking. Comment."

He jammed the helmet over his head and climbed on in front of Maria. They thundered out of the parking lot, leaving the still-staring reporter in a cloud of dust.

4

INVESTIGATION

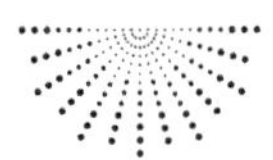

Shizuku watched Maria and Conryu make their way toward the exit of the carnival grounds. It was an absolute miracle the shadow hounds hadn't killed anyone, especially Conryu. Even if the beasts hadn't intended it, a single brush with fang or claw could have seriously injured or even killed someone in the crowd.

And then zombies. Who ever heard of zombies with a dark aura that negated powerful fire magic? If Conryu hadn't been able to deliver the magic physically they might have been in trouble. He certainly had his father's skill when it came to fighting. It would be interesting to see what he could accomplish in the realm of magic.

She brushed loose grass off her knees while Terra watched with an impatient frown. Terra hadn't been thrilled about getting called in on a Sunday, but with a blatant attack on a public venue Orin hadn't had any choice. The police only had one wizard on their staff, a not especially powerful wind mage. This sort of investigation was definitely a job for the Department.

Shizuku didn't mind lending a hand considering it was her

family—and she certainly considered Conryu a member of her family—being targeted. That she had to work with Terra and not Clair was a relief. Clair had been in her grade at the academy and they'd never gotten along.

Shizuku chanted in the divine tongue, "Reveal the hidden darkness." The spell should reveal the source of the hounds as well as the dark aura that surrounded the zombies. She repeated the words over and over, gently directing the white mist that served as the spell's visible manifestation around the area. Soon an inky, insubstantial line appeared.

A wave of her hand sent the mist rushing along in the same direction as the line, following it to its source. Terra fell in behind her as they traced the spell through the grounds. All the visitors had left so they had no trouble making their way to the center of the park.

A gray, stone construct filled an area several hundred yards in diameter. It resembled a small mountain, with a shadowed cave entrance straight ahead. The line went right inside, getting thicker as they drew closer to the source. Beside her Terra muttered a spell of her own, this one in the language of earth. A little quaver ran through the ground in response to the magic.

"It was raised by mundane means," Terra said. "The exterior only looks like stone, it's actually some sort of light-weight composite."

Shizuku nodded. It was hardly likely that the carnival kept a wizard capable of raising such a structure on their payroll.

Terra conjured a ball of flame in her right hand, pushing back the gloom. "Let's head in."

"Whoa, hold on there." A skinny man with a pockmarked face, bald head, and filthy clothes came running toward them waving his hands. "You can't take open flames into the Haunted Cavern."

"Who are you and why can't we?" Terra asked in her official voice, the one that made people who didn't work for the government cringe.

"For one thing, most of the props inside are flammable, not to mention the hydraulic fluid that runs them and the cart. You go in there carrying that ball of fire and whoosh, I'm out three hundred grand and one star attraction and you'll be needing to regrow your hair."

"Is that what happened to you?" Terra asked.

He rubbed his bald pate. "Naw, mine just fell out. There are some flashlights inside you ladies can use. Would that work for you?"

Terra spoke a single, harsh syllable and the flame in her hand vanished. "It will, especially since you'll be joining us to hold one of them."

"I will?"

"Yes, you will. You seem a knowledgeable fellow and we may have questions. Just who are you anyway?"

"Beg your pardon, miss. Wilbur Cullen at your service. I own this carnival. It's been in the Cullen family for over a hundred years. We crisscross the country every year following the island an—"

"That's fascinating, Mr. Cullen, but we really need to move this investigation along so if you'd direct us to those flashlights, that would be great." Terra motioned him toward the ride.

Shizuku watched the interaction with silent amusement. She couldn't speak without ruining her detection spell, but Terra said enough for both of them. Terra herded Wilbur toward the ride like a collie chasing a sheep. Shizuku trusted Terra to keep a look out for any threats while she focused on the line that led ever deeper into the artificial caverns.

Ten feet inside the entrance a track started. Three cars that bore a vague resemblance to mine carts waited for passengers that wouldn't be arriving that day. Wilbur went to a utility cabinet hanging to one side of the tracks and removed a pair of long flashlights. Terra accepted one and clicked it on.

The flashlight's beam did little to dispel the cavern's gloom.

The still-functioning darkness spell must be suppressing the light. Shizuku didn't know why the spell was still active since it had already summoned the shadow hounds and animated the zombies, but it was clearly doing something.

"Which way?" Terra asked.

Shizuku motioned straight ahead. They followed the tracks deeper into the cavern. Plastic demons hung limp from the hydraulic pistons that made them jump out to scare the passengers. The ride looked quite realistic. Whoever had designed the artificial stone had done a good job. No wonder this was a popular ride.

"This is our last carnival until the island returns next year," Wilbur said. "Do you think we'll be able to open back up?"

"I wouldn't count on it," Terra said. "This is the site of an active investigation. Besides, after what happened this morning I doubt you'd find many people willing to return."

"Suppose you're right. We had a good Saturday at least. Everyone wanted to go through the Haunted Cavern. Food sales were good too. We should at least break even on this stop."

"I'm thrilled for you," Terra said. "Please stop talking now."

"Sorry. I talk when I'm nervous."

The black line turned off the main tracks a little ways ahead, where there was a shadowed recess in the wall. Shizuku stopped, grabbed Terra's robe, and pointed at the spot where it disappeared.

"Through there?" Terra turned to Wilbur. "What's in there?"

"It's a maintenance access so we can service the machinery and disassemble the ride."

Both flashlights swung in, illuminating the interior of the maintenance space. In the largest open area a corpse wearing a polka dot dress floated above a spell circle inscribed with dark energy that sparked with red light.

Shizuku released her spell. "Now I see why the spell is still operating. The corpse is maintaining a necromantic loop."

"Aw, Gerty." Wilbur moaned softly.

"Do you know her?" Terra asked with surprising gentleness.

"Gerty's our bookkeeper. I hadn't seen her all day today. Thought she was sick. Her stomach never has worked just right."

"Did she have family?" Shizuku asked.

"We were all her family, but no kids or husband if that's what you mean. She was devoted to the carnival. Gerty worked here since she was fourteen." Wilbur sniffed and wiped his eyes.

"Perhaps you'd like to wait outside?" Terra said. "It won't take us long to deal with this. I'm afraid the police will want to examine your friend's body."

"I understand. And I think I will take you up on your offer and wait outside. Be gentle. Gerty was a good girl." Wilbur fled the maintenance room.

When Wilbur had made himself scarce the two wizards shared a look. "This isn't going to be easy," Shizuku said. "The dark magic has latched on to the body. Whoever set this trap did a poor job of it."

"It's an ugly casting, no doubt, but it did what the wizard wanted it to so you can't call it a complete failure. Whoever is responsible probably didn't care what happened after the hounds were summoned and the zombies raised."

"Maybe not." Shizuku pursed her lips. "But if we don't break the spell and dissipate the necromantic energy properly the body will explode and release a lethal miasma over a square mile at least. It could kill thousands."

"Well, we'll just have to do the job right. How do you want to handle it?" Terra asked.

"I'm weakest in dark magic so you should disable the spell circle. I'll craft a siphon of wind and light to disperse the gathered energy well above the city. Worst case we end up with a few dead birds and acid rain."

"Given the alternative, I can live with that. How long do you need to construct the siphon?"

"Fifteen minutes."

"Let's begin."

Shizuku tried to block out the guttural demonic language Terra used to unravel the spell circle. While she got excellent grades at the academy, Shizuku had never managed even the most basic of dark spells. She simply couldn't get the magic to work for her. It was like her body rejected the Infernal power out of hand.

She began her casting by crafting a framework of light magic running from just above the circle, down the tunnel and out into the sky. That was the easy part. Next she switched to wind magic and conjured what amounted to a contained tornado inside the framework. Finally she bound the two spells together to make a stronger, cohesive whole. Not the most complex spell she'd ever created, but challenging enough given the circumstances.

A chill ran through her and she turned her attention to Terra. The circle had partly broken and wisps of dark energy oozed out of the body's eyes and mouth. The crimson flecks were promptly sucked up into Shizuku's funnel. Everything seemed to be working the way it should. So why was she so worried?

* * *

"Oh, shit!" After twenty minutes of listening to Terra chant in Infernal the human words jarred Shizuku.

It took only a second to figure out what prompted them. Dark energy swirled around the body in red waves, pressing into it instead of getting sucked up into her funnel. It didn't look like an explosion was imminent, but something had clearly gone wrong.

"What happened?"

"I used a conjecture where I should have used a constant. The spell's broken and spiraling out of control."

"Out of control how?" Shizuku asked.

"Best case it will exhaust itself, destroying the body in the process."

"And the worst case?"

"It'll continue to build, eventually exploding and taking the entire park with it."

"Shit."

"Yeah."

Shizuku ran a hand through her hair. "How do we stop it?"

"There's no stopping it now. All we can do is contain it, or try to anyway."

"Okay, I can do a light barrier if you handle earth. Then I'll adjust my funnel to draw anything that escapes up and away from the city."

They hadn't even begun to cast when the body moved. It turned its head toward them, eyes burning with Infernal light. The glow from the circle vanished as all the power rushed into the corpse. The body fell to the ground where it began to rise. A dark aura surrounded it, similar, but different from the zombies. She didn't think this aura would stop their spells, but that begged the question of what it did do.

The creature's teeth and nails lengthened. Green ichor dripped from them, sizzling where it struck the floor. It snarled at them and took a step.

Shizuku chanted, "Divine chains hold all things in place, Heaven's Binding!"

Chains of white light appeared around the reanimated body. It fought, struggling to break free. Dark energy sent cracks running all through the binding.

That answered one question. It was an aura of decay. If it got close to them the magic would rot flesh as easily as the magical bindings.

A chain shattered. At this rate it would escape in moments. She spoke a reinforcing spell, but that wouldn't last long either. The aura of darkness broke down her magic as quickly as she strengthened it.

Pain throbbed at her temples as Shizuku struggled to maintain the binding and the funnel. They needed to end this before the monster escaped. Unlike the shadow hounds, this one wouldn't simply hunt down Conryu, it would kill anyone it encountered. It had gone completely out of control and feral.

"Terra, burn it."

"What about the dark energy?"

"My funnel's still in place." Shizuku grimaced against a fresh spasm of pain. "But I can't hold this thing for long."

Terra chanted in the language of fire, thrust her hands out, and sent a river of flame roaring into the undead monster. Another quick incantation contained the flame so it didn't spread to any of the flammables in the maintenance room.

The magical flames ate away at the undead's protective aura even as the aura rotted Shizuku's binding. The combined magics were wearing it down, but too slowly.

Another chain broke and still the undead fought even as the flames consumed it little by little. Not much remained of Gerty's body, just a charred skeleton, but it struggled with all its might to escape Shizuku's spell.

A third chain shattered, leaving only two. The backlash sent a sharp pain stabbing into her eye.

The light magic binding wouldn't hold. Though she wasn't as strong in earth magic, Shizuku chanted, "Fists of stone, bind and hold, Stone Grasp!" Stone blocks thrust up from the ground and bound the undead's feet in place.

Shizuku's stomach churned and she nearly vomited.

Just a little longer.

Mustering every scrap of her rapidly diminishing strength Shizuku chanted an augmenting fire spell and Terra's flames turned from orange to blue. Thirty seconds later the undead skeleton collapsed and the ashes swirled up the funnel and out of the artificial mountain.

Shizuku released all her spells and fell to her knees, utterly spent, head throbbing with the mother of all migraines. Terra rushed over beside her. "You hurt?"

"Tired. Maintaining four spells is about my limit. I think we underestimated our opponent. That spell wasn't running out of control, it just appeared to be. Whoever set it up used the residual energy to create that undead creature, forcing us to destroy the body before we could examine it."

"If you're right, and I'm inclined to think you are, then we're dealing with an extremely talented wizard." Terra grasped Shizuku's hand and pulled her to her feet.

"Worse," Shizuku said. "A necromancer. Only someone specialized in creating undead could have managed a casting that powerful and subtle."

Shizuku really didn't want to cast another spell right then, but she had to know for sure. "Reveal."

The simple detection spell showed all the dark energy had dissipated. She sighed and relaxed a fraction. They were safe for the moment.

* * *

Lin's stomach finally settled when Conryu's bike roared out of the parking lot. He knew it wasn't the young man's fault that horrible things kept happening in his vicinity, but that didn't change the fact that everyone would be much safer with Conryu elsewhere. As a bonus, most of the reporters appeared to have lost interest now that the main attraction had gone home.

He walked back to the shack where he'd left the welcome clown. She sat on a folding chair, her white face paint smeared from crying. Since the woman hadn't even seen whatever had caused the panic Lin assumed the loss of today's gate had brought on the tears.

Lin flipped open his notebook. "So you were saying everything seemed normal today. You didn't see anyone odd in the area, a strange woman maybe?"

She sniffed. "Why would you assume it was a woman?"

"Because whoever did this had to be a wizard. Think hard."

The clown shook her head. "Sorry, I just don't remember anything out of the ordinary."

Lin nodded. He wasn't going to get anything useful out of her. He dug a card with his number as well as the station's on it. "If you should think of anything, please contact us right away."

She accepted the card and Lin turned to leave. His eyes went wide. A black cloud rose from the center of the carnival. That couldn't be natural.

He tucked his notepad away and ran towards the source. He couldn't do much about magic, but he needed to make sure no civilians remained in the area.

The only person anywhere near the artificial mountain was a bald, middle-aged man sitting on a picnic table rubbing his hands together and staring at the tunnel's opening. He didn't seem aware of Lin's approach.

"Sir." The bald guy finally looked his way. "You should move away. It's not safe."

He laughed, but it sounded more bitter than amused. "You're telling me. My bookkeeper's body is in there floating over some glowing circle and now there's literally a dark cloud hanging over my business. I'm not sure what else could go wrong."

"Are you the owner of this carnival?"

He nodded. "Wilbur Cullen. And you are?"

Lin showed Wilbur his badge. "Do you mind if I ask you some questions, preferably a safe distance from here?"

"Ask away, sonny, but I'm not going anywhere until those wizards come out and tell me what in the world is going on with my carnival."

Lin shook his head in despair. "Did you see anything unusual today?"

"No, everything was the same as every other day. Line formed early, figured we'd have a good take. Shows what thinking gets you. It'll be a miracle if the city lets us come back next year."

"If it's any consolation, Mr. Cullen, since no one was hurt and the incident wasn't your fault I'm confident the city council will let you return next year. That's what I'll say if anyone asks."

Wilbur seemed to see him for the first time. "Thank you for that. I hope you find whoever did this, but there's nothing I can tell you."

"Who's in charge of maintaining the ride? Perhaps they saw something out of the ordinary."

"That'd be the Carrigton boys. Not much brains, but damn good mechanics."

"Where can I find them?"

"Hell if I know. Those things showed up and everybody scattered all over creation. When the ladies finish up I'll run you back to the boys' trailer. If they aren't there I don't know what to tell you."

Lin tried to think of another way to come at this, but nothing occurred to him. Maybe the wizards would have something useful to tell him.

A rumble and roar came from the ride followed by a dull red glow that filled the mouth of the cave. It looked like the mouth of Hell.

"That's a damn good trick," Wilbur muttered. "We could probably duplicate that effect with tinted lights, make the ride look even more ominous."

Apparently Wilbur wasn't so shook up he couldn't still think about business. The glow vanished and the cloud overhead dissipated. Lin let out a breath. It looked like the threat had ended.

As if to prove it the wizards emerged from the ride. The shorter one, a woman of Imperial descent wearing a black suit, looked like every step pained her. Wilbur marched over and Lin joined him.

"Where's Gerty?"

The taller one in gray, a Department wizard for sure, shook her head. "There was a secondary spell that destroyed the body so we couldn't examine it. I'm sorry, but there's nothing left but ash."

Wilbur wandered away staring at the sky and shaking his head.

"And who might you be?" the tall wizard asked.

Lin flashed his badge. "I'm investigating the attempted murder of Conryu Koda. Since he was involved in this incident as well I got the call. Do you think they're related, miss?"

"Just Terra, please. Since the Department assigned me to head the investigation of the magical aspect of the assault, I figure we'll be seeing more of each other."

"You read my mind. Perhaps we can share information and work the case together."

Terra nodded. "Good idea."

The other wizard groaned. "I'm heading home. I need a nap before I talk to Conryu's parents."

"Okay, Shizuku. Will you bring the chief up to date?"

Shizuku nodded and trudged off.

"Will she be okay?" Lin asked.

"Shizuku's stronger than she looks. A few hours' sleep and a good meal will set her back to form. She channeled a lot of power dealing with the undead inside."

"Undead?" Lin tried to wrap his mind around that announcement and failed. He'd studied a variety of magical threats in the police academy, but the instructors always said to let the Department wizard handle them. This case was looking more and more beyond his capabilities.

"Yeah." Terra headed over to a pair of picnic tables. "Let's sit and talk. I think we have a good deal to discuss."

* * *

Conryu swung his bike into the parking garage and down to his space. He'd been tense the whole ride home and now his back and shoulders were killing him. At least nothing had tried to kill them on the road. He almost laughed. What was the world coming to when making a fifteen-minute drive without something trying to kill you seemed like a major victory?

Apparently even crazy wizards and lunatic cultists had their limits. Thank goodness for that. To top it off he'd forgotten to pick up his mother's caramel corn.

He and Maria swung down off the bike and hung their helmets on the handlebars. Maria grinned. "I thought that reporter was going to have a heart attack when you kicked the helmet out of her hands."

"I probably shouldn't have done that, but I couldn't help it. I was so sick of those people and their questions. My life is none of their damn business. Do you suppose she took the hint?"

"For a day or two maybe." Maria took his hand and they walked to the elevator. "You should go straight home. Your parents are probably worried sick."

"I don't know." Conryu hit the button for his floor. "Mom doesn't usually watch the news on Sunday and since my phone isn't ringing I bet she doesn't even know what happened."

The door slid shut and they started up. When they'd gone three floors Maria hit the emergency stop.

"Wha—"

She kissed him, a long, deep kiss that left him struggling to breathe. Her hand slipped up under his shirt and ran over his chest.

He grabbed her wrists and gently pushed her away. "What are you doing?"

"What do you think?" She pressed closer.

Conryu took a step back, but he hit the elevator wall. There was nowhere to run and part of him didn't want to. Another part, the rational part, didn't want to screw things up with the best friend he'd ever had.

"I thought we talked about this last year. We said it was better to stay just friends. That anything more would be too awkward."

"We did." She lunged at him, forcing Conryu to spin around her and slip to the other side of the elevator.

There wasn't much room to maneuver in a six-by-six box. She turned to face him once more, a hungry gleam in her eyes. "We were almost killed today. It was clarifying. I don't want to die without being with you at least once. This is a no-strings-attached thing. If you want to pretend nothing happened after it's fine with me."

When Maria came at him again he didn't dodge. Conryu caught her in a tight embrace. "It's not okay with me. I love you. Whether as a best friend or girlfriend or both I'm not sure. But I know this: a quickie in an elevator is not how we're going to end one phase and begin another. And we're not going to let the stress of the moment ruin a lifelong relationship."

Maria was shaking in his arms and a moment later tears soaked his shirt. He held her for a while, not saying anything.

She looked up at him and he smiled. "You okay?"

"I was so scared those shadow hounds were going to kill you. Then the zombies. Then when you were safe I felt so relieved I was afraid I might pass out. I guess the emotions got the best of me. I'm sorry."

"Don't be." Conryu brushed the hair out of her eyes. "When warriors survive a battle the aftermath leaves them horny as hell. I read in one of Dad's books that it was because in ancient times so many died in battle those who survived had an overwhelming need to rebuild the population. Personally I think it's a mix of adrenalin and other hormones mingling and messing with your brain."

They moved apart and he flipped the switch to start the elevator moving again. Maria smoothed his shirt, her hand lingering a moment on his chest sending a thrill through him. He took her hand and held it. He was only human after all and if she kept that up…

"What are you going to tell your mom?" Maria asked.

"About this? Not a thing."

"You know what I mean."

He shrugged. "The truth. Though I think I'll leave the details to your mom. I don't really understand exactly what happened anyway."

The bell rang and the door slid open on Conryu's floor. "You want to come in and hang out for a while?"

"No, I need a little time to collect myself and take a cold shower. I'll see you at dinner."

Conryu stepped out and the door slid shut, sending Maria up to the penthouse. He gave a little shake of his head and made the short walk to his apartment. What a day. It was only a little after noon and he was completely wiped out. Maybe he could take a nap, and a cold shower didn't sound bad either.

He opened the door and found his mother sitting on the couch staring at the tv. Behind a hot, blond reporter was the carnival with the headline "Chaos at the Carnival!" A moment later Conryu's face came on screen.

"Hi, Mom."

She spun. "You are never leaving the building again."

* * *

Lin and Terra sat across from each other, each sizing the other up. They'd exchanged information and were digesting what the other had said. Lin had worked with the police wizard once before, but only briefly. He wasn't certain about the protocol. Would she take the lead or would they each handle their own aspects of the investigation alone and compare notes occasionally?

He took a drink, trying to gather his thoughts. Wilbur had been kind enough to provide them with bottles of water at cost. The idea of not making a profit galled the man, but given everything that had happened he seemed to think he owed them.

"So what do you make of all this?" Lin asked.

"Beyond the fact that someone wants Conryu dead very badly, I'm not sure of anything. We can't even confirm that the cultist and the necromancer are connected, though it seems beyond comprehension that they aren't."

"Agreed. The cultist, Mr. Call, had contact with someone on an encrypted forum the night before the attack. I'll wager whoever that was is our link. What I'm curious about is, how did the wizard know Conryu would be here today? After the first attack there's no reason to think he'd even leave home."

Terra shook her head, sending her thick, grayish-blond hair flying. "I wondered about that myself. That trap was set a while ago, late last night or early this morning I'd guess. I'm not even certain whoever set it intended the trap for him. It's entirely possible whoever's responsible simply adapted whatever was already here to kill Conryu."

Lin's jaw clenched and he forced himself to relax. This was how it always went at the start of an investigation. He needed to be patient and do the job. "We need more facts and less guesswork. What do you say we go talk to the Carrigton brothers?"

"Excellent suggestion, Detective. We could sit here and bandy ideas back and forth until nightfall, but that's not going to get us anywhere."

Lin stood and waved to draw Wilbur's attention. The carnival owner had been pacing and muttering ever since he'd learned the body of his friend was destroyed. Lin didn't blame him. Finding out the body of someone you'd known for fifteen years had been used in a dark magic ritual would bother anyone.

Wilbur hustled over. His eyes were red from crying, though he appeared under control for the moment. "You two want to go meet the Carrigton boys?"

"Exactly right," Lin said.

They followed Wilbur toward the far end of the carnival, past empty game booths and silent rides, out to what resembled a trailer park. Tractor trailers were parked beside campers with dozens of rusty pickups mixed in for good measure.

Wilbur led them to a small camper, maybe fifteen feet long, still hooked behind a pickup that Lin suspected was older than him. The only discernible color in it was rust. The carnival owner walked up to the slightly askew front door and knocked.

There was no reply or sound from inside. Lin reached for his gun, a twisty feeling in the pit of his stomach.

"Hey!" Wilbur shouted. "Wake up, you two. The police want to talk to you."

Still nothing.

"Mr. Cullen." Lin had his pistol out and ready. "Please step away from the door, sir."

Wilbur stared at Lin's gun, his eyes bugging out. "No need for that. Those idiots probably got drunk and passed out on their couch."

"Mr. Cullen, please."

Wilbur moved aside, shaking his head. When Wilbur had gone fifty feet and taken cover behind a heavy-duty haul trailer, Lin reached for the camper door. Of course it was locked.

"Let me." Terra placed her finger on the lock and spoke some words in what Lin assumed was one of the magical languages. The lock popped open and she moved aside. "After you."

Lin tugged the door open and went up the two iron steps into the camper. The place was empty unless you counted garbage. It only took a minute to clear the tiny trailer. There was nothing much to see beyond a mountain of empty beer cans, several equally empty whiskey bottles, and wrappers from the concession stands. The Carrigton brothers clearly didn't live the healthiest lifestyle.

"It's clear."

Terra hopped up the steps and grimaced. "This day just keeps getting worse. No sign of the brothers?"

"No. Once we have a look around I'll have to get a description from Mr. Cullen. I need to call the crime scene guys out here too. I doubt they'll find anything, but it couldn't hurt to have them check." Lin dug a pair of rubber gloves out of his pocket and handed them to Terra. They looked huge on her tiny hands, but at least she wouldn't leave prints everywhere.

Lin called for the crime scene unit while Terra looked around. They would be there in twenty minutes, which gave them a little time to try and figure out what happened.

"Did you find anything?" Lin asked.

"No. Who lives like this?" She held up a dirty plate with what appeared to be dried cheese on it.

Lin shrugged. He'd seen worse in a flophouse downtown. "The techs will have a better chance of finding something than us."

Lin left the camper. Wilbur was peeking around the corner of the trailer so Lin waved him over. Wilbur rushed to join him. "Are they okay?"

"I don't know, but the trailer's empty. What did the missing men look like?"

"Oh god, not the boys too. Are we cursed, Detective? My people haven't hurt anyone. We just try to make a living the best way we know how."

"There's no curse." Terra came down out of the camper. "I'd sense it if there were. What you have is a serious case of bad luck. Someone has decided to use your carnival for their own evil purposes."

"I'm not certain that's better," Wilbur said.

"The description, sir?" Lin asked.

Wilbur slipped a bottle out of his pocket and took a long pull. "They're twins, dark hair and eyes, usually in greasy overalls."

Terra gasped. "You said they worked on the ride where we found your friend?"

"That's right, why?"

"I guess there's no easy way to say this. Their bodies were raised as zombies by the same spell that summoned the hounds. We were forced to destroy them as well. I'm very sorry."

Wilbur wavered and Lin grabbed him before he fell. "We're cursed." He spoke so softly Lin almost didn't hear him.

"Will you be okay, sir?" When Wilbur nodded Lin sent the carnival owner on his way.

"How is he?" Terra asked.

Lin shook his head. "How do you think? What in the world have we gotten into?"

* * *

Conryu hadn't been able to sleep, but the shower and clean clothes had done him a world of good. He sprawled on the couch half watching some stupid cartoon. Maria had called an hour ago and said dinner was at seven. Dad sat at the kitchen table reading, content with washing his face and putting on a fresh shirt. Mom, on the other hand, had been fussing in the mirror since he hung up with Maria. You'd think it was dinner at the mayor's mansion instead of a casual meal with people they'd known their whole lives.

It was now five of seven and if they didn't step on it they'd be late. At long last Mom bustled out of the bedroom in a blue dress and pearls, her hair done up with some sort of clamps that looked like they could be used to extract a confession.

"Are you sure Shizuku wants us to come? We could have hosted them here."

"Mom, relax. Mrs. Kane definitely invited us up. There's probably some magic book or other she wants to show us after we eat." Conryu clicked the tv off. "We ready?"

Mom grabbed her purse and the three of them made the short walk to the elevator. When they reached the elaborate penthouse door Conryu knocked. Maria opened it a moment later. The scent of meat and spices wafted out, distracting him from the red kimono she was wearing.

"Come on in." Maria stepped aside and motioned them through.

Conryu went first, pausing to kick his boots off in the little depression just inside the door. Five paces beyond the entryway the apartment opened up into a dining room with a cherry table long enough to seat twenty. Six places had been set with pale plates and a selection of knives and forks. A bottle of red wine sat near the head of the table. A crystal chandelier lit the space and gave it an extra air of opulence.

"Is that Giovanni's lasagna I smell?" Conryu asked, his mouth already watering.

Maria grinned and led them into the dining room. "Sure is. Mom didn't feel like cooking so we ordered takeout. I assured her you wouldn't object."

"Good call."

Mr. Kane emerged from a side door, a bright if somewhat forced smile on his face. It was rare to find him in jeans and t-shirt instead of his usual suit. "Conryu, I trust you're recovered from your adventure this morning. Connie, you're looking lovely tonight."

Mom scowled at him, prompting a hurried turn to Dad.

"Sho, always nice to see you."

Dad nodded and they shook hands. "Everything under control, Orin? You're looking a little rough around the edges."

"Yes," Mom said. "What's being done to make sure my son will be kept safe?"

Mr. Kane winced. "I have my best wizard investigating. Rest assured she'll get to the bottom of it. In the meantime, everyone please sit. Shizuku is putting the finishing touches on dinner and by that I mean transferring it from the delivery containers to nice plates. She'll be along in a moment. Can I offer anyone a drink?"

Mom took him up on the offer instantly and downed her first glass in three big gulps. Mr. Kane refilled her glass without comment.

A couple minutes of forced chitchat came to a merciful end when Mrs. Kane emerged from the kitchen with plates full of Italian delicacies drifting behind her. Conryu had trouble deciding whether to focus on Mrs. Kane in her blue-and-gold silk kimono or the food. It was easy to see where Maria got her looks. The food settled on the table.

"Everyone, dig in," Mrs. Kane said. "And no business talk until we finish the cookies."

Twenty minutes and three helpings later Conryu licked the last of the sauce off his lips, savoring the tangy flavor. "That was awesome, Mrs. Kane. I'd fight shadow hounds every day if it ended with a spread like this."

Mom almost choked on her wine. "That wasn't funny, Conryu."

He'd only been partially joking, but decided not to point that out. "Seriously, it was great."

"Thank you, dear." Mrs. Kane gestured and spoke a short phrase in a language he didn't recognize. The dirty plates floated off, leaving the table clean. "I suppose we'd best get down to business."

Mrs. Kane filled them in on everything they'd discovered at the carnival and Mr. Kane chimed in with what Terra and Detective Lin had come up with so far. When they finished Mom was staring in horror and Dad's eyebrows had drawn together, which was about as expressive as he ever got.

At last Mom asked, "What does it all mean?"

"We're not certain," Mr. Kane said. "The investigation is ongoing."

"So what now?" Conryu asked. "I don't really want to spend my whole summer vacation locked up."

"I'm sorry, Conryu, but until we deal with whoever wants to kill you it's best if you stay here where it's safe." Mr. Kane offered an apologetic shrug. "Please understand it's not just you that's at risk. If another attack should happen someplace even more crowded, innocent bystanders might be injured. We must consider their safety as well."

That sucked, but Conryu understood his point. He'd have felt awful if anyone at the carnival had gotten hurt by monsters that were after him.

"There's another matter to consider," Mrs. Kane said.

"There is?" Conryu and his mom spoke at the same moment.

"Indeed. Your magical education is sorely lacking. The academy is set up with the expectation that all the incoming students will have a certain base level of understanding. That is something you'll need to acquire in the next eight weeks."

"Wait, summer vacation ends in ten weeks, not eight."

"For first through twelfth grade it does," Mrs. Kane said. "But for the academy and all the other colleges school starts early and ends late. Next year you'll only have six weeks."

"Great." He glanced over at his mother who was positively beaming. "You seem happy all of a sudden."

"This is perfect! You'll be safe inside studying and I won't have to worry, not with Shizuku's magic protecting you."

"Don't worry." Maria took his hand under the table. "I can help you study. A refresher will do me good."

"I'd be happy to help as well," Mrs. Kane said. "Some of the later concepts are complex. I have a job next month that will take me out of town for a week, but other than that I'm at your service."

Conryu looked at the smiling faces staring at him and choked back a sigh. Eight weeks of intensely studying a subject he couldn't care less about followed by four years of more studying it.

Great.

5
LADY RAVEN

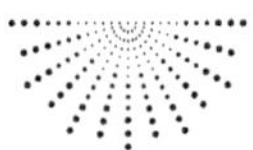

Orin reached the Department lobby and headed straight for the coffee machine. The secretaries hadn't arrived yet so he was forced to make a batch for himself. He yawned as the coffee dripped into the pot. At least it would be fresh; Orin seldom got a fresh cup of coffee at work.

He rolled his shoulders, trying to work the tension out of them. The murders and magical chaos were wearing on him. Not to mention he felt terrible about Conryu being stuck inside for his whole vacation. Maybe he could arrange some guards to watch him during a day trip or something.

To cap off his mountain of problems he'd promised the Department's full cooperation to the police commissioner on an early morning call. Not that he had a ton of resources to offer. Despite the name, the Department of Magic only had four wizards on staff and only two of those were especially powerful.

The attacks had left the city on edge. In addition to keeping him safe, Orin hoped that if Conryu stayed out of sight it would calm the public. The coffee stopped dripping and Orin poured himself a helping in a paper cup.

"I'll have one as well." Terra strolled over. She appeared fully recovered after her adventure at the carnival. Only a slight shadow under her eyes betrayed any weariness.

Orin handed her his cup and fixed himself another. He'd been so intent on his thoughts he'd never even noticed her come through the door. When they'd both taken a good long drink he asked, "Any news?"

"Not yet. Detective Chang is working through statements taken from the carnival workers, but who knows how long that will take and nothing may even come of it. There's nothing left of the spell that summoned the shadow hounds so that's a dead end. I'm not sure where to go next, Chief."

"Let the detective do his work. When he has something I'm sure he'll let you know. Meanwhile, we have another test to administer. Is Clair in yet?"

"Her car wasn't in her spot, but it's early." Terra finished her coffee and tossed the cup. "Are you really going to go through with this? I'm telling you she's not involved with the Society anymore."

"I trust you as much as I trust anyone outside my family and I still made you wear the ring. Even if I didn't harbor doubts about Clair I'd make her do it, just to be safe."

"I'm not sure if I should be pleased by the compliment or annoyed by your stubbornness."

"Be pleased; your annoyance isn't going to affect my decision in the least."

She finally cracked a smile. "Fair enough. It's not like you're treating her any different than the rest of us. I'll let you know when she gets in."

Orin left Terra contemplating a second cup of coffee and headed up to his office. One good thing about getting in early, the halls were quiet.

"Orin!" a thick Scottish accent called from behind him.

He turned to find Angus marching toward him. Orin wanted to slam his head into the wall. So much for the quiet. "Let's go in my office and have a seat, Angus."

"Certainly, certainly." The professor followed Orin into his office and sat in the guest chair. "Is the boy okay? If anything happens to him my work will be ruined."

Orin slumped in his leather chair and blew out a sigh. Nice to see Angus had his priorities straight. If he never had to listen to another word about Angus's precious research it would be a fine thing. "Conryu isn't hurt and I'm sure he'll be thrilled to hear you were concerned. Was there anything else?"

Angus stared off into the middle distance. "It's the Aegis of Merlin. The great wizard's spirit is protecting his successor. This is more proof of my theory. Just watch, Orin. I'll be vindicated and all those who laughed at me will have to eat crow."

"If you say so. Now I have work to do."

"Oh yes, I remember what I wanted to ask you now. When can I talk to him again?"

Orin shrugged. "That's up to him. If Conryu wants to talk to you I don't care, but I'm not going to order him to."

"That's fine. Maybe I'll head over to your building later and try my luck."

Orin nodded. "Fine, just don't make a nuisance of yourself. Conryu's a good kid, but if he makes up his mind to, he's more than capable of throwing you out."

"I saw his display Saturday. I assure you I'll be on my best behavior."

Angus mercifully took his leave. Too bad he had to foist him off on Conryu, but getting the obsessed professor out of the office for the day would be a relief.

An hour later Orin was halfway through the weekend reports when Terra poked her head into his office. "She's here."

"Come in."

Terra and Clair stepped into his office and stood in front of his desk. Orin knew his wife and Clair had their differences, but he tried not to let it influence him.

"You wanted to see me, sir?" Clair adjusted her badge then tucked her hands inside her sleeves.

Orin took the ring of compulsion out of a locked drawer in his desk and held it up. "Everyone that knew about Conryu's press conference has been cleared of involvement in the attack except you. Put the ring on and state that you had nothing to do with the attack on Conryu."

"Is this because of my history?" Clair asked. "I assure you I haven't had anything to do with the Society since I graduated."

"Everyone did it, me included. I have to be sure, Clair. It's not personal." Orin slid the ring across his desk to her.

Clair looked at Terra, who nodded. She slipped the ring on. "I had nothing to do with the attack on Conryu Koda. I haven't been in contact with the Le Fay Society since I graduated from the academy."

Orin nodded, surprised and pleased that he was wrong about Clair. She took the ring off and handed it to him. "Thank you. I'm glad you didn't have anything to do with it. Unfortunately, now I have no idea who might have been behind the attempted murder."

"Oh, god." Clair's hand went to her mouth. "There's one other person who might have known."

"Who?" Orin returned the ring to the locked drawer. He'd take it to storage later. "I questioned everyone that was in the room when we decided to hold the press conference. I didn't even tell Maria and Shizuku about it beforehand. You were the only other person outside the group who knew about Conryu and could have found out about the press conference."

"What about Mercia?"

"Who?" Orin couldn't for the life of him remember someone by that name.

"The wizard who discovered Conryu. Mercia Bottomley, she's one of my testers. She was in the room when we determined Conryu had wizard potential and it wouldn't have been difficult for her to learn about the press conference. The invitation was sent through the unsecured server."

"I totally forgot about her," Orin said.

"As did I." Terra grimaced. "With everything that's happened I never gave her another thought after Orin sat her in that chair in the corner. She simply faded into the background."

"Mercia's good at that," Clair said.

"We need to speak to her at once." Orin stood up. "Where is she?"

"She called in sick this morning," Clair said. "I didn't think anything of it at the time, but now I don't know."

"Damn it! How could we have been so sloppy?" Orin paced and only the fact that he was bald kept him from pulling his hair out. "I assume her address is in her personnel file. You two get over there and bring her in. I don't care how sick she is."

* * *

The Department car raced down the narrow streets, dodging pedestrians and squealing around corners. Terra kept a white-knuckled grip on the handle above the passenger-side door. Sweat plastered her gray robe to her back. The broken air conditioning combined with Clair's driving had her drenched. Clair slammed on the brakes and cranked the wheel, fishtailing and screeching the tires of the sedan.

Horrified onlookers stared for a moment before running for their lives. Terra knew just how they felt, but she didn't have anywhere to escape to. If they ever went out on an assignment together again there was no way Clair was driving, she could give Terra directions.

"Would you slow down?" Terra said. "I'd like to make it there in one piece so we can bring Mercia in for questioning."

"Chief Kane said to hurry. Besides, I haven't had this much fun in years."

"I don't think he's in this big a rush, now slow down before you kill someone."

"Spoilsport. We're almost there anyway." Clair slowed to an only somewhat reckless speed and made a left down Bleak Street. Young men hung around in doorways, wearing tattered clothes and sometimes going shirtless to better display their tattoos. Scantly clad women, girls really, cuddled up against the thugs.

"Are you sure this is where she lives?"

"We don't pay the testers very much, it's probably all Mercia can afford. Maybe that's why she betrayed us."

"She could have just asked for a raise," Terra said. "What are we looking at, power-wise?"

"Between three and four hundred. We only use the weakest wizards for testing, mostly because they can't do much else, magically speaking. She only works two days a week as it is, that's why I was surprised she called in sick. I had her scheduled for two more schools today."

Clair slammed on the brakes in front of a four-story tenement covered with graffiti, bringing them to a screeching halt. The designs painted on the walls appeared geometric and intricate, somewhat like magical runes, but their meaning was lost to Terra, assuming they had any meaning.

They climbed out and locked the doors. Terra put her hand on the hood and chanted a simple warding spell. Anyone that tried to steal or vandalize their car would regret it.

"She's in Apartment C on the top floor." Clair headed for the rusty door.

"Of course she is. What do you want to bet the elevator doesn't work?"

"Even if it does, I wouldn't use the elevator in a place like this."

Terra couldn't argue with that. The lock on the front door was missing and the glass had been smashed out. Not very secure, but then again there was probably nothing worth stealing inside.

Clair shoved the door open and after a quick search they

found the stairs, steep narrow things made from rusty metal. At least they didn't sway or rattle when Terra stepped on them. Sometimes you had to be grateful for small favors.

When they reached the top floor landing Terra was panting and her heart raced. She really needed to get out of the office more and into the gym. To make matters worse Clair didn't even seem out of breath.

Terra straightened, determined not to show any weakness. "Shall we?"

Clair nodded and the door whined when she pushed it open. Crumpled-up newspapers, rotten food, and other things Terra didn't want to look too closely at littered the hall beyond. God almighty, what a mess. And the stink, ugh. If this was the best a Department tester could afford, Terra would advise Orin to give them both a raise.

Terra muttered a simple wind spell to circulate fresh air around her nose and mouth. She took a deep breath of clean air. Much better. Clair continued on down the hall, seeming untroubled by the garbage.

The younger wizard stopped in front of the third door and knocked. "She's cast a simple ward. Probably a prudent precaution given the neighborhood."

Terra nodded in silent agreement. The city should tear the building down and start from scratch.

A minute passed and no one answered the door. Clair knocked again. "Mercia! We need to talk to you."

Still nothing.

"Do you want to break the ward or should I?" Clair asked.

Terra motioned toward the door. "Be my guest."

Clair crossed the fingers of both hands then crossed her arms at the wrist. She spoke the first words of a basic magic negation spell and the hall grew darker. Liquid shadow gathered around Clair as she chanted. When she finished she threw both hands toward the door and uncrossed her fingers, releasing the gathered dark energy.

Her power lashed out, striking the ward and blowing it apart. The light returned to normal and Clair reached out to push the door open. The moment she touched it the wood crumbled to shavings and the doorknob clattered to the floor.

She looked back at Terra, who shrugged. "You might have used too much energy."

"That was the weakest breaking spell I know."

"Your modulation needs work. You could have weakened the spell further by chanting softer or only crossing two fingers instead of all four. It doesn't matter. We can pay for a new door out of petty cash. Let's grab Mercia and get out of here."

Dim light filled the apartment. Heavy drapes covered the small windows and when Terra tried the switch nothing happened. She cupped her palm and whispered, "Light," summoning a glowing white globe.

The empty living room gave no clues about the woman living here. What sort of person didn't even have a chair and tv? The kitchen was just as empty as the living room. A single door on the opposite wall led, she assumed, to the apartment's lone bedroom. If Mercia was here that's where she had to be.

Terra went to the door and toed it open. The bedroom held a single, small end table situated right in the center. It was the first and only piece of furniture in the place. Sitting in the center of the table was an undecorated gold ring.

Terra reached for it then paused and spoke a simple detection spell. The ring registered as magical, but there was no trap. She picked the ring up for a closer look. It was smooth, with no visible runes. That was fairly common if you didn't want the world to know you had a magical item.

"That's Mercia's. She said it was her mother's wedding band."

"Unless her mother wore a magic ring I think we can safely assume that was bullshit. Just like this address. No one's lived here in a long time if ever. I wonder if anything Mercia said on her employment form was the truth."

"What do you think it does?" Clair asked.

Terra shook her head and pocketed the ring. There was no way to know what it did until she returned to the lab and ran a proper analysis. They went back toward the living room. This whole trip was a waste of time. The moment they passed through the bedroom door a tingle of power ran through Terra.

A black energy field filled the door frame leading out into the hall. Something moved in the darkness, almost like the fluttering of wings. Identical energy fields covered the two small windows.

"It's a trap!" Clair raised her hands and chanted a light barrier spell.

Invisible energy swirled around them, ready to block anything that might present a threat. For a moment nothing happened then the glow globe Terra had conjured winked out, plunging the apartment into complete darkness.

She chanted the spell a second time, but the light energy was swallowed the moment she summoned it. Terra frowned and switched to a fire spell. If she couldn't conjure light from her aligned element they were in big trouble.

Terra's fire globe burned away some of the darkness, creating an oasis of light in the pitch-black room. She cast the spell a second time, brightening the room further. Despite the increased light there was nothing to see, only the bare floor and bare wall. A deep snarl came from the bedroom, at least she thought it came from that way. The light didn't extend far enough to reveal the doorway.

"What was that?" Clair asked.

"Nothing good, you can be certain. How did you do in combat training at the academy?"

"Middle of my class. Nothing outstanding. I took a job in the testing division because I thought I wouldn't have to deal with situations like this."

"I transferred to R&D for the same reason. Looks like we're both going to be disappointed." Terra caught a hint of movement. At least she thought she did. It could have as easily been her imagination. "We need to go. Can you maintain the barrier while we move toward the hall door?"

"I think so." Clair chanted again and the light flashed as the spell adjusted to its new parameters. "We can move when you say."

A black form separated itself from the greater darkness. It looked vaguely humanoid, but lacked a face, and the body stretched beyond human proportions with long, skinny limbs ending in oversized clawed hands and feet.

The figure rushed toward them, claws extending as it drew closer. It lashed out, striking the light barrier and getting hurled back into the darkness.

"Was that what I think it was?" Clair's voice trembled.

"If you thought it was a Faceless One then yes." Terra marveled at how calm she sounded. There was a shadow demon out there trying to kill them and she managed to appear unconcerned.

The Faceless One appeared out of the darkness again, slammed into Clair's barrier and was sent flying.

Clair groaned. "Every strike hurts me through the light I called. Its claws are tearing the barrier's essence apart and me along with it. How do we stop it?"

"I believe it's bound to the room. Once we're clear we can destroy it from a safe distance. Let's move." They eased closer to where Terra thought the door waited.

"What if it's not?"

"Then we may end up setting the creature free in the city. The danger's minimal since it's still morning, but once night falls all bets are off."

The Faceless One made another run at them and was again repulsed by the barrier. Clair's knees wobbled and Terra caught her before she fell.

"One more of those and I'm done." Pain and exhaustion filled Clair's voice.

They were running out of time.

A moment later the door to the hall appeared in the light of Terra's fire globes. At least the door frame appeared. The opening was filled with dark energy. Terra reached out to touch it and immediately jerked her hand back. It would melt the flesh from their bones if they tried to force their way out through that.

Their only chance was to unravel the spell and she doubted the Faceless One would give them the time.

"What's above us?" Terra asked.

"This is the top floor. There shouldn't be anything above us."

"Good." Terra chanted in the language of fire, sending more power to her fire globes.

The Faceless One attacked again and was sent flying. The light died and Clair collapsed behind her. They were defenseless now.

Terra finished the spell and hurled the twin balls of flame at the ceiling. They detonated on impact, blowing a twenty-foot hole in the ceiling. Bright morning sunlight shone down into the apartment, stabbing the Faceless One with golden shafts.

The shadow demon threw its head back in a silent scream of pain. Its essence began to burn away at once. Terra sent streams of fire hammering into it to speed its dissolution. A minute later the creature was gone, along with the darkness barriers over the remaining window and hall door.

Terra glanced up at the hole she'd made. Some of the exposed timbers smoldered and several splintered ends burned with enthusiasm. She hissed and snapped her fingers, snuffing out the flames instantly.

Clair scrambled to her feet looking pale, but otherwise unharmed. "That was too close."

Indeed it was. If Mercia had warded the ceiling as well as the windows and doorway their little adventure may have ended much differently.

"No three or four hundred power level wizard set up all this. Either Mercia had help or she pulled an even bigger one over on us than I first thought." Terra glared around the ruined living room.

They left the destroyed apartment and went out into the hall. Clair slumped against the wall while Terra dug out her phone. She needed to let Lin know what had happened. Hopefully he could convince his superiors this was connected to his case and she wouldn't need to deal with another cop.

* * *

Lady Raven stood in the center of her magic circle and adjusted the black raven mask so the eyeholes aligned properly. The shadowy casting chamber held nothing that might distract her. Even the smallest mistake when she was working on a project could mean her end. The upcoming meeting held similar risks. If she couldn't explain her actions to the Hierarchs' satisfaction she might easily end up dead.

It was a shame she had to discard her Mercia persona. She'd gotten comfortable in that one over the last several years. She'd also gathered a great deal of information for her superiors. On the other hand she wouldn't miss having to show deference to those arrogant women at the Department. If they knew her true power they wouldn't have been so smug. Well, they knew it now. She smiled.

When the simple ward she'd woven over the door to Mercia's apartment shattered she'd recognized the magic that broke it as belonging to her former superior at the Department. When the trap she'd left inside activated, Lady Raven assumed she would be down two enemies. To her surprise, Clair and Terra had managed to defeat her Faceless One. Those two were turning out to be tougher foes than she'd expected.

Their time would come, just like the abomination's time would come. She'd failed to kill the boy twice, but when the third time came he'd die just as surely as day turned to night.

Lady Raven tried to clear her mind of irrelevant thoughts. The time for the meeting drew near and her superiors would be able to sense any doubts and weakness. Like the animals whose masks they wore, the Hierarchs would attack at the slightest sign of weakness.

A tingle ran through the mask, prompting her to speak the activation spell, connecting her mind to the group. All around her the shadows seemed to flicker and flow, forming five shadowy avatars of the Hierarchs. Each wore a mask similar to hers. Directly in front of her was the Supreme Hierarch in her dragon mask. Flanking her, two per side, were wizards in animal masks. A tiger, lion, bear, and wolf. Beside the Hierarchs, one on each side, were two Sub-Hierarchs, a bluejay and a mockingbird. Either one of whom would be thrilled if Lady Raven fell flat on her face.

"Lady Raven," Lady Dragon said. "It has come to our attention that you have deviated from the plan. Is everything still on track?"

"Yes, Mistress. I only sacrificed the spare gem in hopes of killing the abomination."

"A task at which you failed." Lady Mockingbird made no attempt to disguise her glee.

"Yes, I admit the boy survived, due to outside influences, but the other sites are secure and the authorities have no idea of their existence. The plan will proceed with no issues."

"And the abomination?" Lady Tiger asked.

"For now he is beyond my reach, but I have other tools that can deal with him when the time comes."

"No." Lady Dragon spoke with finality. "Focus on your mission. In time the boy will come out of hiding. There is no need to rush."

"Yes, Mistress." It galled Lady Raven that she wouldn't have another shot at Conryu, but having failed twice perhaps it was for the best. A third mistake would not be looked on favorably.

"And, Lady Raven." Lady Dragon raised her hand, displaying the Scepter of Morgana for them all to see, a less than subtle reminder that in their true mistress's absence she ruled the Society. "You have already lost your position in the Department. Should you fail to carry the plan to fruition we will have no further use for you."

Lady Dragon vanished, followed quickly by the others, leaving Lady Raven alone in her casting chamber. She pulled her mask off to be sure the connection was fully severed then fell, trembling, to her knees. The chill of her mistress's disappointment sank deep into her bones.

She couldn't fail again, not if she wanted to live.

Lady Raven frowned and considered what her mistress had said. She only commanded that Lady Raven herself not attack Conryu again. It was possible the Hierarchs remained unaware that she'd prompted the zealot to attack the boy at his press conference.

In that case it wouldn't take much effort to convince a fresh batch of the fools to take another shot at him. She even knew the perfect time.

* * *

Lin found Terra and her companion, a wizard he hadn't met before, standing in the hall outside the smoking remains of an empty apartment. Inside, a team of firemen checked for hot spots or embers that might still be a threat. They'd evacuated the fifteen people in the building just to be safe. Considering the damage to the roof he doubted they'd be allowed to stay in their homes tonight or any night until repairs were completed.

The lack of smoke in the hall surprised Lin until he realized the wizards had probably done something to keep it clear. They wouldn't have wanted to stand around coughing while they waited for him.

"You two okay?"

Terra looked his way and smiled. It surprised him how good that felt.

"We're fine, Lin, thanks. Was anyone hurt in the blast?"

"EMTs are checking everyone out downstairs, but they seem fine. What happened?"

Terra told him about the trap and how they escaped. When she finished he asked, "What about your colleague? There was no sign of her beyond the ring?"

"No, and I doubt she ever stayed in that apartment. I'm afraid we need to consider Mercia a suspect in the murders and the attack on Conryu."

Lin tried to smooth his suit and failed. "If you can send me a picture of her I'll put out a BOLO request."

"Of course, but Mercia can alter her appearance with a simple illusion so I don't know how much good it will do you." Terra shrugged her shoulders and worked her neck from side to side. If they'd been alone he would have offered her a massage. "Any luck with the carnival people?"

"No, they've left Sentinel City for wherever they go while they wait for the island to return to the west coast. I'm afraid they were just innocent people with the bad fortune to get mixed up in things that didn't concern them."

"I suspect you're right," Terra said. "It's a shame, but I don't think we could have done anything except what we did."

"Me neither, but that doesn't make it suck any less."

"No, it doesn't. If there's nothing else, Lin, we need to head back and analyze the ring."

"Of course." Lin and Terra shook hands. "Let me know what you find?"

"Will do." Terra guided her still-shaky companion down the hall and out of sight.

Lin sighed. It was a shame Terra was a wizard. She would have made an excellent detective.

"Hey, Sarge," one of the firemen called from the apartment. He'd worked with the guy on an arson investigation a year ago and they'd kept in touch.

"What's up?"

"The room's clear. The wizard did a good job snuffing out all the hot spots. We're going to head out."

"Thanks, guys." Lin took his leave. Outside, one of the uniforms lifted the crime scene tape for him. Lin climbed into his beat-up four-door and headed uptown. The techs had finished analyzing Mort Call's laptop and they traced the person he chatted with to an internet cafe at the edge of a middle-class neighborhood that bordered on a rougher area. Hopefully they had security footage.

Lin didn't bother with his siren as he wove through the midday traffic. Hundreds of people going about their business without a clue that an insane wizard was threatening the city. City Hall wouldn't put it on the news unless they absolutely had to. The panic could end up being worse than whatever the wizard had in mind.

He turned off the main road and into a neighborhood of mixed residential and small businesses. The internet cafe was at the edge of Cliff Street and barely hanging on given the spread of broadband and cellphones.

Speaking of which, Lin's phone buzzed in his pocket. He parked in front of the cafe and dug it out. It was a text message from Terra with Mercia's picture. He'd seldom seen a more average-looking woman save for the deep wrinkles. She wouldn't even need a disguise. Mercia could walk down the street and never draw a second look.

Why couldn't anything be easy? If she had a hook nose, maybe a missing eye and some tattoos, anything to make her stand out would help. Lin slid out of his car and walked up to the cafe. They hadn't opened yet, but a young woman with purple hair and studs running up the side of her ear was fiddling with one of the computers. Lin rapped on the door until she looked up. He pressed his badge to the glass.

She hurried over and opened the door. "Can I help you, Officer?"

Lin showed her the picture on his phone. "Do you recognize this woman?"

"Sure, she gave me my wizard's test last year. I failed."

"I was thinking more recently."

"Oh, then no, I guess not."

"Does this place have security cameras?" Lin asked.

"These days every place does." The girl gave her hair a flip. "We keep three days' worth. You want to take a look?"

"Is it digital?"

"Yup."

"If I give you an address can you download the contents to the police server?"

"I can do better than that, I'll just swap the hard drives and you can take them with you. Be a lot faster than downloading on our crappy connection."

Lin blinked, surprised at how helpful she was. "That would be great, but won't your boss object?"

"Naw, he used to be a cop. If I was anything but helpful he'd toss me out on my ear. Just wait here and I'll bring you those hard drives."

"Thanks." Lin watched as she jogged back through the rows of computers and disappeared through an open doorway into the back room.

The moment she was out of sight he tiptoed along behind her. He stood in the doorway as she frantically tapped commands into a console tied to a server rack.

"You wouldn't be trying to delete evidence, would you?"

She leapt back from the keyboard and looked frantically for an escape. The only way out was through Lin and he had his hand on his pistol grip.

"Please don't do anything stupid. I'd hate to have to shoot you."

"If I let you have those hard drives he'll kill me."

"Who, your boss? You said he used to be a cop."

She smiled and shook her head. "That wasn't the whole story."

"What is the whole story?"

"You have to get me out of the city. Promise me a ticket out of town and I'll tell you everything."

"Deal. May as well grab those hard drives while we're at it."

* * *

Lady Raven had barely finished posting on the fanatics' secure forum when someone banging on the door got her attention. She typed a short command that disconnected her and erased her browser's cache so no one could see what she'd been doing.

She turned to look and found a man in his forties wearing a rumpled blue suit standing in front of the door. He pressed a badge to the glass. Damn it to hell! How had the police found this place already?

It was inevitable that they would, but she'd hoped to get another month or two out of it. Worse, if they'd found the cafe it was only a matter of time before the Skulls came to their attention. The bikers knew far too much for her own good. They were useful tools, but it seemed they had played their parts. It was time to cut them loose.

A plan formed as she made her way to the door. By the time she unlocked it and invited the cop inside she knew exactly what she had to do. It was a small miracle he hadn't arrived ten minutes earlier. If she'd had to send the message to the zealots from her own computer it would have been far riskier. So risky in fact that she might not have even bothered.

"Can I help you, Officer?"

The cop showed her a picture of herself on his phone. "Do you recognize this woman?"

It took all her willpower not to laugh. After a brief interrogation during which Lady Raven did her best to be as helpful as possible, helpful enough to make him suspicious, she went to the back room to retrieve the hard drives.

The moment she left his line of sight she darted to her station at the servers and typed commands that would automatically delete everything she didn't want the authorities to know about. Which was pretty much everything but the contents of three hard drives she'd set up for this exact eventuality.

"You wouldn't be trying to delete evidence, would you?"

As she'd hoped, his suspicious nature prompted him to follow her. She looked left and right, trying her best to appear frightened and desperate, a scared girl caught out of her depth. Lady Raven had honed her acting skills over years of undercover work. In truth she'd spent so much time pretending to be other people she'd almost forgotten who she started out as.

"Please don't do anything stupid. I'd hate to have to shoot you."

His pitiful weapon couldn't have harmed her unless she allowed it to, but she cowered like the girl she appeared to be. She blamed her fear on the dupe that ran the shop for her. He tried to be reassuring and she let him calm her down. They struck a bargain and she pulled the three hard drives she wanted him to have in the first place. It was so much easier to convince someone to do what you wanted when they thought it was their idea.

The cop packed her and the hard drives into the back seat of a car that had seen better days. He jumped in the front and they drove away. Lady Raven kept her hands hidden as she wove a wind spell that would carry a message to Iron Skull. By the end of the day her dupe would be at the bottom of the ocean.

She smiled as they made their way to the police station. What better place to hide than right under their noses?

* * *

Lin guided the purple-haired tech down the hall toward an empty interrogation room. He glanced down at the chipped, filthy black and white tile floor. The station needed to invest in an extra janitor. The mess that was the main corridor from the front of the station to the rear didn't fill a person with confidence about the quality of people working for the city police. A light buzzed and flickered overhead as the bulb slowly died, adding to the ambiance.

"This place reminds me of a mental ward from a low-budget horror film."

Lin wanted to argue, but he had nothing. "Try not to judge the police by the station. There are a lot of good people working here. We do our best with limited resources."

"Hey, Sarge." One of the guys from sex crimes, a three-hundred-pound heap of blubber named Louie that seldom left the office, waved him over to his desk in the maze of cubicles.

"Wait here." Lin left his witness and walked over. "What's up?"

"Got a message from that Cullen guy that owns the carnival. One of his people got so depressed she killed herself."

"What?"

"Yeah, the guys investigating wanted me to let you know since it dovetails with your investigation."

"Thanks, Louie. I'll bring you a Bear Claw tomorrow."

"Fuck you, Chang."

They shared a good-natured grin and Lin went back to his witness. "Sorry for the wait."

She shrugged. "What else have I got to do? Anything exciting?"

"Another body. It seems I'm drowning in them lately. At least this one didn't stand up and start walking around. Come on, I'll get you settled then send those hard drives down to the tech department. It shouldn't take our facial recognition system long to see if my suspects visited your cafe."

"You're going to see a lot more than that."

Lin raised his hand. "Please, don't say anything until we reach the interrogation room. Once we're inside everything will be recorded. That way we avoid any misunderstandings."

Fifteen minutes later Lin sat across from the witness in a dingy, bare room. A single light bulb flickered over their heads. The chipped plastic table between them looked like a reject from a condemned school. Behind the two-way mirror Lin's boss, Captain Connor, watched and listened. He was as eager to crack this case as Lin and had agreed to allowing the girl a deal for anything short of murder.

"State your name for the record, please," Lin said.

"Lacy Winn."

"Again, for the record, you have the right to an attorney during this deposition. Do you waive that right?"

"I do." Her voice sounded steady despite the circumstances. Lacy was clearly a tough girl.

"Okay. Tell us your story."

"Six months ago I took a job doing basic maintenance on the cafe's computers. The job came with a little hole-in-the-wall apartment upstairs. I didn't get good enough grades to qualify for college, not even one of the two-year places. At first it seemed like a sweet deal, but then all these strange guys started coming and going early in the morning and late at night."

"Strange guys?" Lin asked. "Please be more specific."

"I can't give you names, if that's what you mean. They didn't exactly introduce themselves. They were big, biker-looking guys. You know, lots of leather and spikes. Not to mention knives and guns. Five of them showed one night with enough firepower to start a war. Scared the hell out of me."

"Illegal weapons?"

"They had clips as long as my arm. That seems like the sort of thing you guys would frown on."

"What about the tattoos, or patches on their jackets? Anything that could give us an idea who we're dealing with."

She thought for a moment. "There were a lot of skulls. Skull patches, skull tattoos, one guy had a helmet that looked like a skull. They all wore rings that looked like barbed wire. Does that help?"

Lin smiled and tried to look encouraging. "It all helps. You said we'd see a lot on the recordings. What did you mean by that?"

Lacy cleared her throat. "Can I have a drink?"

"Sure." Lin pushed himself out of the chair, poked his head out into the hall, and spotted a uniformed officer walking down the hall. "Excuse me. Would you get my witness a glass of water?"

The officer pulled a face, but nodded. "Yes, Detective."

Lin went back inside and sat down. "It'll just be a minute. Do you want to keep going while we wait or do you need a break?"

"I can keep going. Like I said, they scared me so I reset the security cameras to run during off hours when the bikers were there. Sort of an insurance policy. It reacts to movement so the camera doesn't record all the time and I partitioned the hard drive to keep it from automatically erasing with the rest of the data. The light isn't great, but you should be able to make out all of them, at least a little."

"Clever girl."

The door opened and the officer came in with a plastic cup of water. He set it on the table, nodded once, and silently marched out. Didn't look like he and Lin would be best friends anytime soon.

"Tell me about your boss."

Lacy set the cup down and wiped a drop of water off her lips. "Mr. Connelly? I don't know much about him. He doesn't spend a lot of time at the cafe. It's more of an investment for him. Not an especially good one nowadays either."

"Is there anything else you can think of that might be valuable to us? Even the smallest detail could be vital."

"I'm sorry. I don't really know much. It's not like we're pals or anything. I was just a nobody that kept the computers running."

"Okay. Thank you, Lacy." Lin held out his hand and they shook. "Two officers will take you to a department safe house. As soon as we finish going over the drive and we're sure we don't have any more questions, I'll take you to the airport myself."

Half a minute later Captain Connor and two uniforms stepped into the room. Lacy went with the uniforms leaving Captain Connor and Lin alone in the room.

"What do you think?" Connor asked.

Lin shook his head. "Until we know what's on the tape we only have her word to go on. Certainly nothing I'd want to take to court."

"What's your gut tell you?"

"That she's telling us everything she knows, but that there's a lot more going on here than we know about." Lin picked up the plastic cup by the lip. "I'm going to have this dusted for prints and see what else we can learn about Miss Winn."

* * *

Conryu turned the page of the two-inch-thick book Mr. Kane had given him before they left last night. It was the current edition of The Basics of Wizardry and it was written in the most dry, boring voice Conryu had ever read. He knew they didn't put much effort into making textbooks entertaining, but god almighty it was like the author went out of her way to make this one dull.

Maybe she considered it some sort of test. If you didn't have the focus and discipline to make it through the book you wouldn't make it as a wizard. That was the most charitable explanation he could come up with.

Unable to stand it anymore, Conryu slammed the cover shut and tossed the book on the couch. He switched on the tv. Maybe he could find a replay of last night's ballgame. The clock on the mantle read ten in the morning. He should be out doing something, anything, not cooped up like an inmate. He flipped to one of the news channels and there was his face.

"Who is the real Conryu Koda?" the hostess asked. "The first ever confirmed male wizard, Conryu comes from an unremarkable background."

He switched it off. What the hell did she know about the real him? He'd never even met the woman. Well, when you had twenty-four hours of news to fill you had to talk about something. Conryu hopped out of the recliner and went to the kitchen. Some junk food would take his mind off wizards and reporters. He pulled the refrigerator door open and scanned the awful selection of fruits and vegetables. Where was that last piece of lasagna?

Someone knocked and Conryu closed the fridge. Thank goodness. That had to be Maria. Maybe she'd summarize the book for him. Knowing her she'd read it cover to cover more than once.

He peeked out into the hall just to be sure and frowned at the mass of wild white hair. He knew that hair, but what was that crazy professor doing here?

Conryu opened the door a crack and frowned out at the old man. "Are you lost?"

"No, in fact I was hoping we could talk a bit. I have so many questions. May I come in, please?"

Conryu looked from the professor, to the book on the couch, and back again. Which was the lesser evil? Finally he decided it was a toss up, but he didn't want to offend one of Mr. Kane's colleagues.

He pulled the door open the rest of the way. "You have half an hour, then I need to get back to studying."

The professor, McSomething, Conryu couldn't remember the rest, hustled into the apartment and looked around like he'd never seen one before.

"Looking for something in particular?" Conryu asked.

"Sorry. I was just trying to understand how the most amazing person ever born could come from such an ordinary place. This might be any one of ten thousand apartments in this city. It's inexplicable."

"Yeah. I won't tell my mom you said that as she's quite proud of her decorating." Conryu plopped down into the recliner. "So what do you want, Professor?"

"Angus, please." The professor sat beside the book on the couch. "I've been doing genealogical research on both sides of your family and you know, there isn't a single wizard on either side as far back as I could find records. Would you be willing to give me a blood sample so I can check your DNA for anomalies?"

"No." Angus blinked at his abrupt answer. Conryu didn't especially care. He had no intention of being poked, prodded or tested any more if he could avoid it. "What does my family history have to do with it?"

"Don't you know anything about magic?" Angus pressed on before he could say the sarcastic remark that popped into his head. "Wizards tend to run in families. Not always as directly as your friend Maria, with daughter following mother, but all wizards can find another wizard somewhere in their ancestry, except you."

"How far back did you go?" Conryu asked. He didn't really want to get in to this, but now his curiosity had been roused.

"Things become murky after ten generations on your mother's side, but I traced your father's family all the way back to the second generation after the Elf War, and not a speck of magic could be found. It's absolutely astonishing."

"Huh. Well, was there anything else?"

"Could you tell me what it felt like when you touched the testing device? Did you get a thrill of power when you learned you were a wizard?"

Thrill of power? This guy read too many comic books. "I didn't feel anything, Professor, except my dreams dying. You seem to be the one getting a thrill out of my problems, but for me they're nothing but a pain in the ass. I have to delay starting my job for four years, study a subject that doesn't interest me in the least, all while hopefully not getting killed by any of the nuts that object to my existence. Mr. Kane said that once I finish my training at the academy I'll be free to do what I want. And what I want is to have as little to do with magic as possible."

"No! Don't you see? You have a great destiny ahead of you. You can't simply fade into obscurity. You'll be famous the world over, the most powerful wizard ever. You'll consult with kings and emperors just like your predecessor, Merlin. You'll be a living legend and I'll be vindicated."

Conryu leapt to his feet, marched to the door and yanked it open. "You and Merlin can both take a flying leap. Now get out before I throw you out."

"Please, I have many more questions."

"I'm going to count to five and if you're still here I'll make you wish you weren't. And I promise you I won't need magic to do it. One!"

Angus scrambled to his feet.

"Two!"

He rushed across the living room, out the door, and stopped in the hall. "If you change your—"

Conryu slammed the door in his face and leaned against it. He didn't know what was worse, the people that wanted to kill him or the ones that wanted to use him. At least the killers didn't try and pretend it was for his benefit.

Consult with kings and emperors. Ha! What in the world would he have to tell a king? Maybe if something broke on the royal motorcycle he could help, but his expertise ended there.

A knock sounded on the door. Stubborn old fart couldn't take a hint.

He yanked the door open and found Maria standing there stunning as ever, in a pale blue dress.

"Everything okay?" She shied away from him and Conryu realized he was still scowling like he expected the professor.

He smoothed his expression and stepped aside to let her enter. "Sorry. I had an unpleasant visitor and I was afraid he'd come back."

"Oh?"

He recounted what the professor had to say. When he finished he added, "I wasn't eager to renew the conversation."

"You really don't want to have anything to do with magic?"

Conryu groaned. Not Maria too.

6

THE BLACK SKULLS

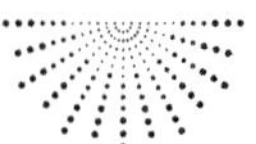

Terra sat in her cramped office surrounded by books of magic both new and old. Despite its small size she was most at home tucked away out of sight. Terra wasn't good with people. She knew she tended to be abrupt and to assume others were as informed about magical matters as her. She'd fought the problem since her time at the academy and still hadn't beaten it.

Lin said he'd call around midmorning and she was anxious to hear what he'd come up with. Who was she kidding? Terra just wanted to talk to him again. She felt like a teenager waiting for some boy to call after their first date.

Two days had passed since she last spoke to the detective though it seemed like longer. Unlike most people she dealt with outside the Department, Terra found the good detective easy to talk to.

For her part, she and Clair had figured out what the ring did: it was a power suppressor. Mercia wasn't a weak wizard after all. Unfortunately, they had no idea how great her true power was. Though based on the trap she set at her fake apartment Terra guessed she was at least as strong as Shizuku and perhaps a little stronger.

They also had no idea why she decided to hide her power in the first place. Clearly she wanted access to the Department without drawing any attention. As a tester Mercia would have known the names of every new student going to the academy, but that wasn't exactly secret information. The academy made enrolled students' names public. The government had determined that regular citizens had a right to know if they were dealing with a wizard.

Terra had made her report to Chief Kane yesterday and he had someone searching the academy records to try and find Mercia's true power level, but so far they'd found nothing, not even her name. The government kept meticulous records when it came to wizards, so the fact that they found nothing about Mercia was odd if not downright sinister. It seemed like every time they took a step forward it was followed by two more back.

Her phone rang, jarring Terra out of her contemplations. She could do nothing about the records so she needed to focus on things within her control, like figuring out who had attacked Conryu.

She picked up the receiver. "Terra Pane."

"This is Detective Chang, Terra. We've made some progress in our investigation. I tracked the person chatting with Mort Call to an internet cafe. It seems a gang called the Black Skulls was using it as a meeting place. Since he hasn't woken up yet, is there any way you can extract information from Mr. Call's mind? Our wizard says it's possible, but beyond her ability."

"A psychic probe, it's not something I have any skill with, but my boss's wife might be able to do it. I'll ask him and let you know. Now, who are the Black Skulls and what do they have to do with Conryu and Mercia?"

"The Skulls are a biker gang that's into drugs and guns. They've also moved into illicit magical items. We have them on tape collecting mundane-looking items from an unknown individual. Our wizard found traces of magical energy at the cafe."

Terra frowned. She knew a little about the underground trade in magical items, but it tended to be narrow and limited to collectors. It didn't seem like the sort of thing that would interest a gang. "Would it be possible for me to have a look at the cafe? We have an amplification device that can give more information about those trace energies you found."

"Certainly. I'd prefer to speak to you in person anyway. Can you meet me there in an hour?" Lin gave her the address.

"I'll be there." She hung up and left her office.

It was a short walk down to the secure storage room. She'd been taking the stairs for the last two days to get a little exercise. Studying the energy patterns and chatting with Lin should be simple enough, no need to bring Clair along.

She reached the thick steel door and placed her hand on a metal plate beside it. Terra spoke a brief incantation, deactivating the wards and unlocking the door. Inside the store room dozens of shelves held hundreds of items: books, scrolls, and other magical paraphernalia.

Terra selected a set of glasses held together with silver wire. They would magnify the aura of any residual magic a hundred times. She reached for a silver ring, paused, then grabbed it. A little extra protection was never a bad idea. She slipped the ring on and headed for her car, locking the door behind her.

* * *

Terra found Lin leaning against his car waiting for her when she arrived. The internet cafe was a rundown dump sealed off with yellow police tape. She'd never had much use for technology. It tended to be more of a distraction than anything as far as she was concerned anyway.

Terra parked her beat-up car behind Lin's equally beat-up

sedan. She didn't know where all her tax dollars were spent, but it wasn't on vehicles for public servants.

Lin opened her door for her, prompting a smile. "Thanks. Did your wizard mention what sort of magic she found?"

Lin opened his notebook. "Fire and darkness, both extremely weak."

"The residual aura might be weak, but whatever left them had to be reasonably strong or she would have found no trace at all." Terra strode toward the cafe door. "I'll know more shortly."

"Do you need the area clear or can I join you?"

"Join me, by all means. Your presence will make no difference one way or the other." She smiled and opened the door. "For the spell. I'll be glad for the company."

He smiled back and her heart did a little flutter. What was wrong with her? She was acting like a silly girl. When the door closed behind Lin she slipped the glasses on and chanted.

"Reveal all things hidden."

Three dark trails appeared between the dingy rows of computers. "Darkness magic for sure."

Terra followed the trails toward the back of the cafe, bumping into chairs as she focused on the magic instead of where she was walking. Lin gently took her elbow and guided her around the various obstacles. The trails led to a blank wall. She touched the smooth, painted surface.

"There's something hidden behind here."

"Are you sure? Our wizard didn't mention even seeing anything in this part of the building."

Terra traced a square on the wall, leaving a glowing path behind. "Right here. I can't say what, but something was here, something powerful."

"Step back." Lin pulled a folding knife out of a coat pocket.

Terra moved aside and Lin stabbed the wall, cutting the wall board around the square she marked. When he finished he pulled the chunk of material out and tossed it on the floor. On the other side was a small niche built into the framing. Runes had been burned into the wood. The whole thing seethed with residual dark energy.

"Something potent was stored here at one time. Those are runes of containment and binding. Whoever used this hiding place didn't want whatever they put here leaking out."

"Can you tell what it was?" Lin asked.

Terra shook her head. "The residual energy doesn't have any real shape. Where did your wizard detect the auras?"

"In the back room where they held their secret meetings. Through the door on your left."

Terra slipped through the door. The filthy office lit up with lines of darkness and fire. The dark magic was the same as whatever was in the niche. She scanned the walls and found a faint aura on the wall that was opposite the hole they just cut in the wall.

"Someone used magic to reach through the wall and retrieve whatever was stored there. The magic looks very similar to what we found at the carnival, only stronger. I can't tell much about the fire magic, but given what you said about the people gathered here I feel pretty confident it was a weapon. What sort of items were they trading?"

Lin consulted the ever-present notebook. "Five boxes and what looked like a glove."

"The glove is almost certainly the weapon, probably a Flame Hand Gauntlet, very dangerous. The five boxes I'm not sure about. The lines continue out the back door." Terra followed the dark energy outside. "They split up here, going in five different directions. The trail dissipates after a hundred yards or so."

"So whatever was in those boxes could be anywhere."

Terra took her glasses off and returned them to their case. "I'm afraid so. When was the tape made?"

"Four nights before the attack on Conryu."

"That's a day before anyone even knew the boy had wizard potential. Whatever we've stumbled into is about far more than Conryu. That's a long time for such potent magical items to be in the hands of people who have no idea how to use them properly."

"We need to find the Skulls and learn what they did with them."

"Absolutely." Terra chewed her thumbnail and frowned. "The real question is: What, if anything, does all this have to do with Conryu and Mercia?"

"Even if it has nothing to do with them, I can't risk criminals having access to dangerous magic. The threat to the city is too great."

* * *

The deep roar of Iron Skull's bike fell silent when he pulled into a parking spot outside Sentinel Central Hospital. He took off his helmet and hung it on the handlebars. The bone-white skull-shaped helmet always made him smile. It was a gift from Mistress Raven. She said it was an actual demon skull and it did always make him feel powerful when he wore it, though not as powerful as his new toy. He clenched his right fist, making the heavy leather of his gauntlet crunch. The pentagram on the back of his hand glowed with an inner fire.

When she first gave him the magic glove Iron Skull couldn't believe it. He'd owned and used all sorts of weapons, but a magic flamethrower, how fuckin' awesome was that? There had been a time when he could never have imagined calling anyone master, but serving Mistress Raven had become the single most fulfilling thing he'd ever done. The fact that she usually wanted him to do all the things he liked best anyway helped.

Take this morning. He got a message telling him to off Mort

Call. Skull had no idea who the fuck Mort Call was and he didn't care. She wanted him dead and Skull liked nothing better than killing people, especially now that he had his flamethrower. He'd already come up with a handful of new ways to kill people with it and he was eager to try out his most recent idea. He'd burned that fat prick that ran the computer place to ashes, but that had ended too quick for him to really enjoy it.

Skull straightened his mohawk and adjusted his black leather jacket, trying in vain to look less intimidating. Not that he had anything against killing everyone in the hospital if that's what it took to get Call, but Mistress Raven had made it clear that when she sent him to kill someone, ideally, he would only kill that one person. A massacre drew more attention than she wanted just now.

He checked his appearance in his bike's polished chrome gas cap. Not bad. He smiled, revealing a jumble of crooked yellow teeth. Skull gave his bike an affectionate pat and headed toward the main entrance. The huge, sprawling complex covered half a square mile if you counted the grounds. He'd need directions if he wanted to avoid searching all day for his mark.

Halfway to the door Skull spotted a man in his late fifties carrying a bouquet of flowers coming from his left. That was handy. Skull had almost reached him when the guy looked his way. The suit's eyes went wide then closed the instant Skull's fist sank into his gut. The guy slumped and Skull helped himself to the flowers.

Perfect. Now he really looked like a proper friend making a visit to his ailing buddy. Skull left the barely conscious man curled up in the fetal position and groaning on the sidewalk. What a wuss. Couldn't even take one punch to the gut.

The automatic doors opened at his approach. Inside was a waiting room filled with sick or injured people. A row of nurses sat behind a long desk, each at her own computer station. All but one was helping someone already. Skull ambled up to the free nurse, a dusky-skinned woman with cornrows and too much eye shadow. She flinched when she noticed Skull looking down at her.

He smiled, trying to set her at ease. The way her eyes widened suggested he failed. "I'm here to visit an old friend of mine, Mort Call. Can you tell me which room he's in?"

"One moment, sir." The nurse typed, frowned at her screen, and typed something else. At last she looked up. "I'm sorry, Mr. Call is in police custody and isn't allowed any visitors. If it's any consolation he woke from his coma this morning. The doctors think his chances of recovering are good."

Skull didn't think his chances were so good, and a pair of cops wasn't going to improve them much. At least now he knew why Mistress Raven wanted him dead. If he knew something and had woken up it was only a matter of time before he spilled his guts.

"Maybe I could just go up and drop his flowers off. The cops could look them over and take them into the room. That wouldn't hurt, right?"

The nurse finally smiled. "I suppose not. He's in room 560 in building C."

She gave Skull directions and he set off drawing the gazes of everyone in the waiting room. Building C waited a five-minute walk from the main entrance. He passed doctors, nurses, janitors, and other visitors on his way and without fail they all did a double take when he strode past.

Skull shook his head and stepped into the elevator that would take him to the fifth floor. He didn't look that unusual, did he? He knew a lot of guys with a mohawk and leather jacket. Maybe it was the tattoos. He had a shattered skull pierced with a dagger inked on the side of his neck. It was pretty hardcore. Though he had a trio of nastier ones on his chest.

The elevator chimed and the doors slid open. An older couple took a step back when they saw him inside the elevator. Of all the people he encountered, the elderly seemed to react like that the most consistently. He held the door for them and they scurried in without a word of thanks. So much for the older generation having better manners.

Skull walked to the nearest hall and checked the first room number he came to: 502. At the far end a pair of boys in blue sat in stiff chairs and sipped from paper cups. He grinned and stalked towards them. As he walked, Skull sent his thoughts into the gauntlet, drawing out the fire spirit's power the way Mistress Raven had taught him. When the back of his hand grew warm he knew it was ready.

He was almost to the room when one of the cops hopped to his feet and raised a hand. "I'm sorry, sir. No one is allowed to visit this patient."

"But I brought him flowers." Skull held out the bouquet. "Can't you at least give these to him?"

When the cop was only three feet away Skull lashed out, driving his gauntlet-covered fist into the cop's gut and releasing a blast of fire. Bright orange flames burst out his back and the cop collapsed.

Skull caught him and hurled the dead cop at his still-living partner. The corpse caught the second cop halfway out of his chair. He scrambled to avoid it, but the weight of the body drove him back down.

Skull rushed over, grabbed the living cop's head and poured fire into it. The cop's skull burst like a ripe melon. That was always good for a laugh.

An alarm sounded and sprinklers sprang to life, drenching the hall. Skull stepped into Mort's room and found his target struggling to sit up with his hand cuffed to the bed rail.

Mort stared at him with wide, frightened eyes. "Who are you?"

"No one special."

Skull lunged across the room and slapped his gauntleted hand across Mort's mouth. He called on the magic again, sending flames down the mark's gullet, incinerating his internal organs. When he finished, smoke was literally coming out of Mort's ears.

Skull couldn't stop grinning. That had worked even better than he'd hoped. The only problem was when you burned up their lungs the target couldn't scream. Maybe next time he'd burn up some less vital organs and leave the target to die slowly.

Then again, if Mistress Raven wanted someone kept quiet, letting them die slowly might not be the way to go. Skull would just have to try it on one of his own victims. Maybe he'd grab someone on the way home. The guys would probably enjoy the show, take their minds off Numb getting his dumb ass killed.

Skull left the still-smoking corpse of Mort Call smoldering in his bed and stepped out into the hall. Voices shouted and nurses hustled patients and visitors toward the stairwell. It didn't look like they'd made it this far or noticed the dead cops yet. Skull considered dragging the bodies into Mort's room, but dismissed the idea at once. It would only delay the inevitable by a few minutes at best.

He stepped over the bodies, doing his best to ignore the streams of water plastering his mohawk flat against his head, and headed for the elevator. He pressed the call button, but it didn't light up. Annoyed now, he stabbed it three more times.

"Sir." A big, broad-shouldered orderly in purple scrubs spotted him and walked over. "The elevators are disabled during a fire emergency. You'll have to take the stairs."

"Of course they are." Skull shook his head. That was the problem with hospitals, too safety conscious.

A gasp from the orderly drew Skull's attention back to him. He was staring down the hall at the dead cops. Too bad, he seemed like a nice-enough guy. On the other hand Skull never passed up a chance to use his gauntlet.

The orderly looked away from the bodies just in time to catch a heavy fist to his forehead. At the moment of impact Skull released a burst of fire. The orderly's head exploded in a shower of blood and flames.

Skull grinned. That was the coolest fuckin' thing ever.

A feminine scream from down the hall caught his attention. A pretty redheaded nurse stood trembling, her hands to her mouth, staring at him. He stomped down the hall toward her, ignoring the scattering of people headed for the stairs.

Skull clamped his bare hand around the back of her neck. "Shame you had to see that. Now, we're going to walk out of here together. Give me any trouble and I'll pop your head like a zit, got it?"

She managed a silent nod.

Skull guided her toward the stairwell where they merged with the flow of people coming from the floors above. It wasn't a particularly speedy group considering they were evacuating a fire. Maybe they thought it was just a drill. Of course all the people with canes and walkers didn't hurry things up any.

The faint whine of sirens approaching reached him. Sounded like the fire department was taking it seriously. The sirens also convinced the healthier people to step on it and several jostled Skull in their haste to flee. Remembering Mistress Raven's lecture about self-control, Skull refrained from burning them all to death.

At the bottom of the stairs people were streaming out the nearest door. For his part Skull turned down the hall that led to the main entrance where he'd left his bike.

"Please don't hurt me," the nurse whispered.

Skull loved it when they begged. It made him want to hurt her even more. Looked like he wasn't going to have to grab someone on his way home. He'd just take—Skull glanced down at her name tag—Janice home with him.

The main waiting area had cleared out by the time they arrived. Through the glass doors four cop cars were visible. Each car had a pair of cops behind it pointing their guns at the entrance. How the hell did they know where he was going?

"Where are all the cameras in this dump?" When Janice didn't answer Skull gave her a shake. "Answer me."

"Everywhere." The word came out more of a whimper.

Great, the cops were probably watching him right now. He looked around until he spotted one of the cameras and flipped it off. Skull had hoped to make this a quick in and out, but it looked like he'd get to have a bit more fun before the day was done.

Skull forced Janice directly in front of him and marched her closer to the door so the cops could take a good look. If there was one thing you could count on it was a hostage keeping the boys in blue honest. If they so much as farted in his direction Skull would burn her to death.

"We have you surrounded." Some asshole must have found a bullhorn. "Come out with your hands up."

They always said that. Skull looked down at the now-crying Janice. "Do you think that line ever works?"

"I don't know."

"Me either, but it's not going to work today." Skull pushed her close enough to trigger the automatic doors. "Clear the fuck out of here or Janice is going from the hospital to the morgue."

A little whimper escaped the captive nurse. It was a nice touch, but he doubted the cops heard her.

"There's nowhere you can go," the asshole with the bullhorn said. "Release the girl before someone gets hurt."

Skull shook his head. "These cops need to catch a clue. There're already four dead guys upstairs."

No comment from Janice. She was probably overwhelmed by all the excitement.

Skull raised his gauntleted hand and called the fire. A stream of flame streaked toward the car nearest where he'd left his bike.

The cops behind it scrambled to get clear.

A moment later the gas tank exploded, sending the car up into the air before it came crashing down on its roof. He adjusted his aim and commanded the fire to come forth again.

* * *

Lin led Terra out of the cafe and toward their cars. She really was a remarkable woman, strong, smart and dedicated. If she worked for the police department he would have been delighted to have her for a partner.

Terra took a deep breath and stretched. "So what now?"

"I need to focus on finding the Skulls. I wish I could help you find your missing wizard, but the gang represents a direct threat to the city and so gets priority."

Terra waved off his apology. "I understand. Finding Mercia is the Department's responsibility anyway. What about Conryu? Chief Kane has him basically on lockdown, but that won't last forever. At the very least he'll have to leave his building to start school."

"Knowing Conryu he won't last seven weeks cooped up inside. The truth is, and I'm reluctant to say this after my earlier mistake, I doubt there's an active effort being made to go after Conryu. As far as I can tell Mort acted alone and the incident at the carnival now looks more like an attack of opportunity."

"That suggests if another opportunity should present itself he might still be in danger."

Before Lin could respond his phone rang. "Excuse me."

"Mort Call has been murdered at the hospital along with his guards," the police secretary said.

"What? You're sure?"

"What is it?" Terra asked.

He held up a finger.

"We're sure. The attacker matches the description of one of your gang members. They have him surrounded. Since you're the officer of record for the case they asked me to let you know."

"I'm on my way." Lin disconnected. "We're in luck. One of the Skulls is trapped in Sentinel Central Hospital. The guys are moving in now to apprehend him."

"I'll come with you. If it's the one with the Flame Fist Gauntlet you'll need my help to subdue him."

"Climb in, I'll drive."

They loaded up and Lin took off at full speed, siren blaring. It only took five minutes to reach the hospital. The smoke was visible after three minutes and the flames after four. Lin followed the smoke to the main entrance. Two police cars were burning. Beside the doors a man with a mohawk held a woman hostage. On his right hand he wore a glowing gauntlet.

The biker pointed the gauntlet at a third car. Terra lowered her window and began to chant in a hissing, sibilant language.

A ball of fire shot from the biker's glove.

Terra snapped her fingers and pointed. The fireball fizzled out halfway to the car.

Lin swerved to a stop behind the two intact vehicles. Terra never took her eyes off the biker and never stopped the chanting. She climbed out of the car and marched straight toward him. One of the uniforms rushed to stop her.

"It's okay." Lin waved him off. "She's a government wizard assisting in the investigation."

Terra snapped and pointed again. Lin looked away from the patrolman as the last sparks of the fireball sputtered in the air ten feet from the cars. She took another step forward.

"Don't go too close," the patrolman said. "He's holding a hostage."

Terra stopped moving, but continued chanting in that strange language. A twenty-foot wall of flame roared to life in front of the biker. Even from a distance the heat made Lin flinch.

There was movement then a figure staggered, screaming, through the flames. It was the nurse and her uniform had caught on fire.

"Don't shoot!" Lin shouted. "It's the hostage. Keep your eyes open for the perp."

Terra snapped her fingers a third time and the flames covering the woman vanished. She raised her voice and the cadence of the chant sped up. Terra threw her hands to the side and the wall of flame disappeared.

She blew out a breath and fell silent. Lin rushed to check on the nurse. No sign remained of the biker.

The nurse had first- and second-degree burns on her hands and face, but the damage wasn't anywhere near as bad as it might have been if Terra hadn't been there.

"Are you alright, miss?" Lin asked.

She nodded, tears streaming down her face. "I thought he was going to kill me."

"You're safe now—"

The rest of Lin's words were drowned out by the roar of a motorcycle. He scanned the parking lot and spotted the bike thundering toward the exit.

Two patrol cars blocked the opening, but he raised his glove and twin blasts of fire streaked ahead of him, blowing the vehicles out of his way. The rumble of the motorcycle quickly faded.

An EMT arrived and Lin handed the burned girl over to him with a final pat on her unburned shoulder.

"We have to get after him," Lin said. "This is too good an opportunity to let him slip through our fingers."

"Don't worry." Terra joined him near the burned nurse. "That gauntlet is putting out enough magical energy that I'll have no trouble tracking him. I'll call Clair. We're going to need all the help we can get."

* * *

What a fucking rush! Iron Skull roared down the street, his gauntlet still hot and glowing from all the fire he hurled. He hadn't had that much fun in years. At least until the wizard showed up. She made the fire do what she wanted instead of what he wanted. He hated her more for that than for spoiling his fun. He revved the engine and put on more speed. The people on the sidewalk stared at him and Skull gave them a one-finger salute.

He glanced over his shoulder. No cops. Too bad, Skull would have liked to blow up a few more of their cheap-ass cars. Despite the lack of pursuit, Skull knew he wasn't in the clear yet. Mistress Raven had taught him enough about magic to know that the wizard from the hospital would have no trouble tracking him.

Well fuck her and the cops. Let 'em come. The boys had been itching for a fight since they got to the city last month. Today they were going to get it. Lucky they had plenty of treats stored up for just such an occasion. He turned down a side street toward the rough part of town where his gang had set up shop in an empty flophouse. Empty now anyway. They'd had to gut a handful of bums and pushers when they first arrived, but the locals quickly learned The Black Skulls were no one they wanted to fuck with.

Bloody Skull was standing watch on the front steps of the boarded-up two-story shack when Iron Skull parked in front of the building. He had his trademark blood-red bandana tied around his face and the grip of an automatic pistol poked out of the waistband of his oil-stained jeans. "All finished, boss?"

Iron Skull ignored the question. "Get the boys ready. We're going to have company soon."

"What kind of company?"

"The heavily armed, blue kind. Go on."

Bloody Skull let out a war whoop and ran inside. Of all the gang Bloody was the only one that liked to fight more than Iron Skull. He'd get his fill today, no doubt.

Iron Skull drove around to the rear of the flophouse. Across the street was an empty garage beside a collapsed house. He pulled his bike inside next to the others. To keep the guys busy while they waited for Mistress Raven's orders Iron Skull had them dig a tunnel connecting the basement of the flophouse to the garage. His mistress had been kind enough to use her magic to reinforce the tunnel for them so he wasn't worried about it collapsing during the fight with the cops.

Iron Skull switched his bike off and closed the garage door as far as it would go. Hopefully the cops wouldn't notice the bikes parked inside. He crossed the street and Grim opened the door for him. "We really gonna fight the cops, boss?"

Grim sounded like a five-year-old on Christmas morning, or as much like one as a six-and-a-half-foot-tall, three-hundred-and-fifty-pound bald man covered in tattoos could.

"Damn right. I want you upstairs on The Pig. How many ammo belts we got for it?"

"Ten, I think. That's five thousand rounds, right?" Grim wasn't quite as good at math as a five-year-old.

Iron Skull patted his leather-clad shoulder. "Close enough, Grim. Take Tough and a box of grenades with you."

Grim smiled, revealing his three remaining teeth, and ran off to find Tough and the grenades.

Iron Skull went deeper into the house, ignoring the exposed framing and the stink of beer and piss. They'd stayed in worse places over the years. Not much worse, but a little.

"Boss." Bone Skull emerged from a side door. He was dressed in all black, his long hair slicked back from his face and only one tattoo visible. Bone was the only member of the gang that, if he walked down the street, wouldn't draw a second look. That made him useful, but his brain made him Iron Skull's second in command. On the bed behind him, Iron Skull caught a glimpse of machine guns and boxes of ammunition. "What kind of opposition we looking at?"

"Every cop they can call in and at least one wizard. She's good with fire magic so my glove won't be much use until we take her out."

"Easier said than done. Wizards are tricky to deal with, especially surrounded by cops."

Iron Skull nodded. "We'll just have to hope we get lucky and a stray bullet blows her brains out."

"And if we don't get lucky?"

Iron Skull lowered his voice. "That's what the escape tunnel's for. You and me'll split while the others hold them off. You know once they get started the others will never run."

"Bloody won't, that's for sure."

Overhead, Grim stomped around, getting his machine gun set up. It wouldn't be easy for Grim and Tough to make their way downstairs once the bullets started flying. Iron Skull blew out a snort. Who was he kidding? Once the fighting started it would be a wonder if he could pull himself away from the battle. He never felt more alive than when he was an inch from death.

* * *

Lin led a parade of cop cars and two heavily armored SWAT vehicles down the street. Speakers broadcast a warning to the people staring at the passing motorcade to stay inside and away from windows until the police gave the all clear.

In the seat beside him Terra stared straight ahead, the magical glasses perched on her nose. She'd been guiding them since they left the hospital ten minutes ago. The second Department wizard, Clair, sat on the back seat muttering in a deep, guttural language. Terra had said Clair was skilled in earth magic so that was probably the language she spoke. What the wizard hoped to accomplish he had no idea. The police wizard was busy with a surveillance job and according to the captain couldn't join them.

"Turn left at the next intersection," Terra said. "We're getting close."

A quick look at the neighborhood would have told Lin that even without Terra's warning. He hadn't expected the gang to set up shop in the money district so it was no surprise they'd moved into the roughest part of the city. It made the tenement they'd visited the other day look positively gentrified. This neighborhood would have looked right at home in a southern border town. The only thing missing was a pack of half-human heart hunters.

"Right there." Terra pointed at a two-story house that was still standing only by a miracle of physics.

The roar of a machine gun filled the street. Lin flinched when bullets clattered off the windshield without penetrating. The armored trucks raced ahead, drawing fire and forming a barricade in front of the house. Men and women in body armor carrying machine guns piled out and returned fire.

Something came flying out of the second-story window.

"Grenade!" a SWAT officer shouted.

It exploded just short of the armored vehicle. Shrapnel clattered off the thick steel.

More bullets bounced off the windshield of Lin's car as he maneuvered into the barricade. He slammed it into park as another fusillade of bullets tore through the air. Lin reached for the door handle, but Terra laid a restraining hand on his shoulder.

"Stay in here. Bullets can't penetrate the car."

"Why not?"

Terra nodded toward Clair who was still chanting in the strange language. "She's created a barrier that stops anything made of earth from passing through. Since the bullets are lead..."

"And the grenades?" Lin asked.

"It'll stop the shrapnel, but if one goes off too close it might cause the gas tank to explode."

"Terrific. What now?"

"Depends. Do you want prisoners or do you just want me to stop them as fast as I can?"

Lin shook his head at the bizarre situation he found himself in.

There was a firefight going on just feet away. Bullets were clattering off his car like raindrops. Yet here he was having a calm conversation just like nothing was happening.

Another grenade went off on the other side of the SWAT van.

"A quick decision would be good," Terra said.

"I'm a cop." Lin grasped the steering wheel until his knuckles turned white. "I arrest people. I don't kill them unless I absolutely have to."

Terra looked out the windshield and raised an eyebrow. "You don't think this falls into the latter category?"

What could he say to that? It looked and sounded like a war out there. He should know, he'd fought in one. "Do what you have to."

Terra nodded, her lips set in a grim line. She began to chant in what he now recognized as the language of fire. The words picked up pace and her tone grew louder.

The roof of the flophouse burst into flame. An explosion from the second floor sent a body flying out the window. It landed in the dirt that passed for a front lawn and didn't move.

A second man stood in the now-missing window. SWAT concentrated their fire and he fell beside his companion, riddled with dozens of bullets.

Through it all Terra never stopped her spell. The flames spread from the second floor to the first. Smoke billowed out the windows. The stream of bullets had slowed to a trickle.

The front door slammed open and a man with a red bandana covering his face stumbled out, firing a pair of submachine guns. A dozen rifles spoke as one and he went down in a heap.

"Where's the guy from the hospital?" Lin asked.

Terra stopped her spell. "He's still in there. His gauntlet is holding back my flames. I'm not sure if he's alone or not."

"I'll tell the SWAT team. We're going to have to dig him out."

"No! Tell them to keep their distance. He may be able to stop the flames, but in about a minute that house is going to collapse. We can dig his body out of the rubble."

* * *

Lady Raven smiled as she watched her minions in the makeshift viewing mirror. One by one they fell to the police and her former comrades at the Department of Magic. It hardly seemed fair, two wizards supported by a small army of cops taking on five bikers with a flame gauntlet. It was a shame. The Black Skulls had been useful pawns, but they'd played their part and like all pawns, there came a time when a sacrifice was necessary. They were loose ends and they needed to be snipped.

It was an interesting, voyeuristic experience, listening to her servants' thoughts as they came to realize they had no hope of winning. Lady Raven had always been closely attuned to dark magic and she fed on despair and negative emotions. She focused her will on Iron Skull and settled in to watch the show.

Iron Skull coughed and raised his gauntlet. He'd stopped the flames from reaching them, but not the smoke. The silence from upstairs announced the deaths of Grim and Tough. Beside him Bone had his sleeve over his face, trying to filter the fumes. By the front door Bloody was still blasting away between coughs.

The rafters crunched above them. "We gotta go, boss," Bone said.

Iron Skull hated running, but he couldn't deny his lieutenant's grasp of the situation. "Bloody! Time to go."

"Fuck that! I'm not running from these pigs." Bloody roared and charged out the door, a gun in each hand.

The roar of gunfire quickly went silent. So much for Bloody. Iron Skull headed for the little closet that disguised their escape tunnel. He ripped the door off and threw it aside.

His concentration faltered and the flames rushed closer. Iron Skull snarled and mentally commanded them to retreat. The fire obeyed, but like a hungry lion swirled around at the edge of his control, eager to devour him at a moment's notice.

"Go, Bone. I'm right behind you."

That surprised Lady Raven. She'd figured Iron Skull would toss his man aside to get through the tunnel first. You found loyalty in the oddest places. Shame she hadn't had more time to discover Iron Skull's hidden depths.

The house shook and rumbled as a portion of the roof collapsed. Bone disappeared down the tunnel and Iron Skull leapt in behind him. The dirt walls still looked solid. Ahead of him Bone belly-crawled like mad toward the bikes.

A tremor ran through the walls and dirt clattered off Iron Skull's head. His breathing sped up as he tried to reach Bone. He needed to stay calm. Mistress Raven's magic wouldn't fail them.

Lady Raven laughed out loud at Iron Skull's faith in her magic. If the biker had any idea what she planned he would have taken his chances with the police. Of course, Lady Raven knew he wouldn't. Psychopaths like Iron Skull weren't capable of giving up as long as they thought they had another option. That's why she'd agreed to help them with their stupid tunnel. It was an insurance policy.

One of the police outside knocked on the cheap motel door. "Everything okay, ma'am?"

Her guards must have heard her laughing. "Yeah, just watching a movie. Thanks."

Bone had almost reached the exit when Lady Raven returned her attention to the image in the mirror. She spoke a single harsh word in Infernal, canceling the earth magic she'd used to reinforce the tunnel. It shuddered and collapsed, crushing her pawns and burying them all in one go. The police should thank her for sparing them the trouble of a funeral. Another short spell severed her link with the bikers and caused the small hidden tattoos on their necks to vanish, eliminating any trace of their connection to her. If all went according to plan the investigation should come to a dead end, freeing her to move on with the next phase of the plan.

* * *

The flophouse collapsed with a resounding crash. The moment it did Terra spoke a short phrase and the fire extinguished and the embers cooled. Behind her Clair fell silent. The fight had been fierce, but short. They had the bikers outnumbered and overwhelmed in terms of both magic and weapons. The confrontation ended the only way possible. It all seemed like such a waste. What had the thugs hoped to accomplish?

Lin climbed out and Terra and Clair joined him. He looked over his car and shook his head. "Not a scratch on it."

Clair raised an eyebrow. "You sound disappointed."

"Maybe a little. A few bullet holes would have been a good excuse to ask for a new car. This one's on its last legs."

"I'll remember that the next time we're in a firefight," Clair said.

"I'm not complaining." Lin waved his hands.

"Hey, Lin?" One of the SWAT team members jogged over. Judging from the bars on his arm he was the team commander. "If you feel the scene's secure my guys are ready to go."

Lin glanced at Terra. She closed her eyes and cast a simple light magic spell. There was nothing living in the rubble. "We're good. It's a recovery mission now."

"You heard the lady." Lin and the SWAT leader shook hands. "Thanks, John. You're the best."

John jumped into the back of the SWAT van and a moment later they rolled out. The side of the van was pocked with bullet holes and slashed from shrapnel, but none of it had gone through to the interior. They really built those things tough. Terra slipped her glasses on and found a faint magical aura around both vans. Magical reinforcement helped too.

"Are you two going to hang around?" Lin asked. "Cleaning this mess'll take a while. We'll need to bring the bomb squad down along with some heavy equipment."

"I need to find the fire gauntlet and whatever they had hidden in that niche at the cafe. Until those items are secured a wizard needs to be on the scene."

"I'll head back to the office and inform Chief Kane," Clair said.

Terra nodded and Lin said, "I'll get an officer to take you."

While Lin got one of the uniformed officers to take Clair back to the office, Terra walked over to the collapsed building and muttered, "Reveal."

When nothing immediately popped out at her she slipped the glasses on to magnify the energy. There was a very weak lingering dark aura that matched the energy from the cafe. Those coffers must have been here either before or after they were taken to the hidden storage niche.

She also picked up a stronger fire aura, but not as strong as she would have expected if the gauntlet was buried under the rubble. Terra traced it to the edge of the ruined house where it vanished. Frowning, she walked all the way around the perimeter of the house and found no energy signature strong enough to be the gauntlet. Even under the rubble it should have glowed like a light bulb to her magical senses.

Terra returned to the last place she saw the magical energy. She stood facing the street. It was headed that way when it vanished. Did the biker from the hospital have some sort of suppressing container? There was no way to know without digging down to the body. She'd just have to be patient.

Lin joined her as the patrolmen began setting a perimeter with yellow tape. "I called in the cleanup crews. It'll take days to sift the rubble and deal with any unexploded ordinance. I don't suppose there's any magic that could speed the process along?"

"Despite what some of the more arrogant wizards like to pretend, there are limits to what magic can do. I'm afraid you'll have to sort this out the mundane way. I'd appreciate it if you started right there." She pointed at the last place she sensed the gauntlet.

"Considering everything you've done for us since this investigation began I think we can accommodate your request." Lin grinned. "After all, we have to start somewhere."

7
PARTY CRASHERS

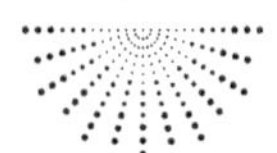

"The wizards killed Mort, just like Black Bird said they would." Michael paced in the close quarters of the tiny apartment that served as the official church of the True Face of God. The four other members of his congregation watched his agitated movements with bright, eager eyes. They knew, as he knew, that the time for their glorious retribution was nigh. "For that heinous act God will punish them. He will punish them through our hands."

"Amen!" Gabriel raised his hands in praise. Brother Gabriel was always the most demonstrative of his little congregation. He'd lost his job as a demolition worker when the company switched to using magical constructs to pull down derelict buildings. For safety, they claimed, but everyone knew the truth. The wizards had enchanted the weak-willed suits into doing what they wanted.

"Though he wasn't a member of our congregation, Brother Call was still a fellow traveler on the true path. As a sign of our faith and to honor our fallen brother we will finish the good work he started. We will kill the boy wizard before his powers can be unlocked and his soul condemned to Hell for all eternity. Though it may cost him his life we can still save him from damnation. It's our duty."

That brought smiles to the faces of men eager to do God's work. These were good men, strong both in body and in faith. They couldn't fail, especially since Black Bird told them everything they needed to know, both when and how to best accomplish their noble mission.

"Brother John." Michael focused his intense gaze on the youngest member of their group, a man of only nineteen years who'd been denied his rightful place at college due to the foul influences of magic. "Did you bring the item?"

John reached into the pocket of his ragged army surplus jacket and pulled out a small device with a screen and several buttons. Michael wasn't a technical person, his skills lay in a more divine direction, but Brother John worked at an electronics store and had a gift for cobbling together technology.

"Are you sure this is right? I felt bad about stealing the components from my boss."

Michael bent down and stared into John's watery brown eyes. "We're doing God's work, son. There can be no crime while we're acting in his name. Will it work?"

"Yes, sir. I tested it with my phone and it blocked the signal from several hundred yards and weakened it for a third of a mile."

Michael clapped the youth on his bony shoulder. "Good man. I knew I could count on you."

John puffed up at the compliment and sat up straighter. He'd do what was necessary. Michael saw it in his eyes.

"Brother Jacob." Michael turned to the oldest member of the group, a still-spry sixty-year-old who ran a pawn shop and found the True Face of God after surviving a brush with cancer. "Did you bring the weapons?"

"Sure did, though a stranger collection of gear I never seen." Jacob unzipped a green duffle bag and laid the weapons on Michael's battered coffee table. First came a baseball bat, then a pair of chef's knives, a three-pound sledgehammer, and last a wrecking bar. "How come we can't just take guns? I have plenty of them at the shop."

"The wizard's vile magic protects the building. Black Bird says only weapons that are also tools can pass through." Michael made the sign of the cross and spoke a prayer in Latin. "With God's blessing these humble implements will see his task complete."

Ezra snatched up the baseball bat. Heavyset and balding, Ezra had seen some rough years before he found his way to Michael and the church. He caressed the grip of the bat. "I was the star shortstop in high school. Feels good to hold a bat again."

Michael smiled and folded his hands together. "It will feel even better when you use it to send the heathen to meet his maker. Take up your weapons, brothers. We go to do God's work."

The congregation left Michael's apartment and piled into his white panel van. He settled in behind the wheel and turned the key. The starter whined and refused to catch. He paused and looked to heaven. "Dear Lord, if you wish us to complete your divine work please make this useless pile of metal start up."

He tried the key again and with a little divine intervention the motor sputtered to life. The guys gave a round of Hallelujahs and Michael pulled out. They drove through the streets, watching the people go about their business, indifferent to the blasphemies surrounding them. That would all change tonight when they announced the abomination's death on the evening news.

Fifteen minutes later they parked in the garage under the wizard's building. There were only a few cars at this time of day so they had no trouble getting a spot close to the elevator. Though Michael had no intention of retreating it always paid to be careful.

"Are you sure we should be doing this in the middle of the day?" John asked.

"Of course." Michael raised his fist. "We will bring judgment in the bright light of day."

"Besides," Jacob said. "Everybody's at work right now. Fewer people to call the police before we finish our work."

"That too." Michael slammed the transmission into park and they climbed out of the van. "Brother John, up to the roof. Call us when you're in position and you're ready to activate the device."

"Yes, Michael." The young man scurried into the elevator and pressed the button for the roof.

When he'd gone Ezra said, "Shame the kid's going to miss the important work."

"John has a gentle soul." Michael pulled his knife and tested the edge. "He would be a liability to us in a fight."

"Ain't going to be no fight." Gabriel slapped the wrecking bar into the palm of his hand making a meaty smack. "It's going to be a slaughter."

* * *

Conryu closed the big book of boring magic and banged his head on the cover. He'd been reading at the dining room table in an effort to keep from falling asleep. It had been a week since he began his house arrest and Conryu finally finished the stupid book.

Much as he might complain, if you looked past the mystic mumbo jumbo it appeared magic was nothing more than a system of energy manipulation that you altered to create the effects you wanted. As long as he looked at it that way he found he could wrap his head around it pretty well. The problem was whoever wrote the book liked to couch everything in supernatural terms instead of just saying straight out what she meant.

The alarm on his phone rang and Conryu glanced at the clock. Eleven exactly. Jonny and Rin were supposed to have lunch with him and Maria. Mrs. Kane had gone out of town for a job so they were all going to watch the opening match of the Four Nations

Magical Tournament together in Conryu's apartment. It wasn't like he could go anywhere.

Maria didn't think much of the North American team this year. Conryu had no idea if the team was any good, all he knew was this was Heather James's last year and the blond team captain was one of the hottest women he'd ever seen. He'd have to be careful not to drool or Maria would give him a smack.

Conryu collected the bag of chips and fresh salsa his mom had picked up for him and spread them out on the living room table. The others were supposed to bring sandwich fixings and more snacks. Five minutes later his doorbell rang. Maria was waiting on the other side with rolls and deli meat. "I'm the first to arrive?"

He grinned. "Yup, though you had the shortest trip. I finally finished the stupid book."

"But did you understand it?" Maria slipped inside.

"I think I understand the principles, how the various types of energy interact, that sort of thing. What I can't figure out is why people who wield certain types of energy wouldn't get along."

"It's not that the people don't get along, it's that the energy doesn't combine well with its direct opposite." Maria put the meat in the fridge and the rolls on the counter. "Some wizards also have a tendency to get mixed up in the politics of elemental spirits which can lead to arguments as well. Those who specialize in one type of magic tend to view the world through the lens of that magical philosophy and it colors everything else. It's stupid on a lot of levels, but then wizards aren't so different than any other group of people."

Conryu sighed, still not really getting it. "It sounds sort of like the arguments Harley guys and Indian guys have."

"That's as good an analogy as any. When are the others supposed to arrive?"

"Any time now." Someone knocked. "Speak of the devil."

Conryu was surprised Jonny arrived first. He figured if anyone would arrive early it would be Rin. Jonny had a cooler with him, hopefully stocked with soda. "Hey, bro. Did I miss anything?"

"Nope, we've got ten minutes before the start. What'd you bring?"

"Root beer, cola, and mineral water for the ladies."

"Bless your heart, Jonny Salazar," Maria said in an over-the-top southern accent.

The boys shared a laugh at that. Maria's phone rang and while she talked Conryu and Jonny broke into the chips and salsa. A few seconds later Maria joined them on the couch.

"Who was it?" Conryu asked.

"Rin. She can't make it, her little brother's sitter had to go home early. It's weird, my phone cut off in the middle of our conversation."

Conryu shrugged. That happened now and then. No big deal. Since Rin wasn't coming they fixed themselves some sandwiches and settled in.

The announcer came on the tv. "Ladies and gentlemen, welcome to the 567th annual Four Nations Tournament. This year's odds-on favorite is the Empire of the Rising Sun's team with four seniors and two juniors returning to compete."

"Who do you like?" Maria asked.

"Heather James," Conryu and Jonny answered together.

He thought maybe that wasn't the wisest answer an instant before she smacked him on the back of the head. The blow didn't surprise him in the least, but it still stung. "I meant which team. All the guys and many of the girls like Heather James. I read online she's got a modeling contract waiting for her after she graduates."

That surprised Conryu less than the slap. "I don't know. If the Alliance doesn't have a chance I guess I should root for the Empire, since that's where Dad comes from."

"Yeah, that's who I'm going for," Maria said.

"I've got twenty bucks on the Kingdom," Jonny said.

The camera shifted to the arena floor and they stopped talking. There were no seats since the people monitoring the event didn't allow a live audience on the off chance a spell went out of control. Outside the arena dozens of lounges had been built with large-screen tvs, bars and restaurants for the patrons, and plenty of gambling halls.

The tournament was being held in the Republic of Australia this year, though no one gave their team much chance of success. A group of girls stood at each of the cardinal directions. They wore robes associated with their element and school patches on the back.

"What are they starting with this year?" Conryu asked.

"Group casting. It's the trickiest discipline and requires the most teamwork." Maria took a bite of her sandwich.

That was one of the last chapters Conryu had read and he hadn't fully understood it. Something about layering spells so opposing energies didn't come into contact.

The Empire team and Australian team moved to the edge of the arena leaving the Alliance to face off with the Kingdom of the Isles team in the first match. Five members of the Alliance team raised their hands. Heather took the lead, chanting a spell, her blue-green robe swirling around her, outlining the exquisite figure underneath as the power built. She was stunning, like someone out of a story.

"Oh man," Jonny groaned.

Maria glared at him then shifted her gaze to Conryu. He kept his expression neutral, barely.

A water dragon appeared above her. Next it was wrapped in a skin of swirling energy by the wind mage, followed by scales of fire and spikes of earth. Last the light mage cast a spell, but nothing happened.

"Did her magic not work?" Conryu asked.

"It worked," Maria said. "Light magic can interact with all four elements. She used her spell to bind the construct into a complete whole. The results aren't visible, but they're probably the most important if the team wants to win."

"What now?"

"Just watch," Maria said.

A single member of the Kingdom team stepped forward. She wore a black robe and carried a rod tipped with some sort of round black gem. She chanted in a language both guttural and entrancing. Conryu had never heard anything like it. Those strange words spoke to him, called him. He leaned closer, his food forgotten.

Beside him Maria shivered and set her snack down. On the screen, power gathered around the gem, throwing off black sparks. The chant built to a crescendo. With the final word the wizard in black thrust the rod at the dragon construct.

An orb of dark energy streaked toward the dragon. It crashed into the stone spikes, smashed through the fire scales, shredded the wind skin and exposed inside the watery center, blowing the construct to shards of energy.

"Told you they were going to lose." Maria hugged herself and tried to act like nothing had happened.

For his part Conryu couldn't get those words out of his mind. He wanted to hear more.

The match went to commercial and a few seconds later someone knocked. "I thought you said Rin wasn't coming?"

"That's what she told me. Maybe something happened."

Conryu shrugged and walked to the door. He looked through the peephole and saw the familiar mass of white hair. He groaned and opened the door. "Can't you take a hint?"

"Sorry, my boy," the professor said. "I just thought you might li—"

"Die, abomination!"

Conryu looked down the hall. Four men carrying an assortment of improvised weapons roared out of the elevator and charged.

Conryu grabbed the professor and yanked him inside before bolting the door. "We've got company!"

* * *

Lady Raven booted up her laptop and logged in to the secure forum using a proxy server. After a few days the tiny motel room had grown confining. It would be a relief when the police finally completed their work and let her go.

She'd sent the zealots all the information they needed to infiltrate the building and kill the boy the day before yesterday. It hadn't been difficult to determine when Shizuku Kane would be out of the city and the rest was simply understanding how the building's wards functioned—child's play for a wizard of her skill.

The question was did the cultists have the courage of their convictions, or were they nothing but talk? Hopefully the death of their compatriot would properly motivate them. If that didn't do it she didn't know what would.

There was a single private message waiting for Black Bird. She smiled and clicked on it. The cultists were attacking today a little before noon. She checked the time. Quarter after eleven. She had to hurry.

She tossed the laptop on the bed and stood up. The only mirror in her piddling little room was in the bathroom. Not ideal, but it would work. She stepped into the cramped bathroom and locked the door behind her. She doubted the cops outside would barge in on her, but why risk it?

A wind spell linked the mirror to a minor spirit and sent it soaring out over the city. What it saw appeared on the mirror. After a number of scouting runs she knew exactly where Conryu's building lay and how to get there. Her will guided the spirit and soon the roof of the building came into view. A young man stood there with a small device in his hand. That had to be the cell scrambler she told them to bring.

Excellent, the attack was either already underway or soon would be. She commanded the spirit to remain in place and chanted another spell. Though Lady Raven preferred to use shadow beasts for jobs like this, the bright daylight rendered that impossible.

Fortunately, sunlight didn't bother actual demons in the least and she knew the true names of two that would like nothing better than to have a chance to rend the flesh from a foolish mortal. Not that the other demons she'd dealt with over the years didn't enjoy a bit of rending. It seemed to be one of the prime pastimes in Hell.

With the wind spirit serving as a focus Lady Raven opened a small portal above the building and called the names of her hunters. The black-winged demons hurtled through the gate, eager to answer her call.

They plummeted toward the cultist on the roof. Their bloodlust washed over her through the spell that connected them. Her face flushed and her fingers curled like claws. Nothing would have pleased her more in that moment than to feel the man's blood oozing through her talons.

She clenched her fists. "No."

Lady Raven refused to let the demons overwhelm her.

The hunters continued their descent. They'd reach the cultist in moments. If they damaged the signal disrupter her true prey might call for help.

"No!"

The demons pulled up short and soared away. Their rage at being denied prey flooded through the link. She forced the feelings away. The demons obeyed her, not the other way around. If she didn't maintain control of herself and of them it would lead to a bloodbath. No bad thing in and of itself, but not what she desired at the moment.

She formed an image of Conryu in her mind and thrust it into the demons' brains through their link, along with an unspoken threat that if they let him escape it would be the end of them. The hunters shrieked their anger to the heavens, but it did nothing to affect her will.

She commanded. They obeyed. Period.

* * *

"Dude, what's going on?"

A heavy blow struck the door before he could answer Jonny's question. A second blow struck and the tip of a crowbar appeared through the wood.

"That door won't hold them long." Conryu turned to the trembling professor. "Do you know those guys?"

"We rode up on the elevator together. I didn't notice the weapons."

Another crash rattled the door.

Jonny and Maria were both on their feet and looking more than a little worried. Conryu didn't blame them. How many times did someone have to try and kill you before it became routine?

Maria whipped her phone out and dialed. She shook her head. "No signal."

"Try the landline. Jonny, help me push the couch against the door."

The boys ran behind the couch and shoved it until the far end hit the door frame.

"No dial tone!" Maria slammed the receiver back down.

"What should I do?" the professor asked.

"Stay out of the way." Conryu brushed past him and went to Maria. "I didn't think you could bring weapons into this building."

"You can't."

A resounding crash blasted one of the panels out of the door.

"Really?"

A face appeared in the opening. It was a man in his late thirties with a full beard and wild, crazy eyes. "Give us the abomination and the rest of you will be spared."

"Eat shit!" Jonny shouted.

The man snarled and withdrew. A moment later the pounding resumed.

"We've got a minute, maybe two." Conryu looked around, but the only weapons were kitchen knives. Hardly ideal. "We'll have to take the fire escape."

"You're not supposed to leave the building," Maria said.

"Inside's looking as lot less safe than it did yesterday." Conryu led the way to his parents' bedroom where the fire escape attached to the building.

Maria dragged on his arm. "The wizard might have sent them in to flush you out. Who knows what kind of monster might be waiting outside."

Conryu went straight to the window and pulled it open. "I'll take my chances with potential monsters over sure-thing murderers." He motioned her through, then the professor and Jonny. Conryu climbed out last and slammed the window shut. It wouldn't even slow a crowbar, but maybe one of those assholes would cut himself.

A hideous shriek was followed by a...something, slamming into an invisible wall inches from the railing. It had black wings like a crow; long, thin limbs that ended in curved talons; and a fang-filled mouth that took up half its face.

Jonny scrambled away from the creature and pressed his back against the building. "What the hell is that?"

"A demon!" Maria and the professor shouted.

A second creature almost identical to the first slammed into the barrier. Three-inch claws scrabbled against thin air as it tried to reach them. Maria shot him her patented *I told you so* look.

"Up or down?" Conryu shouted over the screams of the demons.

"Down," Maria answered without a moment's thought.

"Go, Jonny. I'll bring up the rear."

Conryu didn't have to tell his friend twice. Jonny's sneakers clanged on the metal steps as he ran down them. The professor followed at a slower, but still hurried pace. Maria looked back at him, her eyes wide. He squeezed her shoulder and gave her a little nudge toward the steps.

She'd barely moved when the sledgehammer crashed through the window, missing Conryu by inches. He snapped a kick that caught the guy's wrist as it swung past. He didn't connect cleanly, but he knocked the attacker off balance so he fell halfway out the window and lost his grip on his weapon.

When hands grabbed the attacker's belt to help pull him out of the way Conryu ran for it. Maria had cleared the first landing, giving him a clear path. He bounded down the steps four at a time, catching up with the others in seconds.

"What do we do when we hit the ground?" Conryu asked when he reached Maria. A few feet away the demons soared back and forth, just waiting for them to leave the protection of Mrs. Kane's wards.

"Hug the wall. It looks like Mom's wards extend about three feet from the wall. As long as we stay in that safe zone the demons can't reach us."

"You hear that, Jonny?"

"Loud and clear, bro."

Conryu started to ask the professor, but the old man was busy gagging and tossing his lunch over the railing. The demons lunged for him, but Conryu managed to jerk him back to safety.

"Careful. You don't want to die before you can prove your theory, do you?"

The professor coughed and wiped his mouth. "I'm not used to this much exercise. Even in my youth I preferred the vicarious thrills of a good book."

The heavy tread of boots on metal announced the pending arrival of their unwelcome guests.

"Suck it up, Professor. We need to move." Conryu gave him a gentle shove towards Jonny who'd stopped and looked back. "Keep him moving."

Jonny nodded and grabbed Angus by the wrist, half encouraging and half dragging him along. Conryu and Maria followed as closely as they dared.

Conryu glanced up. There were only two guys behind them. The others must have gone around to cut them off. Only three more floors and they'd reach the pavement. Should he stand and fight when their numbers were divided? It would be tricky fighting armed men given the space limitations.

They reached the final landing and Conryu still didn't know what to do. "Any thoughts?"

"We just need to hold out a little while longer," Maria said. "Mom would have sensed it the moment those demons struck her barrier. She'll call Dad and he'll send help."

"How long?"

She shook her head. "Maybe ten minutes."

"Shit!" Ten minutes surrounded by demons and lunatics might as well be ten hours.

Ahead of them Jonny had the professor smushed up flat against the wall. "Dude, which way?"

Behind them a broad-shouldered guy in his thirties carrying a crowbar started down the ladder to the ground. The nut with the sledgehammer stood on the platform above. Conryu stepped back, set himself, and lashed out with a side kick that struck between the ladder rungs.

The force of the blow sent Crowbar Man flying out into the alley between his building and the one next door. He landed with a dull thud. When the demons didn't immediately fly down and rip him to pieces it confirmed what Maria had guessed. The killers and the demons were working together.

"Head for the garage," Maria said. "At least we'll be safe from the demons."

* * *

At least they'll be safe from the demons. For some reason, as they ran through the almost-empty garage, that thought kept running through Conryu's head. He had the professor by one arm, Jonny had the other and between them they almost carried him. It would be hours before anyone returned home from work. Ninety percent of the residents worked for the government and came and went on the same schedule as his mother.

The professor stumbled and fell to the concrete. "I can't take another step." He held his head between his knees and gasped for breath.

Conryu looked around, but there was nowhere to hide. They'd intentionally run away from the elevator on the assumption that the other killers would be around there somewhere. They'd gotten a small lead on the two that followed them down the fire escape and lost them when they ducked into the garage.

He'd explored the building with Maria when they were kids, but his brain had frozen. There had to be somewhere to hide until the cavalry arrived. He shot Maria a pleading look. She shook her head.

"What now, dude?"

Why did Jonny keep asking that? Conryu had no idea what to do next. Running for their lives was the best he could come up with upstairs and he hadn't thought up anything better yet. Unfortunately the professor was blown and running was no longer an option, unless they were willing to leave the helpless old man to the tender mercies of a group of deranged killers. Conryu didn't especially like the professor, but he couldn't leave him to die.

"Conryu." Maria's voice held a hint of hope and when he looked where she pointed he grinned.

"I love you, you know that?"

He'd completely overlooked the fire hose hanging behind a

glass door on the wall. That thing shot water with enough force to strip the paint off a car. He'd seen it used when a rusty, piece of crap hatchback had caught fire his junior year.

Conryu crouched down in front of the professor. "Climb aboard."

With Jonny's help he maneuvered the professor onto his back and carried him piggyback out of the way. He lowered Angus to the ground and leaned him against the wall. Maria crouched beside him and nodded that she'd look after him.

Jonny smashed the glass out and yanked the hose free. The tread of heavy boots and shouts echoing through the garage hastened them along.

"You want to aim or work the valve?" Conryu asked.

"Aim. I owe these bitches a bath."

Conryu grinned and handed his friend the brass nozzle. They bumped fists and Conryu went back to the round valve. He gave the valve a test twist and found it free and ready to go.

And not a moment too soon. All four guys rounded the corner, spotted them, and charged.

Conryu spun the valve all the way open and a moment later a gusher blasted out, hitting the nearest man in the chest and sending him sprawling. Jonny wrestled the powerful flow into the big guy with the hammer, knocking him to the ground as well.

The bucking hose was giving Jonny all he could handle so Conryu grabbed it a few feet behind his friend to stabilize his aim. Between the two of them they washed the killers down the garage until they were out of range.

The four men scrambled to their feet and looked intent on charging straight into the stream a second time. Conryu hoped they were that stupid.

One of them wasn't. The man with the beard that wanted Conryu to turn himself over grabbed the others and held them back. He pulled out a walkie-talkie and spoke into it. Conryu tensed, ready for whatever they planned next. And where was the backup Maria had assured him would be on the way?

What he wasn't ready for was the water flow to come to a sudden stop. He glanced back, but the mechanism looked fine. Something must have happened somewhere else. Conryu had no idea where the main shutoff was, but apparently someone had found it.

The bearded man brandished a chef's knife and the killers stalked forward. "No more of your tricks, monster. God has decreed that you must die, just like every magic using abomination in this corrupt world. If you don't resist I promise you a quick end."

Conryu bared his teeth. If this prick thought he'd just stand by and let his throat be cut he didn't know who he was talking to. "Let go of the nozzle and move back. I need some room," he whispered.

Jonny looked at the heavy brass nozzle then back at Conryu with a knowing smile. "Fuck 'em up." He moved back beside Maria and the professor, giving Conryu a good fifteen feet of clear space, plenty for what he had planned.

Apparently the boss killer misunderstood. "Your friend has abandoned you, just as God has. You are alone in the world. Kill him."

A middle-aged man with a baseball bat sauntered toward him, looking far more confident than he had any right to. Conryu waited until he was about twenty feet away then he set the hose to spinning. He built up momentum until the killer closed to within ten feet then he let it fly.

The brass nozzle hit the idiot square in the face with the force of a cannonball. Teeth and blood flew everywhere. His nose crushed flat and the front of his face caved in. The bat clattered to the floor followed in short order by the man that had been holding it.

Conryu snapped the nozzle back and set it spinning again. The three killers still conscious and on their feet shared a considerably less confident look. The older man with the crowbar didn't worry Conryu. The long chunk of iron looked far too heavy for him to handle in a fight. The big guy with the sledgehammer was another matter. He held his weapon easily, like someone with long familiarity.

"Come on, boys," Conryu said. "Say a prayer and step right up. See if God is inclined to turn aside my weapon."

The leader looked at the big guy who looked right back, clearly in no hurry to have his face smashed in. Conryu almost wished they'd charge. He couldn't keep the nozzle spinning forever.

The leader pulled his walkie-talkie out again. Conryu felt pressure building in the hose and had just time enough to toss it aside before it went berserk, spraying water every which way and thrashing like a beheaded snake. Looked like the boss had more brains than Conryu had first thought.

The three killers charged. Conryu did the last thing he figured they'd expect: he ran right toward the big guy with the hammer.

The hammerhead came right at his skull. Conryu slid under the attack. His opponent used too much power and lost his balance. Conryu gave him an uppercut to the groin. He didn't care how big the guy was, that would put him out of commission for a while.

Hammer Man's pained, high-pitched squeal was music to Conryu's ears. Even sweeter was the sound of the sledgehammer hitting the concrete floor.

He snatched up the weapon, whirled, and hurled it at the cultist with the crowbar as hard as he could.

The heavy steel hammerhead crashed into the unfortunate killer's left thigh. His leg bent at an impossible angle as his femur shattered from the impact. Conryu turned his cool regard on the leader. He narrowed his eyes and locked gazes with the man like his father had taught him.

Conryu strode forward, ignoring the moans and groans of the

injured men. "You're all alone now. Unless you expect God to show up and save you. Me? I wouldn't count on it."

"You won't shake my faith, abomination. Even if I fall here, I do so secure in the knowledge that I served my God until the end." The leader laid the chef's knife along his forearm and beckoned Conryu forward.

Looked like this one knew how to use a blade at least. Conryu took a step.

"Watch out, bro!"

Conryu ducked in time to see Jonny come flying past. The bat he'd picked up from the unconscious killer crashed into the leader's head and sent him to the ground.

Jonny raised the bat for another stroke, but Conryu caught his wrist. "Fight's over. Thanks."

Jonny's breath rasped and the muscles in his jaw bunched. It looked like a huge effort for him to lower the bat. Conryu gently took it out of his hands before he let go of his friend's wrist.

Conryu kicked the knife away from the unconscious leader. The fight was over, he reminded himself. They were safe for the moment. He didn't know about the next moment, but for now Conryu would take what he could get.

8

A PARTING CLUE

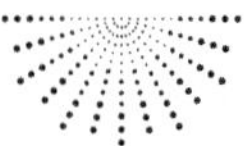

Lin parked in front of the motel the police department used as a safe house. It was nothing fancy, just a cheap, two-story affair with maybe thirty rooms. While it wasn't luxury, Lin had made sure the place was clean and secure. He owed Lacy that much for her help.

A full day had passed since the most recent attempt on Conryu's life. The bomb techs were still searching the ruins of the bikers' base and it looked like they'd need several more days before the excavators started to dig. How many times was he going to answer a call saying the boy had been attacked, show up, and scrape a bunch of idiot cultists off the ground? You'd think if Conryu laid out enough of them the rest would take a hint and find another target. Of course that would be rational behavior, not the sort of thing you thought of where zealots were involved.

In addition to the continued attacks, Lieutenant Smith of the bomb squad had announced an additional delay to the excavation of the flophouse. When he made that announcement Lin had feared Terra might turn him into a frog, assuming wizards could actually do that. When she'd calmed down he'd dropped her off at her car with a promise to call as soon as they got the all clear.

Apparently unable to leave it alone for two or three days she'd called this morning and asked to take another look around.

Two uniformed officers, a big white guy and a skinny black guy, sat in cheap folding chairs on either side of the door to room 1B. They jumped to their feet the moment they recognized Lin.

He climbed out of his car, flashed his badge more out of habit than necessity, and knocked on the door. A moment later Lacy's purple hair appeared in the gap in the doorway. "Hi, Detective."

She closed the door, undid the safety chain, and opened it all the way. She had a cheap white motel robe tied around her. Poor girl looked exhausted. "Miss Winn, may I came in?"

"Always so polite." She stepped aside. "Welcome to my humble home."

Lin stepped inside and she closed the door behind him. Humble was certainly the word for her room. Single bed, night-stand, cheap tv on a cheaper table. If that bed felt as hard as it looked it was no wonder she had circles under her eyes.

"What brings you by?" Lacy asked.

"I've come to set you free." He reached into his jacket pocket and pulled out a plane ticket. "One way to Central City, as promised. Your information was a huge help. Consider your record clean. If you want to get dressed and pack I can take you to the airport."

She hugged him. "That's awesome, Detective. Just give me fifteen minutes."

He left the room and she shut the door. From another pocket Lin removed a folded-over packet of papers. "You guys have been reassigned. Thanks for looking after her."

The officers on duty each accepted a bundle. "Our pleasure, Detective," the black officer said.

"Yeah, though many more days of this and I'd have gone into a coma," the white officer added. "Not that the girl was any trouble, just the opposite, we hardly heard a peep out of her."

Since Lin had been shot at and nearly roasted to death he

wasn't overly interested in their complaints. "I'm sure the duty officer will find something more exciting for you to do."

The officers piled into their vehicle and left the parking lot. Lin watched them until they'd gone out of sight. Maybe he could coax someone into giving him a boring case once he'd tied this one up.

Lacy emerged from her room having exchanged her robe for ripped jeans and a tank top. A green army surplus bag dangled from her shoulder. She was awfully skinny. Maybe he should offer to stop at a diner on the way to the airport.

"All set?"

"Yup."

Lin opened the passenger-side door for her. She smiled and shook her head before tossing her bag in the back seat and climbing in. Lin joined her and fired up the car. It was only fifteen minutes to the airport and they had plenty of time before Lacy's flight took off.

"Do you want to stop for something to eat on the way?" he asked.

"That's sweet, but I already had something this morning. You've been great and all, don't think I don't appreciate that, but I'm ready to blow this town."

Lin smiled. "Fair enough. Want to hear how we found your bikers? They're all dead so I can tell you."

"Thanks anyway. It's all above my pay grade. There is one thing I'm curious about. Did you ever catch up to my boss? That prick still owes me a week's pay."

"I'm afraid not. He probably spotted us at the cafe and took off. We have his picture out everywhere. It's only a matter of time until we find him."

"Maybe you could rough him up a little for me."

Lin laughed. They spent the rest of the ride in amiable silence until he pulled up at the busy main gate. Lacy jumped out then reached back for her bag.

"Are you meeting someone in the capital?" Lin asked.

"I have a sister there. I'll call her before my flight takes off. Thanks again, Detective."

Lacy shut the car door, waved, and ran toward the terminal. Lin blew out a sigh, said a silent prayer that she'd be okay, and drove off to meet Terra at the biker's house.

The crosstown journey took half an hour, not including the fifteen minutes he spent at a sandwich shop picking up two BLTs to share with Terra. As he drove he found himself wondering if the attractive lady wizard would like to join him for a more formal meal, dinner with a nice bottle of wine maybe.

When he arrived the techs were poking the pile of rubble with probes connected to a laptop. Terra stood by the curb beside her car, toe tapping and arms crossed. Maybe she was hungry. Free food always put people in a better mood.

He parked behind her and got out, paper bags in one hand and bottles of water in the other. "Morning. Have you been waiting long?"

"No. What's in the bag?"

"Lunch. You hungry?" Lin offered her a bag and bottle.

"Thank you." She opened the bag and smiled. "I love BLTs. How did you know?"

Lin hadn't had a clue, instead acting on the assumption that everyone loved bacon. "I am a detective. What news from the world of magic?"

"Nothing beyond my boss wanting me to recover the artifacts as quickly as possible and track Mercia while I'm at it."

"Any luck?" Lin dug in to his sandwich.

"No on both counts. What about you?"

"I actually had a good morning. I took our witness to the airport." He smiled and shook his head. "I'd never heard someone her age use the expression 'above my pay grade' before."

Terra dropped her sandwich. "Are you certain that's the exact expression she used?"

"Yeah, why?" Lin took a drink to moisten his suddenly dry throat.

"Mercia used that same expression all the time. Especially when she was bitter about her position in the Department."

"You don't think...?"

"I do think." Terra dug the now-familiar glasses out of her gray robe and slipped them on. "She rode with you this morning?"

"Yeah, like an hour ago."

Terra marched back to his car, muttering as she went. She stopped beside the passenger-side door and scowled. "There are remnants of illusion magic present on the seat and in the air."

Lin had lost his appetite. "Was it Mercia?"

"No way to know for sure, but I'd bet a month's pay it was." Terra slammed her fist on the roof. "Damn it all to hell! She was right in front of us and I missed it."

* * *

Lady Raven jogged into the airport, eager to get out of the detective's sight. She'd enjoyed the Lacy Winn persona, but her usefulness had ended. The cops had been kind enough to deal with all her loose ends and the Skulls had placed the shadow gems where she'd instructed. Now the only living person that knew where they'd been hidden was her and she had no intention of telling anyone.

Hundreds of people ran from gate to baggage claim through security and to the crappy restaurants. None of them had a clue how the world would change and all thanks to her. She'd worked for months under the noses of her so-called superiors at the Department of Magic and they had never guessed. It would be sweet indeed when they finally learned who had brought about their downfall.

Only her failure to deal with Conryu Koda left a bitter taste on her mouth. Lady Raven swallowed a curse. After the zealots had failed and Shizuku Kane had banished her demons she'd severed the connection between the mirror and the wind spirit. Fortunately that attempt hadn't required her to expend any Society resources, just a group of worthless, deluded men and a little of her personal magic. She wouldn't be mentioning the little episode to the Hierarchs when she next spoke to them.

Yes, it would certainly be wise to keep this most recent failure to herself, especially since they essentially ordered her not to even make the attempt in the first place.

Lady Raven made her way to the help desk. Though she doubted it would do anything to improve her mood she decided to make a petty, almost childish gesture. Even wizards got to act childishly once in a while. "Excuse me."

A middle-aged woman with curly brown hair looked up at her with a flat, bored expression. "Can I help you?"

"Would it be possible for me to leave a message for a friend here? He forgot his ticket."

"Sure." She handed Lady Raven a blank envelope and a pen. "Write it on here and I'll log it into the system. If he checks at any of the stations someone will tell him we have it."

"Thanks so much." She jotted a quick note on the inside of the envelope, wrote "Detective Chang" on the front, and sealed the ticket inside. "I can't thank you enough."

The woman accepted the envelope with a disinterested grunt then set to typing on her terminal. Lady Raven left her to it and headed for the ladies' room.

The stall farthest from the door was empty. Inside, she released her youthful illusion and changed into a black dress. A less elaborate spell altered her hair and face enough that no one would recognize her as either Mercia or Lacy. That done Lady Raven headed to the front of the airport where the taxis waited. She'd be long gone before the good detective even considered looking for her, assuming he ever did.

An hour and a half later found her once more standing in a

spell circle wearing her raven mask and facing the Hierarchs. She couldn't judge their emotions behind the masks, but none of them looked angry. That was enough for Lady Raven.

"I trust you've cleaned up your mess," Lady Tiger said.

They didn't seem to know about her most recent failed attempt to kill the boy. Thank heaven for that. "Yes, I'm now the only living person who knows where the shadow gems are hidden. We can activate them whenever you wish."

"You know better," Lady Wolf said. "We can't activate them until the floating island returns."

She had in fact only suspected that. Despite her efforts in enchanting the gems she hadn't developed the spell, only cast it. "What of me? Do the Hierarchs have a task for me in the meantime?"

"You will tend the gems," Lady Lion said. "Watch over them and deploy defenses. We have come too far to risk failure now."

"I assure you the gems—"

"You will guard them," Lady Dragon said. "And you will not fail us in this."

She found her throat had gone dry. "As you command, I obey."

"Yes." Lady Dragon severed the connection, leaving Mercia trembling all over.

* * *

Terra stood, arms crossed, as they finally started digging in the ruin of the flophouse. A week had passed since the fight with the bikers and the bomb squad had finally given the go ahead. No one had seen any sign of Mercia after she left the airport. Lin had gone to search for her and found a note with the ticket he bought her. The note read, "Hope you can get a refund." Terra's fist clenched. When she finally got her hands on Mercia…

She shook off her anger and focused. First the artifacts, then Mercia. The gauntlet at least had to be in there somewhere. Terra had no idea why she couldn't sense it. Maybe some residual energy from her fire spell was interfering with the detection magic.

A huge excavator with a claw on the arm grabbed some of the rubble and spread it out on the ground nearby. Terra examined it through the glasses and found nothing. She shook her head and the operator gathered up the debris and dropped it in a waiting container. For over two hours they repeated the procedure until they reached the concrete foundation. Someone had smashed a hole in it.

Terra examined the hole and found a mixture of earth and dark magic in the dirt. She poked it and found the soil loose. Lin came over and crouched beside her. "Find something?"

"There was a tunnel here, but it collapsed. The magic holding it together was negated. I'll bet you our missing artifact is buried in that tunnel along with the biker from the hospital."

"That would still leave us one short based on the video Lacy, I mean Mercia, provided."

"True, and we still have no idea where those five cases ended up. What do you say we dig out this tunnel and see what we have left to find afterward?"

Lin nodded and motioned the excavator over.

Three tedious hours later they had two bodies and the fire gauntlet. The magical weapon was every bit as powerful as Terra had first thought. In the hands of someone that really knew how to use it, a lot of damage could be done. Not that the thug had been any slouch in the damage department, but in the hands of a fire wizard what he'd done amounted to nothing. She'd feel much better when it was locked up in the Department's secure storage room.

Though they'd stopped digging when they found the bodies, the tunnel clearly continued on to a garage a little ways away. Lin drew his pistol and the two of them eased over to the building. Terra spoke a short incantation and the door slid up out of the way. Lin lunged in, weapon leading. Five bikes, including the one from the hospital, sat in the middle of the dirt floor.

While Lin searched the saddlebags Terra checked for magic. There was just a hint of dark energy around the bags, but that was it. "They must have transported the cases somewhere else."

"There's nothing here but more guns and a dirty bandana. Shit! Another dead end. We're running out of leads."

Terra chewed her thumbnail. "Where's the other bike?"

"What?"

"There are six dead bikers. Did any of those guys strike you as the type that would ride double? Where's the other bike?"

"'Scuse me."

Lin spun and raised his pistol.

A skinny guy with black, lanky hair and covered in tattoos raised his hands. "I surrender."

Lin lowered his gun. "This is a crime scene. You're going to have to leave."

"Okay, but I had some information for you about the gang that lived over yonder."

"If you have some information for us, sir, we'd be most grateful if you passed it along," Lin said.

"I thought you might be. One of them badasses paid me two hundred bucks to give you guys an address on the off chance there was a fight at the house. I thought he was nuts, but it's three weeks later and I assume he's dead and you're here."

Lin and Terra shared a look. "What address?" Lin took out his notepad.

The informant rattled off a warehouse number on the docks. "He said you'd find what you were looking for."

"Why did you follow through?" Lin asked. "He's dead. You could have kept the money and not said a word with no one the wiser."

"Hey, man, when Tito gives his word and takes your money, he does the job."

The sun was low in the crimson sky when Tito wandered off the way he'd come. Lin and Terra headed back to the cars. Terra stretched and yawned as they walked.

"It's getting late," Lin said. "What do you say we head out to the docks in the morning?"

"Good call. If there was trouble I wouldn't be much use, tired as I am."

"I'll pick you up at your office at eight. Okay?"

Terra nodded, climbed into her car, and headed home. She'd be glad when this case was closed and she could return to her regular work. Being a policewoman exhausted her and she didn't even have to do the paperwork. She'd miss seeing Detective Lin Chang. A faint smile curved her lips. She should do something about that, assuming she found the courage.

* * *

The cry of gulls and the stink of a mixture of salt and rotten fish assaulted Lin the moment he stepped out of his car. He put his hand over his nose, but it didn't help. At all. From her grimace Terra wasn't any more pleased with the odor than Lin. She muttered something and swirled her finger around. The stink vanished, replaced by a sweet, cinnamon odor.

"I don't know what you did, but thanks."

"My pleasure, believe me."

They'd parked in an empty lot beside warehouse thirty-two, a rusted-out metal building with three condemned signs nailed to the walls. He sighed. Why couldn't these thugs ever do their dirty work somewhere nice. Then again, if they ran into trouble he was just as glad the nearest people were the longshoremen working a quarter mile up the dock unloading a cargo ship.

Further out to sea another pair of the huge container ships waited their turn to dock and unload. One of them sounded a horn that echoed across the waterfront and sent the birds scattering.

Lin and Terra headed toward the warehouse. The main doors were covered in rust and bird shit. It didn't look like anyone had opened them in a while.

"I think Tito sent us on a wild goose chase." Lin shook his head.

Terra raised her hand, closed her eyes, and cast another spell. "No, there's something in there. It looks like the missing motorcycle. There are two more doors on the back side of the warehouse. We can get in that way."

It was a short walk to the rear of the building. The back doors were every bit as rusty as the front but scratch marks and a few scuffed areas indicated they'd been moved recently. Scattered shafts of light pierced the darkness inside. Lin grabbed the door and yanked it open enough for them to squeeze through.

A light switch hung on the wall a little ways to the left of the door. Lin weighed the chances of getting electrocuted then flipped it. Not so much as a spark.

"I'll handle the lights." Terra held out her hands and spoke a spell. Six glowing pebbles appeared on her palm. She blew a puff of air over them and they flew up to the roof and grew bright enough to reveal everything in the vast space.

Not that there was much beyond the mix of empty beer cans, rotten scraps of food, and a torn mattress stained with god only knew what littering the floor. A little ways further on a black chopper rested on its kickstand. The bike had skull-embroidered saddlebags. Whatever they were supposed to find would be in those.

"Don't touch anything." Lin worked his way over to the bike, careful to follow his own advice.

Lin reached the bike and flipped open the first bag. Another gun, terrific. How many weapons did these guys have? The next bag yielded an envelope labeled "pig."

"I guess it's for me."

While Lin studied the letter Terra crouched and carefully reached inside the bag. "I found one." She spoke so softly Lin barely heard her.

A black coffer identical to the ones from the videos rested in Terra's hand. It shined in the magical light. At first glance there appeared to be no seam. "Can we open it?"

"It's empty."

"How can you tell?" Lin moved in for a better look. He reached out to touch it.

"Stop!"

Too late.

His finger brushed the smooth wood and darkness descended on the warehouse.

The scream of a bird filled the air. Terra grabbed him by the collar and began to chant.

A bubble of white energy surrounded them and pushed back the darkness. Movement flickered here and there.

Lin pulled his automatic, but couldn't find anything to shoot.

"Put that away. Those are shadow beasts. Your bullets won't do anything."

Lin holstered his weapon. "What should I do?"

"There's nothing you can do. This is my fight."

Lin hunkered down behind Terra. His gaze darted back and forth, trying to figure out what sort of creature they were dealing with.

The answer came a moment later when a huge black raven slammed into the barrier and disintegrated. Terra flinched and her barrier wavered for a moment.

She chanted another spell, this one in the hissing language of fire. A dome of flame appeared over the white one already in place.

Lin hated feeling so useless. There was more stuff in the bag and it was within her barrier. Even if he couldn't fight he could still investigate.

He reached into the open bag. Inside was another envelope, a big manila one stuffed to the top and unlabeled.

"We have to make a break for it," Terra said. "Be ready to run."

Lin snatched the envelope and tucked it inside his jacket. "Where to?"

"Outside. If we can make it to the sunlight it will weaken the shadow beasts enough for me to destroy them."

"I like the sound of that. Say when."

She snapped her fingers and the flame dome exploded outward. Lin caught a glimpse of dozens of ravens swirling around. It looked like they were made of living darkness.

"Now!"

They ran for the open door.

Terra stumbled on a pizza box.

The light barrier wavered as she struggled to catch her balance.

Lin grabbed her by the elbow and around the waist and they ran on. The flames holding off the ravens flickered and began to die.

Only a few strides to go.

He put his head down and pushed Terra along as fast as he dared.

A raven slipped through the flames and slammed into the barrier. It burst and cracks appeared in their protection.

Two more strides.

Another raven flew at them. Lin pushed Terra out the door and into the sunshine a step ahead of it. He staggered and spun around. A cloud of shadowy birds swirled around the warehouse. There had to be hundreds of them.

Beside him Terra began another spell. A ball of flame appeared above her head and continued to grow as she chanted.

"Can you really destroy all those monsters?"

She ignored him and kept casting, her voice getting louder as the fireball grew. With a final shout she hurled the sphere at the collection of shadow beasts. It detonated in the center of the group.

Lin looked away from the blinding explosion. When he turned back the ravens and most of the warehouse roof were gone.

Terra fell to her knees and wheezed, her bloodshot eyes leaking tears. Her skin had turned ashen and her lips pale blue. Lin had seen drowning victims that looked healthier.

"You okay?"

She offered a weak nod. "Used too much power with that last spell. This is the backlash. Give me some time."

"Can you make it back to the car? This is no place for a rest."

"Hurts everywhere. You go ahead. I'll be along as soon as I can."

"I'm not leaving you alone in your condition. I can read standing up."

"Thanks." She fell over on her side and curled up in a ball.

Lin didn't have a lot of experience working with wizards, but he'd never heard of one collapsing after using magic. Not that it was probably something they advertised.

* * *

Lady Raven sat at her desk, a tome bound in black leather open in front of her. Two crimson, blood candles burned on either side of the book, shedding a flickering glow over the twisted Infernal script. Her workshop apartment was the only place her enemies hadn't discovered yet.

It was rented in the name of another persona that had no connection to Lacy Winn or Mercia Bottomley, so she had no reason to think she'd be discovered. Still, her hunters had proven disconcertingly adept and determined. She would have to be careful for the next year. One more mistake could jeopardize the project, not to mention her life.

She rubbed her eyes and refocused on the text. The black magic book had been her reward when she achieved the rank of Sub-Hierarch two years ago. Lady Wolf had delivered it herself, a great honor indeed. If—when her current mission succeeded, Lady Dragon would grant Mercia the privilege of joining the true Hierarchs. That would be an even rarer honor, as few ever met the secretive leader of the Society face to face.

Lady Raven's head popped up when a distant ward triggered. Had one of the shadow gems been discovered? No, that was impossible. They were too well hidden.

A full-length, black glass mirror hung on the wall and Mercia walked over to it. It was vastly better suited to scrying than the simple bathroom mirror she'd been forced to use at the motel. She focused on the tingle in the back of her mind and spoke the words of activation. "Show me what lies beyond my sight, Spirit Vision!"

The glass grew cloudy then resolved into an image of the docks.

Her shadow ravens swirled around a decrepit warehouse. Lady Raven frowned. She hadn't hidden one of the shadow gems there, in fact she'd never even seen the building before.

What in the world was going on?

"Closer." The image zoomed in. Detective Chang and Terra staggered out of the warehouse and onto the docks. What was she holding?

The image zoomed further. How had Terra gotten ahold of one of the coffers? Wait, that wasn't one of the ones she hid, that was the sixth that had held the gem she'd used at the carnival to try and kill Conryu. That should have been consumed along with the gem when the spell ran its course.

Goddamn useless bikers.

They must have kept it after removing the gem instead of leaving them together like she told them. But why? Iron Skull would never have disobeyed her. Lady Raven had had the great dumb thug wrapped around her finger. Not the other one though. What was his name, Bone? He'd always looked at her with suspicion. He had to be the one that betrayed her.

Back on the docks Terra cast a spell that destroyed her ravens along with a good-sized chunk of the warehouse. Perhaps she'd underestimated the quiet wizard.

Even if Terra was stronger than Lady Raven had thought, the wards she'd placed around the hidden gems were far stronger than the one she just bested and judging from Terra's condition that effort had about killed her.

If Terra continued to interfere she would finish the job her ravens started.

* * *

Lin draped his suit coat over Terra as she lay moaning softly on the ground. The warehouse still smoldered and every once in a while a steel rafter would come crashing down. He'd called in the incident then turned his attention to the envelope marked "pig." Clearly whichever biker had left it here expected a member of the police to find Tito and eventually track the letter down. That spoke to a level of planning Lin wouldn't have expected from one of the brutal gang members.

He tore open the envelope and pulled out a single folded sheet of paper. A note written in flowing script said:

Dear Pig. If you're reading this the bitch wizard has betrayed us. I knew she would, but Iron Skull refused to listen. She looked at us the way I look at roaches. I've set up this somewhat elaborate treasure hunt both to conceal my work from Lady Raven and to see if you have the brains and determination to carry out my revenge. Since you're reading this I assume you do.

Lady Raven had one major job for the gang and that was to place five boxes like the one you found throughout the city. We each took one to a specific location. After we placed it she must have cast a spell on us, because I can't remember any details. I've spoken to the others, all except Iron Skull, and pieced together as much as I could. It's all gathered in the second envelope.

I don't know what the witch has planned, but I'm certain it's nothing good. Not that I care, you understand, but no one betrays the Black Skulls and gets away with it. One of our boys already died doing the wizard's errands. Stop the bitch and avenge my brothers, Pig.

It was signed "Bone" and beside the name was the image of a stylized skull. It seemed Mercia wasn't as well loved as she might have hoped. Whichever of the dead bikers was Bone Skull, Lin owed him a thank you.

Terra groaned behind him and he turned to find her struggling to her feet. Sirens in the distance heralded the approach of the police and fire departments. The area would be crawling with people soon. Once Lin gave his report he'd leave the cleanup to others. Terra staggered over and returned his jacket. Her lips were pink again and she'd stopped crying.

"You good?" he asked.

"No, but I'm better." Terra leaned on him as they walked back to his car to wait for backup to arrive. He quite liked the feeling. "Anything interesting?"

Lin handed her the paper.

When Terra had finished reading she said, "Lady Raven, huh? That explains the shape of the defensive ward. Though I can't prove it, I'm certain it's Mercia. Have you looked through the other papers yet?"

"No, I was going to wait until I got back to headquarters." The first fire truck pulled in. "I'll have to explain what happened then we can head out. That reminds me. How come the trap went off when I touched the box, but it ignored you?"

"I didn't touch it."

Lin stared. "You picked it up."

"I conjured an energy barrier between my bare skin and the

coffer. It's standard procedure when handling an unknown magical device. You can understand why."

"You might have warned me."

Terra shrugged. "I tried, but I wasn't quite fast enough. It never occurred to me that you might try and touch it. We're trained in how to handle magical items. I guess I assumed you were too. See what comes from making assumptions? From now on we're going to have to be much more careful."

Lin couldn't argue with that.

* * *

"I don't believe the threat is over, Captain." Lin sat in front of his boss's cluttered desk and tried to remain calm. "Just because the bikers are dead doesn't mean we're finished. The letter clearly states that the wizard, Lady Raven, still intends us harm."

Lin had dropped Terra off at the Department of Magic and continued on back to his station. The moment word got out that he was back his commander called him into his office and gave him hell for destroying the warehouse. It was mostly pro forma since the thing had been condemned anyway. What wasn't, however, was his captain's very real desire to have this case be closed. A pile of dead thugs made for an excellent ending, one he could show the mayor and get a pat on the back in return.

The captain liked a good pat on the back, but Lin couldn't sign off on the case when he knew those boxes were still out there.

"Lin, I understand, really. But this is now a matter for the Department of Magic. Our part is finished. Turn over all your information to them and move on. We have a backlog of murders as long as my arm that need investigating."

"Sir, I really don't think we should leave this investigation unfinished. The risks are too great."

"You've been working this case, what, a couple weeks nonstop?

Take the rest of the day off, tomorrow too, then come back in ready to start on something new."

"Sir—"

"This isn't a debate, Detective. Go home."

Lin got up, nodded, and reached for the door.

"Lin."

He turned back. "Sir?"

"You did good work on this case. The Black Skulls were wanted in three other sectors for crimes ranging from murder, to arson, to kidnapping. Getting them off the streets is a huge deal. Don't think I don't appreciate it."

"No, sir. It's just I don't think the job is finished and I hate leaving something half done."

"The wizards will take care of their own. Regular folks like us will only be in their way."

After the mess he'd made of things at the warehouse Lin didn't have a good argument for that one. "Understood, sir. If they need us I'm sure they'll let us know."

Lin took his leave, pausing at his desk to collect the letter and packet. Terra was smart and hard working. He had no doubt she'd get to the bottom of whatever was going on. Probably better than he'd have done it himself.

His battered pickup was parked at the far end of the crowded lot. The long walk helped clear his head. He had a day and a half, maybe he could still help, at least for a little longer. The starter whined when he turned the key, but it finally caught.

The station was only ten blocks from the government complex so five minutes later Lin was parking again. He collected his evidence and marched through the main doors. Only one of the secretaries had a customer so Lin chose the farthest-in slot and walked up to the man behind the desk.

"Can I help you, sir?"

Lin flashed his badge. "Detective Lin Chang to see Terra Pane."

"One moment, Officer." The man picked up his phone and

punched three digits. He murmured something, nodded, and hung up. "She's with the chief. You can head on up. His office is on the top floor."

"I don't want to interrupt."

"It's okay, Chief Kane wants to speak to you as well. The elevators are in the back to your right."

Lin took the elevator up. A short hall led to a closed door. Behind a desk to the left of the door sat an attractive woman in her mid-thirties. She brushed her brown hair out of her eyes and smiled. "You can go right on in, Detective."

"Thank you." Lin nodded to the woman in passing then tugged the door open.

Inside was a spacious office with a glass wall overlooking the city. The floating island was still visible far out over the ocean. Two walls were lined with bookcases. Directly ahead was a huge cherry desk behind which sat a broad-shouldered bald man that had to be Chief Kane. In one of the two chairs in front of the desk he recognized the back of Terra's head.

The chief stood up and walked over to the staring Lin. "Come in, Detective. No need to be shy."

Chief Kane shook his hand and guided him over to the empty chair. "Sit down, make yourself comfortable. We're all friends here."

"Thank you, sir." Lin settled gently into the soft leather chair. It probably cost more than his truck.

"Orin, please. I know you and Terra are already aquatinted. She tells me you've been a tremendous help in trying to locate Mercia."

"That's why I'm here." Lin placed the documents on Orin's desk. "My captain says as far as we're concerned the case is closed. Dealing with Mercia is a matter for wizards."

Orin smile vanished. "Is that right? What do you think?"

"I don't think we should close out the case, but it's not my call.

The plain truth is I'm a very small fish in a big ocean. If the captain says I'm done, I'm done."

"We'll see about that." Orin picked up his phone and dialed a number. A moment later he said, "Tom? It's Orin, I need a favor. Of course we're on for golf this Sunday. I wouldn't miss it."

"Who's he talking to?" Lin whispered to Terra. He was relieved that her color had returned to normal.

"Probably the mayor. They're old friends. I suspect very shortly you're going to be back on the case. And thank god for that."

"Why? I'm sure you could have handled it."

"I'm a researcher, Lin. I don't know the first thing about criminal investigations. I've consulted once or twice, but I never ran one on my own. If the chief dropped this in my lap I wouldn't know where to start."

"Thanks, Tom." Orin hung up the phone. "There, that's all sorted out. You'll be getting a call shortly, Detective. Until then how about you show us what you brought?"

Lin handed him the letter. "I haven't had a chance to even open the packet yet. Have you examined the box at all?"

Terra shook her head. "Nothing more than a cursory look. It'll take me weeks if not months to fully reconstruct the spell from the residual energy. At first glance it strongly resembles the energy from the carnival ritual. I assume at one time it held whatever catalyst Lady Raven used to activate the spell. If I use that as a starting point it might speed things up a great deal, unless I'm wrong, in which case it'll set me back."

Orin shook his head and dropped the letter on his desk. "Not terribly encouraging, Terra. And this letter is too vague to be of much use."

Lin's cell rang, interrupting Orin. He looked at the Department chief who nodded. "Detective Chang."

"No," his captain said. "Lieutenant Chang."

"I don't understand, sir."

"You're being promoted and reassigned as liaison to the Department of Magic. You'll also serve as their chief investigator. Congratulations." The captain hung up.

"Good news?" Orin asked.

"I guess. I've been reassigned to your department as chief investigator." Lin's head spun. He'd worked out of the same station since he joined the force. He knew everyone there and they knew him; some of them were like family.

"We can always use good people at the Department." Orin handed him the letter. "Terra, I believe there's an office up the hall from yours. That should be a good place for the detective. Get him settled in, won't you?"

"Yes, Chief."

Terra groaned and stumbled to her feet. Lin followed her example. Orin shook his hand again and Terra led him out of the office.

Just like that his whole career had changed. Lin had wanted to finish what he started, but what would happen after? How much use did the Department of Magic actually have for a detective?

He followed Terra out and back to the elevators. They rode down to the fifth floor where she guided him to a closed door. Terra opened it and a musty smell mixed with bleach washed over him. Lin stared at the so-called office. It looked more like a storage closet. Someone had shoved a cheap particleboard table and plastic chair into it and rechristened it an office. There wasn't even a computer or shelves. Hell, he didn't even have paper and pencil. On the other hand it had four walls and a door, which put it head and shoulders above the cubical he'd worked out of at the station.

"I know it doesn't look like much," Terra said. "But I can get you a Department laptop and there's a supply closet down the hall, just help yourself to whatever you need. I'm right next door if you have any questions."

Terra ducked into her office down the hall and closed the

door, leaving Lin to his own devices. First things first. He tossed the letter and packet onto the table and went to fetch a notepad and pencil. Getting to the desk was a squeeze, good thing he stayed in shape. If he was ten pounds heavier he doubted he'd fit.

The contents of the packet spilled out onto his desk. Page after page of handwritten notes in the same hand as the letter. Lin scanned the first five, trying to get a feel for what he had. It looked like Bone had simply written down everything the other members of the gang remembered about their missions. There was no rhyme or reason and most of it lacked context.

One said he remembered mostly birds and trees. That could describe any one of a hundred parks in the city. Another described rushing water, but was it the sewer or the Gallen River entering the ocean? How was he supposed to make sense of this?

9

EPILOGUE

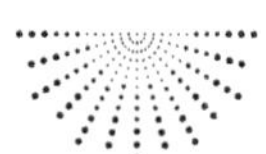

Lady Raven stretched and got up off her couch. For the past ten days, since Terra and Detective Chang had discovered her box in the warehouse, Lady Raven had been going from one hiding place to the next, setting additional wards and preparing guardians. It seemed next to impossible that the hiding places would be discovered, but if they were whoever found them would regret it.

There was one more matter to attend to. While her apartment was comfortable and secure for the moment, she couldn't discount the possibility of her enemies learning about it. If they did it simply wasn't possible to protect it the way she'd like, at least not without drawing attention that she didn't want. She needed a secure fortress she could retreat to when the time came to activate the ritual. Somewhere her enemies wouldn't dream of trying to breach.

She had a location in mind and nearly a year to prepare. However, before she'd fully warded it the building remained vulnerable. Guardians would be necessary for the first month or two, then as a second line of defense. The multiple failures of her shadow beasts had demonstrated their limits in the starkest terms, especially when it came to sunlight.

If she eliminated that weakness, their power was beyond question. What they needed was a shell to protect them from the weakening rays of the sun, and Lady Raven knew exactly where to find such hosts.

She shrugged on her black robe and chanted, "Reveal the way through infinite darkness. Open the path. Hell Portal!" A black disk appeared in the air before her. Lady Raven stepped through it and into the borderland between the mortal realm and Hell. Time had no meaning in this in-between place and distance was simply a matter of will.

With her destination firmly in mind Lady Raven called the name of a demon she knew. A black-winged monster appeared out of the darkness and carried her to her destination. She spoke the spell again and emerged in a darkened corner outside the government building.

It was late and the sky moonless. No figures stirred in the night. Her former place of employment would be empty, but Lady Raven had a different destination. An invisibility spell hid her from anyone she might encounter as she made her way to the city offices. In the basement of that building was the morgue where unclaimed bodies awaited cremation.

There should be a handful of night watchmen patrolling the grounds, not that mere men would have any chance of stopping her, even if they could see her. Five minutes later brought her to her destination. While the guards weren't an issue, the wards protecting the building were another matter. The moment she stepped through the doors her invisibility would be stripped away. Worse, she couldn't open a portal inside either.

She smiled. If there weren't challenges what was the point of doing something? She marched up the steps and stopped in front of the glass doors. Inside, a single guard sat with his chair leaning back against the wall, his feet up on a hard wooden bench.

Lady Raven knew the security routine as well as anyone who had ever worked there. Assuming they hadn't changed anything, another three guards should be patrolling the other floors while this fool guarded the lobby. In reality they were probably all holed up somewhere napping. That's what happened when you hired minimum wage workers to protect your property. As long as she made it past the first man without raising a ruckus the rest would be easy.

A hard rap on the glass got the guard to spring to his feet. He stared at the entrance, but of course couldn't see her. He narrowed his eyes then rubbed them, as if that would make any difference.

Come on, you great buffoon, come investigate.

The guard shrugged and started to settle back in. Lazy, useless excuse for a guard. She thumped the glass again, harder this time. He whirled around and stared again. Finally he pulled his flashlight and started for the doors.

Lady Raven chanted, "Your life is mine." Her hand crackled with necromantic energy as she stepped aside to avoid bumping into him.

The guard unlocked the doors and stepped outside. He waved his flashlight this way and that, trying in vain to figure out what had made the noise. He was a young man, barely older than Conryu.

When he turned back toward the doors she reached out and grasped the back of his neck. The dark energy flowed out of her hand and into his head. Flesh withered and rotted, leaving nothing but a skull sitting atop his broad shoulders.

The guard collapsed and she left him where he lay, stepping over his body and through the now-unlocked doors. Her skin tingled as her invisibility spell was negated. Lady Raven marched through the empty lobby, her hard heels clicking on the tile floor. She went straight to the elevator and rode it one floor down to the basement.

The elevator chimed and the doors slid open revealing a fully equipped surgical suite. The overwhelming scent of disinfectant mingled with a hint of blood. It appeared someone had just cleaned. She hoped her former servants were in good enough condition to house the shadow spirits.

Beyond the operating room was the morgue. Dozens of niches sealed by stainless steel doors covered the back and side walls. She brushed aside the hanging plastic barrier and went straight to the rear wall. A quick scan of the labels revealed the Skulls' resting place.

Lady Raven gestured and spoke a word. Five doors opened and the slabs slid out revealing the pale, tattoo-covered bodies of her former servants. Each of their torsos sported a stitched up Y incision. Two of them had nasty burns covering their arms and back and a different pair was riddled with bullet holes.

They made an especially unattractive group of potential servants, not that they'd been much more appealing while still alive. Still, the corpses were sufficiently intact to serve as hosts for her Faceless Ones and nothing else mattered.

Lady Raven began the summoning spell. "Spirits of death and darkness, faceless foes of the living, appear and serve me."

The already chill air dropped another twenty degrees as she tapped the corrupt energy of the netherworld. Her spell reached a crescendo and five humanoid figures made of living darkness appeared above the corpses. The Faceless Ones oozed into the bodies, filling every pore and orifice until it appeared the bodies had been dipped in an oil slick.

Slowly the nether spirits worked their way into their new hosts. All around her the other niches began to rattle. One door popped open and a foot emerged. Like a sort of bizarre birth, a mindless zombie worked its way free of the narrow slot. In short order a second and third emerged, animated by the residual energy of her summoning spell.

These weak, stupid creatures were of no use to her beyond the annoyance they'd cause her enemies when they came to work in the morning. A simple command spoken in Infernal sent the newly made zombies out of the morgue and out of her way. They'd shamble around in the basement, maybe a few would find the stairs and work their way up, following the scent of the guards patrolling the upper floors.

Before the Faceless Ones finished integrating with their hosts twenty of the lesser zombies had shuffled out of the morgue. The clumsy things sent tools crashing to the floor in the surgical area as they made their way out.

When the last of the crashes sounded and the moans had faded to nothing, Lady Raven checked on the progress of her guardians. The black essence of the Faceless Ones had sunk fully into the bikers' bodies. The wounds had sealed, leaving the flesh smooth and free of punctures. This wasn't done for aesthetic reasons, but to keep any light from reaching the spirits and potentially weakening them.

The process of entering the flesh would also serve to transform it, making the skin durable enough to withstand bullets and the bones hard enough to survive the impact of a truck. When they reached her soon-to-be fortress Lady Raven would make further improvements to her guardians.

"Rise," she commanded.

The five once-faceless spirits forced their hosts up off the slabs. Their movements were stiff at first, though already smoother than the zombies. That was to be expected. The spirits had been bodiless for a long time. It would take weeks for them to grow fully used to having a physical form again.

She grimaced at their thoroughly ugly, nude bodies. That would need to be remedied as soon as possible. "Follow me."

* * *

Orin sat at his desk and held his head in his hands as Adam finished his report. The night before someone had broken into the district office morgue and raised all the bodies inside. The undead had proceed to kill the four night watchmen and a handful of employees before the security forces were called in to destroy them. They'd gotten lucky in that the creatures were among the weakest sort of undead and required only a bullet to the head to put them down permanently.

"So that's it," Adam said. "Five bodies are still unaccounted for. We've searched the whole building so our working assumption is that whoever made the zombies took the bikers' bodies away with them."

Orin looked up. "You mean she, not they. Can there be any real doubt that Mercia is behind this?"

"I agree that she's the most likely suspect, but since we have no proof it's still speculation. Do you have any further orders?"

He sighed and shook his head. "Not for the moment. Though we'll certainly want to increase our patrols and make sure no one walks their route alone."

"I already made the adjustment to the schedules. If there's nothing else I'm going to make a final inspection of the building so everyone can return to work."

Orin motioned him out. When did his life get so complicated? It didn't seem that long ago that his biggest worry was Maria getting another ear infection. Now he had the first male wizard to deal with, a deranged former employee breaking in and stealing bodies, and his little girl going off to college in five weeks.

He rested his head on the cool wood of his desk and sighed. That felt good.

The door opened and he looked up to find Terra striding toward him, looking grimmer than usual. She stopped in front of his desk and leaned forward. "I found where she opened a portal. There were footprints in the grass leading up to it."

"When did you become a tracker?"

"The tracks killed the grass right down to bare dirt. A blind person could have followed them."

"Fascinating, but I hardly think dead grass is our biggest concern right now."

"Then you're mistaken." Terra's scowl deepened. "Whatever Mercia transformed the bikers into has a powerful enough dark aura their presence alone was enough to kill the grass. That means they're also strong enough to drain the life from a person and there are five of them god only knows where out there."

Orin rubbed his face and swallowed another sigh. "What do you propose we do about it?"

Terra's expression softened. "I've been thinking about that ever since I found the tracks. The truth is I have no idea."

"That's not what I was hoping to hear from my chief researcher. Speaking of which, have you made any progress on the box?"

"I understand the function of the box itself. It was designed to hold something, hiding its aura until a specific condition caused it to open. In this case the spell has been modified so only a specific individual would be able to open it. I assume the missing boxes retain the initial enchantment."

"Does any of that help us?"

"Not really."

Orin thumped his head on the table. Of course it didn't. This summer had been a comedy of errors, why should it change now? They just needed a tiny bit of luck and it would break everything open, he knew it in his bones. Luck, unfortunately, had been in short supply.

THE AWAKENING

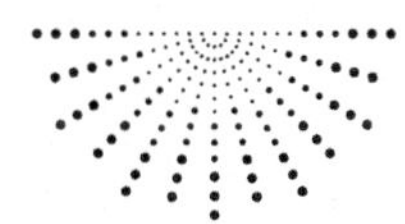

THE AEGIS OF MERLIN BOOK 2

1

ALL ABOARD

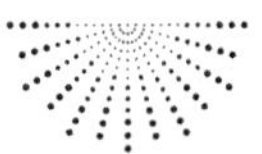

Conryu threw his last clean shirt into his suitcase and clicked the lid shut. Summer vacation had ended yesterday and after the attack on the apartment building no one else had bothered him. Even the press kept their distance for the most part, and thank goodness for that. If they continued pestering him he was going to lose his temper and flatten one of them. Of course they kept sending lady reporters so that made it harder. Maybe the producers thought a pretty face would overwhelm his distaste for their profession.

When a full month had passed without an attempt on his life he'd managed to convince Mom to let him out of the building. It may have helped that being inside didn't keep the lunatics from coming after him anyway. That was the argument he'd made at least.

They let him go to the dojo to train and the shop to work on his bike. It wasn't much, but after a month cooped up an all-expenses-paid world tour wouldn't have made him any happier.

The hours he spent out of the apartment were also hours he didn't have to study some stupid magic book or listen to a lecture from Maria.

He loved Maria, but if he'd had to sit through one more lesson on some esoteric point of magic he would have screamed. At least the crazy professor hadn't returned. That alone was a gift on par with his hours of freedom. Conryu felt he should send a thank you note to the cultists. That near-death experience had really shaken Angus. Conryu doubted it would last, but you had to take what the universe gave you.

He took one last look at his phone and set it on his nightstand. The information packet the school sent over covered all the rules, and there were a ton of them. The most strictly enforced was a ban on most forms of technology. The teachers considered it a distraction from their magical focus. Conryu thought that was stupid, but no one asked his opinion. Apparently there were only six computers in the school office and a handful of phones, land-lines no less. Talk about medieval.

"Conryu!" his mother called. "Let's get a move on. You don't want to miss the train."

"God forbid I miss the train to magic land," Conryu muttered as he grabbed his suitcase.

His parents were waiting by the door, his mother's foot tapping like a mad woodpecker. "Come on, come on!"

"Easy, dear." Dad rubbed her shoulders, prompting a deep sigh.

They rushed down to the parking garage, thankfully encountering no reporters. During his daily jaunt to the dojo he'd run into one of them now and again, usually Kat Gabel, the woman he'd met the day after the press conference. His cold silence combined with the world's shortest attention spans had sent most of them off to find a chattier subject. Poor bastard.

Conryu paused to adjust the cover on his bike. It had pained him when he had to remove her battery and put the tarp over her. It felt like pulling a shroud over a loved one. Riding his bike topped the list of things he'd miss.

"Hurry up, Conryu," his mother said.

He sighed and climbed into the family SUV. The ride to the

train station took half an hour, and when they arrived a veritable forest of satellite dishes greeted them. Networks from all over the Alliance packed the parking lot. A throng of reporters and cameramen had gathered by the main entrance. Ten policemen kept the entrance clear and the reporters under control, more or less. It looked a bit like herding cats, only more chaotic.

Conryu grimaced. Now he knew why they weren't waiting in the garage. Everyone in the world knew where to find him today. He wasn't looking forward to running that gauntlet. Or worse, running into another would-be killer.

Mom's phone rang. She glanced at it and hit connect. "Hello, Orin. Yes, we're looking for a spot now. Side entrance? That's probably a good idea. We'll drop him off there. Thanks."

She hung up and turned to Dad. "Orin says we should go to the side entrance. Go up a street and you'll find an alley that leads to the service door. He's waiting there."

Dad made no comment, simply pulling back out of the parking lot and following Mom's directions until they reached an open area at the rear of the station, the only occupants of which were a pair of overloaded dumpsters and the flies that lived in them. A single door marked "employees only" was situated in the center of the station wall.

"The glamorous life of a wizard." Conryu climbed out of the car and pulled his suitcase from the trunk. The stink from whatever was rotting in the dumpsters almost knocked him over.

Mom was on the phone again and a moment after she hung up Mr. Kane opened the door for them. "Best say your goodbyes here. The platform's going to be awfully crowded."

Mom grabbed him in a bear hug and kissed his forehead. "Be careful and do your best. This is a great honor even if it's one you didn't seek. Write me every week."

Conryu hugged her back and grinned. "How? We don't have access to email."

"With actual pen and paper." She sniffed back tears.

Conryu sent a pleading look at his father. He knew Mom was going to start crying, but he still wasn't comfortable with it.

Dad gently guided Mom to one side and hugged Conryu. "Be sure to keep up your training. We'll see you at winter break. Good luck."

"Thanks, Dad. Love you guys." He hustled through the door, ignoring the tightness in his throat. This was his first time away from his parents for an extended period and while part of him was looking forward to it, another part was anxious. The fact that he was going to a completely unfamiliar environment didn't help.

Mr. Kane spoke to his parents for a minute then joined him in a damp, gloomy hallway. Water dripped from heavy iron pipes overhead and spiderwebs crowded the corners above the door. All they needed was a guy in a rubber monster suit to complete the effect.

"Ready to begin your adventure, my boy?" Mr. Kane patted him on the back and they started up the passage.

"If I say no can I go to vocational school instead?"

"No, sorry." He didn't sound sorry, but Conryu didn't comment. "I have some news about the people responsible for the attempts on your life."

"Good news, I hope."

Mr. Kane looked away.

Bad news, of course. Why did he even allow himself the illusion of something positive? Ever since that test his life had been a series of catastrophes, why should today be any different?

"Don't keep me in suspense."

The distant murmur of voices prompted Mr. Kane to stop. "We're pretty certain the Le Fay Society is behind the shadow beast attack. Mercia is most likely a member. It's doubtful she could have managed everything on her own. It's also a dead certainty they have something bigger in mind. I have people working on it. You should know that the Society has a sorority branch at the academy. I don't believe they'd be so brazen as to actually attempt to murder you, but keep your eyes open for dirty tricks and pranks, some of which may be dangerous. And frankly, just because I think it's unlikely they'll try something lethal, doesn't mean I'm right."

Conryu shook his head, trying to process what Mr. Kane had said. "So I'm walking into a situation where I'll have to be on the look out for pranks and potential murderers? This is the worst college ever. Not only do I have to study a subject I have no interest in, I also have to watch for assassins. Any other good news?"

"Well..."

"Really? There's more?"

"Angus put in a request to serve as your advisor. He argued that as a man you'd need another man to talk to now and then. Since he's the world's foremost expert on male wizards and no one else spoke up they agreed to let him make a weekly visit to the campus."

"Seriously? I have to talk to the professor once a week too? I think I'd prefer to take my chances with the assassins. And how can someone be an expert on a subject that up until two months ago the whole world believed was a fantasy?"

Mr. Kane shrugged. "You don't have to talk to him if you don't want to, but one reason I didn't overrule Angus's request was because I thought he'd serve as a useful courier should I need to pass you information or vice versa. Anything written could potentially be compromised, so I'd appreciate it if you just poked your head in when he makes his visit."

"Fine, but I can't imagine a less likely spy. I doubt he could keep a secret if his life depended on it."

"Depending how serious the Society is," Mr. Kane said. "It just might."

With that cheery thought they continued on out of the hall and up onto the main boarding platform. Several scores of families were gathered in little clumps, saying their goodbyes. There was a lot of crying and hugging which Conryu did his best to ignore.

"How many passed the test citywide?" Conryu asked as they worked their way through the throng.

"Forty-three. It was actually a little below average this year. Sentinel had fifty going last year. Even so, we had the biggest contingent in the Alliance. Central City only had thirty-five."

"What's the total class size?"

"Four hundred and something, I can't remember the exact number."

"So there's going to be around sixteen hundred students, all girls, except me? Maybe this college won't be so bad after all."

* * *

They found Maria and Mrs. Kane waiting beside a pillar near the boarding platform. Whispers and mutters followed them as he and Mr. Kane made their way across the crowded room. All the stares made Conryu feel like a circus freak, or maybe a monkey. He debated between sticking his tongue out at them and ignoring everyone before settling on the latter.

Beyond some turnstiles at the end of the room rested the shining silver high-speed maglev train that would carry them to Central City, then on to the academy campus. He'd never ridden the train, but they said it was so smooth you couldn't even tell you were moving. Conryu didn't fully understand the mechanics behind it, much less the magic, but it sounded fascinating.

Maria frowned the moment she noticed him. What had he done now? He hadn't even said hello.

"You're wearing that to your first day on campus?" She pointed at his black t-shirt.

He looked down at his shirt, jeans, and boots. They were all clean and didn't have any holes. What more did she want?

He glanced around and noticed all the girls had on expensive dresses and jewelry, fancy shoes and purses. Even their luggage looked new. He turned his attention back to Maria, finally taking note of her white dress, silver jewelry, and heels.

"Maybe they'll take one look and kick me out." As if he'd get that lucky.

"You look fine, Conryu." Mrs. Kane smiled. "I'm going to need my ring back though."

Conryu held up the hand with the silver ring. He'd been wearing it for so long he'd forgotten all about it. The ring had become a part of him.

Mrs. Kane spoke a word of magic and the ring enlarged and floated off his finger over to her. She grabbed it out of the air and tucked it into her leather purse. "It's not that I mind you keeping it, but outside magic isn't allowed at the academy. The teachers would confiscate it the moment you arrived. It's more for safety than anything else. It'll be waiting for you when you get back for winter break."

"Thanks, Mrs. Kane. Can we load up or what?"

Mr. Kane handed them each a ticket. "I've arranged a private room for you two. Until you reach the campus you're a target. The Department wizards have put special protections in place, so please try to stay inside for as much of the trip as possible."

House arrest again, swell. Conryu pocketed his ticket and grabbed his bag and Maria's two. She gave her parents one last hug then they walked through the turnstile.

They'd barely cleared it when a familiar voice called, "Conryu Koda!"

He turned and sure enough there was Kat Gabel, dressed in a short skirt and tight top. That was almost enough to make him forget she was a reporter and stop. Almost.

No cameraman with her today. Maybe she was on the outs with her station since she couldn't convince him to do an interview. That would explain the outfit: she was desperate. Whatever, it wasn't his problem. He started for the train.

"Wait! Mr. Koda, a word, please."

Conryu kept moving. "Which car are we in?"

"The last one." Maria looked up from her ticket. "Are you just going to ignore her?"

"That was my plan." Conryu eyed the length of the train. Twenty cars to go and it felt like Maria had packed everything she owned. "Do you have a better suggestion?"

She pursed her lips then shook her head. "I guess not. It just seems rude."

The reporter ran ahead of them then turned to face Conryu. "Just a few questions. Maybe we could talk more on the ride to Central."

Conryu looked at Maria. "I thought this train was just for students."

"No, they set aside four cars for us. The rest is open to the public."

"Great." Conryu tried to step around the annoying reporter, but she moved to block him. "Excuse me."

"Just a quick interview. Please?"

"Go bother someone else. There're forty girls back there who I'm sure would be thrilled to answer any question you might have."

The reporter put her fists on her hips. "No offense to those girls, but they're not news. You are."

"Then you're shit out of luck." Conryu marched forward. She'd either move aside or he'd run her over.

Kat held her ground for a few steps, but when it became clear he wasn't stopping she backpedalled. "How does it feel to be the first male student at the academy?"

Conryu lowered his head and strode on.

"What sort of magic are you most interested in?"

She was stubborn, no doubt about that.

Maria placed a restraining hand on his arm, bringing him up short. "You might want to watch out."

It took him a moment to realize she wasn't talking to him. There was a thump and Conryu looked up. The reporter had tripped on a baggage rack and landed on top of a pile of suitcases.

He grinned. "Let's go."

He and Maria jogged down the platform to the final car where a station employee wearing a red-and-gold uniform waited in front of the car door.

"Tickets please," he said.

Maria showed hers, but Conryu couldn't reach his without putting all the bags down. "Could you get mine?"

By the time he realized he'd asked her to reach into his pants pocket her hand was already digging around. He tried to think about anything other than what Maria's hand was moving around next to, but his mind went blank. It was with a mixture of relief and disappointment that she finally pulled the ticket out.

The guy looked him and Maria over and stepped aside. "Enjoy your trip."

They climbed aboard before the reporter caught up. Inside, a narrow hall ran down the middle of the car, separating two rows of private cabins.

"We're in number ten," Maria said.

She led the way while he struggled to lug the suitcases down the hall. If he ever got ahold of the person that designed these cars, god help them. Maria had the door open for him when he finally reached the end of the hall.

He grunted and heaved the cases through the door. The small cabin was well appointed with two soft chairs separated by a low table. Conryu wrestled the suitcases into the overhead storage compartments. A door led to a private bathroom. Assuming food was delivered they really wouldn't have to leave the cabin.

Conryu plopped into the left-hand chair and was pleased to note it had a lever on the side to put the feet up. Out on the platform students were piling into the other cars. "How long a trip is this anyway?"

Maria sat opposite him. "It's eighteen hundred miles to Central City. So three or four hours, assuming no issues. Then another hour or so while they switch the cars to the academy track and take us the rest of the way."

"The academy isn't actually in Central?"

"Too many distractions. The campus is situated in the wilderness fifty miles outside the city. There's a lake and forest. The pictures I've seen are quite beautiful."

"Great. Hey, I just realized, I didn't see any older girls out there. Where are the upperclassmen?"

"They went in yesterday. It's a tradition that the freshmen arrive a day after so they can get a big welcome. Don't worry, I'm sure it won't be as bad as you think." Maria put her feet up and smiled.

Conryu just sighed. "It'll probably be worse."

The train lurched when it first started moving, then the ride became as smooth as Conryu had been led to expect. The view outside the window soon became a blur as their transport reached full speed. The city vanished, replaced by the wide open spaces beyond civilization. At times it appeared they'd gone back to an age before people lived here. There was nothing but trees in every direction. A small town came and went so fast he barely registered it.

"What does this thing run on anyway?" Conryu asked. "Electricity?"

"Pure magic powers it." Maria put down the book she'd been reading. "The tracks follow a ley line all the way to Central. You know why they built the capital where it is, right?"

"Because it's nearly in the exact center of Alliance territory?"

"That's only part of the reason. The city is built over a convergence. Eight ley lines come together there. Government wizards can work powerful magic by drawing on its energy, more powerful than anything they could manage on their own anyway. The academy is connected to the convergence via a manmade line. That energy powers the various defenses and conveniences on campus as well as making magic in general easier to use for the students."

"How do you know all this stuff?"

Maria held up the book she'd been reading. It was *The History of Central City*. Conryu shook his head. Of course, he should have known.

He raised the footstool and leaned back. "Wake me up when we arrive."

* * *

Conryu felt the train slow and opened his eyes before Maria could shake him. She smiled. "We're here."

He sat up and looked out the window. "Holy shit!"

The Central City skyline filled the window as they eased their way closer to the train terminal. Dozens of skyscrapers dominated the view. Unlike Sentinel City's buildings, which were generally rectangular and utilitarian, Central's were designed in every shape imaginable; some were spires that looked too slender to stay standing, others started out square and turned into spheres at the top. There was one that bristled with antennas, that had to be a tv station.

The walls of the train station cut off the view and Conryu leaned back. If Maria was right, and she usually was, they had an hour before they resumed the journey to the academy.

There was a crackle followed by a metallic-sounding voice. "Attention students, please remain seated while we switch tracks as the process can be rough. We will be connecting more cars to the train so please be patient. All other passengers may disembark as soon as the vehicle comes to a complete stop. Thank you."

Conryu's stomach grumbled. "Isn't there any way to call room service on this thing?"

"I don't see anything. Besides, there's always a big dinner the first night at the academy so all the students can get acquainted. You should save room."

"Since when have I ever had to make a special effort when it comes to eating?"

"You got me there. Unfortunately, I don't see any other options."

He sighed and settled in. Conryu had barely gotten comfortable again when someone knocked on the cabin door. They shared a look before he went to answer it.

"Give me a break." Standing in the hall was the professor in his tweed jacket. "This car's for students only. How'd you get aboard?"

"I showed them my Department of Magic badge and they let me right on. I only have a few minutes though. I'm not scheduled for my first visit to the campus until next week."

"So what do you want?" Conryu asked.

"I just wanted to see how you were feeling, you know, first day at a new school and all. You must be excited. I know I am."

"Yeah, I can hardly contain myself. Was there something else? You don't have anything to eat do you?"

The old man looked away then back. "I also never got a chance to thank you for saving my life that day."

Conryu didn't need any reminding about which day he meant. "You're welcome."

The professor patted his jacket, reached in, and pulled out a container of peanuts. "I grabbed these out of the vending machine on my way here. You're welcome to them."

"Thanks." Conryu tore the package open and ate a handful. They were delicious though unpleasantly warm from the professor's body heat. "So Mr. Kane roped you into being his go-between. How's that supposed to work?"

The professor shrugged. "Just like it sounds I suppose. I'll bring you messages from him and vice versa."

"Excuse me." Maria leaned closer. "What's this about secret messages?"

"Oh, um..." Angus looked everywhere but at her.

Conryu swallowed a mouthful of peanuts and repeated what her father had told him before they left. "Your dad wanted some way to send messages that couldn't be intercepted. So the good professor here got the call."

"Angus, please. We'll be spending a lot of time together, no need to be formal."

Conryu almost gagged on his peanuts. "A lot of time? I thought five or ten minutes a week, tops."

"Oh no, I get you for an hour every session. That way you can tell me about your activities in detail. It will be wonderful research for my next book."

"Next book?" Maria perked up at the mention of a book she hadn't read.

"Yes." Angus puffed out his chest. "*Merlin Reborn*. It'll be an even bigger sensation than my last book."

"What's it about?" Conryu asked even though he already had a pretty good idea of the answer.

"You, of course. It's your biography. Your transformation from ordinary young man into a legend."

Maria giggled and Conryu found he'd lost his appetite. "You should probably get going, Professor. See you next week."

"Yes, yes. It would be awkward if I was stuck on the train. And please, it's Angus."

Angus took his leave and Conryu closed the door behind him and rested his forehead against the cool metal. He didn't know what he was being punished for, but he regretted it.

Maria came up behind him and rubbed his shoulders, drawing a happy groan. "Having your own biographer is quite an honor."

"I'll sell him to you cheap. Would you like to have your transformation from ordinary girl to legend chronicled for posterity?"

They laughed though Conryu's was more bitter than amused. The train shook and the image out the window spun as they switched tracks. Five minutes later they were moving again. The train quickly left the city behind and entered the wilderness. They didn't reach anywhere near the speeds they achieved on the way to the city, but the school was only fifty miles away so it didn't matter.

Before he knew it the woods opened up, revealing a gleaming lake shining in the evening sun. A modern steel-and-glass five-story building sat on the shore and two docks jutted out into the water with three small boats tied to the pilings. An even bigger building was just visible further inland. In addition to the larger buildings a handful of smaller two- and three-story bungalows perched just off the beach.

"The big one on the lake is the dorm. It's divided by element. Light wizards on the top floor and dark wizards in the basement." Maria pointed at a tree-covered island in the center of the lake. "That island is where they do survival and combat training. The big building you can't see very well is the main hall. The little ones are where sorority members live."

"I guess living on the lake will be nice." Conryu pictured bikini-clad college girls splashing in the water and smiled. Jonny would have loved it here. "It's more modern looking than I expected. I thought we'd find a castle with hidden rooms and shit."

"Disappointed?"

He shrugged. A prison was a prison regardless of what it looked like.

2
ARRIVAL

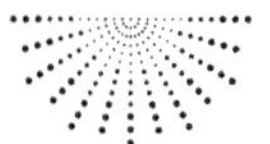

There was no proper station at the academy. The tracks just stopped and the cars emptied out onto a cement platform next to a neatly trimmed open field. It looked big enough to hold a football game no problem. In the distance beyond a low hill the dorm loomed over them. The main hall wasn't even visible from where they unloaded. The whole place looked like someone had plopped the campus down in the middle of the wilderness.

Conryu, Maria, and another four hundred plus girls piled out of the eighteen cars and onto the platform. A woman in blue-green robes stood a short ways away and waved her hands to draw the students' attention, with limited success. Everyone was talking and gawking all at the same time.

A cool breeze blew across the lake, ruffling the leaves and reminding Conryu that fall wasn't that far off. Splashing bikini girls would probably have to wait until the end of the school year. That seemed a long way off.

Conryu and Maria tried to work their way closer to the teacher, but it was tricky with so many others milling around. He tried to ignore the whispers and sidelong glances. He'd expected to run into Kimmy, but if she was there Conryu couldn't spot her.

A piercing whistle brought them up short. Everyone fell silent and turned toward the woman in teal.

"Thank you," she said. "I'm Assistant Dean Hanna Saint. I'll be showing you to the dorm where you can leave your bags, then to the welcoming ceremony where we'll figure out your alignment and potential. Once that's done we'll eat and have a good time. The real work begins tomorrow."

Beside Conryu, Maria was practically dancing with excitement. "I'm going to be light aligned, just like Mom. I can feel it."

He smiled at her enthusiasm and wished he shared it. "I'm sure you'll get what you want."

All around them the girls were laughing and debating which element they'd end up with. A handful seemed to have a preference though the only near-universal opinion was that no one wanted dark. Probably didn't want to live in the basement.

"If you'll follow me." Mrs. Saint walked toward the dorm and the students fell in behind her in a vague line.

Conryu kept his focus on where he was walking as he trudged up the hill lugging three suitcases. When he reached the top a chorus of boos filled the air. He looked up and there were maybe a hundred girls standing in their way, many waving signs, most of them with the word "men" or "boys" with red lines through them. Several chanted, "Abomination, go home."

Since all he really wanted to do was go home Conryu wasn't especially offended. The girls all wore robes of different colors so it wasn't just one element that wanted him gone. His existence was clearly an equal opportunity offense.

"Break it up!" Mrs. Saint shouted. "This is an unsanctioned gathering. Return to the dorm now or I will see you in my office tomorrow morning."

All the freshmen were staring at Conryu. He just shrugged and offered a sheepish smile. What else could he do? It wasn't like he planned on getting protested. At least no one had attacked him with a knife, so it was actually going better than the press conference.

"Don't pay any attention to them, Conryu." Maria put her hand on his shoulder.

The protesters started wandering back toward the dorm in groups of two or three. Several looked back and glared at him. He glared right back, holding their gazes until they looked away.

When the bulk of the girls had left the field Mrs. Saint said, "Let's keep moving. We have a busy night ahead of us."

They hadn't gone more than a dozen steps when something wet and heavy splattered against Conryu's right thigh. Three of the girls, two in white robes and one in red, had returned with their hands full of tomatoes.

The girl in red threw another one. Conryu dodged it easily enough once he saw it coming, though a blond girl behind him wasn't so lucky. She squealed when the tomato splattered all over her pale-blue dress.

A girl in white threw one at him. Conryu dropped his bags, snatched the tomato out of the air, and whipped it back at her. The juicy missile struck the girl right between the eyes. Liquid ran down her face and stained her robes. He stared at the other two, daring them to take another shot at him.

Mrs. Saint chanted something and the three girls went rigid. The teacher marched over to them. "You three will report to my office at six a.m. for punishment. If you're so much as a second late I'll double it. You're a disgrace to this academy. Be grateful we're required by law to train you or I'd have you expelled. Now get out of my sight."

The girls stumbled when the magic holding them was released. The girl in red spat on the ground. "I'd rather be expelled than go to a school that would accept that." She jerked her head toward Conryu.

Mrs. Saint nodded. “I’ll do my very best to grant your wish. Now get out of here.”

With one last glare the three girls scurried away. Conryu brushed the leftover tomato pulp off his pants. He hadn’t known exactly what he’d expected, but that hadn’t been it.

Mrs. Saint walked up to him and sighed. “I’m sorry about that. The administration warned them not to hold the protest, but it seems we weren’t forceful enough. I hope you won’t judge our school by those idiots. Most of us are excited to discover what the first male wizard can do.”

“Thanks, I guess.” Conryu rubbed the stain again, but didn’t make much progress in getting it clean.

“Let me take care of that for you.” Mrs. Saint cast a quick spell and the stain vanished and dried in seconds. She repeated the spell for the crying girl that had gotten hit by accident. “There. As you can see we don’t have much use for washing machines around here. Let’s hurry or we’ll be late for The Choosing.”

* * *

It was with no small amount of relief that Conryu dropped his and Maria’s baggage off in a big, empty room just off the main entrance to the dorm. It must have been put there for exactly this purpose because when everyone had left their bags it was almost full.

Mrs. Saint closed the door and chanted a spell. The door glowed briefly before the light vanished. Conryu caught her attention and raised his eyebrow.

She grimaced. “No, we don’t usually have to ward the door to the luggage room, but under the current circumstances it seems prudent.”

Conryu grinned. “You mean you don’t want anyone messing with my underwear?”

Mrs. Saint barked a laugh and the fine wrinkles around her

eyes crinkled. "Exactly. After the protest I'm not taking any chances."

They followed the assistant dean deeper into the dorm, through a lounge filled with chairs, sofas, and tables, past steps leading to the upper floors, down a hall and finally through a set of double doors that opened into the dining hall. Long tables ran the length of it and hundreds of girls in robes sat waiting. At the far end of the room was a wall of glass. Orange light from the sunset outside streamed into the room, casting weird shadows. A cheer went up when the new students entered. They probably wanted to eat, just like Conryu.

Along the far end of the hall was another table oriented left to right, filled with older women. In the center of the table sat a girl in pale-blue robes that looked far too young to be up among the teachers. In the dead center of the room a pedestal with a rectangular device resting on it waited. The device had six gems fixed to the top. From left to right they were: white, pale blue, blue-green, brown, red, and black.

The young woman in the center of the teacher's table stood up and said, "I'm Dean Emily Blane. Welcome to the North American Alliance's Arcane Academy. Please form a line in front of the Elemental Tester. Let The Choosing begin!"

Another huge cheer filled the room.

Conryu took a step forward, but Mrs. Saint placed a hand on his chest. "Would you mind terribly going last? We don't want the other girls to be overshadowed. This is a big day for everyone after all."

He shrugged. It didn't make a speck of difference to Conryu when he went. If they wanted him to go last that was fine. He moved toward the doors to make room for the others.

When Maria started to join him he held up a hand. "It's okay, you don't have to come back with me. I know you're anxious to find out your alignment."

"I'm going with you. It's not right, making you go to the back of the line like a second-class citizen. If they want you to go last, I'll go second to last." She took his hand and dragged him to the back of the line.

Conryu just smiled and took his place behind her. It seemed like he was always trailing along behind Maria. He wouldn't have had it any other way.

The first girl in line, a bronze-skinned brunette with a killer figure, stepped up to the box. Mrs. Saint stood on the opposite side and offered a reassuring smile to the hesitant girl.

"Don't worry, it works just like the testing device they used to check your magical potential. Just touch each gem in turn and the one that reacts is your aligned element. The strength of the reaction determines your power within that element. Start with dark please."

The girl reached out a shaking hand and touched the black gem. She sighed when there was no reaction. Fire and earth ignored her as well. When she reached the water gem the humidity in the hall went up about ten percent and the air took on a foggy haze.

The student removed her finger and everything went back to normal. Mrs. Saint beamed at the girl. "Congratulations, you're water aligned, same as me. We'll be seeing a lot of each other as I also teach the first year Basics of Water Magic. Please take a seat at one of the empty tables. Next."

The next two girls were fire aligned, followed by an earth-aligned student. So it went until Maria's turn came. She stood before the box and reached out for the dark gem. The instant she touched it she flinched and yanked her hand back. "It burned."

"Let me see." Mrs. Saint held out her hand and Maria put hers into it. The assistant dean muttered something and made a pass over Maria's finger, prompting the girl to sigh. "You have a high sensitivity to dark magic. I've seen it before, but it's rare. Skip right to the light gem."

Maria did as she was bid and the gem lit up followed by a heavenly chorus. She looked back at Conryu, smiling ear to ear.

"Just as I thought. You're strongly light aligned. I doubt you'll be able to cast dark magic at even a basic level. Go ahead and take a seat."

Maria hurried over to the closest empty seat then spun to watch. She wasn't the only one. It felt like every eye in the room was focused on him. Conryu hated the attention, but he supposed he'd have to get used to it.

"Mr. Koda, you're up," Mrs. Saint said.

Conryu took a breath, let it out slowly, and stepped up to the box. He reached for the black stone and rested his finger on it.

The hall went dark. Crimson eyes appeared, all of them staring at him. Conryu stared back in a daze. Nothing like that had happened when the twelve dark-aligned girls had touched the stone. The only reaction they got was a slight dimming of the lights.

"Take your finger off it, now!"

Mrs. Saint's order snapped Conryu out of his daze. He snatched his finger off the gem. The lights reappeared at once, but in his haste he grazed the fire gem. For a moment it felt like they'd stepped into an oven, but the heat passed as quickly as it appeared.

The assistant dean stared at him.

"Can I go now?"

"No. Touch the fire gem."

"Hanna, what are you doing?" Dean Blane asked.

"The fire gem reacted to him when he brushed it."

"Impossible." The young wizard rushed around the table and over to the pedestal. Up close she looked even younger with her blond ponytail and smooth, pale skin. She didn't look old enough to be a student, much less a teacher. She stared at Conryu with sparkling green eyes. "Did you feel the gem react?"

Conryu remembered the heat and nodded.

"Touch it again," the dean said.

He rested his finger on the gem and blistering heat, like someone had opened the door to a blast furnace, bathed the room. Conryu snatched his finger off it, careful not to graze the earth stone. He needn't have bothered.

"Touch the earth gem." The dean's eyes had gotten wider and her smile grew.

Conryu didn't really want to, but he couldn't exactly refuse. He nodded and touched the brown gem. The floor rumbled and shook. He removed his finger at once. "Sorry."

"Sorry? Good heavens, don't be sorry." The dean spun in a circle like Maria did when she was particularly excited. "Before we found you, Conryu, the whole world believed it was impossible for a man to do magic. The world also believed more than one elemental spirit wouldn't react to the same wizard. You have made a lie of two of the fundamental truths of wizardry. To think that something so remarkable would happen in my lifetime is a marvel. I don't know how to thank you."

"I didn't really do anything." Conryu found himself in the deep end and in desperate need of a life preserver.

The dean came around the pedestal and hugged him. He was so shocked he froze. "You will, Conryu, I can feel it. Now, touch the water gem."

* * *

In the end every gem reacted to Conryu to one degree or another. The dark gem reacted the strongest and the light gem the least, but every one of them did something. No one seemed quite sure what it meant, least of all Conryu himself. He was finally allowed to go join Maria at the end of her table. All the other girls inched away from him. Maria frowned at them and moved closer, almost sitting on his lap.

The other girls didn't look disgusted so much as afraid. After the black gem's reaction he didn't blame them. Those red eyes had scared the crap out of him too.

"That went well," Conryu said as platters of steaming food drifted into the hall, borne by invisible spirits. A platter of juicy meat and potatoes landed right in front of Conryu. A little tingle ran through him when the departing spirit brushed up against his arm.

"It could have been worse." Maria filled her plate then handed him a roll off a platter further up the table. "At least no one tried to kill you. I'm curious which floor they'll put you on since you're apparently aligned with every element."

Conryu didn't care which floor they put him on, though of course he would have preferred to be on the top floor with Maria as she seemed to be the only person not afraid of him or angered by his presence. On the other hand, two of the tomato throwers were light aligned so maybe that wouldn't be the best place for him.

The feast went on for over an hour. If the idea was for the students to get to know each other it was a miserable failure for Conryu since only Maria spoke to him. The fact that they were close seemed to make the other girls reluctant to talk to her also. That sucked and made him feel guilty. There was no reason for Maria to be ostracized just because of him.

When the feast wound down Mrs. Saint left the teachers' table and clapped her hands. "All right everyone, let's call it a night. The older students can head to their dorms; freshmen, line up and follow me."

Conryu started to stand, but she waved him back to his seat. "The dean wants to talk with you in private. She'll assign you a room after."

He sat back down and looked at Maria. "Can you manage your bags okay?"

She gave him a thumbs up. "No sweat. See you tomorrow."

"Good night."

When the dining hall had emptied of both students and teachers the dean came around her table and sat beside Conryu. "You, my new best friend, are a riddle."

"I'm a freak. What were those eyes staring at me when I touched the black gem?"

"The gems, or more precisely the portal gems, are a physical manifestation of a connection to the alternate realities from which wizards draw our power. The black gem is a direct link to Hell and the eyes were demons attracted to your power. You, my boy, are the most powerful dark magic user in history. Demons and other dark spirits will be eager to meet you and recruit you to their side."

"Great. The humans here don't have much use for me, but at least I can be friends with demons."

"There's more good news. Since all the other spirits accepted you as well you can make alliances with any of the elemental sprits. That's an unheard-of opportunity. You could be an ambassador between fire and water, earth and air, even Heaven and Hell. Though in all honesty you'll get the most power out of dark spirits."

Conryu rubbed his face. "On a minor issue, what color robe am I supposed to wear?"

"Black," she answered without a moment's hesitation. "You're going to need to focus on dark magic training above all the others."

"Guess I'll be sleeping in the basement then."

"Yup. But don't worry, I've arranged a private suite for you with its own bathroom. Can't have you sharing with the girls, after all. The senior I kicked out wasn't thrilled, but she'll get over it."

Conryu groaned. "So you made me another enemy?"

"Try not to worry about it. Tomorrow morning you and all the other freshmen will go down to the lake at dawn to perform The Awakening ceremony. Once that's complete you will be able to cast spells." She put her hands on either side of his face and forced him to focus on her. "This is very important, for all the new students, but you especially. When you cast your first spells be very careful. If you make a mistake it could be very bad indeed."

"What about the others?"

"It's dangerous for everyone, but you're twenty times stronger than the next strongest dark magic user so the risks are twenty times greater."

The day just kept getting worse. He tried to imagine what else might go wrong, but nothing came to him.

3

DAY 1

The basement room was nowhere near as unpleasant as Conryu had expected. The small suite he'd been assigned was warm and dry, with a chest of drawers, surprisingly soft bed, nice desk and comfortable chair, and the bathroom included a stall shower and pedestal sink. All in all it could have been much worse. No wonder whoever the dean had evicted was annoyed.

There was supposed to be a teacher assigned to each floor as a monitor, but Conryu saw no sign of her. Perhaps in the morning. He was too tired tonight to worry about it. His clothes ended up in a pile on the floor and he was asleep almost before his head hit the pillow.

The next thing he knew someone was shaking him awake. He groaned. "I'm up, I'm up."

He rolled over but no one was there. His clothes were lying neatly folded on top of his drawers and a crisp black robe hung on the back of his chair. How had someone snuck in without his hearing and who woke him up?

"Is anyone here?"

A breeze swirled around him, almost caressing his face. Of

course; they'd sent a spirit to wake him. It had probably just blown under the door.

"Thanks for picking up my clothes." The breeze brushed against him again. It seemed the spirit couldn't communicate verbally.

Conryu stood up, stretched, and headed for the bathroom. He was in desperate need of a shower. Behind the curtain was a shower head, but no knobs.

"How do you get water?" He didn't know if the air spirit could help him, but he figured it was worth asking. If he had to hunt down the teacher or worse, another student, he'd feel like an idiot.

In response to his question a spray of water shot out. He stuck his hand in then pulled it back and shivered. "Warmer, please?" He felt ridiculous talking to a shower stall, but it seemed to be working.

When steam filled the bathroom he checked again. Perfect. Conryu climbed in and pulled the curtain shut. A cloth and all the necessary supplies sat on a small shelf built into the stall. Maybe this place wouldn't be so bad.

Conryu had finished scrubbing his hair and was washing his chest when a pair of hands began to wash his back. He blinked water out of his eyes. It had to be his imagination.

A moment later a distinctly feminine chest pressed against his back and began to rub against him.

Conryu pulled away and spun around. A woman made of water hung in the air in front of him. Her features were indistinct, but there was no mistaking the overall shape. The water spirit smiled and reached for him again.

He dodged around her. "Thank you, but I can manage on my own."

She pouted, and Conryu felt like a jerk. The spirit had only been trying to help after all. "Okay, you can wash my back, but hands only. Deal?"

The spirit smiled again and flowed back around behind him

where she resumed scrubbing. Five minutes later the strangest shower of his life ended and he stepped out onto the bathmat. "Great, no towels."

In response the wind spirit swirled around him like a mini tornado, drying him in under a minute. This was going to take some getting used to. Conryu finished his morning routine, dressed, and threw the black robe over the top of everything.

"Thanks, ladies. See you later." A watery hand waved to him from the bathroom door and the wind spirit swirled around his neck like a cat rubbing his leg.

Conryu stepped out into the hall in time to join a line of girls in black headed toward the stairs. He fell in behind a dark-haired girl with pale skin. She glanced at him then turned away without comment.

He sighed. Maybe he should make an effort to be friendly. "So, do you know what this awakening thing is all about?"

She favored him with a look of cool disdain. "It's a ritual to awaken our power."

"Yeah, I got that from the name. I meant, do you know what's involved?"

She chewed her lip for a moment. "No, I'm not certain."

Conryu nodded, feeling a bit better about his own ignorance. "I guess we'll find out when we get there. I'm Conryu Koda."

"I know." They started up the steps. "You were the biggest news item of the summer. I could hardly turn the tv on without seeing your face plastered on it."

"Tell me about it. Those vultures followed me whenever I left the house. This one reporter even stalked me on the train here. It was a huge relief when I found out reporters aren't allowed on campus. Where are you from?"

"What do I have to do to get you to leave me alone?"

Conryu shrugged. "Ask."

"Would you leave me alone?"

"Sure." Conryu fell silent as they reached the top of the stairs and wandered into the lounge. Girls in red, blue and white were piling down the stairs from the floors above. Conryu blew out a sigh of relief when he spotted Maria in her gleaming white robe. She waved and hurried over.

"Hey." Conryu gave her a quick hug.

"Morning. Sleep good?"

"Like the dead. You?"

"Hardly a wink. Too excited."

He nodded, not surprised. "So, did you have towels in your bathroom?"

She stared at him for a moment. "Of course. What kind of question is that?"

"I didn't. A wind spirit dried me off and a water spirit washed my back. It was one of the odder experiences of my life and considering I've been nearly stabbed to death and attacked by shadow hounds, that's saying something."

"Weird. You might want to mention it to your floor monitor."

"I don't want to cause them any trouble. Both spirits seemed nice enough, nicer than any of the other students I've met so far."

"Just be patient. Once the girls get to know you I'm sure you'll have lots of friends." Maria frowned as she finished. "Just not too close, okay?"

"You bet."

"Attention everyone." Six teachers, one of each element, stood in front of the doors. The wizard in red appeared to be the oldest and she was doing the talking. "If you'll gather by element we'll head out to the beach."

"Good luck." Maria jogged over to the other girls in white and immediately fell into what appeared to be a friendly conversation. Must be nice.

A dozen girls in black eyed him suspiciously as he approached. He didn't know if they were afraid he was going to tear their robes off and attack them or one of his spells might backfire and kill them all. After his conversation with Dean Blane he was worried about the latter.

He smiled, trying to appear friendly, but it didn't work. He ended up standing next to the girl he'd spoken to earlier. She scowled, appearing no more interested in talking to him now than she had before. Looked like he was the odd man out, literally.

The teachers led them down to the beach just as the sun started to peek over the trees. Five glowing circles and one of black so dark it appeared to absorb the morning light decorated the beach.

"Everyone take your place in the circle of your element," the fire wizard said.

Conryu and his reluctant companions marched down to the black circle. The light seemed to dim further as they approached.

"Stop!" The wizard in black ran toward them, waving her hands.

Conryu froze three feet from the circle. He and the girls all looked back at her.

"Mr. Koda, please join me away from the circle. Just to be safe, you'll be doing your awakening on your own after everyone's finished. Dean's orders, sorry."

Conryu shrugged and stood beside the dark wizard as everyone else gathered in the circles. When they were in place the wizards began to chant. Energy from the circles arced over, entering each of the girls and bringing ecstatic looks to their faces. They all stared at each other, eyes wide, with big smiles.

When the ritual finished all but the black circle vanished. The wizard in black turned to Conryu. "Your turn."

Conryu walked down to the circle, every gaze tracking his progress. He'd grown thoroughly sick of being the center of attention everywhere he went. Maybe after this he could simply be another student, no different than the rest, aside from being a guy of course. And maybe unicorns would come flying out his ass. He caught Maria's gaze and she gave him a thumbs up. At least there was always one person he could count on.

As he drew closer to the circle it seemed the black line thickened and the light of the now fully risen sun dimmed. Had to be his imagination. Of course, that's what he thought about the water spirit and she turned out to be real enough.

When he stepped into the circle a feeling of welcome settled over him. Conryu had never experienced anything quite like it, but it felt good all the same.

The teacher began her chant. An odd pressure built in Conryu's chest and it grew as the spell increased in power. After half a minute the pressure became an ache that spread through his whole body, like something trying to claw its way out.

The ache became pain and soon the pain grew to the point that it took all his willpower to stay on his feet. Just when he thought he might faint, whatever was trying to escape exploded out of him.

The world went black. Red eyes surrounded him, like when he touched the gem. Hundreds of voices whispered in a language he didn't recognize. The tone was at times pleading, at times demanding, and yet other times almost hungry.

"I'm sorry." Conryu hoped these spirits understood him like the ones in his room. "I don't know what you're saying."

Some of the eyes vanished and the susurrus of voices fell away until only three remained. One was female, sultry and rich. Another snarled and growled, more like an animal than a person. The last was deep, male and powerful. Unfortunately he couldn't understand them any better than he did the more numerous voices.

He moaned and his arm burned as red letters seared into his flesh. Three words inscribed themselves in the meat of his inner forearm. A bright light blinded him and he knew no more.

* * *

Maria watched Conryu make his way down to the black circle. Just looking at that horrid dark energy turned her stomach. It sucked that Conryu couldn't bathe in the light energy like she had. The warmth and purity of it left her feeling like she'd just climbed out of the best shower of her life. That energy lived inside her now, ready to appear at her command.

Maybe it was the same for dark-aligned wizards. She liked to think so. Conryu deserved a break.

All around her the girls were muttering. None of them seemed certain what to think about Conryu. The range of opinion ran from nervous to outright hostile. Maria had only spoken to a few of the girls in the light magic group, but it was clear that the ones who came from a family with wizards in it were more disapproving than the rest. His existence threatened to change everything they knew and most didn't like it.

He stepped into the circle and a cool breeze sent a shiver up her spine. Maria didn't believe in omens, but if she did that wasn't a good one. The black-robed teacher began the spell a second time. At first he looked fine, standing there, rocking back and forth on his heels, looking bored like he always did. After a minute his face twisted and soon he doubled over.

"Conryu!" Maria started toward him. One of the teachers restrained her. "I have to help him."

"You can't."

Maria looked back into the sad eyes of the fire wizard. "Why?"

"This is his awakening and it's different for everyone. Usually the path is a smooth one, other times it isn't. With one of his power there was little hope of a smooth opening. If he's strong he will survive."

"Survive!?"

Maria's question was overwhelmed when a pillar of darkness engulfed Conryu. The dark wizard had stopped chanting and was looking frantically from one teacher to another. She'd clearly lost control of the spell.

"What happened?" All around Maria the other students were chattering in frightened voices. They stared at the midnight pillar with fear in their eyes, the same fear that filled her.

Indistinct shapes swirled around the column, appearing and being absorbed back into it faster than her eyes could follow. The teachers had all gathered in a little circle and Maria joined them unbidden. If something was to be done to help Conryu she meant to be a part of it.

"There's nothing I can do," the dark wizard said. "The awakening spell's run out of control and changed into something else."

"How is that possible?" the fire wizard asked, just a hint of panic in her voice.

"It shouldn't *be* possible. I've cast the awakening every year for a decade and nothing like this has ever happened. At worst I've had girls faint from the pressure and one threw up." The black-robed woman waved at the pillar of darkness. "But this?"

She shook her head and they all turned toward the pillar. It was clear to Maria none of them was either able or inclined to do anything. Maria didn't know a single spell and even if she did her light magic wouldn't be of much use against whatever that was.

No matter. Her best friend was trapped and she had to try and help.

Maria ran toward the darkness, eluding the grasp of the fire wizard. She stopped ten feet from the circle.

Dark energy washed over her. Maria's body trembled. It was so much worse than back at the carnival.

"Conryu!" If his magic was causing the spell to spiral out of control maybe he could stop it. "Conryu! You have to stop the spell from the inside. Do you hear me? We can't turn it off, only you can."

Maria stopped shouting and watched the pillar. At first

nothing happened then a shudder went through it. Instinct prompted Maria to move back.

A moment later the pillar blew apart, revealing Conryu standing on the beach. His robe appeared to be burning with black flames, or maybe it was made of the flames.

She blinked and the flames vanished. Conryu collapsed on the sand and didn't move. Maria ran to him and fell to her knees.

He was breathing, thank god.

The teachers joined her. The light wizard gently rolled him over and murmured a spell. She flinched back at once. "His innate magic broke my spell. I can't tell what, if any, damage he's sustained."

"Look at his arm," the wind wizard said.

On the inner portion of Conryu's right forearm three words appeared to be burned into his flesh. She couldn't read any of them, but the language was clearly Infernal. What had happened to him in there?

"What do we do?" Maria asked.

The fire wizard shook her head. "I don't know that there's anything we can do except take him to the nurse's office and hope he wakes up on his own. The rest of you should get to class, you're already late for your first lecture."

Maria took Conryu's hand and winced at the dark energy radiating from it. "I'm not leaving him until he wakes up."

* * *

Conryu drifted through the darkness surrounded by red eyes. The pain had faded everywhere except his arm, where the brand seemed to glow with a ruddy light. What did it mean? Nothing like this had happened to any of the girls. Was it some sort of punishment?

It didn't seem like a punishment. Maybe this was the only means the dark spirits had to communicate with him since he didn't understand their language. As soon as he learned it he'd be sure to tell them that burning their message into his arm wasn't a good way to get his attention. Effective, but not good.

When he tried to draw a breath it felt like something was pressing down on his chest. He groaned and the darkness began to recede. Conryu opened his eyes and found the dean's youthful face a foot from his.

"Gah!" He tried to scramble away, but she was straddling his chest. That explained why he was having so much trouble breathing. "Could you climb off me, please?"

She frowned. "You don't like having me on your chest? Perhaps if I move down a little."

She wriggled down closer to his waist.

"That's not better." He looked around. Bright lights shone down on him. He was lying on a thin, narrow bed surrounded by curtains. "Where am I?"

"My office." A plain, middle-aged woman with a kind face wearing a white robe came into view. "I'm the school nurse. Dean Blane, get off my patient."

"I was just getting a closer look." She reluctantly climbed off and stood to one side of the bed.

The nurse shook her head. "A woman your age should know better than to act like that."

The dean glared at the nurse. "I am not that old. So do you know what's wrong with him?"

"Not a thing. Whatever happened didn't make any physical or magical changes to his body beyond the brands. As far as I'm concerned he's fine."

"Excuse me," Conryu said. "What exactly happened and how long have I been here?"

"You've been unconscious for two hours." The nurse took his wrist and checked his pulse. "As to what happened, I have no idea."

Conryu turned his head to look at Dean Blane. "Do you know what happened?"

"According to the wizards that observed The Awakening, the spell ran out of control and you became trapped in a sort of pocket dimension halfway between our reality and Hell." She hung her head like a little girl caught with her hand in the candy jar. "I'm sorry, Conryu. I never dreamed the spell would react so strongly with your power."

"Was there anything else you could have done?"

"No, that is the only spell we know to activate a potential wizard's power."

"Then don't worry about it." He reached out and patted her head. "What about the marks on my arm?"

She brightened at the change of subject. "Now there I can help you. Mrs. Umbra, our Head of Dark Magic, came in to look at them while you were napping. You've been branded by three separate demonic entities. The first one is Cerberus, King of the Hell Hounds."

Dean Blane traced the first letter of the first word. Conryu flinched and pulled away.

"Still sore?"

He nodded. "Why did they brand me?"

"It's their way of offering to make a contract with you. Their name burned into your flesh combined with the correct summoning spell would allow you to bring one of them to this reality and control them."

"Why would a demon willingly give me that sort of power over it?"

"That's a long answer and you'll get to it in your regular coursework."

The curtain flew back. "Conryu!"

Maria rushed over and hugged him. "I was so worried. They said they didn't know when you'd wake up."

He rubbed her back. "I'm fine, really. Shouldn't you be in class?"

"No way. I couldn't concentrate while I was worried about you. Our first lecture was just History of Magic 101. Nothing we can't easily catch up on."

A familiar breeze swirled around Conryu. Dean Blane said something in a thin, whispery voice and the breeze responded, solidifying into an eighteen-inch-tall girl with pale skin, gossamer wings, and a sheer dress.

"This pixie says she knows you," the dean said.

The pixie flew over and sat on his chest, smiling. Conryu ruffled her hair with his index finger. "She woke me up this morning and brought my robe. I didn't know she was a pixie. I thought it was just a friendly breeze. Were you worried about me?"

The pixie nodded and buried her head in his shirt.

"It's okay, little one, I'm fine. Can you tell the water spirit for me?"

The pixie sat up, nodded, and blew away.

"The one that washed your back?" Maria asked.

"Yes."

"The naiad revealed herself to you?" Dean Blane asked.

"Yeah. Is that against the rules?"

"No, it's just that they're usually very shy. They seldom show themselves to anyone except a favorite water wizard." The dean gave a little shake of her head. "If you're up to it you should both go to class. Your first practical magic lesson is starting in fifteen minutes."

How she knew that when there were no clocks Conryu had no idea, but soon he and Maria were rushing across the spreading expanse of lawn toward the main building where they held classes. The steel-and-glass structure shined in the bright morning light. Conryu held one of the doors open for Maria then followed her into the entry hall. A short ways ahead of them a wide staircase led upstairs and to the basement.

Light magic was studied up on the top floor and dark magic in the basement. Maria gave him one last worried look before she began the five-story climb. He appreciated the concern, but wished everyone would not make a big deal out of it. So he got caught in a pillar of dark magic and branded by three demonic entities, big deal.

He sighed and started down the stairs. Who was he kidding? No matter what he might wish, it was clearly a big deal. The dean herself seemed to have taken an interest in Conryu and he doubted that happened often.

The basement was surprisingly warm and well lit. A long hall covered with white tile was lined with doors. The scent of disinfectant lay over everything. Conryu counted until he reached the fourth on the right and pushed it open.

Inside he found a simple classroom filled with fifteen chairs facing a chalkboard up front covered in mystical notations. The girls turned to look at him when he stepped through. He favored them with his best smile, but received nothing but scowls in return.

He started to shut the door. "Wait, please."

He turned and found the dark wizard that had cast the awakening spell on him hurrying down the hall, her dark hair streaming behind her. Conryu opened the door all the way and stepped aside to let her enter. The teacher brushed past him and strode up to the front of the class. She erased the formulae on the chalkboard and wrote her name.

"I'm Mrs. Lenore. Welcome to the Practical Application of Dark Magic. Conryu, give me a hand."

He'd been about to sit down, but caught himself, straightened, and went to the front of the room. The teacher dug out a pile of black leather-bound books and handed them to him. "Are you okay?" she whispered.

"Fine."

In a louder voice she said, "Pass those out and take a seat."

Conryu finished handing out the books before settling at the back of the room with the last book. He flipped it open to the title page, *Infernal Basics*.

"For a dark wizard the first thing you need to learn is to speak Infernal, the language of Hell. Without that you can't properly understand dark spells or bargain with demons for service. Our first ten weeks will be divided between learning the language and studying some basic techniques. Now, who can tell me the primary purpose of dark magic?"

Half a dozen hands went up. Mrs. Lenore pointed at a tall blond girl. "Go ahead, Elizabeth."

The girl stood up and said, "The primary legitimate use of dark magic is spell breaking."

"Very good." Elizabeth sat back down and the teacher continued. "Dark magic is antithetical to all other forms of magic and can therefore be used both to destroy wards and other protective spells as well as negating an enemy wizard's magic in a combat situation. In fact, before I took a job as a teacher I worked as a ward breaker for a demolition company."

Another girl raised her hand. "How did you end up switching jobs?"

Conryu was curious as well. He'd assumed the teachers would have some special training.

Mrs. Lenore looked away for a moment then turned back. "My predecessor retired and the Department advertised the opening on their website. I applied, took a test to prove I understood the course material, and two weeks later got the job. Now, what else can dark magic be used for?"

Conryu raised his hand and she pointed at him. He stood. "You mentioned bargaining with demons. Is that an actual, legitimate use? I would think dealing with demons would be frowned upon."

"Demons have a bad reputation because so many dark wizards

misuse them for evil purposes. A demon is really no different than any other elemental spirit. Each spirit embodies a particular essence. The four physical elements combine to make up all matter. Light magic spirits—angels if you like—represent the physical manifestation of creation, order, and life. Dark magic spirits—demons—represent entropy, chaos, and death. If properly summoned and bound they're basically an extension of their master's will. Combine an evil wizard with a demon and you get bad results."

"What about shadow hounds? Are they demons?"

Everyone turned to look at him. Conryu shrugged. "Just curious."

"I heard about the incident at the carnival," Mrs. Lenore said. "Shadow hounds aren't actual demons. They're nether spirits, vengeful monsters created when a living creature is killed in a horrific way either deliberately by a necromancer, that is an evil practitioner of dark magic focused on the creation of undead, or simply by misfortune. Shadow beasts live in the netherworld, a sort of pocket dimension between the mortal realm and Hell."

Conryu nodded and sat back down, feeling a bit better about his brands.

4
ATTACK

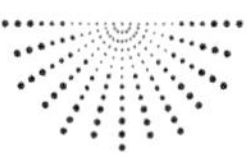

Sunday had finally arrived and with it Conryu's first meeting with Angus, as the goofy professor insisted Conryu call him. It lasted just long enough for the old man to inform him that he had nothing to report from Mr. Kane, but he did have a questionnaire as long as Conryu's forearm that he wanted filled out by next week. Conryu deposited that in the first garbage can he encountered on his way to the campus grounds.

Speaking of forearms, he had been careful to keep the brands out of Angus's sight. They were just the sort of thing that would put the professor in a giddy mood. Angus was surprisingly demanding for someone with no actual authority. He seemed to think Conryu's sole reason for existing was to serve as his research subject. Conryu would disabuse him of that notion in short order.

Since classes ran six days a week this was his first break since the train arrived. All the school clubs and sororities had set up stands out in front of the main hall to show the new students their options for extracurricular activities. Beyond the tents and displays the soft maples were starting to turn red. It wouldn't be long before fall arrived in earnest.

At the edge of what resembled a fairground Conryu met Maria. Her white robe looked stunning with her black hair.

"Hey."

She smiled. "Hey. How'd your meeting go? Any news?"

"Not from your dad." Conryu nodded toward the displays. "See anything interesting?"

"I've gotten offers to join three clubs and the Le Fay Sorority. I turned the sorority down flat, but told the clubs I'd think about it."

Maria grabbed his arm and they started down the path between the displays. A delightful odor of sizzling meat and vegetables came from the cooking club's tent. Conryu guided them that way.

A girl in a red robe with an apron over it stood in front of an open tent passing out hors d'oeuvres. Conryu reached for a puff pastry filled with cheese, but she snatched it away from him. "No boys allowed in the club."

"What are you, five years old?" Maria took a step toward her.

Conryu shook his head. This fight wasn't worth the effort. "Forget it. I can't cook anyway."

They continued on, Conryu getting the cold shoulder at each tent, until he sighed. "Why don't you look around on your own. I'm going for a walk in the woods."

"Conryu."

She reached out to stop him, but he waved her off. "It's fine. I'll meet you at the dining hall for lunch. Have fun."

He strolled on past the displays, leaving Maria on her own. She'd have a much better time finding a group to join if he wasn't there messing things up. At the very edge of the gathering sat a small platform covered in junk metal that had been badly welded into the shapes of a spider and a star fish. Four girls, three in brown and one in red, fussed over the sculptures, seeming oblivious to his presence.

He really should've just kept going, but curiosity got the best of him. "Excuse me."

The girls all looked his way. One of them, a tiny blond in red robes who couldn't have been over four feet tall, squealed and hid behind the brown robes of another girl eight inches taller than Conryu and fifty pounds heavier.

"Got a problem?" a brunette in brown asked.

"Not at all. I was just curious about these statues. I do a bit of metal fabrication myself. Is this an art club?"

"Art club!" the little blond shrieked. "These are golems, you ignorant boy. We're the golem crafting club."

Conryu wracked his brain, trying to remember what the book said about golems. His eyes widened and he looked at the statues in a new light. "Those things are intended to move?"

"Things!" she shrieked again. "Our golems are the finest in the school."

"We're the only ones that even try to make golems," the giant girl said.

"That doesn't make them any less awesome." The little blond scampered out from behind the giant's robe. "Are you saying our golems aren't awesome?"

"They're the first golems I've ever seen so I'm not sure I can judge. I do think that if you adjusted those struts on the spider you'd have a much stronger design. Their angle of alignment is all messed up. Try going at forty-five degrees." He held his hands so they formed a little pyramid.

"We do not need your advice," the little blond said.

Conryu shrugged. "You and everyone else at this school. Good luck."

He ambled off toward the woods to enjoy a little peace and quiet. A dirt path went all the way around the lake. That would make a nice hike. The whole loop was maybe five miles, just enough to get his blood pumping. After a week sitting in classes for eight hours a day he needed the exercise.

Conryu set off at a quick walk and soon broke into a jog. The breeze off the lake was brisk and kept him from sweating too much. At the halfway point he reached for his phone to check what time it was before he remembered it was back in his room at home.

Stupid no technology rule. How was he supposed to keep track of time if he couldn't even have a watch? The wind spirits guided them to class on time, but out here he was on his own.

A branch snapped in the woods. Conryu dropped into a fighting stance just as three girls in masks and matching robes stepped onto the path from either side, blocking his way.

"You ladies out for a run?"

The girl wearing a red mask and robe raised a hand and cast a fire spell. A cat as tall as Conryu's waist made of solid flames appeared before her. "Attack!"

The cat spat fire.

Conryu leapt aside and rolled back to his feet, his back warm from the close call. These had to be the same girls from the night of his arrival. One of them had worn a red robe.

The fire cat leapt at him, claws and fangs blazing.

He dodged again, sliding back onto the path. His opponent was quicker than he expected, turning and giving chase before he was ready. Fiery claws burned shallow grooves in his back.

Conryu hissed and kicked out at it. His foot passed through the cat, accomplishing nothing except singeing his ankle.

Shit!

He couldn't fight it without magic of his own and the only spell they'd taught him so far was a glowing globe that he could make with either light magic or fire magic. He hadn't learned a single dark magic spell, though he did know a few words of Infernal.

Twin blasts like lightning streaked past him, cutting gouges in the earth to his left and right. Looked like the two in white had decided to join in.

He only had one real option. Conryu turned back the way he'd come and ran for it.

* * *

Conryu zigzagged as lightning blasts sent dirt and debris flying all around him. A small tree exploded at the edge of the trail, showering him with splinters.

Damn it! If this was a wizard battle he didn't want any part of it, especially since he couldn't fight back. Being used for target practice sucked.

The fire cat lunged in from out of nowhere, forcing him to skid to a halt and let it fly past.

The moment he stopped a bolt struck at his feet, staggering him and sending needles of pain dancing up his legs.

He was too exposed on the path. Conryu ducked into the woods, darting between the thick hardwood trunks. The only bit of good fortune was that the woods were mature and little brush covered the floor.

He ran as fast as he dared and soon the blasts came less frequently. The light wizards must have lost sight of him. A low hiss brought him up short.

Somehow the fire cat had gotten in front of him. The fire spirit arched its back like a real cat and spit flames. Conryu dodged behind a tree. Streams of flame rushed by on either side. Sweat soaked through his t-shirt and robe.

The moment the flames let up he darted out and raced past the cat. It batted at him, but only shredded his robe. What he really needed was a fire extinguisher.

Idiot! He had a perfect fire extinguisher only a hundred yards away.

Conryu ran for the lake. It would take a while, but swimming back to the dorm wouldn't be a problem.

The moment he burst from the woods onto the trail a blast of lightning slammed into him and blew him ten feet backward where he landed with enough force to knock the wind out him.

Every nerve screamed so that he barely noticed the gravel digging into his back.

As he choked off a moan of pain Conryu came to understand their plan. The girls had waited for him to figure out the lake was his best bet to escape the cat and set a trap. Like a fool, he walked right into it.

While he fought his spasming muscles the three wizards strolled down the path toward him. The fire cat emerged from the woods and pranced over to the red-robed wizard. She patted it on the head and he swore the creature started purring.

They stood in a circle around him, looking down through their masks. "He's not so dangerous, is he, sisters?" the wizard in red said.

"Not at all," a white robe replied. "I'm not sure why the Hierarchs were so concerned about him."

Conryu tried to sit up, but the fire wizard stomped on his chest, forcing him back down, and gouging him with her sharp heel.

"Who gave you permission to move, abomination? Behave and we'll make your end painless." He heard her smile. "Reasonably painless, anyway."

The first name on Conryu's forearm burned. Cerberus. The demon dog's name was one of the words of Infernal he'd learned.

Mrs. Lenore, as well as the dean, had warned him to be careful when he first tried dark magic. He would have loved to obey, but if he didn't do something in a hurry he was going to die.

Conryu concentrated on the pain in his arm.

The fire cat snarled.

"What is—" the fire wizard began.

"Cerberus." Conryu called the demon dog's true name in Infernal.

The temperature around him dropped twenty degrees.

The girls jumped back as dark wisps gathered around him and

took on the shape of a giant mastiff. The nub on its neck split and formed three snarling heads.

The leftmost head looked down at him and whined. Somehow the monstrous demon beast managed to look concerned. The other two heads snarled at the three girls.

The white wizards threw up their hands and blasted Cerberus with lightning. The moment the bolts struck his shadowy form they vanished.

Cerberus's snarling grew deeper, angrier. The head that was looking at Conryu turned back to the now-quailing girls.

"Attack!" The fire wizard pointed at Cerberus and her cat leapt at the demon dog.

Cerberus's bark was more like a roar. The cat's flames were blasted out of existence.

Cerberus took a step toward the girls. The grass under his foot withered and turned brown, like a powerful frost had struck it. The demon dog lunged and snatched the fire wizard off the path and shook her like a terrier with a rat.

"No," Conryu choked out. "Don't kill."

Cerberus released his grip on the fire wizard and sent her crashing into the trunk of a maple just off the path, where she slumped to the ground, unmoving.

The demon dog turned his attention to the light wizards. They spoke in unison and a blinding flash forced Conryu to look away. When his eyes had recovered all three of his attackers were gone.

Cerberus changed from snarling protector to whimpering, worried puppy in an instant. Conryu struggled to his feet and slumped against the giant dog.

"I'm okay."

Cerberus's whine carried a tinge of doubt.

"I'll live. How about that?"

Three heads displayed black tongues as long as his leg and began to pant. At least there wasn't any slobber.

"What do you say we head back? I'm going to have to visit the nurse again."

Cerberus's bark sounded happy this time and he shrank a little to let Conryu drape his arm over his back.

"Good boy." Together man and demon dog stumbled down the path.

* * *

Maria watched Conryu walk through the fair and ignore the withering disdain from every girl he passed. What was their problem anyway? Conryu didn't choose to be a wizard, none of them did. It was just something you were born with. He didn't even want the power, unlike everyone else at the academy. They treated him like a leper just because he was a guy. If they'd just give him a chance they'd see how amazing he was.

She sighed and started walking. Some of the clubs actually looked pretty cool. The astronomy club and the alchemy club especially interested her. Maria's problem was she had trouble getting around the idea that they'd never even consider letting Conryu join with her, not that he'd necessarily want to. Both clubs revolved around math and science, not his favorite subjects except as they applied to motorcycles.

The point wasn't whether he'd like to join, it was that they wouldn't even consider letting him because he was a guy, like that made him dirty or wrong somehow. It made her so angry she wanted to scream. Stupid, arrogant, hidebound girls!

"Maria!" One of the girls from her light magic class, Irene Cohen, waved a hand to grab her attention. Irene just managed to fit in her white robe. Maria guessed she weighed three hundred pounds. She was standing beside the herbalist club's tent.

Even though they'd just met, Maria already liked the girl. Irene had a sweet, shy disposition and of all the girls Maria had spoken to she was the only one that didn't immediately say something bad about Conryu.

Maria waved back and made her way over. "Irene. Everything okay?"

"Oh yes." Her rolls jiggled as she bounced from foot to foot. "I joined the club. The herbalists have their own greenhouse where they grow all sorts of rare plants, even three Elf Orchids. It'll be great fun studying them."

"I didn't know you had a green thumb."

Irene brushed her blond hair out of her eyes. "Oh yes, I love plants. So much easier to deal with than people. Just give them a little water and fertilizer and they never complain. What about you? Join a club yet?"

"No, I can't decide which, if any, I want to join. None of them would even give Conryu a chance. I'm not certain I can hang around with such narrow-minded people."

Irene's face flushed. "He's very handsome. Perhaps the girls fear he'd be a distraction."

"I almost wish that was it. I think they're afraid if Conryu does well maybe more male wizards will be found and they'll no longer be special. It's disgusting. I assumed wizards would be more open-minded considering all the astonishing things they see every day."

"What if you told the dean? She could threaten to ban any club that refused to let him join. That might force them to give him a chance."

"Maybe, but Conryu would hate the idea of the dean giving him special treatment. The truth is he doesn't even want to be here. He thinks once he finishes school he can go back to being a mechanic like he always wanted. I'm afraid he's going to be disappointed."

Irene was about to say something else when a powerful burst of dark magic washed over Maria. She raised her hand to silence her friend and tried to hone in on the source of the energy.

On the far side of the lake dark energy radiated in waves.

There was a path that wound around that way and Conryu said he was going for a walk. It had to be him.

"Maria, what is it?" Irene didn't share her sensitivity to dark magic and so had no idea what was happening.

"Trouble. Have you seen any of the teachers?"

"Assistant Dean Saint is down by the lake doing a water magic display."

"Thanks. I have to go."

Maria left Irene staring and ran down to the lake. Mrs. Saint was controlling a serpent made of water while ten girls in blue-green robes watched with rapt expressions. She hated to interrupt, but this was an emergency.

"Mrs. Saint? Mrs. Saint, I need some help."

The assistant dean let the serpent fall back into the lake and turned to face Maria. "What is it?"

"Powerful dark magic." Maria pointed across the lake. "That way. I think it's Conryu."

Mrs. Saint muttered a spell and her eyes went wide. "I think you're right."

She wove her hands through a complex design while chanting in a clear, bright tone. The surface of the lake nearest them shifted into the shape of a boat. "Maria, climb aboard. One of you girls fetch Dean Blane and tell her Conryu needs help."

The girls all looked back and forth amongst each other. Clearly none of them was eager to carry out Mrs. Saint's request.

"Now!" Mrs. Saint roared.

One of the girls finally ran off toward the school to hunt up the dean. Maria ignored them all and climbed into the magical boat. The dark power seemed to be growing by the second. They needed to hurry.

She sat on the railing and didn't get wet. In fact if she hadn't known the boat was made of water she would have thought it was wood. Mrs. Saint joined her and spoke a word of command. The boat raced across the lake toward the source of the dark energy.

They were halfway across when the power died down and started moving. "I think he's following the trail back to school," Maria said

The boat shifted course to intercept Conryu as he made his way toward home. Please let him be okay, Maria thought over and over as they drew closer.

They had almost reached the far shore when he stopped. The boat pulled up at the base of a steep cliff. Conryu was right at the top, but there was no way to climb up, much less carry him down if they did.

Mrs. Saint cast another spell and the boat shifted under them as a pillar of water lifted them up to the top of the cliff. Twenty feet away on the trail Conryu lay facedown, a huge, black, three-headed dog standing over him.

The beast spotted them and let loose a growl so deep it vibrated in Maria's chest. "How do we get to him?"

Mrs. Saint cast a spell and two jets of water lanced out at the black dog. The instant they touched its hide the jets collapsed.

"Don't bother trying that." Dean Blane flew toward them at the top of a small tornado. "Cerberus has inhabited a body of pure dark magic. Any spell we cast will be canceled at once."

"Then how do we save him?" Maria demanded, forgetting for a moment who she was speaking to. "Ma'am."

"Cerberus is drawing power through Conryu. He has to shut it off. Call to him. Let the boy know we're here and he's safe."

"Safe! How can he be safe with a giant black dog standing over him?"

"Cerberus is there to protect Conryu, not harm him." Dean Blane gave her a reassuring smile. "Once he no longer feels threatened the link should sever and Cerberus's spirit will return to Hell where it belongs. Call to him, Maria. If he was in enough danger to instinctively call the demon spirit to his side, there's no one else he'll trust."

Maria nodded. "Conryu. We're here now, but Cerberus won't let us help you. You have to send it back."

No movement from Conryu, but all three of the dog's gazes focused on Maria. A chill ran down her spine when those crimson eyes bored into hers.

"Conryu, please." Maria rubbed her face. "Come on, we don't have all day. If you don't send that dog away we're going to be late."

Conryu's hand moved and he lifted it two feet off the ground. Cerberus rubbed one of its heads against his hand and whined. Conryu patted the giant beast like it was a puppy and the monster vanished along with the crushing dark presence. The three women rushed to Conryu's side.

Up close his wounds were obvious. Four deep lines ran down his back. They looked like claw marks, but the wounds had been cauterized. Three red, blistered patches of skin covered his legs and chest.

"Someone attacked him," Maria said.

"Obviously." Dean Blane chanted a spell and made several mystical passes over Conryu's body. "The claw marks are clearly from a fire elemental spirit and the red patches are from lightning blasts. Hanna, be a dear and see if you can find where he was ambushed. We'll take him back to the nurse's office."

The assistant dean jogged up the trail to look around while Dean Blane conjured a bigger whirlwind and flew Maria and Conryu back toward the school. Maria took his hand and held it until the nurse ushered her out of the treatment room.

* * *

Conryu didn't hurt anywhere, which was a pleasant surprise. Maybe he'd died. You weren't supposed to feel pain when you were dead, right? On the other hand he doubted either Heaven or Hell smelled of disinfectant.

He opened his eyes and stared up at the familiar lights, which, combined with the thin, hard mattress underneath him said he was once again in the nurse's office. Someone had stripped him down to his underwear and a little chill ran through him. You'd think if they were going to strip a guy almost naked they'd turn up the heat a little.

A quick look around the curtained room didn't reveal any replacement clothes, though his boots poked out from under the bed. He held up his arm and ran a finger along Cerberus's name. The demon dog had saved his life today, no question about that. He didn't know what sort of treat you bought for a dog from Hell, but whatever he wanted Conryu would get it for him.

He tried to sit up and found he had sufficient strength to manage it. He was a little stiff, but considering the beating those three had given him it might have been much worse. The moment he shifted his weight the bed creaked and the curtains were pulled back revealing the school nurse and Dean Blane.

The dean favored him with a lascivious grin which served to remind Conryu that he was almost naked. "I think I'm going to need a new robe."

The nurse reached around behind the curtain and emerged with his robe, looking none the worse for wear. She tossed it to him and Conryu slipped it over his head.

"Did you have to give it to him so soon?" Dean Blane asked. "I was enjoying the view."

"A woman your age shouldn't lust over a young man. Especially one who was almost killed."

"I am not that old. Besides, almost getting killed tends to make men eager for female companionship." The dean licked her lips.

Conryu needed to change the subject, rapidly. "Um, what happened? The last thing I remember is collapsing beside Cerberus. I thought I heard Maria's voice."

"That's easy." The dean sat beside him on the sick bed, her legs swinging. "We found you, brought you back, and Sally healed you.

That was about four hours ago. Maria was here for a while, but I sent her to find some food when I sensed you starting to wake up. Your turn to answer a question. How did you summon the demon dog when we haven't taught you a summoning spell yet?"

"I have no idea. Those three girls were going to kill me. I was scared, desperate. The brand on my arm started to ache and I called to Cerberus. Dark energy gathered around me and he appeared."

"Cerberus appeared through the dark magic or the dark magic transformed into Cerberus?" Dean Blane asked. "Think hard, this is really important."

"The magic transformed into him. Why does that matter?"

The dean let out a breath. "It matters because you didn't cast a spell you don't know. The demon dog used your innate power to create a temporary body so it could protect you."

"Okay." Conryu didn't understand what she was talking about, but since the dean seemed relieved he would be too. "Can I get dressed and go back to my room?"

"Not just yet." Dean Blane inched closer and Conryu inched away. "Did you recognize the girls that attacked you?"

"They wore masks, but it was definitely a fire wizard and two light wizards. At least I assume it was since that's the sort of magic they used. I suspect the three that threw tomatoes at me, but I can't prove it. Going from tomatoes to lightning bolts is a long jump."

"Those three are all Le Fay Sorority members so it's a good bet they're the ones that attacked you. Unfortunately, without evidence, we can't do much about it." The dean's lips twisted in an angry frown. "If we could just find something solid on them I'd ban the whole bunch."

"Cerberus thrashed the fire wizard pretty good. Would that be enough evidence?"

"The others would have had her healed and about her business in an hour or two. I'm afraid there's nothing we can do for the time being."

"There is one thing." Conryu couldn't believe he was about to ask this.

Dean Blane inched closer again and leaned against him. "If it's within my power, just ask."

"I'd like to learn a couple defensive spells, something I can use to protect myself so I don't have to rely on luck. Maybe that summoning spell you mentioned, so I can call Cerberus when I need him."

"That's a dangerous idea. What you saw was just a shadow of the demon dog's true power. If you used a proper summoning spell to bring the beast here physically, and it ran out of control..." She shook her head. "Too risky. That said, I do think you need to learn a spell or two you can use for self-defense. If you're willing to give up your free period I can arrange for our Head of Dark Magic to give you some one-on-one training. With your raw power even a simple dark spell would have a potent effect. I can think of three off the top of my head that would have ended your confrontation as soon as it began."

"I'm in. Where and when?" Much as he hated the idea of getting deeper into the study of magic, Conryu hated being helpless even more.

"You can just stay in the dark magic room after your regular class ends and she'll meet you there. I'll take care of the details."

* * *

In the deepest, darkest corner of the Le Fay Sorority building Lady Mockingbird paced, the four-inch heels of her thigh-high leather boots clicking on the tile floor. The black walls and floor of the punishment chamber were lit by a single crimson glow globe. She considered the three girls tied up in front of her.

They hung naked by their wrists, their clothes sitting in a heap in the corner.

They were lovely girls. So young and firm and sweet. A pity they were so stupid.

Fear sweat dripped from them. She took a deep breath. Lady Mockingbird loved the scent of fear. The black lash dangling from her gloved hand snapped and crackled with dark magic. Though Lady Mockingbird was fire aligned, she had considerable skill in dark magic as well. Unlike a flame whip, the black lash wouldn't mar their smooth skin. The pain it caused might make them wish she'd used fire, but burn scars would be far too obvious.

She twitched her wrist, causing the lash to crack and the girls to whimper. Lady Mockingbird smiled behind her mask. Some claimed the anticipation of pain to be worse than the reality. Those people had never felt the black lash.

"Lady, please." Demarlza, the fire wizard that Lady Mockingbird knew to be the instigator of their little adventure, dared to speak. "We thought you'd be pleased if we killed him."

"And did you?" Lady Mockingbird asked.

"No, but we were so clo—"

A snap from the black lash turned her excuses into a scream of pain. Lady Mockingbird had warded the chamber against any sound escaping so dear Demarlza could scream until her lungs bled for all the difference it would make.

When the screaming stopped Lady Mockingbird said, "I warned you to stay away from him. Even before your foolish stunt with the tomatoes, I warned you. I believe I made it clear that my superiors are always watching, always judging. How does it make me look when my subordinates disobey me?"

"We meant no—"

The lash cracked across Janice's back, drawing a scream. "Do not speak until I tell you to. I've explained the rules to you three before, yet you still fail to obey. I say, you do. I don't require your thoughts, opinions, or notions. And I surely don't need your initiative. I have my own plans in motion. Plans that will end the abomination and raise me above the wretched Lady Raven and into the ranks of the Hierarchs."

The girls all hung silently trembling, none daring to speak. Good. That was much better. Unfortunately for them they'd already proven themselves willful and disobedient. They were going to have to learn a proper lesson before Lady Mockingbird would set them free.

She licked her lips. There was little Lady Mockingbird enjoyed more than teaching lessons. It was why she became an educator after all.

Fifteen minutes later all three girls had passed out from the pain and a thin sheen of sweat covered Lady Mockingbird. Nothing like a bit of exercise to start the blood pumping. Now for a hot bath.

A knock on the punishment chamber door brought her up short. None of her girls would dare interrupt for anything but the most pressing business. She let the black lash vanish and sent a burst of fire to sever the bonds holding the girls upright. They collapsed in a heap of delightful white flesh.

They could clean themselves up and get dressed when they came to. Lady Mockingbird walked over to the door and opened it a crack. A dark-skinned sophomore in pale-blue robes stood outside with downcast eyes.

"What?"

"Dean Blane wishes to speak with you, Lady."

Lady Mockingbird ground her teeth. Of course the dean would suspect her girls and want to talk. She'd been having so much fun instructing her wayward apprentices she'd forgotten all about the consequences of their rash action.

"Tell whoever she sent I'll go to her office as soon as I'm ready."

"She's here, Lady. Waiting upstairs in the lounge."

"Is she? In that case bring her some tea and cookies and tell her I'll be with her presently."

"Yes, Lady." The girl bowed, backed away from the door, and hurried toward the stairs.

Such a demure little servant. Not enough spunk to make it far in the Society, but useful nonetheless. Lady Mockingbird dismissed the insignificant child from her mind and focused on her upcoming encounter with Dean Blane.

In spite of her ridiculous, childlike appearance, the dean was as formidable a wizard as there was outside the Society. Lady Mockingbird underestimated the woman at her peril.

A little magic and a change of clothes transformed Lady Mockingbird, Sub-Hierarch of the Le Fay Society into gentle Amelia Light, First Sister of the sorority. A billowing, red silk robe disguised Lady Mockingbird's lush figure and her confident strut became a meek amble. No illusion magic was required; it all came down to attitude.

She found Dean Blane sipping tea from a bone china mug while she sat in an overstuffed chair, her legs dangling like the child she posed as. Why a fifty-year-old grandmaster of wizardry would waste her power pretending to be a little girl was beyond Lady Mockingbird's understanding.

The dean looked up at her approach and smiled. "Hello, Amelia."

"Dean Blane, always a pleasure to see you." Lady Mockingbird made the lie sound convincing. "Is there something I can do for you?"

"I'd like to speak to three of your members, the girls from the tomato incident."

"Disgraceful. Rest assured I chastised them thoroughly for that wretched behavior. I thought they'd completed their punishment for that unfortunate incident."

"They did. However there's been another unfortunate incident. Three girls, two light wizards and a fire wizard, attempted to kill

Conryu Koda this morning. He's fine, though his faith in our security has been shaken."

"You suspect my girls are the culprits?"

Dean Blane's bland smile turned predatory. "Let's say they're at the top of my list of suspects. Do you know where they are?"

Lady Mockingbird held her hands out to the side. "They went out this morning and haven't returned yet. It's their free day after all. I assumed they went down to the fair."

"No doubt." Dean Blane stood up and set her mug on the table nearby. "I trust you'll send them to my office when you find them."

Lady Mockingbird bowed her head. "Of course."

"Excellent. And Amelia, I expect to see them before the end of the day. I'd hate to have to come back."

"I'll make sure of it, never fear." Lady Mockingbird escorted the dean to the front door and closed it behind her.

How much did she know and how much did she suspect? For a moment only, Lady Mockingbird debated simply making the three girls lying unconscious on the floor downstairs disappear, but she dismissed the idea at once. If the girls went missing Dean Blane would use it as an excuse to start an investigation and that was the last thing she needed.

5
TRAINING CONTINUES

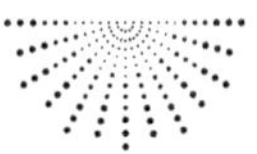

Three days after the attack on the trail Conryu and thirty-nine girls gathered in the gymnasium. Soft mats had been spread over the floor. Today was the first time since he'd arrived that everyone wasn't dressed in robes. Instead they'd all gotten element-colored sweat pants and t-shirts. Facing the group was a similarly dressed wizard in her mid-forties, earth aligned if her brown gear was any indication. She wore her hair cut short and had a chiseled, muscular build.

They were supposed to be learning the basics of combat training and judging by the easy, always-balanced way the instructor carried herself, she was more than capable of teaching them. Not that Conryu needed much in the way of additional combat training. The conversation he'd had with Dean Blane the day before ran on an endless loop in his head.

She'd spoken to the girls Conryu believed were behind the attack, but they swore up and down they hadn't been involved and several other girls from the sorority backed them up. With no other evidence the dean had been forced to let them go with nothing more than a warning. Her next warning was for Conryu to be careful. She promised to arrange extra dark magic lessons as soon as possible.

Conryu forced his mind back to the moment. This was one class where he wasn't behind all the other students. A quick glance revealed many nervous faces and more than one shirt was already sweat-plastered to the girl wearing it. This was perhaps the first time since he arrived that Conryu was the more comfortable one. It made for a nice change of pace.

"My name is Mrs. Grundy," the teacher said. "And this is basic self-defense. Some of you ladies are no doubt wondering why wizards need to learn hand-to-hand combat when you can just blast your opponents with a fireball. Well if your opponent can get in close you'll find most magic useless. You need to learn to disable your enemy quickly and create space to use your spells."

Conryu nodded to himself. This wasn't going to be a comprehensive martial arts class, just some basic strikes and counters that would allow the girls to escape a close encounter.

"Every year when I begin with a new group," Mrs. Grundy continued. "I make the same offer. Anybody that can stay on the mat with me for a full minute without ending up on their back is free to skip my class. Any takers?"

The girls were all muttering amongst themselves, but the teacher's gaze was locked on Conryu. There was a challenge in it he'd seen many times when a student transferred from another dojo to theirs. Some people needed to find out for themselves.

Conryu hopped to his feet. "I'll give it a go."

He walked between the rows of students to comments of "arrogant boy" and "I bet she flattens him." His fellow students seemed to have little faith in him. Shocking.

Conryu stepped on the mat and bowed to the teacher. "Sparring rules?"

Mrs. Grundy thumped herself on the chest and it made a dull sound. "I toughened my body with earth magic. You can go full contact. Don't worry, I didn't enhance my speed or strength. It'll be a fair match."

"My body isn't hardened with earth magic," Conryu said.

"Don't worry, I'll go easy on you. Ready?"

Conryu settled into a neutral, defensive stance, hands raised and feet shoulder-width apart. "Ready."

She lunged at him, going for a leg tackle. Conryu hopped back and struck down, driving her into the mat. Six machine gun punches to the back and ribs followed. Without magical protection his blows would have cracked her ribs.

He leapt over her and spun as she scrambled up off the mat. Mrs. Grundy nodded, some of the arrogance having been knocked out of her. "I felt those even through the magic. How are your fists?"

Conryu grinned. "Good to go. Forty-five seconds more I'd say."

She approached more cautiously this time, fists raised and knees bent in a typical kickboxer's pose. The teacher snapped a midlevel kick.

Conryu dodged back then darted in to close the distance before she regained her balance. Close fighting was a Koda-style specialty. He lashed out with a barrage of rapid-fire punches and elbow strikes.

His opponent blocked some, but a third of them slipped through, scoring hard blows to her face and throat. Her magic protected her, but they both knew that without it she would have been down long before now.

Mrs. Grundy tried to step back and create distance, but Conryu stomped on her foot, locking her in place. That move startled her just enough to create an opening.

He stepped into a double-palm thrust, striking just above and below her breasts and sending her flying off the mat and skidding across the floor. She came to a stop ten feet away, shook her head, and climbed back to her feet.

"You okay, ma'am?"

She rubbed her chest and nodded. "That last one hurt. I feel comfortable saying you don't need basic self-defense training. This is a twice-a-week class. If you have something else you'd like to do, go ahead. I won't be sparring with you again."

"If it's okay, I'd like to help you train. I haven't taught a class since the start of summer vacation and it would be nice to get back into it. Unless the ladies object?"

To Conryu's considerable surprise none of them did. He and Mrs. Grundy moved to the front of the class.

"Okay, everyone on your feet." When the girls had all complied Mrs. Grundy continued. "The most important thing to remember is balance. If you're off balance you're at the mercy of your opponent, as Mr. Koda here so ably demonstrated. Show 'em how."

Conryu assumed the basic stance he'd taken when they began their match.

Mrs. Grundy walked along behind him. "Note the bent knees, wide stance, and weight on the balls of his feet, ready to react."

She snapped a punch at him which Conryu deflected and instinctively countered with an open-hand thrust to her throat. He stopped just short of her skin.

"The next thing to remember is, be ready for anything. Now let's see you."

The girls tried to mimic his pose. Some did well. He suspected they were athletes and used to this sort of thing. At least three clearly had some basic martial arts training.

Conryu walked along the rows, adjusting a foot placement here and a shoulder turn there. He paused by one girl who had so much weight on the balls of her feet a nudge to her back would send her flat on her face.

"That's not going to work." Conryu gently put his hands on her shoulders and the girl went rigid. "Relax, if you're stiff your balance will be even worse."

He adjusted her position until she was in proper balance.

"Feel that?"

She nodded, her eyes wide and nervous. "Thank you."

It came out as more a squeak than actual words, but he appreciated the gesture. They spent the next hour and a half teaching the girls simple tricks and weak spots where a solid hit would do maximum damage.

When the wind spirit arrived to tell them to go to their next class Conryu said, "I don't think it would hurt to give them some exercises they could do on their own. Most of them aren't strong enough to fight anyone off."

Mrs. Grundy nodded. "Go ahead."

Conryu assigned them to do deep knee bends and hold the position until it became uncomfortable, along with push ups and crunches. When they filed out at the end of class several of the girls actually smiled at him. It wasn't much, but it was a start.

* * *

Conryu sat amidst the empty chairs in the dark magic classroom and studied the phrases written on the chalkboard while he waited for his instructor to arrive. Ten days had passed since the attack and Mrs. Umbra, the Head of Dark Magic Studies, finally had some time to train him. He'd begun to wonder if the dean had changed her mind. His palms were sweating and no matter how many times he dried them on his robe it didn't last. He'd heard some of the other dark-aligned students talking about the department head.

The rumor was she'd done a tour down on the southern border where she killed more than her share of heart hunters. While the stories made him nervous they also gave him confidence that his instructor had actual combat experience and would teach him what he needed to know if he wanted to survive a real fight.

A regular tap, tap, tap came from outside, getting louder as it drew closer. A moment later the door swung open and there stood Mrs. Umbra, all four feet ten inches of her. Deep wrinkles lined her face and only a few wisps of white hair clung to her head. Her black robe hid everything beyond hands with swollen, arthritic knuckles. She leaned on a polished black walking stick topped with a silver skull. It was named the Death Stick and served as a potent dark magic enhancer.

Conryu scrambled to his feet. "Ma'am. It's an honor to learn from you."

She closed the door and tapped her way across the room until she was just a few feet away. "Are you afraid, boy?"

"A little, yeah."

She cracked a smile, revealing a mouth full of straight white teeth. "Me too. I've never trained anyone as powerful as you're supposed to be. Even with the Death Stick, you're still easily twice as powerful as me. Since I know what I'm capable of, I also have a fair idea of what you can do. We shall proceed carefully."

"Yes, ma'am. May I ask a question?"

"Yes."

"Everyone tells me how strong I am and that I'm capable of great or terrible things. I don't feel strong, not in magic at least. What exactly am I capable of?"

"That is what we're about to find out. Leena's a good girl, more than able to teach the basics of dark magic, but for someone with your potential a more experienced hand is best. I told Emily that the night of your testing, but she insisted you be treated the same as every other student. I was pleased when she changed her mind."

"So what do I do first?"

Mrs. Umbra walked up to the chalkboard, spun it around to reveal the blank side, and wrote three words in Infernal. Conryu recognized "darkness" and "all" or maybe it was "everything," from his studies, but he'd never seen the third. Next she drew a hand with crossed fingers followed by a figure with its wrists crossed.

When she finished Mrs. Umbra turned back to Conryu. "This

is the formula for the most basic dark magic spell. Do the hand positions, speak the words, then throw your hands in the direction of whatever magic you want to end and uncross your fingers. If you have time you can speak the words multiple times to build up more power. Want to give it a try?"

"I'm not familiar with the second and third words and their pronunciations."

"I'll just recite the whole spell: Darkness dispels everything."

He repeated the awkward sounds until she was satisfied with his intonation.

"I believe I'm ready now," he said.

Mrs. Umbra cast a spell and a flame cat almost identical to the one that attacked him appeared beside her. "Now use the magic to cancel my summoning."

Conryu took a breath to calm his racing heart. He was about to cast his first dark magic spell. After everything he'd been told, he found his hands shaking.

How had it come to this? He should be at the technical college right now learning how to diagnose engine problems. Instead he was out in the middle of nowhere learning magic and worrying about potential assassins.

Well, as Dad liked to say, you had to deal with the problem in front of you. And his problem just now was making a fire cat vanish.

Conryu crossed his wrists and fingers like the drawing showed. "Darkness."

It felt like he'd dropped into a cold, dark well. The room around him looked no different, but in his mind he was back out in the black pillar on the beach.

"Dispels." The darkness gathered around him formed into a sphere between his chest and crossed wrists. He saw the shape of the spell now and understood how to direct it.

"Everything!" The dark sphere solidified.

He hurled it at the fire cat, uncrossing his fingers as he did so.

The cat vanished, but the dark energy didn't. It kept growing, seething like flames and reaching for the enchanted lights in the ceiling.

Mrs. Umbra spoke a single sharp word in Infernal and snapped her fingers. The darkness slunk away like a chastened dog. It gathered around Conryu's feet and he understood that if he wished he could reform the energy into a new spell and fling it out again.

Of course he only knew one spell and had no interest in casting it again.

"What now?" he asked.

Mrs. Umbra tapped her chin and appeared deep in thought. Conryu wasn't sure if that was a good sign or not. "Hold your hands palms up and repeat after me."

She slowly spoke four words in Infernal and Conryu repeated them just as precisely though he had no idea what any of them meant. The darkness leapt up and poured into his hands, through his palms, and into his body. It swirled around inside his trunk and settled in his stomach.

"What the hell was that?" The dark power sat like a meal of greasy pizza in the pit of his gut.

"That was something I've never seen before. When you cast the spell, so much dark energy came through that a demon spirit rode along with it. The spirit possessed the leftover energy instead of letting it dissipate."

Conryu stared stupidly for a moment. "There's a demon spirit in my stomach?"

"Of course not." Mrs. Umbra sighed. "The second spell I had you cast stripped the spirit out of the power and sent it back to Hell. The purified energy remained inside you for future use. That way you can cast spells without drawing spirits through along with the energy you need."

"But I only have the power from a single spell. How long will that last in a fight?"

"You can probably fire three decent shots with what you have stored. You'll need to modulate your casting: whisper the words instead of chanting, cross two sets of fingers instead of four. After that, assuming the fight is still going on, you'll have to chance casting the spell the traditional way and ending up with imps and other minor demons running around afterward. It's not ideal, but you can always clean up the mess if you survive."

"So what now?" Conryu couldn't wrap his head around what had happened. He'd never even heard of modulating spells, though he may have skimmed that section of the book. Maybe if he convinced Maria to explain it he'd understand. He was supposed to meet her for dinner in the cafeteria shortly.

"Do you have your writing pad?"

Conryu flipped open his lined notebook. "Shoot."

She wrote the words to the second spell below the first on the chalkboard. "Copy them both, but don't cast them without me present unless it's life and death. Study them until you know the words by heart. We'll resume our training in two days."

"I thought you were busy until next week?"

"I'll move some things around. We need to figure out how to work around this demon issue if you want to make any progress as a wizard."

Conryu didn't give a flaming crap about progressing as a wizard, but he needed to know how to protect himself and he didn't want demons running around every time he cast a spell so he just nodded. "I'll do my best."

* * *

Conryu left his class with Mrs. Umbra and headed for the cafeteria. He didn't think he was late, but with no way to tell the time he couldn't be certain. The spirits were good about fetching him for a class, but he couldn't exactly ask them for the time. Conryu was still aware of the dark energy inside him, but he was getting more and more used to it as the minutes ticked by. Whether that was a good thing or not he had yet to decide.

The halls were mostly empty as he made his way through the main building and over to the dorm. Everyone was either still in class or they had already arrived for dinner. The scent of roasting meat reached him as soon as he pushed the dorm doors open. One good thing about this school, the food was excellent. Whatever magic they used to make the meals so tasty was one thing Conryu didn't object to.

He spotted Maria sitting at the end of one of the long tables across from a chubby girl in white robes. She'd introduced him to the bashful freshman last week, but damned if Conryu remembered her name. Did it start with an L? No, I. Irene, that was it. She was in his self-defense class, but seldom spoke. If he even looked her way she'd blush furiously.

Maria waved as he approached. Conryu smiled and picked up his pace. Irene started to stand, but Conryu said, "No need to leave on my account."

She sat back down, her face beet red. He slipped into the seat beside Maria.

"Are you sure you don't mind?" Irene asked.

"Of course not." Conryu smiled and she looked away. "It's not like I have any other friends here. Have you been doing your training?" At the moment she was so out of shape that even the most basic moves were beyond her.

"I try, but I get tired so fast."

"That's natural at first. Just do what you can every day and try to add one or two more reps each week. You'll be surprised how fast you can progress if you keep at it."

She nodded eagerly. "I think I have lost a few pounds. If you'll excuse me I'm going to have a salad."

When she'd gone to stand in line Maria said, "That was sweet."

She touched his hand and immediately jerked her hand back. "What?"

"Your skin burned me, like when I touched the dark gem."

"Shit." Conryu explained what happened when he tried casting a spell. "The dark magic is still inside me. I assume that's what you're reacting to."

"I've never heard of such a thing. What's she going to do about it?"

"Your guess is as good as mine. I'm meeting Mrs. Umbra in two days so maybe she'll have something figured out."

"Have you written your mother yet?"

"Not since the attack. I'm not sure what to tell her. Something like, 'Hi, Mom. I'm learning all about magic. Pretty much everyone hates me and I was almost murdered again. Love, Conryu.' I can't imagine that going over well."

"No. I know you can't lie to her, but maybe if you sort of glossed over how much danger you were in. Like you did when you told her about The Awakening."

"What if I told her your dad would fill her in on the details? Do you think he'd mind?"

"Not at all. In fact that's a great idea. Tell her the good stuff and that Dad has some information for her. I'll mail my letter a day before you so he has some warning."

She reached for his hand again before she caught herself and touched his sleeve-covered arm instead. He really needed to sort this magic problem out. Never being able to hug Maria again didn't appeal to him at all.

* * *

Two days went fast and Conryu once again found himself waiting in the basement classroom for Mrs. Umbra. He'd been studying every spare minute to master as much of the Infernal language as possible. He figured the more words he knew the better he'd be able to follow her instructions. He now knew what the words for his second spell meant, though he hoped to never have to use them.

A chuckle slipped out. It amazed him how having a goal he actually wanted to achieve helped his motivation. Before the last two days he hadn't realized how often he and Maria would casually hold hands or she'd grab his arm as they walked down the hall together. Now that they couldn't he found he missed it terribly.

The tapping of the cane heralded Mrs. Umbra's arrival. She pushed the door open and in her hand was a tome as thick as Conryu's palm. It looked like about all the old woman could manage. He rushed over to help her, but she warded him off with the Death Stick.

"You can't touch it until we make the necessary preparations. I think I've sorted out your demon problem, but it's going to be tricky getting everything right." Mrs. Umbra hobbled over to the desk and thumped the book on it. "You've been practicing the spell I taught you?"

"Yeah. I think I've got it mastered."

"Good. A magic detection spell will reveal the ward on this book. I want you to use the magic you have stored to dispel it."

Conryu frowned and spoke a single word of Angelic. "Reveal." It was one of a handful of universal spells his other teachers had shown him so far.

The book lit up with a combined light and fire magic ward. It looked pretty strong, but he hadn't seen enough wards to say for sure.

He cast "Darkness dispels everything!" and hurled all his stored power at the ward. It shattered and dissipated in an instant. The considerable amount of unused dark energy fizzled away as well.

Conryu glanced at Mrs. Umbra, who nodded. "Good. That's the way the spell is supposed to work. No demons running around afterward."

"So how do I get that result with ordinary dark energy?"

Conryu felt lighter than he had in days without the dark energy weighing him down and he wasn't eager to recharge.

"You're going to form a demon contract with Cerberus. Since he branded you the process is already halfway completed. I've written up a basic guardian contract that should serve our purposes."

"What good will that do?" He didn't know much about demon contracts. That wasn't a subject usually covered in a student's first year.

"If you successfully form a contract with him the demon dog's spirit will be constantly nearby. He can chase away any lesser demons that might try to slip through when you cast a spell, thus freeing you to use your magic properly."

"What's the catch?"

She sighed. "That's a complicated question. Maybe I should explain the way things work in Hell. The basics at least. In Hell everything is a competition and demons are constantly jockeying for better position. Battles are constant, the mighty are thrown down and others rise to take their place."

"What's that got to do with me?"

"There are two ways for a demon to grow stronger, destroy a rival and consume its essence or make a pact with a human wizard. The more powerful the wizard the more power the demon gets."

"So I sacrifice a portion of my power to gain Cerberus's help?"

She shook her head. "The relationship is synergistic not parasitic. Cerberus will get power and through him his minions, the hell hounds, will as well. You'll get a powerful guardian who will constantly be close by and ready to appear at your summons. At least those are the terms I put in your contract."

"That's why Cerberus and those other two marked my arm. They couldn't find a more powerful wizard than me."

"Exactly. I recommend you use Cerberus because he's already

proven his willingness to protect you and he's the weakest of the three, though more than adequate for our needs."

"Wait." Conryu remembered how powerful the demon dog was and that was just a fragment of his might. "The other two are stronger than Cerberus?"

"Absolutely. Would you like to meet them?" Mrs. Umbra didn't wait for his reply before she began flipping through the thick book. "Here's The Dark Lady."

Conryu moved closer. On the open page was a pen-and-ink illustration of a female demon with bat wings, curling horns, a pointed tail, and a figure that made Heather James look positively flat-chested. Underneath the picture was the caption, The Dark Lady, Princess of Succubi.

He gave a wolf whistle. "Maybe we should use her."

Mrs. Umbra's laugh resembled a dry cough. "You'd never have another night's sleep if you made a contract with that one."

Conryu thought it might be worth it, but he kept his silence. His teacher flipped through the book until she came to another demon illustration. This one was definitely male. It had a massive chest and shoulders, long smooth horns, a thick, serpentine tail and a black trident. The picture very much resembled drawings he'd seen of the devil. Conryu checked the inscription and about choked. Lucifer, Demon Prince of Lies.

"The devil himself branded me?"

She laughed again. "Hardly. Don't believe all that superstitious nonsense some of the religions spout. Lucifer is just one of many powerful demons. He's clever and sneaky and if the opportunity came to betray you, he'd do it simply because that's his nature. At some point we'll need to remove his name from your arm. A strong connection to that one is not in your best interest."

"No shit."

She glared at him.

"Sorry. So what now?"

"Now you copy the demon contract I prepared exactly. The

wording has to be precise or Cerberus may be free to do things we don't want him doing. That would be bad."

Conryu spent the next however many hours carefully copying the contract. He was surprised to note that he understood almost half of it. Those long nights studying had paid off.

When he finished she took the paper from him, studied it, and handed it back. "Good, now the hard part. You're going to have to shift yourself halfway between Hell and earth. Cerberus can meet you there."

"How will he know to come?"

"The demon dog will sense his brand and come to investigate."

"Okay. But what's to keep Lucifer and The Dark Lady from visiting me as well?"

She tapped him on the forehead with a bony finger. "You're smarter than you look. Nothing is keeping them from paying you a visit. My only hope is that since Cerberus has already answered your summons once, he'll be closer than the other two and you can complete your contract before they show up."

"What do I do if we're not fast enough?"

"Improvise."

There was a cabinet behind the chalkboard that Conryu had never noticed. Mrs. Umbra removed all manner of magical accessories from it: chalk, black candles, a chalice of gold set with rubies. While she fetched supplies, Conryu cleared a space in the middle of the room so she'd have space to draw a conjuror's circle.

He made no comment as the more experienced wizard carefully drew a five-foot circle, then added a pentagram, all the while muttering in Infernal. "Get in the center and don't forget the contract."

He grabbed the paper and stepped into the middle of the pentagram. "What now?"

"Sit down—careful not to touch the lines—and let me finish the circle. When it's complete I'll teach you the words to the transference spell."

She spent the next hour drawing runes in all the empty spaces around the center of the pentagram. Finally she lit the candles and slumped into a chair. "Done."

"What about the chalice? It's empty."

"It's only there for symbolic purposes. Now repeat after me."

"Wait! How do I end the spell?"

"The spell ends when you've completed the contract."

"And if I don't complete it?" Conryu wished he'd skipped lunch.

"Then you'll be trapped between earth and Hell until you do."

"You didn't think to mention that before we began?"

"Would it have mattered?"

Conryu pictured Maria flinching back from him when she touched his hand. "No, I suppose not. Alright, let's hear it."

"Through death's black gate my soul travels to the edge of darkness, Hell Portal!" She spoke the spell using precise enunciation and emphasis. "Clear?"

"Once more please. Hey, how come when you cast the spell nothing happens?"

"I'm going to tell you something, one of the secrets of magic. The words and gestures, they only serve to focus and direct the magic. What really makes it work is your will. That's why, when you were near death, you managed to call Cerberus to protect you even though you didn't know the spell. If you have sufficient will, nothing else is truly necessary. Now pay attention."

She cast the spell again and when she finished Conryu nodded. "I'm ready."

He settled himself and repeated the spell. With each word the darkness around him deepened. By the third word he saw nothing but black in every direction; even the candles vanished. He spoke the final word and it felt like he was rushing through space though he never moved.

When the sensation of movement ended he looked around. Nothing but black and more black. No up, no down, no nothing.

He straightened his legs though it didn't feel like he stood up. In fact he couldn't feel much of anything. What a wretched place. If this was the border of Hell what was the dimension itself like?

Mrs. Umbra hadn't mentioned how he was supposed to attract Cerberus's attention. He assumed the demon dog would simply sense the brand and come... running? Flying? However you moved around in this void.

No sooner had he thought it than he spotted movement in the distance, not that distance meant much with nothing to use as a point of reference. Whatever was out there gradually grew bigger until it resolved into a female figure in a red-and-black dress that left little to the imagination.

The Dark Lady. Terrific.

Where was that dog when he needed it? "Come on, Cerberus, hurry up."

He sensed something moving behind him a moment before a rough tongue licked his cheek. A second tongue licked his other cheek. Thank goodness. Maybe they could get this done before she got too close.

There was a dull thump followed by a whine as Cerberus went flying off into the darkness. A massive figure moved to stand in front of Conryu. Muscles rippled beneath red skin and only a loincloth hid his nakedness. Conryu stared up into the cruel, handsome face of Lucifer and tried to ignore the giant black trident the demon carried in his right hand.

"Come to make a bargain with me, mortal?" Lucifer's deep, booming voice seemed to fill up the space around them, somehow echoing though there were no walls or canyons.

"Of course he hasn't, Luci." The Dark Lady flew up beside Lucifer's left shoulder, wrapped her arms around his bicep and smushed her boobs against him. She looked down at Conryu. "He's come to make one with me."

"Actually—"

"Don't be absurd, woman. All mortal wizards want power, and no one is more powerful than me."

"Hmmm," The Dark Lady purred. "Shall I tell Lord Beelzebub that?"

"The lord of flies doesn't frighten me." Lucifer's boast sounded a little brittle to Conryu, but he didn't think it prudent to say so.

"Of course not." The Dark Lady kneaded his deltoid with her slender fingers. "The Prince of Lies fears no one. Still, I'm sure this boy would prefer to make a pact with me. All the boys want to make a pact with me."

She flew down and hovered in front of Conryu. Her presence was overwhelming. Even knowing it was magic, it took every scrap of his willpower not to rip her flimsy dress off right there. Her tail snaked around his leg, the nimble tip rubbing his thigh inches from his groin.

"You know you want me, mortal. Why the hesitation? With my power at your disposal every woman you've ever wanted, Maria Kane, Heather James, and anyone else will throw themselves at your feet."

Lucifer snatched her out of the air, his huge hand engulfing The Dark Lady from her ankles to her chest. "This mortal is mine, harlot. Be gone before I destroy you."

While they argued Conryu spotted Cerberus slinking closer, staying well out of Lucifer's sight.

Good boy.

If Lucifer and The Dark Lady stayed focused on each other for a little longer, maybe he could complete the contract with Cerberus and escape.

"You might destroy me." The Dark Lady's voice dripped venom. "Maybe. But I'll hurt you enough that your enemies will tear you apart the moment you return to Hell."

Lucifer cocked his arm like he wanted to throw her away, but she dug her nails into his arm and held on like a lioness riding a wildebeest. Conryu motioned Cerberus over and unrolled the contract to let the demon dog read it.

Cerberus watched Lucifer with two of his heads and trotted quickly over. He studied the contract while Conryu risked a glance up at the more powerful demons. Lucifer and The Dark Lady were clawing and hissing at each other like a pair of angry cats. She had the advantage in speed now that she'd somehow broken his grip, but it appeared she could only scratch his skin.

The paper in his hand shifted when Cerberus touched it with his nose. Power flared and a tendril of energy shot from Conryu's chest, connecting him to Cerberus.

"No!" Lucifer screamed and thrust his trident at them.

Conryu shut his eyes and prepared to die.

When he opened them he found he was once more in the dark magic classroom with no trident through his chest. He leaned back and sighed.

He'd done it.

Strange that he didn't feel any different. All around him the magic circle was evaporating along with the last of the magic.

Mrs. Umbra was dozing in her chair, the Death Stick resting across her lap. The candles had burned down to nubs and gone out. Conryu stood up and stretched stiff muscles. How long had he been gone? He looked around, but of course there was no clock. He shook his head. It was a wonder anyone arrived anywhere at the right time.

"Mrs. Umbra."

His teacher snorted in her sleep and sat up. "Oh, you're still alive. Excellent." She muttered a spell and narrowed her eyes. "The connection is complete. I trust you had no difficulties."

"Lucifer and The Dark Lady showed up at about the same time as Cerberus, but other than that it went fine."

She stared at him. "Both of them were there yet you still made the contract with Cerberus? How?"

"Actually it was lucky they were both there. They were so busy fighting with each other that we had time to make our pact. Lucifer nearly ran me through at the end, but the spell concluded before his trident reached me. Strange, Cerberus vanished at the same time."

"Of course he did. The demon dog is right beside you, slightly out of phase. He couldn't very well block the other demons if he was too far away."

Conryu spun around, but there was no sign of the giant beast. "I don't see him."

"I told you he's out of phase, on the other side of the barrier that separates our reality from the six magical realms. He's close enough that he'll be able to watch everything around you, but not so close that he can influence our reality. On the plus side, when you finally learn a summoning spell he'll be quick to respond. That speed may one day save your life."

Conryu yawned. "So when's our next class?"

"Monday. I need time to recover from the ritual."

She needed time to recover? He was the one that almost got run through by the devil.

6

BACK AT HOME

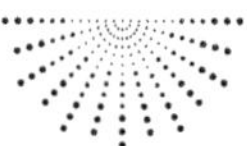

Orin held his phone in one hand and rubbed the bridge of his nose with the other. He'd been in his office for two hours already and it was only eight in the morning. For the past ten minutes Angus had been complaining that Conryu wouldn't tell him every little detail of his life at school and how was he supposed to write his new book if the subject wouldn't cooperate and couldn't Orin do something about it.

In fact Orin didn't think there was anything he could do about it. Conryu had a mind of his own and if he didn't want to talk to Angus there was nothing to be done. At least he was stopping in every week to check for any new information. So far Orin hadn't had any reason to use Angus to ferry a message as he had nothing to tell the boy. Lin and Terra had both hit dead ends in their investigation.

As far as sending information the other way, Dean Blane was an old acquaintance of Orin's and she kept him well informed of events at the school. When he finally had to tell Connie about the attempt on Conryu's life she hadn't taken it well.

And by not well he meant she had demanded Conryu be returned home immediately. That wasn't possible for a number of reasons, not the least being the law. He suspected Sho was upset as well, but the grandmaster didn't show his emotions quite as readily as his wife. Still, he was glad Conryu's father hadn't done anything rash.

It was with considerable relief that Emily had informed him Conryu was studying with Angeline Umbra. If anyone possessed the skill needed to teach him how best to protect himself it was that formidable woman.

"Angus, take a breath." When the professor finally fell silent Orin continued. "I know you want Conryu to spend more time talking to you, but if he doesn't want to have a book written about his life that's his choice. You have to respect it."

He held the receiver away from his ear when Angus started shouting about posterity. The door to his office opened and Terra stepped inside. He waved her to a chair.

"Angus. Angus! I have to go. Just do your best. Yes, I'll talk to him over winter break. Goodbye." Orin slammed the receiver down a little harder than strictly necessary.

"Conryu still giving the good professor fits?" Terra grinned like the idea amused her no end. And why shouldn't it? It wasn't like she had to deal with Angus when he called to complain every week.

Orin nodded and thumped his head on the desk. "What does he expect me to do, order Conryu to talk to him? I thought I was doing good just convincing him to check in once a week."

"Angus wouldn't be satisfied if Conryu let him follow his every move every second of every day. Though if he did maybe Angus would get caught in the crossfire the next time someone tries to kill the boy."

"Not funny, Terra. I thought Connie was going to strangle me when I told her about the attack. Please tell me you have some good news."

"I'm not sure how good it is, but I do have some news. I finally figured out, at least in part, what the object contained in the box was supposed to do."

"I'm listening."

"It's a portal spell keyed to the netherworld. This one was modified and a binding added so the shadow hounds that came through would focus on Conryu. That magic was much newer than the actual portal spell. The magic also looks incomplete, but I can't get any more detail until I open the box."

"Then open the blasted thing. What are you waiting for?"

"I'm not waiting for anything. I tried opening it. Clair tried opening it. Then we tried opening it together. We even tried getting the backup tester to lend a hand. None of us is strong enough to break the seal."

The first twinge of a headache was building behind Orin's eyes. "Plain English, Terra. What do you need?"

"A dark-aligned wizard powerful enough to break the ward. Can you contact Central and ask them to send someone as soon as possible?"

"Will do." He jotted a note on a pad on his desk. "What about Lin? Has he made any progress figuring out where the other boxes are hidden?"

"Not so far, though it isn't for lack of trying. The information is just too vague. It could describe any one of a thousand places in the city. If I can figure out the magic, our theory is it will give us a clue that will unlock the seemingly random information in the packet."

"How likely is that?"

Terra shrugged. "It's all we have to go on."

"Alright, thanks. Anything else?"

Terra shook her head and left the office. When the door closed he picked up his phone again. The sooner he contacted Central the sooner they could put someone on the train out here.

After eight rings one of the secretaries at the Department Headquarters in Central picked up. "Could you transfer me to the dark magic department?" Orin asked when the woman finished her greeting.

The line went silent for a few seconds before a deep, but still female voice said, "Dark magic."

"This is Orin Kane, chief of the Sentinel City office. I need a high-level dark magic user sent out as soon as possible for an emergency breaking."

"Join the club."

"Excuse me?"

"I don't know if you've heard, Chief, but there's a major offensive going on at the Sector Eight border. At least a hundred frost giants have come south and every dark magic user we can spare is up there to negate their ice magic. I don't know what your emergency is, but I doubt it outweighs a hundred frost giants."

"Now look—"

"Sorry, Chief. I'll put you on the list, but I wouldn't count on any help from us until April at the earliest and most likely not before July."

"July?" Orin shouted into the receiver, but the line was dead.

7

THE GOLEM CLUB

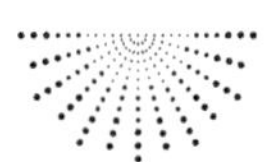

Conryu was beyond grateful that his first class didn't start until nine. After the ritual the afternoon before all he'd wanted to do was sleep. So it was with some annoyance that a dull thud on his door roused him far earlier than he would have preferred. He groaned, sat up, and reached for his phone to check the time.

"Goddamn no technology rule," he muttered for the thousandth time.

He rolled out of bed, threw on his robe, and shuffled over to the door. Outside, the tall wizard from the golem club loomed over him. Hiding behind her was the short blond. He squinted at them in the light from the hall. "Yeah?"

The giant pushed the little one in front of her. "Go on."

The blond twisted her red robe in her hands and stared at the floor. "You were right about the struts."

She spoke so softly he barely heard her. "What?"

She glared up at him. "The struts on Blinky 2.0, you were right, they worked much better when we set them to forty-five degrees. He's way more stable now."

"Great." Conryu looked from the little one to the big one. "Was there something else?"

"Ask him." The giant gave her friend a nudge.

"I'm working up to it." The blond cleared her throat. "Would you like to join our club? You seem to have some practical knowledge that would be useful to us."

"And?" the giant prompted.

"And I felt bad about yelling at you the other day." She looked back and up at her friend. "Satisfied?"

The giant smiled, but didn't comment.

Conryu was all sorts of confused, beyond still being half asleep. "You know if I join your group the other girls will probably hate you, right?"

"We're not terribly popular anyway, as you may have guessed from our location at the fair," the blond said.

"Why? You all seem like… interesting girls."

"Blinky 1.0 went berserk last spring and ruined the cooking club's annual tea party. It's the most popular event of the year." The giant looked down at the fire wizard and shook her head. "It was not my fault. I didn't intentionally mess up the binding just because they didn't invite us to their stupid party."

The big girl gave Conryu a knowing wink. Lucky for them her friend didn't seem to notice.

"So what do you say?" the blond asked. "Want to join up?"

It would be nice to build things again. He'd missed working with his hands in the garage, seeing the bits and pieces of an engine come together into a proper piece of machinery. He didn't know much about golems, but how different could they be?

"Sure, thanks. When do you meet?"

"Sundays, ten until noon. The dean let us convert a storage shed into a workshop about a hundred yards east of the campus. New members always bring the snacks."

The giant cleared her throat prompting the smaller one to sigh. "We rotate every week."

"I'll get this week's." Conryu said. "What does everyone like?

By the way, what are your names? I can't keep thinking of you as the tall one and the short one."

The tall one laughed and the short one scowled. "I am not that short. Sonja Chard." She thrust her hand at Conryu who gave it a polite shake.

He looked up and raised an eyebrow.

"Crystal Conrad." He shook Crystal's hand. "Chips or chocolate would be best for snacks."

"We'll see you Sunday." Sonja stalked up the hall. Crystal shrugged as if to say what can you do.

"Does she have a favorite?" Conryu asked. Sonja looked a little tightly wound and he hoped she'd relax if he brought her something special.

"Vanilla cookies, the little round ones they sell in the cafeteria. I think she might have a crush on you, so be careful."

"Thanks for the warning."

"Crystal! Let's go."

Conryu stared at the girls' backs as they marched up the stairs. What had he gotten himself into now?

* * *

"You joined a club?"

Maria sounded as surprised as he felt. He'd just finished his five-minute visit with Angus and left the professor sputtering and indignant. The old man just couldn't take a hint. If he wanted to write a book about Conryu he'd just have to make up the details and hope Conryu didn't decide to sue for libel.

He'd found Maria waiting for him on the steps to the main building. Since none of the clubs would accept him as a member she'd refused to join one as well. Hopefully now that he'd found a group, she'd go do whatever it was she wanted to do.

"Yeah. The golem club. I thought it might be like shop class. I haven't built anything in weeks so it should be fun. Plus you can go stargazing if you want to without feeling guilty."

"It wasn't about feeling guilty!" she sputtered and looked away.

He grinned and kissed her on the cheek. "If you say so. Anyway, I appreciate the gesture, but now you can join a club of your own."

He glanced at the shadows spreading across the grounds. He had about an hour before he was supposed to meet the rest of the club, plenty of time to pick up snacks and make the short walk over. "You want to come with me? I need to make a stop then head over to the club shop."

Maria chewed her lip for a moment then shook her head. "The alchemy club is meeting in the school lab. They said if I wanted to join I should stop in anytime."

"Cool. See you at lunch?"

Maria smiled. "Absolutely. And be careful. The last time you went off by yourself bad things happened."

"I'm always careful. Besides, I've learned a few tricks since last time. If they want to fight I'm ready."

She grabbed his robe and pulled his face down so their noses were almost touching. "Don't do anything stupid. Even if you have learned a dark magic spell, you're no match for a more experienced wizard. Promise me."

"I promise, okay? Geez, you're worse than my mom."

She stared into his eyes for a moment longer then nodded. "Until lunch then."

Maria trotted up the steps and disappeared into the school. Conryu shook his head and set out for the cafeteria. He picked up two bags of chips, some foil-wrapped chocolates, and a bag of vanilla cookies which he hid in a pocket of his robe. With his supplies gathered Conryu marched out of the dorm and east toward the woods.

It was a short walk to the golem club's workshop. When Sonja said it was a shed she wasn't kidding. He doubted ten people could fit in the building if it started raining. The roof looked sound at least and the rough-hewn boards covering the sides were solid. A barn door on runners concealed whatever was inside. There was no lock, but then again in a school filled with wizards a simple lock probably wouldn't amount to much anyway.

None of the other members had arrived yet and Conryu had a moment of doubt. Maybe Sonja had just invited him out here to give them all a laugh at his expense.

"Oh, hi. You're the first one to arrive." Sonja approached from the north. She looked all around for the others, but there was no sign of them.

"Yeah, I didn't want to be late on my first day."

"Oh." She scratched her head and refused to look at him. "Um, want to have a look at the shop?"

"You bet. I'm excited to see what's going on."

Sonja hurried over and tugged on the door. It didn't budge. A string of loud and virulent curses was followed by a swift kick from the little wizard.

"Let me give you a hand." Conryu reached over her head and yanked on the door. It slid open a foot and Sonja pulled it the rest of the way open.

To say the inside was unimpressive would be an understatement. The spider and starfish sat on a piece of plywood suspended between a pair of sawhorses. A heap of scrap metal fit only for the smelter filled the rear of the shed. There was no welder or power tools. In fact the only tools in the shop were a hammer, some pliers, and a small punch. How the hell could you build anything with that crap?

"It's… something. Don't you have any tools?"

"We're only allowed to use magic. If we need a particular tool we have to make it from scratch. The whole point of the clubs is to improve your magic skills after all."

"How do you weld?"

"A combination of earth and fire magic. I heat the metal,

making it soft enough to shape then Crystal or one of the other girls fuses the two pieces together on a molecular level with earth magic. If you build your golem any other way you're not allowed to enter the Brawl."

Conryu was starting to think he'd made a mistake joining this club. "Brawl?"

Sonja's eyes lit up. "The annual Grand Brawl. Golem clubs from all over the Alliance come here the week before winter break and we pit our creations against each other in a giant battle royal. The winner is the club whose golem is still standing at the end."

"Is there a prize?"

"Just bragging rights and your club members' names on the trophy. Though one year an especially dominant team got a contract from the military to build combat golems for the army. They haven't come back to compete again."

"How did you guys do last year?"

"Terrible." She shot him a fierce glare. "This year's going to be different. Blinky 2.0 is going to crush the competition."

Conryu looked over her head at the ill-made heap of rusty legs jutting at various angles from what looked like two small buckets welded together to make a body. He doubted that piece of junk could crush a soda can. He dug the vanilla cookies out of his pocket. "I picked these up for you."

"Crystal talks too much." She grabbed the cookies and tore them open. "Thanks."

The rest of the club arrived in short order and Conryu was introduced to Onyx Rose and Jade Smith, the other two earth magic users. The girls were polite if hesitant, not surprising given how most of the school seemed to feel about him.

Once the introductions were taken care of Sonja said, "Let's take a look at Blinky."

The little group gathered around the spider golem, filling the shed to bursting. It had metal legs reinforced by struts like he'd suggested. Each leg ended in pointed claws. Its head, if the narrow end of a bucket counted as a head, had eight red stones stuck on it that he assumed represented eyes.

"Pretty awesome, right?" Sonja beamed at him and all but cuddled the ugly metal contraption.

Conryu licked his lips and tried to think of a convincing lie. "It's got potential, certainly. What sort of spirit does it use for power?"

"We went with an earth spirit since it's made of metal," Onyx said.

Jade nodded her agreement. "Earth and fire are the most common spirits for this type of golem and fliers aren't allowed in the Brawl."

"That makes sense. What else were you thinking of adding to the structure?"

They all looked at each other and finally Sonja said, "We thought the structure was pretty well set now that we reinforced the legs. We were going to focus on getting Blinky moving fast and smooth."

Conryu looked the golem over again. The thin metal of its body wouldn't withstand even a glancing blow and the legs were so scrawny he could probably bend them with his bare hands. The claws on its feet were too short to make effective weapons.

"How about you guys focus on movement and I'll see about strengthening the structure?"

His suggestion was met with a moment of silence before Crystal said, "That sounds reasonable. Let's have a snack."

Conryu wasn't hungry. His mind was fully occupied with turning a rusty spider into a real weapon.

* * *

"It's time to begin studying practical dark magic."

The chalk squeaked as Mrs. Lenore stood at the blackboard and drew a circle with a series of magical runes inside it. Everyone leaned forward, eager to learn something besides Infernal. They all spoke enough of the demons' language to hold a simple conversation. Their teacher had deemed them sufficiently fluent to move on to the next phase of their training.

"Okay, this is a basic spell-breaking circle. It is designed to contain and control the dark magic you summon so it only affects the target and none of the people or magic nearby. Any questions before I continue?"

Conryu raised his hand. When she pointed at him he said, "Does spell breaking work like a Dispel magic spell?"

"Mrs. Umbra taught you that one, did she? It's similar, but more focused. The spell you learned has a broad effect designed to end any spell in a large area. Useful in combat, but not focused enough for ward breaking where you might want to eliminate only a portion of a spell and leave the rest intact."

He jotted down her explanation in his notes. He certainly saw the need for something to focus his power. If he cast the spell in the wrong place he'd wipe out all the magic in the room.

"Getting this technique mastered is important for many reasons, the most practical of which is it will be the main component of your midterm in two months. The second is that when you graduate, as dark wizards, this will be the task you are most often called on to perform. There's a huge demand for wizards to remove curses, hexes, and the old wards of buildings in need of demolition or remodeling. You can make an excellent living doing nothing else in most cities in the Alliance."

The girls all perked up at that. Most of them hadn't been thrilled with the prospect of being dark aligned, but now that it seemed they could make a living with it their interest had picked up.

Mrs. Lenore wrote a single word in Infernal under the circle. Conryu recognized it as "break." That made sense, given what they were trying to do. There were a number of Infernal words with similar meanings. Would any of the others work just as well? Probably not if she didn't say so. One thing he'd learned in his brief time at school: precision was everything.

"Who wants to give it a try?"

Everyone looked back at Conryu. He shrugged. "I guess I will."

"Excellent. Take out a piece of paper and copy the circle exactly."

Conryu did as she said. The design of the runes was simple enough and it only took him a minute and change to draw his circle. "Done."

"Good, come up here and let me check it."

He walked to the front of the class and handed her his paper. She studied it for a moment, nodded, and handed it back. "Okay, you're good to go."

She took a wooden block out of a pocket in her robe and set it on the table. A word in Angelic caused it to glow and float seven inches off the table. "Alright, Conryu, slide your circle under the block and place your hands on either side so the tips of your index fingers are touching the circle, but aren't inside it."

He did what she said. "Like this?"

The rest of the class had inched closer to better watch. Mrs. Lenore moved his fingers a hair further from the circle so only the very outer edges grazed the inked line. "That looks good. Now say the spell."

Calling a single word a spell seemed excessive, but he knew what she meant. "Break!"

The block exploded into fine dust. He winced. "Oops."

Mrs. Lenore had her forearm over her eyes and the girls were coughing from the dust. "You used a bit too much power. Next time try whispering the word."

"Sorry."

She shook her head. "It's not your fault. I didn't take into account your unique situation. This circle should limit your power. I forgot that even limited your power is still way too much for what we're trying to accomplish."

"Can I try again?"

She looked away. "Unfortunately I only brought one block. I planned to renew its magic after each of you broke it. I didn't plan on it getting reduced to sawdust."

The girls glared at him as they all returned to their seats. They were the ones that wanted him to go first. It didn't seem fair they were complaining now.

They spent the rest of class practicing drawing the circle until they could do it from memory. When the spirits came to fetch them Mrs. Lenore said, "I'll bring a new block tomorrow, don't worry. One day won't be a big deal."

The girls all left to enjoy their free period while Conryu remained behind to train with Mrs. Umbra. Mrs. Lenore usually hurried off as well, leaving him to wait alone. Instead she sat in the chair beside him.

"It really isn't your fault. I should have known what would happen and warned you to speak softly. Angeline, that is Mrs. Umbra, warned me I wasn't ready to train someone as special as you. She said I needed more experience. I guess she was right."

She looked so glum that Conryu wanted to give her a hug. "Everybody makes mistakes. God knows I've made enough of them. I think you're doing a great job. We'll figure it out together."

"That's sweet of you to say, but she never would have made that error. Maybe it would be best if you studied with Mrs. Umbra exclusively."

Conryu didn't know what to say to that. Certainly the department head was an amazing teacher, but she had other classes and only worked with Conryu twice a week. Add to that the fact that both his teachers were training him in different things and he saw no way forward without both of them.

It surprised him when he realized he really was looking for a way forward. While actually working in the magical field didn't appeal to him, the more he experienced the more he realized he was a part of this world whether he liked it or not and as such he needed to understand it. His continued survival depended on it.

"If you don't mind, I'd like to stay in your class. I've learned a lot and it helps me with my work with Mrs. Umbra."

"Really?" Mrs. Lenore sat up straighter.

"Yeah. She takes too much basic knowledge for granted. I bet Mrs. Umbra hasn't even thought about the stuff you teach for twenty years. It's all as natural to her as breathing. I, on the other hand, often feel like I'm drowning."

"Then I'll be your life preserver." Mrs. Lenore held out her hand and Conryu shook it.

"Deal."

* * *

Conryu strolled through the dorm doors toward the cafeteria. He smiled as he went, feeling better than he had since learning he had to attend the magic academy. His classes with both dark magic teachers were going well and no one had tried to kill him in almost seven weeks. That was a trend he'd like to see continue.

His seventh morning with the golem club had been much more relaxed than the previous ones. The girls seemed to have realized he didn't have fangs or claws and wasn't going to attack them when they turned their backs. He wasn't entirely certain why they'd thought that in the first place. Maybe it had something to do with all the bad things that happened around him. They might have feared getting caught in the middle.

Whatever the cause, the improvement pleased him mightily. The only problem was Sonja and Onyx were both seniors. He'd barely get to know them and they'd be gone, probably along with the golem club. The other girls enjoyed it, but Sonja was the driving force. Without the diminutive fire wizard to motivate them he doubted the rest of the club would stick together. Not that he minded. It hadn't turned out to be at all what he expected when he signed up.

He pushed the cafeteria doors open and spotted Maria sitting at the end of their usual table. She had her head in her hands and he thought she might be crying. She hardly ever cried, so something serious must have happened.

Conryu slid into the seat beside her and slipped his arm around her. "What's wrong?"

"Nothing. I'm just having trouble in class. My wards aren't working the way they're supposed to. My teacher says my angles are messed up and my runes are imprecise."

"You're just getting started. She can't expect you to be perfect after a month and a half."

"She doesn't, I do. I had every advantage coming in here. I've studied more magical books than all the other girls in my class combined. I should be the best and right now I'm middle of the pack. I don't find that acceptable."

Conryu grimaced. Light magic must be really hard if Maria was struggling this much. "Anything I can do to help?"

She smiled and hugged him. "No, but thank you for offering. I'm afraid our disciplines are too different for what you learned to transfer over."

"I didn't really think there'd be anything. The idea of me helping you with schoolwork is pretty funny. Hey, did your teacher tell you about our midterms?"

"Not yet. Why, what did you hear?"

"The light magic class is going up against the dark magic class. You guys will ward something and we have to try and break it. We're studying spell breaking now. It's kinda cool. Seems I have a knack for it. Though it helps that I have the biggest hammer."

She stared at him with wide eyes. What had he said now? "You mean if my wards don't survive I'll fail?"

"From what I understand you only have to make it past one of thirteen students. We have to break at least one ward to pass." He tapped his chin, a habit he'd picked up from Mrs. Umbra. "I didn't think about it before, but that implies at least one person will end up failing."

"I have to go study." She leapt out of her chair and headed for the door.

"Maria? What about dinner?"

"I've lost my appetite," she called over her shoulder without breaking stride.

Conryu groaned. He probably shouldn't have told her that. She was already nervous and now he'd made it worse.

He turned toward the kitchen. Sonja was headed his way, a tray of food in her tiny hands. "Hey, want some company?" She sat beside him without waiting for his answer.

"Sure. So what's the seniors' midterm?"

"Elemental domination. The teacher summons a powerful spirit of our aligned element and sets it free. We have one minute to bring it under control."

"Sounds tough." He imagined trying to bring Lucifer under control and shuddered. "You don't seem too worried."

Sonja swallowed a bite of meatloaf. "I'm good at elemental domination. We've been doing practice runs and I always get mine under control in less than thirty seconds. I'm more worried about finals. We have to show mastery of five elements. I suck at dark magic and I'm shaky with air."

"What do you have to do with dark magic?"

"Cast five spells from first- and second-year classes and then three spells from third or fourth. The first- and second-year spells are a cinch, but the third-year spells focus on demon binding and dismissal. Demons are way harder to deal with than elementals."

"What about fourth year?"

"Itching for a sneak peek?" She grinned at him. "Sorry. Mrs. Umbra says I don't have the aptitude to study fourth-year dark magic. That's fine with me. No offense, but third year was at the outer edge of what I can handle. I can't even imagine what fourth year is like."

He nodded with a mixture of disappointment and relief. "Did you think any more about what I said regarding the golem?"

"You mean reforging Blinky out of solid steel? It's a good idea, but we only have one fire wizard. I don't think I can process that much metal on my own."

"Is the spell difficult?"

"No. Anyone capable of casting fire magic could do it." Her grin broadened into a full smile. "Are you thinking what I think you're thinking?"

"Can you teach me the spell?"

"Ha! I knew it. I sure can. If we work together I bet we can finish Blinky in three Sundays. Once we liquefy the steel Crystal and the others can handle the shaping."

"Shall we give it a try this Sunday?"

"Yes we shall." Sonja hugged him. "This is going to be so fun."

* * *

Conryu arrived at the golem club's shed a few minutes early as was his habit. The days were getting noticeably cooler and all the trees had now turned red and orange. It was a beautiful day and several of the girls from the art club had set up their easels down on the beach to paint the lake and island. Conryu had never been especially artistic, but it looked like a peaceful way to spend the morning.

Maybe Maria should take it up as a hobby. Ever since he'd told her about the midterm and her teacher confirmed it she'd been wound so tight he feared she'd break. It made him glad he'd never worried too much about his grades. As long as he passed, nothing else mattered.

He pulled the door open and studied the pile of scrap metal along with the two semi-finished golems. First he needed to sort out everything that wasn't pure steel.

He pulled one of the battered wooden stools over and got to work. First went the tin and aluminum cans. Apparently the kitchen staff had donated them, in an effort to be helpful or more likely get someone to take the junk off their hands. As he sorted Conryu considered his most recent, pointless, visit to the professor.

Angus had almost pleaded for information about his studies. The professor had been so pathetic Conryu almost gave in. Only the fear that sharing a single sliver of information would encourage him to be even more demanding brought Conryu up short. There was still no information from Mr. Kane. The whole secret messenger thing looked like a bust.

He shrugged and focused on his sorting. He had just started on the brass when Sonja and Crystal arrived. It was Crystal's turn to bring snacks and the tall girl had a bagful.

"What'cha doing?" Sonja crouched down beside him.

"Sorting the junk out of the steel. We don't want to have anything that might weaken the metal when we start forging."

"Good idea." Sonja glanced at his discard pile. "Will we have enough?"

Conryu had been wondering that exact thing himself. "Only one way to find out. Dig in."

Onyx and Jade arrived five minutes later and between them they had the pile sorted in a little over an hour. The steel pile ended up depressingly small. Combined with Blinky they had maybe a hundred and fifty pounds. The max weight for the Brawl was four hundred.

Conryu ate a chip and sighed. "I think we'll have to sacrifice the starfish if we want to get close to our maximum weight."

"If we do that we'll have no backup in case Blinky goes on the fritz again," Onyx said.

She had a point, but as things stood neither golem had a chance of winning. He doubted they had much of a chance even if they used all their metal to make a single construct.

"It's your call, but as it stands now Blinky's going to get squashed by the big golems. Even if we combine them it'll be a hundred plus pounds under the max."

"Let's vote," Sonja said. "All those in favor of making a single golem raise your hand."

Conryu put his hand up as did Sonja. Onyx and Jade both held their hands in their laps. All eyes turned to Crystal. The tall girl looked to Sonja, sighed, and raised her hand.

"Three to two." Sonja beamed. "Out of respect for the sacrifice I hereby christen the combined golem Star Blinky."

They finished their snack and while the earth magic users set about freeing the spirits bound to the golems Sonja took him aside to explain the fire spell they'd be using. It was a simple, two-phrase spell that opened a micro portal to the realm of fire and called forth pure flames hotter than anything on earth outside a volcano.

Considering what happened when he used dark magic the first time he was a little worried about opening a fire portal. Hopefully Cerberus could chase away fire spirits as well as he did demons.

When Sonja had gone over the spell three times and he'd repeated it to her satisfaction she said, "Want to give it a try?"

"Sure." While they were practicing Crystal had made an earthen crucible and filled it with Blinky and half the scrap they'd sorted out.

Sonja winced when she caught sight of her beloved golem in a dirt hole ready to be melted. Conryu gave her shoulder a reassuring squeeze. "He's evolving to a higher state. Just focus on how awesome Star Blinky's going to be."

Sonja nodded and her expression hardened. "Right. Let's do this."

She raised her hand and pointed the palm at the crucible. Conryu mimicked her. They chanted the words in unison. "All things burn to ash, Inferno Blast!" Conryu's hand got warm and what looked like a flame thrower blasted towards the pile of metal. The blueish-white flames forced the other girls to take a couple steps back.

Conryu glanced at Sonja. Her flames were bright orange with a narrower flow. The metal liquefied in minutes. Sonja closed her fist, ending the spell, and Conryu again followed her example.

The moment the flames ended Crystal chanted a spell and the metal flowed, taking on the form of a spider's body. It was fascinating, watching the steel take shape, almost like a sculptor with soft clay. He glanced at Sonja again and found her staring at him.

"What? Did I do something wrong? I know my flames looked different than yours."

"Your casting was perfect. The portal you opened was three times bigger than mine. Compared to the heat of those blue-white flames, my magic added almost nothing to the process. I think I understand now why the other clubs didn't want you to join. You're so powerful you make others unnecessary."

"That's ridiculous. I didn't even know that spell until you taught it to me. I just aped what you did. Without you to guide me nothing would have happened today."

"Thanks."

"Done!" Crystal said.

They turned to find a realistic spider body about as big as Conryu's chest sitting on the shop floor. Everyone stared at it for a moment then they smiled. A good showing in the Brawl now seemed like a real possibility.

8
PRACTICAL MAGIC

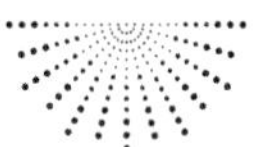

"We're going outside," Mrs. Umbra said as soon as she reached the dark magic classroom.

Conryu leapt to his feet. They were in the middle of an Indian summer and he was delighted at the prospect of spending an hour or two in the fresh air. It was the middle of October and he'd settled into a comfortable routine. History of Magic along with simple universal spells in the morning followed by dark magic in the afternoon and a second class with Mrs. Umbra twice a week. Two other days he helped Mrs. Grundy teach self-defense.

The girls were coming along nicely. He wouldn't want them to enter a tournament or anything, but most of them had gained enough confidence that they could throw a punch without flinching. Even better for him, they'd gotten comfortable enough around him that when they chatted during breaks they included him in the conversation.

Mrs. Grundy had been true to her word, refusing to spar with him again no matter how much he teased her. That was kind of a drag since there were no other trained martial artists at the school. At least none that he'd found.

"So what are we doing today?" Conryu asked as they left the basement and headed for the doors.

"Combat training. I want to find out how well you can use the spells I've taught you in a fluid environment."

"Cool. Where are we going to train?"

"The beach." She glared up at him. "Nothing for you to break if things get out of hand."

Conryu grinned back at her. If there was one thing he had a knack for it was breaking things.

They left the main building and strolled down to the beach. Conryu was eager to begin, but Mrs. Umbra set the pace. When they finally arrived, Dean Blane was waiting, along with a handful of teachers he didn't know.

He hadn't seen the youthful dean in a while, probably since no one had tried to kill him lately. She had on a pale-blue robe and her blond hair in pigtails. It would be far too easy to underestimate that woman.

The dean waved and ran up to him. "Conryu! Isn't this exciting? When I told everyone you were going to be tested today they all wanted to come watch. Every teacher that didn't have a class this period is here."

He glanced at Mrs. Umbra. "I thought you said this was just training."

"It is." She walked across the sand, ignoring the stares that followed her.

Conryu turned back to the dean. "So is it a test, or not?"

"Not the pass or fail sort of test, more like one that measures how far along you are. How many spells has she taught you?"

"Three: Dispel, Cloak of Darkness, and one that strips demons out of excess dark magic energy. I don't know what that one's called. We've been practicing them for weeks. I'm hoping she'll teach me something new. Maybe if I do well today."

"Maybe." Dean Blane patted him on the back. "Do your best."

Conryu took his black robe off, tossed it on the grass, and

followed his teacher out onto the sand. It felt good not having that bulky thing holding him back. Wizards weren't actually required to wear robes so he didn't see any need to train in one.

Mrs. Umbra faced him from thirty yards away, the Death Stick held in front of her. "Ready?"

He nodded, the words of a Cloak of Darkness spell on his lips.

She spoke the first word of the familiar fire cat summoning spell. The moment she did he chanted, "Cloak of Darkness!" Liquid darkness covered him from head to toe. It didn't affect his vision, but the air felt ten degrees cooler.

Instead of one cat, four appeared. Looked like she wasn't going to go easy on him this time.

Conryu crossed his fingers and wrists. Before he began to chant the fire cats spread out so he could only hit one at a time.

All four cats charged. There was no way to dispel one and evade the other three. The Cloak of Darkness negated magic. Maybe if he used that.

He ran toward the rightmost cat. It leapt at him. He met it with a roundhouse kick. His dark-magic-covered foot and shin passed through it, snuffing out the flames.

He didn't have time to inspect his now-unprotected leg as the next cat hurtled toward him. Conryu dodged right and punched it in the head.

The cat vanished in a puff of smoke.

Now his left leg and right arm were bare. The surviving cats circled and charged again. Mrs. Lenore said he wasn't supposed to use a breaking spell without a circle, but if he combined it with the hand gestures of Dispel it ought to stay reasonably under control.

When the cats were ten feet away he threw his hand forward, the fingers crossed. "Break!"

A sphere of dark energy burst from his palm and annihilated both cats.

Conryu renewed his Cloak of Darkness and spun to face his

teacher. Six cats surrounded her, three of fire and three made from sand. He was well acquainted with the fire beasts by now, but the sand ones were new.

All six charged him. He crossed his wrists and fingers again and chanted the spell. He had an idea he'd been considering for a while. Since he doubted Mrs. Umbra would actually hurt him, this would be a good chance to test it.

He made it through the spell five times and summoned a sphere of dark magic as big as a pumpkin before the cats moved close enough. When they were five feet away he dropped the sphere at his feet and willed it to spread in every direction.

In hindsight, chanting the spell five times may have been a little excessive. Darkness rolled out for sixty yards in every direction. The cats were gone in an eye blink. The wave washed over the watching teachers and stripped them of all their protective spells. Dean Blane transformed from a little girl to a grown woman with gray hair and fine wrinkles around her eyes.

When the last of the darkness vanished Mrs. Umbra said, "I think that's enough for today."

Conryu wasn't even out of breath, but decided against arguing. "I got a little carried away."

She waved the Death Stick in an all encompassing gesture. "You think? For future reference you only need to chant 'Dispel' once for anything less than a full elemental. Even then two or three times should be enough. On the plus side you cast multiple spells under semi-realistic circumstances with no trouble and no demons sneaking through. It appears Cerberus is doing his job."

"So did I pass or fail?"

"I told you it wasn't a test. Let's head back in, there's a new spell I want to teach you."

"A moment please." Dean Blane walked over to join them. She hadn't bothered to change back into her youthful shape. Behind her the rest of the teachers were walking back toward the school, muttering and restoring the spells he disrupted.

Conryu rubbed the back of his head and looked at her shoes. "Sorry about that."

"I warned them not to stand that close," Mrs. Umbra said.

"We were fifty yards away. In a million years I never imagined him reaching us with such a basic spell. And the way you combined the command for Breaking with the gesture for Dispel, very impressive. That's a technique taught to third-year dark students. I'd say you have the makings of a fine battle mage. Wouldn't you agree, Angeline?"

Mrs. Umbra nodded. "His combat reflexes combined with the instinctive use of magic indicate an inclination in that direction."

Conryu raised his hand. "Battle mage?"

Dean Blane nodded. "A wizard that specializes in combat, fusing martial arts and magic. It's a potent combination, but limiting if you decide to go that way."

"Limiting how?"

"Well, if you don't want to work for the military, police, or as a private bodyguard you're out of luck." Dean Blane muttered something and her form shimmered until she looked like a kid again. "Don't misunderstand. Just because your options are limited I don't mean to imply there's a shortage of work for battle mages. In the world we live in it might be one of the areas with the most demand."

"He'd make a fine spell breaker if he could get his power under better control," Mrs. Umbra said.

The two women stood there discussing his future like he wasn't present. It was annoying and made him feel like the little control he'd gained over his life was slipping away again. They never even paused to consider that he didn't want to work as a wizard.

* * *

Half a foot of snow covered the academy grounds, but luckily for the golem club Sonja's fire magic kept the area around the shed warm and comfortable. The Grand Brawl was only two weeks away and midterms another week after that. Conryu felt a good deal more comfortable with his chances of passing spell breaking than he did about Star Blinky winning the Brawl.

The now-completed golem sat on a reinforced table where Sonja snuggled up against the thing like it was a puppy and not three hundred pounds of cold steel with fake red gems for eyes. Crystal and the other earth wizards were busy inscribing runes that would enhance the power of the earth spirit they'd summoned.

Conryu frowned and tried to think what else they might do to improve their chances. Now that the design and forging were complete he had been reduced largely to a bystander. He'd only learned two earth magic spells, one that moved a small amount of earth or stone and another that created a weak tremor. The earth magic teacher had been adamant that he not cast the second spell anywhere near a building after his first effort had broken three of the school's windows.

Sometimes it almost seemed the safest thing for him to do was not to cast any spells at all. Which was ironic since that's what he wanted in the first place.

Sonja finally wearied of hugging the spider and came to stand beside him. At this point she was as much a spectator as him.

"Can you bind more than one spirit to the golem?" Conryu asked.

She cocked her head. "I don't think it's against the rules, but if you don't have the two earth spirits in perfect harmony Star Blinky will just run in a circle."

"Actually I was thinking of adding a fire spirit to the head to create a cutting torch to slice up the other golems. Blinky's talons are formidable, but a second weapon might be a good idea. It would also give you something to do during the match besides cheer."

Sonja quivered in place. "That's an awesome idea! I could bind it to Blinky's eyes. How cool would a fire blast from those red gems be? That wouldn't mess with your earth bindings would it, Crystal?"

"It shouldn't." The tall girl straightened up, nearly brushing her head on the low shed roof, and wiped sweat from her brow. "Its head doesn't move anyway."

"This is going to be so great." Sonja leapt up and kissed Conryu full on the lips. She seemed to realize what she'd done and backed away. "Sorry. Overexcited."

"It's fine. Anything I can do to help?"

Sonja shook her head. "I don't think I'd better teach you spirit binding. If you do it we're liable to end up with an elemental lord in Blinky's head and the first time we use his fire blast the stadium will explode."

"Good point." Conryu didn't know the name of any elemental lords so he couldn't very well bind one, but he didn't bother arguing. "I'll just pick up the shed."

Two hours later Sonja announced, "Done."

Blinky's eyes glowed with an inner fire and bright red lines connected the red gems. In the now-realistic-looking spider the effect was quite intimidating.

"Want to test it?" Conryu asked.

"What did you have in mind?" Sonja asked.

He'd saved three cans while he was cleaning and set them up out in the snow. "Try and hit them."

"They're awfully small." Crystal gave the targets a dubious look.

Sonja on the other hand was bouncing with excitement. "But if we can hit those a golem will be a cinch. You guys line him up and I'll look through the spirit's eyes. When it's in position I'll fire."

Crystal muttered in the language of earth magic and the spider twitched then started to move. It climbed down from the table, its six-inch talons digging into the dirt floor.

Conryu scrambled out of the way, hugging the wall in hopes that he'd be clear of the ungainly thing. When the head was facing the general direction of the cans Sonja made a sharp hiss. A lance of crimson energy shot out from the eyes and burned a hole ten inches from the center can. Crystal wiggled her fingers and the golem moved a fraction.

Sonja hissed again and the fire blast struck the middle can dead center, melting it in half.

"Bullseye!" Conryu said.

After a little more adjusting the remaining cans were reduced to slag. Sonja jumped up and down, clapping her hands. "We are so going to win this year."

* * *

After the successful test Conryu was in high spirits. Sonja's enthusiasm was infectious. The little blond got so excited about anything to do with her precious golem it was almost comical. He'd been meaning to ask her why she was so into golem crafting, but he never thought of it until they'd all gone their separate ways. Oh well, it didn't make much difference anyway.

"Conryu Koda?"

He spun, the words of "Cloak of Darkness" on his lips. He hadn't been attacked in months, but he still remained constantly on guard. A woman in a red robe—a teacher not a student unless he was badly mistaken.

"Ma'am?" He relaxed a bit. It wasn't likely one of the teachers would attack him.

"Sorry, I didn't mean to startle you. I'm Amelia Light. I teach third-year fire magic. I saw your display on the beach the other day and I wanted to say how impressed I was. You've learned a great deal in your first semester."

"Thank you. I didn't really want to, but since people keep trying to kill me it seemed prudent to learn enough to hopefully keep myself alive. Was there something I can do for you?"

"No, no. I was out for a walk and spotted you. I haven't had a chance to introduce myself and thought I'd take the opportunity."

Conryu nodded. "I'm on my way back to the dorm. Would you like to walk with me?"

"Thank you. That sounds lovely."

He held out his arm.

She laughed and linked arms with him and the air temperature rose thirty degrees. Probably some spell she'd cast. "Such a gentleman. Did your father teach you manners?"

"Dad's a man of few words. What little I know I picked up from observation and old movies."

They walked along in silence, her hand growing steadily hotter on his arm. Halfway to the dorm it started to hurt. He muttered the Cloak of Darkness spell and focused it on his burning arm. Inky blackness sheathed it from shoulder to wrist. The heat vanished at once.

"Is everything alright?" She looked down at his now-black arm.

"Your hand was getting a little too hot to handle. Thought I'd cool myself down a bit."

She pulled away at once. "I'm so sorry. When I get distracted I sometimes lose focus. I hadn't even noticed."

"It's fine." Thinking of Sonja he suspected that was a trait of fire wizards in general. "Shall we?"

"I'm turning off here. I'm First Sister at one of the sororities. It was nice meeting you." Ms. Light headed toward the lake where the bungalows perched on the shore, leaving Conryu alone on the path.

He watched her for a few seconds then shrugged. What an odd woman. It was only a short walk to the doors and when he pushed them open he found Maria sitting in the lounge, a pale wood box on her lap. The moment he entered she leapt to her feet.

"Hey. Long time no see." He'd hardly said two words to her since the day he mentioned the midterm.

"Yeah, sorry about that. I've been working like crazy on my wards. Mrs. Alustrial says I'm now number three in our class. Not exactly where I want to be, but way better than middle of the pack."

"Congratulations. What's that?" He eyed the box and raised an eyebrow.

"My most recent practice piece. I think it's my best work yet. I want you to test it."

Conryu bit his lip. This wasn't going to end well. "Are you sure you want me to do it? Maybe one of the other girls..."

"No. If my wards can survive you they'll survive anything. Please?" She deployed the sad puppy face and he was defeated.

"Okay. Got a piece of paper and pen?"

Of course, being Maria, she did. Conryu sat at the nearest table and drew out the basic breaking circle. When he finished he placed it flat on the surface. Maria's box barely fit inside.

He placed his hands on either side and whispered, "Break."

Dark magic flared and a hiss rose from the box as wisps of white energy flew off it. He flipped the lid open revealing the empty interior.

He glanced at Maria who was frowning at him. "What?"

"How much power did you put into that?" She sounded angry. He'd done exactly what she asked and somehow he'd still made her mad.

"I don't know. Enough to break the wards and not enough to disintegrate the box. That's what I was going for at least. Why?"

"I thought you were holding back." She sat across from him and studied the box.

"I was holding back. Didn't I tell you what happened the first time I tried that spell?"

When she indicated he hadn't Conryu told her.

"You turned the block to dust?"

"Yeah. I'm under strict instructions never to use full power unless it's an emergency."

"I watched your casting with wizard sight. I'm guessing you used less than five percent of your full power. I don't think the midterm will be a problem for you."

* * *

Lady Mockingbird shivered as she walked back to the sorority house. She liked to get close to her prey before she attacked and to that end she'd sought out Conryu, knowing he'd be leaving his club late in the morning. When he offered to walk with her it had been too sweet an opportunity to let go. The boy had even passed her little test. She could make her hand so hot it would melt steel. His Cloak of Darkness had negated it in an instant.

In that moment she'd gotten a taste of his potential. The power in that simple spell was unfathomable. She'd never experienced anything like it, even when she met Lady Tiger and became a Sub-Hierarch. Besides Lady Dragon and their imprisoned mistress, she'd never imagined anyone could be stronger than a Hierarch. She'd been mistaken. It was well that she was ending him now, before he gained mastery of his magic. Lady Mockingbird doubted anyone would be able to defeat him once that happened.

The door girl opened up at her approach. One of her sweetlings was always watching so she wouldn't have to stoop to opening the portal herself. The pale, dark-haired girl bowed her head as she strode past.

The moment she was inside and out of sight meek Amelia Light vanished and dominating Lady Mockingbird appeared. Her confident stride echoed through the quiet halls as she made her way to the casting chamber in the basement. Her superiors required an update and the meeting was to take place in fifteen minutes.

She entered the dark room and sealed it with a word and a gesture. Her pale-blue mask rested on an ornate end table. Lady Mockingbird tied the mask on and adjusted it until the eye holes were in place.

Time had no meaning in the windowless chamber so she had no real idea how long she'd been waiting when the familiar tingle ran through her. "Take me to the place where all are one." A moment later the shadowy forms of the others appeared, including the most hated Lady Raven.

Lady Dragon appeared directly in front of her and seemed to lean forward. "Report."

"Mistress, I have made all the necessary preparations and will acquire the artifact over winter break. When the time is ripe I will end the abomination."

"And how does he progress?" Lady Wolf asked.

"Given his natural deficiencies as a man, he's making remarkable progress. I've felt his power directly and it is… remarkable."

"How remarkable?" Lady Dragon asked.

Lady Mockingbird knew a loaded question when she heard it. Should she admit that in terms of raw power Conryu was stronger than any of them? No, nothing good could come from that. "As strong as any student I've ever encountered in my time here, that's for sure."

Lady Dragon leaned back. "Indeed. It is well that you're going to deal with him then, isn't it?"

Lady Dragon vanished, leaving the unspoken threat hanging between them. The others faded away until only Lady Raven remained. The hag shot her an insolent grin before she disappeared. No doubt she'd enjoyed seeing the threats directed at Lady Mockingbird for a change. Unlike Lady Raven, she would not fail in her task.

Conryu Koda was going to die at her hand.

9
THE GRAND BRAWL

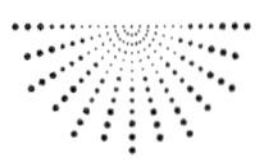

Conryu, Sonja, and the rest of the golem club, along with Star Blinky of course, rode across the lake in a water boat. It was a bitterly cold December morning, and the bright, cloudless day did nothing to add to the heat. Fortunately, Sonja was more than up to the task of heating the air, or at least she would be once they reached shore. As a fire magic user, being out on the water made her seasick in the most noisy fashion possible.

When she finished throwing up for the third time in five minutes Conryu handed her a square of cloth without comment. At the rear of the boat the water wizard tasked with transporting them to the island let out a low chuckle. Like most wizards in her specialty she harbored an irrational dislike of all fire wizards. The glare she shot Conryu indicated she wasn't overly fond of men, or at least male wizards, either.

"Better?" he asked.

"No." She groaned and let out a little burp. "I won't feel better until I'm back on solid ground."

The boat wobbled, and Sonja took his arm in a death grip.

Conryu patted her hand in a vain attempt to calm the terrified wizard.

Overhead a black, dual rotor helicopter came in for a landing near the center of the island. It had a shield and some letters on its side, but he couldn't make out what they said.

Earth magic users had spent the last three days raising a temporary stadium where this year's teams would hold the Grand Brawl. All told thirteen teams would be participating this year, including one team that flew all the way from the Republic of Australia.

It was the first time a team from outside the Alliance had competed. The rumor was they wanted to turn the Grand Brawl into the winter version of the Four Nations Tournament. The Department of Magic had even approved one tv station's request to broadcast the event worldwide. At least no reporters had come searching for him yet. Though he feared it was only a matter of time.

"Do you recognize the emblem on that helicopter?" Conryu hoped a little conversation would help settle Sonja's nerves.

She looked up at the slowly descending chopper. "Never seen it before. Some of the clubs have rich sponsors who pay their expenses and buy the best material in exchange for the teams wearing robes with the sponsor's symbol and name. This may be the first time anyone's arrived by helicopter. Showoffs."

The boat reached the edge of the island and Sonja leapt out, splashing through the foot-deep water and up onto the beach. When she got clear of the water Sonja was soaked from the knees down.

Conryu joined her, moving out of the way to let the others guide Blinky ashore. "You'll catch your death standing out here in those soaked robes."

Sonja chanted in the hissing language of fire and the air around them warmed to a comfortable sixty degrees. Her pants and robe steamed and were soon fully dry. Blinky clambered up the beach and she repeated the spell, drying the golem before it rusted. Conryu figured it would be nothing but scrap in short order, but he wasn't stupid enough to point that out.

Blinky led the way down one of the many paths that went to the center of the island where the arena awaited. Snow-covered branches hung over the path and every once in a while a chill flurry would fall on his head. It melted quickly enough in Sonja's heat, leaving his hair damp.

What sort of designs had the other teams come up with? He doubted there would be any other spiders. The legs made it far too vulnerable. If he'd been in charge of designing a golem he would have gone with a scorpion. The grasping claws and smashing tail would make a formidable combination.

The trail opened up into a wide, empty field with a crude earthen amphitheater in the center. The sides were about twenty feet high and platforms surrounded it. An opening would allow the golems to enter while the teams stood up above and guided them, a safe distance from the action. Wind like a hurricane from the departing chopper sent their robes snapping.

A number of tents had been set around the perimeter of the arena and the various teams were gathered under them, fiddling with their creations. He didn't know what they were doing at this late date. He doubted there was time for much fine tuning.

"Conryu Koda!"

"Aw, shit." He knew that voice. A second later the familiar figure of Kat Gable and a cameraman came running toward them. She was bundled in a heavy parka and her mitten-covered hands grasped a microphone.

Sonja looked up at him. "Friend of yours?"

"More like a stalker. Out of all the reporters in the world why did it have to be her?"

Kat arrived and thrust the microphone at him. "I understand you're on the academy team. How do you like your chances?"

"Sonja Chard is our team captain. I'm sure she can answer all your questions." He nudged the tiny blond closer to the reporter. "We need to set up."

Conryu turned to join Crystal and the others as they headed for the academy tent. Kat lunged for his arm, but he evaded her with ease. He rushed to put as much distance between himself and the reporter as possible.

Despite the distance he heard Sonja chattering on about how awesome Blinky was to the indifferent Kat. Conryu smiled. If anyone could out-talk the reporter it was Sonja. It was like a verbal death match. Conryu knew who he was rooting for.

They reached a multicolored tent with the academy's sigil, a book and scroll, on the side. Waiting for them was Dean Blane, Maria, and the only person he wanted to see less than Kat, Angus.

He hugged Maria and turned to the professor. "It's not Sunday. What brings you here?"

"I rode in with a lovely young reporter in exchange for an interview, though she only wanted to talk about you, which was somewhat annoying. Still, I am the world's foremost expert on male wizards so I suppose it's only natural she'd want to speak to me."

"Of course. In fact I think she was looking for you just now." Conryu waved his hand in the direction they'd just come from. "If you hurry you might catch her."

Angus peered the way he'd indicated. "I can't imagine why she'd want to talk to me again. I thought she'd be eager to speak to you."

"You should go ask her. If nothing else you could rescue our team captain so we can finish our prep work."

"Very well. I'll free the damsel from the dragon." Angus ambled off. Conryu smiled and shook his head. It would be interesting to discover who was the dragon and who the damsel. Once she got going Sonja could talk a blue streak.

"Didn't take you long to get rid of him," Maria said.

"He and Kat deserve each other." Conryu turned his attention to Dean Blane. "What brings you down so early?"

"As the school's representative I have to be here to welcome all the competitors, tell them the rules, that sort of thing. It's boring, but I do get the best spot for the Brawl."

"Who made the dramatic entrance just now?" The departing helicopter had shrunk to a dot in the distance.

"That would be Team Black Viper. They're a military contractor using the Brawl to test a new design. They're the odds-on favorite to take the whole thing every year they compete."

"Don't underestimate Star Blinky." Sonja strutted over to the group looking puffed up after her interview. "We're going to surprise some people this year."

"Did Angus spring you?" Conryu asked.

"Who's Angus?" Conryu described him and Sonja shook her head. "I didn't see him. Kat said she needed to interview some of the other contestants and left. It was kind of a shame. I was just getting going on our new design."

Conryu smiled as their little dragon turned her attention to the golem. If he stayed near her Kat wouldn't dare come too close.

"So at the network's request and with the Department's approval we'll be using a different tournament style," Dean Blane said. "Instead of a single melee we'll divide the competitors up into groups and have an elimination-style battle."

"We don't have the right number of teams," Conryu said. There was no way she'd get it to work out with thirteen clubs.

"It's not ideal, but we'll have to do two groups of three, one in each round, before the finalists go head to head. To make it fair we'll have a random draw to find out who gets stuck in the threesome."

"Would that be considered good luck or bad?" Conryu grinned.

Maria swatted him on the shoulder. "You're awful."

"It's actually a good question." Sonja had a faraway look in her eye. "If two weaker teams got paired up against a stronger team they could gang up and eliminate the stronger contender."

"I have to go talk to the Vipers. They were the last to arrive and I haven't told them the new format yet." Dean Blane started toward a black tent a little ways down from them leaving Maria and the team to their work.

Sonja and the other girls were gathered around Blinky leaving Conryu with nothing to do. He turned to Maria. "So what brings you here?"

"I wanted to wish you luck." She looked away. "I know I haven't been good company lately. It's just I've been so focused on the midterm and—"

Conryu covered her lips with his index finger, bringing her rambling to a halt. "I understand and it's fine. You don't need to explain yourself to me. You used to get focused like this when we were in high school, not so early maybe, but still. It's who you are and I wouldn't change you for anything."

She hugged him again and he stroked her hair. It felt beyond good to hold her, even for a minute or two. Finally she stepped back and smiled. "Think you guys have a chance?"

Conryu glanced over at the girls and found them still engrossed in whatever they were doing to Blinky. "If we make it past the first match I'll be impressed."

"That bad?"

"The design has too many weak points. The fire blasts should help, but I doubt it will be enough."

Half an hour later Dean Blane's voice filled the clearing. "All teams gather at the stadium entrance."

Sonja led the way and when they arrived they found the dean waiting with a hat in her hands and a board behind her. On the board was a tournament diagram with no names. Beside him Sonja was trembling, whether with excitement or fear he couldn't tell.

Last to arrive was Kat and her cameraman. When they were all set up she nodded to Dean Blane.

"Okay. We'll be drawing names to see who goes against who. Since we're the host the academy team will draw first."

Crystal gave Sonja a nudge when she didn't immediately move. The little fire wizard gave a whole-body shake and strode up looking more confident than he knew she felt. Sonja rummaged around in the hat before coming out with the number twelve. That put them in the threesome.

Sonja stuck the marker on the board and rejoined Conryu and the others. "What do you think? Good luck or bad?" Conryu asked.

"That depends entirely on who we're fighting against." Sonja chewed her nails and didn't stop until all the names were up on the board. They were taking on Team Down Under and Team Iron Cross. "I'm still not sure if it's good or bad. At least we didn't get stuck going against Team Black Viper."

Directly across from them a group of eight women all dressed in back robes, their faces hidden by deep cowls, spoke amongst themselves. One of them must have sensed Conryu's interest as she caught his gaze and held it.

Most of her face disappeared in the shadows of her hood, but her green eyes seemed to glow with an inner light. He'd never encountered such a hard, angry glare. Conryu looked away and sighed. It didn't appear they'd be friends either.

With that taken care of the teams dispersed. The matches were scheduled to begin a little after noon. Any students or teachers that wanted to attend were welcome, but they had to provide their own seats as the earth wizards hadn't built any into the stadium. It was deemed far too dangerous for people to be that close to the heavy steel golems. A single mistake had the potential to send a construct flying into the seats, crushing dozens.

While that might be good for ratings it wouldn't do much for the students involved.

* * *

Conryu and the team gathered on their designated platform to watch the first match. A couple hundred students and teachers hung suspended in midair or stood on earth pillars. Conryu spotted Dean Blane and Maria flying about a hundred yards away.

The tv crew had set up on a platform like the ones reserved for the teams. While the cameraman focused on the golems entering the arena below, Kat glared at him. Conryu smiled and waved back. It seemed safe enough since she was on the opposite side of the arena.

The day hadn't gotten any warmer as the sun rose higher in the sky. If anything Conryu thought the temperature had dropped a few degrees. The first match was Team Black Viper against Team Red Scorpion. The Red Scorpion team's golem was, not surprisingly, a reddish-colored scorpion with huge claws and a needle-sharp stinger on its tail. The scorpion was exactly what Conryu envisioned as the ideal golem.

Team Black Viper was equally unimaginative in its name. Their golem was a ten-yard-long black snake with fifteen-inch fangs that gleamed in the bright sun. The body was so smooth Conryu couldn't make out a single seam along its entire length.

"Are they all dark magic users or are they just wearing the robes?" Conryu asked. He'd cast the simple detection spell they taught first-year students, but something blocked it.

Crystal shook her head. "They're using a screen to evade our magic. That snake's still made of metal so some of them have to be earth wizards."

Whatever spell protected the wizards also protected the golem. He couldn't make out what sort of spirit they'd bound to it. He assumed earth since everyone seemed to use that sort of spirit.

On the ground below, the golems circled each other, waiting for the signal to begin the first match. It seemed like it would be an easy win for the scorpion, but Black Viper had won the Brawl before so underestimating them would be a mistake.

"Begin!" Dean Blane's amplified voice rang out.

The scorpion lunged in, claws open and ready. The snake darted aside and snapped at its opponent, leaving deep grooves in its steel skin.

"It's fast." Sonja leaned closer.

Indeed it was. The black snake evaded several lightning-quick strikes from the scorpion's tail before encircling the scorpion, binding its legs and sending it crashing to the ground. Tail and claws snapped and lashed out, but it couldn't reach the snake.

The black golem squeezed ever tighter until the first leg gave a painful screech and ripped free. When a second leg joined the first the Red Scorpion team started freaking out, waving their hands and shouting at each other.

The snake opened its mouth and a black miasma gushed out, covering the scorpion in thick fog. When the darkness cleared the scorpion wasn't moving. It only took a glance to know the magic had been stripped from the red golem.

"They bound a demon to their golem." That was the only thing Conryu could think of that explained the dark, magic-negating mist.

"Does that seem like a bad idea to anyone else?" Jade asked.

"Yeah, but it's not against the rules." Sonja shrugged. "It was only a matter of time before someone tried it. I can't say I'm surprised it was Black Viper."

The black snake slithered out of the arena and Team Red Scorpion rushed down to collect the now-motionless remains of their golem. It was a sad scene, watching them drag the thing out.

The next two teams fought and a sphere-shaped golem covered in blades tore a crab-like thing to pieces. Once the debris was cleared out of the arena it was time for Star Blinky to do its thing. The spider golem clattered its way into the arena followed by a steel kangaroo and a humanoid golem with a sword and shield.

"What's our strategy?" Conryu asked.

"We're going to tear them apart." Sonja glared at the other golems as if she could melt them with sheer willpower.

"No offense, chief, but that's not a strategy. I suggest you stay defensive. If the other two attack each other we can pick off the survivor and move on."

"You don't think they'll double-team us at the opening?" Crystal asked.

"Not unless they arranged it before the match." Conryu wanted to pace, but the platform was too small. "Blinky has the most obvious weaknesses in its design. If I was one of the other teams I'd leave it for last on the assumption it'd be easy to defeat later on."

Sonja opened her mouth to, no doubt, argue Blinky's virtues, but Dean Blane shouted. "Begin!"

The kangaroo leapt straight up, its head flying above the rim of the arena. The knight charged Blinky forcing Crystal to backpedal. A heavy swing of the golem's sword missed Blinky's front-most left leg by inches.

The kangaroo hurtled earthward, long spikes springing from its feet.

The knight raised its shield in the nick of time, but the force of the impact drove it into the sand up to its knees. The kangaroo spun and bashed the knight in the head with its tail.

"What should I do?" Crystal looked frantically from Conryu to Sonja.

"Keep your distance," Conryu said.

At the same moment Sonja countered with, "Attack!"

Before they could decide the kangaroo leapt again. With the knight immobilized there was no way for it to miss.

This time, instead of raising its shield the knight raised its sword. The force of the impact drove the sword all the way through the kangaroo which, it turned out, was hollow. That explained how it leapt so high.

The knight sank in past its thighs. The impaled golem thrashed for a moment then went still, its magic broken.

"Okay, let's slice them up." Conryu pointed to a point directly behind the knight. "If you move there it won't be able to use the shield to block you. Burn its arms off and the match is ours."

The heat ray turned out to be more effective than he'd expected, slicing off the knight's arms in less than a minute. They advanced to the next round where they'd take on the ball golem. The next two matches lasted half an hour combined. The winners were a lobster and another humanoid, this one armed with a war hammer. Those unfortunates would have to take on Black Viper. Conryu didn't envy them in the least.

* * *

"That was a cowardly victory." Sonja stalked around the tent while Crystal and the other earth wizards checked Blinky's bindings. With each step she took, the temperature went up a degree. If she didn't calm down they'd end up in a sauna. Conryu rested on a folding camp chair and tried to ignore her ranting. "Where's the glory in carving up a trapped opponent?"

Conryu opened one eye. "Where's the glory in losing in the first round? When you're in a fight the only thing that matters is winning, and we did. May as well savor it since we don't stand a chance against that spinning ball design."

"What do you mean?" Sonja stopped circling right in front of him.

"I mean the way it spins won't allow you to focus the heat beam on a single spot and if we try and grab it those blades will hook Blinky's legs and tear them off."

Sonja frowned. "Then how do we beat it?"

"We don't. Its design is better than ours. That's why I said you should enjoy your victory, it's going to be our only one."

"You're just going to give up?" She started pacing again. "I didn't take you for a quitter."

"It's not about quitting or giving up." Conryu rubbed his eyes and sighed. How to explain so she'd understand? "It's about preparing yourself mentally for what's about to happen. When I fought in martial arts tournaments there were always three or four contestants I knew I couldn't beat. I didn't fight any less hard against them, but I also didn't get mad when I lost. I learned from those losses and when the next tournament came around I took what I learned and did better until I eventually beat them."

"That's fine, but this is my last Grand Brawl. I don't get to improve and return next year for another try. This is it. I have to win now or not at all."

He had no argument for that. For him the golem club was a fun distraction; for Sonja it was much more important, almost an obsession. That didn't change the essential facts of the situation. Their opponent was simply better designed and more powerful. Sonja's desires and his strategies couldn't change that.

Fifteen minutes later they were back on the platform ready to watch the black snake demolish some more golems. He wondered if it would prove as dominant against multiple opponents as it had against a single foe. There was no way the lobster and knight wouldn't team up against the powerful serpent.

All three golems entered and the battle began. The lobster went right and the knight left so the snake couldn't hit more than one with its dispelling mist at a time. Whichever it attacked, the other would counter with a hopefully critical blow.

Team Black Viper didn't wait for its opponents to get set. The snake rushed at the knight, evading a heavy blow from its war hammer. In an instant it had the knight coiled up from its legs to its shoulders. The heavy golem went crashing to the sand.

The lobster darted in, claws open and ready.

The serpent was prepared. The moment it got close the snake's head popped up and it breathed black mist at the approaching golem.

It wasn't a surprise attack this time and the lobster dodged most of it. One claw was caught in the edge of the mist and fell limp to its side. Conryu tried to study the magic, but it dissipated too quickly. They should have made it so the magic stuck and spread over the construct it hit, stripping the magic as it went. That's what he would have done if he'd known how.

Down below the lobster tried circling around behind the snake, but its head rotated a full circle, allowing the enemy golem no avenue of approach. The snake's coils flexed as the knight tried to force its way free. The black golem was too strong and the knight had no leverage. It wasn't going anywhere without help.

"We should have gone with a snake," Sonja muttered.

"I hate snakes." Crystal shuddered and looked away from the arena.

The lobster made a move toward the viper and black mist rushed from its mouth. The move was a feint and the golem retreated without further damage.

The black snake's mouth remained open and the mist continued to pour out. Soon it covered both the serpent and the knight along with the entire arena floor.

Across the amphitheater one of the Black Viper Team screamed and collapsed. Another followed a moment later.

Something flashed in the light. A member of the viper team had a dagger and was using it on her teammates.

A third wizard went down. They were a third of the way across the stadium, no way he could reach them in time to do anything.

A roar from the arena floor drew Conryu's attention back to the sand. Black mist had filled a third of the battlefield. The mist swirled and formed into a snake ten times the size of the golem. The lobster and knight lay unmoving on the sand.

Dean Blane hurled lightning at the serpent and some of the other teachers and older students joined in. They might as well have shot spitballs at it for all the good their spells did. Every blast fizzled the moment it touched the snake's scales. It reminded Conryu of when his attackers tried to use magic on Cerberus.

Maria fluttered to the ground a few hundred yards away from the arena along with a handful of other first-year students who were flying with teachers. Conryu relaxed the moment he knew she was safe, or at least as safe as it was possible to be with a giant demon snake rampaging through the arena.

The demon serpent's tail smashed into the wall near the news crew, sending them sprawling to the ground. It seemed incidental to the creature as it totally ignored them.

Across the way the deranged wizard continued to stab her way through her teammates.

Sonja grabbed his arm. "What do we do?"

Conryu's gaze shifted from the tiny wizard clutching his sleeve to the giant serpent that ignored every spell thrown at it. He doubted there was anything they *could* do. That said, he had to try.

"Can you get me down there?"

All four girls stared at him as if he'd lost his mind, a perfectly natural response considering what he'd just asked.

"We can't leave those two to be eaten."

"We could make a stone slide." Crystal studied the arena between them and the huddled news crew. "I'll twist it so you land right beside them."

"Perfect." He turned to Sonja. "Move Blinky to the entrance and use his heat blast on the serpent."

"Why would that work any better than a spell?" Sonja was shaking so bad he feared she might faint.

"It won't, but if that thing looks my way a blast might distract it. I'll be counting on you."

She squeezed his arm tighter. "Don't do it. You don't even like that reporter."

"You got me there. But it's a big distance between not liking someone and being willing to let them die. Don't worry, I won't do anything crazy. We just need to get them out of the arena."

Crystal tugged on his robe. "Slide's ready."

Indeed it was. A shiny halfpipe twisted its way down to the arena floor. The serpent was distracted by fifteen flying wizards blasting it with everything from fire to lightning to ice pellets. They all had the exact same effect: nothing.

It was now or never. He hopped onto the slide.

* * *

If he hadn't been terrified that at any moment the big black snake an arm's length away would notice him Conryu might have enjoyed zipping down the smooth slide. It reminded him of the one at the park he used to visit when he was a kid. He and Maria would spend all day climbing up and sliding down.

Deep crimson eyes, each as big as his head, turned Conryu's way. He tumbled off the slide a moment before its tail smashed the stone construct to gravel. The sand broke his fall. Using his momentum he rolled to his feet and ran toward the huddled newspeople.

The snake's tail struck behind him sending sand flying everywhere. He glanced back just as a red ray struck the serpent in the side of the head. It didn't hurt the creature, but it pulled its attention toward the entrance just as he'd hoped.

Conryu slid to a stop beside Kat. Behind her the cameraman moaned and clutched his leg. A splinter of bone poked out of his torn pants. Apparently the sand hadn't been as soft as Conryu had thought.

"What is that thing?" Kat had lost her microphone in the fall, her nice blouse was torn, exposing a lacy bra underneath, and her skirt was ripped up to her hip on one side. It would have been hot if they weren't in danger of being killed at any moment.

"It's a demon. Can you move?" Above them the demon roared and spit black mist in a stream at the flying wizards.

"Demon?" Her eyes about bugged out of her head.

"Yeah, now focus. Can you run?"

"Sure, but Joe isn't going anywhere. Not on foot anyway."

"Shit!" He couldn't carry the cameraman and defend them. How the hell was he going to get the guy out of here?

"Can't you magic him to safety?" Kat asked. "Or heal him or something?"

"Hey, I've been here for three months. I know exactly ten spells and none of them are useful in this situation."

"Then what good are you?" Kat was crying, her mascara leaving long black lines down her cheeks.

Great, now he had a bawling reporter to go with his crippled cameraman. What else could go wrong?

A bright light flashed in his eyes. He followed it to its source and found Maria standing beside the golem club and Blinky. She had a small hand mirror and was flashing the light at him.

Wait. Blinky could carry Joe, no problem.

Maria waved him their way but he shook his head. He couldn't abandon Kat and Joe. He made the phone symbol with his hand and held it to his ear. If one of them summoned an air spirit he could tell them to send Blinky over.

Sonja gave him a thumbs up and swirled her hands around. A moment later a breeze tickled his ear.

"Quit screwing around and get over here." He winced at Maria's tone. Did she think he wanted to be there, just waiting for the demon to swallow them whole?

"The cameraman's leg is broken. Send Blinky over to carry him."

The spider rushed towards them as fast as its skinny legs could carry it. Crystal had it hug the wall in the hope that the serpent wouldn't notice. It took half a minute to cover the distance and

Conryu held his breath the whole way. The serpent never even looked in their direction.

Blinky stopped and bent down so its body was on the ground. "You're going to have to hold him on," Conryu said.

"Me!"

Conryu put his finger to his lips and stared up at the demon. It continued to ignore them as it attempted to blast the other wizards out of the sky, thank heaven.

"Why me?" Kat asked at a more agreeable volume.

"Fine, I'll hold him on and if the demon notices us you can distract it while we escape. Does that sound better to you?"

Kat climbed up on Blinky and wrapped her legs around its head without further argument. Between them they maneuvered Joe up on the golem's back with only a pair of strangled moans from the injured man.

"Okay, Crystal, we're all set."

Blinky started back toward the exit at a much slower pace. Kat held tight to her cameraman, keeping him in the center of the golem, while Conryu jogged along beside them, his gaze never leaving the demon.

Blinky stumbled in the sand and Joe's leg banged off the golem's side.

He screamed.

The serpent spun and oriented on them.

"Go, go, go!" Conryu ran the opposite way, waving his hands to distract the demon. Its head snapped around and focused on him. That worked a little better than he'd hoped.

Its mouth opened and the black spray shot out. Conryu raised his hand, fingers crossed. "Break!"

A ball of dark energy collided with the mist and they negated each other. He let out a breath and kept running. The serpent roared and swung its tail.

Conryu dove under it, rolled to his feet, and ran on. He only managed three strides before he found himself flying up at an alarming rate. Three hundred yards later he stopped beside Dean Blane.

He looked down. "The others…"

"They're fine and in the process of evacuating with the other students too weak to fight. That was a gutsy move, rushing in to save those two." She smacked him on the back of the head. "That was from Maria."

"Yeah. She'll probably give me another one for good measure later, assuming we survive." He gestured at the serpent. "What about that thing? If it gets off the island it could destroy the school."

"It won't. We were just waiting for you to get those two clear of the arena. Now!"

The walls of the stadium trembled and collapsed. Mounds of earth covered the snake for three-quarters of its length. It fought and thrashed, but couldn't free itself.

"That won't hold it for long," Conryu said.

"No." Mrs. Umbra flew over to join them, the Death Stick clenched in her white-knuckled fist. "But it should hold it long enough for us to banish the creature back to Hell."

"We? I don't even know a banishment spell."

"I'll cast the spell, you're just going to provide me with a power boost. Come on, we need to be on the ground for this. The amount of dark magic we'll be conjuring will negate any spells in the area."

Mrs. Umbra flew down and Dean Blane lowered him beside her. She thrust the Death Stick at the still-struggling demon. It had already freed a quarter of its trapped length. Hopefully this wouldn't be a long spell.

* * *

Maria stared, mouth agape, when Conryu waved his arms and coaxed the giant snake to chase him. Half a minute later the golem bearing the reporter and her injured companion came to a stop beside them. The woman started to climb down, but Maria raised her hand. "Don't bother, we're not staying here."

She took a quick look at the injured man's leg. A lot of light magic revolved around healing and she'd been studying basic first-aid since she was a little girl, usually to patch up Conryu after one of their adventures went awry. It didn't take long to realize the man's injury was way beyond her ability.

Lines of people streamed toward the beach where water wizards in conjured boats waited to carry them back to the school. When Maria turned back Conryu was flying up beside Dean Blane. He was safe for now. The pressure in her chest lightened; the dean would keep him safe.

"Let's go." Maria started toward the beach. Out of the corner of her eye she saw something black. When she turned she saw the snake patch on the robe's back. It was a member of Team Black Viper and the woman was running at an angle away from the others fleeing the demon.

"Isn't that the nut with the dagger?" Sonja had moved to stand beside her.

Maria wasn't certain what to think about the tiny fire wizard. She didn't like the way the blond looked at Conryu. There was something in her eye that said she wanted to be more than his teammate.

"What nut with a dagger?"

"One of the wizards drew a dagger in the middle of the match and started stabbing the others. Didn't you see? It's probably why they lost control and let the demon escape."

Maria had been so focused on the match she hadn't even looked at the wizards controlling the golem. "I bet the Department would like to talk with her."

"Hey!" Kat shouted. "Are we going or what?"

"Crystal, you, Onyx, and Jade get those two somewhere safe. We're going to track down that crazy wizard."

Maria bristled when the fire wizard started to take over, but realized at once that she was being stupid. Sonja was a senior and had way more experience using magic than she did. In fact, after having a moment to think about it, the idea of Maria bringing in an experienced wizard on her own was ludicrous.

"Forget it," Crystal said. "Onyx and Jade can handle Blinky on their own. I'm coming with you."

Sonja grinned and turned to Maria. "I don't suppose I can convince you to go to safety? If that wizard turns and fights, things might get ugly."

Maria knew she should do exactly that, but she couldn't back down. "I'll be alright. If it comes to a fight I'll stay out of your way. You might need an extra set of eyes out there."

Sonja shrugged and the three of them set out in the direction the black-robed wizard went. Maria took the lead while the golem headed for the beach. As they worked their way across the lines of fleeing students more than one looked their way, but thankfully no one followed them. Maria stopped at the edge of the forest. One of the narrow paths led through the dense hardwoods.

"This is the last place I saw her."

Crystal muttered in the language of earth and Sonja in the language of wind. A breeze rushed through the trees and Sonja cocked her head as if listening. Crystal crouched and laid her hand on the dirt, her eyes closed.

"She's running east," Crystal said.

"Yes, but the wind spirits don't think she's a she at all. Whatever, this trail ends at a cliff with a narrow trail carved into the side. If we catch her there it'll make our job much easier."

Maria marveled at the ease with which the older women wielded their powers. How could she have even considered going after an experienced wizard on her own? She couldn't even fight like Conryu to say nothing of her limited magical abilities.

The three of them ran down the path. Maria stayed at the back of their formation, content now to let the others take the lead. It was a five-minute run to the end of the path where it opened up into a short, grassy field before dropping off a sheer cliff.

At the edge of the cliff stood a black-robed figure looking out over the lake. Perhaps the wizard had decided to surrender.

"Stay back." Sonja motioned her to remain at the tree line.

Crystal went left and Sonja right as they approached the still figure. Something was wrong. There was no way someone who'd tried so hard to escape would just stand there waiting to be captured.

Maria looked closer and her eyes widened. There were no feet sticking out from under the robe. "Get back!"

Crystal and Sonja both jumped away a moment before the robe exploded with dark energy. The infernal wave sickened Maria, but didn't seem to do any real damage. More importantly the others seemed to have come through the blast unharmed.

A hundred yards away a hunched figure emerged from the edge of the woods. It looked vaguely human, but the ears were long and pointed as was its nose. It opened its mouth and a long, forked tongue shot out and flicked through the air.

Maria shuddered. What manner of creature was it? She'd read many of her mother's books, but she'd never seen anything that looked exactly like this thing.

It threw a hand out and a blast of flame roared toward Crystal. Sonja spoke a harsh word and snapped her fingers, snuffing out the blast.

"You have sssome ssskill, child," the creature said.

"You haven't seen anything yet." Sonja pressed the heels of her palms together and chanted a spell.

A rush of flames streaked toward the creature. It simply stood, arms wide as if embracing the fire, and let the flames wash over it.

When the torrent of fire ended the creature remained unharmed, not so much as a hair out of place.

Maria gaped, unable to believe the monster hadn't sustained any damage when it should be nothing but a pile of ash. What sort of foe did they face?

"Your flamesss are ssstrong and pure. If I had the time I would enjoy corrupting you and turning your sssweet fire harsh and bitter. Alasss I'm in a bit of a rush." The creature slammed its forearms together and thrust its fists toward the sky.

A wall of flames twenty feet high roared to life, blocking their view. A wave of searing heat made Maria break out in an instant sweat even from a distance.

Sonja raised her hands and chanted a spell. The flames wavered, but didn't vanish. The tiny wizard let out a string of curses that would have made a sailor blush.

Maria left her hiding place and hurried closer. They couldn't let whatever that was escape. She didn't know how to help since she knew only a handful of simple spells and couldn't use dark magic, but she had to try.

Crystal laid a calming hand on her friend's shoulder. "Let's try it together."

The girls chanted in stereo and the flames wavered, parted like a curtain, and finally dissipated. There was no sign of the creature. If it had gone back into the woods she would have seen it.

Maria ran to the edge of the cliff and looked down. The thing was halfway down the face, crawling along like the lizard it resembled. Sonja and Crystal moved over beside her.

"That's a neat trick," Sonja said.

"Yeah, but it's not going to help today." Crystal crouched and touched the cliff face while chanting. A tremble ran through the earth and down below a hand of stone snatched the creature off the face and wrapped it up from neck to ankles. "Let's see it cast spells now."

The creature snarled and spat fire at the indifferent stone. It shouted curses at them which the girls ignored.

"Well, we caught him. What should we do now?" Sonja looked from Crystal to Maria.

Crystal just shrugged.

"I say we leave him there and let the teachers deal with him," Maria said.

"That's fine. My spell has done its work. That stone prison will last until an earth wizard counters it."

"Let's go find Dean Blane and tell her we've got an early Christmas present for her." Maria led the way back toward the arena. With any luck the demon snake wasn't still rampaging around.

* * *

The demon serpent wrenched itself side to side sending chunks of rock flying. The creature was tremendously strong and with every twist it freed more of its length from the rubble.

"What do I do?" Conryu looked away from the struggling demon to his teacher.

"Grasp the Death Stick below my hand and imagine dark energy flowing from your body into it. Just focus on that, I'll handle the rest."

Conryu grabbed the shaft of the stick right behind her wrinkled fist and pictured the same energy he remembered from The Awakening on the beach flowing from his body, out his hand, and into the artifact.

He didn't feel anything until a moment later when Mrs. Umbra spoke the first word of Infernal. Something opened up inside him and crackling black energy rushed out. Power pulsed from the skull topper as the spell built to a crescendo. He was so overwhelmed he didn't even hear most of the spell.

A black disk appeared under the serpent and tentacles shot up, wrapping it and pulling the demon back into the portal.

The mighty demon struggled and snapped one of the tentacles. The banishment was failing. He looked down at Mrs. Umbra. She was frowning and chewing her lip. It wasn't just his imagination.

If the demon escaped a lot of people were going to be hurt. An idea popped into his head, more instinct than anything.

"Cerberus!" Conryu focused all his will on the demon serpent. "Kill!"

His arm ached as the demon dog's brand came to life. A head appeared from the portal, a snarling, fang-filled mastiff head with burning red eyes. Jaws that could swallow an elephant whole opened and bit into the snake's side.

A second and third head appeared. Both of them clamped on to the struggling snake. Slowly, but inexorably, Cerberus dragged the black snake down into the dark portal. When the last of the snake's head vanished Mrs. Umbra spoke a final word and the portal closed.

Conryu released the Death Stick and both of them fell to their knees. He'd never been so exhausted in his life. It felt like he'd run back-to-back marathons.

"You okay?" Mrs. Umbra asked.

"Yeah. You?"

"I believe I'm going to have a nap this afternoon, but other than that I'm fine. That was clever thinking, getting Cerberus to aid in the banishment."

He shook his head. "It was just—"

"Instinct?"

He nodded.

"You're a battle mage down to your toes. The magic speaks to you in a way it doesn't to ninety-nine percent of the world's wizards. Trust that instinct, Conryu. It will serve you well."

He stood in time to greet Dean Blane who landed beside them.

"Well done, you two. That could have ended a lot uglier than it did."

"All credit to my student." Mrs. Umbra clambered to her feet. "If he hadn't thought to call Cerberus for help we might have lost it."

"Dean Blane! Conryu!"

They all turned at the sound of Maria's voice. She was running toward them from the edge of the woods with Sonja and Crystal a step behind. She skidded to a stop and wrapped Conryu in a bear hug.

Over her head Conryu saw Dean Blane fix the girls with a glare. "I thought I told you to evacuate?"

"We were," Sonja said. "Then Maria spotted the wizard that was stabbing the other members of Team Black Viper."

She went on to tell them about the battle and capture of the thing that had disguised itself as a member of the team.

When she finished Mrs. Umbra said, "Sounds like a heart hunter, though what one of the southern elf-bloods would be doing here at this time and place is beyond me."

Conryu stepped back and looked down at Maria. "What were you thinking, going after something that dangerous?"

"Me! I'm not the one who ran towards a giant demon snake. You could have been crushed."

She had him there. Somehow he worried less about his risks than he did hers. He always had and always would.

"Let's go have a chat with this heart hunter and see what he has to say for himself." Fifteen teachers had landed while they were talking and they all looked at the dean for instructions. A little growl escaped her lips. "Clean this mess up and search for any surviving members of the Black Viper team. We need more information."

While she was giving her instructions Conryu spotted a flash of red and was surprised to see Ms. Light standing a little ways off by herself, watching the proceedings. He wouldn't have guessed the shy fire wizard was into golem fights. He waved and she wiggled her fingers before rushing away.

"You know her?" Dean Blane asked.

"Yeah, we met a while back walking toward the lake, though I haven't seen her since."

"Stay away from her."

The hard tone in the dean's voice surprised him. "Why?"

"She's the First Sister of the Le Fay Sorority and most likely the one behind the attack on you. That woman's dangerous."

All wizards were dangerous, but the bashful fire wizard seemed about the farthest thing from a threat imaginable. "Really?"

"Really." She turned to Sonja. "Let's go talk to your prisoner."

Conryu and Maria exchanged a look. Sonja and Crystal led the way back toward the woods. The path made for easy walking, though after the fight Conryu's legs felt like limp noodles. Mrs. Umbra wasn't in any better shape, but when he offered her a hand she waved him off.

It took ten minutes at Mrs. Umbra's exhausted pace to reach the cliff. Sonja walked right to the edge and looked over. "What the hell?"

The rest of the group joined her. Halfway down the cliff was the stone fist and inside it was a dead… something. It hung limp, gray, and unmoving between the rock fingers.

The dean hopped over the edge and flew down for a closer look. It didn't take long for her to return. "He's dead. Damn it! I'd hoped we could extract some information."

Conryu shivered at the way she said "extract." He'd never heard the generally happy-go-lucky dean speak in such a harsh tone.

"It was a Red Path Fanatic." Mrs. Umbra leaned on her stick, looking far older than her seventy years. "I fought them on the border. If one is captured it has the ability to stop its heart to avoid questioning. When it realized there was no chance of escape..."

She shrugged. That about summed it up. They'd probably never know what had prompted the insane creature to do what it did.

10

MIDTERM

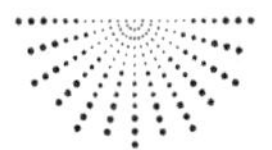

After fighting a giant demon snake Conryu felt a good deal less anxious about the midterm tomorrow. He lay back on his bed and sighed as the pixie sent a cool breeze swirling around him. Good as it felt now he couldn't wait until warm weather to really enjoy it. He wanted to learn the language of wind so he could ask her name and thank her properly, but they didn't study languages outside their aligned element until second year. He just had to make do with thanking her in English since he knew she understood.

Sitting on the bed beside him was his homework, bonus homework in fact, from Mrs. Umbra. The black book contained the names and powers of over a hundred different demons, though not the snake that attacked the Grand Brawl. She wanted him to study and memorize as many of them as possible. If one of them should appear it would be useful for him to know their names so he could better assist in the banishing spell.

Conryu had managed ten listings before his eyes started to droop. It wasn't as bad as the big book of boring magic he'd had to read before coming to school, but it wasn't exciting by a fair bit either. Maria was intent on making one last effort at improving her warded box before the test tomorrow so he was on his own for entertainment.

When someone knocked on his door five minutes later it was with considerable relief and no little curiosity that he jumped up and went over to answer it. Standing outside his door was the pale girl that had blown him off on the day of The Awakening. She was staring at the floor and clasping her hands in front of her.

"Did you need something?"

She finally looked up at him, her pale-blue eyes damp from crying. "I'm going to fail the midterm. I'm the weakest one in our class and I'm going to fail. I just know it."

"Have you been practicing?"

"Every day, but I can't even make the light go out on the training block Mrs. Lenore gave us. How can you disintegrate a cube without even trying and I can't even dim the light?"

Conryu chewed his lip and tried to think of something. "Do you want to come in? It's kind of awkward talking out in the hall."

She scurried past Conryu and stood in the middle of the room looking anywhere but at him. He couldn't tell anything about her beyond her face and hands. It looked like they'd given her a robe one size too big.

"Why don't you sit at the desk and try your spell? Maybe I'll see something."

She sat and took her light cube out along with a pre-drawn breaking circle. Looked like she'd been counting on his offering to help.

When the cube was in the circle she looked to him and said, "Why would you notice something now when you didn't during class?"

Conryu didn't want to say that he hadn't been paying her casting the least attention in class so he changed the subject. "Look... Say, what's your name anyway?"

"Kelsie. I'm from Central. My mom's a wizard and so is my grandma. If I fail the midterm I'll be an embarrassment to the whole family. You don't know what the pressure's like. They're watching everything I do, ready to criticize any little mistake. Sometimes I want to scream or rip my hair out." She was panting and her pale cheeks had turned bright red.

And he thought Maria took this shit too seriously. Yikes. "First thing is you need to get all that crap out of your head. When you're getting ready to cast your breaking, all you should focus on is ending the spell in front of you. Any errant thought will weaken the magic. It's all about mental discipline. Didn't Mrs. Grundy cover this stuff in your self-defense class?"

He didn't think Mrs. Grundy actually talked about discipline as it related to magic, but he didn't want to let on that Mrs. Umbra had shared the secret with him, just in case it really was a secret.

"She might have. I didn't pay much attention."

"Okay, forget the spell. We need to declutter your head first." Conryu dropped to the floor and sat in the lotus position. "Have a seat. Face me."

Kelsie stared down at him from the chair at the desk. "I don't see how this is going to help."

"How long have you been practicing your way?"

"Five weeks."

"How much success have you had?"

"None."

"When's the test?"

"Tomorrow."

He raised an eyebrow. She sighed, left the desk, and sat on the floor facing him.

"Good. Now count backwards from a hundred, taking a breath with each number. If you lose your place you have to start over."

"This is stupid."

Conryu just stared at her.

"Fine."

Two hours later Kelsie finally breathed out a "one." That wasn't actually terrible for a first effort. When his father had taught him that trick it had taken him days to make it to zero. Of course, he'd been five at the time.

"Good. Now go cast the spell. Don't think about anything but the light going out."

She scrambled to her feet and made her way over to his desk. Her hands went on either side of the circle. "Break!"

The light flickered and died, leaving the block as nothing more than an ordinary kid's toy. Kelsie whirled around, her eyes wide. "I did it. I did it!" She jumped up and down and danced around.

Conryu got to his feet. "Congratulations. Remember how that felt tomorrow and you'll be fine."

She stopped dancing and looked at him, maybe for the first time. "Thank you. I know I was kind of bitchy that first day, but maybe we can start fresh."

"Sure, after all, everyone was bitchy to me that first day. You didn't throw tomatoes or try to kill me so that moves you off the top of my avoid list."

She smiled and held out her hand. "To new beginnings."

Conryu shook her hand. "New beginnings."

* * *

A long table had been set up in a conference room that the teachers used when they needed to discuss something affecting the whole dorm. There were thirteen seats, one for each of the dark magic students. The first-year light magic class numbered over fifty so they'd have to stand.

A line of windows covered one wall and let the bright morning light stream through. They'd gotten two inches of fresh snow during the night and the reflection made it almost blinding. Had the light students set the room up so the dark class would have to face the windows, making it harder to concentrate, or was it just a coincidence?

Conryu laughed at himself. After everything that had happened he was starting to see conspiracies everywhere. If he didn't take care he'd end up as batty as Angus.

He leaned against the wall and yawned. He'd arrived a little early so there was only him and two other girls from his class in the room. They chatted about how difficult the test would be while making a conspicuous effort to ignore him. He'd gotten used to it at this point and didn't care enough to take offense.

A few minutes later Mrs. Lenore entered along with three more girls from his class. The girls went to join their friends, but Mrs. Lenore walked straight to Conryu.

"I'd like to ask a favor," she said.

"What sort of favor?"

"When your turn comes I'm going to have you break all the boxes that survive at the same time. I don't want you to hold back when you cast the spell. Give it all you've got."

Conryu frowned. She'd been telling him nothing but hold back, hold back, since they started studying breaking. "Why the sudden change of heart?"

Mrs. Lenore motioned him to follow her and went to the corner of the room, well away from the girls. "Do you know the light magic teacher, Mrs. Alustrial?"

Conryu shook his head. He hadn't spoken to the woman and Maria hardly mentioned her.

"We started teaching the same year and every year she has at least one student whose wards we can't break. Every damn year!" Her voice rose and she glanced over to make sure the others hadn't noticed. "And every year she rubs my nose in it."

"And this year you want to return the favor."

"Yes. This midterm is nothing but a formality for you, that's clear to everyone. But it will be a good way to test just how strong you are."

"If it happens to embarrass your rival that's a nice bonus, right?"

Mrs. Lenore shrugged. "I'm only human after all. And the snooty bitch needs to be taken down a peg."

"If you can find some curtains for those windows it's a deal."

She glanced at the windows as if noticing them for the first time and bared her teeth. "Another of her dirty tricks. I'll take care of it, never fear."

Mrs. Lenore bustled out of the conference room. Where she would find curtains in the half hour before the test began he had no idea. It wasn't his problem. The glare was annoying, but it didn't actually affect the power of their spells.

A little while later all the students but Kelsie had arrived along with Mrs. Lenore who'd found a roll of thick cloth. She shanghaied a pair of girls into helping her hang it over the windows.

They'd barely finished with the makeshift curtains when what sounded like an approaching army stopped outside the door. It opened and a tall, slim platinum blond with gleaming white robes glided into the room. She had the lean, graceful figure of a ballet dancer. Behind her, in perfect lock step, marched the fifty-three members of the light magic class, including Maria, who didn't even look at him.

That was weird. He thought he'd at least get a smile. She must be focused on the test.

Each of the girls carried a wooden box carved with interlocking runes. He wasn't allowed to study them before the test began, but if the other girls had put in as much work as Maria they would all be well protected.

The door hadn't quite closed when it burst open and Kelsie rushed in. "Sorry, sorry."

She looked a mess. Her eyes were red with dark rings under them. Her hair went every which way. It didn't look like she'd gotten a wink of sleep last night. He thought he'd gotten her calmed down yesterday, but apparently not.

"You look like hell." Conryu moved closer and it was clear she was shaking. "What happened?"

"My mom called yesterday, a couple hours after we finished practicing. She warned me not to embarrass her, and said if I failed the test I couldn't come home for Christmas. I've been throwing up all morning."

Conryu moved behind her and put his hands on her shoulders. Everyone in the room was staring at him, but he ignored them. If he didn't calm Kelsie down she really would fail.

"Take a deep breath." He rubbed her slender but well-muscled shoulders. "Do the count. Your mom's not here. Put her out of your mind. Come on, breathe."

Over the next minute and a half the tension gradually left her. The racing pulse in her neck calmed. She'd be okay now.

"Better?"

"Thank you." She squeezed his hand and took her place at the second to last seat on the left.

Despite her claims, Kelsie wasn't actually the weakest girl in their class, just the least focused. Conryu sat at the last spot on the right. They'd funnel everything from weakest to strongest, with him getting anything that made it through to the end.

He worked a crick out of his neck and sighed. Part of him wanted Maria to do really well and make it all the way to the end, but another part didn't want to be the one that broke her wards. Conryu didn't think she'd be too pissed as long as she passed, but there was no guarantee.

Mrs. Lenore and Mrs. Alustrial stepped to the center of the room and all gazes followed them. It looked like a crow had landed beside a swan. The look Mrs. Alustrial gave his teacher, with just a hint of a sneer, finished making up his mind. Conryu was going to annihilate whatever they put in front of him. Mrs. Lenore was entirely too sweet to be treated that way.

"Alright," Mrs. Alustrial said. "Just to be clear, my girls will hand their cases to the first person in line who will attempt to break it. If she fails it will move down the line until someone succeeds or everyone has failed. Questions?"

They'd gone over all this earlier in the week so everyone was already clear on the procedure. For some reason teachers liked to treat students like idiots at times like this.

Mrs. Alustrial turned to her counterpart. "All yours, Leena."

Mrs. Lenore glared at the light magic teacher before focusing on her class. "Everyone take out your paper and pen and draw a breaking circle."

Five minutes later they'd all completed their circles. The first light magic student handed her box to the first dark magic student and the midterm was underway.

Their weakest member managed to break the tenth ward she attempted thus assuring her a passing grade and the girl she defeated a failing one. Halfway through the test Kelsie broke a ward, leapt to her feet, and thrust a fist in the air.

Every light magic user in the room, including their teacher, stared at her until she sat back down. Conryu couldn't stop grinning.

Maria's turn came and she made it all the way to him where her box was added to a pile of three sitting before him. She glanced at him and raised an eyebrow. He wasn't allowed to say anything during the test so he just shrugged. His turn would come soon enough.

* * *

Maria hated ignoring Conryu when they entered the testing room, but Mrs. Alustrial's instructions were explicit. For the duration of the midterm the dark magic students were to be regarded as the enemy and treated as such. She didn't know how to begin thinking about Conryu as her enemy, then he started rubbing Kelsie Kincade's shoulders and it got a little easier.

To be fair it looked like the girl was on the verge of a heart attack or psychotic break. Maria knew as well as anyone Conryu's shoulder rubs did wonders to calm a person down. And was he giving her meditation lessons? When had they gotten so friendly?

The last time she talked to him he claimed none of the girls in his class would so much as speak to him. Now he was getting touchy-feely with one of them. Maybe she hadn't been paying enough attention to him.

Once the instructions were given the test began. It went smoothly until Corrie's wards were broken by the first girl to attempt them. It was a shame, but Maria wasn't too surprised. Corrie had only pulled a four hundred on her test so she was at the very bottom of the scale when it came to wizards. It was unlikely she'd ever move past the most basic spells.

When Kelsie leapt up and celebrated finally breaking a ward Maria had been more interested in Conryu's reaction. He offered the satisfied grin she'd seen so often when something went his way. More importantly, why were there two boxes in front of him? He shouldn't be letting them accumulate like that. What was he playing at?

Maria's stomach tightened when her turn came up. Her nerves lessened with each attempt until her container reached Conryu. He took it and added it to the others. She caught his eye and raised an eyebrow, but he just shrugged. It wasn't like they could talk in the middle of the test, but she really wanted to know what he was up to. Judging from the look on Mrs. Alustrial's face she did too.

When the last light magic student had completed her midterm Mrs. Lenore said, "Well done, everyone. Now we have something special in store. For the first time since this test began one of my students will attempt to break multiple wards in one go. Conryu."

So that was it. She sort of understood. As powerful as he was asking Conryu to break any of their wards was like asking him to crack an egg. But six at once? If he didn't break them all did that mean he failed the midterm, or did he pass as long as one broke?

Conryu didn't look especially concerned either way as he

stacked boxes inside his circle. When the last one was in position he placed his hands on either side of the circle.

"Break!"

A blast of dark energy engulfed the boxes and when it vanished nothing of the containers remained, not even a mote of dust.

Everyone stared at him and Maria realized her mouth was partway open. She knew how strong he was in theory, but even seeing the dark magic hound standing over him on the day he was attacked hadn't prepared her for that display.

She'd spent weeks warding her container and she knew the others had as well. In an instant he'd wiped that all away and with no apparent effort on his part. If he could do that after only half a year, what would he be capable of after graduation?

* * *

Conryu was greatly relieved when he blew away all the boxes like Mrs. Lenore wanted and judging from her big smile his teacher was pleased as well. Fifty-some scowling light magic students, on the other hand, seemed less pleased. Well, if he'd learned one thing it was that you couldn't satisfy everyone. As long as Maria wasn't too mad at him he didn't care what the rest thought.

Mrs. Lenore clapped her hands to silence the murmur of conversations that had sprung up. "Okay everyone, that's the end of your midterm. The train for Central leaves at nine o'clock sharp tomorrow morning. Make sure you're packed and on board before then. Class dismissed."

The moment Mrs. Lenore finished Kelsie jumped out of her chair, ran over, and hugged him. "I can't believe I passed and it's all thanks to you."

He disentangled himself and took a step back. Under that bulky robe she had some nice curves. "I didn't do anything.

Anyone could have taught you that meditation trick. It was your strength of will that got the job done."

"You're too modest. Maybe we can talk more after winter break?"

"Sure. I don't have so many friends here that I'll turn a new one away."

"Great." She started for the door, turned and waved. "Bye."

He waved and when she'd gone shook his head.

"So when did you and Kelsie Kincade get so friendly?" He hadn't noticed Maria approaching.

"Yesterday. Is that her last name? It was the first time the girl had even spoken to me. She shows up outside my room and wants me to help her prepare for the midterm. The day before the test. I taught her the count backwards trick. Seemed to help."

"Was the shoulder rub a bonus?" They headed for the door.

"Did you not notice how upset she was?" Conryu countered. "I don't know what sort of family she comes from, but her mother called last night and it totally screwed her up. Have I told you how much I love our moms? I'm so glad neither of them would do something like that."

Maria stopped in the doorway and turned to face him. "Are you telling me you don't recognize the name Kincade?"

"Should I?"

"Kincade Magic Industries? The world's largest fabricators of custom magical items and enhancements. Her family is the richest, most powerful family in the Alliance if not the world. They could buy Sentinel City and have money left over."

"Wow. Wonder why she didn't mention it?" He shrugged. "Whatever. However much money they have, they still treat their daughter like crap."

11
WINTER BREAK

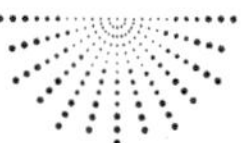

Conryu packed only the minimum he needed for the two weeks he'd be home and to his relief so did Maria. Only having two bags to lug to the train instead of three was a lot easier. Even better, he'd ditched his robe and wouldn't have to wear the stupid thing again until he returned to school. He knew other schools had uniforms, but couldn't they have come up with something a little less bulky?

They'd been assigned the same cabin for the ride home as they'd used on their way to school. Conryu stepped into the cabin and muttered, "Reveal." The wards lit up. It looked like the Department had protected them from everything; every element except dark was represented in the wards. How long had it taken to accomplish that? He hoped whoever cast the spells didn't have to renew them every time he rode to and from home.

"So do we have any plans for winter break?" Maria asked.

"Mom might have something up her sleeve, but all I want is to hit the dojo, make sure my bike still runs, and not think about magic for two weeks."

"I take it you're not planning to study up on the second semester's classes?"

"You take it correctly. I even made a point to forget"—he made air quotes around the word— "the book Mrs. Umbra gave me. I need a break from that stuff. Besides, Mrs. Lenore didn't mention what we were working on when we get back."

"We're doing healing. After wards it's the most important skill for a light magic wizard."

The train lurched and they were underway. Conryu barely got his chair up when someone knocked on their door. It couldn't be Angus. The nutty professor hadn't been back since the Grand Brawl. Conryu had allowed himself a moment of hope that the demon had scared him away for good.

He glanced at Maria who shrugged.

Well, one way to find out. He opened the door and found Kelsie standing outside. She had on a pretty gray dress cut in a conservative style and black pearls. His guess about her curves had been dead on. She filled her dress out nicely indeed.

"I was sitting alone in my cabin and thought some company might be nice." She looked past him at a frowning Maria. "I hope that's okay."

"Of course it's okay." He stepped aside to let her pass. "Right?"

Maria slipped out of her chair. "Maybe I should leave you two alone."

"Don't be like that. You're the one that said I'd make some friends eventually. Now that I have you're going to act jealous?"

She brushed past him without a word, slamming the door shut behind her.

Conryu sighed. "That woman's going to drive me nuts. I've known you for three days and she acts like we're dating behind her back."

"Maybe I should go." Kelsie took a step toward the door.

"No, it's fine. She'll realize she's acting silly and come back. Take a load off. It's only half an hour to Central. If there's something you wanted to talk about we'd better get started."

She perched on the edge of Maria's chair like she was ready to flee at the first opportunity. Conryu sat opposite her. When she didn't say anything for a while he raised an eyebrow.

Kelsie smiled and shook her head. "The truth is I didn't really want to talk about anything specific, I just didn't feel like being alone."

"That's cool." Conryu put his feet up. "After all, once you're home you'll have plenty of company. Are the Kincades a big family?"

She gave him a sharp look. "Maria told you?"

"Yeah. You didn't really think that was the sort of thing you could keep secret did you?"

Her smile faded. "I hoped I might. Once they know who I am people quickly sort themselves into two groups: Those who suck up to me in hopes of getting a job after they graduate and those who are jealous. It splits about fifty-fifty. It was nice pretending I could have a real friend, even if only for a few days."

Conryu laughed. "I assure you I have no interest in working for your family and from the way they treat you I'm certainly not jealous. I wouldn't trade my family for yours if you gave me all the money in the world."

That seemed to set her back on her heels. "But we're rich, powerful—"

"Miserable."

"What?"

"You talked to your mom and then you were unable to sleep. You spent the whole morning getting sick. When you walked into the testing room you looked like the Grim Reaper was waiting for you outside. If a simple phone call did that to you, I can't imagine what it'll be like spending two weeks with her."

"I... No. I mean, it should be okay since I passed the midterm. Mom's not the warmest person in the world, but she loves me, I think. It's complicated. Our family's different than most. It's very competitive. My cousins are always trying to make me look bad so they can become heir to the business. Mom needs me to be strong."

"I'm even less jealous of you now." Conryu leaned back in his chair. "Do you actually want to run your family's business?"

Her eyes went wide. "Um, I..."

"Has anyone even asked you that before?"

"No. It was always just expected that I'd take over one day. It's my destiny."

"Ugh! I hate that word, probably because Angus likes it so well. There's no such thing as destiny. I choose my path and you need to do the same. You don't have to be miserable if you don't want to be."

"Easy for you to say. You don't know my mother."

Conryu grinned. "Thank goodness for that."

Maria returned to the cabin shortly after Kelsie left to collect her bag and disembark. Conryu and Kelsie had spent the last part of the ride discussing minor things of no importance. It was nice and seemed to reassure her that he really didn't want anything from her.

"So did you and Princess Kelsie have a nice talk?"

Conryu blew out a sigh. "We did. Turns out she likes techno dance music, kittens, and not getting yelled at by her mother. Are you going to glower at me the whole way home?"

She ran her fingers through her hair. "No. It's just when I said you'd make friends I didn't think you'd end up with the richest girl on the planet wrapped around you. She's got a serious crush."

Conryu waved his hand. "That's crazy. I've known her for three days. We've spoken for at most four hours and I hugged her once. After two weeks at home she'll forget all about me."

"Uh-huh. How much you want to bet?"

* * *

Kelsie left the train and headed for the front of Central Station. She had no trouble carrying her bag on her own. It was a Kincade carryall and thanks to its magic it would never weigh more than two pounds, even if she filled it with bricks. She hadn't fully appreciated the convenience until she watched Conryu wrestling his and Maria's bags down the narrow aisle.

She smiled as she walked down the front stairs to where her ride was parked. Mom had sent the black limo, of course. She knew Kelsie preferred the red one. It was just the sort of petty snub her mother specialized in. You'd think since she passed the midterm her mother might, just this once, have done something she knew Kelsie would like.

The familiar Central City skyline gleamed in the clear, cold air. It really was a beautiful city. Her mother claimed it belonged to the Kincades in fact if not in name. That was how her family measured everything: what they owned and who they owned. It was a long list.

As she approached the waiting limo the driver got out and opened the back door for her. He wore an all-black uniform and didn't speak as she climbed inside. Kelsie had seen him a few times around the house, but didn't recall his name. He closed her door and they were on their way.

While the limo drove through the slushy streets she thought about Conryu and how nice it would have been to show him around Central. He had a kind, gentle manner and seemed to have no interest in her family or business. That was so odd as to be an almost foreign concept to her.

Kelsie's first thought when he made the claim was that he was pretending to have no interest in order to get close to her before asking for something. He'd been nothing but kind to her and that seemed a terribly unfair thought.

Halfway through the trip from the academy while he was listening to her ramble and laughing at her lame jokes, she decided to take him at face value. They'd be friends until he did something to prove his bad intentions. She hoped he didn't do anything, at least nothing to prove her fears correct. Her cheeks warmed when she remembered how it felt when she hugged him after the test. In truth there were a few things she wouldn't mind him doing.

No, she couldn't let her imagination wander down that path. He was clearly involved with Maria, though the exact nature of that relationship seemed a little vague.

The limo pulled through the iron gates and began the half-mile trek up the driveway to the mansion. They parked, Kelsie got out, and stared up at the seventy-eight-room mansion that had housed fourteen generations of Kincades. The imposing white building had nothing warm or welcoming about it. It served one purpose and one purpose only: to intimidate anyone coming to visit her mother. It did that job very well indeed. Even though it was supposed to be her home she felt thoroughly intimidated.

The driver stood beside her holding the magic bag, waiting for her to lead the way inside as was proper. Now there was a word she'd have to keep in mind every moment of the next two weeks. If she did anything that wasn't proper for the heir to the family her mother would have a fit.

She went up the short flight of steps to an entryway flanked by roman columns. At four strides from the door she mouthed the word that deactivated the wards and caused double doors twice her height to open.

Beyond the doors a marble foyer bigger than some people's houses spread out in every direction. The driver set her bag beside her and withdrew without comment. The groundskeepers and drivers lived in small houses out of sight of the main house and Mother didn't like them hanging around inside.

Kelsie reached for her bag and caught herself. It wouldn't do for her to carry it herself. One of the servants would take it to her room.

Speaking of which. The chief butler emerged from a side door and bowed to her. Tall, gaunt and with a cool, haughty manner, he'd served her mother for longer than Kelsie had been alive. "Welcome home, miss."

"Thank you, Alec. Is Mother in?"

"Lady Kincade is still in the city. I believe she intends to return for the evening meal."

"Oh." Why in the world had Kelsie imagined her mother would be here to greet her? "I believe I'll head up to my room and rest. Are any of the other family members here yet?"

"Lady Amanda and Miss Charlotte arrived yesterday. The rest aren't due until tomorrow."

Ugh, Aunt Amanda and Cousin Charlotte, her least favorite relatives, not that any of them were fantastic. Kelsie was careful not to let any of her distaste show. The trick to interacting with her family was to keep the hate bottled up tight.

"Very good. Have my bag brought up." She left Alec in the foyer and headed up the curved stairs to the second floor.

She walked past the familiar paintings, each of them hideous and worth millions. Would it have killed her mother to buy at least a couple nice landscapes? Probably, since landscapes were over decades ago. Now it was abstract globs of color you had to have cluttering up your walls.

Kelsie reached the door to her room and allowed herself to relax. It was the one room of the mansion her mother allowed her full control over. She reached for the handle.

"Hello, Kelsie."

So close and yet so far.

Charlotte emerged from one of the guest rooms further up the hall. The two of them couldn't have been more different. Charlotte was two years younger, blond haired and rosy cheeked, and with the soul of a barracuda.

"Charlotte. Alec mentioned you and your mother arrived earlier. I trust you're well."

"Perfectly well. I got every question right on my midterm plus the extra credit. I have the best GPA in my class. I'm sure to receive the highest score when I take the wizard test next year."

"You know grades and magical power aren't related. You might not even pass. Nothing to be ashamed of if it doesn't go your way."

Charlotte's pouty lips curled into a nasty smile. "You'd like that, wouldn't you? No family competition until after you'd graduated. No, cousin, I'm going to pass and then I'll show everyone what a Kincade wizard is really capable of."

"Well, I wish you the best of luck." Kelsie opened her door, stepped inside, and slammed it behind her. It was going to be a long break.

* * *

The train pulled into the Sentinel City station an hour after sunset. Bright lights illuminated the platform and the station beyond. The train was only half full on this trip so the crowd waiting beyond the turnstiles was thinner than when they left.

The front of the station wasn't visible as they pulled in, but Conryu allowed himself a moment's hope that the worst of the press had moved on to new stories. He'd been out of sight and out of mind for months now. Surely something had happened, some shiny new story must have appeared to hold their interest.

He grabbed their bags and followed Maria out onto the station platform. About halfway home he'd finally managed to convince her there was nothing between him and Kelsie beyond a simple friendship and she'd finally relaxed.

The platform had been swept free of snow so at least he didn't have to worry about his footing as they headed for the exit. "Do you think everyone came to pick us up?"

"Unless Mom had a job I'd assume so." Maria pushed through the turnstile and scanned the crowd for their parents.

"Conryu Koda!"

"Aw, man."

Pushing her way through the crowd, Joe the cameraman following in her wake, was Kat Gable. She had on a long insulated jacket with a fur-lined hood. The ever-present microphone was clenched in her fist.

"I should have let the snake eat them."

Maria giggled. "I see my dad and your mom. Maybe if we hurry we can beat her to the car."

"Maybe we could run her over."

Maria grabbed his arm and pulled him along toward their parents. They'd covered half the distance when his mom spotted them and ran his way. She caught him in a hug and kissed his cheek.

"Are you okay? Orin told me everything and I saw that snake on tv. Why do these things keep happening to you?"

"Relax, Mom, I'm fine. Where's Dad?" He looked over his shoulder. Kat was tangled up with a knot of people about a hundred yards behind them.

"Your father's waiting in the car. You know how he hates crowds. Shizuku's working late on a consultation." She hugged him again. "It's so good to have you home."

"It's good to be home. Can we get out of here? I'm starving."

"Of course. I've got a chocolate pie in the fridge."

Conryu's mood brightened at once. "With whipped cream and those little shaved bits on top?"

"Yup, just like you like it. And a day-old Giovanni's pizza."

"Conryu." Mr. Kane relieved him of Maria's bag. "I understand you passed your midterm with flying colors."

"He was a total showoff." Maria had her hands on her hips.

"It was Mrs. Lenore's idea." He looked back again. Kat had

gotten free of the tourists and was plowing their way. "Let's step on it."

His mom looked back. "It's that awful woman. She calls once a week to try and schedule an interview with you. I've a good mind to tell her off right here."

"Maybe not on national tv. Let's just go." Conryu urged everyone toward the exit.

As they hustled along Mr. Kane said, "After you've settled in there's a matter we need to discuss."

Tension appeared between Conryu's shoulder blades. "What kind of matter?"

"A magical matter best not discussed outside the Department. Would you be willing to come in the day after Christmas?"

"Sure. I didn't have anything planned." His mother was listening with a worried crease in her forehead. It seemed that crease had gotten deeper over the last half a year.

Mr. Kane must have noticed it too. "Don't worry, Connie. It's nothing dangerous."

"It better not be." She glowered at Mr. Kane. "My boy's been through enough."

Conryu seconded that, but somehow doubted Mr. Kane was being totally honest with his mom. If it wasn't something serious he wouldn't have hesitated to say what he wanted done. And in Conryu's experience serious meant dangerous.

* * *

After a delightful first day of winter break spent looking his bike over and helping his father train at the dojo, followed by an equally nice Christmas, Conryu found himself sitting beside his mother on the way to the Department of Magic to help Mr. Kane with whatever it was he needed. Maria's dad refused to say anything more outside the confines of his building.

When his mother had glanced at him for the third time

Conryu said, "If you don't keep your eyes on the road we're going to crash. After everything that's happened it would be ironic if I died in a simple car wreck."

"Don't joke about that, Conryu. Every day you're gone I wonder if that's the day I'll get a call saying those loonies have finally gotten to you. Sometimes I can't sleep I'm so worried."

"Try and relax. The teachers have taught me some good tricks. I'm nowhere near as helpless as I was this summer. Mr. Kane told you I helped banish the giant demon snake, right?"

"Yes, it gave me palpitations. I saw that thing just before the cameraman went flying. Was it as big as it looked on tv?"

Conryu debated lying to her, but decided against it. Once he started lying about the threats it would never stop. "It was pretty big. Mrs. Umbra and I handled it. The Brawl was canceled though so my team didn't even get credit for participating. Sonja was pretty upset."

In fact she'd been so pissed that she set the letter from the golem committee on fire just holding it. Conryu had suggested if she wanted to try again she should join a golem club after she graduated. He didn't know if she would. Sonja wasn't one to play second fiddle to anybody.

Mom pulled into the government building parking lot and Conryu walked her to the door of the science building before jogging over to the Department. Mr. Kane had given him directions to his office so Conryu didn't need to ask anyone.

He rode the elevator up to the top floor. Mr. Kane's personal secretary smiled at him as he approached. She was cute so it was a good thing Maria hadn't come with him today. She'd gone on a job with her mother. Something about wanting some real world practice.

"Conryu Koda?" the secretary asked. When he nodded she continued. "The chief's expecting you. Go right in."

"Thanks." He pushed the doors open and found Mr. Kane

behind his desk, the blond wizard that saved him at the carnival in one chair, and Detective Chang in the other.

Mr. Kane stood up and offered a tired smile. "Conryu. Thanks so much for coming in. You remember Terra and Lin?"

"Sure. Hey, Sarge." He nodded to the detective. "So what's this all about?"

"We need you to break a ward for us," Mr. Kane said.

Conryu blinked and stared from him to the others. "Why me? This is the Department of Magic. You must have dozens of dark magic wizards that could do it for you."

"We do, but they're all deployed up north to help halt a frost giant invasion. No one we have available is strong enough in dark magic to get the job done. Emily assures me you have the power to do what we need."

"I appreciate Dean Blane's vote of confidence, but did she explain I sometimes destroy the warded item in the process of breaking the wards?"

"Don't worry." Terra got out of her chair. "I've inscribed a special circle that will direct your magic precisely against the wards. All you need to do is apply the spell."

The older wizard sounded too eager. He would have expected her to be resentful of a first-year student doing her job for her.

"What are you guys not telling me?"

"I warned you he was sharp," Lin said.

"Terra's eager for a demonstration of your power," Mr. Kane said. "She's been reading the reports, but wants to see what you can do firsthand."

"Reports? What reports?"

Mr. Kane winced. "All your teachers submit weekly reports about your progress to the Department. You can't be surprised. After all you are the first male wizard. It's only natural that we'd want to keep a close eye on you."

So the teachers were all spying on him. He wished he was more surprised. "Fine, let's get on with it."

The little group left the office, rode the elevator two floors down, and entered an unremarkable hall lined with doors. Terra led the way to a door marked "casting chamber" and opened it.

Inside, the younger wizard from the day of his test stood beside a simple wooden table. On the table was a black box sitting in the center of an elaborate spell circle. The circle looked five times as complex as the one he knew how to draw.

"Conryu, you remember Clair?" Mr. Kane nodded toward the woman.

"Sure, she's the one that didn't think I was human."

Clair shrugged, not looking the least put out. "It was the most likely explanation."

"I take it that box is what you want me to break?"

"Yes." Terra marched over beside the table and they all went to join her. "It contains the remnants of a spell. Until it's opened I can't reconstruct it."

"How much power do you want me to use?" Conryu looked the box in the circle over. He only recognized one in three runes.

"Go all out. I designed the circle to shunt the excess power away the moment the wards break so there's no danger of you overdoing it."

"Okay."

Conryu put his hands on the table the way he'd been taught. "Break!"

Dark energy crackled through the circle and into the box. The wards sizzled and dissolved. A dark ooze, like living oil, sloughed off the box, revealing deep, rich brown wood underneath. The ooze inched toward the circle then flinched back when it touched the first line.

Conryu moved his hands and stepped back. "There you go."

Terra wore a broad smile. "That was impressive. The reports didn't exaggerate your power. All three of us tried to break that ward, alone and together, and we couldn't so much as scratch it."

"What's that ugly ball of black snot that keeps trying to slip through the circle? The wards I broke at school just sort of fizzled away."

"I wish I could tell you." Terra muttered something and flicked a finger at the blob. A spark shot out at it, forcing it back toward the center of the circle.

"Is it classified?" Conryu bent down for a closer look. The blob almost acted alive.

"Not at all." Terra turned back to look at him. "I've simply never seen such a thing. Until I've analyzed it and determined if it's dangerous I don't even dare reach into the circle."

Conryu turned to Mr. Kane. "Did you need anything else?"

"Terra, Clair?"

Terra shook her head. "I'd love to run some experiments, but I need to focus on this. Thanks for your help. It was a pleasure to watch you cast."

"Glad you enjoyed it. Can someone give me a ride home? I don't want to hang around here until Mom finishes her shift."

"I'll do it," Lin said. "We need to discuss some security matters anyway."

* * *

Kelsie had been home for three days before she received a summons to go to her mother's home office. Sometimes she felt more like an employee than a member of the family. She left her room and made her way through the professionally decorated halls, downstairs to the office.

The heavy oak door was closed and if she knew her mother she'd be sitting in her big leather chair facing away from the door so she could slowly turn and glower. Next would come the critique of all Kelsie's mistakes followed by a harangue about what a disappointment she was. It would be neither the first nor the last such visit for Kelsie and she'd endure it as she always did, without comment or complaint.

She took a deep breath, counted backwards from ten to settle her nerves, and knocked.

"Come in." Her mother's muffled voice came through the door.

Kelsie pushed the door open and walked into the opulent room. Leather-bound books lined the walls. A warm, magical breeze kept off the chill. Her mother sat facing her behind a massive cherry desk.

Magic kept her mother's face smooth and youthful despite having passed fifty the year before. Her skin was pale and her hair jet black. It was like looking thirty years into the future every time Kelsie saw her.

"You summoned me, Mother?"

"Yes. I understand you passed your midterm. From the reports I'd received I had my doubts. Congratulations."

Kelsie hesitated. This was different. What was her mother up to? "Thank you."

"Tell me about the boy wizard. I understand the two of you have become close."

Now she understood. "We're in the same class and he helped me with my breaking. I wouldn't say we're close."

"No?" Her mother leaned on the desk, her bright blue eyes intent. "I understand you hugged him immediately after the test then spent the trip to Central alone in his cabin."

"A moment of exuberance. We did nothing on the train but chat."

"Pity. Your task for the second half of the year is to seduce him into your bed. His genetics will make our bloodline stronger. Any child born from such a union will be a powerful wizard. This is your responsibility."

"You would make a whore of me?" The words were out before she could stop herself.

"Not a whore. No money will change hands. I researched your father back eight generations. He came from good stock. Five women in his direct bloodline were wizards, all above average in power. I did everything possible to ensure I gave birth to a strong wizard as was my responsibility as future matriarch of the Kincade family. In the end I failed, but not because I was too squeamish to do what had to be done." Her mother shrugged, either unaware of or indifferent to Kelsie's growing horror.

"What about love?"

"Love?" That drew a harsh, humorless laugh. "Love has nothing to do with it. Your father was a soft weakling from a decadent family, but he had the right genetics. He gave me the best opportunity to succeed. I assure you he didn't complain about the job."

"Conryu's been nothing but kind to me. I can't use him like that."

"If he's been kind then you're halfway done. The only reason a man shows a woman kindness is to get her on her back. If he's already being friendly you can just be patient and when he makes his move, go along with it. Everyone gets what they want."

Kelsie held back her tears with nothing but sheer force of will. Mother was wrong about Conryu. He could have tried something on the train, or when they were alone in his room, but he'd never put a toe out of line. He seemed as sweet a boy as she'd ever met.

The easiest thing to do was to go along with her suggestion. If Conryu turned out to be what her mother suspected and she secretly feared then she'd have no regrets using him. If he didn't then they'd stay friends.

"Very well, Mother. I'll do as you say. When he makes his attempt to seduce me I'll play along with it. After that it's up to nature."

* * *

Lin dropped Conryu off at his building and headed back to the Department. It had come as a considerable surprise when the detective had told Conryu about his promotion and transfer. He didn't seem certain if it was a reward or punishment. Conryu thought the latter, but didn't want to discourage him.

He made the short walk to the elevator and hit the call button. The job at the Department hadn't taken an hour and it was barely nine o'clock. It would have been cool to hang out with Jonny, but the military academy didn't take a winter break. Conryu wouldn't get to visit with him until summer vacation.

The door to the elevator chimed and slid open. Maria and her mother stood facing him, both in identical suits.

"Conryu!" Maria jumped out and hugged him. "I thought you were helping Dad today."

"I did. Job's done."

"That was fast." Mrs. Kane stepped out of the elevator. "What did he want you to do?"

"They were having trouble breaking a ward. I cracked it for them." He shrugged. "It wasn't a big deal. Terra had a circle ready. All I needed to do was cast the spell. Everyone seemed pleased."

"That's good. Do you have plans for the rest of the day? Maria and I are going on a job and you're welcome to join us if you'd like. Get a taste for the business of magic."

Conryu wasn't overly interested in the business of magic, but spending the day hanging out with Maria and her mom sounded way better than sitting around watching tv all day. "Sounds cool. What's the job?"

The little group walked to where Mrs. Kane had her car parked. It was a sweet black sedan with chrome wheels. "I have a client that wants to upgrade his anti-theft wards. Apparently whoever did the original casting left a loophole that allows animals through. A family of raccoons got into his garbage and he decided to call me in to fix things."

"You're kidding." Conryu climbed into the backseat. "He called a wizard to deal with raccoons? Wouldn't a pest control outfit be cheaper?"

Mrs. Kane shrugged and slipped behind the wheel. "I'm happy

to take his money. Don't worry, he's got plenty. Mr. Montgomery owns a string of stores and has a net worth in the middle eight figures. He could hire me to build him a new house and ward it and still not notice the hit to his bank account."

They pulled out of the garage and drove across town to the suburbs, coming to a stop in front of an iron gate leading to a community of mansions. A small guardhouse sat to one side of the gate and a man in a uniform stuck his head out the window.

"Can I help you?"

Mrs. Kane rolled down her window. "Shizuku Kane to see Mr. Montgomery. He's expecting me."

The guard's head disappeared back inside for a few seconds before popping out again. "Yes, ma'am. He called to tell us this morning. You can head on up."

A buzzer sounded and the gate slid open. They drove down the private road to the last house, a sprawling brick mansion on a huge landscaped lot.

Conryu whistled. "Wow. What did you say this guy sells?"

"Furniture and appliances mostly." Mrs. Kane shut off the car.

"Does he stuff them full of drugs?"

Maria giggled. Mrs. Kane shot them both a stern look. How many times had they been on the receiving end of that expression over the years?

"I know you're just joking, but that's the sort of thing that could cost me a client and if he tells his rich friends maybe more than one. I need both of you to act in the most professional manner possible during this job. Understand?"

They both promised and the three of them headed for the door. As they walked Mrs. Kane muttered a spell. Conryu recognized it as a variation of the one they taught freshmen to allow them to see magical auras.

Conryu muttered, "Reveal." The house lit up as wards became visible. A twisting crisscross of light, fire, and earth magic surrounded the house and spilled out over the grounds.

"Do you have to pick that apart or just add a little more to it?" If she had to pick it apart they were going to be here all day.

"Don't worry, I just have to add a simple three-rune figure to the matrix to keep animals out. Shouldn't take more than an hour or two." Mrs. Kane knocked on the door and a minute later it opened revealing a man in his seventies in a plaid robe, leaning on a cane. Infernal runes danced around his head, chest, and hands. "Mr. Montgomery? I'm Shizuku Kane, we spoke on the phone. This is my daughter Maria and—"

"Conryu Koda, the boy wizard." Mr. Montgomery held out a trembling hand to Conryu who didn't dare take it for fear of what the dark magic might do. "I've seen you on the television. Please, can you help me?"

"Yes, sir. Mrs. Kane is here to fix your wards so the raccoons don't raid your trashcans again."

"Maria and Conryu are studying at the academy. I brought them along so they could see real world magic in action. I hope you don't mind."

"Mind!" Mr. Montgomery stared at him with watery blue eyes partly covered with cataracts. "He's going to save me from the curse. Twenty years ago she said it. Only a male wizard could free me from the curse my family has suffered under for generations. Now you've come. God be praised."

Conryu looked to Maria for advice, but she was staring from Mr. Montgomery to him back to her mother. Mrs. Kane didn't look any more certain of what was happening than Maria.

"Maybe we could go inside and you can tell me about it." It was the only thing Conryu could think to say.

"Yes, of course, please." He hobbled to one side to let them in. "The door to your left leads to the living room."

Conryu moved between Maria and the old man just to be sure he didn't accidentally touch her. With all that dark energy swirling around him even a graze would hurt her.

They stepped through the door and into hoarder central. It

looked like every newspaper since the guy had been born littered the floor. Several humps that might have been chairs sat across from a longer hump that was probably a couch. The only uncovered piece of furniture was the tv. He had the news on.

Conryu, Maria, and her mother stood in an awkward little circle, none of them certain what to do next.

"Sit down, sit down." Mr. Montgomery plopped down on the floor, adjusting the papers to make a little nest around himself. "When I saw you on the news last summer I knew it was fate, destiny."

Destiny again, great. Conryu settled on the floor facing Mr. Montgomery. Maria and Mrs. Kane eyed the dirty papers. He understood their reluctance. Their suits probably cost a grand each.

Conryu took off his jacket and spread it over the floor. The ladies settled on it with grateful smiles.

"So tell me about this curse," Conryu said.

"For ten generations my family has suffered from creeping madness. It sets in at forty, the age my many-times-removed great-grandfather stole a book from a witch's library. It's a hideous thing with a pebbly green cover and yellow pages made of human flesh. The words are written with the veins and blood. It has a pulse. You can see the blood moving through the vessels."

Conryu shuddered. "Where is it?"

"In the library. I keep it locked up tight."

"Is that the reason for all the wards?" Mrs. Kane asked.

He nodded. "If someone stole it the curse would afflict their family as well. I couldn't compound my ancestor's crime like that."

"So what is it you want me to do?" Conryu asked.

"End the curse!"

"Yeah, but how exactly?"

"If I knew that I wouldn't need you. All I know is the wizard I consulted said a male wizard was the only one that could break the curse. I thought it a sick joke at the time. Then I saw you and knew hope for the first time in my life. Please. You can name your price. All that I have is yours if you can free my family of this nightmare. My son will turn forty in three weeks. Please, help me."

That was perhaps the most pitiful speech Conryu had ever heard. Unfortunately it didn't bring him any closer to knowing how to help. "Can we examine the book? I might glean some clues from it."

"I can't go near it. It pains me to even be in the same room as the wretched thing. The library is down the hall, third door on your right. The book is locked in a glass case. The key's been lost for a hundred years."

They left Mr. Montgomery muttering to himself in the living room and followed his directions to the library. If the living room was pure chaos the library was the opposite. Bookcase after bookcase, each shelf filled with a single, precise row of leather-bound tomes, covered the walls. In the center of the room was a stand with a glass enclosure.

Conryu stopped in the doorway. "Are you guys sure this is something we should get mixed up in? I mean this is quite a bit more serious than stopping some raccoons."

"It is," Mrs. Kane said. "But unless you're willing to leave Mr. Montgomery in the state we found him, I don't know that we have any choice but to investigate and try to help."

He looked to Maria. She just shook her head. "You don't need me to tell you the right thing. Quit dawdling and get in there."

He smiled. Trust Maria to cut to the heart of the matter. Conryu stepped through the doorway.

"You've come at last, Master." A deep, booming voice filled the room.

Darkness gathered at the corners of Conryu's vision. Maria had taken a step into the room, but he pushed her back before the darkness fully descended. That much dark energy might have killed her.

All around him it looked like someone had spilled a giant bottle of ink, save for the stand and a narrow path over to it.

"Who are you?" Conryu asked.

"I have forgotten. I know only my purpose."

"What is your purpose?"

"To impart my knowledge to you."

"To me? You don't even know me."

"My creator knew you. She made me to serve you."

Conryu massaged the bridge of his nose. The mother of all headaches was building behind his eyes. "Maybe you'd better start at the beginning."

* * *

Maria stumbled when Conryu pushed her and a moment later darkness descended on the library. She shuffled back, her chest aching from the proximity of so much dark energy. If she'd been in there when the barrier fully manifested it could have killed her. Conryu must have realized it and shoved her to safety. What had he stumbled into now?

"Mom?"

"I don't know what to tell you, sweetheart. I can't see or sense anything beyond that wall of darkness. When I agreed to take this job I envisioned a simple demonstration and an easy payday. I never imagined something like this happening."

"What do we do? He might be in trouble." Maria was on the verge of tears and hated herself for her weakness.

It seemed like whenever anything happened all she could do was wait and hope her best friend survived. Why was she so useless?

"I was mean to him on the train home."

"Why?"

"I was jealous. Conryu helped Kelsie Kincade with her breaking and she seemed infatuated with him. She's rich, pretty, and in most of his classes. I've been so busy studying I haven't had much time to hang out with him."

"You were afraid he'd drop you for Kelsie?"

She nodded and couldn't look at her mother. It seemed such a stupid thing to be mad about now.

"What did he say?"

"Conryu says they're just friends and they probably are. You know how he is. If someone needed help he'd do whatever he could. Kelsie definitely has a crush on him. I could tell just by the way she looked at him."

"And you? How do you feel about Conryu?"

"I..." How did she feel? She loved Conryu, of course she did. Maria had always loved him, but was it like a sister or a girlfriend? The truth was it depended on the day. When he hugged Kelsie she felt like a girlfriend, an angry one at that. "I don't know."

"You need to make up your mind. It's not fair to Conryu to make him wait forever. You have him to yourself for another ten days. You need to decide what you want before the competition makes the decision for you."

The house shook and a deep laugh echoed through it.

The darkness beyond the door pulsed stronger, forcing Maria to move back. Conryu was in there, surrounded by that energy. Deep inside it was a part of him. Could she really be with someone when a part of their nature was poison to her?

* * *

The book laughed. That was something Conryu had never expected to encounter. A pulse of dark magic shattered the glass case and the book flew up and out, hovering in front of him. The green cover flowed like wet clay, forming a face, an ugly, scaly, in no way human face.

"You're a demon."

"I was, and I suppose my essential nature hasn't changed. You wanted my story, Master. Here it is. I am a scholomantic, a training aid created to teach you all the secrets of dark magic. My creator was a witch with the gift, or curse, of prophecy."

"Why do you call her a witch and not a wizard?"

"Witch, wizard, warlock, mage, sorcerer: all names for the same thing. What does it matter? Anyway, shortly after the end of the Elf War a vision came over her. She saw that a wizard would be born, the most powerful in history. And that the wizard would be male. She became obsessed with you, while at the same time doubting her sanity."

"Why?"

"How should I know? Have you ever met a seer that was totally sane?"

Conryu had never met a seer of any sort, but didn't comment. "Go on."

"She came to believe it was her destiny to teach you about dark magic since she knew you'd be strongest in that field. She also knew by the time you were born she'd be long dead. To satisfy her obsession she needed a way to preserve her knowledge."

"You."

"Yes, me. Before she summoned me and forced me into this rather unimpressive form, I was an Arcanalite, a demon that studied magic in all its forms. It's an obsession we're born with. I contain all of the knowledge I possessed before my transformation as well as that of the witch. There is very little you could ask me about dark magic that I couldn't answer."

Conryu nodded. "That's cool. How about a little test? There's something I've been curious about."

"I can answer none of your magical questions, save those that will help you decide to accept me as your teacher, until you officially accept me as your scholomantic."

"Would that be like a demon contract? And assuming I agree, will it free Mr. Montgomery from his curse?"

"The agreement is similar to a demon contract, but the

connection is much deeper. And yes, it will free the pathetic mortal down the hall from his curse. In truth, the curse was only supposed to keep whoever took the book from throwing it away. Over time it transmuted into a hoarding and paranoia curse. Once you accept me it will have served its purpose and fade away."

"One last question. Will accepting you mess up the contract I already have with Cerberus?" Conryu rolled up his sleeve to show the book the brands on his arm.

"Well, aren't you popular? No, our agreement will have no effect on your arrangement with the demon dog. So do you accept?"

Conryu walked away and paced along the narrow path in the darkness. Should he accept? Dealing with a creature like this might be dangerous. He dearly wished for a quick call to Mrs. Umbra. He glanced back at the darkness sealing the door. He couldn't even ask Mrs. Kane. He was on his own.

After a minute of pacing he walked back to the book. Whatever else, he couldn't leave Mr. Montgomery and his family to suffer a curse that was intended to help him. He had to accept responsibility, even if it wasn't really his fault.

"Very well. What do I have to do?"

The book flipped open to the first page. It said: "Property of," followed by a blank line. "Just sign on the line."

"I don't have a pen."

The page flicked out, stretched, and sliced Conryu's finger open. "There you go. Just press it to the page."

It was just like something out of a bad horror movie. Conryu pressed his bloody finger to the page. Blood flowed and formed into his signature. Something shifted inside him, like when he'd made the contract with Cerberus, only stronger.

When the feeling faded he asked, "What now?"

"Whatever you wish, Master."

Conryu glanced back at the black wall separating him from the rest of the mansion. "How about you take down the wall?"

"Now that we have formed a contract I can no longer perform magic on my own. If you like I can teach you the spell to remove the barrier."

"Good idea."

The book's pages riffled and stopped about halfway through. On the page was a sequence of Infernal runes above a specific hand position. Conryu studied the runes; luckily he recognized them all.

When he'd committed both the words and gesture to memory Conryu said, "I have it."

The book snapped shut and said, "Show me."

Conryu focused. "The dark winds of Hades blow away all obstructions, Shattering Wind!" The darkness vanished just like a giant gust of air had blown it away. The instant the doorway cleared Maria rushed in and hugged him.

"Are you okay? What is that?" She was staring at the ugly book floating behind him.

"It's a scholomantic. Say, do you have a name? I can't just call you 'book.'"

"I believe I had a name once, but it was so long ago I can't recall. If you wish me to have a name, Master, feel free to make one up."

Mrs. Kane walked up to the book and studied it. The book studied her right back.

"You keep charming company, Master. Who's this lovely young lady?"

"This is Shizuku Kane and the one crushing me to death is her daughter, Maria." Maria took the hint and let him breathe. "How about Prime? You know, short for primer. That would be a good name for you."

"I quite like that, Master."

Prime was about to say something else when Mr. Montgomery

stumbled into the library. "You did it! My mind is clear for the first time in years." He spotted Prime floating beside Conryu and staggered back. "It's alive!"

"It's okay, Mr. Montgomery. Prime's going to be coming with me so you won't have to see him anymore. He's been waiting for me for a long time. I'm sorry your family's had such a hard time of it. The magic became twisted over the years."

"Is it really over?" Tears were streaming down the old man's face.

"It really is. If you'd like I'm sure Mrs. Kane can take care of your raccoon problem before we go."

"Absolutely." Mrs. Kane swept in and guided Mr. Montgomery out of the library, explaining how simple the process would be.

When they were out of sight Maria said, "Was it just chance that we stumbled onto the book in this of all places?"

"Not chance," Prime said. "Destiny. The witch may have been crazy, but she was never wrong about a prophecy. She saw that we would meet, so it was bound to happen. Perhaps her power influenced things over the centuries so it would come to pass when you were just beginning your journey down the path of wizardry. Then again it might have been pure, dumb luck. Who knows. I'm just glad to be awake again after all this time."

An hour later they were on their way home. Once the curse was lifted Mr. Montgomery found he no longer cared about the raccoons, but he did pay Mrs. Kane's $10,000 fee along with a nice bonus. His eagerness to give Conryu anything he wanted ended half a second after the curse, but he did agree it would be best if Prime went with him when he left.

* * *

They stopped for lunch and Mrs. Kane called her husband. As soon as she finished telling him what happened they were headed back to the Department. She dropped him off at the front doors then she and Maria went home. For the second time that day Conryu headed up the elevator and down to Mr. Kane's office. The secretary frowned at Prime, but motioned him through.

Inside Mr. Kane waved him into the left-hand chair beside Terra, who couldn't take her eyes off Prime. "Why don't you tell me about it?" Mr. Kane said.

When Conryu finished Mr. Kane had his head in his hands. "I'm sorry, but I wasn't sure what else to do."

Terra's soft chuckle prompted Mr. Kane to look up long enough to glare at her.

"There's nothing else you could have done," Terra said. "Certainly leaving a family to suffer under a curse wouldn't be in any way ethical. The problem is I'm not at all certain if the school will allow you to bring the book with you."

"They have a library, do they not?" Prime asked. "Why would one more book cause the teachers distress?"

"Because the other books can't fly or talk." Mr. Kane looked up. "You're closer to a magical item than a book and outside magical items aren't allowed, at least not in the hands of a student."

Terra had been staring at him and Prime this entire time. "Actually he isn't a book or magical item. The scholomantic is most closely related to a familiar. Conryu and Prime have bonded their souls like a master and familiar would. I'd say they have a range of a hundred or so yards. If they were to separate by more than that both of them would experience considerable pain."

"A familiar. Well those are allowed, though usually not until second year. I think I can convince Emily to make an exception for Conryu." Mr. Kane closed his eyes and sighed. "What's one more at this point? Besides, we owe you one for opening the box."

"So you'll take care of it?" Conryu asked.

"I'll do my best." Mr. Kane offered a reassuring smile.

"Thanks, Mr. Kane. I should probably go introduce Mom to Prime."

"If you can spare the time," Terra said. "I'd appreciate it if your scholomantic would take a look at the black ooze. If it can identify the substance it would save me a lot of effort."

Conryu glanced at the book floating beside his shoulder. "What do you say? Want to have a look?"

"If you wish it, Master, I'm happy to do so."

"Excellent." Terra jumped out of her chair and led them to her casting chamber.

The lab looked exactly the same as that morning. The little black blob bounced around inside the circle as though trying to find a way out. Terra briefly described the situation then asked, "What do you think?"

Prime flew closer to the circle. "It's necroplasma. Some dark magic wizards use it as a medium to contain potent energy. It's no wonder you couldn't break wards enhanced with this. It's nasty stuff and can only be summoned with a human sacrifice. That little blob could hold enough dark energy to kill several elephants or bind a modestly powerful demon. If the wards were designed properly they'd withstand almost any breaking."

"Why's it still bouncing around?" Conryu asked.

"I suspect it's trying to return to the wizard that conjured it." Prime's cover flexed in a fair imitation of a shrug. "But that's just a guess."

"So if we release it the necroplasma will lead us to Mercia?" Terra looked giddy at the thought.

"It might," Prime said. "Understand, I'm speculating. It's just as likely that if you release it the blob will dissipate into nothing. I have no way to know for certain."

"Fair enough. If worst comes to worst we'll chance using the little booger as a bloodhound."

* * *

"Isn't there something you'd like me to teach you, Master?"

Conryu sat on the couch, his feet up on the coffee table, watching a replay of the previous night's hockey game. He had to return to the academy tomorrow and the last thing he wanted to do was spend a precious minute learning a new spell.

Not to mention it would break his deal with Dean Blane. Conryu had spoken to her last week and she said he could bring Prime to school with him, but he had to promise not to study anything Mrs. Umbra hadn't approved of. That gave him all the excuse he needed to ignore the book's constant nagging.

"You know the deal I made. Now be quiet so I can enjoy the game."

The book fell silent and if he was lucky it would remain that way for an hour or two. The scholomantic had a one-track mind and no hobbies to distract him.

Halfway through the second period someone knocked. Conryu wasn't expecting company and as he walked to the door he said a silent prayer that it wasn't Angus. His life had been blissfully professor free since the Grand Brawl and Conryu was in no hurry to change the status quo.

He looked through the peephole and sighed when he saw the top of Maria's head. They hadn't spoken since what happened at Mr. Montgomery's and he feared she was uncomfortable around Prime. To be fair he wasn't totally comfortable with the talking book yet either, but he had to live with the thing.

He opened the door and grinned. "This is a pleasant surprise."

Conryu stepped aside. Maria didn't smile, she just brushed past him without looking up. He closed the door and turned back. "What's wrong?"

"I've been thinking."

Uh-oh. "Yeah?"

She glanced at Prime. "Is there somewhere we can talk, alone?"

"Sure. Prime, go to my room."

The book obediently floated down the short hall to his bedroom. As he understood the nature of their connection the scholomantic could see and hear everything he did and vice versa, but at least it wasn't right there staring at them.

"So what's up? School resumes tomorrow. That usually puts you in a good mood."

He dropped onto the couch and Maria sat beside him. "Mom said something to me, when you were in the library arguing with that book. She said I needed to decide what I wanted out of our relationship. That it wasn't fair to keep you guessing."

"I've got no complaints. When we're together I'm happy. Whether it becomes something more than what we have now..." He shrugged.

"I know you don't have any complaints. And I know you love me, like I love you, but I think... I think that until we finish school I'd like to keep things as they are now, just friends. I want to focus on my studies. If you and Kelsie or someone else want to try being a couple I promise I won't get jealous."

Conryu knew she was trying to have this deep, meaningful moment, but he couldn't stop himself from smiling. "I know you think you mean it, but you don't. You were about ready to kill me after I hugged her and we talked for half an hour. Imagine if someone told you we were making out in the hall or that you saw us."

Maria flinched, proving his point. Conryu leaned over, kissed her on the cheek, and put his arm around her.

She sniffed and snuggled up closer to him. "You're being drawn into something and I'm not sure I'm strong enough to follow. I want to stay beside you, but I'm so scared. So much keeps happening. I'm totally confused."

"Yeah, but I'm not. Until I find someone I love more than you, an event I can't conceive of, you're the only girl for me. Don't misunderstand. I still plan to stay friends with Kelsie and the golem club. They're all nice girls and Kelsie especially seems like she needs a friend that doesn't want anything from her. As for the rest of that stuff… I'm not sure I want you to follow me. Knowing you're safe will make it easier for me to do whatever I end up having to do."

She buried her face in his chest. "What are we going to do?"

"I don't know, but we'll figure it out together."

12
LADY MOCKINGBIRD

The cab ride was smooth and almost silent as they traveled over the newly paved road. Lady Mockingbird reclined in the back, her spell keeping the driver's mouth shut. She had no use for the idle chatter of fools. The ever so useful spell that compelled his silence would also ensure that ten minutes after she got out of the cab he'd remember nothing of his most recent fare. She considered killing him, but a body would draw more attention than a forgetful cabbie.

It would have been far simpler for her to have flown to her destination, but the magic that protected the target would have detected her arrival. If the Kincade West building went on lock-down even her formidable skills wouldn't be enough to break in. Once Lady Mockingbird was inside, however, all bets were off.

As they drew ever closer to her destination Lady Mockingbird turned her focus inward, ignoring the steel high-rises gleaming in the late afternoon sun and crowds of people making their way to or from the many bars lining the Santa Angeles city streets. Everything that didn't affect her mission was a useless distraction that she had to put out of her mind.

This mission had to succeed. If she failed to secure the device, the rest of her plan would be ruined. She would have only two options then: try and cobble together a last-minute replacement or admit failure and accept the Hierarchs' punishment. Neither of those options was likely to result in her standing victorious over the dead body of Conryu Koda, basking in her superiors' praise. The only reward for failure was death.

The cab pulled over across the street from a black, thirty-story building. Nothing identified it as anything more than a place of business, but Lady Mockingbird had done her research. In addition to the day-to-day stuff, there was a secure arcane research facility in the basement. According to her source the device she wanted was located on the lowest level.

She rubbed the platinum ring on her left index finger. The ring would enhance her light magic spells, allowing her to use magic usually beyond her innate ability. She shuddered when she considered what she'd promised Lady Bluejay in exchange for the loan. It would all be worth it when she was promoted to Hierarch.

Lady Mockingbird stepped out of the cab and made a subtle gesture, sending the cabbie on his way. When her ride was out of sight she crossed the busy street and strode up to the front doors just like she had all the right in the world to be there. Today she was playing the role of a business woman and she had the suit and low heels to look the part. She wore special glasses that generated a field that blurred her features in security cameras.

Automatic doors slid open at her approach. A shiver went through her as she passed through the wards. Despite her best efforts she hadn't discovered exactly what the potent protections did and she wasn't anxious to find out.

Beyond the doors lay a tiled entryway. A security checkpoint blocked anyone entering from moving past that small area and deeper into the building. Three men sat behind a desk beside an old-fashioned metal detector. She'd hoped for only two guards. Dominating the minds of three people, even three halfwit males, was too much for her limited light magic abilities.

As she walked towards the guards she began the first spell, murmuring under her breath, barely moving her lips. If she didn't time this perfectly one of the guards might have time to hit the alarm. That couldn't be allowed no matter what.

"Can I help—"

The center guard slumped face first into the desk, his forehead smacking the hard surface. Just as she'd hoped the other two focused their attention on their fallen companion. She immediately chanted, "My will is your will, my wish your command, Puppet Master!"

The domination spell crashed into their minds like a sledgehammer. Both men's jaws went slack then they stared at her with mindless adoration. She so loved that look on a man's face.

"I need to go to the basement."

"Which level, Mistress?" the guards asked in stereo.

"The lowest."

"We don't have the access codes for that level. Only those assigned to work on B4 have them."

Lady Mockingbird's lip curled and the men flinched at her displeasure. She'd hoped a simple card swipe would grant her entry. Her source didn't actually work in the building so she didn't know all the defenses.

"Is there anyone in the building right now that can enter the secure area?"

"Yes, Mistress, Vice President Lowery is in his office upstairs. He knows the codes for all the secure areas."

"Call him down here."

"He won't come. Mr. Lowery never uses the main doors. If there's a security issue he'll send our boss to handle it."

The guards' dual voices were giving her a headache. She couldn't keep piddling around down here. Every second she wasted with these idiots increased her chances of getting caught.

"Can anyone go up to Lowery's office?"

"Yes, Mistress, though his secretary may not let you in."

Lady Mockingbird smiled. "She'll let me in. One of you show me the way, the other stay here and send anyone that enters away."

Guard A led her toward her destination while B sat back at his station. As long as no one that actually knew what was supposed to be happening showed up she should be okay.

Her desire to hurry must have leaked through the connection with her guide as the man all but jogged to a bank of elevators at the rear of the lobby. He pressed the call button and they rode up to the top floor together. Below the buttons for the floors was a keypad.

As they ascended she asked, "Is there more security upstairs?"

"No, Mistress. The whole top floor is Mr. Lowery's executive suite and only he and his secretary are there most of the time."

She nodded. That should make things easier. Lady Mockingbird took a bullet from one of the clips on the guard's belt before replacing it in its holder. She made a mystic pass over it and cast. "Fragment of earth be my arrow."

The elevator chimed and the doors slid open revealing a hardwood-paneled hall leading to a large desk occupied by a stunning, dark-haired woman of Imperial descent in a revealing black dress. She suspected the secretary's duties included more than typing.

"Who are—"

Lady Mockingbird flicked the bullet at her. "Stone Acceleration!"

The magic hurled the metal casing and bullet at just short of the speed of sound. The secretary's brains splattered all over the wall behind her.

"The door."

Her servant hastened to open the heavy wooden door for her. Beyond it was a sprawling office with windows on three sides so Lowery could look out over the city. The man himself sat behind a glass desk with his back to her. All she saw was his bald head and broad shoulders.

"I do not wish to be disturbed," Lady Mockingbird said.

"Yes, Mistress." The guard drew his gun and closed the door behind her.

"Did you need something, sweetheart?" Lowery didn't bother turning around.

Lady Mockingbird twirled her finger. "Binding Flames." Bands of flame wrapped around his chest, locking him in place. If he tried to move it would result in a major burn.

"Indeed I do, darling." Lady Mockingbird spun her finger again. This time Lowery's chair mimicked the gesture, spinning him around to face her.

"Who the hell are you?"

"Who I am is a good deal less important than what I want. This can end one of two ways. Only one of which results in you living through the night."

Lowery's throat worked as he tried to swallow. "What do you want?"

"Access to the lowest level of the building. You're going to walk with me to the elevator, escort me to the lab, and then back out. Once I'm out of the building you'll never see me again."

"If I help you I'll lose my job, at best. The Kincades aren't known for their generous and forgiving natures."

Lady Mockingbird sent a psychic command and the flames flared brighter. Lowery broke into a heavy sweat. She didn't let the fire burn him, yet, but the threat was obvious. "You have to ask yourself what's the greater risk: them or me? I assure you I'm skilled enough at dark magic to compel your screaming soul to tell me what I need to know if I can't convince you any other way."

"What are we waiting for?" Lowery offered a shaky smile, as if that would save him.

* * *

Lowery gagged and looked away from where his dead secretary was slumped on the floor behind her desk. The pathetic man squeezed his eyes shut and stumbled to the elevator. She expanded the fire rings to allow him to walk, but at a thought from her they'd burn him into charred lumps.

Lady Mockingbird tapped the button for B4. She didn't worry about leaving fingerprints. An invisible energy field surrounded her hands both to prevent exactly that and to avoid accidentally triggering any magical item she may touch.

When the elevator refused to move she looked at Lowery who punched in a five-digit combination. The doors finally closed and the elevator lurched. The guard kept his weapon drawn as they descended, his gaze locked on Lowery. Lady Mockingbird didn't need the weakling's protection, especially from the quivering mass of flesh sharing the elevator with them, it was simply an unavoidable side effect of the spell that controlled him.

It didn't take long for the elevator to make its descent and soon the chime rang again and the doors slid open.

"Is there anyone down here?" Lady Mockingbird asked.

"No, the researchers have all gone home for the day. The job is intense, so they work short shifts."

"Let's hope you're right, for their sakes." She motioned him out first.

The guard started to follow them, but she raised a hand. "Stay here and hold the elevator. We won't be long."

"Yes, Mistress." He took up position between the doors, bracing it with his hands and feet. A bit excessive, but it should do the job.

The lab was a combination scientific research station and casting chamber. Computers sat on desks beside bookshelves lined with leather-bound tomes. She would have dearly loved to explore the contents of those books, but now wasn't the time.

"Where is the Chimera Jar?"

Lowery looked back at her, aghast. "How do you even know about that? It's top secret."

She poked a finger into his cheek, forcing his gaze away from her and back into the lab. "Where is it?"

"The vault." He pointed at a steel door at the rear of the room. "Please, it's still under development. The chimeras it produces are uncontrollable. My best people aren't even sure it's possible to create a stable chimera. If you use it you're more likely to kill yourself than anyone else."

"You concern is touching. Now open the vault and fetch the jar."

He slumped over even further and shuffled over to the steel door. A keypad identical to the one in the elevator hung on the wall beside it. Lowery punched in an eight-digit code this time and the door cracked a few inches releasing a hiss as the pressure equalized. He grabbed the handle and yanked it wide open.

The door was easily a foot thick. She never would have burned her way through. Inside it was lined with niches, the contents of which were hidden behind metal doors. Wards of various elements crackled in her magical vision. Whether they were there to keep the contents in, thieves out, or both, she couldn't say without further study.

At the far end was a safe built into the wall. It had a standard combination lock which Lowery manipulated with practiced familiarity. He pulled the smaller door open revealing a bizarre... something, made from an amalgam of metals. It resembled a trophy with a tight-fitting cap more than anything. The Chimera Jar rested on a slender folder filled with paper, most likely research notes. She'd need those as well.

"Are there any other protections?" she asked.

"The building wards and two steel safe doors not enough for you?"

He screamed when her fire band seared his shoulder with a

third-degree burn. "Best mind your manners. Your usefulness is now at an end. Grab the jar and notes and hand them to me."

He whimpered, but complied.

The moment the smooth, cool metal touched her skin she sensed the power in it. It would do what she needed. Lady Mockingbird knew it.

"Will you let me go now?"

She regarded Lowery with a cool frown, the one that set her girls' knees trembling. "There's one more matter."

"All thoughts of me begone, Burning Eraser." She tapped his forehead.

A microburst of flame seared away a tiny portion of his brain. He collapsed to the floor of the vault, unconscious. She'd burned away his memories of the last twelve hours. Even if they questioned his corpse, the knowledge was gone forever.

Lady Mockingbird left the vault and closed the door behind her, forming an airtight seal. He would suffocate long before he woke up, ensuring that they'd have nothing but a body to question. It wasn't the worst death she could think up, but it would do for the arrogant man.

Her pet guard was still holding the elevator door open when she returned. He immediately moved aside for her.

"Are you finished, Mistress?"

She chanted the spell again and tapped his forehead. The guard collapsed just like Lowery, his memories burned away. "I am, thank you for your assistance."

She rode up to the lobby and repeated the procedure with the other two guards before walking out of the building. The moment she stepped outside a tremendous hue went up as antitheft alarms sounded.

Lady Mockingbird summoned the wind. She'd be well out of the city before anyone arrived to investigate.

* * *

Lady Mockingbird landed in a forest clearing forty miles outside the city. A pair of fire globes appeared at her command and she looked around, not that there was much scenery. Big evergreens surrounded the snow-filled glade. A simple fire spell kept the cold from being a bother.

The trip back to the academy was over a thousand miles, way too far to fly. She'd have to travel by portal to Central, then fly the last fifty miles. The good thing was as a teacher she knew how to bring a magical item through the wards without setting off an alarm.

Before she opened the portal additional protections were necessary. When one traveled through the realm of fire, even a fire wizard had to take precautions. Especially when carrying important papers.

She focused first on herself. "No flames may touch me. No fire may burn me. Fire Shield." When the magic had settled around her she repeated the spell for the Chimera Jar and its research papers. For the duration of her trip through the realm of fire no harm would come to her or her possessions.

"Reveal the way through infinite flame. Open the path. Fire Portal!" A bright red disk appeared before her. Heat rushed out of it, melting all the snow in the clearing and stirring enough of a breeze to blow her hair back.

Stepping into the portal was like stepping into an infinite bonfire. Everywhere she looked there was nothing but flames. She floated, untouched by the heat, and whispered a name. "Metros."

A minute later a great phoenix flew under her and bore her away. She pictured a particular alley in Central and whispered, "Carry me to the convergence." The firebird snapped its wings.

Lady Mockingbird didn't dare speak her desires too loudly. The spirit she was allied with had enemies and a skilled foe could listen through the flames. If she was lucky they'd make the short flight with no trouble.

A shriek drew her attention up and a little behind them. A pair of winged fire lizards, their red scales sparking in the flames, were quickly gaining. Fire lizards were natural predators of phoenixes and she allowed herself a moment of hope that this was just normal hunting behavior.

She raised a hand in their direction and chanted in the language of air. "Father of winds blow away my enemies, Tornado Blast!" A mini tornado swirled out from her palm and sent the two lizards tumbling. If they were just out hunting that should be enough to discourage them into finding other prey.

As she feared, the lizards righted themselves in moments and plunged after them. Her phoenix let out a little shriek, more afraid than fierce. Though it would resurrect if the lizards killed it, being torn apart would not be a pleasant way to end its current existence.

"Don't worry." Lady Mockingbird spoke in a gentle, soothing voice that anyone who knew her well would doubt she was capable of. "I have more potent means to defend us."

This time she raised both hands and cast in Angelic. "Light of Heaven burn away my enemies, Lightning Blast!" Her borrowed ring sparked, lending power to her spell. Twin lightning bolts leapt from her hands and burned through the lizards' wings. They fell, flapping frantically with their uninjured wings, but unable to do anything but spin in a circle.

They would continue to fall until something snapped them out of the air and made a meal out of them. She didn't know if there was anything resembling the ground below them. For all she knew they might fall forever. It would serve the stupid beasts right for trying to devour her beautiful phoenix.

Shortly after the encounter her mount stopped and hovered in the sky. No one really understood how the various spirits always knew exactly where they were in relation to the mortal world, but they were never wrong.

"Thank you, pretty one." Lady Mockingbird hopped off the

phoenix's back and floated using her own magic. Her mount flew off, leaving her to her own devices.

She cast, "Grant me the power to see through realms, Vision Gate!" A one-way viewing portal appeared revealing an empty alley between two brick buildings and not a soul in sight. Exactly as she'd hoped.

At her command the portal opened and she stepped back into her own world. Only seconds had passed in real time. Much as she would have preferred to fly directly to the academy, she had to return Lady Bluejay's ring. She also had to pay the promised price.

The portal had opened into one of the few poor areas in the capital. Of course, no Society member would be caught living in such a dismal place. It was beneath their dignity.

She walked across the quiet city, ignoring a group of drunken young people still staggering about. Soon the rundown buildings gave way to shiny new apartment buildings. Lady Bluejay lived in a modest apartment on the twenty-fifth floor of the Sky Bride complex.

Lady Mockingbird entered the ground floor and rode the elevator up. It would only take two hours to repay Lady Bluejay for the loan. She would do what she had to. The ring had been well worth the humiliation she now faced.

The elevator chimed and she flinched. She stepped into the carpeted hall and walked down to unit six. She stopped outside the unimpressive steel door, slipped the borrowed ring off, gathered herself, and knocked.

The door opened, revealing the slim, almost gaunt form of Lady Bluejay. She wore a suit of black leather that must have taken an hour to pull on. The shiny material reflected the hall light in a harsh glare. Lady Mockingbird held out the ring and Lady Bluejay snatched it out of her grasp.

"It came in handy then?"

"It did."

"You're ready to repay your debt?" Lady Bluejay's lips curled into a satisfied smile.

"I am."

Her host stepped out of the way. "Then come in."

On the dining room table was a leather collar and leash beside a frilly white apron. She grimaced, set the Chimera Jar on the table, and began to strip.

For the next two hours, dressed in nothing but the apron, Lady Mockingbird cleaned the apartment. She began, of course, with the toilet and moved on from there, all while Lady Bluejay held her leash and watched, a huge grin on her smug face.

It took every ounce of her self-control not to burn the flesh from Lady Bluejay's face. Only the fact that the rest of the Society would hunt her down and do far worse stayed her hand.

When the two hours ended and she was dressed and free of the collar, Lady Mockingbird went to retrieve the jar. Lady Bluejay had it in hand, frowning.

"You humiliated yourself for this little bauble? Hardly seems worth it."

She snatched the item back and retrieved the paperwork. "Your ignorance is charming. Good evening."

"Good evening. Come back any time you want to borrow the ring."

Lady Mockingbird slammed the door behind her and stalked to the elevator. When she was a Hierarch she'd settle things. If all she made Lady Bluejay do was clean her home she could consider herself fortunate.

13
BACK TO SCHOOL

Conryu opened his eyes and found Prime staring at him from about ten inches away. "Gah! What the hell are you doing, trying to give me a heart attack?"

"No, Master, I sensed your parents moving around and assumed that meant it was time for you to get up as well. We're returning to the academy, are we not?"

"Yeah, I guess we are. Can you make yourself look like a normal book? Your face makes it kind of obvious you're not what you appear to be."

"Certainly, Master. After all I spent centuries appearing as a simple book. I'm not eager to repeat the process, but if you command it, I will obey."

"Good. At least until we get to school. I don't want the whole world knowing what you are. Not to mention you'll probably freak out the regular people at the train station. Most folks aren't used to flying, talking books."

Prime bobbed back and forth in the flying book equivalent of a nod. "Yes, I can see where I'd be overwhelming to an ordinary human. My splendor can't be underestimated."

"Right." Conryu rolled out of bed, stretched, and threw on some clothes. "I haven't seen you eat anything. Do you get hungry?"

"No, Master. As a magical entity I draw sustenance from the magic that permeates this world. Though I do enjoy the taste of human bones."

Conryu grimaced. "Pretty sure we don't have any of those in the fridge. Let's go see what Mom's cooking for my last breakfast at home for a while."

Prime sniffed. "I believe I detect cooking meat."

"That's bacon, the greatest human invention after the motorcycle." Conryu left his room and made the short walk to the kitchen. Prime flew along by his side.

Sure enough his mother was frying bacon and mixing pancake batter. He kissed her on the cheek. "Morning."

Dad had his face buried in the paper. He lowered it long enough to nod at Conryu. Positively chatty for Dad. He took a seat across from his father and waited for breakfast.

"Good morning, mother of my master."

Mom squealed when Prime flew up to her. She hadn't gotten totally used to the scholomantic and tended to react to him like she would a rat scurrying across the kitchen floor.

"Conryu, keep that thing away from me when I'm cooking. Or doing anything else for that matter."

Conryu patted the table beside him and Prime landed there. "He was just being friendly. Since we're probably going to be together for the rest of my life you guys should try and get along."

"I'm working on it." She plated pancakes and bacon and handed it to him.

The rest of the morning went quickly and they were soon on their way to the train station. Maria rode with them as both her parents had to work.

She snuggled up beside him in the back of the SUV.

"Is this female your mate, Master?"

"Mate!" Maria glared at Prime.

Conryu groaned. The scholomantic might know about magic, but that seemed to be about all it knew. "Prime, it might be best if you stop talking for a while."

"Like forever," Maria said.

"Apologies, human relationships have always been a mystery to me. Even when I was still a proper demon I never had what you would call a friend, much less a mate; the ideas are alien to demons."

"They work for us, now be quiet."

Prime flew back to the trunk and landed on his bag. Conryu shook his head. "Sorry."

Maria relaxed again and he put his arm around her. "It's fine, I'm just annoyed neither of my parents saw fit to see me off."

"What's up with that? I figured your dad would come along anyway."

"He was gone before I got up this morning. Whatever's going on at the Department has him really worked up. He gets home late and leaves early. Last Sunday he fell asleep in his chair and was muttering about finding mercy. Mom's worried about him and she never worries. Do you think it might have something to do with whatever he had you helping with?"

"Maybe. They all seemed pretty anxious to have me break into that box, not that they told me anything beyond that." He shrugged. "I figure if they wanted me to know they'd have said something. It's probably a bureaucratic thing. Mom says being in charge of a government department is like working in a daycare. That's why she never accepts promotions."

She rested her head on his shoulder. "I hope you're right."

Conryu hoped he was too, but he doubted it. That black ooze screamed evil. Anything created from a human sacrifice had to be serious. He never thought he'd be glad to return to the academy, but that stuff gave him chills. The less he had to do with it the better. At least at school he understood most of the threats.

He glanced out the window. A light snow had started to fall. The city looked so peaceful. He hoped it stayed that way.

THE CHIMERA JAR

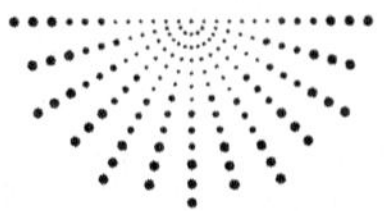

THE AEGIS OF MERLIN BOOK 3

1

TEAMWORK

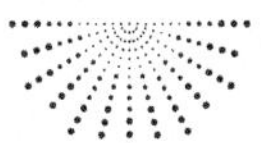

Conryu walked down the familiar hall to dark magic class with a mixture of relief and disappointment. Winter break had been a pleasant change of pace after months of magic studies, but he hadn't been able to avoid magic all together. The business with the Department remained fresh in his mind. Hopefully Mr. Kane would have the situation straightened out soon, if for no other reason than Maria was worried about him.

Prime wriggled in his grip. The scholomantic didn't like being carried and kept fidgeting in his hand. Right now Prime looked like nothing but an ugly green book. Conryu hid him between his notepad and *Infernal Basics* book.

So far he'd been able to keep Prime a secret from the other students, though he had no idea who Dean Blane had told. Only Mrs. Umbra had asked to see the scholomantic and that had been a brief inspection conducted ten minutes after he got back to school. She seemed neither impressed with Prime nor disappointed in Conryu for claiming him. That was about as good a reaction as he dared expect.

Prime had strict instructions to remain silent except when

they were in his room and even then Conryu wasn't allowed to study any of the many secrets the book held, except as applied to whatever his teachers had him working on.

In addition to checking out Prime, Mrs. Umbra had said that they'd turned the investigation into the Grand Brawl incident over to the Department in Central. The only clue they'd found was a small fragment of necroplasma that had been made as hard as steel. It seemed the viper golem had been made of the stuff, but most of it dissolved when the demon escaped. He shuddered to think how many lives it took to create that much of the crud.

"Conryu!" Kelsie jogged down the hall to catch up to him.

He slowed and she fell in step beside him. When he hadn't run into her on the train or in their dorm Conryu feared she may have decided she didn't want to be friends after all. Her bright smile as she walked beside him argued otherwise.

"How was your winter break?" he asked.

"I survived. You?"

"It was interesting." No reason to give her too many details, especially since he had no idea what he could and couldn't talk about. "I did some fieldwork with Maria's mom, you know, to get a taste of the business of magic. Can't say I'm much more interested in it now than I was."

"I don't blame you. It seems like all my family talks about is business. I feel more like my mom's employee than her daughter sometimes."

"That's harsh." Conryu opened the classroom door for her.

The others turned to look when they entered. No one said anything, they just stared. It couldn't be just him. They had to be used to having a guy in the class by now. Maybe it was because he was hobnobbing with the rich and famous.

He shook his head and took his seat at the back of the class. When Kelsie sat beside him instead of in her usual spot up front Conryu raised an eyebrow.

"What? I can't sit beside my friend?"

"Sure you can. I was just surprised."

The door burst open and Mrs. Lenore hustled through. "Sorry, I got mixed up in something. Welcome back, everyone."

She set to drawing on the chalkboard. When she finished there was a group of stick figures around a spell circle. "So for the second half of the year we'll be focusing on group castings. Group castings allow individual wizards to combine their power to create more potent effects than they'd otherwise be able to. With each person added to the casting it grows more complex so we'll be limiting our groups to five."

Mrs. Lenore wrote out two words in Infernal, *break* and *shatter*. "We'll start working in pairs to create a combined breaking."

From behind her desk she took out metallic spheres covered in runes. "These will be your practice targets. One member of the group will chant 'break' to destroy the wards while the other chants 'shatter' to smash the orb. The spells protecting them are much more potent than those used in the wooden blocks we trained with earlier. Everyone pair up."

Before Conryu had a chance to look Kelsie's way Mrs. Lenore continued. "Conryu, you'll be working with me. For safety reasons you understand."

Conryu sighed, nodded, and walked down to the front of the class to join her. While the girls were talking and sorting themselves out Mrs. Lenore leaned close so no one could overhear. "It won't do any good to pair you up with one of the girls until you can modulate your power enough to match a weaker partner. As it stands now your power would do all the work and she'd get nothing out of the experience."

"So what am I really going to do?"

"I'll explain once the girls have started."

The groups were soon set and Mrs. Lenore watched them for a few minutes to make sure they were doing everything correctly.

When she was satisfied she rejoined Conryu in the front of the room.

"So you were saying?"

"Right, modulation. You need to hold back enough of your power so you don't overwhelm your partners."

"That sounds kind of pointless. If the idea is to combine our powers to create a more potent effect why would I use less than my full power? I mean to match Kelsie I'd have to use like ten percent of my full strength and the combined casting would amount to less than a quarter of what I could do on my own. How is that beneficial?"

Her mouth opened and closed but no words came out. She looked a bit like a fish caught on the beach. After a moment she pulled herself together. "When you put it that way it makes no sense at all. Combined casting is what I always teach during second semester. It never even occurred to me that it wouldn't work for you."

She slumped and fell silent. He glanced back at the girls, but they were all engrossed in their practice. He put a hand on her shoulder and Mrs. Lenore looked up.

"What are we going to do? If the final is all about combined casting I guess I need to learn it."

She shook her head. "That's not really what it's about. It's just the breaking is of an order of magnitude stronger than what a single dark wizard can handle."

Conryu raised an eyebrow at that.

"Okay, an ordinary dark wizard. Sometimes I don't even know why you're in my class. If you took the final today you'd pass it with ease."

"For the sake of argument and the fact that we don't have enough people for only two groups, how could I work with weaker partners? We've established that lowering my own strength is useless. What could a second and third person do to make me stronger?"

She sat on the edge of her desk and rubbed her temples. "I'm not sure. A standard circle casting wouldn't work. It's designed to unite wizards of similar strength. The problem is fusing the energy flows into a coherent whole."

"When I helped Mrs. Umbra banish the demon serpent she drew out my power and directed it with a spell of her own. Would something like that work?"

"If you had the Death Stick and fifty years of experience, sure." Mrs. Lenore closed her eyes and sighed. "I don't know what to do. I'm a horrible teacher."

"Don't say that. This is new for everyone. I have class with Mrs. Umbra later. Would you mind if I mentioned the problem to her? She might have a suggestion."

"By all means. God knows you need someone other than me to help you."

* * *

Class ended and everyone but Conryu left for their free period. The moment the last girl closed the door behind her Prime shook the notepad off and flew in front of him.

"That woman is incompetent. I should be overseeing your instruction. Imagine, telling the most powerful wizard in the world that what he really needs to know is how to make himself weaker. Of all the stupid ideas I've heard over the millennia that one's right up there with 'Let's call Lord Beelzebub *Bug Eyes*.'"

"Don't be so critical. Mrs. Lenore's a good person. I'm afraid she's just a little out of her depth."

"I didn't say she wasn't a good human, I said she's an idiot. If she'd given it even a moment of thought she'd have realized her idea didn't even bear contemplation."

The ominous tapping of Mrs. Umbra's Death Stick sent Prime flying back to hide under his notepad. The head of dark magic was the only person Prime seemed to fear, not that Conryu blamed the scholomantic. She certainly had an intimidating presence. Despite that, Conryu found he was eager to see her again.

The door opened and the short, wrinkled figure in black hobbled in.

"Afternoon, Mrs. Umbra."

"Conryu. I trust that ill-mannered book has been behaving itself."

"Prime's been on his best behavior. I haven't told anyone about him yet. Is that the plan or can I let others know?"

"Up to you, but until you learn to cast spells through it, the scholomantic will be a point of vulnerability."

"Is that what you're going to teach me?" He sat up straighter. Anything that eliminated a potential weakness was of interest to him. "Before I forget, I have a question."

She hobbled down and sat behind the desk. "Oh?"

He briefly explained what had happened in his first class. "Anyway, it sounds like combination casting won't be of much use for me. I need to figure out some way to work with my classmates, if only for the final."

She nodded and tapped her chin. "Hey, book."

Prime flew up off the desk, but didn't speak.

"Do you have anything on fusion magic?"

Conryu had never heard of such a thing, but Prime flipped his pages before finally stopping. On the open page was an image of three wizards standing in a triangle formation. The two in the back rested their hands on the one in front's shoulders and the text described how to merge the three powers into one. It looked like exactly what he needed.

"Can I show this to Mrs. Lenore? She seemed really upset that she didn't know what to teach me."

"Let me see."

Prime flew over to allow Mrs. Umbra to read the pages. After a minute she nodded. "Very complete. That should solve your group casting problem. You have my permission to study those pages in your spare time, though don't experiment without one of your teachers present."

"Never crossed my mind."

Prime flew back and landed on the desk.

Conryu patted his spine. "Thanks."

The scholomantic's pleasure flowed through their link.

"So what are we going to practice?"

"As you guessed we're going to work on you sharing your spells with your book. Ordinarily this isn't something we teach freshmen. Not much point since you're technically not allowed to have a familiar until your second year. But in your case we'll have to make an exception. That happens a lot, doesn't it?"

Conryu grinned. "Yeah, but what can we do?"

"Indeed. Ready to begin?"

He spent the next two hours trying to force a Cloak of Darkness spell to cover himself and Prime. After twenty castings Conryu was exhausted and the best he managed was a scattering of black spots so it looked like Prime had a fungus infection.

"That's enough for now," Mrs. Umbra said. "Feel free to practice that as much as you like. By that I mean for at least an hour a day. We meet up again in three days. I expect you to be able to cover both yourself and the book in darkness."

Conryu nodded and stood up. "We'll get there."

* * *

Maria reached the top-floor landing and made the short walk to the light magic classroom. She was eager to find out what they'd be working on this semester. She assumed healing since along with warding it was a light wizard's primary area of expertise. It would be nice to be able to have something concrete to offer Conryu.

She'd told him she doubted she was strong enough to join him on his journey, but if she learned to heal that would be something he couldn't do, even with all his power. That thought made her smile. It was nice to think there was something magical Conryu couldn't accomplish.

Inside the classroom about two-thirds of the others had arrived and were sitting at their desks. Mrs. Alustrial was standing at the front of the class, looking especially stern with her face twisted in a deep scowl. She glared at Maria as she made her way to the desk she shared with Irene.

"What did you do to get on her bad side?" Irene asked.

"No idea. This is the first time I've seen her since midterms. Congratulations on passing by the way."

"Thanks, you too. Shame about Corrie."

"Yeah." Maria hadn't seen the weakest member of their class since she arrived, but the girl had to be upset. If Maria was ever demoted to the lowest rungs of magical study she'd have cried herself to sleep for weeks. Conryu probably would have done backflips, but the odds of him getting demoted were about as good as the sun not rising in the morning.

The last of the class entered with seconds to spare and took their seats. Mrs. Alustrial tapped the chalkboard with her pointer and everyone fell silent.

"Thank you, ladies. For the rest of the year we will be working on healing."

There were murmurs and Maria did a mental fist pump. Healing, just as she'd hoped.

Mrs. Alustrial cleared her throat. "Before we begin I want to discuss what happened at midterms, especially the shameful display by Conryu Koda."

This time the mutters had an angry tone. Everyone had been embarrassed when Conryu had demolished their best work with no visible effort. Maria had been a little annoyed too, but considering the way most people treated him she didn't blame Conryu for showing off a little. Besides, he claimed it was his teacher's idea.

"That sort of showboating has no place in our fine school. I complained to his teacher as well as Dean Blane, but since he didn't break any rules no punishment was levied. Mrs. Lenore even had the gall to note that a little humility would do me… that is, us, good." Mrs. Alustrial started pacing as her face grew red. "As though it were my fault that every year for the past ten years her students haven't been strong enough to defeat my best students. Her bitterness was hardly attractive."

Looked like her teacher had a bruised ego. Talk about not attractive. When her classes first began Maria had looked up to Mrs. Alustrial, now she was starting to wonder.

"So," Mrs. Alustrial continued. "As long as you're in my class you will have no contact with Conryu and as little contact with the rest of the dark magic class as possible. We wouldn't want their negative attitudes rubbing off on you. Understood?"

Maria heard nothing after the order to avoid Conryu. It was ridiculous and she had no right to tell them who they could hang out with after class.

Mrs. Alustrial fixed her gaze on Maria. "I said, understood?"

"No, ma'am, it is not understood. I'm not going to stop seeing my friend just because he upset you and I doubt you have the authority to make me."

The muscle at Mrs. Alustrial's jaw bunched. "As your primary teacher I have all the authority I need. You will avoid that boy even if I have to assign you to detention every free moment you have."

Maria glared back. "I wonder what Dean Blane will have to say?"

"This is not her concern, you will say nothing about it."

"I won't mention your threats if you back off your order to avoid Conryu."

The two women engaged in a staring match for half a minute before Mrs. Alustrial looked away. "Do what you want. But if you need extra help with healing, like you did with wards, I suggest you find someone else to ask."

Bitch!

At this point Maria wouldn't have asked her for help if her life depended on it. It was going to be a long second half of the year.

* * *

After an agreeable dinner with Maria, Conryu headed back to his room. He needed to talk to Mrs. Lenore, but he wasn't sure if he should tell her about Prime. For the moment he'd copy the pages on fusion magic and say Mrs. Umbra gave them to him, which was close enough to the truth.

The moment he stepped into his room the pixie swirled around his neck in wind form, then turned into a tiny girl and settled on his shoulder.

Prime flew out of his grasp and snarled at the pixie. She pressed herself against his cheek and trembled.

"Stop that, Prime. This is the first friend I made when I arrived and I'll not have you scaring her. You two are going to have to learn to get along."

The pixie flew up near the ceiling and stuck her tongue out at Prime. The scholomantic rushed toward her, but Conryu snatched him out of the air. "Enough. Open up to that page about fusion magic so I can copy it."

Prime glared once more at the pixie and landed on his desk, open to the page he needed. It took the better part of an hour for him to copy the three pages of Infernal along with the images. His drawings weren't as nice as the originals, but they got the idea across.

Satisfied with his efforts Conryu stood up and headed for the door. He paused when he reached for the handle and turned back. "I trust you two will behave yourselves while I'm gone."

Prime slammed himself shut on the table while the pixie transformed into wind and blew out of his room. So much the better if they weren't in there alone. Conryu stepped out into the hall and shut the door. It was like trying to keep a pair of angry feral cats apart with those two. They'd only known each other for a day and already seemed to hate one another. Didn't he have enough to worry about?

He put that minor annoyance aside and headed toward Mrs. Lenore's room. It was convenient for him that his teacher was also the dark magic dorm supervisor. She had the center room so no one could claim she played favorites by being closer to one side or the other. He had a hard time imagining that was an issue, but then again he'd heard of stupider things.

Conryu knocked and a moment later Mrs. Lenore opened the door. She'd traded her black robes for soft pink pajamas that draped over a slim, but still curvy figure. He was so surprised he took a step back. Mrs. Lenore slammed the door in his face.

A few seconds later it opened again and she'd thrown her robe over the pajamas. Her cheeks were bright red and she refused to meet his gaze. "Conryu. Can I help you with something?"

Probably best not to mention the PJs. "Yeah. Mrs. Umbra had an idea about the combination magic thing. Is this a good time to talk?"

"Of course, of course, come in." She stepped aside and he went in.

Her room was identical to his, except for some extra decorations. A pair of pink bunny slippers that were a perfect match for the pajamas peeked out from under her bed. He couldn't restrain a smile.

Mrs. Lenore noticed where he was looking, hurried over, and kicked the slippers out of sight. "What did she have to say?"

"Right." Conryu handed her his copied notes. "She thought fusion magic might be the solution to our problem."

She'd barely started looking at the pages when something whistled in the bathroom. "Damn it! My tea."

"I'll get it." He started for the bathroom door.

"No!" She stumbled in her rush to block him.

Conryu didn't know what to do when Mrs. Lenore fell right towards him and in his moment of hesitation their feet tangled up and they ended up in a heap on the floor.

She lifted her head up out of his crotch and offered a shaky smile. "This isn't going very well, is it?"

"Not very. Why don't I sit on the bed and when you're ready we can talk?"

"That's an excellent idea."

They separated and regained a modest amount of decorum. Conryu sat on the edge of the bed while Mrs. Lenore disappeared into the bathroom to deal with the whistling teapot. Why there was a whistling teapot in her bathroom was a subject he didn't want to explore.

A short while later she emerged with a steaming mug. "I'd offer you a drink, but I only have the one cup."

"That's fine. I don't like tea anyway. So, about fusion magic. Do you think that would work?"

She sat beside him and spread out the pages he brought. "I won't lie, I'm not at all familiar with this sort of magic. I've never taught it or even seen it performed. I'm not saying it wouldn't work, but the ritual is so far outside my area of expertise..." She shrugged.

"That's cool. Like you said, I can probably do the final on my own, I was just thinking since we don't have the right number of girls for five-member teams this might be a way for the two odd ones out to work with me. Maybe it would be best to go with six-person teams and me alone."

"No, it won't be." She scrubbed a hand over her face. "Six is too many for such inexperienced wizards. Some of the girls have the skill to pull it off. I think I might go with one group of six and one of five, but that still leaves one girl out."

"I think Kelsie would be willing to work with me on the fusion magic. What do you say I ask her and if she says yes, we give it a try?"

"Can I keep these notes? If it's not too complex I should be able to figure it out in short order, at least enough to help you two. Make sure you tell her she'll have to learn circle casting along with fusion magic so it'll be extra work."

"Will do, thanks. I'll go try and hunt up Kelsie." Conryu started for the door then turned back. "By the way, those are cool slippers."

Mrs. Lenore pointed at the door, but the hint of a smile played around her lips.

* * *

Kelsie didn't have a room of her own. She stayed in a group room with the other freshmen girls on the opposite end of the floor from his suite. This could be awkward if all twelve of his classmates were around. Well, there was nothing for it.

He left Mrs. Lenore's room and made the short walk down to the... barracks? That didn't seem like the right word. Quarters maybe? He sighed and quit trying to distract himself. Going to the girls' room was perfectly innocent and nothing to be concerned about.

Conryu gathered himself outside the door and knocked. A minute later a glowering blond who'd never introduced herself to him opened the door. At least she still had her robe on.

"What?"

"I was looking for Kelsie."

"Why?"

He was half a breath from telling her it was none of her business when Kelsie rushed up to the door. "Conryu. This is a surprise. What brings you here so late?"

He was pretty sure it wasn't that late, but that was beside the point. "I have a proposition for you. Got a minute?"

"Sure, we were just practicing circle casting. Let's take a walk."

They left the still-frowning blond behind and headed back toward his room. He didn't say anything until they were halfway there.

"So I was talking to Mrs. Lenore and we've come up with an idea that will let me team up with someone for the final. It's called fusion casting."

"Never heard of it."

Conryu held his door open for her then closed it behind them. "Basically it does just what it sounds like. One person fuses their power to another's to create a more powerful whole. I haven't gotten too heavily into the details yet, but if you're interested I thought we might team up for the final."

"Absolutely!" Her enthusiasm surprised him for half a second before she added, "If I team up with you there's no way I can fail."

"Before you get too excited I have to tell you that you'll also have to study circle casting. This will make extra work for you."

She waved a hand. "That's fine. One of the things my mom taught me is how to spot a sure thing. You and anything to do with dark magic is a sure thing. I'm in."

"Cool. I'll tell Mrs. Lenore and we can figure out a practice schedule."

2
SUNDAY AT SCHOOL

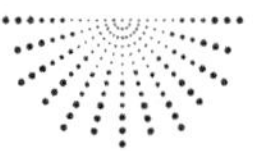

The rest of the first week went by in a hurry. He divided his time between practicing with Prime and with Kelsie. He could now cover both himself and the scholomantic in a Cloak of Darkness. Mrs. Umbra had them working on a calling spell that would bring Prime to him through a dark portal if they were separated. That trick made the Cloak of Darkness seem like child's play.

When his day off finally arrived it had been a total relief until he remembered he had to visit Angus. Now Conryu found himself approaching the door to the office where they stuck the professor during his visits. The halls were silent in this part of the school, especially on a Sunday.

The office was a little space, barely big enough for the professor and his desk, much less a spare chair and Conryu. It smelled faintly of ammonia and was at the opposite end of the floor from the administrative area. He secretly suspected the so-called office was actually a converted storage closet. Not that he blamed the staff for sticking Angus in a hole in the wall as far from them as they could manage without putting him outside.

The door was open and Conryu poked his head in. "Any news?"

Angus looked up from the book he'd been reading. "Nothing from Chief Kane."

"Cool. See you next week."

"Please, can't you give me just a minute of your time?"

The professor sounded so depressed Conryu stepped into the room. "What is it?"

"Is there nothing I can say to impress upon you how important it is for your story to be told?"

"You don't care about my story. You talk about how you're this big expert, but you don't know shit about wizards, male or female. All you have is a stupid theory that I had the misfortune to prove partially possible and now you've latched on to me like a tapeworm in hopes of making a buck and getting your good name back." Conryu was panting and his face burned. He shouldn't have said anything, but he'd been wanting to get that off his chest for a while.

"Do you really believe that?" Angus sounded genuinely hurt.

"Is there some reason I shouldn't?"

"Come in and sit down." Angus sounded as old as he looked. "Maybe I should tell you my story."

Conryu hesitated then went in. Stupid curiosity. He should just leave, but now he had to know. He squeezed himself into the tiny room and sat on the little plastic chair.

"When I was a boy in Scotland I wasn't the strongest or healthiest, so I spent most of my time at the little library in our village. I think I was twelve when I stumbled on a story about Arthur and Merlin. The wizard fascinated me, haunted me even. I read everything I could find about him and when I ran out of books I went online and did more research. Everything about him was labeled fiction, but I wondered."

"Wondered what?"

"If everyone knew male wizards were impossible, why did

someone bother to make up such a character, even for a work of fiction? And it wasn't just Merlin. Many other books featured a male wizard as a character. Why, if it was impossible? I couldn't stop pondering the question. I devoted my life to trying to tease out the answer and I came to one inescapable conclusion: all the male wizards, of which Merlin was the first, were patterned after a real person. I based my efforts around that premise and was roundly mocked, even losing my professorship over it. Then you come along and prove that my theory isn't impossible."

"Lucky me."

"No, lucky me. Don't you understand? If I can figure out how you came to be it might prove the rest of my theory, that Merlin's spirit lingered after death and influenced your birth. I don't know how to prove it, but I have to." Angus's eyes almost glowed with strength of his obsession.

Conryu got up and shook his head. "That's a great story, but your fantasy doesn't interest me. I'm stuck being a wizard. I've made peace with that, more or less. What I'm not willing to be is a research subject. All the teachers already send weekly updates to the Department. I suppose I can be grateful they didn't want to dissect me. I'd thank them for that, but I don't want to give them any ideas. I need to go."

He stood up and headed out, leaving the silently staring professor behind.

* * *

Conryu stalked through the quiet halls in a foul mood. How dare the professor expect him to validate a theory he didn't believe in or understand? The old man's obsession was his problem, not Conryu's. He badly wanted to punch something, but knocking a hole in the wall wouldn't do any good.

He looked around again, but found himself alone in the hall. He took a deep breath and did the first movement of the most basic kata. He worked his way through it, remembering his father's advice and letting the anger flow out of him with each breath.

Angus and his crazy ideas were beyond his influence, just like having to come to this school was beyond his influence. As his body moved through the familiar forms he came to understand that what really made him angry wasn't Angus, but his lack of control, the world's complete indifference to what he wanted.

Once the reason became clear the tension melted away. Instead of fighting he needed to accept his situation. His anger wouldn't change anything. He needed to forget about the future and focus on the moment. If circumstances required him to learn to be a wizard, he'd be the best damn wizard they'd ever seen. After he graduated he could put that all aside and do what he wanted. No one would have any claim on him beyond those he allowed.

He finished the last movement and sighed, his mind clear and focused for maybe the first time since he arrived at this school. He continued down the hall at a quick walk. Maria was probably wondering where he was. His meetings with Angus usually only lasted a minute or two.

He found her pacing in the entryway, arms crossed and scowling. "Sorry I'm late." He leapt down the last four steps.

She stopped and turned to face him. "What took you so long?"

"Angus wanted to tell me his life story and like an idiot I agreed to listen. Kind of pitiful actually."

"So do you know what the dark magic final will be yet?"

"Circle casting. Not for me though. Naturally my power doesn't allow me to do the same thing as the rest of the people in my class. I have to do something called fusion magic. Kelsie and I are teaming up for the final."

"You and Kelsie, huh?"

"Yeah. Remember, no getting jealous. So what about your final?"

"The whole second semester is focused on healing with the final being the construction of a healing ward around a badly injured animal. If it lives we pass, otherwise we fail."

"Ouch, poor critter." She swatted him on the arm. "Hey! I didn't mean yours, but I wouldn't want to be stuck with the girl that failed the midterm."

"Don't worry, Corrie's not going to have to take the final. Once she failed the midterm she was downgraded to basic instruction only. All she'll learn from now on are the simplest universal spells with no further testing."

"Geez, that's rough."

"Yeah, but the theory is if she can't manage the first-year midterm then she doesn't have much hope of learning more advanced techniques. There were seven other girls from the remaining classes that got downgraded with her, so at least Corrie isn't on her own." Maria cocked her head as if listening to something he couldn't hear. "I'm late for alchemy. See you for dinner?"

"You bet."

She kissed him on the cheek and trotted off. One of the older students must have sent a wind spirit to fetch her. Conryu watched her until she was out of sight, enjoying the hints of her figure visible under the flowing white robe. He stretched and yawned. He hadn't spoken to Sonja or the other girls from the golem club so he had no idea if they were still planning to meet up.

He headed for the door. The easiest thing would be to go over and find out for himself. If they were there, great, if not, well, he'd deal with that when he had to.

* * *

They needed to make the robes thicker, or maybe add a fur liner in the winter. Conryu shivered as he quick-stepped down a narrow path through the snowy grounds toward the club's workshop. On days like this he especially missed home. Being right on the ocean Sentinel City never got this cold. Hopefully Sonja would have the shed all heated up when he arrived.

"Do you ever get cold?" He had Prime tucked under one arm like a football.

"No, Master. Demons are much more durable than mortals. Only magical cold causes me any discomfort."

"Lucky you."

As he walked he kept his head on a swivel. Everyone was holed up inside where it was warm so if someone wanted to try something this would be an ideal time. He hadn't been attacked in months, not that he was complaining, but he also doubted the people that wanted him dead had simply given up. Every day that went by without an event made him even more nervous.

"Shit!"

The shed was closed up tight, no steam rose from the roof, and no tracks marred the snow in front of the door. Where was everyone? He scratched his head and began to retrace his steps.

Why had he imagined anyone would be there in the first place? The Brawl had come and gone, so they didn't really have anything to work towards. Maybe he'd been foolish to think someone would let him know, but he found it annoying all the same.

He had only gone a few paces when an explosion shook the ground. It wasn't coming from nearby and he dismissed the notion of an attack at once. A second, larger blast caused the snow to fall from some nearby trees.

"Reveal." He scanned the area and soon spotted magical energy coming from down by the lake. All the elements were represented.

Curiosity and cold warred within him before curiosity won. He jogged toward the lake and several hundred yards later the trees opened up, revealing a gathering of several hundred students. Conryu paused at what he considered a safe distance and watched the proceedings.

A girl in blue-green robes stood at the edge of the lake and waved her hands. He was too far away to make out what she was saying, but soon a dragon made of water rose up out of the lake. Another girl, this one in black, assumed the position for Dispel. A black orb shot out and struck the dragon. Another boom sounded as the mass of water splashed down in the lake.

He didn't know what sort of test they were taking and he didn't especially care. Conryu rushed back to the dorm and went down to his room. Inside it was nice and warm. A hot, dry breeze swirled around him, driving the cold out. When he was nice and toasty the pixie settled on his shoulder. Prime flew over and landed on his desk, apparently too cold to even muster a growl for the little wind spirit. So much for the durability of demons.

What was he supposed to do now? He could practice summoning Prime, but he'd been looking forward to a break from magic. He turned to look at the pixie, who smiled at him.

"Do you know Sonja Chard? She's a senior, fire wizard, came to visit me a few weeks back."

She hung her head and gave it a shake. A moment later she perked up and whistled something in the piping language of the wind.

Conryu sighed. "I don't understand."

She stared at him for a handful of seconds then turned into a breeze and blew out the door. Maybe he offended her.

"Pixies are flighty creatures." Prime flew up off the desk. "A random thought probably popped into her empty little head and she flitted off to explore it."

"Why do you dislike her so much? As far as I can tell she's an absolute sweetheart yet you've done nothing but growl and snap at her since we got here."

Prime flexed his cover in what Conryu had come to recognize as his approximation of a human shrug. "I'm a demon."

He said it like that was the only explanation required. "Would you care to elaborate?"

"Demons and other spirits have never gotten along. Just being in their presence makes my pages crawl. I can barely tolerate the wind spirit and the water spirit peeking at us from the bathroom."

Conryu turned his head just in time to catch a glimpse of the naiad vanishing out of the doorway.

"But only because you command it, Master. To put it simply, demons do not play well with others."

"Great."

The pixie blew back in and turned into a girl. She grabbed his robe and tugged him toward the door. He started to ask what she was doing before he remembered he wouldn't understand even if she told him. Conryu held out his hand and Prime flew into it, shifting as he went so he resembled an especially ugly leather-bound book.

"I'm coming."

He followed her up and out of the basement, down the long hall to the cafeteria. Sonja sat by herself in an ill-lit corner, a bag of vanilla cookies on the table in front of her. She nibbled one with a distant look on her face.

"You found her for me, thanks."

The pixie rubbed her cheek against his and blew away.

Now he had to figure out why Sonja looked so depressed. Conryu had always favored the direct approach so he walked over, laid Prime on the table, and sat across from her. "Hey."

Sonja looked up at him. She had dark ridges under her eyes. "Go away."

He grabbed the bag of cookies out from under her nose. "Can't do that. There's a new rule: depressed people aren't allowed to eat cookies, it just brings the rest of us down and insults the cookies."

He grabbed one and popped it in his mouth. It was dry, bland, and way too sweet. Why on earth did she favor the nasty things?

"I refuse to be cheered up. Now give me my cookies and leave me alone."

"At the very least you owe me an explanation. I half froze on my way out to the shed. And when I arrived, instead of my favorite fire wizard, I find a closed door and not so much as a note."

She reached for the cookies, but he pulled them further back. "If you're a good girl and tell me why the only club that would let me join has disbanded I'll let you have one."

"There's no point to meeting anymore. The Brawl's over and I'm graduating this summer. I am sorry I forgot to tell you."

"So, what, you're going to spend the rest of your Sundays alone in the cafeteria moping and eating cookies?"

"That was my plan."

"Fine, but if we're going to mope we are going to do it properly. Just a minute." Conryu went over to the kitchen and bought a pair of ice cream cups and grabbed two spoons. He opened one and set it in front of Sonja. "There. According to my mom you can't have a proper mope without ice cream. Now, do you want to eat in silence or do you want to tell me about it?"

Sonja grabbed a cookie, nibbled it, and blew out a sigh. "It's my family. They want me to come work for them as soon as I graduate. I love my parents, but I really don't want to work at the factory."

"Did you tell them?" Conryu took a bite of ice cream. Much better than the cookies.

"No. They were so excited about me joining the company I didn't have the heart. I don't know what to do. If I tell them I want to work with them I'll be miserable and if I tell them I don't I'll feel like a shit-heel. It's your classic no-win situation."

Sounded like Sonja had the same problem as Kelsie. Did anyone have a good relationship with their parents besides Conryu and Maria? "Do you get along with your parents?"

"Oh, yeah. They're great, a little workaholic maybe, but otherwise great. I never planned on working with them you know. I was going to go into engineering, but senior year I passed the wizards' test with a decent score and they immediately began planning how I could help out. It was like they forgot I had other plans."

Conryu smiled, thinking of his own plans, now on hold. A burst of inspiration struck. "You ever think about building a motorcycle with an engine that runs on magic?"

She stared at him. "Why would anyone build an engine that ran on magic? A gas engine is much simpler."

"Just to see if it was possible. You'd need earth magic to make the parts move. Water magic for lubrication."

"No, earth magic would handle that as well, oil comes from the earth after all. You could use fire magic for extra thrust and wind magic to keep the bugs out of your teeth."

"What about something for safety?" He took another bite of his ice cream and struggled not to smile.

"The wind bubble could probably handle that too." She dropped her cookie and frowned at him. "I know what you're trying to do and it won't work. I'm determined to be miserable."

"Right. Do you think fire magic in the combustion chamber would work better than earth magic to power the engine?"

The discussion lasted for another hour and by the end he doubted he could have kept Sonja from trying to build a magic engine even if he wanted to. "Do you think Crystal, Onyx, and Jade would be interested in working on it?"

"Crystal for sure, as long as she doesn't make the academy team. The others were pretty pissed when I closed up shop so they may have moved on."

"Wait, the academy team? You mean for the Four Nations' Tournament?"

"Yeah, they're holding tryouts today down by the lake. Crystal wanted to give it a shot, but I don't think she can beat the earth magic wizard from last year's team. Crystal will be a senior next year and the current girl will have graduated so she should have a good chance if she wants to try again."

"Why didn't you try out?" Conryu asked. "You're pretty strong in fire magic."

"One of the girls in my grade is way stronger than me and she's trying out. I'd have no chance against her."

"Oh, well, we'll just have to focus on the engine. I can handle the repairs if you two take care of the magic. It shouldn't be hard to lay my hands on a motor and tools. Shall we get started next week?"

"Might as well. We're out of cookies and ice cream." She jumped up, ran around the table, and hugged him. "Thanks. This should be fun."

He grinned, thrilled at the prospect of working on a motor again, and even more thrilled to see Sonja back to her usual self.

* * *

Lady Mockingbird's heels clicked on the stairs as she led her four strongest girls down to the basement casting chamber. She'd spent her every free moment the past week poring over the research notes taken from the Kincade's lab. She'd never admit it, but some of the magical theory was way over her head and she considered herself well read when it came to advanced wizardry.

Nevertheless she felt confident that she understood the process sufficiently to begin the summoning and binding portion of the project. She would, however, be taking all necessary precautions, thus the line of girls following with bowed heads.

At the bottom of the steps she turned left and entered the austere casting chamber. Everything had been removed, even her full-length scrying mirror, to be certain no stray magic would interfere with her casting and to protect the valuable item from out-of-control spirits.

Following the directions in the lab notes, she'd spent hours after her classes inscribing a spell circle. The complex mix of runes intertwined and covered most of the floor. She had to be careful not to stare as the runes had a tendency to twist and writhe in her vision, filling her with nausea and a hint of vertigo.

"Places, ladies." She'd gone over the project often enough that the four girls hurried to the four corners of the room and settled in to await her next command.

Lady Mockingbird stepped to the center of the circle and placed the jar at her feet before tiptoeing back, careful not to disturb any of her delicate runes. She would start with fire as that was her strongest element.

She threw her hands up and to the sides, a dramatic and unnecessary gesture, but one that pleased her nonetheless. This was a moment to savor, the moment when Conryu Koda's life ended and her ascension to Hierarch became reality.

"Begin."

The girls chanted the same spell, each in the language of their aligned element. Lines of energy climbed the walls and ceiling; red, white, brown, and blue intertwined and fused, creating a massive protective barrier around the chamber.

When all the lines had appeared and the girls had fallen into a monotonous, sustained chant, Lady Mockingbird began her summoning. "From the hottest realm I call you, child of fire. Appear and serve a loyal ally of flame. Fire Summoning!" The power built slowly as the heat in the room rose. Sweat drenched her body, running down her back and legs, and soaking her red robe.

She ignored all the distractions, focusing on her will and desire. A flaming gate appeared in the middle of the chamber directly above the jar. She called the name of a spirit well known to her. "Azoth Blazewing."

It was a shame to sacrifice such a valuable servant, but she wanted to be certain her first summoning went smoothly and the blazewing was of sufficient power for her needs.

The flames shifted and swirled before a shining, translucent wing emerged, followed by a second. The moment they cleared the flames the wings beat so fast they became a blur. Wind rushed around Lady Mockingbird, drying the sweat for a moment.

A dragonfly as long as she was tall pulled itself free of the portal. The moment the blazewing cleared the gate she collapsed it. The giant, flaming insect zipped around the room a couple times before hovering in front of Lady Mockingbird.

She crooned to it in the language of fire, soothing the spirit's distress. With gentle coaxing she positioned it directly above the Chimera Jar. She offered it a gentle smile and spoke the activation phrase for the artifact. "Make many into one."

Black tentacles shot up out of the mouth of the jar and dragged the blazewing down. It buzzed and spat flames, all to no avail. A minute later it was gone and the temperature of the room had dropped back to normal.

Lady Mockingbird wiped her brow. One down, three to go. "Take five, ladies."

The students fell silent and slumped against the wall. They'd done well. None of her girls had faltered when the blazewing appeared nor had they fumbled a single word during the lengthy summoning. She expected no less, but was still pleased that they met her high standards.

Ten minutes later, when the girls had caught their breaths and her strength had returned enough to resume, Lady Mockingbird clapped her hands. "Positions."

They all scrambled up and restored the wards. When they'd fallen into a comfortable rhythm she chanted in the language of earth. It was essentially the same spell only in a different language. As a fire wizard Lady Mockingbird knew far fewer earth spirits than she did fire, but one whose name she'd found in her research should closely match the blazewing in power.

The lab notes had been very definite that all four spirits used in the chimera had to be of like power. That was why she used the blazewing instead of one of the more powerful fire spirits she'd met over the years.

The floor rumbled as the spell reached its conclusion and the earth portal opened. She called the name of the spirit. "Prima Basilisk." A moment later the knobby, horned head of the basilisk emerged from the gate. It dragged itself into the chamber using eight heavily muscled legs that ended in talons as long as her forearm.

The basilisk turned its yellow gaze on Lady Mockingbird and loosed a roar that shook the chamber. She ended the spell, closing the gate and trapping the earth lizard in their reality. Unlike the blazewing, the basilisk didn't look on her with a gentle expression.

Though earth and fire got along most of the time, summoning the beast into the close confines of the casting chamber put the basilisk on its guard and her at a disadvantage. She couldn't give it time to attack. It had appeared close enough to the jar that she risked speaking the activation phrase.

The tentacles shot out again, and the ends flailed against the basilisk's pebbly hide. Damn it! The earth spirit was just out of range.

Lady Mockingbird raised a hand. "Burn my enemies to ash. Flame Blast!" A jet of fire streaked toward the basilisk. Her spell splashed against its tough skin, but instead of driving it closer to the jar it only enraged the beast.

The basilisk roared, lowered its head, and charged toward the wall. The house trembled, but the wards held.

Many more blows like that and the building wouldn't survive. Even from a distance the tension on the face of the girl protecting that wall was clear. One more solid hit would knock her out.

Lady Mockingbird chanted another spell. "Flames of protection!" A wall of flames shot up between the basilisk and the wall it had just struck. The beast shook its head and turned toward her. It wasn't the brightest creature in existence, but it had just enough intelligence to recognize her as the source of its problems.

It snarled and charged right at her. Its crest horn looked far bigger when it was pointed right at her chest. A quick wind spell empowered her leap and carried her over the beast's back. She whistled once in midair to adjust her trajectory, avoiding the flailing tentacles and coming to a safe landing on the opposite side of the jar.

The basilisk slammed full speed into the wall behind her last position, shaking the building and making the wards tremble. If she couldn't force it into the jar soon she'd have to send it back to its home dimension or risk losing the building.

It turned to face her and she dared hope it might be stupid enough to charge right through the tentacles in its rage to reach her.

That hope was thwarted when it stalked to the left, keeping well away from the jar. At least it hadn't decided to attack one of the girls. If even one of them lost her focus the wards would collapse allowing the basilisk to smash its way out with ease.

The basilisk didn't have the right sort of magic to read her mind, but as it passed one of the girls its tail lashed out. The casual blow couldn't penetrate the barrier, but it startled the young wizard enough that she stammered through a portion of the chant.

The line of energy fluctuated and collapsed. Dumb though it was, the basilisk was still a magical creature. Its head perked up the moment the wards collapsed.

It was no use. Lady Mockingbird chanted the portal spell again, this time opening it right under the beast's many feet. It fell through the opening and back into its own realm. She sealed the gate, not giving it a chance to climb back out. Another quick incantation deactivated the jar.

Though she hated to admit it, even to herself, Lady Mockingbird was going to need some help if she wanted to secure the remaining spirits required to complete the chimera.

3
SENTINEL SEARCH

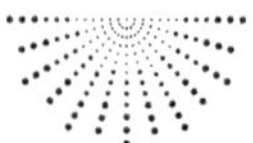

Terra slowly coaxed the residual energy out of the open box and away from the blob of necroplasma. She'd turned off every light save one in the casting chamber to minimize distractions. She'd been fiddling with the ugly blob since Conryu opened the box for them. Every trick she'd tried failed to coax it to do anything but slam itself over and over again into the containment circle. She'd finally given up and returned to her original plan of determining the purpose of the artifact once contained in the box.

The cloud of dark energy rose above the blob and when it was high enough she opened a small gap in the containment field and brought it out. She breathed a sigh of relief when the energy cleared the opening and the field had resealed. Though she had absolutely no experience dealing with necroplasma, Terra didn't want her first effort to be chasing the mad blob all over her casting chamber.

Now that she didn't have to divide her focus Terra used wisps of dark energy to nudge the cloud of energy into its former shape, using the fragmented lines running through it as a guide. It was a tedious task combining optimism and guesswork.

Hours passed, or so she assumed from the stiffness in her back, but at last the final line fell into place. Her heart skipped a beat when she recognized what the spell did. The five artifacts would tap into the power of the floating island to open multiple portals to the netherworld to summon god knew how many shadow beasts into the city. If it worked tens of thousands might die.

At least now she knew why nothing had happened since the battle with the bikers and the theft of their bodies. Mercia couldn't trigger the summoning until the island returned this summer. That was their one advantage. If they somehow located and destroyed the boxes before the island returned, Mercia's plan would fail. If even one remained she could still summon dozens of monsters capable of killing scores or more people.

That was beyond contemplation.

The cloud of energy dissipated and she switched the lights back on. The blob appeared less energetic when she left the room fully lit.

She strode out of the chamber and down the hall to Lin's office. Hopefully he'd finished mapping the potential hiding places. She paused outside the unmarked door, knocked once, adjusted her hair and robe, and pushed it open.

Lin sat behind his desk hunched over a cheap laptop, the pile of notes beside him. He looked up and smiled. "Hey. Any progress?"

"Some." She told him what she'd discovered and when she finished Lin stared at her, his mouth hanging open.

"You're saying she could summon hundreds of creatures like those things that attacked Conryu? How would we even begin to deal with something like that?"

"If it happens, all the wizards in the city wouldn't be enough to stop every shadow beast before it killed someone. We need to handle this before the island returns. Have you finished mapping all the potential hiding spots?"

"All the ones the computer and I could come up with." He typed a command and an aerial map of the city appeared on the screen. Hundreds of little red dots littered it.

"Can you overlay the path of the floating island?"

Another command produced a wide gray path over the city.

"You can eliminate anything outside of that swath."

Dozens of little dots vanished, leaving far too many behind. Lin hung his head. "That's still a hell of a lot of spots to check."

"She'll want to open the portals in the most densely populated part of the city, so you can eliminate everything outside the city center."

"Okay, that leaves around sixty left to check. That's a lot, but manageable. If we deploy the city police we should be able to clear the lot of them in a week."

Terra shook her head. "We'll need to send wizards. Mercia will have hidden the boxes behind illusions and magical defenses. If you send regular cops and they trigger a trap… No, that might be almost as bad as a portal opening."

"So, you and me, maybe Clair and the security guy...Adam, right? If we can coax the police into loaning us the department wizard she could check a few locations."

"That should work. Once we find one box I can calculate the approximate location of the other four. I'll round up Clair, you call your former boss. We'll meet downstairs in an hour. Oh, and be sure to print out a list of all the addresses."

* * *

Lin guided the car through the early afternoon traffic. After months of frustration they were finally close to cracking the case. In the time since his reassignment he'd had more than a few doubts about whether they'd ever make any progress, or if Mercia was too clever for them. He never should have doubted Terra. That woman had determination to spare. Though if he never had to look at that list of descriptions again that would be okay.

Beside him Terra stared out the window. They were still a ways from the park where they hoped to find the first box, so he doubted she'd detect anything. Maybe she was mentally preparing herself for whatever they'd have to deal with. Lin felt far out of his depth most days at his new job. Sometimes it came as a relief that they'd just stuck him in an office with his packet of clues. If he'd had to comment on some magical matter he'd have sounded like an idiot.

The light turned red, forcing him to ease to a stop. He glanced at Terra again. She seemed to be in her own world.

He enjoyed the profile of her face and neck for a moment then said, "What's on your mind?"

She jumped as though she'd forgotten he was there. "I was thinking about the warehouse and what sort of trouble we might find when we track down the rest of the boxes."

Lin grimaced. It had been a near thing last summer when he accidentally triggered magic protecting the box they recovered. Only Terra's power had allowed them to escape with their lives, though she'd paid a high price for the effort.

"Maybe it won't be that bad."

"Wishful thinking. Mercia has had months to prepare her defenses and unlike the first one we found, these boxes still have their artifacts inside. No, if all we encounter is a swarm of shadow ravens I'll consider us lucky indeed."

Lin tried to think of something encouraging, but the light changed forcing him to focus on the road. That was probably just as well. Only inane words of encouragement came to mind and she'd see right through them.

Five minutes later he pulled into a space beside the park. It was only half-hour parking, but his government plates should keep them from getting a ticket. He waited for a break in the traffic, climbed out, and joined Terra on the sidewalk.

The park only covered four blocks and according to his research had a single fountain. If the information the biker left was accurate, then the box had to be near it.

"What should I do?"

Terra took her magic-enhancing glasses from a pocket of her gray robe and slid them on. "Just keep your eyes peeled and don't touch anything."

He laughed. "Don't worry, I learned my lesson."

The air was bitter as they walked down the path toward the fountain. The bare branches of the trees cast a spiderweb of shadows across the trail. Lin was glad he had on his heavy wool jacket. He assumed Terra used some sort of magic to keep the air around her warm as her robe seemed far too thin for the weather.

One advantage of the cold, it kept all the people inside and out of their way. If this went sideways, the fewer people around the better.

Terra muttered under her breath as they walked, her gaze flicking back and forth. He doubted they'd find anything this far from the fountain, but she appeared to be taking no chances.

They spent the better part of ten minutes at their deliberate pace to reach the center of the park. Some kids had built a pair of snowmen off to one side. The fountain was a simple octagon of gray stone about hip high and filled with ice. He wanted to draw his pistol, but there was no threat visible and he doubted it would be much use against anything they might encounter.

Terra strode over to the fountain, her chanting rising in volume as she worked her way around it. She examined the sides and top before making a mystical pass that evaporated the ice to allow a better view inside the bowl.

Finally she fell silent and turned to face him. "This place is a bust. There's not even a hint of magic."

Lin shrugged. It was too much to hope they'd hit it on the first try. "Shall we head to the next one?"

They had barely gotten in the car when Terra's phone rang. "Clair? You did? We're on our way."

"What is it?" Lin fired up the car and cranked the heater.

"They found one of the boxes. Clair says it's warded six ways from Sunday and her magic can't touch it. She wants me to come over and lend a hand."

"What's the address?"

* * *

Terra spotted Clair and Adam outside the door of an abandoned building. The sign over the door said "for sale by owner," but there was no name or number written on it. The derelict building sat between an apartment complex and a mini-mart. A trickle of people eyed the unusual pair loitering around the old building as they made their way up and down the street, but no one took the time to talk.

Lin pulled in behind Clair and Adam's car and they climbed out. Terra marched straight over to Clair. "What did you find?"

"You'd best have a look yourself." Terra followed her inside.

Beyond the door was a large open space covered in graffiti and littered with cigarette butts and empty beer bottles. It looked like the local youth used the place as a hangout. If they couldn't do something about the box, they'd have to make sure no one entered the building.

Clair pointed to a spot on the wall near the ceiling. Terra slipped on her glasses. "Reveal."

A section of the wall shimmered in her enhanced vision and revealed a cutout. A wooden crate sat below the opening. When she climbed up for a better look Terra flinched. A web of dark magic filled the space, the black box barely visible through all the threads.

"Not screwing around, is she?" Terra asked as she climbed back down.

"No. I cast my best breaking spell and it didn't even draw a twitch from the wards. Even together I doubt we'd penetrate it."

"I agree. And even if we did we couldn't open the box itself."

"So what do we do?" Clair sounded nervous and Terra didn't blame her. Despite the evidence it was hard to square what they knew of Mercia from her time at the Department with what she'd accomplished here.

"We need to set up stakeouts at all five locations. If Mercia comes to check on her handiwork they could potentially follow her back to wherever she's hiding out."

"That's a pretty thin plan. She can trigger the spells from anywhere. And whatever else she is, Mercia isn't an idiot. No way she'd do anything to compromise her hiding places or headquarters."

"All true." Terra ran a hand through her hair. "Maybe we should just cordon off the place to keep the locals out. I doubt anyone would bother this box given its location and the illusion hiding it, but if they got to partying and smashing stuff you never know what might happen."

"What do you think, an aversion ward around the building? That should keep any non-wizards out of the area, and if it's broken, it will give us warning that something was happening."

"Good call. Can you handle it? I want to try and figure out where the remaining boxes are most likely hidden."

"No sweat." Clair limbered up her fingers.

Terra left Clair to her casting and walked out of the building. Adam and Lin stood on either side of the door, hands thrust into pockets and steam coming out their mouths. The poor guys were way out of their depths and she felt bad reducing them to chauffeurs and bodyguards. Not bad enough to send them home. It was pretty handy to have someone good with a gun if they should run into any of the more corporeal undead.

"So what's the deal?" Lin asked. "Can you two handle it or not?"

"Definitely not. Clair's going to fix it so the local kids can't go in there anymore. Let's see if we can figure out where the other four are hiding."

"I'm up for anything that gets me out of this cold."

While Lin started the car and cranked up the heat Terra turned to Adam. "She won't be long if you want to wait in your car."

Adam shook his head. "I'll guard the door until she comes out. How are we going to resolve this crisis, Terra?"

Terra offered a tired smile. "When I figure that out, you'll be one of the first to know."

Adam grunted.

Terra climbed into the car beside Lin who already had his computer open and the map on the screen. He highlighted their current location and marked it "number one." "Now what?"

"Eliminate anything further from this point than the diameter of the island."

Lin typed and over half the remaining points vanished. Terra studied them. It didn't take long, using the one position they'd confirmed as a starting point to find the four points that completed a pentagram.

She pointed them out one by one and Lin highlighted them. "It seems so simple now," he said.

"Getting rid of ninety percent of the false locations helped a lot." Clair tapped on the window and she rolled it down. "All done?"

"Yup. Anyone getting too close will have an overwhelming urge to puke their guts out. That ought to convince them to party somewhere else. How about you?"

Lin turned the laptop to show Clair what they'd discovered.

"Standard pentagram layout, nice. You want to ward the other four like I did this one?"

Terra nodded. "For now that's all we can do. Which ones do you want?"

Clair shrugged so Terra gave her the two closest, a church and a funeral home. "Shouldn't take more than an hour or two. We'll have to update the chief when we're finished."

Terra sighed. "Yes. He's not going to be thrilled with our results."

"I'm not thrilled with our results."

Terra couldn't argue with that.

* * *

"Well the clue was right," Lin said as he pulled the car off the access road and parked beside a chain link fence. "It's certainly dark and wet."

They were approaching the location of the final box, a culvert seven feet in diameter that directed storm runoff to the ocean. This was the one he was looking forward to the least. He'd fished more than one body out of these drains over his years on the force.

Lin slid out of the car and shivered. Sunset wasn't for another two hours, but the temperature was dropping already. He walked around the car and joined Terra beside a gate in the fence. It had a padlock of course, but a wave of Terra's hand combined with a muttered command popped it open in a jiffy.

It was a short walk from the gate to the culvert. A wide, concrete gully funneled water from all over the city to this drain. More than one person had drowned over the years when they were caught in a flash flood. One good thing about doing this in the winter was they didn't have to worry about a flood. Pneumonia, on the other hand, seemed a distinct possibility.

"How about sharing a little magical heat over here?"

Terra glanced at him like she'd forgotten he was even there. "Sorry."

She put her hand on his back and warmth flooded through him, drawing a long sigh. "Thanks."

"No problem. Let's get moving. We don't want to do this after dark."

"No, but we have over an hour of daylight and we don't want to slip and break our necks."

The warning proved apt. You could hardly take a step across the snow-covered concrete without hitting a hidden patch of ice. Lin feared he really would break his neck before they reached the culvert.

An iron ladder hammered into the stone granted access to the drainage gully. Lin eyed it and frowned. The black opening of the culvert gave off a bad vibe. "I don't suppose you can ward it from here?"

"Afraid not. First we have to confirm the box is actually down there. Just because we got the other locations right is no guarantee on this one."

"Come on."

"We have to be sure. If it makes you feel better I'll hold your hand when we reach the dark part." She whistled and hopped off the edge of the gully. Terra drifted like a leaf in a breeze to the icy floor.

Must be nice.

He crawled down the ladder, testing each rung as he went. When he reached the bottom his hands ached from the tight grip he'd held on the freezing rungs.

"Shit! I left my flashlight in the car."

Terra hissed and waved a hand. A handful of fire orbs flashed into being. "I think we can manage with these."

She gestured and the balls of flame flew into the culvert opening. Icicles hung from the top and a foot-wide path of brown ice ran down the center. He really didn't want to know what was mixed with that water. At least the cold held down the stink.

He blew out a breath and marched toward the opening, determined to complete the job as quickly as possible. He'd barely taken three steps when Terra grabbed his arm.

"What?"

"Something's not right. The dark magic feels different here, less contained."

Lin reached for his pistol, taking his time, waiting for her to reassure him that it wouldn't be necessary. Terra remained silent, her focus on the still-hidden recesses of the culvert. That told him all he needed to know about the seriousness of the situation.

The flaming orbs drifted deeper into the culvert. He caught a glimpse of pasty white skin and yellow teeth then the moans rang out.

"Aim for the head," Terra said. "I need to stop the overflow of energy so you'll have to deal with the zombies."

"Right." He worked the slide, putting a bullet in the chamber.

Terra whistled and flew up into the leaden sky.

"Hey!"

"Draw them away from the entrance so I can get inside. You'll be fine, zombies are slow."

"Great," he muttered. "Zombies are slow. That's her big piece of wisdom."

The first of the undead shambled out of the culvert and into the light. It was an ugly thing; most of its face had been eaten by rats. Where there had once been eyes there were only black pits.

Lin drew a bead on its head, then lowered his weapon. She wanted them away from the opening, so dropping the first one a step away from it wasn't the best plan. He waved his arms. "Hey, you ugly fucks. Come and get me."

The lead zombie oriented on him and picked up the pace, speeding up to a quick walk.

Lin backpedaled, maintaining the distance between them. One after another walking corpses emerged from the culvert until five of the hideous things were chasing after him in a slow-motion race.

When they were a hundred feet up the gully he put a bullet in the forehead of the closest zombie. It collapsed like a puppet with its strings cut.

But only for a moment. The zombie sat up and the hole in its head closed as he stared in horror.

This was going to be harder than he thought.

* * *

When the first zombie Lin shot sat back up Terra stared in disbelief. When he dropped a second one and it climbed to its feet again she knew she had to hurry. They were far enough up the gully now that she could land without fear.

She conjured more flaming spheres and surrounded herself with a light magic barrier. With her defenses in place she landed and eased her way into the culvert. Behind her more shots rang out.

The zombies were drawing power from the energies of the box and using it to heal wounds that should have destroyed them. Until she sealed that leak Lin couldn't defeat them.

Terra positioned her flame spheres every ten feet as she made her way deeper into the cold darkness. There was really nowhere to hide anything in the culvert, it was just a metal tube with no shelves or hollow walls. She couldn't imagine Mercia simply tossing the box on the ground. A flood would wash it out into the ocean.

Something moved at the edge of her light. She pointed and a flame sphere flew toward it.

"Ugh." She gagged and put her hand over her mouth and nose.

A lumpen mass of flesh sat off to one side of the culvert. Pale, putrefied, and covered in bristly hair, once upon a time it might have been a pig. Deep, slowly regenerating gouges covered the thing. In the center of the mass sat the box.

Disgusting as it was, all she needed to do was conjure a sealing circle around the mass. That should weaken the zombies enough for Lin to finish them off.

"Mine," a guttural, inhuman voice said. From behind the mass an emaciated, hunched-over figure emerged. It had an elongated jaw filled with enough teeth to do a shark proud. A foot-long slime-covered tongue flicked from side to side.

The ghoul ripped a hunk of flesh from the lump with a taloned hand and stuffed it into its dripping mouth. "Mine," it said as it slunk closer.

Terra threw a hand out. "Flames of destruction incinerate my enemy, Fire Blast!" A searing jet of flame shot out.

The ghoul lunged to one side, faster than she expected. The stink of seared flesh indicated that she hadn't missed altogether.

It circled around her, forcing Terra to spin to keep it in sight.

"Fire Blast!"

It dodged a second jet of flames then a third. It was too quick for such an imprecise spell.

She switched to wind magic. "Father of winds lend this unworthy fire wizard the gift of your protection, Tornado Trap!"

A small tornado lifted the ghoul up and smashed it into the top of the culvert, pinning it in place.

She raised a hand. Now that she had it trapped she couldn't miss.

Something snaked around her ankle and yanked her off her feet. The impact broke her concentration and the ghoul fell to the floor.

A fleshy tentacle from the pile of ghoul food had her by the ankle. The light barrier kept it from hurting her, but it was pulling her closer.

Behind her the ghoul's talons scrabbled against steel as it climbed to its feet.

Terra pointed at the tentacle and hissed. A dart of flame severed it six inches from her foot. She rolled over, cupped her hands, and chanted. "Flood the world with flames, Fire Surge!" A river of flames gushed from her hands and roared into the ghoul's mouth. Its head exploded in a shower of gore.

She sighed and climbed to her feet. More shots rang out.

Right, Lin was counting on her. A piece of the ghoul's skull had landed on her shoe. It slid off and worked its way toward the unmoving body. Other pieces were doing the same. Even with its head completely destroyed the ghoul was trying to heal.

She needed to focus. At the rate it was recovering she had maybe five minutes to complete the sealing spell. That should be plenty. Hopefully.

Terra raised her hands and began to chant in Angelic. "Seal the darkness, bind the evil." Glowing runes appeared one after another around the flesh heap. She chanted the phrase over and over as she circled the fleshy mass and drew runes with her fingers.

It extruded more pseudopods and sent one flying at her.

Terra stepped to the side and kept casting. She couldn't break her rhythm or the warding would fail and she'd have to start over.

She crouched down to avoid another attack. The circle was halfway complete.

Two tentacles shot at her this time. Terra dodged one and took a grazing blow to the ribs from the other. She ignored the pain and kept going.

Four tentacles formed. No way to dodge all those and continue the spell.

She had to finish first. Terra picked up the pace of her casting, risking a mistaken enunciation.

The last syllable fell from her lips a moment before the first tentacle shot out. It slammed into her barrier, but failed to smash through.

Good.

She turned to the ghoul and found the remaining pieces of its broken skull had stopped moving.

Shots rang out in quick succession then there was silence.

Terra stumbled toward the entrance to the culvert. Lin still needed her.

She stepped into the fading sunlight. Lin was walking toward her, tucking his pistol back into his shoulder holster. He was okay.

Thank god.

* * *

"So after I finished warding the culvert Lin called the police to retrieve the bodies and we came straight back here."

Terra finished her report leaving Orin with a pounding headache. He'd been sitting in his office all day drinking coffee and waiting for news. Now that he had the news the waiting didn't seem so bad. At least Terra and Lin hadn't been seriously injured in the confrontation.

Clair had given her report half an hour ago. She and Adam hadn't run into any monsters, but neither of his wizards had been remotely successful in dealing with the actual problem. He shouldn't have been surprised given how ineffective they'd been with the first box, but it was still a disappointment.

"So what do you suggest we do about it? Your wards won't stop Mercia from activating the artifacts when the island returns, will they?"

"No, they're very simple defenses designed to keep ordinary citizens from wandering into a dangerous location." Terra slumped in her chair. "We need to call him back. There's simply no other option."

"You realize how it looks, the Department of Magic having to rely on a first-year academy student to solve our problems for us?"

"It looks terrible, but given the alternative…" She shrugged.

There it was. That simple, exhausted shrug spoke volumes. However much Orin would have liked to spare Conryu any more trouble, he had no choice. With the northern incursion stretching their wizards thin, he had to rely on the assets available.

"Do you think we could wrap it up in a day?"

"With Conryu's power he could break the wards in an afternoon, but that assumes no traps are activated when he does. I have no certainties to offer you save one. If we do nothing, on June 25 the city will be flooded with nether spirits. Enough that it will probably take every wizard the Department can muster to destroy them all and even then I'd expect massive casualties."

"I'll call Dean Blane and make the arrangements. If we can bring him in Sunday morning and get him back before classes on Monday, no one will even need to know about the threat. The last thing we need is to start a panic."

4
CHAOS ON SUNDAY

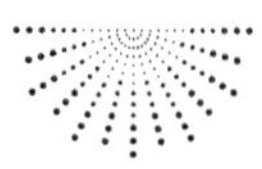

Another Sunday had rolled around, once more forcing Conryu to make the walk to Angus's dinky office to check in. Conryu's mind was a million miles away. Who would have thought it would be so difficult to find an engine? Everyone he asked turned him down. Over and over the same thing: it was against the no technology rule. He wanted to turn it into a magic item, but that didn't do much to convince them. It looked like his experiment was going to end before it began.

Sonja would be so disappointed. She'd really been looking forward to the project, so had he for that matter. He really hoped the professor didn't feel the need to share any more of his life story. He didn't have the patience for it today.

Conryu adjusted his grip on the scholomantic. Despite another two weeks of practice he still hadn't managed to summon Prime through a portal yet. Mrs. Umbra assured him that it was the most complex thing he'd attempted so far and he shouldn't be disappointed if he couldn't master it right away.

He frowned when he reached Angus's office. The door was closed tight. Usually he left it open until Conryu arrived.

Conryu's knock was met with a quick, "Come in."

He pushed the door open and stuck his head in. Dean Blane was sitting in his chair.

"Get in here and shut the door," she said.

He complied at once, shutting the door tight. "What—"

She pressed a finger to her lips. When he fell silent she cast a spell in the whispery language of the wind. "Okay, we can talk now."

"What's going on?"

Dean Blane took a breath, but Angus cleared his throat before she spoke. "Fine, you tell him."

"Thank you." Angus smoothed the front of his tweed jacket. "I have a message from Chief Kane. You're needed back in Sentinel City. The rest of the boxes have been located and you're the only one strong enough to break the wards protecting them. Isn't this wonderful? People are already starting to recognize how special you are."

Conryu resisted the almost overwhelming urge to punch Angus in the face and turned to Dean Blane. She shook her head. "There's no one else. Don't worry, it'll be a quick trip. You'll be back before classes on Monday."

"How? The train ride there and back takes most of a day."

"You'll only be taking the train as far as Central. From there you'll go the rest of the way by dark portal. We receive regular deliveries so it won't seem strange for the train to come and go an extra time today."

"Well, maybe I can arrange to have an engine delivered while I'm out. That way the day won't be a total loss."

"I got word you were trying to find one. What's that about?"

Conryu explained and when he finished she grinned. "That's about the most impractical thing I've ever heard of. Technically it violates the no technology rule, but I'll grant you an exemption since you're conducting a magical experiment. It'll be interesting to see if you can make it work. More importantly, it makes a perfect cover for your outing. Let's go, time's a-wasting."

"I can't just disappear without telling Maria and the club, they're all expecting me."

"I'll tell everyone what they need to know." Dean Blane stood up. They were almost pressed together in the small space. "All you need to focus on is your mission. I'll walk you to the train."

"Good luck, my boy." Angus was positively beaming at him.

At least someone was excited. Regardless of his wishes to the contrary, it seemed he was getting drawn deeper and deeper into the magical world. Mr. Kane had told him last summer the government regarded him as a valuable resource. They certainly weren't shy about using him. At least it was to help his home town. If they'd asked him to go to North Port or Santa Angeles on the west coast he might have complained more. Not that it would have probably done much good.

He followed Dean Blane out of Angus's office and down the hall. "Don't say anything about the mission outside of a warded room. There's no way to know who might be listening. I've assured our privacy in case you have any more questions. Listen to Terra and don't do anything they don't ask you to do."

"Don't worry about that. The last thing I want is to do more than necessary. Do you have any idea how long I'm going to be on call?"

"You're, what, eighteen? Given an average life span—"

"Okay, okay, I get it."

He followed Dean Blane down some back halls he didn't even know existed until they emerged from a small side door. She whispered something and a chill settled over him. The next thing he knew they were flying.

"Jesus!"

They went just high enough to clear the trees before landing on the train platform. Today only the engine and a single car waited on the tracks. The door was open and inside were piles of crates, sacks, and a bunch of shelves.

"Looks comfy."

"It's only half an hour. This train doesn't go to the station, but a warehouse. A Department car will meet you there. Good luck."

He stepped into the train and before he knew it they were moving.

* * *

Maria paced just inside the main doors of the lecture hall. Everyone else was busy with their clubs or studying so she had the large foyer to herself. Conryu was late again. That was getting to be a habit. She hoped the professor wasn't telling him more of his life's story. Conryu was one of the more patient and gentle people she knew, but even he had his breaking point.

Speaking of breaking points Maria was approaching her own with Mrs. Alustrial. Her light magic teacher wouldn't look at her much less acknowledge her questions in class. If there was a point she didn't understand she was out of luck. It didn't seem like a very professional attitude, but when ego was involved sometimes nothing else mattered.

"Maria." Dean Blane approached at a quick walk.

A queasy feeling settled in Maria's stomach. "Have you seen Conryu?"

"As a matter of fact I have."

"Oh?" Please let him be okay.

The dean muttered a spell. "He had to return to the city. An emergency came up and your father needed him for another breaking."

"Oh god. Is it something dangerous?"

"Not at all. It's just the magic involved is a little more than the wizards at the Department can handle. Don't worry, he'll be back by Monday."

She forced herself to take slow breaths. Dad wouldn't put Conryu in danger. "Thanks for telling me. I should probably get to my alchemy club."

"Actually." Dean Blane moved to block her when she took a step. "There's something I need you to do for me. While Conryu's task isn't dangerous, it is something we want kept quiet. I need you to take a message to the girls in his club. If I do it they might grow suspicious."

"Of course." If they were asking for favors this might be a good chance to get Mrs. Alustrial to straighten up her act. Maria hated dragging someone else into her problems, but there was nothing she could do on her own. "Maybe you could help me with something as well."

"Like what?"

Maria told her what was happening in her class. "I was hoping I could switch teachers."

Dean Blane frowned. "All the other light magic teachers have other classes. I'll have a talk with Mrs. Alustrial. I assure you when Monday rolls around, you'll have no further problems from her."

Maria shivered at the dean's cold tone. She wouldn't want to be on the receiving end of a lecture from the dean, not when she was in that mood. "So what did you want me to tell Conryu's club?"

"Tell them he's gone to Central to arrange an engine and that he won't be back until late." She gave Maria directions to the club's shed and they parted ways.

She left the lecture hall and trudged across the campus to the ragged little shack sitting right at the edge of the woods. Steam rose from the roof and all the snow was melted in a ten-yard circle around it. The promise of heat quickened her pace.

Maria knocked on the door and it slid open revealing Sonja and Crystal.

"Conryu?" Sonja sounded far too eager. "Oh, Maria right? He's not here."

"I know. Conryu asked me to bring you a message. Dean Blane gave him permission to go to Central to pick up an engine for your project. She's suspending the rules and calling it a magical experiment."

Sonja grinned. "It's about time. I was starting to wonder if this job was ever going to begin. How come he didn't tell us himself?"

Maria's heart raced. She hated lying. "It was a spur of the moment thing and he had to rush to catch the train. He won't be back until late tonight."

"Huh." Sonja looked up at Crystal. "Guess there's nothing to do today. Want to go to the cafeteria and have an ice cream?"

"Sure."

Sonja returned her attention to Maria. "You can join us if you'd like."

"No, thank you. I have to get to alchemy club." She fled before she had to answer any more questions.

* * *

It seemed like they'd barely gotten moving when the train began to slow down again. Conryu held on to the shelves until the final lurch. The door slid open at once and a middle-aged woman in a gray robe glared up at him.

"Well, come on then."

She moved to one side and he hopped down. Ten yards from the track was the biggest warehouse he'd ever seen. The black sedan parked next to it looked like a toy. The Department of Magic's pentagram logo was painted on the side of both car and warehouse.

The wizard marched toward it and he fell in step behind her. Not much for chit chat, these Department wizards. This one was every bit as friendly as the one that tested him.

She pointed at the back seat door and climbed in behind the wheel. He hadn't even gotten his seatbelt fastened when she stomped on the accelerator and they went screeching out of the lot. The buckle finally clicked into place and not a minute too soon the way his chauffeur drove. At least the soft leather of the seat was more comfortable than the sack of onions he sat on during the train ride.

"So is it safe to talk in here?" Conryu asked.

"Yep." She swerved around a dump truck, zipped past it, and pulled back in front.

"Do you know any more about what's happening?"

"Nope." She stepped harder on the gas.

Conryu caught a glimpse of the speedometer as it crept past eighty. "Did you by any chance ever drive a race car?"

That drew a laugh. "Boss wants you at HQ double quick. When the boss says jump you by god better jump."

"Who's the boss?"

She looked at him in the rearview mirror. "You kidding?"

"No, ma'am. Everything in this business is new to me. I assume you're talking about the Central Station Chief."

"Not just the Central Chief, Malice Kincade is the head of the whole Department. She answers only to the president, and some say he answers to her, at least on magical matters."

"Kincade, you mean the famous Kincades?"

"If it has to do with magic they're the only Kincades. Malice turned the business over to her middle daughter ten years ago when she took over the Department. I'm not the least ashamed to admit she scares the shit out of me."

The Department wizard fell silent after that. Conryu looked out the window at the Central City skyline. The various designs looked even more impressive up close. One in particular drew his eye, a black, cylindrical skyscraper maybe forty stories high. A ten-story pentagram was engraved in the glass. Talk about an intimidating building.

Ten minutes later they were parking in a connected garage. Conryu scrambled out, relieved to have made it in one piece, and followed his guide through a set of automatic double doors. Inside, the halls were gray and undecorated. Not so much as a single piece of art cluttered the walls. They stopped in front of a bank of elevators and she pressed the call button.

"So what's with the book?"

Conryu glanced down at Prime. "It has some notes Dean Blane thought might be useful."

The scholomantic sent its annoyance through their link, but the wizard appeared to accept his explanation. The elevator chimed and the doors slid open. She motioned Conryu in first then followed.

The control panel had four basement levels and thirty-eight above-ground levels. The Department wizard waved her hand in front of the panel and spoke a short phrase. It wasn't Infernal so he didn't know what she said. A basement level five button appeared and she pushed it.

She caught him staring and grinned. "We don't want just anyone to have access to the portal chambers."

The ride down took less than a minute. The doors opened on a long corridor. She motioned him out. "Just follow the hall to the central chamber then go through the black door. The boss is waiting for you."

Conryu stepped out and the door shut behind him. He blew out a sigh and started down the empty hall. Stupid wizards and their creepy hangouts. It felt like at least a hundred yards before the hall opened into a round chamber with six doors, one for each element.

The black door wasn't even like a painted black, it was more like the absence of all light and Conryu found he didn't want to touch it.

"Don't be such a coward," Prime muttered around his arm.

"Be quiet. No one's supposed to know about you."

The door didn't have a handle so Conryu reached out to give it a shove. When his fingers were six inches away a burst of dark energy leapt from his hand to the door. It didn't so much swing open as fade away.

Inside was an almost empty room with a circle carved into the stone floor nearly identical to the one from his awakening. Standing beside it was a woman in gray robes, her white hair pulled up into a severe bun. She held her hands clasped behind her back and stared at him with green eyes as hard as gems. Her wrinkles weren't quite as deep as Mrs. Umbra's, but it was a near thing.

"Conryu Koda."

He nodded and stepped into the room. His instincts said not to show this one any fear. If she caught so much as a hint of weakness he was doomed. "Malice Kincade, nice to meet you. Your granddaughter's in my class."

"I know. I know everything about you. I haven't decided whether you're the greatest threat this world has ever known, its best hope for the future, or both."

Conryu cocked his head. "Why would I be either? I have no ambitions beyond a hope, a vain one it seems, to live a quiet life. As long as the world leaves me alone, I'm content to return the favor."

"A man without ambition, how unusual. Perhaps you'll grow into it or maybe you'll be manipulated into serving the ambitions of others. Whatever the case, know this: if you become a threat I'll see you dead."

"Great. Maybe next time you people need some breaking done you should call someone else. You think I can't find a better way to spend my Sunday? And by the way, you should be nicer to Kelsie. She's a sweetheart and you and her mother both seem to stress her out. She's doing her best."

"Her best isn't good enough. She's a Kincade."

Conryu waited for more, but Malice seemed to consider that all the explanation required and in her mind maybe it was.

"In any case," Malice continued, "it's no concern of yours."

"You're wrong. Kelsie's my friend and I don't wish to see her in pain."

Malice glared at him and he glared right back. Conryu refused to let the vicious old woman intimidate him.

She finally looked away and moved closer to the circle. "Enough of this useless banter. You have a task to perform. The circle will carry you to the border of Hell. Call Cerberus and ride him to the end of the path. You'll emerge in the Sentinel City Department's portal chamber."

Conryu held up his forearm. "What's to stop Lucifer and the Dark Lady from interfering?"

"The path is warded against demons. Cerberus will only be able to enter because of your connection. Now go."

Conryu stepped into the circle. Malice took a clear crystal key on a thong out from around her neck and touched the edge of the circle.

Everything went black. He blinked and once again found himself a step from Hell.

* * *

Conryu looked around at vast amounts of nothing and sighed. It would be okay with him if he never had to come back here.

"Cerberus."

A pool of darkness gathered beside him and in moments the demon dog formed a body half again as big as a horse. All three heads panted, their tongues hanging out. The center head leaned down and licked him.

"Good to see you too. Crouch down so I can climb on, please." Cerberus lay down on his belly and Conryu leapt up onto his broad back. "We'd best be on our way before any unwelcome guests arrive."

Cerberus whined and his body trembled under Conryu.

"What is it?"

"Back again, mortal?" a familiar, deep voice said. Lucifer

emerged from the endless darkness, the demon shining with his own inner light. He held the massive trident over one shoulder like Paul Bunyan with his ax.

Conryu didn't want to get into a discussion with the demon. "I'm just passing through. Come on, Cerberus."

The demon dog set out at a trot that soon accelerated into a full run. Lucifer kept pace easily. "No need to rush off, boy."

Conryu ignored him, drawing a rumbling growl from Lucifer. The trident rose and plunged down at them.

Conryu flinched, but it struck an invisible barrier a foot above his head. He blew out a sigh. Malice hadn't lied about the ward anyway.

Lucifer hammered the barrier several more times with equally futile results. "The Department of Magic's wards are as impressive as always. Wouldn't you prefer make a contract with me rather than that puppy?"

Cerberus's left-hand head growled, but Lucifer ignored it. Conryu ignored the demon's looming presence. It felt like they were covering vast distances with each stride. Hopefully they would reach the exit soon.

"Come now, be reasonable. If I were to contract with you I could lend you a portion of my power. Strong as you are now, teamed with me you'd be invincible. You can't ask for more than that."

Conryu finally looked at Lucifer. "Until you decide to betray me? I've been warned about your nature. You weren't christened the Prince of Lies for nothing. I don't trust you and I can't very well team up with someone I don't trust. Cerberus has proven himself a loyal partner and that's worth more than raw power."

Up ahead a light appeared. That had to be the exit gate.

"Deny me, boy, and Hell will never be a safe place for you. Every time you enter I'll be waiting. One of these days you'll make a mistake and when you do I'll rip the screaming soul from your body and drag it down to the darkest pit I can find." With that final threat Lucifer vanished.

Cerberus's right head looked back at him and whined.

"Yeah, he's a real charmer. Don't worry, we'll be extra careful." Cerberus came to a stop six feet from the disk of light and lay down to let Conryu climb off his back. He patted the demon dog on his flank. "Thanks for the ride."

Conryu stepped into the light and left Hell behind.

* * *

Lady Raven reclined on the soft velvet of her couch and sighed. In the five months since she'd been forced to abandon two of her identities she'd turned her lair... She smiled to herself. Calling the place a lair made her sound like a witch in a storybook. Hideout perhaps? No, that carried a sort of gangster feel. Redoubt perhaps, that had a properly secure sound to it.

She turned her head to regard Iron Skull's reanimated body. It stood silently against the stone wall. "What do you think? Shall we call this our redoubt?"

Of course the Faceless One occupying the body was incapable of responding. It simply stared straight ahead with its empty black gaze. Though powerful and obedient, her new servants weren't much for company. Six more months and she could leave her dingy temporary home for a place befitting a newly risen Hierarch.

She'd sensed it when the weakling Department wizards approached her hidden boxes along with their feeble attempts to dispel her wards. They were both pathetic, but she gave them credit for at least hunting the boxes down. She'd harbored doubts that they were capable of that much. Terra and Clair had even been kind enough to add an extra layer of protection to her hiding places.

How frustrating it must be for the Department to know the

locations and still be totally powerless to do anything. She almost laughed aloud, but instead sighed. She should summon a familiar to share her victory with. It was terribly unsatisfying having no one but undead to whom she could gloat.

The familiar tug from her mask drew Lady Raven's attention to the end table in the corner of her lounge. It wasn't time for the monthly report, she'd just spoken to her superiors last week. She rolled off her couch, walked over, and grabbed the mask. What did they want?

A door in the left-hand wall led to her new casting chamber. She entered and sealed it behind her. When she reached the casting circle in the center of the room she cleared her mind and slipped the mask on.

Lady Raven was instantly taken to the meeting place where she found only Lady Wolf waiting. She'd never been summoned by less than the full group. "Hierarch?"

"Your hiding places are compromised. The boxes must be moved at once."

"As I said last week, the Department wizards are powerless to damage my wards. I assure you the artifacts are in no danger."

"They've summoned the abomination. Are you so confident your defenses will hold against his power?"

Lady Raven swallowed. If the boy was coming he'd destroy her wards in a second. "I'll move them at once. May I ask how you learned of his arrival?"

"Our agent in Central alerted us. He's traveling by dark portal if he isn't there already. Your time is short, Lady Raven. Do not fail us."

Lady Wolf vanished and she was alone in her casting chamber. Conryu Koda again. The boy wizard was turning into the bane of her existence. Fortunately she'd made arrangements for just such an emergency. Five months was a long time to prepare and she hadn't spent all her time on interior decorating.

When he arrived at the first location she'd have a surprise waiting for him and his friends.

* * *

Conryu stepped out of the light, leaving Lucifer and Cerberus behind. When his vision cleared he found himself in a chamber very similar to the one in Central. The black disk he was standing on had the exact same rune pattern.

"Conryu! This way."

He spun and found Mr. Kane waving to him from beside the room's only door. Terra and Lin were with him. Conryu jogged over. The moment he cleared the dark circle the power vanished. Though he knew Lucifer couldn't break through the wards he felt a good deal better now that the portal had closed.

He reached Mr. Kane and the little group hustled through the door. "I trust your trip went smoothly."

"I'm not sure smoothly is the word I'd use, but I made it." Conryu followed Mr. Kane to the nearby elevators with Lin and Terra bringing up the rear. "So you need me to break some more wards?"

"Yes. The team finally tracked down all five boxes, but we can't access them."

"How strong are the wards?" Conryu asked as they rode the elevator upstairs.

"I estimate twice as strong as the one you broke for us last time," Terra said.

Conryu nodded. That shouldn't cause him any problems.

Prime wriggled free of his grasp and flew up to look Terra in the eye. "What did you do with the necroplasma?"

"It's still in my casting chamber trapped in the spell circle. I'll figure out how best to deal with it once we've collected Mercia's gifts."

The doors opened and they stepped out into the lobby. "I'll

leave you with Lin and Terra. Thanks again for your help, Conryu." Mr. Kane started back into the elevator.

"Will I have a chance to visit my parents?"

"I don't think so. We need to get you back to school ASAP. Dean Blane called me after you left. I've made arrangements for an engine to be sent to the academy."

Conryu frowned at that. He'd planned to choose the motor himself and he needed his tools. Terra grabbed his sleeve and pulled him toward the exit, not giving him a chance to complain. "We don't have time to waste on idle chatter. The longer those boxes remain in place the more opportunity for something to go wrong."

Mr. Kane waved as he was dragged away. Conryu freed himself from Terra's grasp and followed her and Lin in a more dignified posture. They stepped out into the bright morning sun.

A tan four-door Department sedan idled by the curb. Lin slipped behind the wheel and Terra sat beside him leaving Conryu stuck in the back seat. At least with Lin driving Conryu didn't fear for his life.

They pulled out and headed east toward the docks. Conryu stared out the window. It was good to be home, even if only for a day.

"I never understood you humans' fondness for your home towns." Prime settled on the seat beside him. "It's not like demons pine for home every time some wizard summons us."

"You live in Hell. Who'd be eager to return there?"

"Good point. Lucifer certainly didn't seem pleased to see you again."

"No kidding. We have to figure out how to remove his name from my arm, the Dark Lady's too. Not that I wouldn't mind seeing her again."

"Did she leave a lingering enchantment on you?" Prime flew up and looked him all over.

Conryu was pretty sure the only enchantment she left was in his overactive imagination.

Terra looked back at him. "What's this about seeing Lucifer?"

"He tried to kill me again on my way here, but the wards held. I was just saying I need to get his brand off my arm so he won't be able to tell the moment I enter a portal."

"I noticed some fluctuations in the magic while we were waiting for you. That must have been what I detected. You seem rather calm considering you were almost killed by the devil."

"Yeah, well, I wasn't anywhere near this calm the first time. So do you want me to do a proper breaking or just use Dispel?"

"Dispel," Terra answered at once. "I want every bit of magic in the vicinity wiped out."

"I chanted the spell five times before releasing it once and negated every spell within sixty yards. Will that be enough?"

She stared at him for a moment. "That should do it." She turned back around, muttering, but he couldn't make out what she said.

Half an hour later Lin pulled in beside a chain link fence with a door in it. Beyond the fence was a flat expanse of concrete with a gully running through it. Conryu said, "Reveal." The culvert at the end of the gully lit up. Maybe that was the wrong way to describe the inky black lines running everywhere, but that was how he thought of it.

"I take it the box is down there."

"Yes. Mercia left it on a living pedestal along with a bunch of zombies to guard it." Terra opened her door and climbed out. Conryu and Lin joined her with Prime bringing up the rear.

"Speaking of the zombies," Lin said. "I spoke to my contacts at the morgue. They were all killed by a single stab wound to the chest. Missing persons is trying to match them to any outstanding cases."

"They must have been Mercia's sacrifices." Terra shook her head and led the way over to the culvert.

They stopped well back and Conryu eyed the dark opening. It certainly looked like a place you'd hide a dark magic artifact. "Shall I get on with it?"

"Please. Hurl your spell as deep into the culvert as you can. Don't hold back as we may not have a second chance."

Don't hold back. There was something he didn't hear very often. Conryu crossed his wrists and fingers and began the chant. When he hit five repetitions and the dark sphere was as big as a pumpkin he hurled it at the opening.

Seconds later a wash of dark magic shot out of the culvert, dissipating five feet from them. The wards were gone and he was about to ask where they were headed next when a flash of power burst from the opening.

Shrill screams came from the culvert followed a moment later by a pair of black-winged demons just like the ones that had tried to attack him last summer. The demons flew into the air and spat dark energy at Terra.

She hurled flames and the two energies negated each other. Conryu cast, "Cloak of Darkness!" and dark magic covered both himself and Prime.

Lin drew his pistol and put half a clip into the rightmost demon. If the creature felt the bullets it gave no sign, though it did turn to look at Lin. It opened its fang-filled mouth.

Conryu crossed his fingers and raised a hand. The moment dark energy shot from the demon's mouth he shouted, "Break!"

A sphere of dark energy streaked from his hand and negated the blast.

"Thanks." Lin put his gun away and turned towards Conryu. "What can I do?"

"Not a thing," Prime said. "Only magic can hurt demons."

Lin looked hopefully at Conryu. "Sorry, Sarge, they don't teach offensive spells to first-year students."

Terra was busy exchanging blasts with the first demon leaving the second to focus on him and Lin. Conryu negated another attack. At least the demon hadn't gotten it in its head to fly down and tear them apart.

"Prime, how do we stop them?"

"You could banish them. I have the spell here." Prime started to flip to the proper page.

The spell Mrs. Umbra had used took half a minute to cast and he hadn't even recognized a quarter of the words she used. No way could he memorize and cast such a complex spell under these circumstances.

"That's no good. All I really need is to make them stop attacking."

They ran from another blast. The concrete steamed where the dark energy touched it.

"Try commanding them," Prime said. "A powerful dark wizard can sometimes dominate a demon if they focus all their will on it."

"Your will makes the magic happen, not the words or gestures," Conryu muttered.

That's what Mrs. Umbra had said. It was time to test that theory.

He focused his mind on the demons and having them cease attacking. "Stop!" he shouted in Infernal.

Both demons shuddered and twitched, but their mouths shut and they stopped breathing those dark blasts. Terra ran over to join them.

"Don't break your concentration. I'll open a portal then you order them through."

Terra moved a little ways away and chanted an unfamiliar spell. A black ring appeared and slowly filled in until it became a disk. The demons saw it and struggled harder.

Conryu grit his teeth. "Be still!"

The demons quieted again.

"Okay, Conryu. Order them through."

He pictured the demons flying through the portal. "Go to Hell!"

The demons plunged down out of the sky and vanished through the portal. The instant they vanished Terra spoke a word and the gate closed.

Conryu fell to his knees, the mother of all headaches pounding behind his eyes.

* * *

Terra stared for a moment as Conryu knelt and grasped his head. She knew enough about the academy curriculum to know they didn't teach freshmen how to control demons. In fact she was fairly certain that was a third-year subject. He'd done it with nothing but sheer force of will and raw magical power. Absolutely stunning.

Unfortunately for him, Conryu was now paying the price. Wizards used spells for a reason and one of them was to avoid a backlash from channeling too much unrefined energy. The fact that he used chaotic dark magic made it even worse. On the plus side they were all still alive because of him. If he hadn't been here Terra doubted she'd have defeated both demons on her own.

"You okay?"

Conryu looked at her with bloodshot eyes. "Sure. You don't have any aspirin, do you? I have a horrible headache."

"Sorry. If it's any consolation it wouldn't have helped anyway. Your headache is from magical backlash. Only time or proper application of light magic will make it go away."

"I don't suppose you know how to apply it?"

"Nope. All I know are the basics of light magic." Terra shook her head. "We should have brought Shizuku. She'd have you fixed up in a blink."

"I'll survive either way. If you don't need me I'm going to sit in the car."

"No problem. I'll collect the box and we'll get out of here."

She headed for the culvert and Lin took a step to follow. Terra shook her head and mouthed, "Stay with him."

He turned back to help Conryu to his feet. The two of them started for the car and Terra put them out of her mind. Her spell didn't reveal any lingering magic, but that didn't mean she was in the clear. The moment she let her guard down was the moment she might die.

At the mouth of the culvert she conjured a trio of flame orbs. She sent one to fly ahead of her and kept the others by her side. The walk to the rear of the culvert took only seconds. Where the fleshy mound had once sat there was nothing but a rotten, misshapen heap of stinking gobbets of flesh. Terra devoutly hoped the box wasn't buried in the mess.

She narrowed her eyes and looked closer. There wasn't so much as a hint of magic to be found. As powerful as Conryu's spell was it should still have spared the contents of the box. If she couldn't detect anything...

"No, no, no. Scream, winds from beyond, Gale Gust!" She conjured a focused blast of wind that sent gobbets of flesh flying everywhere. No box. "Damn it!"

Somehow Mercia had moved it to a new hiding place. That begged the question of how she managed it and more to the point, how did she know she needed to.

Terra left the culvert and stalked over to the car. Conryu was lying down in the back, his arm over his eyes.

"Where is it?" Lin asked.

"Gone."

"Gone? Where?"

"Damned if I know. Let's head to the next location. I need to check something." She craned her neck to look in the back seat. "How you holding up?"

Conryu lowered his arm. "I'm better, thanks. So did I half melt my brain for nothing?"

"I wouldn't say for nothing. We would have had to deal with

that trap at some point, but we didn't recover the box. It's been relocated. For the life of me I can't figure how she did it."

"Maybe she moved it through a dark portal. Mrs. Umbra's had me and Prime working on that so if we're separated I can call him to my side."

Terra nodded. "Maybe. The problem is the clues that led us to these hiding places made no mention of backups. I suspect Mercia didn't tell her thugs. Wise move on her part."

Conryu sat up, groaned, and lay back down. "So what now? You need me to clear those other locations?"

"Afraid so, but first I'm going to look and see if the box is still there and your Dispel triggered its disappearance or if it's already gone. We might be able to work around the former, but if it's the latter we're screwed."

* * *

Conryu shuffled through the doors and down to the elevators. Midnight had come and gone and they'd finally made it back to the Department of Magic. He'd dispelled all the wards and traps, helped banish five more demons, and convinced Lin and Terra to buy him three slices of Giovanni's pizza. That had easily been the highlight of the trip.

Though Terra insisted the work he'd done was important and he might even believe it after ten hours' sleep, right now it felt like he wasted the day. The whole point of this mission was to recover those stupid boxes and there'd been no sign of them. No one would even tell him why they were so important.

Worse, at least for Conryu, if Terra and Lin somehow found them again he'd probably have to come back to repeat the process.

"Jesus, Conryu, you look horrible."

He glanced up to find Mr. Kane standing beside the elevator. He had a key that appeared to be made out of crystal and the mate to Malice's.

"It's been a long day. If I never see another flying demon it'll be too soon."

Mr. Kane looked to Terra. "Boxes?"

"No sign of them, Chief. Mercia must have known we were coming and relocated them."

Mr. Kane pressed his palms to his forehead and Conryu wasn't sure if he wanted to scream or cry. "So we're back to square one."

"Actually we're in worse shape than before as we now have no clue where to resume our search." Everyone turned to glare at Lin which made Conryu smile. It was always a nice feeling not to be the one in trouble.

"I'm sure you guys will sort it all out. I either need to get back or find somewhere to sleep." Conryu yawned for emphasis.

"Right." Mr. Kane pressed the call button. "You have classes tomorrow."

"Today. In about seven hours as a matter of fact. I may take a sick day."

"Don't do that." Mr. Kane stepped into the elevator and Conryu followed. They started down to the basement. "Anything out of the ordinary may attract unwanted attention."

"Me falling asleep in class would be out of the ordinary and if I had to cast a spell I might faint. I'll just put it down to food poisoning or something."

They left the elevator and entered the portal chamber. Mr. Kane touched the edge of the circle with the crystal key and it turned black. "Do what you think best. And thanks again for your help."

Conryu took a step toward the portal then turned back. "Be sure they send a full set of tools with the engine. I'm going to have to tear it all the way down."

Mr. Kane gave him a thumbs up and he stepped into the portal.

5

BACK AT SCHOOL

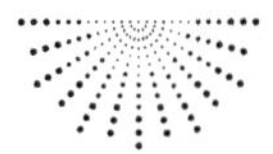

Conryu staggered into his room around four in the morning. He couldn't even remember the ride through Hell beyond Cerberus's worried whining. Kelsie's grandmother may have made some vague threat, but he was so tired he just ignored her. The train wasn't ready when he arrived so he ended up sitting around by the warehouse for three hours. All in all he'd had better days.

"At least you survived." Prime flew over to his desk and settled in his usual spot.

Considering how much he felt like a zombie, he wasn't sure he had survived. He collapsed on the bed, not even bothering to undress. Some time later he was vaguely aware of Prime snarling at the pixie that came to fetch him to class until she fled. Conryu sent mental gratitude to the scholomantic and fell back asleep.

When he woke up again it was an empty stomach that did it. He had no idea what time it was, though well after lunch seemed a fair guess. Conryu rolled out of bed, staggered into the bathroom and let the naiad wash his hair and back.

Clean clothes combined with the shower had him feeling almost human again. The next order of business was hunting up something to eat. The thought had barely crossed his mind when someone knocked.

When he opened the door he couldn't say what pleased him more, seeing Maria waiting outside or the overstuffed sandwich she had in her hands. "Please say that's for me."

"It's for you. When you missed lunch I figured you'd be hungry." Maria brushed past him and into his room. She looked around and shook her head. "What a mess."

"Give me a break. I had a busy day yesterday."

"Yeah, Dean Blane gave me the short version. How'd it go?"

"Not as well as they hoped. You know I can't say much here, right?"

She nodded and handed him the sandwich, ham and cheese with extra mustard, just the way he liked it. Conryu took a bite and sighed. "Have I told you lately that I love you?"

"It's been a few days, but I'll forgive you. The girls in your club were excited when I told them you'd gone to arrange an engine. You didn't forget, did you?"

"Nope. Should be here by the end of the week."

"Are you really going to try and make it run on nothing but magic?"

"Sure, why not?" He polished off the sandwich and found himself looking for a drink.

"Do you want all the reasons why not, or just the obvious ones?"

"I don't actually want any of them. I was just looking for a project to cheer Sonja up. Though the idea of a motorcycle with a magic engine sounds way cool."

Maria wiped a spot of mustard off his face. "Well it took you half the year, but you managed to incorporate mechanic work into your studies. I figured it would take longer."

He grinned. "What time is it?"

"Around three. You slept through all your classes."

He shrugged. "Other than the one with Mrs. Umbra I could

take or leave the rest."

"Not if you want to graduate."

She had him there.

* * *

Twenty minutes after Maria left a pixie arrived with a rolled-up message. He read it while she waited. It was short and to the point. "My office, now." Signed Mrs. Umbra. Conryu handed the note back to the pixie, grabbed Prime, and waved her out. "After you."

He followed the tiny elemental out of the dorm, across the snow-covered field to the main hall. Once they were inside he was surprised to head upstairs instead of to the basement. He'd assumed the head of dark magic would have her office downstairs.

They left the classrooms and continued on past the administrative offices. Several secretaries stared at him as he passed by, but since he had the pixie guiding him they must have assumed he had permission to be there. After what felt like a half-mile hike they stopped in front of a black, rune-covered door. That was more like it. He almost didn't want to knock.

Luck was on his side and the door opened before he had to touch it. Beyond the door was a small office with a desk, chairs, and book-stuffed shelves. He restrained a sigh. Every time he expected to end up somewhere ominous it ended up being normal. All the weird shit seemed to happen when he least expected it.

Mrs. Umbra sat behind her desk. She waved him over to one of the empty chairs and when he'd sat she said, "I heard all about it. How's your head?"

"Fine. I slept off the worst of the backlash. I don't remember it hurting that much when I summoned Cerberus."

"You were barely conscious that time. It's way worse when

you're aware of what's happening."

"No kidding, but I survived, that's what counts."

"How did you manage the other five demons without losing consciousness?"

"Please don't get mad."

The wrinkles in her forehead deepened. "Conryu?"

"I had Prime teach me the domination spell." He winced, but she didn't blast him where he sat. "I know I'm not supposed to study anything without your permission, but it was an emergency."

"Did it give you any trouble?"

"Not really. It was longer than the spells I've cast so far, but the increased power didn't bother me. I had a little trouble with this twisty, flip thing you have to do with your off hand halfway through, but I figured it out after a couple practice runs. I'll be honest, it doesn't seem hard enough to be a third-year spell."

She shook her head. "That's because you're so much stronger than average. Domination requires you to channel ten times as much energy as Cloak of Darkness, for example. The spells aren't the problem. The reason it's a third-year spell is because it takes two years to build up enough capability with dark energy for most wizards to cast it and remain conscious."

"Oh. I have to say it was way easier than using willpower to control the demons. Once I hit them with it they went as docile as kittens. I wish I'd known it to begin with. Would have saved me one hell of a headache."

Mrs. Umbra groaned, opened her mouth like she was going to say something, then closed it again. After a moment she said, "I hear you met Malice Kincade."

"Don't get me started on her. Why is it that so many people feel the need to include a threat when they first speak to me? And I told her she should be nicer to Kelsie."

Mrs. Umbra laughed and leaned back in her chair. When she'd wiped a tear from her eye she asked, "How'd she take it?"

"Not seriously. I don't think I convinced her, but I still had to say something."

"Don't worry about it. You understand you can't talk to anyone about what happened yesterday, right?"

"Yeah, not that I really know all that much. Demons being summoned inside the city doesn't seem like the sort of thing the Department would want getting around. I hate not being able to tell Maria though. It feels like I'm lying to her."

"I'm familiar with that experience. If it's any consolation it's not your fault you can't tell her."

"It's not, but thanks."

Conryu's chat with Mrs. Umbra ended with her promising to teach him more advanced spells in such a tone that he broke out into a sweat. He went back to the dorm ready for another nap. At the bottom of the steps he found Kelsie standing outside his room.

"Hey."

She jumped and spun to face him. "I thought you were inside."

"No, Mrs. Umbra wanted to talk with me. How are you?"

"Worried about you. When you didn't come to class this morning I figured you must have been sick." She was kneading her hands and fidgeting.

She really did seem concerned. He felt a little bad about worrying her, not that he'd had much choice. "It was a stomach bug, something I ate didn't agree with me. I'm fine now. Would you like to come in?"

He opened the door and she ducked inside. Kelsie sat on the edge of the bed. Conryu put Prime on the desk and plopped down in his chair. "So what did I miss?"

"Not much. We practiced circle casting the whole time. Mrs. Lenore was going to start our fusion magic lessons, but she said tomorrow would be fine."

"Since I wasn't there. Sorry."

"No, no, it's okay. I'm just excited to give it a try. What did Mrs. Umbra want?"

"Just to discuss what we are going to work on for the rest of the year. Boring stuff, really." Yet another lie, but he didn't have any choice.

* * *

Kelsie's hands trembled as she walked down the steps to dark magic. She'd gotten pretty good at working with her partner in the casting circle. Between them they'd managed to dispel the light, but not shatter the sphere. It was a beginning at least. Today she was supposed to start fusion training with Conryu. He was so strong the idea terrified her. Why did she even agree to work with him?

Because he was her friend, maybe the only one she'd ever had. The evening before, when he'd invited her into his room, for a moment she'd feared her mother had been right and he was going to try something, but he couldn't have been more polite.

She blew out a sigh and reached for the classroom door. Part of her was annoyed that he didn't try anything and another part knew she'd be furious if he did. What a screwed up way of thinking.

Kelsie stepped inside and found she was the last one to arrive, even the perpetually late Mrs. Lenore had arrived ahead of her. Her cheeks burned when everyone turned to look at her. Conryu just grinned and pulled out the chair beside him for her. She rushed to sit down.

"Okay, now that we're all here," Mrs. Lenore said. "We're going to try something different. Some of you, I've noticed, seem to have the two-person circle casting down, so you'll be trying three-person circles. Meg, you and Caitlin will continue as a pair. Conryu and Kelsie will try fusion casting."

Mrs. Lenore set about instructing the girls on a three-person circle. Kelsie tried to pay attention since she'd have to do it at some point as well, but she couldn't get her mind off Conryu. He sat beside her with the most indifferent expression. He clearly couldn't have cared less about circle casting. For him it must be like a tiger listening to a bunch of house cats receive instructions on hunting mice.

Once the circles were going Mrs. Lenore motioned them over to the corner of the classroom. She set one of the glowing spheres on an empty table. "So the way this is supposed to work is, Kelsie, you stand behind Conryu and put your hand on the center of his back. When he casts the spell you'll feel like something is pulling at you. You just need to relax and let your power flow so it melds with his. If this works the way it's supposed to, you two should create a more powerful result than Conryu would on his own. Shall we give it a try?"

Kelsie moved to stand behind him. She tried to dry the sweat off her hand, but it only lasted for a second. She put her palm on Conryu's back.

He glanced over his shoulder. "Ready?"

"Yes." It came out as more of a squeak than a real affirmative.

"Here we go." He raised his hand. "Darkness bind..."

A thrum of power ran through her, shaking her to the bone. She could no longer make out what he was saying. The psychic vibrations increased with each word until he completed the spell. In her mind's eye a deep, black pit appeared and six glowing red eyes stared back at her.

The pulling Mrs. Lenore described felt more like her soul being wrenched from her body. The darkness inside him was trying to devour her.

Kelsie broke the connection and fled the room. She stumbled down the hall, her heart racing and her breath coming in gasps. A few feet from the door she fell to her knees and tried not to hyperventilate as tears poured from her eyes.

A hand on her back returned her to the moment. She looked up to find Mrs. Lenore staring at her.

"What happened, dear?"

Kelsie described the darkness and the eyes. "It was so overwhelming I panicked. I'm sorry."

"It's my fault. I didn't expect you to be able to see into his portal. Those eyes were Cerberus. Conryu was forced to make a pact with him to keep minor demons from slipping through the gate every time he casts a spell. You don't need to be afraid, the demon dog can't affect anything in our world."

"But it felt like he was trying to pull my soul out of my body."

"I didn't expect that either. Maybe I should have practiced this with Conryu myself before I tried to instruct you." Mrs. Lenore hung her head. "I'm a terrible teacher."

Now Kelsie felt equally bad about upsetting Mrs. Lenore and jealous at the idea of someone else practicing with Conryu.

She straightened and pulled Mrs. Lenore with her. "I'm okay now. I'd like to give it another try."

"Are you sure? I don't want to force you."

She nodded once. "I'm sure."

* * *

Conryu stared as Mrs. Lenore ran after Kelsie. He didn't know what had her so upset. Everything was going smoothly then bang, she broke contact and ran off. It screwed up the spell and now the glowing sphere sat on the table mocking him. While he had no doubt about his ability to destroy the thing on his own, that wasn't the point of the exercise.

The other girls had stopped their practice and were glaring at him. People seemed to enjoy glaring at him and he was getting sick of it. He hadn't done anything wrong. At least he didn't think he had.

Finally Kelsie and Mrs. Lenore returned. Kelsie's cheeks were red and she'd been crying. He still couldn't figure out what had bothered her.

She didn't say anything, simply moved around behind him and

put her hand on his back. "Let's try again."

He looked at Mrs. Lenore who nodded.

Well, here goes. "Darkness bind our power as one, Break and Shatter!" He focused on the sphere and compelled the magic to affect nothing else. When he finished Kelsie stiffened, but didn't run.

A black lance of energy shot out and struck the sphere. One second it was there and the next not even a pile of metal shavings remained.

He grinned. That's the way it was supposed to work.

Kelsie took her hand off his back and peeked around him. "Where's the sphere?"

"Gone. We obliterated it. Good work, partner." He gave her hand a squeeze and she managed a weak smile.

"Let's call that good for today, you two," Mrs. Lenore said. "Kelsie, why don't you try working with Meg and Caitlin on a trio casting."

Kelsie looked up at him then nodded and went to join the other girls. When they were fully engrossed in their practice Mrs. Lenore said, "She caught a glimpse of Cerberus and it scared her."

Having seen Cerberus up close he understood how she might have that reaction. "What did you say to calm her down?"

"Beats me, I'm glad she pulled it together though. How did the spell feel?"

"I didn't notice much difference. I know I'm not supposed to ask, but what did she score on the test?"

"I guess it couldn't hurt to tell you, but keep it to yourself. She pulled a nine hundred, respectable but not above average."

"That's less than ten percent of my full power."

Mrs. Lenore nodded. "We're just going through the motions here, I recognize that, but I don't know what else to do."

Conryu didn't either. Maybe Mrs. Umbra would have some more ideas.

Class wrapped up and the girls all left. Ten minutes later Mrs.

Umbra arrived. She had a scroll in her left hand, bigger than the one the pixie brought, but still not huge.

"Did you bring me a present?"

"No. This is a diagram of how a normal wizard develops." She spread it out on the big desk and when it tried to roll back up she muttered something that made it go rigid. "Now pay attention."

Conryu moved up beside her and examined the scroll. It didn't make for very exciting reading. There was a series of four bars, each more full than the last.

Mrs. Umbra pointed at the first one. "This represents a typical first-year student. She would be able to use about a third of her power safely by the end of the year. The percentage increases each year until the new wizard reaches her full potential in her final year. That is our most important task, shepherding young wizards through these critical first four years. We've chosen the spells and techniques we teach carefully so as not to overwhelm new wizards."

"What does that mean for me?"

"It means following our standard curriculum is pointless. I don't need to ease you through the process because, for some reason, you're already operating at full strength. If I taught you the most powerful spell I know you could cast it without batting an eye. There's one problem. Regardless of its pointlessness, we only have the one lesson plan and you'll graduate before the Department approves a new one."

Conryu's headache was coming back. "So, what, I just show up, put in my time, and pass whatever the final is?"

"Basically. Feel free to learn anything you like from your book, just don't cast any new spells without me. The only reason I restricted you was for your safety. Now that it's clear you're in no danger you may as well learn whatever you can."

An overwhelming urge to beat his head against the wall came over Conryu. Not only was he stuck learning a subject that didn't interest him, now his teacher tells him the whole process was pointless. If not for the law he'd be just as well off studying at home in his spare time and coming in to take the tests.

Four years of his life flushed down the toilet to no apparent purpose. Fantastic.

* * *

The rest of the week passed quickly. Conryu and Kelsie worked on fusion magic for ten minutes every day before she went to practice circle casting with the other girls, leaving him free to study his Infernal. There were still a lot of words he didn't know and until he was fluent in the language his dark magic potential remained limited.

Sunday arrived at last and with it his weekly visit with Angus. The boring visits used to annoy him, now he hoped the professor didn't have any news for him, especially today as he was supposed to meet the supply train and collect the engine and tools Mr. Kane had arranged for him. He was a little nervous, not knowing what style of motor he'd find. Hopefully it would be something simple, without a lot of computer-controlled components he'd have to work around.

Angus's door was open when he arrived which was a good sign. Conryu poked his head in and relaxed when he found the professor alone. "Please tell me you don't have any messages?"

"No, though I'm curious how you made out on your mission." Angus looked at him, all bright-eyed and eager.

"I'm not sure how much I'm allowed to say so you'd better ask Mr. Kane about it. See you next week."

Conryu left the crestfallen professor behind and jogged toward the train platform. Maria said she was working with her light magic teacher today so he didn't have to meet her until dinner. He didn't know what had happened last week, but Maria seemed more content than she had since winter break. She was also determined to be at the top of her class after finals.

He smiled. No one could fault Maria's dedication when it came to schoolwork. He hated it, but when a bunch of crazy wizards wanted you dead there wasn't much to be done. Not to mention it seemed he'd be on call to lend the Department a hand anytime they needed him.

That didn't seem right, but according to Mr. Kane he was the only one available powerful enough to do what was required, at least until the northern incursion was sorted out and god only knew how long that would be, summer at least. So for now he was their only option. With any luck it would be a temporary thing.

After a short, cold walk he arrived at the platform. His engine, a mercifully simple, single-cylinder job that looked like it came from a dirt bike, was sitting on a black pallet beside a large toolbox. Off to one side the delivery people unloaded boxes of food and other supplies. One of the teachers, a water wizard in her mid forties with a stern air about her, was overseeing the unloading, marking items off a list as they were brought out.

He was reluctant to bother her, but Conryu had no idea how he was supposed to transport the engine without a forklift or something.

Conryu bit the bullet and walked over to the teacher. "Excuse me?"

She looked at him wearing the same expression with which you might regard a puppy that shit on the rug. "I was told to expect you. You should know I don't approve of violating the no technology ban."

"Well, we're turning the engine into something that runs on magic, so that will make it a magic item when we're finished and that won't break any rules, right?"

She grunted.

"Anyway, how am I supposed to move it to our workshop?"

"No one explained to you how the lift pallets work?"

He wanted to tell her that if someone had explained to him

how the pallets worked he wouldn't have asked her, but instead he just shook his head.

"Just touch the master rune, that's the biggest one on the pallet, and it will lift off the ground and follow you until you touch it again. Simple."

"Thank you, ma'am."

Conryu followed her instructions and was soon trudging toward the club's shack with the pallet following along behind like a dog at heel. A path had been cut through the snow, so it only took him a few minutes to make the walk.

When he arrived steam was rising off the roof and the door was cracked open, a warm glow leaking out. The moment he opened the door Sonja bounced to her feet and rushed over to the pallet. She pushed it in and touched the rune without so much as a hello.

Crystal was seated on the floor, still looking glum about not making the team, her hands held out toward the fire orb that was heating the place. She stood up with obvious reluctance and ambled over to the pallet which now rested on the ground.

"You got it, awesome." Sonja circled the engine, a huge smile on her face. She looked up at him. "What now?"

"Now I'll tear it apart, clean everything, and show you how it all works. Unless you guys are familiar with engines already."

Crystal shook her head. "All I know is that they start when I turn the key. You really think we can make this thing run on magic?"

"I don't see why not. One type of energy should motivate it as well as another."

"The only reason we might fail is a lack of imagination," Sonja said. "And that's one thing I have plenty of."

Conryu started working on the engine and by the time noon rolled around he had it mostly torn down. He explained what everything did as he went and by the time they parted ways the girls seemed confident they could have it going no problem.

6

THE HUNT FOR MERCIA

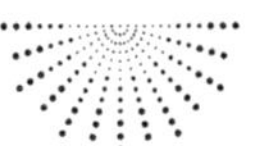

Terra scratched the final rune in the side of her lantern. She'd been working on the artifact twelve hours a day every day for the past three weeks. At last the task was complete.

She tossed her tiny chisel onto her workshop table and wiped the sweat from her forehead. She called the device a lantern because it almost exactly resembled an old-fashioned metal-and-glass hurricane lamp. The difference was this one didn't give off light, instead it would hold the blob of necroplasma that bounced incessantly against the unseen walls of the spell circle that still held it.

With any luck her creation would act like a compass, leading them to Mercia. After their failure last month to secure the boxes they had no other hope than to locate Mercia and capture or kill her before she triggered the summoning. Failing that… Terra didn't want to think about it.

Taking up the device Terra went to the opposite side of the room and studied the erratic black blob as it struggled to escape its prison. You'd think the thing would wear out after a while, but so far it hadn't stopped moving since she captured it.

She set the lantern beside the spell circle and frowned. Though preparing the artifact had taken the most time, transferring the necroplasma was the most difficult part of the project. The fact that she was completely unfamiliar with the substance didn't make the task any easier.

Why hadn't she taken the time to consult with Conryu's scholomantic when it was here? She reluctantly admitted it was her overconfidence, thinking that they'd be able to retrieve the boxes and thus wouldn't have any need of the blob that had led to her mistake in judgment. Well, stuff happened, now she had to deal with it.

She removed the glass portion of the lantern revealing the rune-inscribed chamber that would hold the blob. A deep breath cleared her mind and she began a dark magic domination spell. It wasn't powerful enough to control a demon, but she should be able to use it to coax the necroplasma from one prison to the other.

As she chanted the blob finally went still. She completed the spell and willed the necroplasma to move left. When it complied she gave herself a mental high-five. A second command moved it to the opposite side of the circle.

So far so good. Now was when it might get tricky. Using her thumb she rubbed out a portion of the spell circle, just enough for the blob to pass through. She commanded it to move into the lantern.

The blob extended a pseudopod out the gap then inched out. It oozed over to the lantern and stopped.

It fought her control. It was nothing but a fist-sized gob of mindless evil and it still resisted her. Terra ground her teeth and focused all her will on the necroplasma.

"Do it, now!"

With a final quiver the blob entered the lantern. Terra slid the glass back in place and relaxed. The pressure in her mind receded and she let out the breath she'd been holding.

The blob slammed back and forth in its new prison, but her work had paid off. It couldn't escape.

Terra allowed herself ten minutes to recover from the transfer then grabbed the lantern and headed for Chief Kane's office. It was already late afternoon, but she knew he'd want an update at once.

The moment she stepped out of the elevator the chief's secretary waved her through. Terra pushed through the doors and found her boss standing at the window staring out over the city. It was pretty, with a fresh coating of snow over everything.

She'd only been vaguely aware of the weather since she'd been sleeping in her office while she worked on the lantern.

"Sir?"

Orin turned to face her. He was nothing more than a silhouette standing in front of the bright window. "Please tell me you have some good news."

"Well, I'm not sure if it's good or not, but I finished the artifact and transferred the necroplasma. We can begin the hunt first thing in the morning."

He stepped away from the window and sat in his chair. This crisis had aged him. There were new lines around his eyes and she was certain he'd lost weight.

"That's something. Are you certain you can't start today?"

She shook her head. "Too close to nightfall. If we have to deal with shadow beasts it'll be better to do it in the daylight. Besides, I'm so tired I can't see straight. I'll get a good night's sleep and be ready to go in the morning."

He rubbed his face. "Of course. I didn't mean to sound unreasonable. It's just I need this sorted, sooner rather than later."

"I think we all feel that way, at least I know I do. But there's only so much you can do in a day." She debated saying more then shrugged. "Why don't you have an early quit, sir? Go home, see Shizuku, take a little rest. No offense, but you look like hell."

His laugh held no amusement. "That's better than I feel. I have some things to finish up then I'll head out, okay?"

"Yes, sir."

* * *

Lin, Terra, and Clair were gathered in the chief's office. Light poured through the window in an almost blinding glare. On the desk the blob in Terra's lantern was still for once. The nasty thing didn't like the sun. Lin wasn't all that thrilled to see it this morning either. It meant it was hunting time again and so far he hadn't been much use when dealing with these supernatural threats. Other than shooting a few zombies he'd been more hindrance than help.

Chief Kane peered at the lantern then looked up at them. "So this thing's going to lead you to Mercia?"

"That's the theory according to Conryu's scholomantic," Terra said. "I'm in no way ashamed to admit that this is all outside my area of expertise. However, given my complete lack of other ideas, I didn't know what else to try."

"Don't give it a second thought. All avenues must be explored." Chief Kane opened a drawer in his desk and pulled out a long box. "Lin, this is for you."

The chief opened the box revealing a shiny silver pistol and six full clips. They looked like 9mm, the same as his service weapon.

"Thank you, sir, but I'm more familiar with my current weapon."

Chief Kane thumbed one of the cartridges out of its clip and tossed it to Lin. "Look at the bullet."

Lin squinted at the tip. There was something drawn on it. "Sir?"

"Those are rune-marked bullets ordered from Chard Manufacturing: magic bullets. I understand your weapon has been less than effective in your previous outings so I made arrangements for an upgrade. The pistol is designed to handle the bullet's power. A standard weapon would explode the moment you fired it."

Lin looked the bullet over again. An enchanted weapon. With this he would be able to fight and have a hope of accomplishing something instead of hiding and letting Terra handle everything. That idea pleased him a great deal. "Thank you, sir."

Lin swapped his old pistol for the new one then switched out the clips on the opposite side of the holster. The fit was a little tight, but not too bad. The four extra magazines went in his jacket pocket.

"Now." Chief Kane got to his feet. "Go find this psycho and bring her in. I'm not supposed to say this, but if she's not still breathing when you do that's fine."

They left the chief's office and made their way down to the lobby and out to the waiting car. It was, as always lately, a bitterly cold day. Lin couldn't remember a winter this frigid in his forty plus years of living in Sentinel City. He turned the heat all the way up and pulled out of his parking space.

Beside him Terra held her contraption with one hand and touched one of the numerous runes covering it with the other. The lantern lit up and the blob poked up into the glass enclosure.

He drove to the parking lot exit. "What now?"

"Give it a minute," Terra said.

A minute later Lin asked, "What now?"

She glared at him and tapped the lantern glass. The blob wobbled and leaned left. "Go left."

Lin obliged, not daring to go too fast lest he miss a turn. In the back seat Clair snorted. "Do you really think that little ball of snot knows where it's going?"

"If you have a better idea I'd like to hear it," Terra said. "Next right."

Lin made the turn and tried to ignore the ladies' bickering. He had yet to decide if they really didn't like each other or if arguing was just a habit.

For the next hour they drove at an agonizing pace through the crowded city streets, drawing honks and middle-fingers from annoyed drivers. Eventually they left the center of the city behind and headed into the manufacturing district on the outskirts. He drove past a cement factory, then a recycling plant before Terra said, "Stop."

Lin looked out the window at a rundown smelter. It looked like the place hadn't been used in years. A thick layer of soot covered the windows so that he couldn't see anything inside.

"This is the place," Clair said. "I can sense it."

Terra nodded and Lin pulled over and parked on the side of the road. They piled out of the car and stood looking at the huge building.

"You think she's here?" Lin had his doubts. He couldn't imagine anyone living in a place like this.

"Don't judge a book by its cover." Terra held up the lantern and the blob strained to get to the building. "There's definitely something here. With the right magic you could turn the inside into a comfortable residence and no one would know from the outside."

Lin drew his new gun and worked the slide, chambering one of the enchanted bullets. "Well, let's check it out."

* * *

Terra led the group toward the only visible door on this side of the giant factory. The necroplasma struggled to escape, constantly lunging toward the deserted building. The crash of steel getting smashed into cubes at the recycling plant next door made it hard for her to concentrate, but Terra kept the words of a defensive spell on her lips. If this really was Mercia's base then she expected a hard fight.

Terra grabbed the doorknob, but it didn't budge. Lin moved

closer, but Clair brushed him out of the way. She chanted in the language of earth and flicked her wrist. The steel-core door ripped free of its hinges and went flying. At least they wouldn't have to worry about anyone barring it behind them and the noise from the plant covered anything they might do.

Clair ducked through first, followed by Terra, with Lin bringing up the rear. The inside stank of grease and burnt metal. Thin shafts of light filtered through the filthy windows. Terra was afraid to summon fire globes in case something flammable still lingering in the building. It would be a shame to blow themselves up and do Mercia's work for her.

Clair summoned a pair of globes using light magic, revealing a pair of massive crucibles hanging from a system of rails attached to the ceiling. Further down the smelters sat cold and black, like giant lumps of coal.

"What now?" Lin asked.

Terra raised her lantern and watched the blob. It wanted to go deeper into the building so she obliged, easing her way down the soot-covered path between the equipment. An occasional groan or pop echoed through the vast space as the sun heated the cold metal roof. She had to force herself not to look at every squeak and focus on the blob. If there was any threat Clair and Lin would handle it.

The necroplasma grew more frantic the deeper she went until it was positively berserk about a third of the way to the rear of the building near a hydraulic pump that appeared to run the rail system. "We're close. There must be something hidden nearby," Terra said.

Clair cast a seeing spell. The chill in the air changed from physical to psychic. Her casting must have triggered a trap. Something growled from Terra's left followed a moment later by a snarl from her right.

They were surrounded.

"Back to back!" Terra dropped her lantern so she'd be free to cast.

Lin dashed over and stood behind her, his pistol raised and ready. Clair reached them half a second later. Crystal protrusions covered her like a suit of armor.

From the dark recesses between giant machines, glowing red eyes glared. A trio of hell hounds stepped into the light. Fire dripped from their jaws and black teeth like saliva.

Behind her Lin said, "I have two targets. Do I shoot?"

Terra weighed the risk of blowing them to bits with the risk of getting torn apart. It didn't take long to make up her mind. "Yes."

The word had barely crossed her lips when Lin's pistol cracked followed half a heartbeat later by an even bigger explosion.

As if he'd fired a starting pistol, all hell broke loose. Terra chanted, "Flames of destruction incinerate my enemy, Fire Blast!" and hurled flames.

Clair enchanted a nearby chain and used it to flail at the hell hound nearest her while Lin's pistol cracked again and again.

Terra's first target was pushed back until it slammed into a support column, a huge patch of skin charred and burned away. Despite the damage the hell hound showed no sign of being out of the fight.

The two uninjured hounds gathered themselves.

"Flames of protection appear before me, Fire Wall!" A ten-foot-tall wall of blazing flames sprang up between them and the hounds. "Lin?"

"I took out one, but I needed a full clip to do it. The second one decided to hide behind a pile of scrap. I can't get a clear shot."

Clair shifted and chanted. A loud clatter was followed by explosions and an even louder clatter.

"We're clear on this side." Lin spun to stand at her shoulder.

"I'm lowering the fire wall in three, two, one." She thrust her hands down and the flames vanished.

Behind it the hell hounds were gone.

"Shit! Clair?"

Clair crouched down and rested her palm on the floor while muttering. "They're circling, two left and one right."

"Lin, take the right." Terra raised her hands. "Flames of destruction answer my call."

Blue-white fire danced around her fingers, ready to be hurled at the first sign of the monsters.

"They're coming." Clair straightened and cast a spell of her own. The chain she'd used earlier stiffened into a spear that hung in the air above her.

Lin's pistol spoke first. Terra didn't even have time to glance his way before the remaining two hounds leapt at them. She threw her hands forward, focusing all her power on the nearest demon. The inferno scoured away skin and flesh and bone, leaving nothing but a charred pile of ash.

Clair's spear impaled the second hound and pinned it to the floor. The demon struggled but couldn't free itself.

Terra pointed at the spear. "Light of Heaven burn away this darkness, Lightning Blast."

A crackling bolt of electricity arced down the spear and into the hound, burning it from the inside out until it burst into a puff of black smoke.

"Clear!" Lin said.

Terra wiped the sweat from her brow. They'd survived the first test.

"I have only three clips left," Lin said. "I hope those bullets aren't expensive."

"Only a hundred dollars apiece." Clair bent down and touched the floor again, chanting in the language of earth.

While she was casting Terra retrieved the lantern. Her magic had protected the glass from the drop leaving the necroplasma still trapped and growing more agitated by the second.

"There's a large space under the floor." Clair straightened. "It's three-quarters the size of the factory. I can't get a sense of what's in it."

"Are you being blocked, or is it just too hard to say for sure?" Terra asked.

"There's definitely some sort of ward interfering with my earth magic. All I can tell is a rough idea of size and depth."

"So we're going in blind?" Lin slapped a fresh clip into his pistol.

"Believe it or not," Terra said. "That's a good thing. There must be something important down there if Mercia spent time and magic to protect it."

"I believe it not. If there's one thing I've learned in my years as a cop it's that going into a situation blind is the single most likely thing to get you killed."

"We'll just have to hope you're wrong, because we're going down there just as soon as we find the entrance."

* * *

"Found the release." Clair pulled something behind the pump. A vibration ran through the whole structure as the floor slid open revealing a long staircase.

Terra studied the path down. "I don't see any traps from here."

"I jammed the lever with a piece of scrap." Clair gestured and the light globes flew down the stairs. They'd been hacked out of the bedrock and were far too narrow for Terra's taste. "Those almost look like someone carved them by hand, either that or they were made by an unskilled earth magic wizard. I did better work as a freshman."

Terra looked at Clair. "Do you want to take the lead? You have the best chance of detecting a trap underground."

Clair nodded and started down the steps. Terra followed, picking her way down the narrow path while holding the lantern. The stone had a slight sheen of moisture that made the steps even more treacherous. Lin brought up the rear. When Terra looked back she found him looking over his shoulder more than ahead.

They moved ever deeper into the darkness. Soon the light from behind them vanished and they had nothing but Clair's globes to show them the way. If they had to fight shadow beasts with no sun to weaken them they might be in trouble.

She grit her teeth and kept going. Terra knew going into this it was risky. The three of them would deal with whatever they had to in order to keep Mercia from activating the boxes.

"It levels out up ahead." Clair's voice echoed in the narrow stairway.

Terra picked up her pace and soon she and Lin joined Clair in a wide open space. At the center rested a stone table in a spotlight. "This must be where Mercia sacrificed those unfortunate people to create the necroplasma."

"You were always a clever woman, Terra." Mercia's voice filled the chamber. An illusion of her head appeared in the air above the table. "It's a shame I couldn't be there to greet you in person. We could have had a reunion."

"We know what you're planning and you won't succeed," Terra said.

Mercia laughed. "And who's going to stop me? You three, stuck in a hole with no way out?"

The floor shook as the stairs collapsed, sealing them in. Clair ran back, but flinched away a few feet from the rubble. "There's a dark magic barrier."

"If not us, then someone else. The Department will not let you get away with this." Terra clenched her fists so hard her nails cut into her palm.

"Your faith in your employer is charming, but misplaced. The government doesn't have enough wizards to put out all the fires burning in the Alliance. Once you're dead there will be no one to stand in my way. Have fun playing with my servants." Mercia's head flickered and faded away.

The floor under Terra's feet shook again, harder this time. Lin grabbed the neck of her robe and yanked her back. A second later a black slab shot up to the ceiling followed by another and another. Hundreds of them filled the chamber creating a maze with the table in the center.

"Thanks." Terra straightened her robe.

"No problem. So how do we get out of here?" Lin eyed the imposing black structure and frowned.

"Not the way we came in, that's for sure." Clair joined them near the entrance of the maze. "I couldn't so much as crack the barrier she put up. If we can't dispel it then I can't clear the stairs."

"Our options appear quite limited," Lin said.

"If by that you mean we only have one then I agree." Terra rubbed the bridge of her nose. "My guess is that table, or perhaps more accurately altar, is the key holding all the wards and constructs down here together. If we destroy it, maybe we have a chance."

"That's a lot of guesses." Clair glared at the maze as if trying to knock it down with sheer force of will.

"Guesses are all I have at this point." Terra set the lantern down and pointed at the necroplasma bouncing around inside. "This thing's done enough damage. Light of Heaven burn away this darkness, Lightning Blast."

A pencil thin beam of electricity shot out, shattered the glass, and incinerated the blob.

"Feel better?" Lin asked.

"Not really. Come on."

* * *

This time Terra took the lead, with Lin in the center and Clair bringing up the rear. Terra claimed it was to allow him to quickly engage an enemy to the front or back, but Lin suspected she just wanted him in the safest place since he was the weakest member of the group. He couldn't even argue. His new gun let him do some damage, but it lacked the versatility of true magic.

All around them warped images followed along. The black stone walls were shiny and reflective, like funhouse mirrors, only without the fun. Everywhere he looked it was like something was moving. Lin didn't know how to separate the false movement from a potentially real threat. He was really starting to regret that transfer just now.

The first turn they came to was a left. Two paces later they reached a three-way intersection. Nothing distinguished one choice from another in his eyes. Terra took the right, looking more confident than he felt.

Lin took one step after her. Another rumble shook the floor and a black panel shot up, separating them from Clair. The maze went pitch black as the light orb died.

Terra hissed a spell and a reddish-orange fireball appeared, filling the air with light. Lin rapped the grip of his pistol on the wall drawing a dull thud.

"Clair!" Terra shouted.

Lin held his breath, but only silence filled the air. Further shouts brought identical results. He groped around where the walls intersected, but they fit so tight he couldn't so much as slip a fingernail between them.

"Shit." Terra slammed her fist into the wall and her fireball flared brighter.

"That sums up our situation beautifully. What now?"

Terra sighed. "We keep moving forward. It's not like we have a lot of other options."

With those words of reassurance they set out once more. Lin stayed as close as possible without stepping on the heels of her shoes. Whatever else happened he didn't want to be trapped alone in the darkness. He was the only one that couldn't make his own light.

"I'm never leaving the car without my flashlight again," he muttered.

"What?"

"Nothing. Think Clair's alright?"

"I hope so. She's a stronger wizard than me so if she's defeated then we're screwed."

"You're not very good at offering reassurances are you?" They came to another intersection and Lin practically draped himself over Terra when they went through it.

"Do you need reassuring?"

An explosion sounded from back the way they'd come. "I do now."

* * *

"Fuck!" Clair slammed her fist into the black slab separating her from Lin and Terra. She made no impression on the unyielding substance. Clair didn't know what the slabs were made of, but it wasn't stone. If Mercia had used rock she'd have knocked the maze flat with a simple spell, as it was, her earth magic didn't so much as touch the stuff.

She ground her teeth and turned her back on the barrier. It wasn't like she didn't have options. There were two other ways to proceed. The question was, which one led her out of this maze?

Straight seemed most likely to take her in the same general direction as her companions so she went that way. Half a dozen steps later a chill presence approached from behind. She spun as a black minotaur lumbered into view. It towered ten feet above her, with curving black horns that sprouted from its bull's head.

Though it was clear what the construct was supposed to be, the minotaur more closely resembled an unskilled child's attempt to make one from clay. The basic shape was correct, but the details were either off or nonexistent. It looked like it was made of pure dark magic, but Clair had never heard of such a thing.

The minotaur stomped the floor and lowered its head. Nothing subtle there.

Clair held her hand palm down. "Oh mother of earth and stone form a weapon to protect your daughter, Earth Spear."

When the minotaur charged Clair punched out at it. The ground shifted and a two-foot-diameter spear of stone burst up through the floor and into the monster's chest.

The force of its charge battled the power of her spell and it was sent flying back. For an instant after impact, the darkness was pushed aside, revealing bronze underneath.

So it wasn't a construct of pure dark magic, but a golem covered in the stuff to protect it from magic. Lucky for her it couldn't protect the statue from impact.

The minotaur picked itself up off the ground, seeming no worse for the tumble. She needed to scrape the dark magic off in order to blast the statue apart. Unfortunately it recovered so fast she didn't have time to cast another spell before the gap she opened sealed itself.

The black statue pawed the ground again. It would drain her, but Clair saw only one option. She placed both hands on the ground. "Oh Mother Earth give birth to a child of stone to serve this unworthy wizard, Stone Behemoth."

The floor shook like an earthquake as a humanoid figure of solid stone pulled itself from the ground. The maze spun around her as she fought the aftereffects of casting two powerful spells in such close succession.

Her behemoth was even cruder in appearance than the minotaur, but it equaled the statue in mass and height. The two constructs came together, fingers locked, chest to chest. Their feet dug into the ground as they pushed and stomped.

It was an even match, but her spell had a limited duration. If she couldn't defeat the minotaur before it ended she'd be on her own again.

The maze finally stopped spinning so she prepared her next

spell. She gathered power slowly to avoid another bout of dizziness. Once she was prepared Clair sent a mental command to her behemoth to tear the dark coating off the minotaur.

The stone construct formed a mouth in its crude head and bit into the minotaur's neck. It pulled back with a mouthful of darkness, stretching the covering like rubber until it tore revealing a patch of bronze.

"Shatter and collapse, Earth Breaker." She hurled a shard of earth energy at the exposed metal the moment it appeared.

Her spell struck before the dark magic sealed up. The minotaur trembled. Its left arm and head fell to the floor and smashed to pieces.

What remained of its body continued to struggle. "Crush it, behemoth!"

Massive fists like pile-drivers rose and fell, blasting off chunks of the statue with each impact until nothing remained but a pile of rubble. Only seconds later the behemoth crumbled on top of it. Her spell had lasted just long enough.

Clair slumped to the floor, her body trembling and exhausted.

* * *

The booms and crashes finally ended. Lin wasn't sure if that was a good thing or not and when he'd asked Terra he'd gotten only stony silence in reply. After that he hadn't dared ask if they were lost.

He thought they were. In fact he thought the walls of the maze were shifting behind them. Now that the battle had ended maybe he'd hear if one of the black slabs rose or fell.

They took another right and after fifteen steps came to a dead end. Terra punched the wall then massaged her hand. Lin kept quiet while she paced the narrow path.

When it became painfully obvious she had no idea what to do next he said, "I think the panels are shifting."

"I wouldn't be surprised."

"Their rise and fall is controlled by magic, right?" He was working out his thoughts as he spoke. Lin knew next to nothing about magic so the process was slow.

Terra finally stopped and looked at him. "Yeah, what about it?"

"Well if magic controls them, why can't you mimic the spell to make the one you want go down?"

She opened her mouth then closed it without comment. It was a stupid idea. He should have kept his mouth shut.

"That's not a terrible idea."

Lin must have misheard. "It isn't?"

"In fact it's brilliant. I'm not sure why I didn't think of it myself. Too busy thinking about how to find our way through the maze to consider anything else I guess." She smacked her forehead and muttered a seeing spell. He didn't know what the words meant, but he'd heard them often enough to recognize it.

Terra worked her way slowly along the path, her gaze focused on the junction between the panels and the floor. He wished he could see what she saw, just once.

At last she stopped at the panel blocking their path. "It's so simple I feel like an idiot."

She cast a short spell and dark energy gathered around her hand. She tapped the wall and it slid down into the floor.

"You did it."

She shook her head. "I claim no credit. It was your idea. Let's go."

Terra made a straight line for the center of the maze, tapping each wall as needed to open the way. In less than five minutes the final wall slid down revealing a thirty-by-thirty-yard space with the altar in the middle.

They stepped into the square and Terra nodded. "Just as I thought. All the magic originates from that altar. Once we destroy it the magic holding the panels up will fade along with the barriers."

Lin pointed his pistol at the stone slab, but Terra raised her hand. He lowered his weapon. "What?"

"Your bullets don't have enough punch for this job. I—"

A tortured moan cut her off in mid-sentence. From behind the altar a corpse clambered to its feet and turned to face them. It wore leather biker clothes and had black pits for eyes.

"Does that zombie look familiar?" Lin asked.

"It's one of the Black Skulls and it's not a zombie, there's too much dark energy in it."

Lin gave the undead thing a second look. "If it's not a zombie, what is it?"

The dead Skull leaned toward them like it was about to fall over then it charged, way faster than the zombies he'd fought before.

"Fire Wall!"

The heat from the wall seared Lin's face and forced him to take a step back. The undead burst through the wall of flames with little more than a few scorch marks.

Lin tried to draw a bead on it, but the thing moved too erratically.

He jumped back to avoid a backhand and fired off a pair of rounds. The first missed, but the second hit its left shoulder. The enchanted bullet exploded, tearing a chunk out of it.

Inside the body was flowing darkness like necroplasma.

"Light of Heaven burn away this darkness, Lightning Blast."

Terra's blast sent the creature sailing back through the fire wall. She gestured and the flames vanished. They hadn't been very effective anyway and Lin preferred being able to see.

"You okay?" Terra asked.

He nodded. "Damn, that thing is fast."

The creature had skidded to a stop near the altar. It surged to its feet. The wound he'd put in its shoulder was already closing.

"How do we kill it?" Lin asked.

"Excellent question. Try to take out its legs while I think of an answer."

The undead charged again. How was he supposed to hit something moving like that monster's churning legs? He'd barely hit its body.

He fired a shot at its hip, but it lunged to the side. Lin had its full attention now.

He backpedaled and shot. Fireballs burst all around the thing, but none of them made a solid hit.

It was only yards away, its open mouth revealing inhuman fangs. Lin gave up on its legs and took aim at that open mouth.

Only one shot left so he'd better make it count.

He squeezed the trigger and its head disappeared in a ball of flame.

The still-moving body stumbled past him. Lin ejected his empty clip and slapped a fresh one in. When the smoke around the undead's head cleared it revealed a featureless black oval that immediately sank back into the body.

The undead stopped staggering and oriented on him, the lack of a head seeming to pose no difficulties for it.

Lin had two clips left. Hopefully it would be enough.

* * *

The moment Terra saw the black blob that served as the creature's head she knew what Mercia had done. "Lin, I know how to kill it."

He glanced at her, the relief in his expression palpable. "Don't keep me in suspense."

"You need to blow away the flesh and expose the Faceless One inside so I can sear it away."

Lin grimaced then nodded before returning his full attention to the quickly recovering undead. He raised his pistol and took aim.

"Flames of destruction hear my call." Terra opened a path to the realm of fire. Maintaining it would tire her more quickly, but she wouldn't have to keep chanting the primary phrase each time she wanted to cast her spell, only the words of shaping would be necessary.

Lin fired and the enchanted bullet blew the undead's arm off, revealing the skinny black twig that served the Faceless One.

"Fire Arrow!" She thrust her hand forward and a yard-long bolt of blue flame shot out, incinerating the arm before it withdrew back into the body.

The Faceless One let out a moan. She doubted the thing felt pain, but to have a portion of its essence burned away must have had some effect.

It charged again, this time at her. As Lin said, it was fast, but the damage had slowed it by half a step and she managed to dodge a clubbing blow from its remaining arm.

It stopped to regroup and the moment it did Lin fired again, this time blowing off its right leg below the knee.

"Fire Arrow!" Another section of the monster was burned away.

It bounced in place and flailed with its remaining arm. Lin raised his pistol again, but she lowered it. It couldn't move or attack them now. Terra could finish it herself and save a few of Lin's precious bullets.

Terra raised her hands and sighted through them, centering the bouncing undead. "Flames of deepest earth consume all things in your path. Flames of creation and flames of destruction rise and devour, Volcanic Core!"

The ground shook and a pillar of glowing white flames blasted up through the hobbling monster. Everything was burned away. Flesh, bone, and darkness were all consumed by the pure white flames.

When nothing remained but her own magic in the pyre she lowered her hands and ended the spell. Sweat plastered her hair to her face and she stumbled when she tried to take a step. Lin caught her and eased her to the ground.

"Thanks."

He nodded and sat beside her. "That was impressive. How come you didn't use that spell to start with?"

Terra blew out a sigh. She was right on the edge of backlash. If that spell hadn't ended it they would have been fully screwed. "It's too slow to hit a moving target and I can only cast it once before I need to take a long rest."

"Well, since there's nothing trying to kill us at the moment I'd say you've earned that rest." Lin gave her a pat on the back.

"Thanks, but I'm worried about Clair. It seems like she should have caught up to us by now."

"If she didn't figure out how to lower the panels she's probably still wandering around lost. We certainly would be."

"I guess, but I'm in no shape to do anything about it one way or the other."

* * *

Terra allowed herself a full three hours to recover from the battle. Even in the sunless chamber she had an excellent sense of time. After four years at the academy she'd mastered telling time in her head. It was a necessity if you wanted to arrive anywhere when you were supposed to and a useful trick for wizards, some of whose spells lasted for a specific length.

She climbed to her feet and stretched. The weakness and dizziness had passed and her body felt strong enough to channel magic again. Lin joined her and together they eyed the altar.

"You up to smashing that thing?"

Terra had no intention of admitting it, but she wasn't entirely certain she was up to it. All the room's magic was flowing from the stone out to the maze and barriers. There was bound to be potent protections in place. She would have much preferred to tackle it in combination with Clair, but the other wizard hadn't made it to the central chamber yet. Terra didn't much like Clair, but she was starting to worry.

"One way to find out, right?" Terra rolled up her sleeves, flexed her fingers, and tried to think which spell to use to destroy the altar. Her best hope had to be with fire magic since it was her aligned element, making her twice as powerful in it as any other. Ideally she'd like a dark magic wizard to strip away the wards first, but that was out of the question.

Finally she made up her mind. "Stay back near the wall."

When Lin had moved as far from the altar as possible, she raised her hands and focused her will. "Oh flame of god's forge, swirl, rage, and consume all things, Vulcan's Tornado!"

Heat gathered as Terra spun her hands, shaping the burgeoning fire into a vortex. Over the course of half a minute a full-fledged funnel cloud of flames gathered around the altar. The stone grew red hot, but didn't melt. She needed to kick up the heat.

"Father of winds grant this unworthy servant of fire the loan of your breath, Gust!"

She directed the hot dry winds into a matching vortex. The heat tripled and the edges of the altar liquefied, dripping onto the floor.

Just a little more, oh winds.

In answer to her mental plea the gust grew in intensity. Her enhanced vision revealed the web of magic holding the wards together growing unstable as the stone broke down.

Terra grabbed Lin and dragged him behind the panels. Seconds later the altar exploded. Gravel rained against the makeshift barrier. When all had gone silent they inched their way back into the chamber.

The altar was nothing but a pile of half-melted rock. The wards were fading fast. A minute later all the panels crashed back into the floor. She slumped, but remained on her feet. Terra doubted she could cast another spell today if their lives depended on it.

Lin gave her robe a tug. "There's Clair."

She looked where he indicated. Clair was lying on the hard floor, dead or unconscious Terra couldn't tell. They ran over and Lin knelt and checked her pulse. "She's alive."

"Backlash. She must have had one hell of a fight."

"What now?"

"Now we rest. No way are we getting out of here before tomorrow at the earliest. If I have to clear all the rubble myself it might take two days.

* * *

In the end it took a day and a half for the tired, hungry, and thirsty people to dig their way out. Lin carried the still-unconscious Clair out of the factory and to their car. Terra followed along behind in only slightly better shape.

He started the car and cranked the heat before pulling out and heading back to the Department. The return trip went way quicker and twenty minutes later they were parked and Lin was carrying Clair in to the infirmary. He put her on the hard cot and Terra covered her with the thin rags that passed for blankets.

"How long do you think she'll be out?" Lin asked.

Terra shrugged. "No idea. Wizards handle backlash differently. I'm surprised she hasn't woken up already. If she doesn't wake up in another day they'll have to put in an IV to keep her from getting dehydrated. The longest backlash coma I've ever seen lasted three weeks and the wizard couldn't cast for six months."

"Let's hope Clair isn't out of commission for that long. I have a strong feeling we're going to need her before six months are up."

7
REMOVING THE BRAND

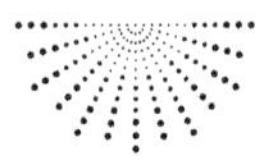

Conryu eyed the most recent target Mrs. Lenore had prepared for them. It looked like a bowling ball someone had covered with geometric designs. On the other side of the classroom Mrs. Lenore was giving the girls some instructions for their training. He didn't pay any attention since he was never going to have to do circle casting.

For the past month he and Kelsie had obliterated everything she'd put in front of them with no discernible difficulties. In fact their practice time lasted less than five minutes at the start of each class. It was yet more going through the motions, but at least it was fast. As soon as they finished he'd settle in with his Infernal study guide and Prime would help him practice telepathically. Having a demon as a study buddy made learning the awkward language much easier.

Beside him Kelsie was fidgeting and trying to focus on Mrs. Lenore's instructions while darting glances at today's target. Every time it seemed she was afraid they'd fail. So far they hadn't, but if they did he feared she'd blame herself.

"Will you relax? If you tense up your power won't flow as easily."

"Really?"

He had no idea if that was true, but she was making him nervous and that wasn't helpful. "Yes, now calm down. Try the backwards counting trick."

She fell into the easy breathing rhythm he'd taught her and soon her fidgeting stopped. She couldn't have gotten past twenty numbers when Mrs. Lenore came to join them. The rest of the class was up to four-person circles and she seemed very pleased with their progress.

The moment she stopped in front of Kelsie and Conryu her smile vanished. She'd been trying for weeks to find something that would challenge them and so far had come up short.

"So whose bowling ball are we sacrificing?" Conryu asked.

"It's not a bowling ball, it's an earth density orb. The earth magic seniors use them to practice altering the density of stone without changing its mass. This one has had its density maxed out. I doubt a drill with a diamond bit would scratch it."

"Cool. Anyone ever try to blast one of these things with dark magic before?"

"Not as far as I know. If you two destroy the orb, that's it. I have no idea what else to give you as a target."

"We still have three and a half months of school left," Kelsie said. "What will we do for the rest of the semester?"

"You'll work on circle casting and he can work on whatever Angeline, that is Mrs. Umbra, has him practicing."

Conryu rubbed his hands together. "Let's crack this egg. Ready, partner?"

Kelsie gave the orb a dubious look then took her place behind Conryu. When her hand settled in place Conryu began the spell. "Darkness bind our power as one, Break and Shatter!"

The ebony ray lanced out and struck the orb. It resisted for an instant before crumbling to gravel. Conryu grinned and thrust a fist into the air. "Yes!"

Mrs. Lenore's shoulders slumped. "I thought I had you for half a second there. Congratulations, you two can officially handle anything you'll encounter in the final."

Kelsie went and joined a circle while he settled in to study. Prime's telepathic voice appeared in his head. *You could have destroyed that orb on your own. That girl is unnecessary*. The scholomantic sounded the same whether it spoke out loud or mentally.

Conryu still had to mutter, but he could keep his voice low enough so the others didn't hear, not that they'd be apt to, given their chanting. "I suspected as much, but I'd appreciate it if you didn't run down my partner."

Prime's disdain came clearly through their link, but the scholomantic refrained from further comment. They spent the next hour and a half in mental conversation. He got comfortable with a handful of new words before everyone left him to wait for Mrs. Umbra.

She tapped her way in five minutes later. "I trust you two have been practicing the summoning spell?"

"Yeah, we can manage about fifty yards now. But I've been worried lately about what will happen if Lucifer senses Prime passing through the gate and grabs him."

"The transition over such a short distance is instantaneous. It would be like trying to pluck a bullet out of midair with your bare hands."

"I get that, but I'd feel a lot better if we removed this stupid brand from my arm."

She sat on the edge of Mrs. Lenore's desk. "As would I, but I haven't come up with any way of doing it."

"What if I just forced Lucifer to take it off himself? After all he put it there."

"That's a bold plan, but I fear you're not strong enough even knowing the domination spell." She tapped the head of the Death Stick on her palm. "But maybe if I teach you how to use this."

* * *

Despite the cold Conryu and Mrs. Umbra left the nice warm school and walked down to the beach. She informed him there was no way he was starting his practice inside since she didn't want him bringing the building down on them when he screwed up. Which he would, since everyone screwed up their first time using a magical artifact to enhance their casting.

They stopped at the edge of the frozen lake. He couldn't stop his teeth from chattering so he didn't know how he'd cast a spell. Mrs. Umbra took pity on him and hissed a fire spell. Warmth rushed into him and he sighed.

"So what do you want me to do first?"

"I want you to listen while I explain how this works. The Death Stick allows a dark-aligned wizard to channel twice as much energy as they'd be able to otherwise. You understand the implications for you?"

Conryu shook his head. He didn't fully understand what all the numbers they used to describe power levels meant. He used magic more instinctively than intellectually.

"I'll use myself as an example. If I were to take the wizard's test again I'd pull around 3,000 as a base and 6,000 in dark magic. If I channel through the Death Stick that dark magic number goes up to 12,000, making me one of the most powerful dark magic users in the world."

"Wow."

"I'm not saying that to impress you." He flinched at her angry tone. "I need you to understand. My maximum power is a hair lower than your base. If you use the Death Stick your dark magic potential approaches 50,000, four times greater than mine."

"Sure, that's a lot, but the numbers don't mean anything to me. They're just words."

"Let me put it this way. If you cast Dispel with the Death Stick you could probably negate every spell and ward on campus."

Conryu's jaw dropped. "Holy shit. Seriously?"

"Seriously. That's why we're going to proceed with great caution. Any spell you cast will be directed out over the lake and away from the school. You want to try it?"

He swallowed the lump in his throat. If he wanted to force Lucifer to remove the brand he needed to figure this out. "Let's do it."

She handed him the Death Stick and the handle vibrated in his grip. When he told her, Mrs. Umbra said, "It's responding to your magical potential. The vibration's in your mind not your hand. Don't worry, it's a good sign. The artifact has accepted you as a viable user. That's the first step."

"Right, okay. What would have happened if it rejected me?"

"Nothing. You would have felt no vibration and when you cast it wouldn't have enhanced your spell. The Death Stick only responds to those with a dark magic potential over 5,000. Now, we're going to start with a spell you're familiar with." She pointed out over the lake toward the island. "I want you to cover the island in Cloak of Darkness."

The island had to be over a mile long. He'd only ever covered himself and Prime in the cloak. "The whole thing?"

"Yes. Remember, don't think you can, know you can."

Right, he had to believe it was possible to have any hope of getting the spell to work. He took a breath and settled himself. When he spoke the first word of the spell it felt like someone had breached a dam. Power unlike anything he'd ever imagined rushed into him.

He focused through the rush and finished the spell, waving the Death Stick towards the island as he did so. Liquid darkness fell across three-quarters of the island before the last of the energy left him. He felt hollowed out. He'd never experienced anything like it.

When he described it to Mrs. Umbra she nodded. "That's not uncommon when using an artifact. Wait until you cast a spell without it for the first time. It'll feel like the most pitiful thing ever. Don't worry, it's only because of the proportion. You're not any weaker."

He looked out over the mostly covered island. "I couldn't cover the whole thing."

She laughed. "I didn't think you could. In fact I doubted you'd manage half, so this is better than I expected. With time and practice you'll be able to draw out the Death Stick's full potential."

Conryu recalled the massive power and shook his head. "That wasn't full strength?"

Mrs. Umbra's face crinkled when she smiled. "You only tapped a little over half your maximum. When you reach one hundred percent I doubt you'll have any trouble convincing Lucifer to remove your brand."

* * *

Conryu watched as Crystal adjusted the runes covering the piston and cylinder. Her earth magic created oil with no trouble, just way too much. He wasn't concerned though. If there was one thing working on Blinky had taught him, it was to expect to make adjustments. They'd been working on the engine every Sunday for six weeks now.

Sonja had inscribed a steel cylinder with fire magic to replace the spark plug. Once Crystal fixed the lubrication problem he'd reassemble the motor and see if it worked or if they'd made a bomb.

"So what are you guys studying now?" Sonja asked. The two of them were keeping their distance so Crystal could better focus.

"Nothing but Infernal in my regular class, but Mrs. Umbra is teaching me how to use the Death Stick."

She perked up at that. "Third year my class got to try the Ashen Scepter, but I didn't have a strong enough potential to make it work. Actually only one girl in my class succeeded in awakening it and she's a prodigy. Like you I guess."

Conryu laughed at that. He was no more a prodigy than he was a duck. "Is this the girl you couldn't beat at the team tryouts?"

"Yeah. Her fire magic potential is the strongest in a hundred years so I don't feel bad about it."

He nodded. "It was pure chance I was born with enough power to wield the artifact. Mrs. Umbra says only someone with dark magic potential over 5,000 can use it. I've still only managed to draw out about three-quarters of its full strength."

Sonja patted his knee. "Just keep at it. If anyone can master it, you can."

"Thanks." The little fire wizard's vote of confidence meant a lot to him. It surprised Conryu how much he'd come to value Sonja after such a short time knowing her. Maybe it was because she acted more like a middle-schooler sometimes than she did a twenty-two-year-old that made him protective of her.

"I think I have it," Crystal said.

Sonja sprinted over to the workbench and he joined her a moment later. Conryu ran his finger down the piston. There was just a thin sheen covering it. When he checked the fit in the cylinder it slid in and out without any friction.

"What do you think?" Sonja was bouncing in place.

"I think when I finish putting it back together we can test it."

"Yes!" Sonja jumped up and spun around.

An hour later the engine was reassembled and sitting upright in the cradle he'd built for it. "So how do we start this thing?" he asked.

Sonja hopped up on a stool to get a better look. "See that big rune beside the fire cylinder?"

"Yeah."

"When you touch it a link will be created between you and the engine. Your magic will power it the same way you maintain a spell like seeing, though this will drain you faster than such a basic spell."

"That's it?" It sounded too simple.

"That's it. Bear in mind that what seems like no big deal for you would exhaust me in half an hour. That's why a magic engine really isn't practical for most people. A non-wizard couldn't even use it."

"Cool." He touched the rune.

A little jolt ran through him and the engine fired. The piston cycled and turned the drive shaft. He let it run for half a minute. It looked like Sonja had it set for about a hundred rpm. Nowhere near enough to make it useful, but enough to prove the concept. As a nice bonus it didn't blow up and kill them all.

"How do I switch it off?"

"Touch the rune again."

Conryu did so and the engine shut off. A little tingle passed through him as the link vanished. "I'd call that a successful test. You know what we need to do now?"

Sonja's smile had her face stretched tight. "What?"

"Build something for it to run. Maybe a go cart or dirt bike."

"I vote go cart." Sonja was waving her arms around. "All of us can ride in that."

"If you guys think I'm getting in anything powered by an experimental magic engine you're both nuts," Crystal said.

Sonja and Conryu shared a look. "So a two-seater?" he asked.

She grinned and they bumped fists.

* * *

Conryu bounded down the stairs and into his room. He'd left Prime in the library and now he was going to try and summon him. He'd managed the spell over shorter distances, but the library was right at the outer limit of their link. If this worked he could summon Prime from anywhere.

He cleared his mind and focused on the tether that connected him to the scholomantic. He pictured it as a black thread running from his chest to Prime's spine. When he had the link fully visualized he took a breath.

Before he spoke the first word of the spell someone knocked. Conryu blew out a sigh. He wasn't expecting anyone. He sent a thought of patience to Prime and opened the door. Maria was waiting outside and hanging her head.

"Hey, what's up?"

She slipped past him and sat on the edge of his bed. When she finally looked up he took a step back. A full beard covered her face.

"Holy shit! What happened to you?"

She sniffed back a tear. "In alchemy club I reversed the order of two ingredients and the potion blew up in my face. You can see the results."

"Yeah. What are you going to do about it?"

Maria gave him the most pathetically hopeful look. "I thought maybe you could use dark magic to negate the potion's effect."

Conryu winced. Maria was highly sensitive to dark magic so if she was willing to have him use it on her she must have been desperate. The problem was he had no idea if Dispel would work on something like this and if he used breaking he might blow her head off. Delicate magic was in no way his strong suit.

"Maybe we should ask Mrs. Lenore. Having me blast you willy-nilly with dark magic might not be the best idea."

"No!" She grabbed his arm before he could take a step toward the door. "Bad enough the alchemy class knows I screwed up the potion, but no one knows about the beard but you. I took off as soon as I felt it start growing."

He understood how she wouldn't want anyone to know about this. He snapped his fingers. "I bet Prime will know what to do. I was just about to try summoning him. Hang on."

Conryu moved as far from Maria as the room would permit and repeated the visualization process. When he was ready he chanted, "Come to me through darkest paths, Familiar Summons!"

A black disk appeared in the air and Prime emerged through it before it shut. "Well done, Master. Even that terrifying witch will be impressed with this."

"Thanks, but we have a more pressing problem."

Prime flew over and studied Maria from head to toe. "This was caused by a misfired potion, yes?"

She nodded.

"It can't be dispelled by dark magic. You either need to use the correct counter-potion or wait for the effects to end. It shouldn't last more than a week."

"A week!"

Prime flew around behind him. "At most. It might only last three or four days."

"Why can't we dispel it?" Conryu asked.

Prime peeked over his shoulder at the still-fuming Maria. "Potion magic works by infusing power into a person's entire body. It's not just a matter of zapping her face. You'd have to remove every trace of the magic from her entire body without damaging her cells. No offense, Master, but you still lack sufficient control for such a delicate operation."

He couldn't argue with that. While his control had improved he would never dare anything that delicate, especially on Maria, with her low tolerance for dark magic. "Maybe there's another option."

Maria perked up. "Anything."

Conryu ducked into his bathroom and returned with his disposable razor. "You could shave."

She stared at him for a moment. "Shave? That's your brilliant idea?"

"I didn't say it was brilliant, but there's a long tradition of using these to remove facial hair. It has to be safer than me blasting you in the face with dark magic."

She crossed the room and took the razor from him. "I guess it couldn't hurt to try."

Five minutes later she emerged, clean shaven, from the bathroom. "How do I look?"

"Gorgeous. How's it feel?"

"The skin's a little sensitive, but other than that not bad."

"Cool. You can keep the razor if you want."

"Thanks, but I have a pack in my room."

An image of Maria shaving her legs in the shower popped unbidden into his head. He sighed and shook it off. "I forgot to tell you. We got the engine running."

"That was fast. I thought it would take you longer to figure out how to replicate all the mechanical issues."

"We simplified everything so all that was left was basically the cylinder, piston, and drive shaft. Next week we're going to start working on a go cart."

She smiled. "If you were half as enthusiastic about magic as you were about your toys, you'd be the greatest wizard since—"

"Don't say it."

"Merlin."

* * *

Conryu couldn't stop pacing as he waited for Mrs. Umbra to arrive. Three days ago he'd managed to cover the entire island in Cloak of Darkness and she pronounced him ready to confront Lucifer. He'd been eager at the time, but now that the moment was here, fear had replaced excitement.

After another ten trips up and down the aisle he stopped and sat on the nearest desk. He needed to follow the advice he always gave Kelsie. Slow breaths. Focus on the goal. He knew what he was capable of when using the Death Stick. He'd pop in to Hell, force Lucifer to remove the brand, and be back before he knew it.

Right. That's why he hadn't mentioned anything to Maria over dinner last night. At least her beard had stopped growing. Thinking about those soft, smooth cheeks covered in thick, bristly hair brought a smile to his face and eased his nerves.

It was easy for him to think of Maria as perfect when it came to schoolwork so it was heartening that even she made an occasional mistake. Not that she saw it that way, but with a perfectionist you had to make allowances.

When Mrs. Umbra finally arrived he'd calmed down enough to think he had a chance of succeeding. A frown made her wrinkles deepen. "Are you certain you want to go through with this? The risks are tremendous."

"I know, but the risk of doing nothing and then having to travel by dark portal… I don't know. As long as I know he's just waiting on the other side for me to arrive makes it hard to concentrate on anything else. I need to do this as much to get it off my mind as anything else."

She nodded and held the Death Stick out to him. "I understand. I'll prepare the circle, you work on strengthening your link to the artifact."

Conryu focused all his attention on the Death Stick. What had once been a vibration when he first picked it up had now evolved into an almost electric current running between them. It approached the intensity of his connection to Prime.

While Mrs. Umbra drew on the floor he did the visualization exercises she'd taught him. Over and over again he imagined the enhanced domination spell overwhelming Lucifer and forcing him to obey.

Sometime later he was brought back to reality when Mrs. Umbra said. "We're ready."

He opened his eyes and studied the spell circle she'd drawn. It was different than before, simpler. When he commented on it she said, "It's a simple portal containment spell. You're not going to form a contract after all."

"Right, so is there some way for me to retreat if this doesn't work?" When he'd gone to form a contract with Cerberus he couldn't return unless he succeeded. That was pressure he didn't need while dealing with Lucifer.

"Don't worry, I left an escape valve this time. Just say 'return' in Infernal and you'll be yanked back to our reality."

"That's a relief, not that I intend to fail."

"No one intends to fail, but it still happens. Good luck."

She patted him on the knee as he and Prime stepped into the center of the circle. He touched the Death Stick to the central rune and willed it to activate.

He blinked and found himself surrounded by darkness. A rough, dry tongue licked his left cheek while a giant head rubbed his right side.

"Good boy." Conryu rubbed Cerberus behind the ears and the giant demon dog groaned like a puppy. He really needed to introduce Cerberus to Kelsie. If she saw him like this she wouldn't be at all afraid of him.

Cerberus's heads all popped up and a deep growl rumbled through his chest. Something moved out in the darkness. "It's okay, boy. I was expecting him."

Cerberus whined and Conryu knew how he felt. Just because he was expecting Lucifer didn't mean he was looking forward to the confrontation.

When he could make out the horns on the demon's head he began the domination spell. "By my will be bound, oh child of Hell. Your thoughts are my thoughts, your desires, my desires, Domination!"

The massive power gathered in the Death Stick by his spell lashed out and crashed into Lucifer's mind. Unlike the weaker demons he'd subjugated, the Prince of Lies resisted with more strength than even Conryu had expected.

Lucifer clutched his skull, his handsome, arrogant face twisted in pain. Over and over in his mind Conryu commanded the demon to submit.

Lucifer snarled. "You think you can command me, mortal. Me! Who is more akin to a god than a demon. I will break your spell and rend you limb from limb."

Conryu ignored the threats and continued to press his commands with everything he had. Lucifer continued to resist just as fiercely.

Cerberus's head brushed his hand and a jolt of power ran through him and out into Lucifer as the demon dog joined his will to Conryu's.

Lucifer howled and thrashed. For a moment he feared their combined power wouldn't be enough. Then Lucifer's face went slack and the spell settled into place.

Conryu didn't dare let out so much as a sigh of relief lest he break his fragile spell. "Remove your brand from my arm."

He raised his arm and pulled the sleeve of his robe back revealing the mark underneath. Lucifer raised his trident like a zombie and waved it over Conryu's arm. The mark burned even worse for a second then it was gone.

"Leave this place and never show yourself before me again." He combined that command with an overwhelming desire for Lucifer to be gone.

The giant demon fled back the way he'd come as fast as he could fly. Conryu held the Death Stick up and ready until Lucifer had moved fully beyond his sight. Only then did he release the sigh he'd been holding back.

"That was impressive." Soft hands massaged his shoulders while a tail wrapped around his thigh and worked its way up toward his groin.

They'd been so focused on Lucifer neither he nor Cerberus had noticed the Dark Lady's approach. That she hadn't interfered was a point in her favor, but she was still a demon.

Conryu pulled away and spun to face her, the Death Stick between them.

She raised her hands and her perfect lips curled into a smile. "I have no wish to fight you. Your display with Lucifer got me all excited." She ran her hands down her breasts and stomach.

Conryu had more trouble concentrating now than he did when Lucifer burned his mark off. "What do you want?"

Her lips parted revealing elongated eyeteeth. "I want to be your friend, your special friend."

He raised an eyebrow at that. If Maria was jealous of him and Kelsie how would she react to him being special friends with the Dark Lady? "I'm not really looking to form another demon contract. Cerberus is a fine partner and Prime is an outstanding familiar."

Cerberus barked once as if in agreement. She glowered at him prompting the demon dog to shy away and whimper. "I can offer you far more than these limited allies you've chosen."

He allowed himself another long look at her perfect figure. That brought her smile back.

"I know you desire me, mortal. Accept me in Cerberus's place and I shall give you pleasure beyond anything you can conceive of. We can seal the bargain with a kiss."

She leaned in, her lips glistening. Conryu's head swam and he couldn't focus. This was wrong, but for the life of him he couldn't figure out why.

Prime flew in front of him, blocking off his view of the Dark Lady. The moment he did Conryu's mind cleared.

Bitch! She'd used some sort of magic on him. "Cloak of Darkness."

The anti-magic coating covered him and Prime a moment before the scholomantic went flying. When she saw Conryu covered in darkness the Dark Lady bared her fangs and hissed. "You would have had much more fun if you'd just played along."

"I will not be your slave." He raised the Death Stick between them and held his free hand out for Prime.

Her expression smoothed as though nothing had happened. "Perhaps I was a bit forward. It is my nature after all. What if we tried something else, sort of a getting to know you phase. I could be your agent. All powerful dark wizards need a demonic agent to keep them abreast of what's happening in Hell. If I was your agent I wouldn't be able to work against you."

Prime slapped into his hand, but he never took his eyes off the Dark Lady. "What's in it for you?"

She pressed a hand over her heart. "I only want to help."

"Then don't lie to me. If you say there's nothing in this for you then I call bullshit. You're looking for a power boost."

"Such a charming mortal expression. Fine, I want a power boost. The stronger the wizard the more powerful I become. Why do you think Lucifer was so eager to kill you after you refused him?"

"He didn't want anyone else to form a contract with me and grow stronger."

She nodded. "With your power you'd have your pick of demonic servants. Now that you've cut ties with Lucifer others will come calling. With me as your agent you'll have someone to warn you when the next one decides to try and strike a bargain."

Conryu lowered the Death Stick slightly. If she was telling the truth there was certainly something to her suggestion. It was simply too much for him to decide in his exhausted state.

She seemed to sense his wavering and leaned closer, giving an up-close look at her exquisite chest. "I have much to offer."

No kidding. "I'll think about it. Return!"

In a blink he and Prime were back in the dark magic classroom. Returning to the real world drained the last of his strength. He wobbled and barely made it to a nearby chair before his legs gave out.

"Is it done?" Mrs. Umbra hobbled over to him and reclaimed the Death Stick from his nerveless fingers.

"Yeah, but there's something else we need to discuss when I'm less exhausted."

"My office, after the evening meal tomorrow."

He nodded and fell asleep in the chair.

* * *

Conryu's head throbbed, though he was pretty sure it wasn't from magical backlash. He was sitting in the cafeteria waiting for Maria to join him for dinner. The voices of the other students chattering about this and that, none of it remotely serious, set his nerves on end. What he wouldn't have given to talk to Jonny for an hour about sports or bikes or just about anything besides magic or demons. He might as well have wished to visit the moon, he had about as much chance of having that granted.

He'd woken up half an hour ago in the dark magic classroom, alone and with a blanket draped over him. He'd have to remember to thank Mrs. Umbra tomorrow, which brought him back to the source of his current headache. Despite his most earnest wish to have as little to do with the politics of magic as possible he kept getting dragged deeper into it.

Between the Department and the Dark Lady's warning it was like he'd gotten stuck in quicksand. At least whatever they were serving tonight smelled good. He was about to check it out when Maria pushed through the doors. She waved and smiled, making her way over to join him at their usual table.

"Have you been waiting long? I was practicing bone fusions and totally lost track of time."

"I've been here maybe fifteen minutes. How's your…?" He brushed his cheek with his index finger.

"Not a single hair in twenty-four hours. I think it's run its course. Thank goodness for that. What about you? You're looking a little rough around the edges."

"It was an eventful afternoon." He filled her in on his confrontation, careful to keep his voice low. It wasn't necessarily a secret that he was having demon issues, but he didn't want to announce it to the whole world either. When he finished Maria was staring at him. "I'm supposed to talk to Mrs. Umbra tomorrow about the whole agent thing. Do you know anything about it?"

Maria shook her head. "Mom never wanted to get mixed up in politics, either human or spirit. It's one of the reasons she doesn't work for the Department. That and private practice pays better."

"I never wanted to get mixed up in it either, but from the sound of it, now that I've chased off Lucifer, I'm going to have a bunch of other demons looking to make use of my power. I swear I wish I could rip this power out of my body and stick it in someone else."

Maria reached out and took his hand. "I'm glad you're the one who got it. I know you don't want it, but can you imagine what someone inclined to evil could accomplish with your magic? The world should be grateful someone as kind and honorable as you were born with it."

Conryu kissed her cheek. "Thanks. Let's find something to eat."

They collected their food and while they ate Maria told him about her studies. She'd healed a bird's wing, enabling it to fly again. Only her and two others had succeeded at that complex ritual. He smiled as she went on and on in fine detail as only Maria could when she was fully engrossed in a subject.

Her absolute delight in her studies was infectious and his headache faded away. She said it was lucky that he was born with the power, but Conryu thought it would have been much better if Maria had been the one to get it. On the other hand, he doubted she would be as happy if she had to spend her afternoons in Hell or worrying about whether the religious nuts, the crazy wizards, or the devil would be the one to succeed in murdering her.

The thought of Maria having to deal with all that made him glad, just for a second, that he was the one with the power and not her.

* * *

As Conryu made his way upstairs to Mrs. Umbra's office he wondered for the hundredth time why he bothered going to dark magic class at all. He sat there for two hours watching the girls doing circle casting and studying Infernal with Prime. He gained nothing from the former and could easily do the latter in the library or his room.

If nothing else he could now carry on a reasonable conversation in the demonic language. He wasn't fluent yet, but he was getting there. Mrs. Umbra's door opened at his approach. It was like the doors at the grocery store only with magic instead of electronics. Probably shouldn't make the comparison to his teacher.

Mrs. Umbra was seated behind her desk scowling at the Death Stick which rested in front of her. She looked up when he entered and waved him to an empty chair.

"Everything okay?" He settled into the guest seat.

"I'm just reminding this ungrateful artifact who its proper master is. You spoiled it and now it's trying to refuse my magic."

"Sorry."

She waved him off. "It's fine. I sorted it out, but you can't use it again. If you do I fear there'll be no getting it back."

"I didn't want to use it the first time, but circumstances forced my hand."

"Shit happens, as the kids like to say. So what's so important?"

He gave her the gist of his conversation with the Dark Lady. "She seems to think other demons are going to come calling. I'd really like to dismiss that out of hand, but I can't. Everything she said makes too much sense.

"You're right and I should have considered the repercussions of driving off Lucifer more closely. That said, I don't see any alternative to removing his brand since he kept trying to kill you."

"Agreed. But that begs the question of whether I need an agent in Hell or not. Do you have one?"

"I do. An imp I call Zippy because he's always flitting around like a humming bird. He keeps me abreast of what's happening in a general way, armies of demons gathering, two of the princes going to war, that sort of thing. Zippy doesn't have the access to find out detailed plots so he's less useful than he might be. I made the deal with him when I was young and never bothered ending it."

"So what should I do? Do I take the Dark Lady up on her offer or do I find an imp or some other minor demon?"

"An imp wouldn't do you any good." She sighed. "I hate to let that harpy get a single talon into you, but I fear she's your best bet. You're already partially connected anyway. If you form a proper contract she'll be unable to take any action against you and likewise you'll be unable to harm her."

"I wasn't planning on trying to harm her." In fact he'd prefer to have nothing at all to do with her.

"I know, so the contract gains you a great deal and costs you nothing. I'll write it up for you like I did with Cerberus then you can copy it and show it to her during our next class."

"You're going to have to teach me that spell circle you use so you won't have to keep drawing it for me."

"Your book should have the circle, it's a standard spell." She snapped her fingers. "That's your homework. Memorize the circle so you can draw it when we meet the day after tomorrow."

That'd teach him to open his big mouth.

* * *

Conryu appeared once again on the border of Hell, contract in hand. He'd drawn the circle to Mrs. Umbra's satisfaction on the first try, which both pleased and surprised him. As always Cerberus was on the other side waiting for him. The demon dog seemed anxious and he suspected he knew why.

He scratched the central head behind the ear. "Don't worry,

I'm not going to end our contract. She's going to be busy spying on the other demons so your job isn't in danger."

Cerberus barked and gave him a playful butt with his right head. Conryu laughed and gave him a swat on the flank.

"A boy and his dog, how sweet." The Dark Lady appeared from above and to his right. Her flimsy black dress swirled around her as her wings flapped and she landed in front of him. "I assume you've considered my offer."

"I did. Here's my counteroffer." He handed her the contract.

The Dark Lady's expression went from cool to bright and back again as she read the various clauses Mrs. Umbra had included. The whole thing was only a page long. She said the simpler the contract the less chance a wily demon might find something to pervert to her benefit.

At last she lowered the paper and looked at him. "This is more generous and detailed than I expected. I assume you had help writing it?"

"I consulted a more experienced wizard, yes. So is it a deal?"

"It is. With this I'll move into the upper echelon of Hell." She scratched her finger and let a drop of thick black blood drip onto the paper.

A cord of power shot from his chest to hers. For a moment his mind was overwhelmed with visions of lust and power. Every act of domination or perversion conceivable flooded into him. There was no rhyme or reason to it, just a riot of images coming and going so fast he could hardly separate one from the next.

It was over in seconds. When he recovered his wits he found the Dark Lady licking her lips and smiling. Her presence had expanded, that was the only way to describe the feeling he got when he looked at her. The contract had served its purpose and been consumed.

"Was that your mind I saw?"

"Only the tiniest piece of it." She glided closer and rested her hands on his shoulders, her face just inches from his. "I could teach you so much more. You've only scratched the surface of your capability. It's going to be a dark and glorious journey, Master. I am eager to begin."

"You're eager to show off your new power."

Her smile grew and her grip tightened. "I can't keep any secrets from you, can I. You're right. I'm looking forward to returning to the Black City and putting several of my ill-mannered former peers in their proper place. With the power I've gained it will not be difficult."

"How much has our bargain increased your strength?"

"I'm half again as powerful as I was. Alas, you won't receive a similar boost. Your gains will be much more focused. You will find spells that affect the minds of your targets simpler and more potent than they otherwise would be. That is my area of expertise after all." She leaned closer and kissed his cheek. "Call me some evening, Master, and I will be happy to instruct you."

Prime flew closer. "I will handle the master's instruction."

The Dark Lady flicked a glance at the scholomantic and immediately dismissed him. Conryu had the impression using magic was the last thing she planned to instruct him in.

He needed to move this conversation in a different direction. "How will you contact me if there's a threat?"

"In your dreams. When your mind is free our link will allow me to create a lucid dream where we can interact."

"Okay, good luck. Return!"

He was once more back in the classroom. Mrs. Umbra was staring at him while leaning on the Death Stick. "How'd it go?"

"She accepted and seemed well pleased with the terms. She plans to use her newfound power to put some rivals in what she considers their proper place."

Mrs. Umbra snorted. "Typical demonic behavior. You've made a lot of progress this year and we still have months to go. If anyone had told me how far you'd advance in seven months I would have said it was impossible."

If someone had told Conryu how deep down the magic rabbit hole he was going to be yanked in seven months he'd have said the same thing. Yet here they were. He tried to think how to get his life back on track and failed.

What in the world was going to happen to him? He didn't know the answer to that question and it scared him more than a little.

8

IN BETWEEN

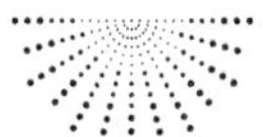

"Woo-hoo!" Sonja shouted as the go cart leapt over a hill and went airborne. When the cart landed Conryu wrestled with the steering wheel, trying to keep them out of the woods. He was doing his best to stay near the edge of the grounds so they didn't tear up the soft earth. The frost had only gone out a week ago and this was the first day they'd deemed it warm enough for a test drive. That combined with the fact that finals started in three days meant it was today or never.

The controls were loose jointed and had at least six inches of play whichever way he turned the wheel. Still, considering they'd slapped it together in about twenty hours, the Blinky Mobile, as Sonja christened it, was handling her maiden voyage pretty well. They hadn't flipped, crashed, or exploded so Conryu was happy.

What they had done was gather an audience. Scores of students and teachers had come outside to watch their mad rush around the grounds. Conryu grinned, for once not caring that everyone was staring at him. They hit the beach, fishtailed a couple times in the sand, and roared on.

"Can it go any faster?" Sonja's blond hair was blowing in the wind and he hadn't seen her this happy since the Brawl.

They'd altered the magic so the engine's speed was controlled by the one who activated it. Conryu wasn't overly confident in his crude transmission, but then he didn't really care if the cart survived beyond today's joyride so he willed it to rev up and the motor obliged.

Sand flew and they shot down the beach like madmen. He slowed a fraction and turned back onto the grounds. The plan was to make a full circle and end up back at the shack. If they survived Crystal said she might go for a ride too.

Sonja braced herself as they went flying over another hill. The second half of the trip was a little smoother than the first as he grew more comfortable with the steering. They finally skidded to a stop beside the shack. The earth magic brakes Crystal had dreamed up worked like a charm.

"That was awesome!" Sonja leapt out of the cart and danced around like a six-year-old.

Conryu couldn't argue. It wasn't his bike, but the cart was a hell of a lot of fun to drive.

"Did you write your parents yet?" He wanted to ask when he had her in a good mood.

"I sent the letter Monday, but I haven't heard back yet. I hope they don't get mad."

Conryu had finally convinced Sonja to tell her parents she wanted to do something besides work at their factory. She'd sent their engine designs to a magical engineering firm and they'd been impressed. Sonja thought they might offer her a job.

Crystal watched them, smiling and shaking her head. Before he could ask her if she wanted to go for a spin Dean Blane landed a few feet away and marched over.

He winced. They'd torn the lawn up a little, but it was nothing ten minutes of earth magic couldn't fix.

"So you got it running." The dean looked the go cart all over. "I have to say, when you told me about the magic engine I had my doubts, but it works."

"Sonja and Crystal deserve all the credit." Conryu leaned back in his crude seat. "I'm just a mechanic."

The dean jumped in beside him. "Take me for a ride."

He glanced at Sonja and Crystal who gave him the thumbs up. "Hang on."

Conryu willed the engine to life and they went roaring down the path. Now that he was getting comfortable he took the turns even faster, one time getting up on two wheels. When they finished Dean Blane's hair was going every which way and she had the biggest grin he'd ever seen.

"I think I may appropriate this for my personal use. Switch places with me, I want to drive."

Conryu hopped out, deactivated the engine, and moved to the passenger seat. When Dean Blane had settled in the tires spun and they shot down the path. Though she didn't set as furious a pace as Conryu, Dean Blane went right along and two minutes later they were back where they started.

Despite the breeze sweat covered her forehead. "That really drains you, doesn't it?"

Conryu hadn't noticed much of a drain and when he said so she smiled and shook her head, muttering about youth.

"Just don't overdo it. You have finals in three days." With that she flew back to the main building.

Conryu spent the next hour giving rides to anyone that wanted one, including Maria and Kelsie. When he finished he collected Prime from the shack and headed to his room, suddenly in need of a nap.

* * *

A revving engine drew Lady Mockingbird to the window. The idiot boy had built a go cart and was racing the thing around the grounds. She'd heard the rumors that the golem club had moved on to making a magic engine and dismissed them as foolish gossip. It appeared it wasn't gossip after all, but the project wasn't any less foolish. Why would anyone bother to create something that only one in ten thousand people could use?

She slid the curtain shut. Let the abomination enjoy himself. By the end of the week he'd be dead and forgotten. It was time to place the final ingredient into the Chimera Jar.

Her three strongest light magic wizards were waiting for her in the casting chamber. After the debacle with the basilisk she'd made a point of having multiple wizards of the proper alignment on hand to control the spirit she summoned.

It galled her to have to rely on her subordinates, but there was no way around the fact that she simply wasn't strong enough on her own, outside of fire, to handle the bindings. It was the nature of magic regardless of what her ego would have preferred.

She descended the stairs and entered her casting chamber. The jar sat in the middle of the chamber, right where it had rested since she acquired it months ago. It glowed red, brown, and blue. All she needed now was the unifying light element. An angel would be far too risky so she'd decided to settle for a golden lion.

The standard four girls were in place to maintain the wards and three more in white robes were waiting to seize control of the lion when it appeared. Everything was as ready as possible.

"Wards!" She raised her hands and the girls began their chant. When the protections were in place Lady Mockingbird glanced at the light wizards and they each nodded once that they were ready. "Here we go."

"Through Heaven's light I call the golden guardian. Appear before me, guardian of Heaven's gates, Divine Summoning!" Lady Mockingbird completed the spell and a disk of light appeared.

Through the portal walked a lion as tall as she was and shining with golden light. "Now!"

The light magic wizards chanted as one. "Divine chains hold all things in place, Heaven's Binding!"

White chains shot from small portals and wrapped around the lion's neck and limbs. It roared at near-deafening volume and struggled to break free. Inch by inch the chains pulled the divine spirit closer and closer to the jar.

Her part of the casting was done, but Lady Mockingbird did her best to will the lion closer. Just a few more feet. Her jaw clenched so tight it ached.

The lion's glow intensified and one of the chains shattered. It pulled away from the jar and one of the girls let out a low moan. Her light wizards' faces contorted as they fought to control the spirit. Their hands and knees trembled.

Her girls were too weak. This was why she hated relying on others. For the most part they were useless.

She stepped to the side and raised her hands. Lady Mockingbird would have preferred to avoid damaging the spirit, but if the alternative was failure then she had no choice. "Burn and batter my enemy, Flame Fists!"

She punched both hands toward the lion and a pair of fists made of fire the size of pumpkins lashed out, striking the spirit in the chest and driving it back.

With its balance unsettled the girls managed to drag it just short of the jar.

Just a little more. She punched out again and the fists pounded the lion's chest. It staggered back another step.

With a thought she activated the jar. Black tentacles shot out and wrapped the spirit up before dragging it inside.

The girls collapsed, but she paid them no heed. Lady Mockingbird had eyes only for the jar. The separate colors swirled and became one even as they grew continuously brighter. For a full minute the surface of the jar resembled a whirlpool of paint.

At last the light faded. She rested her finger on the jar and probed the power inside. She'd done it. The chimera was ready to be released at her whim.

"Mistress?" One of the girls that had maintained the barrier knelt beside the unconscious light wizards. "The backlash has knocked them out."

"They served their purpose. Put them to bed. If they're strong they'll recover quickly. If not..." She shrugged. They wouldn't be the first bodies she'd disposed of over the years.

* * *

Clair sat in the corner of the Department's spare casting chamber and tried to calm her raging mind. The room contained only the hard, plastic chair she'd brought with her. Everything else was white and silence. It almost reached the level of sensory deprivation. In theory it should help her push past whatever had blocked her access to her magic. In theory.

She stood up, raised her hands, and focused her will. The moment she did blinding pain crashed through her brain and made the casting chamber spin. Three months and she still couldn't cast. So much for theories. What good was a wizard that couldn't use magic?

Terra tried to assure her that eventually her power would return, but the pity in her fellow wizard's eyes sickened her. She accepted pity from no one, least of all a colleague with weaker magical potential.

"Still no good?" Speak of the devil. Terra stood in the doorway watching.

Clair shook her head. "How long can this last?"

"It's only been three months. Try to be patient." Terra walked over and gave her a pat on the back.

Clair almost punched her. She didn't need sympathy, she needed her magic.

"The chief wants to see us."

"Why include me? I'm useless right now."

"Have you forgotten everything you know about magic?" Terra's voice turned hard. "You're still a member of this office, try and act like it. Orin's at his wit's end. The island's in sight of the city and in a week will be within the area we projected was most likely Mercia's target. If there was ever an all hands on deck moment, this is it."

Clair straightened. "Alright, let's go."

The two women made the short trip upstairs. Inside the chief's office Lin was already waiting. Orin watched them from behind his desk. He looked like he'd lost twenty pounds and gained a bunch of new wrinkles. Clair shook off her self-pity. She wasn't the only one with problems.

"Clair?" He raised an eyebrow.

"No change yet, sir. What's the situation?"

He waved them into the empty chairs and sat behind his desk. "I've asked yet again for reinforcements and been told yet again they have no one to spare. Shizuku's offered to help however she can and I've gotten in touch with a handful of the most powerful local wizards. I was vague on the details, but received promises of aid should the worst happen. I never realized just how few wizards of real power there were in the city."

Terra sighed. "Wizards with high combat potential are rare everywhere. That's what makes them so valuable. Will you bring Conryu in when school ends for the year?"

"He's already in this up to his neck. If there's trouble I'll call him, but until something overt happens, I doubt his abilities will be much help. Hopefully he'll get at least a week to enjoy his summer break."

Clair snorted a laugh. The floating island would be in the contact zone less than a week after he returned home. If nothing changed this was going to be a miserable summer for everyone.

"I've received a shipment of five hundred explosive rounds and ten pistols capable of using them. Not nearly enough, but with the conflict in the north still going strong it was all they could spare. Lin's going to take care of distributing them to a small group of officers with the intention of deploying them in the affected area. I have no idea how much difference they'll make, but every little bit helps." Orin favored them with a desperate look. "Any other ideas? Feel free to speak up."

"What about providing emergency shelters?" Clair asked. "Your building and the Department offices are both warded against magical intrusion. Could we move people in the affected area to safe houses like that?"

"Some, certainly, but if our estimates are correct close to half a million people live in the target zone. There aren't enough secure places in the city to protect everyone and we don't want to start a riot."

"And remember," Terra said. "Once the shadow beasts appear they'll be free to move anywhere in the city after the sun sets."

Though she wouldn't admit it, Clair hadn't even considered the monsters simply spreading out as they pleased. Once the gates opened no one would be safe anywhere in the city.

9

SET THE TRAP

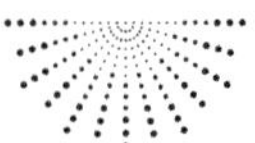

Lady Mockingbird stepped out onto the dock behind the sorority house, the Chimera Jar in her hands. She'd traded her red robes for gray to better blend in to the dark night. Not that she expected to run into anyone out on the island, but better safe than sorry. All three of her light magic girls had woken up with no lasting damage from the ritual. That was a blessing since she had already drawn too much attention to the sorority. Three missing students wouldn't be any help.

Tomorrow was the last day of finals and the abomination would be going to the island to take his test. She called the wind and took to the air. All she had to do was put the jar in a place he'd be sure to approach and set the terms of activation. Once she'd done that, his fate was sealed.

Below her stars sparkled on the lake's surface. It was nice to fly without worrying about the cold or snow. She hated winter. When she received her promotion to Hierarch she planned to ask for a posting somewhere warm, maybe the Republic of Australia.

The flight only took seconds. She started to descend to the central clearing when she spotted movement. Lady Mockingbird halted and hovered silently above. From the edge of the woods a small, dark figure emerged.

What was Angeline Umbra doing out here this late at night? Probably making one last check to be sure everything was safe for her precious protégé. Lady Mockingbird went higher. She'd just wait until the crone finished her rounds then set her trap.

She couldn't help smiling. Wouldn't the old bat be surprised when the Chimera Jar opened and the beast slaughtered her favorite?

Angeline puttered about in the clearing. Lady Mockingbird was too high to make out what she was doing, but whatever it was she wished Angeline would hurry up. She didn't want to fly around all night. Angeline went rigid and started to look up.

She sensed me!

Lady Mockingbird flew as fast as she could in the opposite direction to which the head of dark magic was looking. She dove toward the forest, landed on one of the paths, and canceled every spell she had running.

Shit!

Even without her magic Angeline would sense the Chimera Jar itself. She ran down the path to give herself a little more time. When she found a little niche between a pair of twisted evergreens she stuck the jar in it and raised both hands in front. "Sprits of earth and stone hide this object from all prying eyes, Earth Screen."

The jar sank into the ground. Her spell would block even magical sight from locating it. She dashed off again, angling away from the hidden jar. It would be easier to fly, but if she did that Angeline would be sure to know someone was out here and given the numerous attempts on Conryu's life, she might call off the test tomorrow or move it elsewhere. Neither option would give her the opportunity she needed.

Best to stay on the ground and run and hide like she was a little girl playing hide and seek. It never crossed her mind to confront the withered master of dark magic. Not that she was afraid, certainly that wasn't it. She just didn't want to give away the fact that she was present on the island.

She ducked off the trail and into a thick patch of evergreens. She debated another concealment spell, but decided to take her chances.

Five minutes later the tapping of a walking stick on stone drew her attention. Lady Mockingbird held her breath.

Her hunter was right there, twenty feet away, back on the path. Surely the old wizard wouldn't venture off the smooth trail and risk getting tangled up in the brush and vines.

Seconds felt like minutes and minutes like hours. Her heart hammered in her chest and she wished Angeline away like a child trying to frighten away a monster. At long last the tapping resumed and slowly grew fainter.

Lady Mockingbird blew out the breath she'd been holding and slumped to the ground. She rested for a few seconds then scrambled to her feet. She'd shadow Angeline and be sure she'd gone before retrieving the jar and setting her trap. That was the safest way. There was too much riding on this to take unnecessary chances.

* * *

Angeline shrugged and continued down the path. The magic she'd sensed earlier was gone and she couldn't find anything that might be the source. It was probably just a passing pixie and her paranoia combining to lead her on a wild goose chase.

She never used to be this jumpy, but since Conryu arrived it seemed her life had gotten many times more complicated. Not that she blamed the boy. He hadn't put a toe out of line since he arrived, unlike the members of a certain sorority.

No, just being who he was made him a target and she'd be

damned if she let anything happen to him. He was her hope for a proper retirement. When he graduated she planned to offer him the Death Stick and the academy her resignation. She was getting too old for this. It was time to find somewhere warm, and do a little consulting and a lot of lying on a beach.

She walked down the path as fast as her achy legs allowed. She'd left some surprises for Conryu and still had one to go. She smiled as she climbed the path. There was no question he had the raw power to deal with her surprises, the interesting thing was whether he had the smarts to figure the right way to use it.

A twig snapped and she paused. That wasn't a pixie. The little wind spirits couldn't be noisy if they wanted to. She doubted anyone would be pulling a prank on her, none of the students had the nerve to try it. After several seconds of silence she continued on her way.

Ten minutes later she reached a clearing on one of the island's plateaus. She drew a circle and delayed summoning. This would be a fun one for him. And even better for her as it was the last thing she had to do before returning to her bed.

When the circle was complete she listened once more for any movement and found all quiet. She shook her head and called the wind. She was definitely getting too old for this.

* * *

Lady Mockingbird feared Angeline would hear her heart pounding when she snapped that twig, but it appeared she worried for nothing. She watched until the old wizard was out of sight then finally relaxed. That had been far too close.

She retreated back the way she'd come, pausing long enough to collect the jar. Back in the clearing she set the jar a little ways away from the pillar that controlled the shield around the island. She crouched down in front of the jar and placed her hand on it.

The magic awakened at her touch and she set it to activate

when the abomination entered the clearing with all three crystal keys. The idea of killing him in the moment of his assumed triumph amused her greatly.

She straightened up, her knees popping in protest. Just one more thing to do. She placed her hand on the pillar and willed the runes controlling it to appear. An alteration here and an extra rune there would assure he couldn't escape and help couldn't arrive in time.

Lady Mockingbird wiped her sweaty brow. She'd done everything she could. Time would tell if it was enough. She flew back to the sorority and a hot bath. Tomorrow promised to be an interesting day.

10

FINALS

They were the last to go, of course. If there was one thing Conryu had gotten used to over the past year it was going last, that and getting ugly looks. The rest of his class had passed their finals yesterday and the day before. Maria was doing her light magic final today as well. Conryu had wished her luck before joining Kelsie on the lakeshore.

Speaking of whom, beside him in the rocking boat Kelsie looked like she wanted to throw up. It wasn't motion sickness, there wasn't enough chop on the lake to say so. In fact it was a beautiful spring day, the sun was warm on his face, the leaves were out, and a light breeze filled the air. They each had packs with a day's worth of supplies.

The dark magic final lasted a maximum of twenty-four hours. In fact the first group had needed most of that time to complete the test, whatever it was. They weren't allowed to talk about it beforehand. They'd receive their instructions when they landed on the beach.

"Are you okay?" Assistant Dean Saint sat at the rear of the boat as she guided them to the island.

"Fine." Kelsie didn't make the lie sound believable. Her ordinarily pale complexion had gone ghost white, the black robes she wore heightening the effect.

"Let me guess," Conryu said. "Your mom called yesterday to offer some unwanted encouragement?"

Kelsie nodded. "She said not to disgrace the family name any more than I already have."

"Charming. Don't worry, we'll knock this out of the park. Your mom will be so proud she won't know what to think."

Kelsie reached across and held his hand. He squeezed back, trying to send reassuring thoughts. They'd gotten pretty comfortable working together over the last three months. Kelsie no longer flinched when they used fusion magic. He'd hoped to introduce her to Cerberus, but hadn't figured out how to go about it yet.

Their boat slid up on the beach and they all piled out. He and Kelsie shrugged their packs on and turned to face Mrs. Saint.

The assistant dean pulled a folded piece of paper out of her robe and handed it to Kelsie. "Here are your instructions. That paper is a map. Three locations are marked, each containing a key hidden within protective magic. Your test is to retrieve the keys and insert them into the column you'll find in the exact center of the island. You have one day to complete the test. For the duration a barrier will be raised over the island to prevent anyone coming or going. When all three keys are in place the barrier will fall and I'll return to pick you up. Questions?"

Sounded simple to Conryu. When Kelsie shook her head Mrs. Saint continued. "Then good luck. The barrier will go up as soon as I clear the beach and your time will begin."

Mrs. Saint hopped back in her boat, backed off the beach, turned, and sped away. A shimmer went through the air as the barrier fell into place. Conryu muttered, "Reveal." The shield looked strong, but nothing he couldn't blast through if it became necessary.

He turned back to Kelsie. "Let's have a look at the map."

She unfolded it and he moved closer. Their landing point was marked with a black star. An X indicated the pillar in the center of the island and the three keys were shown as little red triangles. The nearest key was maybe a quarter mile from their starting point. Shouldn't take long to walk that. According to the map it was hidden in a cave.

"Which one do you want to try first?" Kelsie asked.

Conryu pointed at the cave. "May as well do the closest one first, don't you think?"

"Okay." She folded up the map and tucked it in her pocket.

They set out at a steady march, a pace Conryu could keep up for hours if need be. They soon left the beach behind and entered the thick spruce growing at the edge of the forest. The prickly needles scratched his arms through his robe as he tried to break a trail for Kelsie.

"If I'd known how thick the underbrush was I'd have packed a machete." He spat out a mouthful of needles. "You okay?"

"Fine. I'm not as frail as I look."

He grinned. It was good to see Kelsie showing a bit of spunk. He'd feared talking to her mother might have messed her up like at the midterm.

A hundred yards from the beach the thick evergreens thinned out and gave way to mature trees. He blew out a sigh of relief. If they'd had to walk all the way in that scrub it would have been rough.

Now that they had some space Kelsie moved up beside him. A little further inland the ground rose into hills. That was where they'd find the cave.

"So are we going to bother with the fusion thing or do you just want to dispel the wards yourself?"

"I think we'd better do the fusion thing."

"Why? At this point I realize my power is a meaningless addition to your strength."

He glanced over at her. She wasn't frowning or angry, thank goodness. "Mostly I was thinking that the teachers might be watching in a magic mirror and if I do all the work they might not give you credit for the final."

Her eyes widened. "I hadn't considered that. We'll definitely do the fusion magic. Thanks for not lying and saying you couldn't do it without me."

Conryu stopped and turned to face her full on. "I'm never going to lie to you, not unless I'm ordered to. You're my friend and I respect you too much to do something like that. There may be times when I can't tell you everything that's happening, but that will be because others have cautioned me against it or the information might put you in danger."

She blushed and looked away. "Sorry. I'm not used to the truth unless it's couched in an insult from my family."

"Your family sucks. You should spend a couple weeks in Sentinel with me and Maria this summer, see what a normal family looks like."

"Really? I'd... I'd like that. You know I don't think I've ever visited anyone without my mom and that was just business."

"Sure, we'll have pizza at Giovanni's, I'll take you for a ride on my bike, it'll be awesome." They stopped at the base of the foothills. "We have to be getting close. What's the map say?"

Kelsie dug it out again. "It says there's a lightning-scarred oak near the cave."

Conryu searched the treetops. The half-dead oak stood out like a sore thumb amongst the evergreens. It almost looked like someone had put it there intentionally to mark the key's location. Considering they were at a school for wizards that wasn't beyond the realm of possibility.

The oak was about a hundred yards to their left. He set off again. They hadn't taken more than a handful of steps when Kelsie asked, "You don't think Maria will mind if I come for a visit?"

"Why would she? I've already explained to her, several times, that we're just friends. Besides, she'll be busy working with her mom."

"Do you not have to work?" Kelsie asked between gasps as they climbed up a steep slope.

At the top he spotted a cave and since it was the only one remotely in the vicinity of the oak it had to be their target. It was so dark he couldn't see past the entrance. Kelsie was panting beside him so better to wait a little while before they explored further.

"I'll help Dad in the dojo and putter around my friend's garage, but without a work certificate of some sort my options are pretty limited. I don't have any overwhelming desire to spend my summer vacation working a fryer or waiting tables. I tried that two years ago and it sucked."

"No, that doesn't sound terribly appealing. The hard part now will be getting my mom to let me go."

"Let you? You're an adult, you don't need permission."

"I do if she locks me in the house."

He almost laughed, but from her grim expression he realized she wasn't kidding. What a screwed-up family. At least his mother only locked him up for his own safety. "Why don't you just come straight over from school? You're already packed and she can't lock you up if you don't go home."

"I don't know if I could defy her like that. My mom doesn't take that sort of thing lightly."

"Well, think it over. Whatever you decide I'll back you up. Shall we go collect that first key?"

Kelsie stood up straighter than he'd ever seen her. "Yes we shall."

* * *

As they strode down the hill toward the cave Conryu moved a little ahead of Kelsie. It was instinctive and he did it all the time when he was with Maria. Overprotective she liked to say. Better over than under he always countered. In this case it turned out to be a good decision. Halfway to the opening four fire cats appeared in a swirl of flames.

Conryu chanted Cloak of Darkness, dropped his pack and charged. The cats spread out to surround him.

He took out one with a roundhouse kick. The moment he did a second one sprang at his now unprotected leg.

Conryu leapt over it and pointed his right palm with the fingers crossed at its back. "Break."

He landed, rolled to his feet, and spun. Both hands came up in matched gestures. "Break!"

Two spheres of darkness struck the remaining fire cats, snuffing them out in an instant. No threats remained so he canceled the Cloak of Darkness.

"That was impressive." Kelsie had taken cover behind the massive oak tree. "I didn't expect to encounter any physical threats."

"I suspect Mrs. Umbra left them for me as a bonus test. They didn't even look at you, did they?"

"No, not so much as a glance. You think the summoning spell required them to focus on you?"

"Yeah. You don't know any defensive magic, do you?"

Kelsie shook her head. "Only the basic stuff they've taught us. Most of us don't get special training with the head of dark arts."

"If you want to sit in on one of my classes the only requirement for joining is a minimum of two attempts on your life. I think I'm up to four."

"I'll stick with the standard course of study, thanks. Besides, Mrs. Umbra makes me nervous."

"Why? She's been great with me."

"She reminds me of my grandmother." Kelsie shuddered.

Having met her grandmother Conryu seconded the emotion. Mrs. Umbra, on the other hand, was nothing like the domineering master of the Department of Magic. "I think if you got to know her you'd find she's really nice and I'm not just saying that because she's probably watching us."

Kelsie looked all around like she expected to find Mrs. Umbra hiding behind one of the nearby trees.

"Maybe we should go get the key," Conryu said. "I doubt we'll have any more to worry about at this site. Do you want to handle the light?"

Kelsie chanted and an orb of fire about the size of his fist appeared in the air beside her. He waved her toward the opening. "After you."

"I wouldn't want to be rude. Please, go ahead." She sent the ball of fire in ahead of them.

Conryu shrugged and walked in after it. Kelsie clutched his arm and walked along beside him until it became clear the cave was strictly a single-file proposition.

The cave appeared freshly dug. Some earth magic wizard had probably made it last week when they were working on the preparations for finals. Crystal said she'd done some casting to help the teachers get ready, though she wouldn't give him any details.

He brushed dangling roots out of the way. The tunnel didn't extend very far into the side of the hill and they soon reached a circular chamber. A low pedestal rose out of the ground and in the center sat a crystal key. Wards crackled in his enhanced vision, light and fire magic mingled together.

"I think we can handle this," Conryu said. "How about you?"

Kelsie studied the wards and nodded. "No sweat."

She moved behind him and put her hand on his back. Conryu cast the spell, careful to target only the wards and not the key itself. The protective magic sparked and vanished when his ray of darkness struck it.

Kelsie darted in front of him and snatched the key. "One down, two to go."

They retraced their steps and the moment he cleared the

entrance the cave collapsed with a whoosh. Kelsie squeaked and grabbed his arm again.

He patted her hand. "Relax, we're the last team remember? The cave was no doubt designed to be sealed when we finished our test."

She released him and brushed a stray hair out of her eyes. "They might have waited until we were a little further away."

He shrugged. "Where to next?"

She tucked the key away and dug out the map. "Ugh! Looks like the next key is on the northern tip of the island. Three-quarters of a mile if we set a straight course."

Conryu looked over her shoulder. "That's rough country." He pointed at two paths on the map. "If we take this one, then that one, it'll be easier walking."

She frowned and looked from the little marker on the side that said "half a mile to the inch" to the paths. "I'd say that route is more than twice as long, but I agree, thrashing through the shrubs is for the birds."

* * *

Kelsie trudged along behind Conryu. The path made for easier walking, but it was still uphill the whole way and she wasn't the world's greatest athlete, unlike her partner. She thought about how he handled those four fire cats and shook her head. It was like they were nothing to him.

He had very little in common with the other freshmen. She wished she could wield her magic with so much confidence. Though at the moment what she most wished was that she could climb the path without her legs and lungs burning. Maybe she should have taken those exercises the self-defense teacher assigned more seriously.

Five minutes later she couldn't take it anymore. "I need a rest."

Conryu stopped and glanced back at her. He wasn't even

breathing hard, damn him. "Sure. I'd say we have another half mile or so. Best to be rested in case Mrs. Umbra left another surprise."

"Do you think she might have?"

He grinned. She loved that expression. "I'd count on it. She wants to see how much I've learned."

"You've done pretty well so far."

Conryu looked around then motioned her to follow. A little ways off the trail was a fallen tree. He sat and patted the rough bark beside him. She settled in and sighed, delighted to get her weight off her feet. After a second she dared to lean against him. He felt safe and solid and warm.

"We've done pretty well so far."

She tilted her head up at him. "What?"

"You said I'd done pretty well, but what you meant was we. You and me are a team after all."

She restrained a laugh that would have sounded humorless and bitter if she'd let it out. It was sweet of him to say so, but they both knew she was more of a burden than a help. That he never treated her like a burden made Kelsie like him more than she should.

Sometimes she pretended he might like her as something more than a friend, then she saw him with Maria and knew she was dreaming. When they were together he looked so happy she wasn't certain what the right word was to describe it. That they argued like an old married couple only added to the impression.

"We are a team, at least for a day, though I don't think I bring much to the partnership."

"You're wrong. You bring something important: trust. When you put your hand on my back I know you won't do anything to put me at risk. That one fact makes you the perfect partner. There's only one other person I trust that much and she can't be near me when I use dark magic."

"Thanks." She stood up. Knowing he trusted her sent a jolt of energy through Kelsie. Whatever it took, she wouldn't let Conryu down. "Shall we move on?"

"Yeah." He led the way back to the path and they resumed their trudge.

Fifteen minutes later the path leveled out onto a plateau. She took the map out again. "It should be right around here somewhere."

They took three more steps away from the path. The stink of sulfur filled the air a moment before a black circle appeared on the ground. Conryu stepped in front of her.

Kelsie peeked around from behind him. In the center of the circle was a two-foot-tall humanoid with a tail and bat wings. She might not be the world's best dark wizard, but she knew an imp when she saw one.

It didn't attack, so clearly the test wasn't combat related. She stepped out from around Conryu and they moved closer.

"What do you think?" he asked.

Kelsie didn't know what to think. Clearly there wasn't a key in the area. "Beats me."

Conryu turned his gaze on the imp. "Do you have the key?"

The little demon stuck its tongue out at him. That wasn't very helpful.

Conryu nodded once. "I believe I know what's required."

He chanted a spell she'd never heard before. Dark power gathered and a shiver ran through her. This spell was of an order of magnitude greater than anything she'd ever experienced.

When he finished he thrust his hand at the imp. Its glowing eyes dimmed and its expression went slack.

"Do you have the key?" Conryu asked again.

"No," the imp answered in a dull monotone.

Kelsie swallowed the sudden lump in her throat. She might not have recognized the spell, but she recognized the effect. He cast Domination. That was an insanely high-level spell, certainly higher level than a first-year student should be able to use. What exactly was he learning in his extra class?

"Do you know where the key is?" Conryu asked.

"Yes."

"Where?"

The imp pointed to a spot further down the way. "Buried under a juniper bush." The instant it fell silent the imp and the dark magic circle both vanished.

"Guess he finished his task." Conryu shrugged and started toward the spot the imp pointed out.

Kelsie shook off her surprise and followed. "Where did you learn that spell?"

"That's a long story and I'm not sure I'm allowed to tell it to you. Suffice it to say there was an emergency with a demon and I had to learn it in a hurry."

She stared. Kelsie didn't know anything about an emergency involving a demon so whatever happened it couldn't have been at school. But if not at school, then where?

Conryu stopped and knelt down beside an evergreen bush about a foot around. He tipped it to the side and yanked out a box that resembled the ones the light magic class used in the midterm only it didn't have a latch or seam.

"No wards, but there's something magic inside."

Kelsie renewed her seeing spell. Sure enough the box was ordinary enough, but something was radiating magic from inside. "How do we open it?"

"I'm not sure we do. I think we're supposed to shatter the box without damaging the key inside."

She moved to stand behind him, but Conryu stopped her. "What?"

"You should cast the spell on your own."

She blinked, not certain she'd heard him correctly. "You think I should shatter the box?"

"Yeah. There are no wards protecting it, it's just a simple pine box. The truth is, I'm not certain I can cast the spell gently enough not to harm the key."

She chewed her lip then nodded. "I can try."

"No. Don't doubt yourself. Remember what I said before the midterm. You have to believe the spell will work." Conryu set the box in front of her and took a step back. "You can do it. I know you can."

Kelsie nodded and knelt in front of the box. If he believed in her then the least Kelsie could do was believe in herself. She took a deep breath and focused. Her hands crossed just above the box. Now or never.

"Shatter!"

There was a sharp snap and fissures ran through the pale wood. Kelsie held her breath and the cracks spread. The surface of the box resembled a spiderweb when the snapping finally stopped, but it was still in one piece.

She hung her head. "I blew it."

A strong arm draped around her shoulders. Conryu knelt beside her and nodded toward the damaged box. When she looked he tapped it with his index finger and it fell into a dozen pieces.

He fished out the crystal key and grinned. "Good job, partner."

"I did it." She breathed out the words so softly she doubted Conryu heard her.

"What?"

His face was only a few inches from hers. Before she could think better of it Kelsie kissed him full on the lips.

* * *

When Kelsie's lips pressed against his Conryu was so surprised he didn't pull away for a second. Once he regained his wits he gently moved her back. "That's the sort of thing that might give Maria the wrong idea about us."

"Sorry, I, uh, sorry." Her gaze darted all around, anywhere but Conryu's face.

He sighed and held out the key. Clearly Maria had been right about Kelsie having a crush on him. Had he been unable or just unwilling to see it? Probably the latter. He'd inherited a tendency to ignore anything he didn't want to deal with from his father and any feelings she might have for him certainly fell into the category of things he didn't want to deal with.

"Where to next?"

Kelsie took the key and dug out the map. She unfolded it and frowned. "Almost all the way across the island. I thought this was supposed to be a magic test not a fitness test."

"If you ever find yourself in combat you may have to use your magic when you're tired. I'd say it's a pretty legitimate test."

"You're only saying that because you're in good shape already."

"Look on the bright side," Conryu said. "We're near the highest point on the island. It's all downhill from here."

"You have a sick sense of humor, you know that?"

"So I've been told." Conryu studied the map. "Looks like we need to pass through the central clearing. It'll be a good chance to take a look at the pillar. Maybe find out if there are any surprises waiting for us there."

"You think Mrs. Umbra left a trap at the pillar as well?"

He shrugged and headed towards the nearest path. "Beats me, but I wouldn't put it past her."

Kelsie fell in beside him and they started down a steep trail. Roots jutted out and the tops of rocks poked clear of the dirt. He hadn't expected smooth walking, but this trail was worse than the one they came up.

Beside him Kelsie's toe caught on a vine and she staggered. Conryu shot his hand out and grabbed her before she fell into a patch of raspberry vines. Unfortunately, in his rush to catch her, his hand ended up right between her breasts. Kelsie's face turned bright red.

Conryu let her go as soon as he got her back on balance. “Sorry.”

She shook her head, unable to look at him. “It's fine, thanks.”

He held out his hand. “Maybe you better hold on until we reach level ground.”

“Okay.” She grasped his fingers with surprising strength considering how small her hand was.

He had no idea how long it took to reach the base of the hill, but it felt like hours. Kelsie was wheezing like Mr. McShane after a long day in the bike shop. When he tried to let go of her hand she held on for an extra second.

“What do you think about a lunch break?” he asked.

“Any kind of break is okay with me.” She slumped to the ground in a thick patch of old spruce needles just off the trail.

Conryu unslung his pack and joined her. He hadn't grabbed much to eat, mostly junk he snagged from the cafeteria before rushing out to the beach. He settled on a piece of jerky, some chips and a bottle of water. Kelsie was busy peeling an orange.

They ate in awkward silence for a few minutes before Kelsie said, “About that kiss, I really didn't mean anything by it. I was just so excited.”

Conryu washed down a mouthful of dried meat with a long swig of water. “Forget about it. Nothing's changed as far as I'm concerned. Though I don't think you should do it again.”

“I won't, promise.” She peeked at him from behind her hair. “Unless you want me to.”

Conryu clenched his jaw. Why did everything have to be so complicated? Regardless of what she said over winter break, he knew Maria would be heartbroken if he took Kelsie up on her offer. He couldn't deny a certain attraction between him and Kelsie. She was a pretty girl, but he didn't love her.

They finished their meal and Conryu helped her to her feet. When she tried to keep holding his hand Conryu gently disengaged. He didn't want to hurt Kelsie's feelings, but he also didn't want to encourage something that couldn't happen. He was seriously starting to regret inviting her for a visit over summer break.

Ten minutes from their picnic site the forest path opened up into a wide clearing. At first glance you'd never know there'd been a stadium or that a giant demon snake had appeared and fought half the faculty five months ago. The earth wizards had done an excellent job smoothing everything over.

In the center of the clearing was a square black pillar devoid of decoration. From this distance he couldn't see the slots for the keys, but that had to be their final objective.

"What's that?" Kelsie was looking a little off to one side.

There was something there, smaller than the pillar. He squinted in the bright sun. It looked like a jar or vase maybe. "I have no idea. Maybe it's Mrs. Umbra's last surprise."

He took a step toward it, but Kelsie grabbed his arm. "Let's find the last key first. It's probably best to do things in the right order."

She had a point, but Conryu was eager for a closer look at the jar. Kelsie gave him another tug the opposite way and he sighed and let her lead him away. He had plenty of time. Another hour more or less wouldn't matter.

* * *

Kelsie and Conryu skirted the clearing before starting down another trail that led to the final key. She didn't know what that weird jar near the pillar was, but it gave her the shivers. Maybe she could get Conryu to warm her up. No, damn it, she couldn't keep thinking that way. All she'd end up with was disappointment.

This path was flat and relatively free of obstacles. She would have liked an excuse to hold Conryu's hand again, but couldn't think of one. Maybe if she faked another stumble, but he'd probably see right through that.

Conryu walked ahead of her, setting a slow but steady pace. She licked her lips and found them still salty from when they kissed. Or more likely the salt came from the sweat that poured down her face as the heat of the day increased.

God, what had she been thinking? He was uncomfortable around her now. It was clear in the way he carried himself. She'd screwed up the only real friendship she'd ever had just because she couldn't keep her hormones under control.

Maybe she hadn't ruined things completely. If they passed the final and she didn't do anything else to make him nervous, maybe she could salvage their friendship.

All she knew without a doubt: she didn't want to face a life without him in it.

"Did the map say anything about the last hiding place?" Conryu had paused a little ways up the trail and was waiting for her to catch up.

She must have slowed while her mind wandered. Kelsie jogged over to him, her aching legs swearing at her with each impact. She refused to be a burden. Somehow she'd keep up, even if it killed her.

Kelsie stopped beside him and pulled the map out. The final location was in a forest clearing and judging by how far they'd come it couldn't be far off. "All it says is, 'Enter the clearing and leave with your prize.'"

"That seems straight forward enough. How much do you want to bet it doesn't end up being that simple?"

"No bet. Nothing about this test has been simple, why would it change now?"

He grinned and a thousand-pound weight lifted off her chest. "I thought I saw the turnoff just ahead. Come on."

Sure enough twenty paces further on a narrow trail branched off the main path. It couldn't have been a hundred yards before they reached the clearing described on the map. It looked like a tornado had touched down and tossed trees around like matchsticks.

Conryu peered around the clearing. He must have renewed his seeing spell without her noticing. Kelsie frowned as she cast her own spell. She hadn't seen him renew it up on the plateau either. Was he just maintaining the same spell all the time? An hour of maintenance would exhaust her. If he'd kept his active since they landed on the island, that was hours ago.

She shook her head. It was another example of just how different he really was. She focused on the task at hand.

The whole clearing radiated magic, a mixture of light and water. That didn't exactly help her narrow down the key's location.

After a minute of staring she threw up her hands. "I can't tell anything with all that background magic, can you?"

"Nope. Looks like water and light."

"That's how I read it. What are you thinking?"

"I'm thinking illusion magic is primarily light and water. Maybe this clearing isn't as cluttered as we think."

She smacked her forehead. Of course it was illusion magic. Kelsie needed to screw her head on straight. How'd she miss such an obvious conclusion?

"That doesn't help us find the key, does it?"

"Sure it does. Now that I know the problem, I know what they want me to do. Mrs. Umbra wants me to dispel the illusion. It's the only spell she hasn't had me cast yet so it makes sense."

Of course it made sense. Why wouldn't the teachers expect him to dispel a giant illusion? Conryu crossed his fingers and wrists and began to chant. He went through the spell three times then hurled a sphere of dark magic the size of her head into the clearing.

An ebony wave washed over everything. When the magic cleared the tumbled trees were gone. The only thing remaining in the clearing was a single stump with the crystal key resting on it.

Kelsie walked over, grabbed the key, and did a pirouette that ended facing Conryu. "I'd say that's that."

"Yup. I think we passed. What about you?"

"Considering we collected the last key in under five hours I think we should get the best grade in our class."

"Let's head back to the pillar so Mrs. Saint can come fetch us."

The walk back seemed to go faster. They went straight to the pillar, though Conryu never took his eyes off the jar. Up close she realized the thing was made up of an amalgam of different metals. Why did it look so familiar and leave her trembling every time she looked at it?

Three vertical slots were cut in the pillar. She pulled the first key and inserted it. A rune lit up above the key.

A deep roar filled the clearing. Kelsie leapt back into Conryu's chest. "What was that?"

"The jar." He nodded toward the now-trembling vessel.

"The jar roared?"

"I sure hope so."

The lid blew off and multicolored energy poured out. The streams of energy gathered, forming first a body then three heads. Each head was made of a different type of energy. Earth was in the center with fire and water on either side. All three heads roared to the heavens.

"Oh my god." Kelsie could hardly believe her eyes. "It's a chimera."

"A what?"

A stream of fire rushing toward them cut off her answer.

Conryu raised his hand. "Break!"

A sphere of dark energy negated the fire blast. The other two heads orientated on them.

Conryu scooped her up and ran for the trees.

* * *

"He really is amazing." Emily stood beside the head of dark magic as they watched Conryu and Kelsie in the magic mirror hanging in her office.

The two students emerged from the woods after collecting the last key and headed for the pillar. They'd managed to clear a finals course far more challenging than any Emily had ever seen for first-year students in under six hours. The fastest an ordinary final had ever been cleared was ten hours and that was over twenty years ago.

"I'm not certain why we even bothered making him take the final." Angeline tapped the Death Stick against her chin. "Even with my extra surprises I could have told you the result."

"It's tradition. We're a school after all. Not having our star student take a final exam would be unfair."

Angeline snorted. "You think Conryu would care? As far as I can tell all he wants is to learn what he needs to keep himself safe. Beyond that I don't think he gives a damn."

Emily sighed. Conryu certainly wasn't the most enthusiastic student to ever pass through her school. That was a shame. If he really dedicated himself he had the potential to do almost anything with magic. She could hardly wait until next year when he started getting seriously into the other elements.

"What's that jar? Another of your surprises?"

Angeline shook her head. "I thought maybe you added it."

"No, I didn't. And if you didn't..."

"Shit!"

In the mirror Kelsie put the first key into the pillar. A few seconds later a three-headed monster appeared out of the jar.

"What is that thing?" Emily asked. The monster had traits of three different elements, including fire and water. Which should have been impossible.

"I don't know, but we need to get them out of there. Use the emergency override to lower the shield."

Emily rushed behind her desk and dug a six-inch rune-marked stone cylinder out of a locked drawer. "Got it. Let's go."

They didn't bother with the door. Emily opened her window and jumped out, chanting wind magic as she fell. The wind caught her and soon she was flying full speed toward the island. Angeline joined her on her own mini tornado a moment later.

They flew over the grounds and toward the lake. From up high she could just make out the towering figure of the monster from the jar. It was smashing around the clearing, breathing fire and raising a cloud of dust.

Occasionally a sphere of dark magic would cancel one of the blasts. That had to be Conryu. He was still alive and knowing him he was protecting Kelsie. She clenched her jaw and willed the wind spirit to fly faster. No student had died in training since she took over as dean, now two of the most famous students to attend the academy were in danger at the same time. How had this happened?

They reached the island and hovered over the central clearing. Every so often a streak of flame or jet of water would splash against the barrier. When she lowered the shield they'd be subjected to the monster's attacks as well.

She glanced at Angeline. The head of the Death Stick crackled with dark magic. What had she expected? Of course Angeline was ready for a fight.

"Hurry, Emily. We don't want to lose those kids."

Emily tapped the runes in a particular sequence until they all lit up. She waited for the barrier to lower, but nothing happened. The runes started flashing and the cylinder vibrated. She threw it away a second before the stone exploded.

"Someone's interfered with the failsafe. I can't lower the barrier. Can you dispel it?"

"No. I helped design the barrier and we made it so no one could interfere with the test. As long as we had the emergency deactivation control I didn't worry about it."

"Can he dispel it?" Emily winced every time the monster smashed another tree flat.

"Probably, but he won't."

Emily couldn't believe what she heard. "Why?"

"Conryu has an overprotective nature. He wouldn't risk that creature running wild and maybe hurting everyone at the school. He'll try and figure out some way to deal with it himself. We need to find out who messed with the barrier and stuck that monster in there."

"I know where to start looking. The Le Fay Sorority."

* * *

Conryu ran through the woods, leaping fallen trees, and generally trying to put as much distance between them and the chimera as possible. Kelsie felt almost weightless in his arms. Nothing like a burst of adrenaline to make you feel strong.

Behind them the monster roared and toppled trees. When they reached one of the many clearings on the island Conryu stopped and set Kelsie down. His lungs were burning and his heart raced.

"Are you okay?" She put a hand on his back as he gasped for air.

"Yeah. Just give me a minute to catch my breath. How did you know what that thing was?"

"My family made it."

"What?"

"The Chimera project was commissioned by the military. They were looking for a weapon they could deliver behind enemy lines and activate remotely. We had a team researching it at Kincade West. They'd managed to fuse multiple elemental spirits and hold them within a jar. What they hadn't figured out was how to control the monster they'd made. Fusing multiple elements into a single creature drove it insane."

"I didn't think you were all that involved with your family

business." Conryu had his breathing under control now. He turned back toward the clearing where the mad thing was tearing up the forest.

"I'm not, but Mom couldn't stop talking about it over winter break. The company has a lot of money invested in the project and it looked like she was going to have to pull the plug. The day before I left to return to school someone broke into the lab, stole the prototype, and killed several employees. No one could figure out what happened to it. I guess we know now."

"I guess we do. So how do we kill it?"

Kelsie hugged herself. "I don't know. The team never made one this powerful. They only used minor spirits. When they finished the experiment the wizards blasted it with dark magic until it burst."

"So I just need to hit it with enough dark magic to break the bonds holding it together?"

Her laugh held a hysterical edge. "Yes, that's all you need to do. But I doubt even you could conjure enough dark magic to destroy a chimera that size."

The roars and crashing were getting louder. "We need to put some distance between us and that thing. There's someone I want you to meet. He might be able to help."

They started down a trail at an angle away from the rampaging chimera. Conryu unslung his pack and dug out Prime. Kelsie gasped when Prime flew up on his own.

"Kelsie, this is Prime, my scholomantic. Prime, Kelsie, my dark magic partner."

"Charmed," Prime said. "What sort of mess have you gotten into now, Master?"

"I thought you'd know, given our connection."

"You stuffed me in that sack so I decided to take a nap. The mess?"

Conryu gave Prime the short version of Kelsie's story. "Any idea how we can crush that thing?"

"I assume it's held together with light magic?"

"That's right." Kelsie ducked under a tree branch. "It has a light magic core inside the earth body."

"Then we need to blast a hole through the body then hit the core with Dispel." Prime said it as if this would be the simplest thing in the world.

"I don't know any magic that would blow away that much earth."

"Not yet you don't." Prime opened and flipped through pages.

Conryu stopped and studied the page Prime settled on. "Death Spiral. A dark magic spell designed to smash through magically hardened defenses."

Kelsie moved to stand beside him. "That's a new one to me. Looks complicated."

It certainly did. The chant was twenty words long and needed to be repeated three times. At least the gesture was simple, a twirl of the finger to give the magic the appropriate shape. Under ideal circumstances it would take him days of practice to master the spell. A distant roar indicated he didn't have days.

"Never fear, Master. Since it's an emergency I can feed the words of the spell directly into your mind. All you need to do is repeat after me."

"Alright, but how big a hole will this spell make? The chimera is huge. I could blast through it and never reveal the core."

Prime chuckled. "With your power behind it the spiral will hollow the beast out. The important thing to remember is, you need to hit it chest on. That way you'll bore through the narrow way."

"And you'll have to be quick," Kelsie added. "The chimeras were designed to heal rapidly."

"Okay, but the real question is how will I avoid getting blasted to bits while I'm chanting that crazy-long spell?"

Prime flexed his cover. "That's outside my area of expertise."

* * *

They settled on the simplest plan possible. They'd sneak closer to the chimera and Conryu would cast the spell as quietly as he could in hopes that the monster wouldn't notice. There was a good deal of hoping in their plan, but given their limited knowledge and experience it would have to do.

They left the trail and entered the woods. Moving amongst the trees should make it harder for the chimera to spot them.

"Are you sure you wouldn't rather stay behind?" Conryu asked.

Kelsie was thrashing around through the branches behind him and making enough noise for a small army. "We're partners, right? Where you go, I go."

He figured she'd say that, but he wanted to at least make the offer. This wasn't a simple test anymore and the chimera wasn't one of Mrs. Umbra's extras. It wouldn't ignore Kelsie the way the fire cats did.

Conryu glanced back and met her gaze. There was no doubt or hesitation in her eyes, only determination. Good, anything less would likely get her killed and him along with her.

The monster's roars grew louder and louder the closer they came. It almost sounded in pain.

"Of course it's in pain," Prime said. "Forcing all those different spirits into a single body creates pressure and tension. It's trying to tear itself apart while the light magic tries to hold it together."

"What sort of lunatic would create such a thing?" He looked back at Kelsie. "No offense."

"None taken. I often think my family is more or less all mad. My hope is that it isn't something we grow into."

Conryu grinned. At least she hadn't lost her sense of humor.

They were getting close now. He slowed his pace and eased up between the trees. He crouched down beside a big fallen spruce and peeked around it.

Kelsie came up next to him, their cheeks almost touching. The chimera was in the middle of a new clearing, stomping on the trees it had knocked down. The water head snapped at the fire head which roared back.

The earth head in the center came down between them. The monster was literally at war with itself.

"It's kind of pitiful."

"Yes. Put it out of its misery, Master."

Conryu nodded. Seeing the thing up close, watching it writhe and twist... Destroying it would indeed be a kindness.

He raised his right hand. Prime sent the words into his mind. "Deepest darkness twist and writhe. Grind and smash what I despise. Break through bonds and destroy all barriers, Death Spiral."

He made it through once with no trouble; the chimera was too distracted to notice him. When he began the second pass and real power started to gather around him, the earth head popped up and looked around.

Conryu focused on the spell, but didn't take his eyes off the monster. If it made any move toward them he'd have to abandon the casting and run for it.

Three-quarters of the way through the second chant the fire and water heads popped up. All three heads swung this way and that. They sensed his magic, but couldn't figure out where it was coming from.

He finished the second recitation and began the third. He only made it through three words before all three heads focused on him. Not good.

Kelsie broke cover and ran to the right. The chimera turned its gaze on her.

Sensing his anxiety Prime sent the words faster.

The fire head extended toward Kelsie.

Conryu spoke the last word and twirled his finger.

Flames belched from the chimera an instant before his Death Spiral crashed into its chest. The impact of the spell shoved the chimera aside. The flames struck behind Kelsie, but the force of the blast sent her flying into the brush.

Conryu started to go to her.

"Master, the core."

Conryu turned back. The spiral had bored a tunnel through the chimera's body and revealed a pulsing sphere of light magic. He raised his hand, fingers crossed. "Break!"

Conryu put all of his will into it and a bigger than usual orb of darkness streaked out. Dark magic hit light and snuffed it out. The water head splashed to the ground, the flames fizzled, and several tons of earth and rock collapsed in a heap.

He blew out a breath. "Kelsie!"

Smashing his way through the brush Conryu reached his partner's side. She lay on the ground, limp and unmoving. Her left side was a mass of burns and her calf was pierced by a shaft of broken wood. Only the weak rise and fall of her chest gave any indication she still lived.

They hadn't brought any first aid gear. Conryu tore off his robe and bundled it under her head. What was he supposed to do? He was good at breaking things, not healing.

Maybe he should pull that piece of wood out while she was still unconscious. He grasped the shattered end, pulled the foot-and-a-half-long shaft out and tossed it away. Blood immediately started to ooze out of the hole.

He put his hand over it and pressed hard. The blood "Shit!"

Conryu adjusted her head and tore one of the sleeves off his robe. He wrapped it around her calf several times and tied it tight. The burns were completely beyond him.

"Prime! Do you know any healing magic?"

"I'm sorry, Master. Light magic is anathema to me."

"Damn it!" He took Kelsie's hand. "You can't die. Come on."

He closed his eyes and focused. Magic was all about willpower. If he could control demons with nothing but strength of will, surely he could heal his friend.

Come on, come on.

In his mind Conryu pictured the burns healing and the wound on her calf closing. Warmth flowed out from his hands as pain throbbed in his head.

"Master."

Conryu opened his eyes. Where before there was only charred and blistered flesh now pink heathy skin covered Kelsie's side. He untied his makeshift bandage. Only a small round scar remained where the wood had pierced her.

"How is this possible, Master? You are a dark wizard of immense might. You shouldn't be able to use light magic beyond the most simple spells, and certainly not with force of will alone."

He sat beside Kelsie and held his pounding head in his hands. While he waited for the backlash to subside Conryu told Prime about his Choosing.

"All six gems reacted? Even my creator didn't foresee such a possibility. You are truly a worthy master."

"Thanks. Now stop talking before my head explodes."

11

SORORITY BATTLE

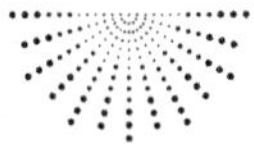

Lady Mockingbird lounged on a velvet sofa in her otherwise empty casting chamber and watched the abomination run from her chimera. She was pleased she'd taken the time to leave a wind spirit behind when she placed the jar. This show was far better than anything on television.

The monster that emerged from the jar far exceeded her expectations. It made all the effort she'd expended summoning and binding spirits worthwhile. With a bit of luck she might rid the world of the Kincade brat as well.

The image on her magic mirror flickered as the wind spirit fought her mental command to move closer to the chimera. Lady Mockingbird couldn't really blame the little pixie, she wouldn't have wanted to fly close to the rampaging creature either.

Someone knocked on her casting chamber door. She scowled. Lady Mockingbird had left strict instructions that she didn't wish to be disturbed.

The image in the mirror vanished and she stood up. She wrenched the door open and standing there with her gaze lowered was one of her second years. "What?"

"Apologies, Mistress, but Dean Blane and Mrs. Umbra are here. They do not appear to be in good spirits."

Lady Mockingbird growled. If they were here they either knew or strongly suspected she was behind the chimera. She might talk her way out of this—might—but the odds weren't in her favor. "Warn Demarlza and the other more zealous members. It may come to a fight."

The sophomore dared to look up. "Is a fight with the dean and the head of dark magic a good idea, Mistress?"

Lady Mockingbird backhanded the girl hard enough to spin her around. "Of course it's not a good idea, but there are only two of them. We may eliminate an additional pair of the order's enemies. Now go warn the others. If I can deflect them, fine, if not we need to be ready."

"Yes, Mistress." The second year whimpered and ran off.

Stupid child. Did she imagine Lady Mockingbird didn't realize a fight with two of the most powerful wizards in the world, much less at the school, wasn't a prudent move? If the dean discovered what she'd been doing Lady Mockingbird would end up in the Lonely Rock beside the order's leader and all the other wizards guilty of inappropriate use of magic. That was a fate she couldn't accept.

Better to die killing enemies of the order. She only wished she could have witnessed Conryu's death at the fangs of her chimera or better yet killed him herself with her own magic.

* * *

Emily and Angeline stood in the tiled entryway and waited for Amelia to show herself. The First Sister of the sorority would be full of excuses, but this time Emily didn't plan on leaving until she'd checked every nook and cranny of the building. If they'd put so much as a hair out of line she'd ban the whole bunch. Emily couldn't actually kick the students out, but she could fire their poison-tongued mistress and keep them from gathering and plotting. That alone would make this exercise worthwhile.

"Rather gaudy place, isn't it?" Angeline waved the Death Stick in an all-encompassing gesture.

Though Angeline kept her emotions fully in check Emily recognized the subtle crinkling around her eyes along with a little extra hardness in her generally stern expression. The head of dark magic was furious that someone had taken another shot at her prize pupil. Emily pitied anyone that crossed her today.

"I think they decorated the place like a Kingdom cottage. Or at least what they thought one should look like."

Angeline grunted and turned to her left. Emily heard the approaching footsteps a moment later. Amelia swept into the entry hall, her red robe swirling behind her. Something was different about her today. She seemed more confident, almost eager to see them.

Every bit of intuition in Emily screamed that something was wrong, but she couldn't act based on a feeling.

"Emily, Angeline, what a wonderful surprise. What brings you fine ladies to our humble sorority?"

She was mocking them, but in a polite way. Emily wiggled her fingers and drew down her focus. It would come to a fight, she knew it.

"There's been another attack on Conryu. Since your sorority is at the top of my suspect list I intend to search the premises.

"Your theories aren't sufficient cause to poke your noses into our sorority."

"I'm dean of this school and my authority is all I need to examine any building or room on campus. You should know that. It's spelled out clearly in the student manual."

"So it is. Where would you like to start?"

"Your casting chamber," Angeline said in a tone that brooked no argument.

Amelia offered a brittle smile. "Certainly, right this way." Her gaze darted left just for a second.

Emily caught a glimpse of half a dozen older students gathered in the drawing room. They all wore angry, eager expressions. In the middle of the pack was Demarlza, the fire wizard she was certain had led the first attack on Conryu.

They followed Amelia along a short hall to a door that led to stairs down to the basement. This might complicate things—fighting in an enclosed space would let the enemy concentrate their magic. At the bottom of the steps Amelia went to the first door and opened it for them.

"Right through here."

Emily went in first. There wasn't much there, just a sofa and magic mirror. Casting chambers were usually kept empty. Why was there a sofa in here?

"Watching something interesting?" Angeline walked over to the mirror and tapped it with the Death Stick.

An image flickered to life. A black spiral blasted through the chest of the monster exposing a glowing sphere. A moment later an orb of dark magic streaked in and destroyed it. The creature collapsed into so much rubble.

Angeline grinned and tapped the mirror again, breaking the connection. "Impressive, the boy learned Death Spiral. And under adverse conditions as well."

"No!" Amelia shouted. "He was supposed to die."

In the doorway behind her the students from upstairs had gathered.

"I don't suppose you'll come along quietly?" Emily asked.

Amelia thrust a hand forward and hurled a stream of fire. The blue-orange flames struck an impenetrable black barrier.

Angeline held the Death Stick horizontally in front of her, dark magic crackling around the silver skull. "You think you can threaten my student and get away with it?"

She slashed the Death Stick toward the group blocking the

doorway. A wave of dark magic blasted Amelia and her followers back and stripped away the defensive magic they'd already cast.

Amelia was the first to her feet. "You think you can best a Sub-Hierarch of the Le Fay Society, hag?"

Angeline snorted a dry laugh and crooked a knobby finger. "This one's mine. Can you handle the pups?"

Emily nodded and eyed the handful of students collecting themselves after the blast of dark magic. There were two seniors, they would be the most challenging. The rest were a mix of third- and second-year students.

Demarlza was the first to her feet. She snarled and summoned a pair of fire cats. She wasn't an especially attractive girl to begin with and the ugly expression she wore did nothing to help.

Emily summoned a pair of wind wraiths. The invisible spirits hung in the air beside her. Since it was six against one she'd have to fight defensively.

Her pulse pounded in her ears and power crackled around her fingers. Emily hadn't been this excited in years.

* * *

Conryu sat in the brush and held his throbbing head. The effects of the magical backlash had let up a little, but damn little. Prime was floating well above them keeping a look out for any approaching threats. After the chimera he had serious doubts that anything nasty remained on the island, but at this point he wasn't prepared to take it for granted. Considering the shape he was in at the moment Conryu doubted he could handle a fire cat, much less a stronger opponent.

Beside him Kelsie groaned. He raised his head in time to watch her trying to sit up. Conryu held out his hand.

She took it and he pulled her to a sitting position. "How are you feeling?"

"Better than I have any right to be. You healed me."

He nodded and winced as the movement brought on another stab of pain. "Yeah. You were in pretty bad shape after that blast."

"I felt your concern. You were really afraid I was going to die."

"If you'd seen how you looked you'd have been afraid too."

"I'm glad I was unconscious. Thank you for saving me. I don't know what I can do to repay you, but whatever you want just ask."

"If you hadn't distracted the chimera when you did I wouldn't have been able to kill it. I'd say we're even. Besides, I don't keep scores with my friends."

She smiled. "How did you heal me?"

"Light magic channeled with willpower." He rubbed his temples. "I don't recommend it."

"Don't worry, I doubt I could channel enough light magic to heal a paper cut."

"If you're up to walking we should lower the barrier for Mrs. Saint. I'll feel better once the school nurse takes a look at you."

"I'm good to go. My leg doesn't even hurt." Kelsie wiggled her foot around as if to prove it.

Conryu climbed to his feet without fainting, then helped Kelsie up. The pain behind his eyes was already receding, thank goodness. He broke a path through the brush and branches back to the nearest trail.

Prime flew down beside them. "There's smoke coming from one of the little houses on the lakeshore."

"The sorority bungalows?" Kelsie said. "Which one?"

"The farthest from the school."

"The Le Fay Sorority." Conryu clenched his jaw. He'd bet his bike they were behind the attack. Someone else must have figured it out as well. "We need to get over there."

He stumbled as a fresh pain stabbed through his brain.

Kelsie slipped his arm around her shoulders. "You're in no condition to go anywhere and I'd only be in the way."

He couldn't argue with that, at least for the moment. The two of them stumbled along like the walking dead until they reached the central clearing. The jar sat in the same place near the pillar, both seemingly undamaged by the monster.

Kelsie went to the pillar while he continued on to the jar. For such a small thing it certainly caused a lot of trouble.

He pointed his hand at it. "Shatter!"

It blew into a dozen pieces. There, no one else would have to worry about fighting a chimera for a while and no spirits would be tortured into such an obscene form.

"Conryu."

He winced. "Did you want to take that back to your mom?"

"I don't care about the jar, we have another problem."

He suppressed a groan. There was always another problem. Conryu joined Kelsie beside the pillar. She held up one of the keys. It had snapped in half.

"Shit! Looks like we're stuck here until morning."

"Do we still pass if we break a key?"

Conryu couldn't have cared less if he passed or failed. Mrs. Umbra had all but admitted the classes and tests didn't really apply in his case. Kelsie, on the other hand, seemed genuinely worried. Given her family situation he wasn't surprised.

"I suspect defeating an unknown magic beast will get us enough extra points to make up for the broken key. How do you want to kill the next eighteen hours?"

"Let's go down to the beach and see what's happening at the sorority."

Conryu shrugged and started out. It wasn't like there was anything else to do.

* * *

Angeline twirled the Death Stick, creating a shield of dark magic that negated the stream of flame roaring out of her opponent's hand. So complete was her defense that she didn't even notice the heat. She hadn't been in a real fight in years. The rush of adrenaline mingled with a burst of fear set her heart racing. Angeline had missed that rush these past years teaching.

Finally the fire ended. Angeline was only distantly aware of roars and explosions coming from other areas of the building.

"Cloak of Darkness!" Angeline covered herself in liquid darkness.

"Shroud of Flame!" Flames swirled around Amelia as she countered with a defensive spell of her own.

"By your name I call you, by my will I bind you. Rise, hell hounds!"

A hell gate opened on either side of Angeline and two dogs as black as a moonless night stalked out. Each of them stood as tall as her, their eyes burning with a red glow. The servants of Cerberus snarled.

"Attack!"

The hell hounds lunged towards Amelia who leapt. A burst of fire from the soles of her feet launched her higher and farther than an ordinary woman could manage.

As she flew over the hellhounds she pointed both hands at them. "Burn to ash!"

A torrent of flame consumed the demon dogs. Amelia landed and turned her flames on Angeline who negated them with another dark shield.

Amelia panted and leaned with her hands on her thighs.

She had skill, but no stamina. Pity.

"Oh sweet death, lend me your strength." The Death Stick pulsed with dark magic. "Dread Scythe."

Her artifact transformed into a black-handled scythe with a silver blade. Black wings grew from Angeline's back and what appeared to be a billowing black cloak covered her from head to foot.

Amelia took a step back. As well she might when faced with an avatar of the reaper. Dread Scythe was Angeline's ultimate trump card.

She kicked the floor, her wings beat the air, and she launched herself at the woman that had caused her favorite student so much grief.

"Flames of Protection!" The hastily chanted spell called a wall of flames into being between Angeline and her target.

She might as well have not bothered. A casual slash cut the spell apart. With her barrier gone a wide-eyed Amelia stared at the descending blade. The shining silver was the last thing she saw before the Dread Scythe cut her in half.

Wisps of dark magic rose from Angeline as she slumped to the floor, her spell ended. For all its power, Dread Scythe took a toll and she wasn't as young as she used to be.

An explosion shook the building. Sounded like Emily was getting serious. She forced herself to her feet and hobbled toward the door. If she didn't fancy getting buried under a heap of gaudy decorations she needed to leave the basement in a hurry.

* * *

Maria settled into her chair. On the table in front of her was a rabbit with a deep gash in its side. Its ribs quivered as its heart raced. All around her the other students had nearly identical animals before them.

Poor little thing. It was a shame they had to hurt the animals intentionally, but as her teacher said, it was no different than a scientist injecting an animal with some disease so they could test the cure.

She stroked the rabbit's head in a vain attempt to calm it down. "Don't worry," she whispered. "I've gotten good at healing. You'll be right as rain in a little while."

She glanced out the window toward the island. Conryu was out there now, with Kelsie, just the two of them. She swallowed a little growl. She trusted him completely, yet part of her worried that despite what he said Conryu secretly had feelings for Kelsie.

Maria gave a little shake of her head and looked away from the window. Whatever was happening out there was beyond her control. Right now she needed to concentrate on her own final. Bugs was counting on her after all.

At the front of the class Mrs. Alustrial tapped her pointed stick against the chalkboard. Since her conversation with Dean Blane, Maria's teacher hadn't given her a moment of trouble, as long as you didn't count the glares when she thought Maria wasn't looking. On the table beside her was an hourglass filled with red sand.

"All right, class," Mrs. Alustrial said. "This is where you put what we've been studying to practical use. You have three hours to construct your healing ward and repair the damage to your test subject. I have every confidence in you all, but should anyone fail I guess we'll be having rabbit for dinner."

When no one laughed her expression went flat. "Three hours. Begin." Mrs. Alustrial flipped the hourglass.

Maria took a breath and centered herself. She'd been studying the spells so much the past months she saw them in her dreams. The rabbit gave a twitch and she put her hand above it. "The light of Heaven is the light of healing. Take that which is injured and make it whole, Healing Ward."

A white glow spread from her palms down over the injured rabbit. When it was fully enclosed tendrils of power snaked down from the dome and entered the rabbit. As she watched the ugly red wound begin to close, the muscles knitted themselves together over the animal's ribs. Its breathing calmed and its pulse slowed.

Maria grimaced as the effects of the spell began to drain her. Though the power came from Heaven it passed through her and was given shape by her magic and will. Maintaining the flow at the correct pace took great mental focus.

The wound was fully closed and the skin was growing over it when the explosion sounded. At least she thought it was an explosion. It sounded distant.

Her ward wavered along with her concentration. She refocused long enough to restore it, then risked a glance out the window. Smoke was rising from the lakeshore. It looked like one of the bungalows had caught on fire.

A second explosion, louder this time, rattled the windows. Some of the other girls muttered, but Mrs. Alustrial slapped her pointer on her table. "No talking."

She looked back to her rabbit. It was sitting up, nose twitching, and seemed free of pain. The skin had grown back. There was a nasty scar on its side, but she was certain it would survive.

Maria released the magic and raised her hand. "My healing's complete. May I go see what's causing all that noise?" She was the first to finish which pleased her greatly.

Mrs. Alustrial stood up and walked over. She examined the rabbit, running her finger over the scar. Her face twisted into an angry scowl, but she nodded. "You pass. Congratulations on making it to your second year."

Her teacher leaned in closer and whispered. "I'm relieved to be done with you. Mark my words, your boyfriend will be the death of you. Go if you wish. I couldn't care less."

Maria got up, grabbed her books, and strode for the door. She wouldn't say anything, wouldn't give Mrs. Alustrial the satisfaction of provoking her, but she was relieved not to have to deal with the woman any further. Her irrational dislike of Conryu was every bit as stupid as the other girls' attitudes. You'd think someone her age would know better.

She closed the door behind her with a little more enthusiasm than necessary and turned down the hall. She'd passed and that was what mattered. Hopefully her second-year teacher would be more reasonable.

At the bottom of the steps a group of girls had gathered. They had packed in four deep in front of the lecture hall doors. "Excuse me." Maria elbowed her way to the front.

Thick smoke billowed up from the lakeshore. She shoved the door, but it was locked.

"The teachers initiated a lockdown."

She glanced to her left and a little down. Conryu's friend Sonja was standing there and staring out with everyone else.

"What does that mean?" she asked.

"It means we're stuck in here and we'll miss out on the excitement." Sonja sounded like the little girl she resembled.

A pair of teachers flew towards the lake. Maria frowned. How had they gotten out? The roof! "Can you cast flying magic?"

"Sure, why?"

"I think I know how we can get out of here and find out what's happening."

Sonja grinned, reminding her for a moment of Conryu. "What are we waiting for?"

They slipped past the still-gathering students and rushed up the stairs. Maria set a brisk pace, but Sonja kept up despite her shorter legs. Once they reached the top floor Maria went to a door in the northern wall and yanked it open. Inside was a ladder up to a hatch that opened to the roof.

"How did you know about this place?" Sonja asked as she climbed up behind Maria.

"My light magic class is on this floor so I've had time to explore. I caught a glimpse of the ladder when one of the teachers opened the door last month. I figured it had to be the roof access."

"Cool!" Sonja ran over to the edge of the roof. "Check that out."

Maria joined her and her eyes widened. A huge wall of fire blazed in front of the Le Fay Sorority. A small crowd had gathered, but they couldn't move past the roaring flames.

Sonja put her arm around Maria's waist. "Ready?"

The question proved to be rhetorical. Sonja chanted a spell and they were airborne before she thought of an answer. Maria yelped, but the short flight was smooth. From their position above the fire she could see girls pouring out of the sorority house.

A few seconds later the roof blew up amidst a torrent of dark energy. Two figures emerged, but she didn't see them well enough to figure out who they were before Sonja lowered them to the ground.

The little fire wizard released her and wiped her brow. "Whew, flying two people is way more work than just transporting myself."

Maria had just time enough to wonder if Sonja was implying she was fat when the wall of fire vanished. Dean Blane and Mrs. Umbra were herding the students into a group. Beyond them the house had collapsed.

"Guess the show's over," Sonja said.

"Yeah." Maria doubted they'd seen even half of what really happened. Part of her wasn't sure she wanted to know what was going on. Deep inside she knew it had something to do with Conryu.

* * *

Emily had complete confidence in Angeline's ability to handle Amelia. As flames burned into her wind barrier on one side and lightning crackled into the other she had a little less confidence in her own situation. Demarlza's fire cats charged in between the flame blasts.

The fire cats bared their fangs and leapt. Her wind wraiths flew in and scattered the flames until only embers remained.

"No!" Demarlza redoubled her flame's intensity.

Emily staggered under an especially intense burst of lightning. If she kept playing with these kids, they might actually beat her. While she didn't want to kill any of her students, this bunch might not give her a choice.

"Father of winds blow away my enemies, Tornado Burst." She

threw her hand forward and a mini twister sent all six girls flying out the door and into the hall beyond. One of them hit the wall with enough force that she didn't get back up.

Emily risked a glance at Angeline. The head of dark magic was under assault from a river of flame, though none of it pierced her shield. She shook her head and stalked out of the casting chamber. Angeline could take care of herself. She needed to convince these kids to surrender before someone got killed.

"If you give up now, I promise the court will take your age and inexperience into account during the trial. The longer you fight the worse it will look for you."

"You think we'll surrender to someone that let an abomination into our school?" Demarlza forced herself up. "Better we die as true wizards than accept such a thing."

Emily shook her head to hear one of her pupils spout such utter nonsense. "True wizards keep an open mind when they encounter the unknown, they don't condemn it out of hand. Only an ignorant, closed-minded fool judges a person by nothing but their sex. Girl good, boy bad. That's primitive thinking and unworthy of a student attending this academy."

Two of the younger girls were muttering to each other. Demarlza must have heard them. She gave the nearest a bat to the side of the head. "We will not betray our mistress. Burn!"

A blast of flames was deflected by her wind barrier.

"Go upstairs and gather the others, I'll hold her here," Demarlza ordered.

The other girls hesitated and for a moment Emily dared hope they might come to their senses, but it wasn't to be. Four of them rushed up the stairs, leaving their unconscious companion behind.

"Just you and me." Demarlza offered a cruel smile. "You don't seem so tough now."

Demarlza raised her free hand and a ball of fire appeared. The instant the spell formed Emily pointed. "Jet Gust."

A focused line of wind struck the fireball and detonated it. Demarlza's concentration broke and the torrent of flames vanished. This one was clearly beyond redemption. "Your breath is your life. Cease to breathe and cease to be, Asphyxiation."

Demarlza scratched at her throat as the wind magic stole the air from her lungs. She clawed and gasped and fell to the floor where she kicked around before going still. Emily shook her head again. What a waste. The girl had such potential.

The tap, tap, tap of the Death Stick alerted her to Angeline's approach. She eyed the two bodies in the hall and sighed. "It couldn't be helped."

"No. Amelia?"

"That also couldn't be helped. Not that she was worthy of our help. The other pups?"

"They ran upstairs, I assume to set a trap."

"Perhaps a display of sufficient force will knock some sense into them." Angeline had a wicked gleam in her eye.

"What did you have in mind?"

"I'll blast a path out of here and you fly us through. Once I saw the boy use Death Spiral I got an itch to try it myself. I haven't cast it since I came to teach."

"I suppose that might work. Did you teach the spell to Conryu? Death Spiral seems a bit stronger than what we'd discussed."

"No, I suspect his book taught him. There isn't much regarding dark magic the scholomantic doesn't know. I'm impressed he managed to cast it so well so quickly."

"I agree. Perhaps next year we should design a new course of study for him. I won't bother submitting it to the Department for approval. As long as he passes the midterms and finals they won't care how we go about teaching him."

"That's an excellent idea. Have we given them enough time to get nervous?"

"I think so. Whenever you're ready." Emily moved back to give

Angeline some extra room as well as making sure she wouldn't get caught in any magic spillover.

Angeline chanted and spun the Death Stick in a slow circle. Dark magic gathered around the silver skull. When she'd built up the necessary power she thrust the Death Stick at the ceiling. A spiral shot out, smashing through the ceiling and carrying the debris along with it.

Emily moved back beside Angeline. "Father of winds, carry us into your domain. Air Rider."

The wind gathered around them, strong but gentle, and carried them through the floor and up out of what remained of the roof.

A group of sorority members had raised a wall of flames to hold off the approaching students and teachers. Girls poured out of the collapsing house and onto the field outside.

Emily guided them to the ground between the students and the house. The remains of the building collapsed at the same moment they landed. It was an unintentional but powerful bit of symbolism.

The girls faced them, hands raised and ready to cast.

Emily held her hands to the side in a gesture of peace. "Your leaders are dead as is the sorority. Whether you face a wizards' tribunal or we bury you at the bottom of the lake is up to you."

At that moment Assistant Dean Saint rose up behind them on the head of a water serpent. That was the final straw. The rebellious students threw up their hands in surrender and the wall of flames vanished.

Teachers rushed down to join them and Emily directed the new arrivals to take the sorority members into custody.

Now that everything seemed under control Hanna landed beside them. "Looks like I missed the excitement."

"On the contrary, your timing couldn't have been better. Your water serpent knocked the fight out of them and allowed us to avoid any more deaths. I'm grateful beyond words for that."

"How's the boy?" Angeline asked.

"Conryu and Kelsie are fine. They were sitting on the beach watching the fireworks. He lost his robe somewhere on the island, but other than that they didn't have any visible damage."

Emily sighed. "All and all as good a result as we could have hoped for. Did you take them to the nurse's office?"

"No, the barrier is still up."

Angeline frowned. "I know they collected all their keys. What's the hold up?"

Hanna shrugged. "I couldn't get close enough to ask."

Emily patted Angeline on the shoulder. "We'll find out in the morning. Right now we have a mess to clean up."

* * *

The pops and flashes from the sorority bungalow had ended hours ago. The sun hung low in the sky as Conryu dragged the last dry branch into the pile he'd made on the beach. Kelsie lounged on the sand and stared up at the sunset. She'd offered to help him gather wood, but he didn't want to risk her injuring her leg again.

He heaved the stick into the pile and nodded. The pile was almost as tall as he was. The nights were still chilly so a fire would be nice.

Kelsie rummaged through her pack for a drink and walked over to him. "It's a nice pile of wood, but I don't think my lighting spell is going to be enough to get it started." She flicked her finger and a little flame appeared on the tip.

"Getting it going won't be a problem." Conryu moved a safe distance away and raised his hand. "All things burn to ash, Inferno Blast."

A stream of blue-white flames streaked out. After a few seconds he had a roaring bonfire going. Conryu ended the spell and turned to Kelsie. "See, no sweat."

"Where'd you learn that? The only fire spells they taught us in universal magic class was a light globe and how to ignite and snuff out a candle."

"A girl in my club taught me. Maybe you know her, Sonja Chard?"

"I don't know her personally, but my mother regularly curses her family for stealing a portion of our military business. That alone is enough to make me think I'd like her."

"I think you would too, she's spunky. Remind me to introduce you when things calm down."

"She might not be so friendly since our families are in direct competition."

Conryu laughed and lay down on the sand near the fire. "Sonja's about as enchanted with her family's business as you are with yours. It's amazing how much you two have in common."

Kelsie lay down beside him and rested her head on his shoulder. When he didn't say anything she snuggled in closer. It had been a crazy day and he understood if she needed a little reassuring.

When he turned his head to look at her Kelsie was already fast asleep. That struck him as an excellent idea and the moment he closed his eyes he was dead to the world.

The next thing he knew someone was kicking his foot. Maybe if he ignored them whoever it was would go away.

"Wake up, sleepyhead."

Conryu opened one eye. The youthful face of Dean Blane was staring down at him. He started to sit up, but found his movement restricted. He opened the other eye. Kelsie had draped herself over him and his arm was pinned under her, and her leg draped across his thighs.

"I don't want to get up," she grumbled in her sleep and moved closer.

"You didn't bring Maria with you, did you?" The fact that no one was strangling him at the moment argued that she hadn't, but he wanted to make sure.

"Nope, it's just me and Hanna and she's waiting by the boat. You had quite an adventure yesterday."

"Yeah."

Conryu gave Kelsie a shake and she finally opened her eyes. The moment she realized who was there and how she was wrapped around him she scrambled to put some space between them. "Sorry. I was asleep and I didn't realize what I was doing." Her face was bright red.

"Relax." Conryu patted her knee. "Time to go back."

"Almost time to head back." Dean Blane plopped down beside them. "There are a couple matters we need to discuss and there are far fewer ears out here. Tell me what happened."

Conryu did as she asked, with Kelsie chiming in here and there. When he finished Kelsie asked, "Do we still pass even though one of the keys was broken?"

"Absolutely. The fact that you survived that monster would earn you a passing grade in my book." Dean Blane fixed Conryu with a serious look. "You really channeled light magic with nothing but willpower?"

He nodded. "The backlash made the headache I got from dominating those demons feel like a tickle, but Kelsie's okay, so it was worth it."

"I assume you saw the battle at the sorority house?"

"Yeah. Let me guess, they left the chimera for me?"

"Exactly right. Apparently Amelia Light was a Sub-Hierarch in the Society. We'll have to search through the rubble, but I hope to find out more about the group."

"I thought they were a political committee that supported women looking to advance to high positions in the government and at companies," Kelsie said.

Conryu didn't pay much attention to politics, but Dean Blane seemed to know what Kelsie was talking about.

"The Le Fay Society has two groups. The one you're talking about claims to be a nonprofit dedicated to women's issues and unaffiliated with their more aggressive sister organization. The second group is more of a terrorist organization determined to change the world directly with violence and fear."

"Why do they hate me so much?" Conryu asked.

Dean Blane sighed. "The Society believes the world should be ordered in three tiers. Wizards at the top, non-magic-using women below them, and men as slaves and breeding stock at the bottom. The appearance of a male wizard elevates a being they consider little better than an animal to a status equal to theirs. That isn't something they can accept. Hence you need to die."

"Is it me or is that a little harsh?" Conryu grinned, hoping some humor might lighten the suddenly serious mood. It didn't. "Right, so what now?"

"For you two it's a full examination by the nurse. Graduation is in two days. Then you return home for summer vacation."

"I was thinking more about what we were going to do about the crazy people trying to kill me."

Dean Blane clambered to her feet. "I don't know about that, but I think we've rooted out all the snakes here."

Kelsie raised her hand as though asking permission to speak. "But you didn't actually know Ms. Light was a member of the bad Society, did you?"

"Not with certainty, though I had my suspicions. Until she made her move I couldn't prove anything."

No one said it out loud, but Conryu at least was wondering whether there were any other snakes hiding in their midst.

12

END OF THE YEAR

Maria stared in growing horror as Conryu explained what had happened on the island. She'd seen the battle with the Le Fay Sorority, the whole school knew about it at this point, but she'd had no idea what precipitated it. She shouldn't have been surprised it was an attack on Conryu.

"So I destroyed the chimera and healed Kelsie—"

"Wait." Maria was certain she must have misunderstood. "You healed her? How? You're a dark wizard."

She tried to comprehend what he was saying, but her brain refused. If Conryu could heal he really didn't have any use for her. All her hard work this semester had been for nothing.

"Willpower. Anyway, you remember the light gem reacted to me as well. Dark magic is my focus this year, but I have the potential to use all types of magic at a fairly high level, at least Dean Blane seems to think so. You should have seen how excited she was when I told her. You'd have thought I'd given her a million dollars."

They were standing outside the nurse's office waiting while the nurse checked Kelsie out. Conryu had come through with a clean bill of health. In fact, he barely had a scratch on him. It was easy for her to think of him as indestructible, but Maria knew just how near a thing it had been.

"So what happened next?"

Conryu told her the rest including how they ended up on the beach sitting beside a bonfire. Sounded a little too romantic. On the other hand she didn't want him shivering through the night and getting sick either.

"The dean and assistant dean came to fetch us when the barrier went down. Sorry if I made you worry."

Since no one had told her what happened she wasn't as worried as she might have been. "It's not your fault."

"How'd you do on your final?"

"I passed and no one tried to kill me. That's how finals are supposed to work."

He laughed. "Yeah, well, maybe next year. I forgot to tell you. I invited Kelsie to come for a visit this summer. Seemed like it would be nice if she saw what a normal family looked like."

Maria stared at him, her brain not fully processing what he just said. "What?"

"I said I invited Kelsie to come for a visit this summer."

"What?"

"Don't be that way. She's a sweetheart. If you gave her half a chance I bet you two would get along great."

Maria heartily doubted that. She saw the way Kelsie looked at Conryu even if he wasn't willing to acknowledge it. That girl wanted more than to be just friends. "Where's she going to stay?"

"I figured on the couch. The apartment's only got two bedrooms after all."

"She's staying with you?" Maria's voice went up three notches. This had to be a bad dream. She was going to wake up in her bed any second now.

"You don't trust me?"

"With a beautiful girl sleeping twenty feet from your bedroom door?"

"What? You used to sleep over all the time when we were kids."

"Focus on the last part of that sentence. We were kids. You two aren't kids."

The door to the nurse's office and Kelsie emerged. She glanced at Maria and ventured a faint smile. "I couldn't help overhearing. If it's going to be a problem I don't have to visit."

She wanted to tell Kelsie it absolutely was going to be a problem, but Conryu said, "No, no problem. We sorted it all out. Assuming you don't mind sleeping on the couch."

"No, I don't mind. Though I don't think I've ever slept on a couch. It couldn't be any less comfortable than the beach, right?"

"Not at all. I nap on it all the time."

Maria looked from Conryu to Kelsie and back again. They were chatting and smiling like they were perfectly comfortable together. When had all this happened? At least before they'd been a little awkward around each other. Maybe it had something to do with the battle and his healing her. Sometimes using light magic on someone created a powerful bond.

"Are you going to send your mother a note?" Conryu asked.

"Yes, this afternoon. I wouldn't want my driver to come to pick me up and not be there. I'm afraid Mom won't be very happy with me." She grinned in a near-perfect imitation of Conryu. "But that's part of the fun."

Kelsie acted more like his girlfriend than Maria. Standing there with them she felt like a disapproving sister, looking for reasons why they shouldn't do what they were planning.

It sucked.

* * *

Conryu and Maria walked side by side toward the cafeteria. Graduation wasn't an especially big event at the academy. Since only students were allowed on campus they didn't bother with handing out diplomas or making speeches. Instead there was a big group gathering with food and games where the seniors could say goodbye to their fellow students and the teachers.

This year the staff had decided to go all out, with fancy catering arriving by train that morning. Dean Blane said it was to help take everyone's mind off what happened at the sorority. Conryu thought it would take more than appetizers to do that, but he didn't want to sound negative.

The members that surrendered had been taken to Central where they'd face a wizards' tribunal led by Kelsie's grandmother. He shivered, not envying the girls that encounter. He felt bad for anyone that had to deal with that woman, even people that wanted him dead.

"So what's your mom got planned for you this summer? Will you be able to hang out with us a little?"

"I'll just be helping her with whatever I can. I wouldn't want to get in you and Kelsie's way."

He groaned. "Are you still going on about that? What's it going to take to convince you we're just friends?"

"I think you believe you're just friends. If you still believe it at the end of summer break I'll be convinced."

Conryu sighed and pushed the cafeteria doors open. He couldn't figure out why Maria imagined he'd change his mind about Kelsie after her visit, but maybe when he didn't that would convince her. He certainly hoped it did. Things had gotten far too uncomfortable between them.

Inside most of the students and faculty had gathered. As usual Conryu was among the last to arrive. He caught a flash of red out of the corner of his eye and the next thing he knew Sonja leapt at him and wrapped her arms around his neck.

"I did it," she said far too loudly right next to his ear. "They didn't even yell, just like you said they wouldn't. I'm so relieved."

Maria muttered something about him being popular with the ladies before wandering off toward the laden tables to find a snack.

"What's with her?" Sonja asked as he lowered her to the ground.

"Long story. So what were you saying with such enthusiasm?"

"I hadn't heard back from my parents so I called and told them I was taking a job with a magic engineering company. The company was really impressed with what we did on the engine and offered me a good salary. It's so exciting. I may even have a chance to work on golems there."

"Congratulations. What did your parents say?" Conryu guided her toward the food. He'd skipped lunch and was eager to eat.

"They were disappointed, of course, but they said if that was what I really wanted to do it was okay and if it didn't work out I could always come work at the factory later."

"That's about the best you could have hoped for."

Sonja nodded and hugged him again. "I never would have had the guts to tell them if you hadn't encouraged me. Thank you, thank you, thank you."

He gave her a pat on the head. It was good to see Sonja excited.

"Oh, there's Crystal. I haven't told her yet since I wanted to let you know first. Later."

And she rushed off again. Sonja was a lot like a tornado. She appeared and disappeared quickly, but left an impression.

Conryu examined the nearest table and only recognized half the offerings on it. He settled on a deviled egg. The moment he popped it in his mouth Dean Blane approached.

"How would you rate your first year at the academy?"

He swallowed the half-chewed egg. "I lived through it. If the next three are anything like the first, I'll be the first student to graduate with a combat citation."

She laughed. "Next year won't be anywhere near as bad as this one. With the sorority gone and the worst offenders removed you should be safe."

"Emphasis on should."

She shrugged. "There are no guarantees in life. You've come a long ways, I can't wait to see what you accomplish next year."

He spotted Kelsie approaching as Dean Blane left. How was he ever going to get something to eat? She stopped in front of him and hung her head. "Mom found out I was planning to visit you and said I couldn't go."

"And?"

She blinked. "What do you mean?"

"I mean you're an adult, right? It's your decision not hers. What do you want to do?"

She looked away then back. "I want to go with you."

"Then do it. When the train stops in Central tomorrow stay onboard. Show her you have a will of your own."

"Mom'll be furious." Kelsie offered a little smile. "Let's do it."

13
ALMOST TIME

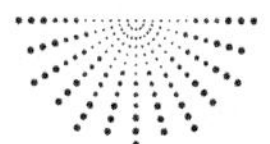

Conryu stepped out of his suite and set his bag beside the door, gently so he didn't shake up Prime. After a moment of indignation the scholomantic had agreed to hide amidst his laundry, all clean, thank you very much. He'd come to the conclusion that he'd introduce Prime next year as his familiar since sophomores were allowed to have one, but for now he'd keep it a secret.

Several upperclassmen rushed past him on their way to the train. They still had an hour before departure so Conryu had decided to wait and walk with Kelsie. Maria was supposed to meet them in the lounge upstairs. She still wasn't thrilled that Kelsie would be spending two weeks camped out on his couch, but she wasn't scowling at him all the time at least.

A little ways down the hall Mrs. Lenore's door opened and she stepped out into the hall. Conryu waved. She had on her black robe instead of the pink pajamas.

She smiled and crossed the hall. "Looking forward to your vacation?"

"You know it. What about you, any plans?"

"I'm visiting my family on the west coast. We'll hang out at the beach, surf, fish, all that sort of stuff."

He grinned. The idea of Mrs. Lenore as a surfer chick never crossed his mind. "Sounds fun. I've never been surfing. The beaches in Sentinel City aren't the cleanest. There are a few stretches you shouldn't even walk on without boots."

"That sounds awful. Two blocks from my parents' house is the most beautiful white sand beach you've ever seen. We live in a little town so far off the beaten track hardly any tourists come to visit so we often have it all to ourselves."

"Cool. I have to ask. Why was there a teapot in your bathroom?"

She blushed and looked away. "Students aren't allowed to cook in their rooms so the teachers don't either. Sometimes at night I like a cup of tea and I don't want to go to the cafeteria so I made a little stove with a fire spirit. I keep it in my bathroom so no one will see it."

"That doesn't strike me as a big deal, but rest assured your secret is safe with me." Kelsie emerged from the group room and headed their way. She had on a simple blue dress and black shoes and carried a bag in each hand. "Until next year."

"Have a nice summer."

Conryu left his bag and went to help Kelsie. "Can I carry those for you?"

"No need."

"Are you sure?" If she had as much stuff as Maria those bags had to weigh a ton.

She held one out to him. "See for yourself."

He took the bag and found it weighed next to nothing. "How?"

"Magic. These are Kincade Carryalls. You can put whatever you want in them and they never weigh more than two pounds."

"Now I know what I'm getting Maria for her birthday. How much are they?"

"Ten grand each."

He winced. "Jesus. On second thought I'll just buy her those hair clips she's been hinting around for since April. You ready to go?"

"Yup, all set."

Together they went upstairs. The lounge was almost empty so he had no trouble spotting Maria. After so many days of seeing her in the white robes it almost came as a shock to find her in a black sundress and wearing her favorite silver jewelry. Her bags sat on the floor beside her and she rose as they approached.

Conryu kissed her on the cheek. "You look gorgeous."

"Thanks." She nodded to Kelsie. "Shall we head out? It would be a shame to miss the train."

"You got that right." He hefted her bags in his right hand and groaned. "Are these heavier than when we arrived?"

"They might be. The librarian said I could take a few books home with me. I found three that Mom doesn't have in her collection."

"What are they printed on, slate?" Conryu led the way through the doors and down to the train platform.

Hundreds of girls stood waiting. The babble of voices almost immediately made him long for the quiet of their cabin. The glint of silver caught his eye a moment before the train eased up to the platform.

He glanced back at the school. He wouldn't miss the place, but on the other hand his first year of school hadn't been quite as bad as he'd feared. Close, but meeting Sonja and Kelsie had helped balance out the repeated murder attempts.

He found he was curious to discover what next year would bring.

* * *

Lady Raven stood in the light of one of the two windows in her redoubt and watched the floating island drift ever closer. The edge of the shadow was touching the city now. In a couple more days it would be in place and the Le Fay Society would put the Alliance on its knees begging them to spare Sentinel City.

Maybe they would. If the world's leaders met the Society's demands the island could continue on its way and no one would be worse off for the little scare they'd receive. And if the leaders gave in this time, when next year rolled around the Society would make new demands. It would continue on until the artifacts were found or the trick stopped working.

She smiled. A large piece of Lady Raven hoped the powers that be refused to yield to their demands. How many lives could her shadow beasts take before they were destroyed? It would be exciting to find out. Either way she would have completed her mission. The Hierarchs would have to recognize her efforts and promote her. It was a win-win situation and those were her favorites.

She stretched, enjoying the warmth. Not much longer now.

Lady Raven could hardly wait.

THE RAVEN'S SHADOW

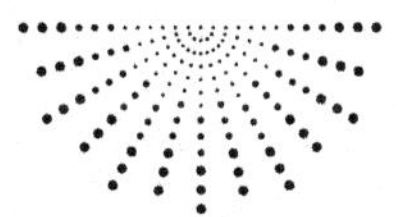

THE AEGIS OF MERLIN BOOK 4

1
HEADING HOME

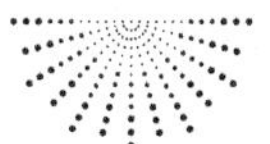

Conryu yawned, snuggled deeper into his soft chair, and glanced out the window. The train was pulling into Central Station. In the distance the black Department building drew his eye. Despite being only half as tall as some of the surrounding skyscrapers it still managed to dominate the skyline. It was probably the aura of the unnatural that surrounded it. Either that or the presence of Kelsie's grandmother inside twisted reality.

Speaking of which, he'd offered to let Kelsie ride with them, but she'd insisted on staying in her private cabin. She claimed to be tired, but Conryu suspected she felt like a third wheel when Maria was around. He really hoped the two girls eventually learned to get along. He was very fond of both of them and it would make his life a lot easier if they liked each other at least a little.

Across from him Maria had her nose buried in one of the books she'd brought home with her. Why on earth she'd want to do more studying after all they'd done at school this past year baffled him. The only reason he'd brought Prime was because he had no choice. A powerful bond connected him to the scholomantic. If they were separated by more than a hundred or so yards the results would be painful for them both.

The brakes whined as the train slowed and came to a stop. The majority of the students would disembark here before boarding trains to other parts of the Alliance. Conryu and Maria had the good fortune—at least, good fortune in terms of avoiding potential assassins—not to have to leave their cabin. The whole car would be added to the train headed for Sentinel City.

Maria looked up from her book. "Are we there?"

"We're at the capital, but we've still got a long way to go."

"Oh." She lowered her face back to the book and was instantly lost in her own world.

Conryu shook his head and smiled. Must be nice.

Of course, Prime would like nothing better than to spend every moment cramming his head full of new spells. Conryu was a good deal less enthusiastic about studying, preferring to learn what he needed when he needed it. His hope was that he wouldn't need any magic this summer.

In the hall outside, a door slammed and a moment later a muffled voice protested.

Maria looked up again. "What was that?"

"Beats me." Conryu strode over and opened the door.

A big guy in a black suit had Kelsie by the wrist and was dragging her toward the exit. A second man had her bags.

"Hey!" All three turned to look at him. "What the hell are you two doing?"

The man with the bags scowled through his goatee. "Ms. Kincade is coming home with us. Return to your cabin and there won't be any trouble."

"You think you can kidnap my friend and there won't be any trouble?" He stepped out into the hall. "Let her go and get lost. Then there won't be any trouble."

"Conryu, these are my mom's private security guards. If she told them to bring me home they won't let me go."

"Do you want to go with them?"

"No."

He glared at the men in black through narrowed eyes. "Then we have a problem."

The nearest man tossed Kelsie's bags to the ground and reached under his coat. When Conryu saw the pistol he threw his hand forward. "Shatter!"

The gun burst into a handful of metal filings. In the guard's moment of surprise Conryu stepped in with a snap kick to the side of his knee.

When the guard's knee hit the hall floor Conryu spun into a slashing elbow to his opponent's temple. The guard's head thumped off the wall and he collapsed in a heap.

The second guard appeared uncertain whether he should release Kelsie and fight or try and drag her out of the train car. Conryu stepped over the unconscious figure and advanced down the hall.

The still-standing guard thrust Kelsie in front of him. "Don't come any closer."

"Or what? You expect me to believe you might hurt your employer's daughter?" Conryu concentrated on Kelsie. "Cloak of Darkness!"

Liquid black covered Kelsie from head to toe.

"Gah!" The guard thrust her away from him. He clearly had no idea what the spell did, just as Conryu had hoped.

Conryu pulled Kelsie behind him. Maria stood in the doorway and held out her hand. "Come on."

Kelsie hesitated for just a moment before ducking into the cabin. Maria nodded to him, slammed the door shut and snapped the lock.

Conryu stared at the still-conscious guard. "Just you and me now. If you want to leave I promise I won't tell anyone."

The guard fell into a fighting stance. "You took Freddy by surprise. I won't go down so easy."

"Did you see what I did to his gun? I could do that to your head just as easily."

The guard's Adam's apple bobbed as sweat poured down his face. Conryu didn't actually know if such a simple spell would blast the guard's head to bits, though it stood to reason the spell affected living flesh as well as it did nonliving material. The truth was even if it did work that way, he wouldn't do it, but Freddy's pal didn't know that.

The guard lowered his fists. "You don't understand. If we go back without Lady Kincade's daughter she'll fire us at best."

Conryu didn't have much sympathy for men who would kidnap a girl just because their employer told them to. "Try to look on the bright side. At least you'll still be alive to search for a new job."

He stepped back over Freddy, who was now groaning on the floor, and stood beside his cabin door. Conryu raised his hand. "Take him and go. Last warning."

"Alright, alright. Just so you know, I'm blaming you for all this." The guard collected his partner and the pair of them stumbled off the train.

Conryu sighed and lowered his hand. They'd bought his bluff. Thank goodness.

* * *

Conryu waited until the two goons were off the train before he turned and knocked. "They're gone, let me in."

A second later the lock clicked open and he slid the door aside. Maria returned to her seat across from Kelsie, who was still covered in his Cloak of Darkness spell. Conryu waved his hand and the darkness vanished.

The guard's tight grip had raised a set of nasty bruises on Kelsie's wrist. "You okay?" he asked.

"Yeah, but Mom's going to be really mad. I mean, I knew she

wasn't going to be happy I ignored her order, but I never thought she'd send two of her personal bodyguards to drag me home."

"Let me see your arm." Maria gently took Kelsie's bruised wrist in her hand. She chanted a spell and a bright glow surrounded her hand. She rubbed the injuries and Kelsie sighed.

"You know," Maria said. "I wasn't thrilled when Conryu invited you to come for a visit, but if this is how your family treats you I'm starting to think he should have offered to let you stay longer. There."

The glow disappeared revealing smooth, healed skin.

"Thank you." Kelsie lunged across the little table and hugged Maria. "For everything."

Conryu grinned and went back out to collect Kelsie's bags. He'd have to thank Kelsie's mother. Her thugs' attack had done more to make Maria sympathetic to her problems than anything he could have said. Maybe, just maybe, the two of them would start getting along better now.

He brought the bags inside and set them in the corner. There wasn't room enough in the overhead storage for two more suitcases. There also weren't enough chairs for all of them. He shrugged and sat on the floor, using her bags as a backrest.

"I'm sorry." Kelsie started to get up. "I'm taking your chair."

"Don't worry about it." He waved her back into the seat. "I doubt Dumb and Ugly will be back, but I'll feel better if I know where you are."

"I heard you talking through the door." Kelsie sat back down. "Would you have really killed that guy?"

"Naw. I'm not even sure if Shatter will work on living flesh."

In the storage area Conryu's bag shifted and bounced. He sighed, stood up, and unzipped it. A t-shirt flew out and zoomed around the cabin like a cheap Halloween ghost. Prime's muffled voice was unintelligible.

"Hold still." Prime hovered over the table and Conryu pulled the shirt off him. "What did you want?"

"I eavesdropped on your conversation and since it is my duty to educate you I attempted to escape and do so. Shatter isn't an effective spell for killing. That said, it's a simple thing for a powerful dark wizard to kill. All you need to do is focus on your target and say 'die' in Infernal."

"That sounds way too easy," Conryu said.

"The spell is simple, making it work is hard. You have to genuinely want the spell's target to die with all your will. The least bit of doubt and the spell will fail. I hesitate to find fault, Master, but I fear you lack the capacity to kill with magic. You're too kind hearted."

Maria shook her head. "That's not a fault. If Conryu could casually kill someone he wouldn't be who he is."

The cabin fell silent for half a minute before Kelsie asked, "So how long to reach Sentinel City?"

The mood lightened at once and Conryu settled back on his makeshift couch. He really didn't want to kill anyone, but as a warrior he knew enough to realize the day would come when he'd have to make a choice. He wouldn't always be able to win while leaving his enemies alive.

"Four or five hours on the train, plus however long it takes to drive to our building." Maria reached for her bag. "I have extra books if you'd like something to read."

"No, thank you. I don't think I could concentrate. I'm just going to rest my eyes and try to take a nap."

That sounded like an excellent idea, but Conryu was too keyed up to sleep. After half an hour or so the train got underway again. When they moved out of sight of Central City he finally allowed himself to relax.

Sometime later the train jerked. Conryu's eyes popped open and he was halfway to his feet before he noticed the station out the window. He must have dozed off after all. He twisted his neck from side to side to work the stiffness out.

Kelsie was softly snoring and he hated to wake her, but he

didn't have enough hands to carry her and the bags. He gave her shoulder a shake and she groaned.

"Come on, wake up. We're here."

She blinked and sat up straight. Maria held out a napkin and tapped her chin. Kelsie wiped the drool off while turning beet red. She crumpled up the napkin and climbed out of her chair while Conryu collected his and Maria's bags.

"Think your parents will be here?" Conryu asked.

Maria shrugged and opened the door. "No idea. I can't get a straight answer whenever I ask about what's happening. I can tell Dad's stressed to the max and it's rubbing off on Mom. I hope at least one of them's here, but I'm not holding my breath."

"At least your parents aren't going to send someone to try and kidnap you," Kelsie said.

Maria laughed. "True, but not sending kidnappers is a pretty low bar. From what Conryu's told me I wouldn't trade parents with you for the world."

They made their way to the car door and climbed down to the platform. Since they were in the last cabin in the last car everyone had already disembarked and was making their way toward the lobby. The trio followed along at an easy pace.

"Think we can coax Mom into taking us to Giovanni's for dinner?" Conryu adjusted his grip on Maria's bag.

"I don't know, but that's an excellent plan. When's Jonny getting in?"

"I'm pretty sure he said the day after tomorrow."

"Who's Jonny?" Kelsie asked.

"Another old friend." Conryu grinned. "He's attending military school. His plan is to be deployed to Florida and defend scantily clad beach babes from zombies."

"That doesn't sound very likely." Kelsie glanced back at him. "He knows that, right?"

"He should, I've told him often enough. Jonny—"

"Conryu Koda!" Running down the platform was Kat Gable and her unlucky cameraman, Joe.

"Oh, for Christ's sake. Can't I get off the train just once without that lunatic waiting for me?"

Kelsie turned to face him. "You know Kat?"

"Sort of; she's my personal stalker. The woman is incapable of taking no for an answer."

"Do you know her?" Maria asked.

"Sure, she's interviewed me and my mom half a dozen times. Kat handles all the magic-related interviews for her network. She's tough, but fair, though one time my mom threatened to buy her station and fire her."

Kat reached them and thrust her microphone in Conryu's face. "How did you enjoy your first year at the Arcane Academy?"

Conryu glared into the camera. *Shatter!* The lens cracked and sparks shot out the back.

"Fuck me!" Joe dropped the camera and danced away a second before it burst into flames.

Conryu turned his gaze on Kat. "No comment."

She lowered the microphone and frowned. "How long are we going to have to play this game? Why don't you just give me the interview and we can both move on."

"If you want it to be over all you need to do is stop showing up wherever I am. I don't owe you a thing."

Kat shook her head then her eyes went wide. "Kelsie Kincade? I didn't even notice you there. What brings you to Sentinel City?"

"Visiting friends. Nice to see you again, Kat."

"We need to go. I imagine my mom's getting impatient." Conryu stalked past the now-silent Kat.

"Bye." Kelsie waved to the reporter and fell in behind him with Maria bringing up the rear.

When they were outside of Kat's range of hearing Maria said, "Did you make his camera explode?"

Conryu offered his best innocent look. "Me?"

"Yeah, you."

"Did I cast a spell?"

"No."

"There you go."

They left the platform and after a quick search through the many hugging families spotted Conryu's mom standing near one of the pillars on the right side of the entry area. She saw them at the same moment and waved before running over and hugging him.

After half a minute and several kisses Conryu wiggled free. "Hey, Mom. Dad waiting in the car?"

"Of course." Mom turned her attention to Kelsie. "Aren't you going to introduce me?"

"Sorry. Mom meet Kelsie Kincade. Kelsie, my mom."

They shook hands and Kelsie said, "Thanks so much for letting me stay with you. I hope I won't be too much of a bother."

"Not at all, dear. Sho and I are always glad to meet a friend of Conryu's. And such a famous one. I'm afraid you'll find our little apartment smaller than you're used to."

Kelsie smiled. "At school I share a room with eleven other girls, so rooming with three people won't be a problem."

"Did my parents not come?" Maria's disappointment came through loud and clear.

"No, Orin asked me to give you a ride home. Your mom was called out of the city on an emergency consultation and he's been working crazy hours at the Department. I have no idea what's happening, but everyone's nerves are stretched tight."

Maria slumped and Conryu wanted to give her a hug, but his hands were overloaded as it was. He couldn't have been more pleased when Kelsie did it for him. Even better, Maria didn't shrug her off. Summer was looking to be a good deal more pleasant than he'd first feared.

* * *

Kelsie screamed when Conryu opened the throttle on his bike and they roared down the highway. She'd never ridden on a motorcycle before, her mother said they were too dangerous. As she clutched Conryu's chest and watched the cars whiz by she thought she might have finally found something she and her mother agreed on.

What Kelsie couldn't deny was the thrill of it. Her heart raced and tears streamed down her face both from the wind and the excitement. It also provided an excellent excuse to hug Conryu which was something she'd never pass up.

He shot past a bus and she tightened her grip. When he'd shown her the gleaming black bike this morning she never imagined flying down the road at ninety miles an hour, her hair snapping behind her in the wind.

Last night had been her first experience sleeping on a couch and it was much nicer than she'd expected. Conryu's mother had fixed it up like a proper bed with soft sheets and a warm, snuggly blanket. She'd been so sweet, doing everything short of tucking Kelsie in to make her feel at home.

Kelsie couldn't help contrasting the welcome she'd received from these total strangers with the one her family gave her whenever she came home after a trip. Generally all she got was a combination of complaints and indifference. She'd been tempted to ask Mrs. Koda to adopt her on the spot and after the incident on the train that might still be an option. If nothing else she now understood why he said he wouldn't trade families with her for all the money in the world.

Conryu slewed the bike into the right lane, slowed, and pulled onto the off-ramp. They hadn't really had a destination, the trip was just an excuse for him to take his beloved bike for a spin.

After his parents and Maria, Kelsie was pretty sure Conryu loved his bike the most. When he'd uncovered it this morning he whispered to it and stroked it in a way that made her jealous.

Kelsie would have loved to woken up that way. With his parents in the kitchen and Maria four floors up that didn't seem likely.

He wove through crowded city streets, to where, she couldn't say. Ten minutes later he pulled into a dirt lot. In the nearby park workers were building a fence around the perimeter. Conryu switched off the motor, put down the kickstand, and pulled off his helmet.

She copied him and shook out her hair, trying to restore some semblance of order. "What is this place?"

"This is the site of the annual Shadow Carnival. It's also where I was almost murdered for the second time. I'm not entirely sure why I came back here. It was like something drew me."

The flap on his saddlebag rustled and Prime flew out. She'd been so excited by the ride she'd forgotten all about the book.

"It's not unusual for the site of past trauma to haunt a person for years afterward. Don't be concerned, Master, there's nothing wrong with your mind."

"As always, Prime, you're a great comfort."

"So what happened here?" She'd never heard the whole story about Conryu's many brushes with death even though she'd lived through one of them.

When he finished telling her she shook her head. "So that's why you were curious about shadow beasts in our first class. I admit I was wondering."

"Why didn't you ask?"

"I was wary of you right up until my desperation got the best of me. Looking back, I can't believe how many weeks I wasted. If I'd just taken a chance that first day when you talked to me we could have become friends so much sooner."

"We're friends now, that's what counts." He patted her knee.

His gaze shifted to the sky. Hanging above them was the huge floating island. She'd seen this one before, though it didn't fly directly over Central. It looked like it was headed right for them, sort of a slow motion meteor from a movie.

"When's the carnival?" Kelsie asked.

"This weekend, when the island is directly overhead. It'll be so dark you'll think it's night at noon."

"Can we go?"

"I don't know if they'll let me in after what happened last year, but we can try. Maria and I have been going since we were little so it's a tradition and Jonny would never pass up a chance at junk food."

"How long have you known him?" Conryu had mentioned they were friends, but she didn't know anything else about him.

"Since third grade. He arrives from military school tomorrow for a one-month break." Conryu sighed. "And I thought we got screwed on vacation time. So what do you want to do after lunch?"

She shrugged. Kelsie was happy to do anything as long as it was with him.

* * *

Lady Raven stood on the small balcony of her redoubt and watched the island creep across the sky. It wouldn't be long now. After a year of sitting on her hands, hiding, and making preparations, at last everything would come together. And not a moment too soon as far as she was concerned. Another month cooped up with nothing but undead for company and she feared she might go mad.

Her black silk robe swirled around her as a warm summer breeze caressed her skin and carried the salty scent of the nearby ocean to her. The blue-green water lay on the opposite side of the building from where she stood. Lady Raven imagined it, the waves, the birds. The mental exercise soothed her for a few seconds before the blast of a ship's horn jolted her out of her reverie.

Just as well, really. The final meeting with the Hierarchs was due to begin in ten minutes. She needed to go back inside and prepare. Three steps carried her through the French doors and into her bedroom where two of the undead bikers she'd taken as her personal bodyguards stood against the wall waiting for orders. She'd left three of the others to guard the entrance to her base and the last was destroyed by Terra and her flunkies.

She brushed past her bed, pausing long enough to collect the black raven mask from her nightstand. On her way out she paused to look at herself in the dressing room mirror. Still old, still wrinkled, but still alive and more powerful than ever. That was an exchange the younger members of the Society wouldn't understand for many more years.

Satisfied, Lady Raven opened the door and stepped out into the hall. It was a short walk from the bedroom to her casting chamber, intentionally so, as she had to be available day or night for her superiors, especially now that the culmination of their work was so close at hand. Her guards fell in behind automatically.

There was no danger to her here and it seemed foolish to have the lumbering things following her everywhere, but better safe than sorry. The only rule was they weren't allowed in her casting chamber. The nature of their dark magic messed with her spells in unpredictable ways, so they stood guard outside while she stepped into the Spartan chamber.

When she first arrived she'd taken the time to inscribe a permanent spell circle in the floor, thus freeing herself from having to draw it again and again. The mask slipped over her head and settled into its familiar place. When this mission ended she'd miss the raven mask, but Hierarchs all wore animal masks; only Sub-Hierarchs wore birds. It was an upgrade she was eager to make.

Once inside the circle she cleared her mind and prepared for her superiors to make contact. Five minutes later a faint tingle was followed by the appearance of the Hierarchs and Lady Bluejay. Of the horrid Lady Mockingbird there was no sign.

"All is in readiness?" Lady Dragon asked.

"Yes, Mistress. There has been no activity near the new hiding places and I've seen no activity at the Department that concerns me."

"Excellent. Tomorrow we release our demands. The weak men will do what we require or see the streets of their city choked with the dead."

"As you say, Lady Dragon." Lady Raven's eyes flicked to the spot usually occupied by her rival.

Lady Dragon didn't miss the minute gesture, precisely as she'd hoped. "Lady Mockingbird is dead."

The blunt admission set her on her heels for a moment. Had she so badly failed the Hierarchs that they felt the need to eliminate her?

"No, we didn't kill her." Lady Dragon leaned back in an unseen chair. "Her attempt to slay the abomination failed and her cover was pierced. She fell in battle with the head of dark magic, Angeline Umbra."

"A worthy foe. Pity about Lady Mockingbird."

Lady Dragon's laugh filled the space. "Spare us your false concern. The hatred between the two of you was well known. To pretend otherwise is an insult to all of us."

Lady Raven bowed her head. "I meant no offense. But I do have a suggestion."

"We will hear it," Lady Dragon said.

"What if we included turning over the abomination to us as part of our plans? We could let the fools in the Department do our work for us. That would be a small thing compared to releasing our leader."

Lady Dragon's mask covered her whole face, hiding her expression, but from the way she leaned forward Lady Raven hoped her idea had been well received.

"An excellent idea. It will be a simple matter to add it with potentially great gains. You will make a fine Hierarch, Lady Raven."

Her heart raced upon hearing Lady Dragon's compliment. She had never shown such open favoritism before.

"Be ready." Lady Dragon's figure started to fade away. "When the time comes it will be your responsibility to punish the city should their leaders fail to do as we require."

A second later Lady Raven was alone. None of the others had made so much as a sound. She didn't know what to make of it. Were they distancing themselves in case she failed or had Lady Dragon given orders for them to remain silent?

There was no way for her to know and that fact frightened her almost as much as the completion of her mission excited her. In a few days her fate would be sealed one way or the other.

2

ULTIMATUM

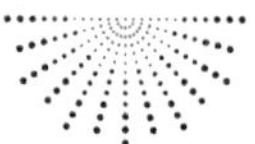

"Long time no see, bro!" Jonny stepped through the door and bumped fists with Conryu.

In the ten months since Conryu'd last seen his second-oldest friend, Jonny had traded his ripped jeans for fatigues, gotten a military-spec buzz cut, and put on about ten pounds of muscle. His already bronze skin had darkened and unless Conryu was mistaken he'd gotten a new scar on his right arm.

"Looks like the army agrees with you." Conryu motioned him to the couch and shut the door.

Jonny managed two steps before he froze. Kelsie was sitting on the couch with a slightly nervous smile. She had on a scoop-neck red dress that hugged her curves in a way that would annoy Maria when she arrived with the food.

Conryu smacked his forehead with his palm. He'd forgotten to mention Kelsie would be visiting in his last letter.

"Who's the babe and does Maria know she's here?" Jonny couldn't stop looking, not that Conryu blamed him.

"Jonny Salazar meet Kelsie Kincade. Kelsie, this is Jonny." They shook hands and Conryu gave his friend a playful shove toward the recliner before sitting beside Kelsie. "So how was your first year?"

"Boring. Dude, you wouldn't believe it. Every day, marching, calisthenics, shooting, and more marching. On the plus side they give us three squares a day and the guns were fun. So was the hand-to-hand combat training. I learned some good tricks."

"Yeah? Maybe a sparring match is in order."

"Maybe give me another year to practice. What about you, anyone try to kill you lately?"

"Not for a week or so."

Jonny's laugh slowly died when no one else joined in. "Shit, you're serious. What was it this time, more religious nuts?"

"I wish. It was a giant three-headed elemental monster called a chimera. The monster tried to burn me, drown me, and crush me. I came through it okay, but it was a near thing for Kelsie."

Jonny turned his gaze on Kelsie. "He's a dangerous guy to hang around with. Did he tell you about the time we were almost eaten by these big black dogs?"

Prime chose that moment to come flying out of his bedroom. "Master, your friend's lack of knowledge regarding the shadow hounds is appalling. I felt it was my duty to come and explain."

To Jonny's credit his reaction to seeing a talking book with the face of a demon was limited to his eyes nearly bugging out of his head. "What the fuck is that?"

"I thought I mentioned Prime in my last letter. He's my scholomantic slash familiar. Long story. Let's just say my year was a good deal less boring than I might have liked. On the plus side I picked up several great friends." For the sake of not totally overwhelming his already overwhelmed friend Conryu didn't mention Cerberus or the Dark Lady.

Kelsie blushed and Prime cleared his nonexistent throat. "Thank you, Master."

"Don't mention it, or the shadow hounds for that matter, but if you want to hang out in the living room it's fine."

Prime settled on the coffee table just as Maria pushed the door open. Her arms were laden with bags and a pizza box. Conryu and Jonny both jumped up to help her with her burden. To no one's surprise Jonny made off with the pizza box.

Jonny took a deep breath and sighed. "This is what I missed the most."

"Hey!" Conryu punched him in the arm.

"Sorry, second most."

Kelsie came to join them in the kitchen as they emptied bags of food on the counter. She whispered, "You are so lucky. I never had friends like this. Jonny seems nice."

"Yeah, he's awesome."

Everyone gathered their snacks of choice. Pizza and chips for Conryu and Jonny while Kelsie and Maria swapped the chips for a salad. Everyone settled around the tv. He sat between the girls on the couch and Jonny returned to the recliner.

Conryu switched the baseball game on. The Sentinel Soldiers were down three runs to the Stark Sturgeons.

"Good to see some things never change," Jonny said around a mouthful of pizza. "The bums still don't know how to play ball."

The Soldiers hadn't made it to the Alliance Series since before Conryu was born and they hadn't even made it to the playoffs in ten years. The screen went black for a second before a giant, flashing alert sign appeared followed by a sternly attractive female anchorwoman.

"We interrupt this broadcast with an important announcement. This station has received a recording from the terrorist organization known as the Le Fay Society. We made this available to the city government one hour ago and after they viewed it we were assured everything is under control. Please keep that in mind as we play the message. Some of you may find it disturbing. If there are small children in the room now would be a good time to take them out."

Thirty seconds later the screen flickered and the image of a woman in an Imperial-style dragon mask appeared on the screen. "I am Lady Dragon, interim leader of the Le Fay Society. My agents have planted a number of magical weapons in Sentinel City. If our true leader, Morgana Le Fay, is not released from the Lonely Rock Prison and the abomination Conryu Koda handed over to us within forty-eight hours we will unleash an army of shadow beasts that will slaughter your people by the thousands. There will be no negotiations. You will comply or die. We will contact you every twelve hours until our demands are met."

The anchor reappeared. "The mayor has assured us that the Department of Magic has this matter well under control and the people of the city are in no danger."

When she started talking about him, Conryu turned the tv off.

"Is this what Dad had you working on?" Maria asked.

Conryu found his appetite gone despite the steaming slice of pizza in front of him. "That seems like a safe bet, though he never told me anything specific about a threat."

"He wouldn't have. Dad wouldn't want you any more deeply involved in something like this than was absolutely necessary."

Outside, sirens came screaming closer and his phone rang. He answered while Kelsie ran to the window.

"There're six cop cars out here and men with machine guns are spilling out," she said.

"Hello." Conryu only half listened to what Kelsie was saying. "Angus? Calm down. What do you mean I need to get out of the building?"

* * *

Orin watched the recording for the fifth time. He was sitting in the Department conference room, waiting for the mayor and his crisis team to arrive. City hall had sent the Society's ultimatum over ten minutes ago demanding to know if it was a hoax and if it wasn't what he was doing about it.

He'd put them off by claiming he didn't want to talk about it over the phone. That bought him however long it would take the officials to make the trip from City Hall three blocks north of here. He turned the computer off and leaned back in his chair. They'd all known something like this was coming, despite his assurances to the contrary. He hadn't exactly lied to the mayor, but he had indicated they were making more progress than they actually were.

Beside him, Terra, Lin, and Angus sat in stunned silence. Finally Terra said, "The other world governments will never agree to free Morgana. She's the most dangerous terrorist on the planet. Nothing we, the mayor, or the president for that matter, can say will change anything."

Orin rubbed his face. "I don't disagree. What I need now is something I can tell the mayor that will give him confidence that we can handle this without giving in to their demands."

He looked desperately at each of them, but found nothing to give him hope. Lin looked exhausted, his eyes black and bloodshot with three days of stubble on his chin. Terra was only a little better, her complexion paler than usual and her gray-blond hair in disarray. Angus just looked totally confused.

Terra shook her head. "I have nothing to offer you, Orin. We've done everything possible and it came up short. What we need to do now is plan for the upcoming battle, try to figure out how to save as many lives as possible."

"That's not what he's going to want to hear."

Orin's secretary spoke through the loud speaker. "The mayor and his team have arrived, sir."

"Speak of the devil." Orin heaved himself out of his chair.

The others joined him and a moment later the doors swung open. The mayor strode through looking for all the world like he owned the place. Tom Corbin was a hale and fit fifty-year-old who favored gray suits and expensive shoes. The Corbin family had been the heart of Sentinel City politics for the past hundred years and if Tom had his way it would continue to be for another hundred.

Behind him were the commandant of police, fire marshal, a pair of security guards, and two others, a man and a woman, that Orin had never met.

"Tom." Orin held out his hand, curious to find out if his old friend would take it.

"Orin." They shook and Orin had a moment of relief. "Please tell me these lunatics are bluffing."

"I'm sorry, Tom. Despite our best efforts we've been unable to neutralize the threat."

Tom sat in the nearest chair and waved his people down. When everyone had settled in he said, "That's not remotely acceptable. I've spoken to the president and there's no way they'll free the witch Morgana. Even worse, the war up north is still raging. We can expect no help from Central."

"That was our thinking as well, sir. I've contacted all the combat-worthy wizards, not that there are many, in the city, including my wife. They're ready to fight at the first sign of danger. We also have an estimate of the most-threatened areas. Evacuations may be prudent."

The unfamiliar woman put her hands on the table and leaned forward. "Our view is that evacuations will be ineffective if shadow beasts are involved. Once summoned they will be free to hunt anywhere in the city once the sun sets."

"Who, exactly, are you?" Orin asked.

"Maggie Chin. My colleague and I are magical risk consultants. Analyzing the potential threat of a large-scale event is our specialty."

"Are you a wizard?" Terra asked.

Orin had been wondering the same thing since she didn't have a gray robe, though Shizuku often wore suits when she was working.

"No, I'm an analyst, not a wizard. But that in no way invalidates my conclusion. The risk of panic outweighs any gain from an evacuation."

Orin drew a breath to continue the argument but Tom raised his hand. "We're of one mind on this matter so let's leave it there."

Orin clenched his jaw and nodded. "Of course. What about organizing a defense?"

Tom glanced at his consultant who looked at the tablet on the desk in front of her. "Conventional weapons are useless against magical threats and our inventory of enchanted weapons is exceedingly limited as is our force of wizards. We will do what we can, but unless the terrorists can be convinced to stay their hand, our options are limited."

Orin looked from the consultant to Tom. "I'm not certain I understand what you're planning."

"Tell me about Conryu Koda," Tom said.

Acid burned the back of Orin's throat. "Conryu's a good kid. He's been of great help in our efforts to resolve this matter."

"And you think he'll continue to be willing to help?"

"Absolutely. Why?"

"We're planning to take him into protective custody. If we can't come up with an alternative solution we'll offer him to the Society in hopes of convincing them to give us more time to meet their other demand."

"You're going to sacrifice him?" Orin kept his emotions under control by the narrowest of margins.

"The life of one or the lives of thousands. It's not a difficult decision." Maggie's emotionless tone grated on his nerves.

"And if you turn over our best hope of defeating this enemy and they activate the spell anyway, what then?"

Tom shook his head. "Even if it's one in a million, it's a chance we have to take."

Angus leapt to his feet. "This is madness. That boy's value is beyond measure."

The mayor didn't even spare Angus a glance. "The decision's

been made. We've already sent officers to take him into custody. I know you're fond of the boy, Orin, but I have to do what I think is best for the city."

Angus's face had turned red and he was working himself into a fury. Orin wasn't far behind, but he'd learned better control. He also had an idea. Before Angus blew his top Orin grabbed the professor by the collar and dragged him toward the door.

"If you can't control yourself you can wait in your office." Orin leaned in close and whispered, "Warn him, Angus."

He tossed the professor out into the hall and pulled the door shut. "Sorry about that. Angus has always been a little temperamental. Shall we discuss contingency plans?"

* * *

"They're coming for you, my boy. The mayor means to use you as a bribe to convince the terrorists to spare the city, though Orin assures me there's no hope of that happening. You need to hurry. The police are already on their way."

"Actually they're here. Thanks for the warning, Angus." Conryu disconnected.

"What's going on?" Maria asked.

"It appears I'm to be a sacrificial lamb. We need to split, now."

"No way we're sneaking out." Jonny had joined Kelsie at the window. "Those guys are the city's elite counter-terrorism unit. They're the best."

"Shit! Well, there are other options. I can go by dark portal."

"Mom's wards won't let you open one in the building."

"Reveal!" A shimmering wall of light magic appeared beyond the window. "Is your mom home from her job?"

Maria nodded. "She got in late last night. I don't think she's up yet and even if she was it would take hours to open a gap in the barrier."

"Not for me it won't. Would you apologize for me?" Conryu

motioned Kelsie and Jonny away from the window and held up both hands. He wasn't supposed to do a breaking without a circle, but under the circumstances he didn't have any choice.

Maria grabbed his arm. "What are you going to do?"

"I'm going to blow a hole in the wards and split."

"Not without me," Jonny said.

"Or me," Kelsie added.

"This is nuts," Maria said. "But I'm with you too."

"No. I doubt you'd survive a trip through Hell. Go to your mom and tell her what's happening then head to the Department. I'll be in touch as soon as I can." Conryu tossed his cellphone on the couch where it sank down between the cushions. It'd be too easy for the police to track him with it. "Prime!"

"Coming, Master."

Maria grabbed the front of his shirt, yanked his head down, and kissed him hard on the lips. When they finally came up for air she said, "Don't you dare get yourself killed."

"I sense people coming, Master. Six, no ten."

"A breaching team," Jonny added.

"Right, time to go." Conryu raised his hands again. "Break!"

The barrier shattered.

"Your friend will need protection, Master. He has no alignment to dark magic."

Conryu grabbed Jonny's arm. "Cloak of Darkness!"

When the liquid darkness had covered Jonny from head to toe Conryu turned to Prime. "Portal spell."

"Yes, Master."

The words of the spell appeared in his mind and he chanted. "Reveal the way through infinite darkness. Open the path, Hell Portal!"

The swirling black disk appeared in front of him. Conryu grabbed Jonny and Kelsie, pulled them through, and willed the gate to close behind them.

* * *

Maria's nausea faded along with the dark portal. He was gone and once more she couldn't follow. How many times was she going to have to watch Conryu run into danger without her? Though she understood there was no way she'd survive a trip through Hell with him. One step through that portal and she would have dropped dead.

There was a knock on the door. "Police! Open up!"

She sighed, crossed the room, and opened the door. The shiny black barrels of two guns were pointed straight at her head. She yelped and took a step back.

The officers pushed the door open and rushed into the apartment. Two men in bulletproof vests, dark-blue fatigues, and helmets held her at gunpoint while the rest searched from room to room.

The Kodas' apartment wasn't huge and a minute later someone shouted, "Clear!"

The living room was filled to bursting with ten large men and Maria. One of the officers removed his helmet and approached her.

"Where is he?"

"Conryu left."

"Bullshit! There's no way he snuck past us. Where's he hiding?"

"Maria! What's going on?"

She slumped with relief at the sight of her mother approaching from down the hall. It looked like she'd just thrown on a robe and slippers. She must have sensed when Conryu broke her wards.

The officer that had been interrogating her spun and leveled his weapon at her mom. A flick of her wrist sent the machine gun flying along with both of the weapons pointed at Maria.

The officer started to reach for the pistol at his side. Mom just glared at him as if daring him to try it.

He seemed to decide discretion was the better part of valor. "You need to keep your distance, ma'am. This is an active scene."

"I don't appreciate people pointing guns at my daughter, Officer." Mom waved her over and Maria ran out of the apartment and hugged her. "Now what's this all about?"

"I have orders to take Conryu Koda into custody. I believe your daughter has relevant information."

Mom looked down at her. "Do you know where he is?"

"No. I tried to tell them. Conryu left."

"As I said, there's no way he slipped past my men." The officer crossed his arms. "Now tell me the truth."

"How did he leave, Maria?"

"By dark portal."

"That's what I thought." Mom turned her gaze on the officer. "Did your superiors fail to mention Conryu is a wizard? Traveling by dark portal he could be anywhere in the city in half a second."

"I was told he's only a first-year wizard and advanced spells were beyond his current ability."

Mom laughed. "Conryu is the most powerful wizard in history. No spell is beyond his ability. Whoever gave you your briefing was woefully ignorant of who you're dealing with."

"Sir," one of the other officers said. "Ops reports they've tracked his cell phone to the apartment."

"You still claim he's not here?"

Maria let go of her mother and turned around. "On the couch."

A third officer bent down and pulled it out of the cushions. "Cellphone, sir. Locked."

The muscle in the officer's jaw bunched. "Fuck! Wrap it up, boys. As usual, the brass gave us bad intel. I'm going to have to ask you to come with us."

He reached out to grab Maria. Mom moved in front of her. "Do you have a warrant to arrest my daughter?"

"No, ma'am, but she's a material witness. We may have more questions."

"If you do we'll be at the Department of Magic with my husband. Feel free to contact us there."

He let out a little growl but finally nodded. "Alright."

The commander and his men retrieved their weapons and filed past Maria and her mother down the hall. Mom kept her arms around Maria until they were all out of sight. "Tell me everything."

Maria did as her mother asked and when she finished she added, "He wanted me to tell you he was sorry about smashing your wards."

Her mother waved her hand. "He didn't destroy them, just opened a hole in them. I can fix them in an afternoon. We need to see your father. Clearly more is afoot here than we know."

* * *

Conryu, Prime, Kelsie, and Jonny hung in the black nothingness of the area between the mortal realm and Hell. Kelsie grabbed on to him and trembled while Jonny spun in a slow circle, taking it all in.

Cerberus barked as he ran up to them. Kelsie squeaked and tried to hide behind him. The giant three-headed dog towered over the little group.

"Dude, please tell me that's a friend of yours." Jonny and Cerberus eyed each other.

"Cerberus is my guardian demon. Aren't you, boy?"

The demon dog barked again and lowered one of his heads so Conryu could give him a scratch. Conryu looked down at Kelsie. "You can pet him. Cerberus won't bite unless I tell him to."

Kelsie reached out a hesitant hand and stroked Cerberus's massive chest. Cerberus panted as she rubbed him. When Jonny moved closer the demon dog let out a deep growl, stopping his friend cold.

"He has no connection to dark magic," Prime said in answer to

Conryu's unspoken question. "Demons and ordinary humans don't always see eye to eye. You shouldn't dawdle here, Master. Even protected, spending too much time in Hell isn't a good idea for non-dark-aligned individuals."

"I second that," Jonny said.

Conryu looked up at Cerberus. "Can you guide us to my father's dojo?"

Cerberus barked and trotted off. They flew along behind him for half a minute before he stopped.

"This is a bad idea," Jonny said. "Those cops will look there for you next."

"I have to let Dad know what's happening. Five minutes tops. He should be between classes so no one will see us."

Conryu cast the portal spell again and they stepped out onto the sparring floor. Dad was kneeling in front of the room facing the ancient swords in his black training uniform. He stood and turned to face them, a deep frown creasing his usually calm face.

"What has happened?"

"Long story, Dad." Conryu gave him the condensed version. "So basically I'm being hunted by the police so they can turn me over to the people who've been trying to kill me for the last year. I figure the only way out of this mess is to deal with the terrorists myself."

"Can you?"

Trust his father to come straight to the point. "Not sure. Mr. Kane was a little vague with what was happening when I helped him this winter. I believe the boxes we were looking for are the weapons they mentioned on the news. If I can neutralize them then I should be safe, along with the city. Whatever I do, I have only two days to get it done."

"How can I help?"

"I need to talk to Terra and Mr. Kane. Can you carry a message to them?"

"Of course. I need to speak to your mother as well. If she finds out about this some other way she'll be even more upset. I'll take your message to the Department."

"Actually, Mr. Koda, if you pick up a cheap prepaid cellphone and sneak it in to them we could keep in touch without the police knowing."

Everyone looked at Jonny. "What? We studied urban escape and survival in school."

"How will I get you the number?" Dad asked.

"We need one as well. Why don't we go together? That way we can just exchange numbers." Jonny pulled out his wallet and opened it. Moths didn't fly out, but it was empty just the same. "I'm broke."

Conryu had thirty bucks. They looked at Kelsie who shrugged. "I left my purse at your apartment."

"I have enough for both," Dad said. "Let me change and we'll go. Put the closed sign up."

Jonny jogged over to the door while his father went to the locker room. When he'd flipped the sign Jonny said, "We shouldn't all go together. I'll go with your dad and meet you guys at Giovanni's."

Conryu shook his head. "We had their food boxes all over the apartment. If the cops are on the ball they'll be keeping an eye out for us there. What about the Burger Shack on Third?"

"That'll work."

Conryu and Kelsie left by the back door. He had until Jonny rejoined them to figure out how to do in two days what the Department of Magic had failed to do in a year.

3
SPY STUFF

Maria and her mom drove to the Department and went upstairs to her father's office. They'd only taken long enough for her mother to dress and collect her satchel before they left. She didn't even take time to restore the wards. Mom insisted they were sufficient for the moment and she was eager to talk to Dad.

Maria had been to the Department building several times over the years and it was always a bustling place. Today everyone was subdued, their heads hanging, and unwilling to make eye contact.

Outside the office Dad's secretary was gone. There was no sign of the woman's purse and her computer was turned off. Maria glanced over at her mother. "Something's really wrong."

"Yes. I've never seen Daphne away from her desk. She's devoted to your father." Mom strode forward and shoved the door open.

Inside, Dad, Terra, and a man she didn't know sat around her father's big desk staring out the window. Of all the things she'd expected Dad and Terra to be doing, "nothing" was at the bottom of the list. Dad came around his desk and hugged them.

"What are you two doing here?"

"A better question," Mom said, "is what were a bunch of cops with machine guns doing at our building? What's this stupidity about handing Conryu over to the Society? And why aren't you doing something about it?"

Dad looked so exhausted at that moment Maria hugged him again.

"Thank you, sweetheart. We've been removed and confined to my office following Conryu's escape. The mayor and his people are handling matters now. They seem to think we're too sympathetic to their prey."

"Is Tom really foolish enough to think handing Conryu over will accomplish anything? I saw a replay of the recording. He's just a bonus. Morgana's who they really want."

"I know and I explained it to Tom in just those terms, but the president made it clear there was no way they'd free Morgana. At this point he's desperate enough to believe whatever those two advisors tell him. He sees Conryu as his only hope of saving his city. When he escaped, well, Tom didn't take it very well."

"So what are we going to do to help Conryu?" Maria stood with her hands on her hips. She knew her father was in a difficult position, but she'd rather die than sit there and do nothing.

"I'm not certain there's anything we can do." Dad went back around his desk and dropped into his chair.

"That's nonsense." Maria needed to get everyone off their asses and working again. "We're a formidable group. You've been investigating this business for a while, right? No one tells me much, but I've picked up enough details to know this isn't something that just came up."

"The problem is," Terra said. "We've exhausted all the avenues of inquiry and come up empty. The boxes remain hidden and until they're neutralized Conryu remains in danger."

"Great, so he has two days to save himself and the city with no one but Jonny and Kelsie to help. All we can do, the people who care about him most, is sit on our hands and hope." Maria wanted to cry.

"Two days, you said." Terra pursed her lips. "That's not right. Lin, we need your laptop."

"It's in my office. The mayor said we aren't supposed to leave this room."

"There aren't any guards," Maria said.

"It's not that far away," Terra added. "I can't see why they'd care. If you're too scared I'll go."

She started to stand, but Lin waved her back. "I'll go. If one of us is going to be locked up, better me than you."

Terra snorted. "As if they could hold a wizard that didn't wish to be held."

Lin left the office and Dad asked, "What are you thinking?"

"Based on the speed of the island it will enter and exit the potential zone of activation over the course of a day. If I'm right Mercia could possibly activate the boxes within twenty-four hours rather than forty-eight."

Mara stared. "You mean Conryu only has one day?"

"Less than that actually. I can't give you any accurate numbers until I run my theory through Lin's program."

* * *

Conryu conjured a tiny Cloak of Darkness spell and shaped it to look like sunglasses. As disguises went it was pretty pathetic, but just walking around without so much as a hat made him feel exposed. Prime had shifted so he resembled a simple, if ugly, book and Conryu carried him tucked under one arm.

The streets were quiet as they made their way toward Third and the Burger Shack where they were supposed to meet Jonny. Conryu hoped they didn't run into any trouble. Not that Dad and Jonny couldn't take care of themselves, but against guns they'd be in a tight space.

They stopped at a crosswalk and waited for the light to change. "You have a plan, right?" Kelsie asked. She sounded so optimistic he hated to burst her bubble.

"I have an idea, whether it's nonsense or workable we'll have to wait and see. Either way I don't intend to give myself up."

"I don't think you should. I can't imagine the government being willing to turn an innocent citizen over to terrorists on the off chance they might do the right thing. It seems as criminal as what the Society is pulling."

The light changed and they crossed over along with the small group that had gathered. Five minutes later the restaurant came into view. Across from it was a green bench beside a trash bin. The bench offered a good view in both directions and no one was close enough to eavesdrop on them.

"Let's sit here."

They settled in to wait for Jonny. Conryu held Prime on his lap, angled away from the street so no one would notice him speaking. Kelsie sat close to him like she was his girlfriend, letting him keep his voice down while they talked.

"Okay, Prime, we need to find those boxes. This winter we theorized they were moved through dark portals. Is there any way we can track where they went?"

"No, Master."

"Damn it." That had been his one good idea.

"Not in the human realm at least. If we go to the starting location Cerberus may be able to track where they went through Hell. We can then emerge and recover the items in this world."

"Are you sure that will work?" Kelsie asked.

"Not at all. I'm not aware of something like this ever being done before."

"It gives us a starting point at least. Next problem. Will the spells I know be enough to deal with any shadow beasts we encounter?"

"No, Master. Dark magic works mainly through entropy.

Shadow beasts are already dead and have no physical form to decay. Domination will allow you to control them, but I have no spells that will destroy them. Fire and light magic would be best."

"I can work with that. Last thing. If we run into those cops again I need a nonlethal way to disable them quickly."

Prime opened and flipped through his pages, eventually landing on a spell called Reaper's Gale. Just the name gave Conryu a chill. He started to read and Kelsie moved in closer to follow along.

The spell drained the life force of anyone caught in the effect. He read the words over and over, committing them to memory.

"This looks lethal," Conryu said when he finished memorizing the spell.

"If you cast it at your full power it absolutely is." Prime snapped shut. "But if you modulate it, whisper, use a flick of your wrist instead of a full swing, and most importantly, focus your will on not killing anyone, it will serve your needs admirably."

Kelsie glanced at him. "Do you have any idea how terrifying it is to know just how easy it would be for you to wipe out scores of people with a wave of your hand?"

"Yeah. I think about it before every spell I cast."

Jonny ambled down the street ten minutes later and waved to them. When he reached the bench Conryu and Kelsie got to their feet and they started down the sidewalk. One of the locations he'd helped clear this winter was only half a mile away. It wouldn't take them long to figure out if his theory was workable or not.

"Did you have any trouble at the electronics shop?" Kelsie asked.

"Not a bit, though your dad's wallet is lighter by a hundred and twenty bucks."

"I didn't think prepaid phones were that expensive."

"They're not." Jonny dug the cheap little flip phone out of his pocket and showed it to Conryu. "He offered me an extra forty to help tide us over."

That gave them seventy with what he had in his wallet. Since Conryu didn't expect to have to do much shopping it should be plenty. One way or the other this business would be settled in two days.

* * *

As the little group walked along toward the abandoned building Conryu found his gaze darting left and right, checking every person they passed for a reaction. Either no one watched the news or they all had other things on their mind. It helped that the majority of the people around them kept their heads down and were absorbed in whatever was on their phones.

As much as his father hated it when everyone was distracted, right now it struck Conryu as the best trend ever. If they'd had to travel everywhere by dark portal it would have been hard on Jonny. Should it come to that, Conryu planned to ask his friend to sit the rest of the mission out.

The condemned building looked exactly as he remembered only without snow. Yellow police tape blocked the entrance, but Jonny just ripped it off and shoved his way inside. The little niche that had held the box was now plainly visible and a fresh selection of beer bottles littered the floor. The sour stench of alcohol and piss perfumed the interior. Without the ward the punks that partied here must have returned.

Kelsie put her hand over her face. "Oh my god, it stinks in here. Who would come to such a place for fun?"

"The smell's a lot easier to tolerate if you're drunk or high." Jonny looked at the dump and crinkled his nose. "Pity I'm completely sober right now."

"Can you stand it for a little longer?" Conryu asked. "It would probably be safest if I try and locate the box on my own. If I find it I'll come back for you two."

"Not planning on ditching me again are you, bro?"

"I want to go too," Kelsie said.

"I appreciate that, guys, really, but if it takes me a while to find the new location I don't want you to have to spend any more time in Hell than necessary. Especially you, Jonny. I have no idea what excessive exposure to dark energy would do to a non-wizard."

"Accelerated aging and cellular breakdown." Prime flew up out of his grasp and hovered in the middle of the room. "Long-term exposure will literally rot a normal human from the inside out."

Kelsie grimaced. "Yuck."

Jonny crossed his arms and for a moment Conryu feared he might want to argue. "Fine, but you better come back and get me before you do anything stupid."

Conryu held out a fist and Jonny bumped it.

"Promise," Conryu said. "If there's stupid stuff to be done, we'll do it together."

He turned and held his hand out. "Reveal the way through infinite darkness. Open the path, Hell Portal!"

The black disk appeared and Conryu stepped through it with Prime beside him. When the portal had closed Prime turned to face him. "Those two are a liability, Master, especially the boy."

Conryu sighed and reached out to stroke Cerberus's side. He didn't know exactly how the giant dog appeared beside him without Conryu noticing, but he'd become so used to it he didn't even jump.

"I know, you're right, but they're my friends and they're trying to help. If I tell them they're just in the way I'll damage two very important relationships."

"If you don't, you might get them killed."

"Yeah." No arguing with that. "Let's focus on the matter at hand. If we can't locate the boxes this problem is moot. Cerberus."

The demon dog focused all six eyes on him.

"I need you to track something for me. A magical artifact was moved from here through a dark portal. Can you follow it?"

Cerberus raised his heads and waved them around, mouths

open and noses sniffing. He padded around, a little this way, a little that way, until he finally barked and crouched down.

It didn't take a genius to interpret that. Conryu leapt onto Cerberus's back, snatched Prime out of the air, and they were off. Cerberus bounded through the darkness, sniffing as he ran.

It seemed they hadn't gone any distance when Cerberus stopped and barked again.

"Here, huh?" Conryu looked around, but it wasn't like there were any landmarks to help him figure out where he was. He didn't know how demons did it. "Guess we'll just have to take a peek."

Conryu raised his hand to cast the portal spell again, but Prime stopped him. "If there are protections in place it would be wise to look before we leap."

He climbed down off Cerberus. "Okay. How do we do that?"

Prime opened and his pages flipped. When he stopped, Conryu read the spell. Vision Gate. That sounded useful. "Grant me the power to see through realms, Vision Gate!"

The darkness swirled, though the effect was more psychic than visual. Three seconds later a round portal appeared and through it he saw a pedestal with one of the boxes sitting on it. He reached up and patted Cerberus. "Good boy. Reveal!"

Lines of dark energy appeared in his enhanced sight. Plenty of wards, though considerably less than he'd expected. He willed the view to pull back. The new location had stone walls and was almost as dark as Hell. The view shifted again, this time top down. Beside the pedestal was a channel with brackish water running through it.

"Great. Of course it's in the sewer." Something moved further down the tunnel and a moment later a pair of great black hounds padded into view. "They look familiar."

Cerberus growled deep in his chest.

"Shadow hounds, Master. It's good that we scouted the area first."

"It certainly is."

A couple minutes passed as he sent the viewing portal all around the area near the box. There was no sign of any more guardians. Two shadow beasts wouldn't be a problem for him now.

"Let's do this." Conryu raised his hand.

"What about your promise to retrieve your friends before going after the box?" Prime asked.

"I will, but first I'm going to kill those shadow hounds."

He opened the portal twenty yards from the hounds and stepped through. They must have sensed his presence. Conryu had barely cleared the portal when two pairs of red eyes raced towards him.

"All things burn to ash, Inferno Blast!" Searing white flames blasted from his hand, filling the tunnel and obliterating the hounds. He allowed a full minute before he stepped back into the portal.

"That was impressive, Master. I've seen fire wizards that couldn't conjure flames that intense."

"Thanks."

Cerberus took them back to where they started and Conryu opened another portal.

"Did you find it?" Kelsie asked the instant he emerged in the condemned building.

He nodded, feeling a little queasy. Casting that many spells in such close succession was enough to exhaust even him. He needed to rest, but first the box. He'd be damned before he let whoever was behind this move it again.

"There are some wards protecting it so you two need to stay behind me until we deal with them. Hold still, Jonny."

His friend stopped pacing long enough for Conryu to cast Cloak of Darkness.

"I should warn you the box is in the sewer. If you think it stinks here just wait a second."

Moments later they were standing a safe distance from the pedestal. Kelsie summoned a flame sphere to light the place up. Jonny shook his head. "All this fuss over that thing?"

Conryu had to admit the black box wasn't terribly impressive on its own, but he knew the power of the artifact inside. He crossed his fingers and wrists. "Darkness dispels everything."

He hurled the black sphere, which exploded on impact, wiping all the protections away. He waited ten seconds more just to be sure.

"I think we're good," Kelsie said.

Conryu agreed and they strode over to collect their prize. His spell had blasted off the necroplasma, revealing the clean wood beneath. He flipped the lid open and inside was a black gem half the size of his fist. Instead of sparkling in the firelight the gem seemed to absorb it.

"It must be worth a fortune." Jonny reached out to touch the gem.

"Stop!" Conryu, Kelsie, and Prime all shouted at the same time.

Jonny jerked his hand back. "What?"

"Never touch a magical artifact until you're sure what will happen," Conryu said.

"It's one of the first things they teach us," Kelsie added.

Conryu put his hand over the gem. "Shatter!"

It burst into tiny black flakes. All the magic stored in the gem vanished.

He snapped the lid shut. "I bet Terra would like to have a look at this. What do you say we get out of here?"

* * *

When Lady Raven felt something drawing near one of her artifacts she assumed it was another sewer worker and her shadow hounds would deal with the intruder shortly. Sure enough seconds after she became aware of the presence it vanished. That was the third unfortunate to stumble on her hiding place. Not too bad considering it had been there for six months.

She stretched out on her couch and returned her attention to the tv. It had been an amusing few hours, listening to the city's leaders lie and make excuses as they tried to reassure the people that there was really nothing to worry about. That the Society wouldn't do something so horrible. Even the idiot men running the city couldn't be stupid enough to believe the threat was a bluff. All the mayor needed to do was ask the Department of Magic and he'd learn the truth.

No, it was all propaganda to keep the people calm. If the leaders of the world failed to do as they were told, they'd learn what the Society was capable of. While Lady Raven dearly wanted to help release their imprisoned leader, a part of her wanted the deadline to pass, freeing her to activate her artifacts and watch hundreds of shadow beasts overrun the city.

She sensed another presence and less than a minute later gasped as a sharp pain stabbed her chest. One of the artifacts had been destroyed.

Even if the incompetents from the Department somehow located her new hiding places they didn't have power enough between them to overcome the protections she'd woven around them.

Her stomach twisted. It had to be him.

Lady Raven leapt off the couch and marched to her casting chamber. Ignoring everything else she went straight to her scrying mirror. She focused her will, but when the cloudy depths of the mirror cleared, only an empty pedestal appeared.

With a massive effort she restrained herself from smashing the mirror to shards. If the boxes were in danger she needed to increase her defenses. She paced from one end of the chamber to the other. What could she do that would slow the abomination down?

Two shadow hounds were obviously not enough. It would be a simple matter to summon more, but she doubted that would do it. It was time to call in a few markers. Lady Raven had made more than her share of allies in Hell, done them favors, and it was time to cash in her IOUs.

That left one more matter. Did she dare tell the Hierarchs that the project was in danger now that they were within hours of success?

Not yet. If the boy forced his way past her enhanced defenses once more then she'd alert her superiors. Better to seek help than allow the enterprise to fail completely. It might cost her a promotion, but that was a small price compared to a swift execution.

* * *

Maria paced while Lin and Terra fiddled with the computer. Despite the warnings no one had bothered Lin on his trip to and from his office. In fact, he said he hadn't seen another soul. It appeared those in charge had ordered the building cleared. For some reason Maria found that disconcerting. A couple hundred people worked for the Department. Even—make that especially—if there was a crisis you'd think there would be plenty for everyone to do.

It felt like they were trying to hide what was happening.

"Would you please sit down?" Dad said. "You're making me even more nervous."

"Sorry, but if I sit I'll fidget. I just realized I haven't seen Angus. He's the one that called Conryu. I figured they'd have him locked up with the rest of us."

"I haven't seen him since this morning." Dad sighed and shook his head. "Angus is surprisingly sneaky and has a tendency to show up or disappear when you least expect it. My guess is he's holed up somewhere, staying out of sight. Hopefully, just this once, he'll keep out of trouble."

Terra slammed her fist on the desk. "I knew it! Based on my calculations Mercia will be able to activate the boxes in sixteen hours and the island should move out of range in another forty."

Maria stopped in her tracks. "Conryu thinks he has two days."

Terra nodded. "If he finds one of the boxes and neutralizes it Mercia will know and she'll activate the other four as soon as she's able."

Lin started typing and Terra looked down at him. "What are you doing?"

"Research. I'm curious about the mayor's advisors. Something about those two struck me as off."

"I didn't sense anything magical."

"It's a cop thing, instincts maybe, I don't know, but I've learned to trust the feeling. Besides, it's not like we have anything else to do."

Twenty minutes later the office doors opened. Every gaze turned to watch Conryu's father walk through. He carried himself with this sort of Zen calm, even in the face of calamity.

"Is he okay?" Maria asked the moment the doors closed.

Sho turned his gaze on her father and raised an eyebrow.

"It's okay, we checked for bugs and magical eavesdropping. You can talk freely here."

"My son is fine and determined to do what he can to set this business right." Sho dug around in his pants pocket, finally emerging with a small flip phone. "This is prepaid and has the number of a matching phone programmed into it. I don't know what he intends. This magical business is beyond me."

"How's Connie taking it?" her mother asked.

"As well as can be expected when her son is being hunted by the police so he can be made into a sacrifice." Sho's voice was as hard as Maria had ever heard it. "How has this fallen on Conryu's shoulders? Surely there are others better equipped to handle such a crisis."

"Mr. Koda, my name is Terra Pane. I'm a wizard working at

the Department. I tested your son when he was first discovered to have wizard potential and later I saw him using that power. Despite his youth and inexperience I believe Conryu has a better chance to resolve this matter than anyone. Frankly, if he fails, this city will be turned into a charnel house."

Sho gave a slight shake of his head. "It's too much to ask of him. He's still just a boy."

Maria closed the distance between them. "You're wrong. I've seen firsthand who Conryu's become over the past year. He can do this. I believe in him and you should too."

The phone rang cutting Sho off. He handed it to Maria who flipped it open. "Conryu? Okay, I'll put it on speaker."

She hit the button and set the phone on her father's desk. "Go ahead."

"I found the first box. It was hidden about a mile from its original location. The wards were minimal, but there were two shadow beasts guarding it. Nothing too powerful."

"How did you find it?" Terra asked.

"Cerberus tracked the residual energy of the transference spell. Don't ask me how exactly."

"You summoned the demon dog to our realm?" Terra's voice rose and her eyes grew wide.

"No, sorry, I should have been more specific. We tracked it through Hell. Prime says enchanted energy lingers longer in the magical realms. Anyway, I'm feeling pretty good about our chances of finding the rest of the boxes."

"Conryu, this is very important," Terra said. "Don't disturb or dispel the boxes until you've located all five."

"Uh, wish I'd known that five minutes ago. I already broke the wards and smashed the artifact inside. Is that bad?"

Nervous looks were passed around the office. Finally Terra said, "It's not bad, but it does start the clock ticking. Mercia will know you've destroyed the box. I fear she will now activate the summoning as soon as the island is within range."

"I've got like forty hours left, no sweat."

"No, you have sixteen hours."

"Shit! Are you sure?"

"It might be less, but certainly not more," Terra said. "You have to hurry."

"No kidding. You want me to send you the box and what's left of the artifact?"

"Please. Leave it outside somewhere and we'll retrieve it."

"I can leave it under Mom's car beside the back wheel."

"That's fine. Hurry, Conryu. We're counting on you."

"And be careful," Maria added before the line went dead.

4
RECOVERY

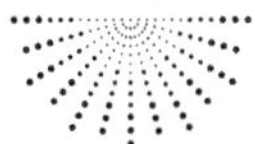

Conryu disconnected the phone and fought a sudden wave of exhaustion. They'd left the sewer by the nearest manhole, rather than by portal, and made their way to a park across the street. He'd feared on the walk over he might not make it. His relief upon seeing a bench was pathetic.

The first hint of a backlash headache was forming behind his eyes. Kelsie and Jonny were both looking at him with nervous gazes. If he looked as bad as he felt he doubted he projected confidence.

"That didn't sound good," Kelsie said. "Sixteen hours isn't very long to track down four more boxes."

"No. I need to minimize my magic use so I'll have strength enough when I really need it. Jonny, could you do me a favor and run the box over to the Department? You know Mom's car. She parks in the Science Department's lot. You shouldn't have any trouble finding it." Conryu handed him the phone and box.

"No problem. What about you two?"

"I need to rest. By the time you get back I should be good to go after the second box."

"Cool, later." Jonny gave him one last look and jogged off toward the street.

Kelsie patted her lap. "Lie down and close your eyes. I'll keep watch."

Conryu took her up on the suggestion, letting his legs dangle off the end of the bench and holding Prime on his chest. He sighed and closed his eyes, thoroughly glad Maria couldn't see him right then.

"Can we do this?" Kelsie asked.

Conryu opened one eye and looked up at her. "Do we have another choice?"

"We could hide. She said we had less than a day. It wouldn't be hard to avoid the police for that long. When the time was up they'd be too busy to bother with us."

"Too busy trying to keep regular people from getting killed by hundreds of shadow beasts. Which I know from experience is impossible for someone without magic. It's the responsibility of those with the power to make a difference to do so."

"You don't even want to be a wizard and I'm not much of one. Why should it fall to us to fix this mess?"

Conryu smiled and closed his eye. "We have to do it because we're the only ones who can. You're right, I'd just as soon never cast another spell as long as I live, but I can't stand aside and let innocent people die if I can stop it. In the end, I'm a warrior and it's a warrior's responsibility to protect those who can't protect themselves. So my dad says anyway."

She sniffed. "You're braver than me. I just want to bury my head in the sand and pretend everything will be fine."

"Don't sell yourself short. You could have stayed behind with Maria, but you chose to come with me. That took guts and I appreciate it."

"You must tell her, Master."

"Quiet, Prime."

Kelsie wiped her eyes. "Tell me what?"

"Prime."

"I'm sorry, Master, but part of my task is to protect you. He's expending extra energy to keep you and his other friend safe. Before he retrieved you, Master eliminated the guardian beasts, casting two extra dark portal spells for no other reason than to spare your feelings."

"Is that true?"

Conryu sighed, mentally cursing his disobedient scholomantic. "Yes, it was safer for you if I dealt with the shadow beasts before I returned to collect you. I didn't think an extra spell or two would make this much difference. You and Jonny were so eager to help, I didn't have the heart to tell you."

Kelsie smacked him on the forehead. "You said you wouldn't lie to me."

"I didn't."

"You weren't completely honest."

"No, but I didn't keep any important secrets from you. If Loudmouth here hadn't spoken up you'd have never known."

"That's a thin line. No more, Conryu. If you need us to stay out of your way just say so. This is bigger than our feelings."

"Okay. Sorry."

* * *

Jonny left Conryu on the park bench looking gray and worn down. In all the years he'd known his best friend, Conryu had never looked as bad as he did today. Even when they both caught the flu after splashing through the river in the middle of winter five years ago and he had a fever of a hundred and three.

Maybe a good rest would set him to rights. Jonny didn't know much about magic or wizards. They only spoke about them at school to warn the regular soldiers to avoid them. Weaponized Humans, which was how the military referred to wizards like Conryu, were looked at the same way as tanks or jets. Any grunt stupid enough to take one on directly deserved to get squashed.

Jonny refused to think of Conryu as a weapon. That giant three-headed dog on the other hand… He shuddered. He reached the sidewalk and soon spotted a taxi. A piercing whistle got the driver's attention.

He climbed in and gave directions to the government plaza. The driver took off and he settled back in the seat. The cushions and springs had long since given out and he sunk in a foot. He planned to have the taxi stop outside the parking lot and make his way on foot.

It would be easy enough to find Conryu's mom's car, but he needed to go inside and talk to someone about what was happening to his friend. Maybe one of the other wizards would have an idea how to help him.

The ride took fifteen minutes. Jonny directed the driver to pull over half a block from the entrance. The cabbie looked back at him like he was nuts then shrugged and pulled to the side. Ten dollars lighter Jonny hopped out and set off for the plaza.

Since it was early afternoon on a Wednesday there shouldn't be any problem getting in. Dozens of people came and went all day every day. He carried the box under his arm like a courier and strode down the sidewalk and up the blacktop just like he had every right to be there.

The Department of Magic wasn't hard to spot what with the giant pentagram on the side. He stopped and looked from the magic building to the science building. He could hunt up the car, drop the box and let Maria know it was there in five minutes.

No, he needed to find some way to help his friend.

Jonny turned firmly toward the magic building and marched forward. He hadn't even reached the door before his hair started standing on end. Something was wrong. No one was coming or going. He figured the place would be buzzing like a kicked hornet's nest. Maybe everyone was busy trying to figure out what to do about the crazy wizards.

Inside the doors the entry area was abandoned. All the little cubby holes where the secretaries waited to greet visitors were empty. His footsteps echoed as he walked across the tile floor. Creepy.

He fished the phone out of his pocket and dialed Maria. "I'm in the lobby. Where are you? We need to talk. He isn't hurt, but I wouldn't say he was okay either. I'm on my way."

Jonny followed Maria's instructions, taking the elevator to the top floor and walking down the empty halls to her father's office. When he reached the door he hung up and pushed it open.

Maria ran over. "What's wrong?"

"I don't know. After we retrieved the box Conryu looked kind of gray and worn out. There wasn't a mark on him and we didn't have much of a fight, but he looked like he'd gone ten rounds in the cage."

"How many spells did he cast?" A woman in a gray robe made her way around the desk and relieved him of the box.

"I don't know, three or four of those black portal things, a couple others to clean the black gunk off your box and smash the gem inside. That's all I saw."

"Terra?" Maria switched her attention from him to the woman.

"Casting four portal spells in an hour would have me in the hospital for a week. The only way to recover from excessive casting is to rest. How long Conryu will need is impossible to say, but we know how long he has. It's extremely important you minimize his casting."

"Yeah. But we need some way to move around and if we can't go by portal..."

Maria's mom tossed him her keys. "Take my car. If I can contribute nothing else I can offer that."

Jonny snagged the keys. "Thanks. I'll be gentle with it."

"You'd better be." She smiled to show she wasn't serious.

"What's going on around here? This place is like a tomb. There's an emergency out there. We could use a little help."

Maria's dad offered a helpless shrug. "The mayor has placed us under house arrest, though it appears he isn't overly concerned about enforcing it. If we tried to leave the building it would probably be a different matter."

"I have to head back," Jonny said. "Wish us luck."

* * *

Lin didn't pay a great deal of attention when Conryu's friend delivered the box and gave an update on his condition. Whatever was happening on the magical end of this crisis was beyond his influence. After many years of experience, first in the military then the police department, he'd learned to move anything outside his control to the back of his mind and focus on the task at hand. And that task was figuring out who was in the conference room advising the mayor.

Whoever they were, they didn't appear to have existed two years ago. Since his police access code had never been revoked he could still use the department's files and research programs. One of them swept the web for any and all information about a given person.

Whoever created the woman's persona had done an excellent job for the past eighteen months, but beyond that they'd become lazy. Lin found a tidbit here, another clue there, obviously fake information planted to make it look like Maggie Chin had existed before a year and a half ago. There was enough to stand up to a cursory search, but if anyone really dug into her past it was clear the identity was a fraud.

Lin glanced up from his computer. Terra was absorbed in the remains of the artifact that Conryu had found. Maria was pacing again while her mother tried to massage some of the tension out of her husband's shoulders. Master Sho sat with his back straight, eyes closed, and breathing even. Lin recognized the simple meditative pose. Sensei had to be worried about his son, but like Lin he'd learned to control himself.

He hated to put more stress on his already careworn supervisor, but Chief Kane needed to know what he'd discovered. "Sir? It appears the mayor's advisor isn't who she claims to be."

Chief Kane patted his wife's hand, got up, and walked around the desk to look at Lin's computer. "Show me what you've found."

"As far as I can tell Maggie Chin didn't exist before a year and a half ago. Do you know who handles background checks for the Department in Central?"

"The security department, same as here. I have no idea which individual is responsible or even if it's just one person."

"Okay. Do we need to let the mayor know his advisor is a fraud?"

Chief Kane scratched his head. "Yes, but without proof of who she actually is he may not believe us given our status. Did you find anything that proves she's not who she claims to be?"

"No, sir. It's a lot of little things that add up to a big thing. I can make the case, but it's not going to be written in flashing neon."

"What about the man?"

"Without his name I can't even begin to start a search."

"How about a picture?"

Lin nodded. "I can work with that."

"Scoot over."

Lin moved aside and watched as Chief Kane accessed the security camera footage. It took most of five minutes, but he rewound to when the mayor arrived. Next they went super slow-motion until the man looked up. "Gotcha, whoever you are."

Lin resumed his seat and took a screen capture of the image. He ran the scanning program and in short order came up with a match. "Uh-oh."

"What is it?" The chief looked over his shoulder.

"Apparently our mystery man is a model. I found about twenty images of him on a stock photo website."

"I seriously doubt he's moonlighting as a male model. Terra, did you notice anything magical about the male advisor?"

Terra looked up from the box. "I didn't even think to check him. Basing an illusion on a photograph isn't unusual."

Chief Kane straightened up. "Ladies and gentlemen, I think we have a serious problem."

* * *

Even from a distance it was clear to Jonny that Conryu had regained some of his strength. He was sitting up and the ashen look to his skin had gone away. That was a relief. Nothing like resting on a hot girl's lap to set a man to rights. He needed to find one of his own. It wasn't fair that Conryu had two girlfriends and he didn't even have one.

He pulled up beside the park, rolled down the window, and blew a sharp whistle. When they looked his way he waved. Conryu and Kelsie hurried over and climbed in, him in the front and her in the back.

"Did you steal Mrs. Kane's car?" Conryu asked.

"No." Jonny pointed at the keys dangling from the ignition. "She loaned it to me with the admonition not to damage it. I also received strict instructions that you're not supposed to use any more magic than absolutely necessary. So where to?"

"Pendal's Funeral Home. I can't remember the address."

"No sweat. This baby has a state-of-the-art computer." Jonny fiddled with the touch screen in the dash, typed in the name of the funeral home and a minute later they were on their way.

He drove carefully, never breaking the speed limit or ignoring even minor traffic laws. The last thing they could afford was to get pulled over by the cops. By now every officer in the city probably knew what Conryu looked like and that he was wanted. It would be interesting to see what crime they were claiming he'd committed.

Despite the fact that he dressed like a delinquent and liked to ride a bike, Conryu had never been in serious trouble in his life. If anything, Conryu was the sort of person that would keep others from getting into trouble. He'd steered Jonny clear of a problem or two over the years.

Jonny darted a look at his best friend. Conryu held that creepy book to his chest like he was afraid someone might want to steal it. As if there was a huge market for talking, demon-faced books that could fly. Jonny wouldn't have taken the thing if offered it for free.

From the back seat Kelsie said, "Isn't it strange? Everyone's going about their business just like there was no danger of the city being attacked at the end of the day."

"Never underestimate the power of denial," Conryu said. "Look at me. A year ago I would have denied the possibility of even being a wizard. Now here I am running around trying to save a city that wants to kill me to protect themselves and using a ton of magic to do it. My protests to the contrary didn't make much impact on reality."

Jonny winced. Talk about bitter. He'd never heard Conryu say anything like that.

They rolled up and parked behind a white hearse. "What now?" Jonny asked.

"Now I portal in, track down the second box, and deal with whatever protections are waiting."

"Cool." Jonny unbuckled his seatbelt and reached for the door.

"We'll wait here," Kelsie said.

"What?" Jonny must have misunderstood. "We can't just sit here."

"Conryu will need to expend extra power to protect us. It'll be safer for everyone if we stay behind and keep watch on the funeral home. Does this model have a built-in phone?"

Jonny tapped the touchscreen. "Yeah."

"Conryu can just call us to pick him up when it's done."

"I'll be quick." Conryu slid out of the car and chanted in that weird language that made Jonny's skin crawl just listening to it.

One of those black disks appeared and he was gone.

Jonny twisted around and stared at Kelsie. "What's the idea? We're supposed to be helping him."

Her pretty lips gave a sad twist. "We are helping him. Staying out of Conryu's way is the best thing we can do. My magic is too weak to make a difference and you don't have any at all. Every bit of power he doesn't have to expend protecting us is that much more he'll have to fight with."

"He's my best friend. Just sitting here while he goes into danger makes me sick."

"I know. I love him too."

5
THE SECOND BOX

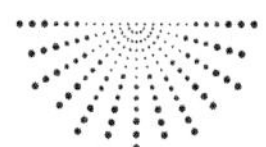

Conryu left Jonny and Kelsie behind and entered the endless darkness of Hell. Cerberus appeared beside him and Conryu laid a hand on the demon dog's massive flank. Power flowed into him.

He looked up at Cerberus's panting heads. "Thanks."

Prime flew up out of his grasp. "That's part of a guardian demon's job, to protect you when you're weak. Or in this case to loan you a little extra power so you hopefully won't need protecting. It is good that you left the others behind. The girl understands and your other friend will as well."

"I hope you're right." Conryu turned his focus on Cerberus. "Okay, boy, time to hunt. Just like before."

Cerberus barked and began sniffing. It took a little longer this time as Conryu wasn't right at the site of the missing box, but soon enough Cerberus was running through the dark with Conryu on his back. Seconds passed before Cerberus pulled up and growled.

A little ways ahead of them a trio of raven-winged demons flew around a central point. The demons turned crimson eyes on them, but didn't attack.

"Corvus demons," Prime said. "Bound to protect that location. Our enemy has taken added precautions."

"How strong are they?" The demons had skinny arms and legs that ended in talons and emaciated bodies covered in thick feathers.

"Not overly, as demons go, but they're fast. Cerberus will have difficulty killing them. Fortunately, they're so weak they have no hope of causing him real harm. Under normal circumstances even a large group of Corvus demons would flee at Cerberus's approach. This lot has been bound so they have no choice but to fight."

"So it's a delaying tactic."

"Most likely, Master."

"Well, we don't have time to waste. Prime, keep your distance." He patted Cerberus. "Ready, boy?"

The growl deepened, vibrating Conryu's legs. He took that as a yes.

"Go!"

Cerberus lunged toward the demons, causing them to scatter. One swung wide and tried to come at them from the rear.

Conryu threw his hand out. "All things burn to ash, Inferno Blast!"

The stream of flames forced the Corvus to swing out wider. Cerberus raced after another of the demons, which beat its wings furiously to stay clear of three snapping jaws.

Another stream of fire forced the demon to flinch left. The sideways movement slowed it just enough for Cerberus's head on that side to bite down on its leg.

Cerberus gave a great shake and ripped the limb off. Reddish-black ichor gushed out as the demon spiraled down and out of sight, whether dead or dying Conryu didn't know.

They skidded to a stop and spun. Through the fight and wild movements Conryu never felt in danger of losing his seat on the demon dog's back. Some additional magic he didn't understand must have held him in place.

The Corvus demons came in from above, one to the left and one to the right, as they raced back toward the box's hiding place. Conryu raised both hands and pictured flames coming from them. "Inferno Blast!"

Twin streams of flame surged out. He missed the one on the left, but burned a wing off the one on the right. It spiraled out of control and disappeared into the darkness. That left one more. "After him, boy."

All three heads barked in unison as Cerberus put on a burst of speed. The terrified-looking Corvus tried to flee, but after a certain distance it was like it hit a wall and veered sharply right. For the second time, the turn did in their prey.

Cerberus snagged a wing with each of his outer heads and bit down on the demon's body with his central head. Several wet crunches later the remains of the Corvus vanished in a puff of noxious smoke.

Conryu scratched between the central head's ears. With Cerberus's help he'd only had to use a minimal amount of power. The demon dog groaned and padded over to the point where the trail ended. Conryu hopped off. "Good job, boy."

Prime flew over to join them. "You two fought well together."

"Thanks. Let's have a look at what we're dealing with this time. Grant me the power to see through realms, Vision Gate!"

The window into the mortal realm appeared in the darkness. An identical box sat on an identical pedestal in a very similar-looking stretch of sewer. He guided the window around the vicinity. There were six shadow beasts that resembled lions guarding this location along with a dead guy dressed like a biker.

"What do you make of him?" Conryu asked.

Cerberus growled and Prime said, "Just looking at it I'd say zombie, but why would anyone bother with adding such a weak creature to the mix? A single shadow beast would be more effective than a dozen zombies."

The three of them watched the odd collection of monsters for another minute as Conryu tried to think of a good way to deal with so many enemies. The shadow beasts didn't hold up at all well against his fire blasts, but he had no idea how tough the new monster was.

"Suggestions?" he asked.

"We don't have enough information, Master."

He shrugged. They'd just have to go in and do their best, the same as always. "Will Cloak of Darkness offer me any protection from the shadow beasts?"

"Yes, the creatures are basically pure magic given a sort of life. The spell should offer as much protection against them as against the fire cats you trained against."

"Should?"

"With magic nothing is certain."

"So I've noticed."

* * *

Terra closed the lid on the box. The material that remained of the artifact was fascinating. Her preliminary tests indicated it was crystalized necroplasma. How many lives had Mercia sacrificed to create her artifacts and their various protections? Not nearly as many as she intended to slaughter if the Society's demands weren't met, that was certain.

As horrible as it was to summon a horde of monsters and set them loose in the city, it somehow seemed even worse to intentionally murder someone and use their life force in a magical ritual. Maybe it was the personal nature of the act.

Orin was talking and Terra wrenched her focus back to the problem at hand.

"It's clear to me now that the people advising the mayor aren't who they claim to be," the chief said. "As I see it we have two choices: We can try to figure out who they are or we can challenge them directly and expose them in front of the mayor."

"I've done all I can as far as research goes," Lin said. "Our next move is to contact Central and talk to whoever handled the primary vetting."

Orin shook his head. "If the job was as sloppy as you say then whoever did it may be working with our imposters."

"If that's the case then our only recourse is confrontation," Lin said. "Where's Clair? I haven't seen her all day."

"She's locked up in her casting chamber meditating and trying to restore her magic." Terra shook her head. The poor woman was obsessed with getting her power back. Terra had tried to tell Clair that only time would set things right, but that didn't reassure the impatient wizard. "As she is now Clair would only be in the way."

"So it's just us?" Orin asked.

"We are not without resources." Terra met Shizuku's gaze and received a faint nod. "Two wizards along with Lin's magic gun are a potent combination. Besides, they only brought two guards."

"No sense wasting time." The chief started toward the door.

He only managed two steps before Shizuku laid a hand on his shoulder. "You and Maria should stay here. We'll return when it's safe."

"This is my responsibility," Orin said.

"Yes, dear, but if it comes to a fight it'll be better if we don't have to worry about the two of you." Shizuku turned to Conryu's father. "Sho, maybe you too—"

"These people are hunting my son. I will join you."

Terra had never been the fearful sort, but when she heard Sho Koda speak in that tone, a chill ran down her back. His expression never flickered, but if pure, cold rage had a sound it was Sho's voice.

Shizuku must have heard it too. "Alright, the four of us then."

Orin dug his access card out of his pocket and handed it to

Shizuku. "This will open any door in the building. My lock code is our anniversary plus Maria's birth month. Be careful."

Shizuku kissed him and nodded. "We'll be back before you know it."

Terra wished she had someone to kiss goodbye. She glanced at Lin, but he was checking his weapon. Sho stood and led the way to the door. Terra had never seen anyone move that smoothly. He reminded her of a hunting cat, all power and balance.

Outside the office Terra assumed the lead, heading towards the stairs. The conference room was two floors below them. At the landing she opened the door a crack and peeked out. The two guards were standing on either side of the entrance.

She could take them out with magic easily enough, but if either of the imposters were disguised wizards they'd sense it. "There are two guards. No way we can sneak past them."

"I will deal with them." Sho slipped out into the hall, not giving her a chance to stop him.

He strode toward the guards, making no effort to conceal his approach, not that there was anywhere he could have hidden were he so inclined. As he moved closer, the nearest guard, a big, broad-shouldered man whose suit was at least one size too small, stepped away from the wall and raised his hand.

"You can't come any closer, sir. Please turn back now."

Sho darted in, grabbed the guard's extended hand, and twisted it. The joint locked. Sho stepped closer and drove his elbow into the side of the guard's head. He wouldn't have gone down any harder if he'd been hit with an ax.

The second guard went for his gun. The pistol came out just in time for Sho to grab the barrel and wrench it to the side. Terra heard his trigger finger snap from the stairwell. Sho jerked the pistol from the guard's maimed hand and cracked him upside the head with it, sending a second body to the floor.

Sho looked her way and motioned the group to join him in the hall.

* * *

Conryu conjured a pair of fire globes then opened the portal thirty yards up the tunnel from where the guardians congregated. That should give him time to react to whatever they did. The instant he emerged, four of the shadow lions charged straight at him while the other two ran the opposite way. The dead biker thing just stood beside the pedestal.

"All things burn to ash, Inferno Blast!" The flames streamed down the tunnel at the charging monsters. One was obliterated instantly. One got singed and the remaining two avoided any damage by leaping up and running along the ceiling.

He waved his hand back and forth, up and down, trying to burn them all away. This bunch was more nimble than the hounds and he only destroyed one more before they forced him to backpedal.

"By my will be bound, oh child of Hell. Your thoughts are my thoughts, your desires, my desires, Domination!"

The surviving shadow beasts shuddered as the spell settled over them.

"Stop!"

They went rigid. Conryu let out the breath he'd been holding.

"Master, the other two are coming from behind us."

Clever things. He focused his will on his bound servants. "Kill the approaching beasts."

The shadow lions fought him for a second, but his magic held. Baring black fangs they charged past him down the tunnel.

"Can shadow beasts actually destroy each other?"

"Your guess is as good as mine, Master. I've never heard of them fighting one another. Their hatred is reserved for the living. Rending shadowy flesh will give them no pleasure."

"Well let's at least hope they can keep the others busy. Somehow I think I'll need all my focus if I want to beat this new guy. Keep an eye on the kitties and let me know if they finish up before I do."

"Yes, Master."

Conryu left Prime to watch his back and eased closer to the box. When he was twenty feet away the undead biker shifted to block him. It leaned forward and for a moment Conryu hoped it was about to fall over.

It charged.

The hulking corpse ran faster than the shadow beasts. Only a lifetime of training allowed him to dodge a fist the size of a bowling ball. The punch skimmed by him and crashed into the tunnel wall, crushing a chunk out of the stone and sending gravel clattering against his face.

He ducked the backhand that took a piece out of the opposite wall. Conryu leapt away and focused on the exposed arm. "Shatter!"

The spell blew a hunk out of its bicep revealing a line of liquid darkness running down the middle of its arm. He'd expected the whole arm at least to disintegrate so that wasn't a good sign.

"Master, the body houses a nether spirit. It will be resistant to low-level magic."

Conryu did a backflip, narrowly avoiding a kick that would have crushed his chest. "I only know low-level spells for the most part. Shatter!"

His spell blew a fist-sized piece out of the undead's thigh.

It raced forward, seeming unbothered by the injury, and landed a glancing blow that sent Conryu flying into the tunnel wall. He rolled aside an instant before a size-twenty boot came crashing down where his head had been a moment before.

Conryu scrambled to his feet and threw out a hand. "All things burn to ash, Inferno Blast!"

The stream of flame hit the undead square in the face. When the torrent stopped, its face had been burned down to the skull. The stench of roasted meat almost covered the sewer stink.

As with all his other attacks the monster seemed unperturbed by the damage. It opened its mouth and smoke emerged. A massive right cross came too fast for Conryu to dodge.

He managed a cross block, but it only minimized the impact. The blow still carried enough force to send Conryu sprawling and sliding through the filth that ran down the center of the tunnel. His forearms ached from the force of the blow, but at least his chest hadn't been crushed.

"Master, I fear you're not strong enough to defeat this enemy."

Conryu was starting to fear that as well. Unfortunately he didn't have any choice.

Wait, he did have a choice. He wasn't strong enough to kill this thing, but he'd bet his bike Cerberus was.

He focused on the ground at the monster's feet. "Reveal the way through infinite darkness. Open the path, Hell Portal!"

The black disk appeared directly under the guardian's feet. It fell most of the way through before its fingers caught the tunnel floor.

"Cerberus." Conryu focused all his wrath on the undead. "Kill!"

Like some unfortunate swimmer in a horror movie, the biker thing was dragged down into the dark. He doubted it would last five seconds against Cerberus. He willed the portal to close just in case it tried to escape.

"Master, the shadow beasts approach."

Conryu threw his hand up just as the first black lion came into view. "All things burn to ash, Inferno Blast!"

The beast was burned away in an instant. He adjusted his aim to sear the one running along the ceiling. It tried to drop to the floor, but he kept the flame on it until the creature burst into black mist.

"That's the last of them, Master."

Conryu closed his fist, ending the spell. In that moment he wanted nothing so much as to slump to the ground and sleep for a week. That wasn't a luxury he could afford just now.

He crossed his wrists and fingers. "Darkness dispels everything."

The basketball-sized sphere of dark magic blew away the wards and necroplasma protecting the box. Five steps closed the distance between Conryu and the pedestal. He placed both hands over the box. "Shatter!"

Splinters and shards of dark crystal went flying down the tunnel.

Conryu staggered over to the filthy tunnel wall and leaned against it. He barely had strength enough to raise his arm, but the thought of resting his face on whatever slime covered the stone gave him a boost of energy.

"Master, this is not a good place to recover. If our enemy sends more shadow beasts you'll have nowhere to hide."

"I know. Just give me a minute to get my wind back."

He closed his eyes and took slow, deep breaths, trying in vain to ignore the rank odor. It felt like the filth coated his tongue and the back of his throat. After a minute or two he started down the tunnel. Hopefully he'd find a manhole, along with the strength to open it.

* * *

Terra and the others joined Sho in the hall outside the conference room. She stepped over the body of the nearest guard and eyed the door. "Reveal."

No wards glowed in her enhanced vision. Maybe her initial impression had been correct and the advisors from Central were just ordinary liars. And maybe pigs could fly. Shizuku put her hands on Lin's and Sho's shoulders and murmured in Angelic. Both men lit up as the light magic shield sprang into place around them. Shizuku repeated the spell on herself.

She should cast a protective spell of her own, but fire magic wasn't subtle like light magic. If they marched in there and she was wearing a cloak of flames it might lead to a fight and right now Terra was more interested in talking.

Lin drew his pistol, but held it at his side out of sight. Shizuku nodded and Terra pushed the door open. The conference room was dark save for the light from a computer screen. The mayor sat in front of it, watching the feed from three different news channels. Terra flicked the light switch, but nothing happened.

Beside him the fake female advisor rested her hand on his back and whispered in his ear. A faint aura of magic leaked from between her fingers.

"She's a wizard," Terra said.

"Where's the guy?" Lin asked.

Shizuku raised her hands. "Let there be Light!"

Bright white orbs flew to every corner of the room. In the far corner a massively muscled creature in the tattered remains of a suit was hunched over a pair of mangled, partially consumed bodies. Bits of flesh dangled from its fangs. It was a demon of some sort and radiated dark magic.

Terra swallowed the lump in her throat. Whatever it was, it looked strong. When she'd led the group here she hadn't expected to confront a demon and a wizard.

The woman left the mayor's side and turned to face them. "You were told to remain in the executive office. Your services are not needed here."

Her words held the power of magic. They washed over Terra like a wave trying to force her out of the room. She clenched her jaw and focused her will. No one could control her unless she allowed it. After a few seconds that felt more like hours the spell faded and her mind cleared.

"You are strong willed, stronger than this weakling at least." She gave the mayor a casual swat across the back of the head. "Pity for you. If you had submitted this would have gone much easier for you."

Dark magic burst from the advisor. Maggie Chin vanished and

a bat-winged female demon appeared. Exquisitely feminine with tiny horns on her forehead and a long, twitching tail, the succubus was stunning. Terra's heart raced and she wasn't even into that sort of thing.

Delicate white fingers grew six-inch black talons. From its place in the corner the second demon roared.

"Lin, you're with me. Shizuku, you and Sho handle the big one."

"Flames swirl and roar. Guard me from all enemies, Fire Armor!" Flames surrounded Terra from head to foot. It would take a potent attack to break her defense.

To her left a lightning bolt cracked. She spared the others a quick glance. Sho was racing to close with the demon while Shizuku blasted it with a second bolt.

They were on their own for now. The succubus sauntered around the table, hips swaying from side to side, only strategically placed black flames covering her nakedness.

"Are you certain you wouldn't rather surrender your will to me? I'm a generous mistress. I promise I won't even kill you when this business is settled."

"All things burn to ash, Inferno Blast!" Terra threw her hand forward and a torrent of flames streaked toward the demon.

A dark aura sprang up at once around her, parting the fire, and keeping it from burning her. Lin fired two shots, but both bullets exploded before impact.

"You'll have to do better than that." The succubus flicked her wrist and a black blade streaked toward Terra.

Lin tackled her and the blade flew over their heads. "We're out of our league," he whispered into her ear.

Terra was quickly coming to that conclusion as well, but she wasn't ready to give up yet. From the floor she chanted, "Flood the world with flames, Fire Surge!"

A rush of flames, twice as powerful as her first spell, poured from her cupped hands. They plowed into the succubus's dark barrier and forced the demon back one step, then another.

For half a second she imagined the spell might penetrate, then the flames guttered and died. Beyond them the demon remained unharmed.

"That was better." The succubus raised her hand and a ball of black energy gathered.

Lin raised his pistol and put three rounds into the ebony sphere. The dark magic devoured the bullets like they were nothing. If that spell hit them it would do exactly the same thing.

* * *

Sho had heard the reports of his son's battles with demons and other magical threats, but until this moment he hadn't fully appreciated what that meant. His roundhouse kick struck the red-skinned monster in the side of the jaw with enough force to break the neck of a normal man. The demon didn't flinch.

It opened its mouth so wide Sho thought its head might split in half. He jerked his leg back before the demon had a chance to bite his foot off. Sho ducked two slashes from taloned hands big enough to rip him in half.

He danced back and a third lightning bolt struck the demon in the chest. The red skin darkened, but beyond that the attack had no effect. He darted in again, landing a dozen machine-gun punches before leaping clear to avoid a backhand.

It was like punching a concrete pillar and every bit as effective. Only the demon's relative lack of speed kept Sho alive. His son had fought creatures like this and won. He had a whole new respect for what Conryu's magic could do.

Shizuku sent a lance of white energy crashing into the demon's chest, doing every bit as little damage as she had with the lightning. The demon took a step toward them and Sho took a step back.

This was pointless. If he pounded that thing until his fists broke it wouldn't accomplish anything. As a warrior Sho feared nothing, but he knew when he was in a fight he couldn't win and this was it.

He risked a glance over at the government wizard and Lin. They were lying on the floor with the female demon standing over them. The creature had a ball of energy in its hand.

An idea popped into his head. A foolish, desperate idea, but if ever there was a time for foolish desperation this was it. He sprinted across the room toward the female demon, ignoring Shizuku's confused look as he went past.

He'd covered most of the distance before the creature noticed him. It swung his way, doing half his work for him. He leapt and kicked at its head, missing intentionally.

The instant he landed Sho spun and kicked the wrist above the black ball, knocking it away from Lin and toward the other demon. He so startled the female that she released the ball.

It streaked toward her hulking companion, exploding on impact. The conference room shook. In the chaos Sho grabbed Lin and Terra and pulled them to their feet.

"We need to go," he said.

Terra nodded and muttered something in one of those nonsense languages the wizards used. A wall of fire sprang up between them and the demons. Shizuku had already reached the doors and was motioning for them to hurry as they ran.

The group darted out into the hall and Terra led them back toward the stairwell. Inside, they went down instead of up.

"We need to return for Orin and Maria," Shizuku said.

"No, we need to lead the demons away from them, not back." Terra took the steps two at a time.

"Would that blast have killed the male?" Sho couldn't imagine anything surviving an impact like that, but he also wouldn't have believed it could live through three lightning strikes, so he had little confidence in his theory.

"No, that orb was pure dark magic. It might have stunned the demon, but it wouldn't have done any real damage." Terra pulled up at the third-floor platform. "We need some extra firepower."

* * *

Kelsie really wanted to move around, but she didn't dare leave the car lest she draw unwanted attention. Conryu had been gone fifteen minutes already. Given that no time passed when he was in Hell that meant he'd been trying to deal with the box and its protections all this while. It had only taken him five minutes to handle the first one. Something must have gone wrong.

Had she made a mistake, not to insist on going with him? No, she knew what she was capable of and her feeble magic wouldn't even be enough to stop a single shadow beast. And Jonny couldn't do magic at all. If they'd gone they'd have only slowed him down. Nonetheless she wished she knew what was happening.

"Do you think he's okay?" Jonny asked, speaking her thoughts out loud.

"Conryu's the strongest wizard ever. If he can't handle this no one can." God, she wished she felt as confident as she sounded.

"He's only one man. No matter how strong he is, Conryu doesn't have eyes in the back of his head."

"He has Prime and Cerberus. I'm worried too, but we have to trust that he'll be okay."

Jonny twisted around and looked at her. "I swore to myself after that business at the carnival, when he put himself in danger to protect everyone, that if it ever happened again I wouldn't run. That I'd stand beside him and fight. Now here I am, just like last time, useless and waiting. What kind of friend am I that I let him face this alone?"

"The same kind as me, I suppose. While I wish with all my

heart I could help, I know I can't. And neither can you. It isn't a matter of not caring, it's about knowing your limitations."

The car phone rang and Jonny spun back around. An icon of a handset was flashing on the screen. He touched it. "Conryu?"

"Yeah." He sounded so weak. "I'm at Seventh and Maple. There's a little cafe."

"Got it. We're on our way." The line went dead and Jonny shook his head. "He sounded worse than last time."

"Must have been a harder fight. That can't be a surprise after he destroyed the first box." Kelsie glanced at the time. Twelve hours to go.

Jonny pulled out and made his way through the busy streets. She wasn't familiar with Sentinel City, but Jonny seemed to know right where he was going. Five minutes later she spotted the cafe and Conryu, sitting slumped at one of the tables. He looked asleep.

Jonny double-parked right across from him, leapt out, and helped him back to the car. Several cars behind them honked, but they paid no attention. Conryu fell into the back seat beside her, Prime clutched in his grasp.

When he blinked and looked up at her his eyes were so red she expected blood to run down his cheeks. And what in heaven's name did he have on his clothes? The stink filled the car. Jonny got in behind the wheel and took off.

"Was it bad?" Kelsie adjusted his head so it rested on her lap. She murmured the cleaning spell in hopes of getting whatever the mess was off him.

"Demons, shadow beasts, and this weird zombie thing that almost took my head off. It's good you two didn't try and come with me. It was all I could do to protect myself."

"Where we headed?" Jonny asked.

"Nowhere for a while." Conryu tried to sit up but she pulled him back down. "Find a parking lot or something. I need to rest for a couple hours."

"One port in the storm coming up."

"Is two hours going to be enough?" Kelsie stroked his hair. The spell had cleaned the worst of the crud off his clothes and the seat. The mess now sat in a pile on the floor.

"We have three boxes to go. I don't dare take any longer."

Prime worked himself free from Conryu's grasp. "If you keep this pace up you'll kill yourself, Master. You need at least six hours' rest or a direct infusion of life energy."

"Six hours is out of the question," Conryu said. "What about the second one?"

"There's a spell, it's actually a variation of Reaper's Gale, that drains your target's life force, but instead of dissipating it draws it into your body. It's another one you'll need to be careful with. Drain too much and your target dies."

"Great, show me. I don't know if I'll use it, but it never hurts to be prepared. I need a spell that will make it easier to kill those zombie things too."

While Conryu studied the book Kelsie studied him. He looked pale and weak, but the determination in his gaze never wavered. She knew he wouldn't give up while he had breath in his body. She'd make sure he kept breathing, even if it killed her.

6

REACTION

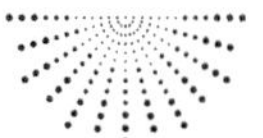

Lady Raven snapped her fingers and the image on her viewing mirror vanished. She understood everything now. It was clear from the moment he stepped out of the dark portal. Conryu was somehow tracing the path her boxes took through Hell.

How was he doing it? She knew of no spell that created such an effect. Regardless, he was doing it and in the process slowly destroying years of work along with her hopes for a long life as a Hierarch in the Society.

The defenses she'd put in place at the last location were the strongest possible given the time she had. She'd increased the number of shadow beasts at the remaining locations, but refused to sacrifice any more of her Faceless Ones. Galling as it was, she had to admit mere shadow beasts wouldn't be enough to hold the abomination off.

Lady Raven reached for her mask. If the mission was to succeed she needed to ask for help.

With her mask in place she stepped into the circle and cast the calling spell. The others had to be waiting near their own casting chambers. With the time of activation so close they'd want to be available in case of emergencies.

Well, this certainly qualified as one. It took less than a minute for the room to go hazy. The first to appear was Lady Wolf. Lady Tiger and Lady Dragon appeared shortly after that.

"What has happened?" Lady Dragon asked.

"The abomination has interfered and destroyed two of the artifacts."

The weight of Lady Dragon's regard pressed down on her. The anger and disappointment in her gaze burned Lady Raven's skin.

"I thought you put protections in place," Lady Wolf said.

"I did and I increased them after his first success." Lady Raven took a deep breath. "They were inadequate. I acknowledge that. If the mission is to have any hope of success I'll need help."

"We have no magic to offer you." Lady Dragon slapped the Scepter of Morgana against her palm.

"What about our other agents in the city? They were supposed to be helping capture the abomination."

"Yes, well, you're not our only disappointment today. Rennet has also been a spectacular failure with regards to capturing him. Apparently the police can't arrest someone they can't find."

Lady Raven couldn't suppress a faint smile. "If you can put me in contact with her I believe I can solve both our problems. And if I may add, perhaps elimination would be better than capture."

"Approved." Lady Dragon rattled off a phone number. "You can reach Rennet at that number. Be certain to tell her this is the last chance for both of you."

The Hierarchs vanished and Lady Raven found herself back in her casting chamber. She took off her mask and scrambled to reach her cellphone before she forgot the number Lady Dragon gave. Somehow she doubted it would be repeated if she asked.

* * *

Maria sat beside her father and stared at the laptop screen. He'd tapped into the building security cameras, allowing them to watch the others confront the imposters. Her heart had skipped a beat when the woman turned into a demon. Everyone had fought bravely, but in the end they'd been forced to flee.

Dad tapped a key, opening multiple windows in the screen. One showed Mom and her companions running down the stairwell, another stayed on the conference room. The male demon shook off the effects of his partner's blast and went after them. It crushed one of the unconscious guards' heads before turning down the stairs. Maria shuddered and looked away.

"Clever Terra," Dad muttered.

Maria looked back. "What's she doing?"

"Terra led them to the magical artifact storage room. There are plenty of things in there that will give them an edge over that monster."

"What's the other one doing?" Maria pointed at the window showing the conference room. The female demon had moved toward the door and stepped out into the hall.

Dad tapped another key and the view shifted. The demon headed for the stairs, but turned up instead of down.

"Uh-oh. Looks like we're going to have company." Dad closed the lid on the laptop and handed it to her. "Time to make ourselves scarce."

"Where are we going to go?" Maria's heart raced. She didn't know a single spell that would even make that thing blink if it came to a fight.

"Don't worry, sweetheart." Dad walked over to the left side of his office and groped around a blank section of wall. There was a click and a secret door slid aside. "Come on."

She slipped in ahead of him and a light came on overhead. A narrow corridor extended as far as she could see behind the wall. Dad joined her and secured the door.

"I didn't know this was here."

"Only the station chief knows about it. The old chief told me when I took over. No one has ever used it since the building was constructed. It was a fine tradition I had hoped to follow. These passages run all through the building. The idea was to have a way to escape and counterattack if the Department was ever assaulted."

"I don't know about counterattacking, but escape sounds good."

He took her hand and squeezed.

Out in the office an explosion was followed by crunching footsteps. Dad held a finger to his lips and nodded his head toward the far end of the passage. Maria tiptoed away from the door.

"I can smell you, mortals. Wherever you're hiding, I'll find you."

Nothing that evil should have such a beautiful voice. The demon could have been a professional singer. Maria choked off a hysterical giggle when she imagined the monster on one of the popular singing competitions. She had to focus.

"Hurry," Dad whispered. "There's a right turn just a little ways further then a ladder down."

She made the turn a moment before another explosion sounded behind them. Dad urged her on and Maria broke into a trot. If the demon had found the hidden passage there was no point in keeping quiet.

"So we have rats in the walls." The demon's voice echoed through the passage. "Good thing the exterminator's here."

Maria tried to swallow, but her throat was too dry. The ladder was just ahead. If they put some distance between themselves and their hunter, maybe they had a chance of escaping. She put her foot on the first rung and clambered down. Aside from a slight vibration the ladder was secure.

She made it to a small chamber at the bottom. There didn't appear to be an exit.

Her breath came in ragged gasps as she scrambled around for an exit. There had to be one. Dad wouldn't have led them to a dead end.

Dad hit the floor beside her and went directly to a section of wall no different from any other. He pressed a particular spot and a panel slid up revealing a number pad. When he input the code another door slid open.

She darted through it and he joined her a moment later. Another long hall greeted them. They'd barely taken a step when something heavy landed in the now-empty chamber. Maria froze, terror gripping her heart. It was a magical effect, her rational mind recognized that, but her primitive mind screamed at her not to move. If she held still maybe the monster wouldn't see her.

The muffled ring of a cellphone broke the spell. It was clearly coming from the other side of the door. What she couldn't understand was why a demon would have a phone in the first place and where the naked creature kept it.

"I'm a little busy right now." Maria heard the demon just as plain as day.

Silence, followed by, "Are you certain? Hold on. No, I don't want to disappoint Lady Dragon."

More silence.

"Very well. My rat problem will keep for the moment."

The clang of the demon's feet on the ladder climbing back up out of the hole set Maria free. She leaned against the wall and tried to calm her still-racing heart.

Dad rubbed her back. "Are you okay?"

"Yeah. What was that about and who's Lady Dragon?"

"I couldn't tell anything from the demon's side of the conversation, but Lady Dragon is the leader of the Le Fay Society. She's the one that delivered the ultimatum this morning. No one knows her true identity. If you're up to it we need to move."

Maria pushed away from the wall and took a step down the hall. Ahead of them a panel clattered open.

She took a step back before Angus's white-haired head popped into view. "Thank god. I was beginning to think I'd never find a way out of these cursed passages."

* * *

Conryu draped his arm across his eyes and tried to sleep. The back seat of a car wasn't the best place in the world to rest. His knees were almost touching his chin, the seatbelt was digging into his hip, and the sewer stink still lay over everything. Assuming they lived through the next day Conryu was going to have to spring for an auto detailing for Mrs. Kane. At least Kelsie's lap made a good pillow.

The car stopped and he looked out the window. Nothing but concrete walls and a pillar filled his vision. "Where are we?"

"Parking garage." Jonny switched the car off. "Figured it would be more out of the way than an open lot. Anything I can do?"

Conryu covered his eyes again. "Not right now. Once I get my strength back we need to go to St. Sara's Cemetery."

"No sweat, bro. Just say when."

Conryu raised his fist and Jonny gave it a bump.

He didn't think he actually slept, it was more a half-awake sort of thing. Conryu's mind wandered, trying to make sense of the situation he found himself in. Sometimes it felt like only days ago when the government wizard told him he had wizard potential and other times it felt like a whole different life.

"Master, I sense many people approaching."

"Probably shoppers returning to their cars." Jonny yawned. "There's a mall connected to this garage."

A gunshot rang out and a bullet slammed into the car. Conryu sat up, a blast of adrenaline washing away his exhaustion.

More shots clattered against the door and windshield. Ten guys with machine guns and bulletproof vests were advancing up the ramp toward them.

"How the hell did they find us?" Jonny had slid over into the passenger's seat and hunkered down amidst shards of the window.

"Beats me, but we can't stay here. Kelsie, scoot out the door. Careful not to expose yourself."

She opened the door and slipped out. Conryu crawled across the seat and dropped to the ground. Jonny joined them a moment later. "What now?" he asked.

Conryu flinched as a bullet ricocheted a little too close for comfort. "I was hoping you'd have a suggestion. You're the soldier."

"Sorry, dude. Soldiers have guns and armor. I'm a civilian today."

"Master, this may prove to be a fortuitous turn of events." Prime floated inches off the floor.

"What?" Kelsie's voice had turned shrill with fear.

"Those men will provide you with an excellent source of life energy. You can put them out of commission and restore yourself at the same time."

He wasn't thrilled about the thought of draining the life out of anyone. Another burst of gunfire made him duck. He wasn't thrilled about getting shot either.

Jonny lay on the ground and looked under the car. "They're almost on us. Five seconds and we'll be surrounded."

Kelsie clutched his arm. "Conryu."

This was no time to be squeamish. He eased free of Kelsie's grip and focused. He wanted to drain the police enough to knock them out, not kill them. "Fingers of the Reaper, black and twisted. Reach for my enemies and claw the life from them. Feed me their souls that I may be strong, Reaper's Grasp!"

A wailing moan filled the air and black spirits exploded from Conryu. The nearest cop came around the car just in time to have a formless cloud of darkness pass through his body.

The cop collapsed, twitching, to the concrete. Beyond the car the frightened cries mingled with the spirits' moaning. Full auto sprays of gunfire went off seemingly at random.

He sensed the first spirit returning before he saw it. The apparition slid through the car door like smoke and slipped into his chest. First cold then heat assaulted him. He stiffened as one after another of the spirits entered his body.

Weakness was burned away and a power unlike anything he'd ever experienced filled him to bursting. When the final bit of energy entered him he gasped and leaned forward. "What a rush."

Jonny peeked over the hood. "I don't see anything moving. I think we're good for now."

Conryu pulled himself to his feet using the bullet-riddled car for leverage. He glanced at the collapsed officer. The man's face was ghost white, but he was breathing which was more than they were willing to allow Conryu.

He helped Kelsie to her feet. When she looked over the car roof at the bodies sprawled across the pavement she buried her face in his chest. He held her for a moment then stepped back. "It's okay. I didn't kill any of them."

Jonny cleared his throat. "I don't think we should hang around here."

"Good call. Think you can find us a car?"

Jonny grinned. "No problem."

While Jonny went car shopping Conryu sat on the hood of their current ride. Prime flew up beside him. "Are you well, Master?"

"Better than that. I'm so buzzed I think I could tear that zombie thing apart with my bare hands."

"That's a side effect of this particular spell. It's also highly addictive. More than one dark wizard has fallen from the righteous path on a quest for ever more life energy. I wouldn't recommend using it more than necessary."

Jonny pulled up in a beat-up blue coupe that looked older than Conryu. "Jump in."

Conryu grabbed the handle and gave it a yank. It came free in his hand. Jonny leaned across and opened it from the inside. It was so tight Kelsie practically had to sit in his lap.

"Is this the best you could do?"

"Give me a break. All the new cars have antitheft devices. This was the only one I could hot-wire. Beats walking, right?"

"Barely."

Jonny shot him a middle finger and took off. They hadn't gone a hundred yards when they found a heavy truck with police emblems on the side blocking their way.

"Think they left the keys in it?" Conryu asked.

"I'll check." Kelsie hopped out and ran over to the truck. A few seconds later she was back. "No dice."

"Looks like we're walking after all." Jonny reached down to untwist the wires.

"Wait." Conryu focused on the ground under the truck. "Reveal the way through infinite darkness. Open the path, Hell Portal!"

The familiar black disk appeared under the front half of the truck. It teetered and fell in. The instant the rear end fell out of sight the portal snapped shut.

Jonny grinned and they bumped fists. Conryu turned to Prime as Jonny drove off. "The demons won't get mad if I drop a truck in their realm, will they?"

"Hell is infinite, Master. The vehicle is a speck in an endless ocean. I doubt anyone will even notice it."

Conryu hoped so. The fine for littering in Hell was probably stiff.

7
DEMONS AT THE DEPARTMENT

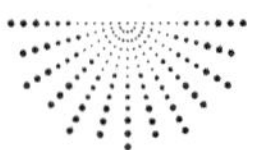

Terra stopped in front of the sealed storage room door and panted for breath. It had been a long run and she wasn't as young as she used to be. At first she'd been concerned that the imposters had ordered everyone home early, now the empty halls came as a relief. The only way this could be worse was if she had to worry about the staff getting caught in the crossfire.

Shizuku stared back the way they'd come. Terra sensed no pursuit, but the light magic user was more sensitive to dark magic than her. "Anything?"

"It's faint but getting closer. The male is definitely on our trail."

Terra swallowed a curse, placed her hand on the metal plate beside the door and spoke the release spell. The door popped open revealing shelf upon shelf covered in magical artifacts.

"What is this place?" Sho asked.

"Storage. We keep potentially dangerous or valuable magical items here." She went in and soon came up with the Flame Fist Gauntlet. "This, for instance, will increase my fire magic a great deal."

The gauntlet was still sized for the biker that had last worn it.

Terra slipped it on and like all magical items it altered itself to fit her hand as if it had been made for her.

"Anything in there for light magic?" Shizuku asked.

Terra rummaged around, looking for the crystal amulet they'd brought in last year. She knew it was here somewhere.

Behind her Shizuku said, "Hurry, Terra, it's coming."

Her search grew more frantic. Where was it? Something flashed in one of the bins. There! The clear crystal amulet had sunk to the bottom of the container. She fished it out and stepped into the hall.

"Here." Terra handed the artifact to Shizuku who slipped it over her neck. The demon was so close now Terra sensed it even with her limited awareness of dark magic.

"This is a potent item." Shizuku fingered the central gem.

"Yeah, if we live through this I'll tell you the story of how we ended up with it. Lin, Sho, stay behind us." When the men had moved a safe distance back she said, "You bind it and I'll burn the bastard to the ground."

Shizuku nodded and raised her hands. The heavy thumps of the demon's tread vibrated the floor. It rounded the corner, its head brushing the ceiling. Had it gotten bigger? Muscles rippled under red skin stretched so tight it looked like it might tear.

Shizuku chanted in Angelic. Light gathered around the amulet and when she finished, the light released. White portals appeared all around the demon and golden chains shot out, wrapping up its arms, legs, and neck.

It thrashed and roared, snapping one of the chains immediately. Shizuku gestured and a new chain shot out to replace the broken one.

Terra clenched her gauntlet-covered hand. "Flames of deepest earth consume all things in your path. Flames of creation and flames of destruction rise and devour, Volcanic Core!"

She opened her hand and thrust it toward the ceiling. The floor trembled and tore open under the demon's feet. White-hot flames spewed forth, hiding the demon from view. Terra squinted, but her focus never wavered. Deep in the heart of the inferno a dark figure struggled.

The demon pressed through the flames, breaking more chains as it went. It was going to escape and if it did they'd never stop it before it tore them all to pieces.

The steel beams her spell exposed twisted and wrapped around the demon, keeping it from moving beyond the fire. Shizuku sent still more chains. Despite all that it continued to struggle to free itself.

Terra focused her will on the gauntlet and demanded it give more power. She had to end it now. The flames intensified until she couldn't even make out the shadow of the demon.

The floor above came crashing down, smashing through their floor and continuing on until the debris hit the lobby. Terra ended the spell. Nothing of the demon remained.

On the opposite side of the hole she'd burned in the floor stood Clair who, despite the danger, wore a huge grin. Terra understood completely. The moment the metal twisted she'd known Clair had regained her magic. For a wizard there was no greater joy.

"Excellent timing." Terra blew out a sigh and started to pull the gauntlet off.

Lin laid a hand on her shoulder. "You should keep that until we deal with the one upstairs."

The one upstairs. For half a minute she'd forgotten the succubus. She tugged the gauntlet back on tight. Dealing with that one would be tricky since it was holding the mayor hostage. She certainly wouldn't be able to use Volcanic Core on her.

"Maybe you'd better fill me in," Clair said.

"We'll talk as we walk. I need to check on Orin and Maria." Shizuku made no move to take off her borrowed amulet.

It went against protocol to let her keep using it, but under the circumstances Terra figured it was the best option. "Let's go."

* * *

Maria's heart about stopped when Angus's head appeared in the passage. She was starting to think she really wasn't cut out for adventure. A quiet little business far away from anything anyone would ever want to hold hostage sounded really good right now. She brushed a cobweb aside and did her best to ignore the musty, stale air.

"Angus." Her father had assumed the lead since he was the only one that knew his way around the passages. "How did you get in here?"

"I found the hidden access one day quite by accident when I stumbled against the wall and it slid open. Imagine my surprise. I had no idea the Department building even had hidden paths. I never did anything about it, but after I called Conryu it occurred to me that making myself scarce would be a prudent decision. I retreated to my office and entered the passages whereupon I got utterly lost."

"Don't feel too bad. I spent the better part of three weeks memorizing the layout of these passages. They're designed in an intentionally haphazard way to make it hard for those not familiar with them."

"I'll happily attest to their effectiveness. By the way, how is Conryu?"

"Okay as of a couple hours ago," Maria said. "He's disabled at least one of the artifacts and most likely a second by now."

Angus shook his head, sending white hair waving in every direction. "The boy's a marvel. Just imagine, after he saves the city he'll be even more famous. A true hero in every sense of the word, just like Merlin."

Maria wanted to slap him for bringing up his pet theory even when they were running for their lives. The last thing Conryu wanted was to be more famous. He was only doing this because no one else could.

An explosion sent dust raining down on her. "Dad?"

"Sounds like your mother and the others are back at it. Let's pick up the pace. I don't want to be in here if something collapses."

"Like what?" Angus's question came out as more of a croak.

"Like the building."

"What?" Angus staggered against the wall when another blast shook the floor.

Maria knew enough about the design of the Department's wards to know the odds of the whole building coming down on their heads was vanishingly small. She allowed herself a small smile. It was good that her father could still tease Angus, even in these circumstances. For some reason that, more than anything, made her believe they had a better chance to win this than they probably did.

They went down another floor before Dad finally led them to an exit. They stepped out into an office filled with books and papers. A green-and-red tartan hung on the wall above a cluttered desk.

"You found my office." Angus rushed over to his chair, slumped into it, and let out a groan. "God, that feels good. I was afraid if I didn't get off my feet soon I was going to faint."

The two guest chairs were filled with notebooks and papers. Maria cleared them off so she and her father would have a place to sit. "What are we going to do now?"

"That depends on Terra and your mother." Dad took the laptop and opened it. He searched through the various camera feeds until a smoke-filled image filled the screen. "Uh-oh."

A huge hole had been blown in the floor. There was no sign of Mom or the others, but there weren't any bodies either. That was something.

"They won't know where to find us."

Dad waved a hand. "They have a pair of skilled wizards with them and the three of us, along with the mayor and Clair, are the only humans in the building. I suspect they'll be along shortly."

* * *

The high from the infusion of life energy had faded to a faint buzz. As fantastic as it felt, Conryu was glad to return to normal. The giddy rush left him feeling invincible and that was a good way to do something stupid. He couldn't afford any mistakes. They only had nine hours left.

Jonny stopped and pulled over to the side of the road, dragging Conryu from his contemplations. Ten cop cars surrounded the cemetery and heavily armed officers patrolled the perimeter. There was no way to sneak through and Conryu wasn't eager to lay out more cops. They were supposed to be on the same side after all.

"What now, dude?"

"Reveal." Conryu squinted at the crumbling mausoleum where the box had been hidden during the winter. Dark wards crackled around it and the aura of one of the boxes was just visible through the walls. "She moved them back."

"What?" Kelsie turned to look at him.

"She moved the boxes back to their original hiding places, this one at least. It's smart; now her artifacts are protected by people I don't want to hurt instead of monsters I'd be happy to destroy."

"Or perhaps both," Prime said. "Shadow beasts could be hidden inside the crypt as a second line of defense. Mingling with the living would make them more difficult targets for you."

Conryu canceled the seeing spell. "Let's try the culvert. If they have that one on lockdown as well we can assume the police are working with the Le Fay Society and not against them."

Jonny did a U-turn, drawing several annoyed honks which he ignored. As they roared down the street Kelsie asked, "Couldn't you just portal in, deal with the box, and escape without the police noticing?"

"Maybe, but what if something goes wrong and I need to retreat? Having twenty plus machine guns pointing my way isn't very appealing. I wish I'd thought to borrow Mrs. Kane's ring when I got home from school."

"Why, what does it do?"

"She said it stopped bullets."

Kelsie chewed her lip and nodded. "That would certainly be handy."

It took almost half an hour to drive across town through the afternoon traffic. Jonny didn't even bother pulling down the street leading to the culvert. The police cars were visible from where he stopped.

"Goddamn it!" Conryu slammed his fist into the car door.

Wasn't it enough to have to deal with wards, shadow beasts, and demons? Now he had a bunch of cops who should be out evacuating people in the danger zone standing between him and the very things that put those people in jeopardy. It was a bad joke.

Conryu dug out the phone, flipped it open, and dialed Maria. She answered after the third ring. A stream of worries slammed into his ear and he held the phone away.

"Maria. Maria! I'm fine, really. Is your dad there? I need to talk to him. No, I'm not trying to get out of talking to you, I'm in a bit of a situation here and I need some advice. Please?"

A couple seconds later Mr. Kane came on. "Conryu, what's the problem?"

"The problem is a bunch of cops that are trying to stop me from getting to the boxes. A SWAT team damn near shot me twenty minutes ago, and the less said about Mrs. Kane's car the better. I need the police out of the way if I'm going to do my job. I can take them out if there's no other option, but the only spell I know that'll do it might kill everyone if I make a tiny mistake."

The silence stretched until it grew uncomfortable. "We have a bit of a situation here as well."

Mr. Kane filled him in on their demon problem. As he talked a headache built behind Conryu's eyes.

Mr. Kane added, "So the mayor has the police convinced you're the primary threat and they've deployed accordingly. Until we deal with the demon controlling him there's no way we can convince the police to back down and even then they might think it's a trick."

"I assume you have a plan."

"No. Terra and Shizuku think they can kill the creature, but there's every possibility of the mayor getting burned in the crossfire. I'm not sure that's a chance we can take."

"What if I come and use Domination to force her to release the mayor and return to Hell? It's that or I risk killing the police between me and the boxes. That's not a decision I'm comfortable making on my own."

"Alright, take the stairs up to the fourteenth floor. After Terra destroyed the second and third floors the elevators aren't working."

"Great. I thought your office was on the sixteenth floor?"

"It is, but we were forced to escape. We're working out of Angus's office for the moment."

Conryu groaned. A demon and the professor, fantastic.

* * *

Smoke was pouring out of the second-floor window when the car pulled into the Department parking lot. Why there weren't people pouring out of the other nearby government buildings was beyond Conryu. The lack of fire trucks was another mystery. There was a station three blocks north. They should have spotted the smoke from their front door.

The almost-empty parking lot gave them ample options, but

Jonny parked as far from the doors as possible. Probably a good idea. If Conryu failed to keep the demon under control and it became a fight, well, better to have their ride a safe distance away.

They piled out of the car and Jonny looked around the empty lot. "You'd think it was a holiday."

"Yeah, Demon Apocalypse Day. Come on." Conryu led the way to the front doors.

When he pushed them open they found a heap of rubble in the lobby. The secretaries' desks were crushed under tons of steel and concrete. A haze of dust filled the air. Conryu covered his face and made his way around the debris and over to the stairwell.

The path was clear and he quickstepped it up to the fourteenth flour. By the time they reached the door Kelsie was gasping and Conryu's pulse raced. Only Jonny appeared unfazed. All that training must have paid off.

When Kelsie had stopped wheezing like a bellows with a hole in it, Jonny pushed the door open and they stepped out into an empty, undamaged hall.

"Shit! I forgot to ask which office belonged to Angus." Conryu pulled out the phone and dialed. "Hey, we're here. Which office is Angus's?"

Three doors to their left a door opened and Maria poked her head out. "This one."

She stepped into the hall and leapt into his arms the minute he came within reach. They shared a kiss and Conryu sighed. "I missed you. Though I'll admit I'm just as glad you weren't with me for the last two fights."

"Bad, huh?" She took his hand and led the group into Angus's office.

The professor was behind his desk, chin on chest, sound asleep. Thank god for small favors. Everyone else was sitting, standing, or leaning as was their preference.

"Hey, Dad."

His father nodded, but made no comment.

"Conryu," Mr. Kane said. "We're in a real mess here. That creature has complete control of the mayor and it's standing right next to him. Any offensive move will hurt him as much or more than her."

"Can you show me?"

Lin had a computer on his lap which he spun so Conryu could see the screen. There was an image of a room with a long table. Seated at the end of it in front of a computer with two monitors was a man in a suit and beside him was a pale, bat-winged demon. Both of them faced away from the camera, but from the curve of her hips it was clear the demon was a succubus. It might even be someone the Dark Lady knew.

He didn't expect that to help him any. From what she'd said it didn't seem like the Dark Lady got along especially well with others of her kind. Of course, if she'd gotten as strong as she claimed since becoming his agent, maybe he could use her as a threat against this succubus.

"So is there a plan?" Conryu asked. "Or do you just want to march up there and see what happens?"

When the silence had stretched to a breaking point he looked from Mr. Kane to Terra to Mrs. Kane before sighing. "Right. Let's go. Kelsie, stay close and be ready to put your hand on my back. A little power boost might be the difference between success and failure."

Maria glared and Kelsie beamed, walking right beside him as they left Angus's office. The old professor had slept through the whole discussion.

It was a short walk up to the next floor. When they stepped out of the stairwell Conryu grimaced. Two bodies lay on the floor, one of them with his head crushed flat, a pool of blood spreading around him.

"Looks like the demon wasn't careful where he stepped," Terra said.

Kelsie grabbed his arm and buried her face in his shoulder. He could almost feel Maria's gaze boring a hole through his back. She was clearly not over the jealousy thing yet.

Dad moved to the front of the group, stepped over the bodies, and shoved the door open. Conryu moved in front of Kelsie and brushed past his father. The rest of the group joined him just inside the door.

The demon stood and turned to face them. She rested her clawed hand on the mayor's neck in an unsubtle threat. Kelsie's hand felt warm on his back.

"I didn't expect to see you fools again. And you brought friends, how nice. The Society will give me a fine reward when I kill you, boy."

Conryu ignored her and focused. "By my will be bound, oh child of Hell. Your thoughts are my thoughts, your desires, my desires, Domination!"

Kelsie's power mingled with his as the spell surged out and settled over the succubus. It was stronger than the last time he used it and not just because of Kelsie's added power. It must have been the power boost the Dark Lady mentioned when they signed their agent contract.

The succubus snarled and twitched her head.

"Be still!" he commanded.

He focused the order on her body rather than her head as he had questions to ask before he sent her back. When her legs and arms went rigid he moved closer, his focus on the spell absolute.

"Release the mayor."

She growled and fought, the mayor staring straight ahead, seemingly unaware of anything happening around him.

Conryu took a step closer and locked gazes with her. "Do it!"

She screamed. A full-body shudder ran through the mayor and he slumped in his chair.

"Dad, Sarge, you guys want to pull him out of here?"

His father and Lin eased around the demon and slid the

mayor's rolling office chair away from her before pushing him back behind the rest of the group.

"Where is the wizard in charge of the artifacts hiding?" Conryu pressed down on her with every bit of focus he could muster.

"I don't know."

With the spell on her the demon was incapable of lying. Her masters probably hadn't told her anything more than she needed to know for just this sort of eventuality. That meant she probably didn't have much in the way of useful information.

"You're the Dark Lady's new pet." The succubus sneered. "I can feel her presence running through your magic. She was never more than a second-rate whore. I don't know how she convinced you mortals that she's some sort of princess of demons."

"What is your name?"

The demon struggled but in the end his magic was stronger than her will. "Rennet."

"Rennet. I'll remember to mention you to the Dark Lady the next time we speak. I think you'll find her stronger now, a true princess. Terra, would you open the portal please?"

Behind him Terra chanted. "Reveal the way through infinite darkness. Open the path, Hell Portal!"

When the dark power from the open portal reached him Conryu said, "Back you go."

Rennet rose jerkily to her feet and shuffled over to the black disk. "You'll never find the last three boxes in time. This city will fall."

She jumped into the portal and Terra shut it behind her.

* * *

While Mr. and Mrs. Kane tried to bring the mayor back to the realm of the waking Conryu motioned his father off to one side. "How's Mom doing?"

The corner of his father's lip quirked up, about as strong a reaction as he ever gave. "You know your mother. She wasn't thrilled when I told her, but she's hanging in there. They have her working on a new project and it's helping her focus on something other than your problems."

"Do you think I should visit her now, or wait until this is over, one way or the other?"

"I don't know. If she sees you she'll get upset. That's just the way your mother is wired. But if things grow worse… I just don't know. Whatever you decide is fine with me."

"Thanks, Dad." Not that he'd been a great deal of help but it was nice just to talk about something other than magic and crazy wizards.

The mayor's groan drew Conryu's attention to the collection of people gathered around the semiconscious politician. Mrs. Kane was applying light magic healing in an effort to wake him faster while Maria looked on with a rapt expression. Whatever Maria's mom was doing, it appeared to be working.

Conryu took a step toward the group, but his father caught him by the arm. Conryu raised an eyebrow. "What's up?"

"I fought a demon today, son. For the first and god willing the last time. I wanted to tell you I have a whole new respect for the things you've done this year. Until I felt the creature's power with my own fists I didn't fully appreciate what fighting such a monster meant. I consider myself a strong warrior, but I couldn't even make it flinch."

Dad shook his head and Conryu wasn't certain what he should say. His father had never made such a long speech before, much less admitted any sort of weakness. The weirdness of it struck him dumb.

A few seconds later a louder groan from the mayor shook Conryu out of his stupor. "Don't worry, Dad. Dealing with things like demons is a job for wizards. Did you know the military considers us living weapons? Apparently that's all we are, weapons. Mr. Kane admitted the government regards us as assets more than individuals. I understand where they're coming from. Some of the things I can do now make me think they're right."

"No. You're not just a weapon, any more than I am. To an untrained person, what I can do is frightening, but it doesn't define me. We are more than the sum of our skills."

Conryu hugged his father. "Thanks, Dad. I think I will go see Mom before I go out again."

"What happened?" The mayor's mumbled question sounded like he was talking with a mouth full of marbles.

Conryu gave his father one last pat on the back and went over to join the others. The mayor was awake now and alternately staring and blinking at those around him. It didn't look like he was fully with it yet.

Mr. Kane crouched down in front of the mayor. "What's the last thing you remember, Tom?"

"Ugh." The mayor rubbed his eyes. "That woman. She said she came from Central to advise me on the current threat. She touched my shoulder. The next thing I know I'm looking at you lot."

"Loss of memory isn't uncommon in cases of psychic manipulation," Mrs. Kane said. "Demons are especially indifferent to any damage they may cause."

"Psychic manipulation? Demon? Maybe someone better tell me what's going on."

Conryu had heard enough. He slipped out the door to make the short run over to the science building. If the worst should happen he wanted to talk to his mother one last time.

8

ON THE RUN

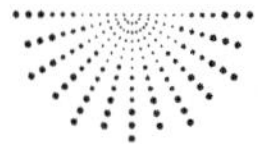

Conryu jogged back to the Department building having spent a weepy ten minutes with his mother. Just as Dad had said, the moment she saw him Mom burst into tears and hugged him. When she finally brought herself under control Conryu gave her the sanitized version of his work so far. Even with the worst of the fights edited out she still almost started crying again.

Eventually, in desperation, he'd asked her about the project Dad mentioned. Changing the subject had worked wonders. She went on and on for ten minutes about how they were trying to fuse a nonmagical vehicle with a magical weapon, in this case a tank that shot fireballs. The military wanted to deploy it on the northern border to help deter the frost giants the next time they marched south.

He'd finally given her one last hug and made his escape. If he had any luck the others would have gotten the mayor up to speed and an order sent removing him from the city's most wanted list. The sun was hanging low in the sky and they didn't have a great deal of time left.

When he reached the conference room and opened the door everyone was seated at the long table. They all looked his way.

Maria stalked over. "Where have you been? We were trying to make plans, but without you we weren't sure of our next move."

"I went to see Mom. Anyway, what's to plan? Order the cops out of the way and I'll go smash those last three boxes and that'll be it."

"Just that easy?" She crossed her arms and stared.

"Simple, not easy, believe me. So are we good to go or what?"

Conryu looked over Maria's head. The mayor climbed to his feet, looking none too steady. "Come here, young man."

Maria took him by the hand and led him over to the mayor. He felt like a little kid being led to the principal's office. "Yes, sir?"

"Orin tells me I owe you my freedom as well as any hope that my city might survive the next day. I wanted to thank you and apologize for all the trouble you've been having with the police. I've spoken to all the station commanders. They'll have their people pulled back within the hour."

"That's a relief as we're getting low on time." He turned to Terra. "Just how long is left?"

She opened their laptop and clicked on something. "Eight hours."

"It's going to be close." Conryu scrubbed his hand across his face. "Jonny, Kelsie, let's get out of here. The cemetery isn't that far away."

"We'll be coming with you." Terra stood and was joined a moment later by Clair and Mrs. Kane.

"Me too." Maria moved to join the group, but her mother waved her back to the table.

"I know you want to help, sweetheart, but your magic isn't strong enough yet. Stay here with your father. We should have this wrapped up in an hour or two."

"Kelsie's weaker than I am and Jonny can't even use magic. How come they can go?"

"They can't." Terra glared at his friends. "We appreciate your help, but it's time to let the professionals handle this."

"You've done a bang-up job of it so far." Jonny crossed his arms and glared right back at the formidable wizard.

"I should go too." Kelsie sounded meeker, but no less determined. "If Conryu needs a power boost I can help."

"It's too dangerous," Terra said.

Jonny and Kelsie both looked at him like he had something to say about it. He sighed. "Kelsie did give me a boost when I dominated the succubus and Jonny's an excellent driver. I doubt I'd have gotten as far as I have without their help."

Part of him wanted to argue in Maria's favor too, but the bigger part would be happy knowing she was somewhere out of the immediate line of fire.

Terra's jaw clenched and relaxed as she grumbled under her breath. "Fine. We don't have time to argue anyway."

Maria hugged him and whispered, "Be careful."

He held her for a moment, soaking in the moment of peace. He doubted he'd have many more of them for the next little while. They broke apart and Maria hurried over to say goodbye to her mother.

Dad stepped closer, distracting him from the others. "You bring honor to the Koda Dojo and I am very proud of you, son."

They bowed to one another then Dad surprised him by taking him in a fierce embrace. "Come back safe."

The six of them left the Department building and headed to the parking lot. Conryu, Jonny, and Kelsie angled toward their stolen car. They hadn't gotten three steps when Terra said, "Where do you think you're going?"

"Our car?" Jonny raised an eyebrow.

"Speaking of cars." Mrs. Kane looked around the parking lot. "Where's mine?"

"It didn't explode," Conryu said. "But the cops shot it up pretty good. We had to abandon it in a parking garage. Jonny liberated that fine vehicle over there."

"You stole it?" Terra sounded horrified.

Conryu didn't blame her, but they hadn't had a ton of better options. "It was that or walk."

"Leave it there. It'd be a shame if you got arrested for driving a stolen car after we convinced the police to stop looking for you." Terra grimaced like she wanted to pull her hair out. His mom used to look like that all the time when he was a kid. "I'll ask Lin to deal with it later. We'll take Department cars. You three ride with Clair. I'll go with Shizuku."

* * *

Lady Raven paced in her casting chamber. She twisted her mask between her hands. On the scrying mirror the police were abandoning their posts protecting her artifacts. As soon as they moved out she switched the boxes back to their secondary hiding places, but that was only a temporary measure. Without the police present Conryu would make short work of locating the boxes and destroying the meager protections she'd put in place.

What the hell had happened to the council's agent? Everything was supposed to be under control on that end. If this was what passed for under control they were in big trouble.

Finally, the expected vibration ran through her mask. She tied it in place and rushed to the spell circle. The Hierarchs and Lady Bluejay were waiting.

"Our agent has been revealed and banished," Lady Dragon said without preamble.

"How?"

"The abomination dominated her and forced her to return to Hell," Lady Bluejay said. "Rennet contacted me as soon as she was able and alerted me to the situation."

"It's clear the leaders of the world have no intention of freeing our mistress or handing over the abomination." Lady Dragon's anger struck Lady Raven like a physical blow. "The artifacts must be activated at once, before any more of them are put out of commission."

"The island isn't yet in position," Lady Raven dared point out. If she activated them now all she could hope for was a handful of shadow beasts that would be instantly destroyed by any modestly powerful wizard that encountered them. They might kill fifteen or twenty people before they were hunted down, but not nearly enough to make a real impression.

"We are aware of that. With two artifacts already gone, there's no way we can complete the ritual as intended. Your new orders are to collect the remaining artifacts, carry them within range of the island, and activate them. I'll leave it up to your judgment where and how to accomplish your new task."

The connection was broken and Lady Raven was once more alone in her casting chamber. Things just kept getting worse. She tossed her mask onto the empty workbench and marched out of the chamber. At least it didn't appear that Lady Dragon held her personally responsible for the plan's failure. It was good fortune that another of the Society's agents had also come up short. That made her own failures less obvious.

Her guards fell in silently beside her as she made her way to the sewer access in the floor. She hardly even noticed the stink of rot surrounding the Faceless Ones' hosts anymore. That made Lady Raven wonder about her own smell, but only for a moment. If she succeeded in this final task it wouldn't matter if she smelled like a pigsty. The Hierarchs would be sure to forgive her earlier setbacks.

Outside the three rooms she'd prepared for her living quarters, the warehouse she'd chosen as her redoubt looked like you'd expect: filthy, run down, and filled with debris abandoned when the company that had owned it went out of business. The building was currently being argued over in court and neither the former owner nor his creditors had legal claim to it. That was one of the reasons she chose it as her base of operations: no one ever came to visit the place.

The other reason was built into the floor. At her mental command one of the Faceless Ones tossed aside a half-full crate revealing a steel manhole cover. The undead lifted the two-hundred-pound disk like it weighed nothing and set it aside.

In addition to their legitimate business operation the owners also ran a drug-smuggling business that used the hidden portal to come and go unseen. Lady Raven found it very useful for the exact same purpose.

She leapt down the concrete tube, whispering to the wind to slow her descent. A small platform rose above the muck and provided a relatively clean place for her to land. Beside it was a floating chariot big enough to hold her and her two guards. She'd made the thing over the winter, as much to alleviate her boredom as anything, but it had turned out to be a useful toy.

When she'd moved to one side two of her guards dropped down beside her, landing with bone-jarring force. The undead didn't even blink as they straightened up. The third remained behind at her mental command. If the worst happened she wanted at least one protector waiting for her return.

The three of them climbed aboard the chariot and with a thought Lady Raven activated the light spells carved into the front of the transport and sent it hurtling down the tunnel.

* * *

The little group reached the cemetery ten minutes later. The sun had set leaving them with nothing but twilight to work with. Conryu didn't know much about shadow beasts, but he knew enough to realize fighting them at night wasn't ideal since they were weaker in daylight.

Clair pulled the beat-up sedan off the road in front of a

wrought iron gate leading into the cemetery grounds. He dearly wished she'd let Jonny drive. The woman was a menace behind the wheel. Conryu pulled his fingers free of the handle on the backseat door and flexed his stiff hand. She hadn't killed them all, but that was the only good thing about the trip.

There were no cops, but when Conryu checked there was no sign of the box either. The crypt that had once crackled with protective magic was now dark and empty. He scanned the rest of the cemetery, but found no magic of any sort.

"Are you seeing what I'm seeing?" Conryu wanted to be certain it wasn't just him missing something due to lack of experience.

"If you're seeing nothing but an empty cemetery then yes." Clair opened the door and they all piled out.

A few seconds later Terra and Mrs. Kane pulled up behind them and joined the group. They both stared out over the gravestones. "She moved it again," Terra said.

"Yeah." Conryu pushed the gate open and started up a low hill toward the crypt with Prime floating along beside him. "I'll have to track it through Hell."

Terra fell in beside him with the others bringing up the rear. "I'm interested to see how you follow the residual energy."

"I don't, I use Cerberus's nose." Conryu stopped in front of the crypt door. "There's nothing dangerous. She must have moved the box, protections and all."

"Yes, I suspect Mercia's been watching every move we make. When the police left the boxes probably did too." Terra's hands opened and closed as she talked.

"Mercia, huh? So I finally have a name for the woman that's caused me so much trouble." Conryu yanked the door open.

Mrs. Kane conjured light globes and sent them in. They revealed an empty chamber and three walls lined with rectangular doors labeled with the names of the bodies inside.

Conryu stepped inside, ignoring the musty, dust-filled air. "So who's going with me and who's following in the cars?"

Jonny immediately said, "Car."

Kelsie and Mrs. Kane agreed with him leaving Terra and Clair to join Conryu. When the others had retreated from the crypt Clair said, "I'll open the portal."

"No, I'd better do that. Cerberus will sense my magic and know it's me approaching. We really don't want to startle him.

Clair shrugged and didn't argue.

Conryu chanted, "Reveal the way through infinite darkness. Open the path. Hell Portal!"

The black disk appeared and he led the way through. Behind him Terra and Clair muttered unfamiliar spells then followed.

"Protective spells, Master," Prime said in answer to his unspoken question. "Neither of the wizards is dark aligned so traveling through Hell is as dangerous for them as it is for your friend."

Clair and Terra were both surrounded by glowing light magic auras. They looked around at the endless darkness, but neither appeared especially disconcerted.

A deep growl vibrated in his chest as Cerberus appeared beside him. Three pairs of eyes stared at Terra and Clair and he bared his fangs.

Conryu swatted his side. "Behave. These are friends."

"Cerberus doesn't care for their aura of light magic," Prime said. "That sort of energy is like a thorn in a demon's brain."

"Well then we need to do this as fast as possible. Cerberus, let's hunt."

All three heads barked and raised their noses in the air. It didn't take long for the demon dog to pick up the scent. A second bark preceded Cerberus crouching down to let Conryu climb up on his back. The moment he did Cerberus leapt into motion, racing through the darkness.

Conryu glanced back to make sure Terra and Clair were keeping up and relaxed when he saw they were. Before he knew it Cerberus skidded to a stop and barked a third time.

"Right here, huh? No demons at least." Whether that was a good thing or not Conryu couldn't say. He waited until the others were floating beside him. "Shall we take a look? Grant me the power to see through realms, Vision Gate!"

The window appeared, revealing a flying chariot racing down another sewer tunnel. "What the hell was that?" Of all the things he'd expected, a chariot soaring through the sewer was way down on the list.

"I didn't get a good look," Terra said. "But it had to be her."

"Why would she be fleeing the hiding place of one of her artifacts?" Clair scratched her head. "Shouldn't she want to defend it?"

"There's only one way to know for sure." Terra cast the portal spell.

They stepped into the damp stink of the sewer. Conryu was getting heartily sick of splashing around in shit rivers. When this was over he was never going underground again.

In front of them sat an empty pedestal. No wards guarded it and no shadow beasts roamed the area.

"She took the box with her." Terra slammed her fist into the slime-covered wall.

"What's she going to do, run around until the island is in place?" For the life of him Conryu couldn't figure out what Mercia's play was.

"She doesn't have to wait. Mercia can take the boxes to the island and activate the artifacts immediately." Terra dug her phone out. "Clair, make us a stone boat while I call Shizuku."

* * *

Lady Raven forced herself not to gloat, not even to herself. She'd beaten the Department wizards to the first box. She hadn't even seen any sign of them. The fools were so far behind they wouldn't know what happened until her shadow beasts ripped the life from them.

The chariot raced down the tunnels as smooth and silent as the wind. In the darkness beside her the shadow tigers effortlessly kept pace. It had been only a moment's work to alter the binding that compelled them to guard the box into one that made them protect her. She doubted the creatures would last long in a fight, but having them might be the difference between success and failure.

Up ahead the sewer split left and right. A mental command turned her transport down the right-hand branch. Another advantage she held was Lady Raven already knew where the boxes were hidden while her hunters had to track them down individually. She smiled as she pictured the frustrated grimace on Terra's face. It would have been nice to be there in person, but that would most assuredly not prove wise.

The next pedestal waited many miles away. Now that she had to collect the artifacts Lady Raven found herself wishing she hadn't hidden them so far apart. Of course, that had been less a personal choice and more a necessity of the ritual she'd planned. If everything had gone according to that plan, she would have opened the largest dark portal in history. For the crime of denying her that honor she'd rip Conryu Koda's heart out and feed it to her pets.

A pair of the shadow tigers surged ahead and a moment later a man in a hardhat and coveralls appeared in the chariot lights. A second later he went down under the insubstantial claws of her guardians. She rushed by the corpse and the two tigers fell back in place. The worker hadn't been a threat, but she didn't chastise the creatures. Giving them a snack now and then made the beasts easier to control.

She continued on for a couple more minutes, nothing and no one disturbing the darkness ahead of her. A mile from the next hiding place she sensed something approaching from behind. She darted a glance over her shoulder. Way behind her a dot of light glimmered in the dark. It was too far away to make out anything, but instinct said it had to be her enemies.

They must have stumbled on her trail at the first pedestal. Lady Raven grinned. She was far enough ahead to collect the next box and leave a nasty surprise for the fools trailing her.

* * *

The tunnel walls blurred as the stone boat raced through the sewers. Conryu had never seen a stone boat much less ridden in one before today. The thing looked like exactly what the name implied, a canoe made of stone that hovered six inches above the tunnel floor.

Clair tried to explain how she charged the stone of the floor with a different frequency of magic than the one she used on the boat and that the two powers pushed against each other causing it to levitate, but his eyes just glazed over. It worked and that was enough for him.

Since she was directing the boat Clair sat in the front with Terra behind her and Conryu in the rearmost seat. The back of Terra's head and her streaming hair obscured his vision. He caught an occasional glimpse of the wall as they whipped by, but otherwise he was blind. Terra muttered constantly as she tracked the energy of Mercia's chariot. Conryu wanted to help, but such finely tuned magic was still beyond him. If they needed something smashed he was ready to step up.

"I see a light," Clair said.

Conryu moved left then right, trying to look around Terra. He caught a glimpse of something—he thought he did anyway, it might have been his imagination.

"It's her." Terra had stopped her muttering. Maybe now that they were closer she didn't need the spell to help her track Mercia. "Step on it."

"I'm giving it all I can. It's not like there's a gas pedal."

"Conryu, switch places with me."

Conryu and Terra shifted and shimmied around each other, causing the boat to wobble and drawing a barely audible curse from Clair.

When they finally swapped positions Terra put her back against his. "Hang on. Father of winds grant this unworthy servant of fire the loan of your breath, Gust!"

Terra slammed into his back and the boat rushed forward at almost double the speed. The light ahead quickly grew brighter.

"Too much, Terra!" Clair had to shout over the roar of the wind. "I can't control the boat. Your wind magic is destabilizing my earth spell."

The shadows ahead shifted. Conryu had seen that before. "We've got company coming."

He'd barely gotten the warning out when a shadowy tiger lunged into the light of the flames. With both women fully occupied it fell to him to protect everyone.

Conryu thrust his hand toward the lunging beast. "All things burn to ash, Inferno Blast!"

The flames incinerated the tiger in a second.

"There are more, Master," Prime said from where he huddled under the lip of the boat.

Conryu's gaze darted left and right, trying to pick out the beasts' movements from the flickering shadows. He shot another burst of flame, but hit only stone.

Clair screamed and the boat spun out of control. They slammed into the right wall, bounced off, and crashed into the left side. Conryu's brain rattled in his head. He caught a glimpse of a dark claw withdrawing from the front of the boat.

"Are you okay?" Conryu didn't dare look at her.

"Yeah, my light barrier held, but that still hurt like a son of a bitch."

Behind him Terra had ended her spell. She hissed and the light grew brighter. Circling them at the edge of the shadows were five more tigers.

He scrambled to his feet and hurled a stream of fire at one, but the beast easily dodged. "Any suggestions, ladies?"

"I can deal with the tigers if you can keep them at bay for a minute," Terra said.

"I'll do my best."

Terra didn't reply as she'd already fallen into the rhythm of her spell. Conryu threw both hands forward and waved the flames around, simulating a wall of flames. Behind him the power of Terra's spell grew.

Clair stayed huddled in the stone boat with Prime, rubbing her temples, and giving her head an occasional shake. Looked like she'd gotten the worst of it in the crash.

"Duck!" Terra shouted.

Conryu clenched his fists and dropped back into the boat. A rush of flame that filled the tunnel from ceiling to floor streaked down the monsters. After its passing the stone gleamed and there was no sign of the shadow beasts.

"You destroyed them all," Prime confirmed. "However I sense more up ahead, their presence is faint but I believe it's another six beasts."

Conryu looked up at a sweating, limp Terra. That spell must have taken a lot out of her. He turned to Clair. "I think we'll have to handle the next bunch."

"Earth magic is useless against insubstantial enemies and my fire and light skills aren't what I'd like them to be."

"You can help a little though, right?" If he had to rely on the simple fire spell Sonja had taught him they might be in trouble.

"I'll do all I can. Climb aboard, Terra. The boat's ready to go."

They took their seats. Conryu remained in the middle in case he needed to blast anything while Terra slumped in the rear, eyes closed and panting for breath.

Clair guided them down the tunnel at a more cautious pace.

No one wanted to fly straight into another ambush. The only thing that reassured him was the knowledge that Prime would warn him if the shadow beasts attacked.

A few minutes later, after who knew how many hundreds of yards, they spotted another light ahead of them. It didn't seem like they'd gone fast enough to catch up to Mercia, so who knew what type of trap she'd left this time.

"Reveal." The light was magical, but his spell revealed nothing else. He squinted, trying to make out what was glowing. "It's not moving."

"It's not Mercia." Terra shifted behind him. Her voice sounded strong; he took that as a good sign. "She's further away."

"As are the shadow beasts," Prime added.

"Want me to dispel it?" The closer they inched to the light the itchier he felt. It had to be a trap. Of course it might be a trap that went off when he tried to dispel it, like last winter with the demons.

"No. Clair, stop well back from it and we'll approach on foot. I don't want to blunder into anything."

"Every minute we waste, Mercia's lead grows." Conryu couldn't see Clair's expression, but the frustration in her voice came through loud and clear. He understood that. Sometimes it seemed like every step they made was in the wrong direction.

"We won't stop her if we're all blown up."

Clair grumbled, but eased the boat along until the head-sized sphere of light came into view. Conryu frowned. Why would a dark wizard like Mercia set a trap using light magic? It didn't make sense.

"Okay, Conryu," Terra said.

He crossed his fingers and wrists. "Darkness dispels everything."

The orb of dark magic struck the sphere and it vanished in an instant. The moment it did a magical vibration ran through him. A wall of flames sprang to life and came rushing at them.

Conryu raised his arms and hoped he lived through the next five seconds.

* * *

Jonny drove along at twenty miles an hour, following Maria's mom's directions. He hated the Department car. The steering was loose, the suspension sucked, and every pothole sent a spring up his ass. Surely they had better cars than this for their employees. It wasn't even an improvement over the piece of shit he hot-wired in the garage, leaving aside the fact that it wasn't stolen.

He sighed. Cars he understood, the whole magic thing, not so much. Apparently Mrs. Kane was following Conryu and the others' path through the sewers. He glanced in the rearview mirror. Kelsie had her nose pressed to the window as if she could somehow peer through the pavement down to the tunnels. The girl had a serious crush on his clueless best friend.

Whatever trick Mrs. Kane was using, it wasn't one Kelsie knew. Not surprising given she was only a freshman. Then again, Conryu was a freshman and he could open portals to Hell, had a pet giant three-headed demon hound, and whatever spell he'd used in the parking garage that gave Jonny chills just thinking about it. The noises the cops had made when those black spirits passed through them would haunt his dreams for the rest of his life.

Jonny thought of Conryu like a brother, but damn. The shit he could do wasn't right.

"Turn left," Mrs. Kane said.

He frowned. There wasn't a street to turn down. A little later they reached an intersection and he made the left. Hopefully it wouldn't screw up her spell.

Two blocks later she said, "Stop."

He parked under a light across the street from a pizzeria. His mouth started watering. The army was good about getting them their three squares a day, but the food left a great deal to be desired.

Mrs. Kane left the car and Jonny and Kelsie joined her.

"Did they stop?" Kelsie hurried around the car and stood beside Mrs. Kane. "Are they fighting?"

"They did stop, but I don't sense any fighting. It's possible they lost her trail. Do either of you see any manhole covers?"

Jonny scanned up the street. There was usually one every few hundred yards. Of course it could be in the shadows between street lights.

The ground shook and something exploded. He spun just as one of the thick steel disks went flying into the air about fifty feet before crashing into the street.

"There's one."

The ladies ignored his attempt at humor and ran for the opening. Kelsie reached it first and started for the ladder hammered into the side of the shaft.

Mrs. Kane grabbed her collar. "Let me check and make sure we're not dropping down into a trap or the middle of a battle."

She muttered something in one of those weird languages the wizards spoke and nodded. "It's clear."

Before she could resume her descent Conryu's face appeared at the bottom of the shaft.

"You okay, bro?"

"Yeah, but Clair's pretty banged up. She took the brunt of the blast. I can't climb up with her and Terra's too exhausted to cast."

"Move her into position, Conryu," Mrs. Kane said. "I'll use a wind spell to lift her up."

Conryu didn't immediately move. "She's earth aligned. Will wind magic be okay?"

"For the three seconds I'll need to lift her it'll be fine. Hurry now."

He nodded and disappeared back into the darkness. A minute

later he returned carrying Clair in his arms. He stood her up against the ladder and held her in place while Mrs. Kane cast another spell.

Wind swirled and carried the unconscious woman up along with the stench of the sewer. Jonny's appetite died in an instant. When Clair had flown all the way out of the opening Jonny caught her and carried her to the car. Kelsie ran over and opened the back door. He laid her on the seat and wiped the sweat from his brow.

Mrs. Kane nodded to Jonny. "Help Conryu. Terra's in no shape to climb on her own."

"Got it." He jogged back to the opening, ignoring the people that had gathered to stare, and looked down. A moment later Conryu appeared with Terra's arm around his shoulders. The wizard's head lolled around like her neck had turned to rubber and her eyes fluttered, half open, half closed. "What can I do?"

"Reach down and grab the back of her robe. I'll push from this end."

Terra muttered something, but it was nonsense to Jonny. Real nonsense, not the magical nonsense he'd gotten used to over the last day. Between them he and Conryu pulled and shoved the incoherent wizard out of the sewer. It was an absolute miracle no cars came along while they were in the middle of the road.

"I have her," Conryu said when she was out. His creepy book flew up beside him a moment later. "Can you slide the cover into place? We don't want someone busting an axle in the hole."

"No problem."

Jonny dragged the cover back where it belonged and joined the others beside the car. In the back seat Clair was encased in a glowing box of white energy. It was just transparent enough to allow him to watch her bruises and scrapes fading away.

Conryu had Terra in the passenger seat and Mrs. Kane held a glowing hand over the woozy wizard's heart. When the light faded Terra's eyes were closed and she started snoring.

Mrs. Kane turned to Conryu. "What happened?"

Conryu sat on the hood and rubbed the bridge of his nose. Though he looked tired, he was in way better shape than the other two. Jonny wished there was something he could do to help, but when it came to magic he was just a bystander.

"We ran into a trap. There was a sphere of light magic which drew our attention, but it was a decoy. When I dispelled it another spell activated which caused the blast. I thought we were going to get roasted alive, but I summoned a dark magic barrier, by instinct more than anything and it negated the worst of the blast. Terra turned aside some of the heat I missed, but Clair was struck by flying debris."

"We were stupid." Terra's eyes had opened after her brief nap. "I assumed since Mercia is a dark-aligned wizard she'd set a dark magic trap and that's what I searched for. I never imagined she'd combine light and fire magic. My overconfidence almost got us killed."

"Clair and I didn't think of it either." Trust Conryu to try and shoulder his share of the blame. He couldn't help himself. For as long as Jonny had known him Conryu had believed he was responsible whenever anything happened, even if there was nothing he could have done to stop it.

"You're a freshman, barely into your training, and Clair doesn't have the experience I do. I've been a government wizard for twenty-seven years and I walked into that trap like a first-year rookie. We're going to have to do a lot better if we want to survive and stop Mercia."

Jonny was suddenly glad, for the first time today, to be a bystander. If it had fallen to him to figure this mess out he didn't know how he'd handle it.

9
HIDE AND SEEK

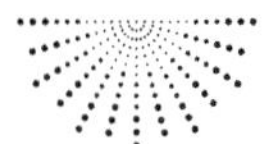

Conryu paced and tried to ignore the faces pressed up against the glass of the pizzeria window across the street. Clair had been under the effect of the healing spell for fifteen minutes and the worst of her visible injuries had disappeared. Mrs. Kane was pouring energy into Terra to counteract the backlash that had turned her brain to mush.

He glanced at Kelsie who was watching every move he made as if she feared he might collapse at any moment. He wasn't in that bad a shape, but it had been a long day and it showed no sign of ending soon. There was still one box to go, the one from the culvert. At the rate she was flying he figured Mercia should be there soon if she hadn't arrived already.

There was no way to stop her from collecting the last one. What they needed now was to figure out how to keep her from activating them. Unfortunately, Conryu hadn't a clue how to go about it. Assuming Terra was right and Mercia was planning to go directly to the island's shadow and activate the artifacts they didn't have much time.

Conryu patted his pockets. Where was that stupid phone? "Hey, Jonny, do you have the phone? I need to talk to Lin."

Jonny dug the little flip phone out of his pocket and tossed it over. Conryu autodialed and a moment later Maria picked up. "Are you okay? Is everything alright?"

"I'm fine, but we've run into a roadblock. Is Lin there? I need to talk to him."

There was a clunk and a pair of taps then Lin said, "Conryu? What do you need?"

"Do you have the map with the island's path on it handy?"

"Just a second." Silence was followed by the faint clattering of keys. "Okay, go ahead."

"Draw a circle one mile in diameter around the culvert location. When you have that overlay all sewer exits. Assuming she can't activate the artifacts underground she'll have to come out of one of them."

More tapping was followed by, "I have three potential exit points between the culvert and the island. Seven if you branch out further."

"Awesome, thanks, Sarge. Can you email all seven to Terra's phone?"

Jonny approached as he hung up. "We got a plan?"

"That might be generous. How are the patients?"

"Still breathing, though I think Terra fell back asleep. So what now?"

"Now we find a high place where we can see most of the exits Sarge found and hope she doesn't come flying out before we arrive."

* * *

Lady Raven couldn't stop smiling as she collected the final box. When those fools had blundered into her trap the heat from the explosion had singed her back and warmed her heart. With a fire wizard and a dark wizard amongst them it was unlikely she'd managed to kill anyone, but she'd gotten them off her trail and that was all she really needed. A smoldering pile of corpses would have been a nice bonus though.

She climbed back onto the chariot between her two guardians. The section of sewer where she'd hidden the final box didn't connect to the section under the island and she needed to be above ground to trigger the artifacts anyway. With just a little luck she might be able to form a proper magical triad and still open a decent-sized portal. It wouldn't be as impressive as what she originally planned, but it would get the Society's point across.

With a mental command she sent the chariot hurtling down the tunnel. It was a short flight to the nearest access and a few seconds later she stopped again. Directly ahead was a grate that led to a processing plant. She hardly thought it possible, but the stench from the plant was worse than the sewers themselves. When her mission was complete Lady Raven planned to take a week-long bath with scented water.

She chanted, "Rust and rot, all things become nothing, Entropic Wave!"

A wave of her hand sent dark energy toward the grate. When the energy had passed by, all that remained were flecks of rust. The chariot shot through the opening, flying over tanks of filthy water, and smashing through a skylight and into the clean, fresh air.

Lady Raven took a deep breath of the cool night air. If she never had to go in another sewer it would be a fine thing. She turned the chariot towards the island. It wasn't much beyond a mile to the outer edge of the shadow. As soon as she reached it she'd land and finish her task.

* * *

They were three blocks down the road when Terra woke up again. Conryu was smushed in the back seat between Kelsie and Mrs. Kane—not the worst pair to get sandwiched between now that he thought about it—while Clair remained in the healing field. He didn't know for sure, but it seemed like she must have had some internal injuries from the blast if she wasn't out of it yet.

Prime rested on his lap. The scholomantic had stayed uncharacteristically quiet since the explosion. Given their connection, Conryu assumed he'd know if Prime sustained any serious damage. Not that there was anything he could do about it. Light magic healing didn't work on demons.

Jonny had Terra's phone open on the dash in front of him, the map Lin had sent pulled up on the screen. A quick search had turned up a twelve-story apartment building with a rooftop garden situated within sight of five of the potential exits. While it didn't offer complete coverage it was the best option available.

"Where are we going?" Terra yawned and rubbed her eyes.

Conryu gave her the gist of his very sketchy plan. When he finished she looked back at him. "I'm impressed. Your plan shows initiative and quick thinking. It's far from perfect, but given our circumstances I can't come up with anything better."

"Thanks, I guess."

Terra's gaze shifted to Clair. "How is she?"

"I don't believe she's in any danger." Mrs. Kane made a mystic pass over the field. "The magic will end when all her injuries are fully healed. It takes as long as it takes."

"That's about what I figured." Terra turned back around.

Fifteen minutes later they parked in front of the apartment building. Lights shone from most of the windows and a low buzz of music filled the air. Just normal people on an ordinary weekday night. Conryu envied them their ignorance, for a moment anyway.

He'd come to realize over the past year that with ignorance came helplessness. Should a shadow beast show up he doubted anyone in the building would be able to do anything but scream and die. It was up to him and the others to make sure that didn't happen. It was a heavy responsibility and one that set his stomach churning whenever he thought too hard about it.

Terra, Jonny, Kelsie, and Conryu started toward the building, leaving Mrs. Kane with the still-healing Clair. It was a short walk to the front door.

As they walked Conryu asked, "Can I control the path of the Dispel spheres I throw or do they only go in a straight line?"

"As always, Master, your will controls your magic. Simply focus on the path you wish the spell to take and it will oblige. The only reason you shot them straight up to now is that it never occurred to you there was any other option."

"Are you okay? You've been quieter than usual today."

"Too many people, Master. Demons like me are solitary, seeking new knowledge on our own. Being around so many others is uncomfortable so I entered a state of reduced awareness."

"From now on I'm going to need you on your game, so no napping. Right?"

"Yes, Master."

They reached the doors and Terra pushed through. Inside was a lobby with a fat, middle-aged man sitting behind a desk sipping coffee. He looked up when they entered, his eyes bugging out when his gaze settled on Prime.

"You lot aren't residents, so you visiting someone?" His gaze darted to and from Prime, as though he feared the book might bite his face off.

"We require access to your rooftop garden," Terra said in that official tone that added a silent *or else.*

The security man seemed to hear it, but he still said, "It's against the rules for anyone but building residents to go up there."

Terra leaned in so their noses were almost touching. "I'm with the Department of Magic and this is a citywide security emergency. Pursuant to City Code Twenty-Three A, all city officials shall have access to any nonresidential space necessary to complete their duties. Anyone obstructing said activities will face a fine of not less than twenty thousand dollars or five years in prison."

"Okay, okay." He dug through the drawer in his desk and came up with a key. "Here. This unlocks the roof door."

Terra snatched it out of his hand and marched towards a nearby bank of elevators. When everyone had gotten onboard and the doors closed Conryu said, "I'm impressed you had that law memorized. I've never even heard of it."

"Of course you haven't. I made it up just now. I've discovered over the years that quoting a law, even one that doesn't exist, will generally convince civilians to do what you want."

Conryu grinned. He didn't think the uptight wizard had a sneaky bone in her body.

"What happens if he looks it up?" Jonny asked.

"Who cares? We'll be on the roof already. Besides, have you ever tried to look something up on the government website? This will be settled before he can figure out for sure I was lying."

"He didn't strike me as the type to go out of his way," Kelsie said. "I bet he just closes his eyes and tries to pretend we were a dream."

The elevator chimed and the door opened revealing a hall that ended in a door labeled "roof access." A pair of big sodium lights illuminated a rooftop garden consisting of a mixture of vegetables, flowers, and lawn. There was a picnic table with an umbrella where people could have lunch.

Floating over the city, the island was a dark area blocking the stars. That's where Mercia was headed. Conryu tried to orient himself. Which way would she be coming from? He turned left. That way, he was pretty sure.

"I need to teach you a spell," Terra said. "It's a simple water spell that will enhance your vision so you can better aim at Mercia."

Terra spoke three words that sounded sort of gurgly, like she was trying to talk with a mouth full of water, and made a pass across her eyes with her left hand.

Conryu mimicked her. His eyes tingled and when he looked at the sprawling city it was like looking through powerful binoculars. "Neat trick."

"The spell warps the water particles in the air, creating a magnification effect. Simple, but very useful in this line of work. Everyone pick a corner and keep your eyes open. If you see anything flying give a shout."

They had barely gotten in position when Kelsie shouted, "I see something!"

Conryu ran over to her and squinted in the direction she was pointing. In response to his desire the spell zoomed in. There she was. Mercia and her two zombies riding in that flying chariot. "Are you up to giving me a boost?"

Kelsie beamed, ducked around behind him, and put her hand on his back. Conryu raised his own arm and focused his will on Mercia, or more precisely, the chariot. "Break!"

The globe of dark energy streaked out, guided by his will, tracking her like a heat-seeking missile.

* * *

Lady Raven sensed a tingle from a spell an instant before it struck. The chariot disintegrated under her and she was falling.

She tossed the boxes away and began the swirling gestures of a wind spell. The pavement was approaching rapidly when the spell kicked in and slowed her descent. Her feet slammed into the ground, sending pain running up her calves and into her thighs.

A short ways away her guardians picked themselves up off the pavement looking none the worse for the fall. Short of powerful magic the undead were nearly indestructible. She took a limping step and winced. Pity she couldn't say the same thing about herself.

"Hey, are you alright?" A young man and his girlfriend came running towards her.

She didn't know if they witnessed her fall from the sky, but her limp was pretty hard to miss. The pair paused a short ways away, frowning with concern.

She took another step and stumbled. The man reached out to steady her. The moment he made contact she said, "Your soul is mine, Lifetaker!"

He shriveled up to nothing and the woman screamed.

Lady Raven winced. She needed to draw more attention like she needed a hole in the head. She gave the nearest undead a mental command and it caved the woman's head in with a single blow from its massive fist.

Lady Raven straightened and took a pain-free step. Much better. Now to collect the boxes. The necroplasma coating would have protected them from any damage, the trick would be discovering where they'd landed. They shouldn't be too far away at least.

She had to hurry. Only one person was strong enough to cast a Dispel that powerful. It seemed her hunters had recovered and were once more on her trail.

* * *

Conryu and the others rushed back to the elevator. The security guard looked up at their approach, but they just waved, tossed him back his key, and kept going. When his Dispel blast had twisted and followed Mercia's chariot just like he wanted it to Conryu had been so excited he almost lost his focus.

Terra hadn't allowed them a moment to celebrate, insisting the fall would at most inconvenience their prey and slow her down a little. They made a rough note of where she should've landed and ran for the elevator.

Outside, Clair and Mrs. Kane were leaning against the car. Clair still looked pale, but she no longer had any visible injuries. Hopefully her magic was restored as well. They'd need everyone to hunt down the elusive Mercia.

"Get in!" Terra shouted. "She's down, but not out."

Jonny leapt behind the wheel and started the engine. This time Conryu got stuck between Clair and Kelsie. Also not terrible if you overlooked Clair's scowl.

Tires squealed as Jonny pulled away from the curb and accelerated down the street. Conryu estimated they were two miles from where Mercia went down, but that was as the crow flies. Taking the streets it might be double that.

Conryu glanced at Clair. "You okay?"

"Yeah. Shizuku said you carried me out, thanks."

"She's being modest. I only carried you as far as the ladder. Mrs. Kane lifted you out with wind magic then Jonny carried you to the car for healing. It was a total group effort."

"You're supposed to say 'you're welcome' and shut up."

"Oh, you're welcome." He shut up which brought a giggle from Kelsie. He turned her way. "Thanks for the power boost up there. Was it me or did it feel stronger than during the finals?"

"I thought so too, but I feared I was imagining things so I didn't want to say anything."

"You're getting closer to your full potential. That can only be a good thing."

Jonny took a hard corner, throwing them together and making him wish they had four seat belts in the back instead of just three.

"And she says I drive too fast," Clair muttered around a faint smile.

"Slow down, we're getting close." Terra had donned a pair of wire-rimmed glasses that would have looked right at home in a picture from a hundred years ago.

Jonny eased off the gas. A horrible shriek of crushed steel

grated in Conryu's ears a moment before the car went tumbling sideways.

Metal crunched and he just managed to grab a hold of Kelsie's shoulder strap. Conryu braced himself enough to keep from bashing his head in. The car rolled twice before settling on its crumpled roof.

Upside down and dazed, Conryu tried to figure out what just hit them. A dull roar was followed by the opposite side door being ripped off its hinges. A big man with black eyes and a slack expression appeared in the opening.

Conryu thrust his hand at it. "All things burn to ash, Inferno Blast!"

The flames shot past Mrs. Kane and struck the undead monster square in the chest, forcing it back. They used the momentary respite to pile out of the car on the side farthest from the creature.

Conryu peeked over the wreck. His blast had burned the shirt off the ugly thing and nothing more. The undead grabbed the car, crumpling the steel with its bare hands, and pushed it toward them.

Clair laid a finger on the car and spoke a short phrase. The car stopped and despite its moaning efforts the monster couldn't budge it.

Terra took advantage of the distraction to point her still glove-covered hand at the undead and chant. A fist made of flame as tall as Conryu hammered the monster and sent it flying back across the street. It crashed into the side of an apartment building, taking a chunk out of the concrete.

A skinny bald man stepped out onto the stoop. "What's going on out here? People are trying to sleep."

The undead ripped a chunk of cement the size of Conryu's head out of the side of the building and drew back like it planned to throw it. Conryu pointed. "Shatter!"

The stone collapsed to dust.

"Get back inside!" Jonny waved his hands as though shooing an animal the direction he wanted it to go.

The man didn't need any more encouraging. He rushed back in, slamming the door behind him. With any luck he'd warn the other tenants and keep them out of harm's way.

The undead tried to climb back to its feet, but Terra's flaming fist smashed down on it again. It didn't look like it was doing much damage, but at least the thing wasn't trying to rip them apart. The undead struggled yet again to rise and yet again the fist came crashing down, this time smashing a piece out of the side of the building on its way down.

"This isn't going to work," Conryu said. "If you keep it up you'll bring the building down."

"I doubt even that would stop it." Clair had ended whatever spell she'd used to keep the car from moving.

"Yeah, I imagine the people living inside wouldn't appreciate it either." Conryu moved around in front of the car. "Let it up for a second. Cloak of Darkness."

As the protective magic settled over him, Terra's flaming fist went up into the sky. This time the undead clambered to its feet without interference.

Conryu pointed at its head. "Shatter!"

Flesh and blood disintegrated, leaving only the bare skull. That got its attention. The monster charged, its heavy tread cracking the pavement with each stride.

When it was in the middle of the street Conryu said, "Now!"

The fist came crashing down. The undead dodged at the last second and kept coming. A fist like a Christmas ham came for Conryu's head far faster than it had any right to. He dodged left and struck the passing forearm with a double palm thrust. His bare-fisted blow didn't do any damage, but the force of the impact launched him clear of the undead and gave him breathing room.

Instead of punching, Terra's fist opened and wrapped around the undead's torso, pinning its arms to its sides. A lightning bolt lanced in, staggering the monster a step. The pavement at its feet turned into a pair of hands that grasped its ankles.

They had it immobilized, but that wouldn't last. As if to prove it the monster shrugged massive shoulders and ripped the flaming fist apart. It punched the first stone hand to gravel and reared back for the second one.

"Reveal the way through infinite darkness. Open the path, Hell Portal!" Conryu opened a gate directly under the undead's feet. At the same moment Clair released it from the remaining stone hand, sending the monster tumbling out of sight.

"Mercia can just call it back to her with a portal of her own," Terra said. "We'll end up fighting it a second time."

"Cerberus! Tear it apart!" Conryu let the portal close. "If she can make any use of the scraps of flesh left over when Cerberus finishes, she's a better wizard than I thought."

Terra didn't comment, instead turning her gaze up the street. "The boxes are on the move. This way."

With no other options, they jogged after her.

* * *

Lady Raven felt the Faceless One she'd sent to ambush Terra and her companions vanish. She'd hoped the powerful undead would have lasted longer, at least long enough for her to reach the shadow. Regardless, it had done enough. She had a sufficient lead that there was no way for her pursuers to catch her before she activated the first artifact.

She ducked down a garbage-strewn alley and glanced up at the island. The base of the island was so dark she could make it out more by the absence of stars than anything. Light from the apartments above filtered down into the alley. It wasn't much, but the meager glow allowed her to save her magic and at this point every speck of power she could hold back was precious.

Only a few hundred more yards. Her last guardian thumped

along beside her, the three boxes tucked under its massive arm, as impassive as a moving statue. That was the best thing about working with undead. They didn't care if one of their comrades was destroyed. In fact she wasn't even sure if the dim-witted creature was aware of its fellow's demise.

At the end of the alley she paused, trying to figure out the best location for the first point of the triangle. The wall beside her exploded, showering her with stones.

"Mercia!" Terra and her group stood at the far end of the alley. The bitch was wearing the gauntlet Lady Raven had provided for Iron Skull when the biker still lived. It would have been a delightful irony if she wasn't the one getting hit with it. "Surrender now and I'll do my best to make sure you aren't executed."

"Ha. That'll be the day." Lady Raven pointed and wiggled her fingers. "Threads from the deepest pit bind my enemies and crush them to nothing, Black Tentacles!"

Dozens of black, amorphous threads like worms a foot in diameter rushed down the alley. Halfway to Terra a monstrous burst of dark magic consumed them all. When the midnight energy cleared the abomination appeared, standing beside Terra.

He was too strong for her to fight head on and anyway she only needed two or three more minutes. She turned to her guardian. "Give me those and stop them."

She took the boxes and ran, leaving her final protector to buy her time.

* * *

"Why'd you give her a chance to surrender?" Conryu asked Terra as Mercia disappeared around the end of the alley. He wasn't a bloodthirsty person, but with everything on the line even Conryu recognized Mercia had to be stopped regardless of what it took.

The undead thing turned to face them and charged. He was

really getting to hate those monsters. Lucky for him this was the last one she had with her.

"Reveal the way through infinite darkness. Open the path, Hell Portal!" The disk opened in front of the monster, but it leapt over the portal and kept coming.

That was new. The ugly thing hadn't even seen him cast that spell before. He closed the portal and Terra sent a flaming fist roaring at the monster. The undead brought its hands together and smashed the magic aside like it was nothing.

Ten feet from them hands of stone sprang up and grasped its ankles. It hit the ground hard, sending vibrations through the soles of Conryu's boots. A second later golden chains wrapped around the monster, holding it down.

"Go after her!" Clair said. "We'll deal with this one."

Conryu shared a look with Terra, who nodded. They ran down the alley and hooked a left. Mercia couldn't have gotten that far ahead of them.

Outside the alley the street was pitch black. No light shone from the streetlights and the island blotted out the moon and stars. Jonny and Kelsie pounded up behind them.

"Which way?" Conryu asked.

Terra peered left and right through her old-fashioned glasses.

"Can you even see anything?" Conryu could barely make out Jonny's silhouette against the light from the alley.

"Don't distract her," Kelsie said. "She's searching for magical energy, not footprints. No extra light needed."

A crash sounded from behind them. He hoped Clair and Mrs. Kane could handle the undead on their own.

A pair of flame globes sprang into being. Conryu squinted against the sudden glare.

"She went right." At Terra's gesture the globes drifted off down the street.

They ran after the globes, Conryu straining to hear anything that might be an attack, but the area was silent.

They hadn't gone far when the already cool night grew even colder.

"No!" Terra picked up her pace.

A hundred yards up the street was a small park, not much more than a patch of grass with a small fountain and a pair of benches. A figure in black stood beside the fountain, on its lip rested a dark, rectangular object that radiated dark magic so strong he could sense it without using the detection spell.

Terra threw her hand forward. "Flames of destruction incinerate my enemy, Fire Blast!"

A line of flames streaked toward Mercia, but struck a dark magic barrier a foot short of their target. "Mercia! Don't!"

There was just enough light to allow Conryu to catch her smile as she opened the lid.

10
THE PORTAL OPENS

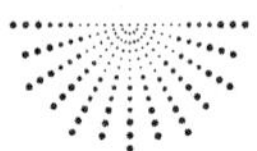

Maria tapped her toe and stared out the huge window in her father's office. It was almost midnight, but thousands of windows, headlights and streetlights lit the city below. The tiny dots of brightness soothed her and filled her with hope, like each one represented a life out in the emptiness of the night.

Conryu's parents sat together in the guest chairs. Sho had his arm around his wife and while his face remained impassive the tightness at the corners of his eyes betrayed his worry. Conryu's mom, on the other hand, was a bundle of nerves, alternating between rocking back and forth, kneading her head, and rubbing her bloodshot eyes.

Maria knew how they felt. Waiting and worrying about Conryu had gotten to be her new hobby. The mayor had appropriated her father's desk and was shouting into the phone with no more success than he'd enjoyed for the past hour. It looked like the city really was on its own.

"Why don't you take a break, Tom?" Dad guided the mayor to one of the spare chairs they'd dragged in to accommodate all the extra people.

"How can they refuse to send anyone?" The mayor sounded baffled. "We're facing one of the gravest crises in the city's history. If Central can't help us now, what good are they?"

Her father clearly didn't have any answers for the mayor. Maria blinked. Maybe she did. "What about calling in the academy teachers for backup? Everyone's on break so they should be free."

Dad rushed over to his desk and grabbed the phone. "That's a great idea, sweetheart. I don't know if any of them are still at the school, but it's worth a shot."

Maria clutched her chest as a shooting pain ran through her. Someone had just unleashed powerful dark magic. She looked back out the window and her eyes widened as a black pillar shot up into the sky. It struck the bottom of the island and immediately tripled in diameter.

"Tell them to hurry. We don't have much time."

Dad looked up from the phone. He dropped the receiver and reached for her. "What's wrong?"

Maria nodded toward the window.

Her father turned and gasped. "What is that?"

"I don't know the name for it, but Conryu was trapped in one during the Awakening ceremony. I think it's a sort of dark portal."

"Mercia must have activated one of the artifacts. Lin!"

"Sir?"

She'd forgotten all about the laconic detective leaning against the wall off by himself. He pushed off and ambled over to the desk.

"Did you take those enchanted guns out to the police stations?"

"Sure, but with everyone focused on Conryu I doubt they were ever deployed."

"Well get out there, round them up, and head to the portal. The wizards are going to need backup. I'll have the civilian casters I contacted earlier meet you in the field. You have full authority to deploy everyone however you need to, right, Tom?"

The mayor nodded then went back to holding his head in his hands. Poor guy looked totally overwhelmed. Not that she blamed him. This wasn't exactly the sort of thing you expected to have to deal with when you were sworn in.

"What if they don't believe me?" Lin asked.

"Tell them to call the Department and I'll have them busted down to traffic cop in the morning."

"I'll go too." Maria gasped as a fresh pain shot through her.

"No you won't." Her father came over and put his arm around her. "Outside the Department's wards I doubt you'd be able to stay on your feet, much less help."

"We'll direct any civilians in the area to come here," Lin said. "There's bound to be wounded. They'll need your help."

Maria clenched her jaw and nodded. They were both right. Her sensitivity to dark magic made her useless in a situation like this.

Lin rushed out of the office while her father returned to the phone. Sho helped Connie to her feet and turned to Maria. "Let's go down and prepare. People will need places to lay down, blankets, and medical supplies."

"We have emergency gear in the Science Department as well," Connie said. Having something to do seemed to take her mind off Conryu.

Maria looked one last time out the window. The black pillar continued to grow in diameter and shadowy shapes flew out of it at random intervals.

* * *

The moment Conryu felt the dark magic surge he cast Cloak of Darkness. His desire to protect everyone caused the spell to cover the others in protective energy as well as himself. Jonny flinched and turned his head away. Kelsie moved behind him and buried her face in his back.

When the initial surge evened out into a mere gusher of power Conryu relaxed. A moment later the first shadow beast emerged, a crimson-eyed hound as tall as his shoulder. A blast of fire from Terra destroyed it.

"How do we close the portal?" Conryu asked no one in particular.

Terra shook her head and blasted another beast. "I have no idea. We need to capture Mercia alive so we can rip the information from her mind."

"Speaking of which, where'd the psycho run off to?" Conryu looked around, but found no sign of her.

"Master, I can sense her moving northeast."

"Go, I'll hold the monsters here." Terra hurled more flames. "Remember, we need her alive now."

"Right, I'll do my best. Prime, you're on point."

The scholomantic flew across the park and Conryu and his friends fell in behind. Take her alive, she says. It would be a wonder if he could stop her before she opened a second box.

"Master, there are ways to extract information even from a corpse. I can instruct you in the proper spell if it becomes necessary."

"Great. I'll be able to mark talking to a dead person off my list of creepy things to do. Any thoughts on how I might take her alive?"

"Your current spells are enough if you use them correctly. Blasting one of her legs off should take the fight out of her."

"Thanks, Prime, you're an inspiration."

They left the park and ran across a street filled with people gawping at the black pillar. Everyone was muttering and several terrified people clung to each other. He doubted they knew what they were seeing, but even the uninformed knew enough to realize it wasn't good.

Conryu forced people out of his way as he tried to keep up with Prime. It was a mark of how the nether portal transfixed everyone that a flying demon book didn't draw so much as a second look. He debated trying to herd them inside, but walls of stone and steel wouldn't slow shadow beasts.

Once they'd left the crowd behind, Conryu picked up the pace. It was probably more than Kelsie could handle, but he didn't dare take it any easier.

"Are we gaining, Prime?"

"Yes, Master. She's stopped."

"Shit! Where?" There was only one reason Mercia would have stopped and that was to open a second box.

"A hundred or so yards to your right."

He turned and sprinted, trusting his protective magic to stop any stray spells she might hurl his way. At the edge of the sidewalk a chain link fence stopped him cold. The light wasn't much better here and he could hardly see past the tip of his nose.

"Prime, where?"

"Keep going, Master, you're close."

There was probably a door in the fence, but he didn't have time to look for it. He focused his will on the fence. "Shatter!"

A whole section disintegrated into flecks of rust. He ran through the opening and promptly slammed into a crushed car. He must have entered a junkyard. Terrific, she could be hiding anywhere amidst all this crap.

He conjured a small fire globe and continued on. Jonny and Kelsie were somewhere behind him, but he didn't dare spare them a moment's thought. Hopefully they'd keep far enough back that he wouldn't have to worry.

A pool of sickly green light to his left caught his attention. He turned toward it, eager to catch up to Mercia.

"Careful, Master. That's necrotic light and it usually signals the presence of undead."

"Can you see in the dark?"

"Of course, Master. I'm a demon."

"Fly ahead and scout the area. I don't want to walk into another trap. And be careful."

Prime flew straight up and then towards the eerie light. Conryu closed his eyes and focused on his link with Prime. It took a moment, but then he could see through the scholomantic's eyes, though everything had a washed-out gray tone.

The light came from a huge mastiff with its head half severed from its neck. The undead dog didn't appear overly troubled by its current condition. It paced between two piles of crushed cars. That had to be where Mercia went.

"What's going on?" Jonny asked.

Conryu flinched and spun around. "Are you trying to give me a heart attack? I think we have a line on her. Wait here, stay behind the cars. I shouldn't be long."

He left his friends crouching behind the junk pile and snuck over toward the undead dog. At least he snuck as best he could considering he was standing in a pool of light in an otherwise dark night. Mercia couldn't have done much to the poor dog, there hadn't been time. He told himself that over and over as he approached.

He caught a glimpse of the mastiff at the edge of his light a moment before it charged. The zombie dog was slow and clumsy compared to the undead biker. He raised his hand, fingers crossed. "Break!"

The black orb flew out and struck the zombie square in the chest. It fell over on its side, truly dead once more.

That was too easy.

Familiar dark power washed over him as another pillar shot up into the sky to strike the bottom of the island. It expanded just like the first one and soon a pair of crimson eyes appeared in the dark, followed by another and another.

"All things burn to ash, Inferno Blast!" He swept his arm from left to right and burned the shadow beasts away.

"Master! She's fleeing west."

Should he stop the shadow beasts or pursue Mercia? Conryu wanted to tear his hair out. He couldn't be in two places at once. What was he supposed to do?

* * *

Shizuku hurled another lightning bolt into the undead monster's chest. So far she'd managed to burn its shirt off. Not the most promising results. She knew her light magic was weak against monsters like this, but she'd never imagined it being completely useless.

A boulder shaped from broken pavement slammed into the monster and staggered it sideways. Clair's magic was somewhat more effective, but not much.

"How are we going to stop it?" Shizuku asked.

"When Terra destroyed one she and Lin disabled it by blowing off its leg and burning the Faceless One inside to ash."

The undead regained its balance and stalked toward them again. Shizuku didn't have any magic capable of disabling the creature for more than a few seconds to say nothing about destroying its host.

She called a golden chain from behind it and yanked the monster back. Its dark magic nature degraded her spell in seconds.

A moment later a second pillar of darkness shot up into the night sky. Shizuku ground her teeth. They'd failed again to stop Mercia. Shadow beasts would be pouring out of that portal as well. They needed to wrap this up in a hurry.

"I think I can take off a leg, if you can burn away the shadow creature inside," Clair said as if reading her mind.

"No problem." If she could target the shadow creature directly, her magic would be much more effective.

Clair chanted and a chunk of the fire escape above them tore off with a high-pitched shriek of protest. The hunk of metal twisted and fused at her command, forming a blade which began to spin. With a sweeping gesture Clair sent it rushing in at the undead's legs.

The creature once again proved its agility, leaping over the spinning blade before coming crashing back to earth.

That didn't save it.

The instant the blade was past, Clair crooked her finger, calling it back. The second pass slashed the undead's leg off at the knee, exposing a twisted black leg inside.

"Light of Heaven burn away my enemies, Lightning Blast!" Without the flesh to provide insulation Shizuku's attack annihilated the exposed shadow limb.

The undead hopped and flailed, but could move no more than a foot or two per second.

Clair's blade came rushing in again, hacking off the second leg, and Shizuku again burned away the exposed inner limb. The stubborn creature attempted to crawl over to them.

The blade came flying down. It slammed through the undead's back, pinning it to the ground.

That steel blade gave Shizuku an idea. "Get back."

When Clair had moved a safe distance away she raised both hands to the sky. "Oh lord of the sky and king of Heaven, cast your might crashing down upon my enemy, Zeus's Lightning!"

Thunder cracked and a bolt of lightning that made her earlier attacks look like a stun gun hurtled down from the sky, striking the steel blade. Power crashed through the corpse, making the flesh translucent and exposing the bones. The energy burned away the Faceless One inside the body and the monster went still.

Shizuku bent over and gasped for breath. She fought the first hint of backlash that caused her vision to blur at the edges. That was the most powerful offensive spell she knew. If it hadn't worked she didn't know what they would have done.

"I know you're tired," Clair said. "But the others need us."

She straightened. "Let's go."

They left the alley and made the short trip to the first portal at a shuffling walk, which was all Shizuku could manage. When they arrived they found Terra frantically burning every shadow beast that appeared.

It was a losing battle. Even if she destroyed every one that appeared on the ground, there were black birds emerging higher up. The shadow ravens were spreading fast. They needed to close the portal before many more got out.

"How do we shut it down?" Clair cast a weak fire spell that burned away a shadow cat.

"No idea," Terra said between blasts. "I tried Dispel, but it absorbs dark magic like a sponge."

"If not dark magic, then what?"

"Maybe I can seal it with a ward?" Shizuku said.

"That much dark magic would eat through your spell in seconds." Terra grimaced. "I just don't see a way through this."

"If I maintain it by feeding a constant stream of light magic it might last longer, maybe ten minutes." That might have been way optimistic on Shizuku's part, but she was determined to do something.

"Then you collapse and get eaten by shadow beasts." Terra shook her head. "I can't allow that."

"You don't have a choice. If I can contain this threat you two can go help Conryu capture Mercia and maybe figure out how to close it permanently."

"Alright. I'll raise a wall of fire then you lay the ward. I know the chief was mobilizing the city's wizards. Hopefully someone will be along to help soon."

With Terra's spell destroying anything that tried to pass through, Shizuku began to chant and weave her ward, adding a silent prayer that she wouldn't pass out before she finished.

* * *

A chill ran through Lin when he gazed up at the second black pillar. The team had arrived near the portal in three cars and he'd immediately sent six officers armed with the magic guns out in pairs to patrol the area for shadow beasts. They hadn't seen any yet, but it was only a matter of time.

It didn't appear that the rest of the team was having very much luck bringing Mercia down. Shadow ravens, like the ones that attacked him and Terra down at the docks, flew out of the upper portion of the pillar. He drew a bead on an especially large specimen, more pterodactyl than bird, but lowered his weapon. It was too high and he didn't want to waste one of his precious magic bullets on a likely miss.

Lin and the other five cops headed straight for the second pillar. He'd noticed flashes of fire. Terra was fighting the invasion on her own and he didn't intend to let that stand.

"When we arrive, encircle the portal and shoot anything that looks like it's made of smoke. Be sure of your targets as there are friendlies and possibly civilians in the area."

Lin reached a chain link fence and began working his way around it looking for a gate. Beyond the fence, visible in the occasional flare of fire, was an auto junkyard. At least they didn't have to worry about damaging anything with stray rounds.

He hadn't gone far when he found a missing section of fence. He motioned two officers left while he took the other three with him to the right. Thirty yards in two figures huddled behind a pile of crushed cars.

Lin whistled. The two looked at him and he recognized Conryu's friends. That was two allies accounted for. He rounded another junk pile and there was Conryu himself, ten feet from the portal and busy burning everything that came within reach. There was no sign of anyone else.

It wasn't like seeing Conryu alive and well came as a disappointment, but where was Terra?

"Conryu!"

Conryu looked over his shoulder for a second at Lin. "Good timing, Sarge. Can you and your guys take over here? Mercia's getting away."

"We can hold them for a little while, go."

Conryu backed away from the pillar while Lin and his men moved in. The book flew down and hovered beside Conryu. The sight of the ugly thing sent a shudder through him.

"Don't get too close, Sarge. All that dark energy isn't healthy for regular people."

A shadow hound emerged from the pillar and Lin blew it away. "Don't worry about us, just capture the target."

Conryu collected his friends and jogged off after the book. Lin put them out of his mind and focused on the steady stream of dark monstrosities emerging from the portal. They didn't pour out in a gusher, but even at one every few seconds they'd burn through their limited supply of bullets in minutes. Once that happened, god help them.

* * *

Conryu hated leaving Sarge and the other cops on their own, but if he couldn't stop Mercia from opening that last box who knew what might happen. He'd hesitated for half a second about bringing Jonny and Kelsie with him, but they really wouldn't be any better off with Lin once the cops ran out of magic bullets. Not to mention they wouldn't have stayed even if he'd wanted them to.

"Where is she, Prime?"

"Not far away, Master. She's moving more slowly now."

"Why?" Jonny asked. "She's almost done. I figured she'd be rushing to finish the job."

"Mercia's expended a lot of power over the past half a day,"

Kelsie said between gasping breaths. "She has to be on the verge of a major backlash herself by now."

"Don't make assumptions," Conryu said. "Everyone's made assumptions about this woman and they've all been wrong."

Outside the junkyard the street lights were still working and apparently Mercia hadn't wanted to waste time or magic to douse them. That at least somewhat argued in favor of Kelsie's theory. He thought he saw a flicker of movement up ahead and muttered the vision-enhancing spell Terra taught him earlier.

It was Mercia, staggering up the street, the last box clutched to her chest. "There she is."

"Why doesn't she just open the stupid thing now?" Jonny asked. Conryu couldn't deny a certain amount of curiosity about that as well.

"Rituals are designed so that the key components must be in a particular formation for maximum effectiveness." Prime spoke like a professor giving a lesson. "Given that she has three boxes I assume she's planning to use a triangular formation. This box will no doubt go equidistant between the other two, forming the final point of an equilateral triangle."

"And if she succeeds?" Conryu wasn't sure he wanted to know and at the same time he needed to.

"Then the area between the three artifacts will become a single, giant portal allowing mass quantities of shadow beasts, as well as larger and more dangerous creatures from the netherworld, to enter the city. That would be exceedingly bad for the humans living here."

"No kidding." Conryu stopped and focused on Mercia. He had to risk taking her out from here. He honed in on her right leg. If he crippled her she wouldn't be able to move. "Shatter!"

A blast of dark energy raced toward the target. She must have sensed it as a counterblast negated his attack and she kept going.

"Shit! We're too far away." Conryu sprinted forward. Jonny kept pace, but the exhausted Kelsie soon fell behind.

"Master, I calculate she only needs another two hundred yards before she can activate the last artifact."

"I'm giving it all I've got." He barely had breath to speak. Mercia ducked between two dark businesses and out of his sight. "Son of a bitch!"

"She stopped, Master, and I sense power gathering."

Conryu lunged through the gap between the buildings. Mercia was bent over the box, making mystic passes over it.

He still had a chance.

Conryu focused all his will on the box. "Shatter!"

The dark wood exploded along with the gem inside and took at least one of her fingers with it.

"I got her!" Jonny lunged past him and leapt at Mercia.

Conryu caught a glimpse of her hateful expression and mumbled words of Infernal.

He concentrated on Jonny. "Cloak of Darkness!"

The spell came into being half a second too late. Jonny screamed and collapsed as the darkness covered him.

Mercia chanted a portal spell and disappeared through it. Conryu ignored the quickly closing disk and ran over to his friend. The Cloak of Darkness's effect vanished at his approach.

He knelt beside Jonny and checked his pulse, faint but still there. His bronze skin had taken on a pale, sickly hue.

"She's drained his life force." Prime flew down beside him. "Your friend should recover, but it will take time."

"*Should?!*"

"I'm sorry, Master, but without proper light magic healing nothing is certain with a spell like that."

He was going to kill that bitch when he got his hands on her.

"Conryu." Kelsie squeezed his shoulder and knelt beside him. "I heard what Prime said. I'm sure he'll be okay."

"I know he will, because you're going to stay with him. When Terra and the others show up, you tell them what happened and have Maria or her mom heal him."

"What about you?" She looked at him with wide, frightened eyes.

"I'm going after Mercia. She's the only one that knows how to close the portals." Conryu patted Jonny's chest and forced the tightness in his throat away. He was going to be fine. He had to be. "You'll take care of him?"

Kelsie nodded. "You can count on me. Go get her."

Conryu nodded, stood up, and opened a portal of his own. Cerberus was waiting and it was time to hunt.

* * *

Terra jogged toward the second portal with Clair in tow. She had to find Conryu and catch Mercia. She didn't care what Shizuku said, there was no way the exhausted wizard could maintain her ward for more than five minutes before backlash overwhelmed her. If that happened it was game over for the whole neighborhood.

The sound of gunshots and explosions reached her, but she couldn't pinpoint the origin. Terra frowned. She knew that noise. It sounded like Lin's enchanted pistol, only more than one. She picked up the pace. If Lin was fighting the shadow beasts then Conryu must have been incapacitated.

"How are we going to plug this one?" Clair asked as they ran.

"I'm open to suggestions."

"That's not what I wanted to hear. Say, where are all the wizards the chief was calling in to help? Seems like we should have run into at least one of them."

Terra shook her head. "You, Shizuku, and I are the strongest registered wizards in the city. We can't rely on any of the weaker casters to bail us out. If they can hunt down stray shadow ravens and protect the civilians I'll take it."

They reached a junkyard and at Clair's gesture the fence

ripped apart. Terra glared at her, but she just shrugged. "I'm sure the owner has insurance and we're in a hurry."

It was a short trip to the edge of the portal. Lin and three other cops had the thing surrounded. There was no sign of Conryu or his friends. A fourth cop lay on the ground thirty yards from the portal. He'd been overwhelmed by the dark energy.

"Lin, what happened?" Terra asked. "Where's Conryu?"

Lin shot a shadow lion and it exploded. "He went after Mercia and left us to deal with the monsters. Man, I'm glad you're here. We're almost out of bullets."

Terra turned to Clair. "I can handle this. You go help Conryu."

Clair hesitated then nodded. "Which way did he go?"

Lin pointed to his left then returned his attention to the portal as the biggest shadow beast Terra had ever seen emerged in the form of a bear. He shot it twice before it exploded. "I'm out."

Terra raised her gauntlet-covered hand and chanted. "Flames of deepest crimson form a barrier to stop my enemies, Fire Wall!"

Enhanced by the power of the gauntlet, her barrier went all the way around the pillar and halfway up its height. An occasional shadow raven snuck out, but it stopped all the bigger beasts. The gauntlet would protect her from the effects of magical backlash, but only for a little while.

Hurry, Clair. She clenched her jaw and focused, determined not to let a single monster out.

* * *

Cerberus stopped and barked. As always there was nothing in the darkness that indicated to Conryu that this was where Mercia had exited, but he'd come to trust Cerberus's nose. If the demon dog said this was it, then it was.

He climbed down from Cerberus's back and cast the viewing spell. They were just outside a rusty warehouse on the waterfront. Why would she have come here of all places? At this time of night he wouldn't have to worry about any bystanders getting hurt. That was a small break.

"Be careful, Master. She may have left a trap."

Prime must have been reading his mind again. Conryu took a step back and found his view had shifted a hundred yards. That should be far enough.

He opened a portal and stepped through. When Prime had joined him he closed it and turned his attention to the dark warehouse. The windows were all blacked out so he had no idea where she might be inside.

"Reveal."

As expected, dark magic wards crackled around the outside of the building. He crossed his fingers and wrists. "Darkness dispels everything!"

The protections vanished under his assault.

* * *

Lady Raven emerged from the portal in her temporary living room. Damn the boy! He destroyed her final artifact and two weren't enough to complete the ritual. A pair of limited portals would be all they accomplished. Years of work down the drain. They might kill hundreds of people, if everything went well, but not nearly enough. She marched through the door and down the hall to where her last Faceless One waited. She was glad she hadn't brought all the undead with her, though she doubted this one would be any more effective than the others.

"I do not want to be disturbed." She stepped into her casting chamber and slammed the door behind her.

He'd be coming after her. There wasn't the least bit of doubt in her mind, especially after she'd nearly killed the other boy. Lady Raven had caught a glimpse of Conryu's face just before she fled. Yes, he'd definitely be coming after her. Hopefully her remaining guardian would be able to hold him off long enough for her to summon help.

Lady Raven snatched up her mask, tied it on, and entered the spell circle. Her thoughts went out to the others as she tried to get someone's attention. A shiver went through her when her wards were dispelled.

He was here already.

While she waited for one of her superiors to answer, Lady Raven focused her will on the spell circle and activated the emergency defenses she'd woven into it. They might slow him down at least.

The air grew hazy and Lady Dragon appeared. "You have failed."

"I opened two portals," she dared to point out. "The city will suffer. If Rennet had bought me a few more hours I'd have won."

"Blaming others for your failure is pathetic. However, you did partially succeed. If you can defeat the abomination I will allow you to retain your position as Sub-Hierarch."

That was at once far more generous than she'd dared hope and a mockery. There was no way she could defeat Conryu on her own. "Can you send help?"

"No. You succeed or fail on your own merit. The Society has expended all the resources on this that we can." Lady Dragon vanished.

She was truly on her own.

* * *

Conryu waited a second to make sure there were no delayed-reaction traps. When nothing happened he marched across the concrete toward the small side door. It was clear of magic and a quick inspection showed no other surprises. Still, better safe than sorry.

"Shatter!"

The door disintegrated and he stepped into the dark interior. A pair of fire globes appeared at his command and lit up the interior. It was a vast, empty space. He stepped inside and walked toward the center of the building. He found a round sewer access with the lid removed.

"Now we know why she used the sewer for her backup hiding places. But where is she now?"

"I sense someone above us, Master."

He turned his gaze to what appeared to be a collection of offices that looked down on the warehouse floor. It wouldn't be hard to convert those rooms into temporary housing and a workshop. He found a set of stairs leading up to the offices and jogged over to them. His boots clanged on every rung no matter how carefully he stepped.

"Don't be concerned, Master. I'm sure she sensed it when you broke her wards."

"Thanks, Prime. You really know how to reassure a guy."

The stairs ended in a rusty catwalk that led over to the office door. What sort of crazy manager would lay out his building like this?

Conryu studied the narrow path, checking for signs of weakness or traps. It looked clear, but just to be safe… "Cloak of Darkness."

He extended the spell to include Prime and set out across the path. When he reached the door without getting blasted or dropped to the cement below he let out a breath. So far so good.

Another spell disintegrated the door and he stepped into a living room. There was a couch, a pair of chairs and a coffee table with gossip magazines strewn across it. To his left was a set of French doors that led to a balcony. That area glowed with a combination of water and light magic which explained why he hadn't noticed it from the outside; it was hidden by an illusion. Straight ahead was another door that led deeper into the complex.

"I sense magic, Master. She's casting a spell."

Conryu ran across the living room and blasted away the door. A short hall led to a pair of doors, one to his left and a second straight ahead. Another of the zombie things stood beside the door on the left which radiated dark magic.

The undead did the trick where it leaned then charged toward him. Conryu was ready this time. He focused on the floor in front of it. "Shatter!"

He blew a hole in it just as the monster's foot came down. It fell through, but caught the edge with a massive hand. Conryu stomped down, smashing the brittle wood and sending the undead crashing to the floor below.

That should buy him some time. He threw his hand up and pointed at the door it had been guarding. "Break!"

The magic wasn't fazed so it must be coming from the room beyond. His next spell blew the door to splinters. On the other side was a Spartan casting chamber with Mercia in the center of a spell circle wearing a black mask.

He sent a spell at her leg, hoping to end the fight quickly, but the spell broke at the edge of the circle.

"Your magic can't penetrate my spell circle. We can keep each other company while this city dies." She cocked her head. "Either that or my Faceless One can tear you limb from limb when it arrives."

The undead's heavy tread on the metal steps was barely audible. He had at most a minute.

"Watch her."

He left Prime and Mercia facing each other and ran back to the living room. Through the doorframe he watched the monster step off the stairs and onto the catwalk. It spotted him at the same time and charged.

When it was halfway across he pointed at the steel walkway. "Shatter!"

A ten-foot chunk of catwalk disintegrated into flecks of rust and the undead went down. It wouldn't be coming that way again.

Satisfied that there would be no more interruptions, Conryu returned to the casting chamber and found everything the way he'd left it.

"Where were we? I remember, you were about to tell me how to close the portals."

"No, I believe you were about to flail ineffectively against my spell circle."

She sounded so smug. He knew just the spell to wipe that grin off her face. "Deepest darkness twist and writhe. Grind and smash what I despise. Break through bonds and destroy all barriers, Death Spiral!" He twirled his finger and released the spell.

The protective shield resisted for a second before it blew apart. The spell continued on, annihilating the rear of the room and exposing the ocean beyond. Mercia fell to the floor and stared up at the ceiling, mouth partway open and drooling.

Conryu crossed the room in a second, knelt beside her, and slapped her across the face, knocking her mask askew. "Wake up!"

Mercia didn't so much as flinch.

"What's wrong with her?"

Prime flew down beside him. "Her consciousness must have been tied to the spell circle in hopes of making it stronger. When you broke one you broke the other."

"Fuck! How do we wake her up?"

"She may never wake up. If you kill her I can teach you a spell to capture her spirit and force it to tell you anything you want to know."

Conryu looked down at the unconscious woman. No one would blame him if he finished her off right now, not after everything she'd done. It wouldn't take much.

He wrapped his hands around her neck. Just squeeze, maybe break, her neck. She'd hurt Jonny. Maybe even killed him.

It would be so easy.

He let go, got up, and walked away. He couldn't just murder her in cold blood, no matter what she'd done.

"Let's have a look behind that last door. Maybe we can find something."

* * *

Kelsie knelt beside the unconscious Jonny and looked from him to where Conryu had disappeared into the portal. For a moment she wished she was Maria so she could do something to help Conryu's friend. She'd only known him for a little while, but he seemed like a nice guy.

She put her fingers to his neck like she'd seen them do on tv. His pulse was weak, but steady, the same as it was when she checked it a minute ago. Part of her wanted to pace while another part didn't dare leave Jonny's side for fear that the moment she did he'd die.

It was a ridiculous notion, almost as foolish as the overwhelming terror that filled her whenever she imagined Conryu's reaction if his friend died while she was taking care of him. The rational part of her knew he'd never blame her, but deep inside she wasn't sure. The thought of losing his trust and friendship made her stomach twist.

A chill ran up her spine. Something supernatural was nearby. She scrambled to her feet and looked around. Nothing was visible.

She looked up, and staring down at her with shining red eyes was a shadow raven. The creature was bigger than any natural bird outside of maybe a turkey. Its shape wavered like smoke in the wind, as if she needed another reminder that it wasn't a living creature she could scare away with a wave of her arms.

And that was about all she had to fight it off, strong language and gestures. Her magic certainly wasn't enough to accomplish anything. Kelsie flexed her fingers. Maybe she could hit it with a Shatter spell. When she'd teamed up with Conryu earlier they'd agreed that her magic had grown stronger.

Whatever happened she wasn't going down without a fight. The raven spread its wings and leapt from the roof. She focused on its head and forced all the doubts from her mind. This would work.

She raised her hand like she'd seen him do so many times. "Shatter!"

The shadow beast was knocked off course, its insubstantial body wavering as it fell to the ground. For a moment she dared to believe she'd done it, then the creature gave a whole-body shudder and spun to face her.

Its eyes were glowing brighter and she'd have sworn it looked angry. She moved between the grounded bird and Jonny. Kelsie pointed at it again.

Before she could cast, a fire arrow streaked past her and burned the raven away. She almost collapsed to her knees in relief. Clair stood in the mouth of the alley, a little wisp of smoke coming from the tip of her extended finger.

"Thank you." Kelsie knelt beside Jonny and checked his pulse again, not because she thought anything would have changed so much as to just do something.

Clair strode over, crouched down, and cast a light magic spell while passing her hand over Jonny. The school nurse had done the exact same thing to her when they returned from fighting the chimera so she knew what Clair was doing.

"Is he okay?"

"No, but he's not about to die either. Where's Conryu? Terra sent me to help him."

"I don't know. After Mercia did this to Jonny he went after her through a dark portal. They could be anywhere."

"Great. How am I supposed to help if I don't know where he is?"

* * *

Conryu disintegrated the last door, not so much because he needed to as because he wanted to burn off a little anger. It didn't help.

Beyond the doorway was a bedroom done all in black. The sheets, blanket, bed frame and cupboard were all painted glossy black. A quick glance didn't reveal anything beyond bad taste.

"Reveal." A section of the back wall glowed with illusion magic. That had to be something important. He pointed. "Break!"

The black sphere smashed the spell, revealing a niche with a large book bound in black leather. No wards protected it, which wasn't a huge surprise. In fact the bigger surprise was that she bothered with the illusion in the first place. If this was her home, even temporarily, it struck him as a waste of effort. It must suck being that paranoid.

He strode across the room and snatched the tome from its compartment. It had to weigh five pounds. Conryu threw it on the bed. It would take Maria a week to read a book that thick and he was way slower than her.

"Master, I can absorb the knowledge contained in its pages and summarize for you."

"Really?"

"Yes, it's a unique ability of demons like me. Shall I proceed?"

"Absolutely."

Prime landed on the book and dark energy flowed from him and into it. Conryu paced, arms crossed, and urged him to hurry. A minute later Mercia's book vanished and Prime grew an inch thicker.

"That was not a nice book, nothing there but black magic."

"You mean dark magic?"

"No. Well, yes and no. Yes, it's dark-aligned magic, but it's all spells and rituals that can only be used for vile and evil ends, primarily creating undead and nether spirits. A necromancer would—"

"What about the portals?"

"Right, once open they can only be closed from the inside or after the island has moved beyond their range."

"Great, you can tell me more on our way back." Conryu ran to the casting chamber with Prime right behind him.

When they arrived Mercia was still lying right where they'd left her. Conryu bent down, picked her up, and tossed her over his shoulder. He winced at the stench. She clearly hadn't bathed since her trip through the sewers, not that he was in much better shape. There was no sign of the undead thing and he had no intention of hunting it down. Someone else would have to take care of that.

He opened a portal and stepped through to find Cerberus waiting. He slung Mercia over the demon dog's back drawing a growl.

"I know, I don't like her either, but this is just temporary. I'll be back to collect her as soon as I can." He turned to Prime. "So how do I close the portals?"

Now that they had moved out of the normal flow of time he felt comfortable taking a minute to get a proper explanation.

"At the center of the pillar is a magic circle that maintains the spell. All you need to do is rub it away and the portal will instantly close."

"That's it? I don't even need to use Dispel?" If that was all he had to do he was going to feel exceedingly stupid for spending all this effort.

"That's it. However, to reach the magic circle you need to walk through a dense flow of pure dark magic. An ordinary human would be annihilated before he could even get within five feet of the pillar. I doubt even you'd survive entering it now that the portal has integrated with the island's magic."

Conryu clamped his jaw tight against a string of curses. "So there's no way I can get in there and turn it off? What about Cloak of Darkness?"

"A spell that weak wouldn't even get you through the first step. To even have a chance... Never mind."

"Don't give me 'never mind.'" He snatched Prime out of the air. "If you know something, spill."

"It's very risky, Master. It would be far more prudent to simply travel out of the city and wait for the spell to run its course."

He gave Prime a shake. "And sacrifice Jonny and Kelsie? Sacrifice Maria and her parents and my parents and god only knows how many strangers? How can you even suggest that?"

"I am your familiar, Master. Part of my duties are to do my best to keep you safe. Not strangers or your friends. You."

He spoke so calmly Conryu wanted to punch him in his scaly face, but it really wasn't Prime's fault. He was a demonic familiar, not the sort of combination from which you'd expect much sympathy.

"I appreciate your concern, but that's not a sacrifice I can accept. I'm going to walk into the nearest portal. The question is, are you going to tell me how I can have the best possible chance, or not?"

"As I said, I'm your familiar. If I can't persuade you to the most rational course, my next imperative is to help you survive your folly. The only spell that gives you even a fraction of a chance to live inside one of those pillars is called Reaper's Cloak. It literally summons a fraction of the Grim Reaper's cloak and wraps it around you. With the cowl up it should protect you from even the most powerful magic."

"Show me."

Prime opened and flipped to the proper page. "Remember, I said 'should.'"

* * *

Conryu stepped out of the hell gate fifty feet from the junkyard portal. He'd tried to open it closer, but the spell simply refused to function within that radius. The bottom half of the pillar was surrounded by a wall of fire which lit up the whole area. Terra stood well back, her gauntleted hand raised.

"Conryu." Lin jogged over from behind a pile of cars. "Did you get her?"

"Yeah, Mercia's with Cerberus, unconscious, but breathing. I know how to shut down the portals. Just in case I screw this up, it's been an honor to go to battle with you, Sarge."

He left the silently staring Lin and walked over to Terra. "I'm going to need you to open a gap for me."

"You can't go in there." The flames wavered when Terra spoke, drawing a grimace. "That much dark energy will kill you."

"Finally, someone who talks sense," Prime muttered.

"I can only shut it down from the inside. Unless you can maintain that wall of fire until the island moves out of range we don't have a choice. That would be, what, ten more hours?" Judging from the sweat pouring down her face he doubted Terra could maintain the spell for ten more minutes.

"Closer to fourteen. Alright, just tell me when."

He nodded and moved a short ways away. Conryu focused his will. If ever there was a spell he didn't want to screw up, this was it.

"I cannot go with you, Master. Reaper's Cloak only affects the caster. Just remember, we're still connected. If you need to draw on that link don't hesitate."

"Thanks, Prime." He blew out a sigh. Now or never. "Shroud of all things ending. Cowl of nightmares born. Dark wrap that looks upon the world's doom, Reaper's Cloak!"

The chill that enveloped him reached to his core. It wasn't physical cold, it was more like what ran through you when you knew someone was about to die. He raised his hands, reached back, and pulled the cowl up over his head. The world fell into black and white, all color and life washed away.

He didn't bother having Terra open a gap in the flames for him. Instead he simply strode over to the pillar and stepped through them. He didn't even feel warm.

Beyond the flames was a gap of several inches. A clawed length of arm thrust out into the fire and was quickly burned away. He tried to think of a good way to avoid those claws, but in the end there didn't seem to be any rhyme or reason to their appearance so he simple stepped out of the flames into the pillar.

The shock of cold caused his muscles to clench. He squeezed his eyes shut as every nerve in his body screamed with a single voice. If any of the shadow beasts struck him in passing he didn't register it over the overwhelming pain of just being in the portal.

He opened his eyes and kept moving. Only the knowledge that the longer he took the longer it would hurt allowed him to put one foot in front of the other.

Step by agonizing step he marched toward the center of the pillar. It couldn't have been more than ten yards across yet it felt like ten miles.

After five steps he reached a circle of runes spinning in the air. He didn't see them so much as become aware of them, since they were black against black. Some sense greater than sight told him where the runes waited.

Conryu trudged three more steps and swiped his hand through them. The spell dissipated instantly. It hardly seemed possible something so powerful was controlled by something so delicate.

The instant his hand passed through the runes the oppressive weight surrounding him vanished, yet the darkness remained. He looked around, but of course there was nothing visible.

After his second full turn he sensed something approaching, a powerful presence that made Lucifer feel like a child. He tried to flee, but was frozen in place. Not by fear, though he had enough of that, but rather by some force beyond his comprehension.

The presence grew stronger by the second and he soon figured out where it was coming from. He spun to his right and there it was, a figure carrying a scythe and wearing a shapeless black robe with a deep cowl. Like every other demon he'd encountered this one seemed to glow with its own inner light.

It stopped in front of him. The apparition was much taller than Conryu yet it appeared far less substantial. He held no illusions of what would happen should they come to blows. After all, it wasn't like you could fight Death.

"I have heard of you." Death's voice echoed, cold and emotionless. "You are the main subject of conversation of half the demons in Hell."

Conryu had no idea what to say and wasn't capable of speaking at that moment in any case.

"When you called my cloak I felt it. Your power is everything the others have claimed and more. I doubted, but having experienced it myself, I doubt no longer."

He needed to leave this place and close the second portal, but how did one bow gracefully out of a conversation with the Grim Reaper? "Thank you for the loan of your robe, sir. It saved my life and the lives of many others."

"It doesn't matter. All lives belong to me, sooner or later. And I don't loan my cloak. Only those with the power to seize it can do so."

A skeletal hand emerged from the fold of his robe and a finger crooked. Conryu's right arm rose of its own accord and the robe drew back, exposing his scarred forearm. The scythe rose. He tried to close his eyes, but found he was denied even that much control.

The gleaming blade swept down, passing through his arm like it was made of air. Conryu winced, expecting the limb to fall away. Instead what was left on his arm was a small mark that resembled the very weapon that had made it.

"I will be watching you, mortal. I expect you will provide me much amusement before I collect your soul."

The Reaper vanished and Conryu found himself standing in the middle of the junkyard.

11

FINISHING UP SENTINEL

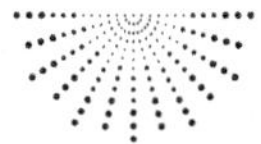

Conryu emerged, having closed the second portal, from what he hoped would be the last portal he had to open for a long time, in the Department parking lot. Dozens of cars jammed the lot, none of them resembling the pieces of junk the government employees usually drove. If he hadn't been so utterly exhausted he might have cared what they were doing there. As it was, all that mattered to him was that they were in his way.

He carried the still-unconscious Mercia like a sack of potatoes. Cerberus had been thrilled when he took her off his back. Conryu trudged the short distance to the front doors, shoved them open, and inside found a makeshift hospital set up with whatever supplies they had on hand, blankets, desks, chairs, you name it.

He spotted Maria right away. She was focused on a little girl with a shriveled right hand. She must have gotten grazed by one of the weaker shadow beasts.

"Drop the horrid woman, Master, and let's find you somewhere to rest."

That was the best idea he'd heard in a long time, but he

couldn't just drop her and leave. If she woke up and escaped, the powers that be would probably want him to hunt her down again. Damned if he was going to provide an excuse for them to give him more work.

"Conryu!" Mr. Kane bustled over. He had his shirt sleeves rolled up and sweat dripped from his face. "You got Mercia."

"Yeah. Where can I stash her? She's getting heavy."

"Stick her in a chair and I'll find something to tie her up with. That's the best we can do for the moment." Mr. Kane went to find rope or whatever.

Conryu spotted a hard plastic chair near the wall and dumped Mercia into it. She slumped and tried to fall to the floor so he ended up having to hold her in place. That became a good deal more difficult when his mother tackled him from behind and started crying.

He couldn't make out what she was saying between sobs, but he assumed it was how happy she was that he was still alive. He would have loved to hug her back, but he lacked enough arms.

"Where's Dad?"

Mom gave one final sniff and let go. "Your father is helping move those too injured to walk. You know, more people were hurt trying to run from the monsters than anything. Lots of broken bones, bruises, concussions, that sort of thing. When the Department was announced as a safe zone they just started showing up. Poor Maria's been working nonstop."

He could relate to that. He finally spotted Mr. Kane returning with a pair of bungee cords. It had to be some sort of joke. At least they'd hold her in place, freeing him to lie down somewhere.

"Have you seen Shizuku?" Mr. Kane asked as he wrapped the cords around Mercia and the chair.

"She's okay," Conryu said. "But suffering from serious backlash. She maintained a light magic ward around one of the portals all by herself. It took a lot out of her."

"I'll be sure to fix her favorite breakfast when she wakes." He straightened up. "There, that should do for now."

Conryu forced himself not to shake his head. He'd locked his bicycle up better than that when he was ten. Right now all he cared about was finding somewhere to lie down before he fell down.

"Conryu." Maria had finally noticed him. She rushed over and hugged him.

He sighed and rested his cheek on her brow. This was why he'd pushed himself so hard. "Hey."

"What happened?" She stepped back but kept a grip on his hands. "Clair brought Jonny in and he's in bad shape. I did what I could, but he's going to be out of it for a while."

"It's a long story and I'm beat. How about I tell you tomorrow?"

"Deal." Maria kissed him and hurried back to help a woman with a deep cut on her forearm.

He smiled. She seemed to have found her place in all this chaos.

"Want me to drive you home?" his mother asked.

"God, yes, but first I need to check on Jonny. Did you see him?" As soon as he asked he spotted Kelsie sitting beside a glowing box. "Never mind. I'll just be a minute."

He picked his way through the people lying on the floor until he reached Kelsie. Her eyes were closed and she was snoring softly. He shifted his gaze to the box. Jonny's motionless form appeared here and there through the energy field. No way to tell how he was doing so he just watched his best friend breathe for a minute and sent him good thoughts.

"You're okay." Kelsie took his hand. "I was so worried. I stayed with him like you asked, but I was useless."

"No. Since I knew you were with him I could concentrate on dealing with Mercia. Thank you for that. I'm heading home. You want to come along?"

She looked from him back to Jonny. "Maybe I'll stay here for a while. I don't want him to be alone if he wakes up."

"That's sweet. I'll let his parents know where he is when I get home."

Conryu left her and rejoined his mother. He allowed himself a moment to hope Kelsie was transferring her crush to Jonny. It would be nice to have that off his plate at least. No doubt Maria would be pleased as well.

He hugged his mother. "Let's go home."

* * *

Conryu rolled out of bed at noon and debated going right back to sleep. His stomach snarled that it was time to rise and shine. He threw on jeans and a t-shirt before stepping out into the hall. He hadn't taken a step before voices, and not those of his parents, reached him.

No, one was his mother, the other Mr. Kane. Didn't he ever take a break? He probably needed sleep worse than Conryu. A couple steps brought Conryu to the end of the hall but kept him out of sight. Kelsie was lying on the couch. She looked at him, but he held a finger to his lips.

"Hasn't he done enough?" Mom asked. If it was possible to shout a whisper she managed it.

"I understand, Connie, but the mayor was insistent. He saved the city after all. The president also wants to offer him a commendation in Central. The whole Department of Magic will be there to observe."

Conryu bit his lip to keep from screaming. Why couldn't they all leave him alone?

"What if he says no?"

"They're not going to seize him at gunpoint, Connie."

"Really?"

"That was a complete misunderstanding. You have to make

allowances for demonic interference. Remember, Conryu's a big deal, not just because of this, but because of what he is. A male wizard is beyond anyone's experience. That fact makes the people in charge nervous. Turning him into a hero is for Conryu's protection. The people need to view him as a protector and not a threat."

"Why would anyone see my son as a threat?" Dad asked.

"Because he's an unknown. And when something is unknown the default is to assume it's dangerous until proven otherwise. And, frankly, Conryu *is* dangerous, all wizards are. There's no way around that. But a dangerous hero, in the end, is better than the alternative. This isn't optional. The ceremony's tomorrow and the mayor expects him there, the Kincade girl as well. They're to be the stars of our little show. Please convince him, for everyone's sake."

A chair pushed back and a moment later Mr. Kane walked to the door and left. Fortunately he never looked Conryu's way.

"You can come out now, son." Of course Dad knew he was there.

Conryu nodded to Kelsie and walked around the corner. She sat up and smiled. "Morning."

"Afternoon actually, but whatever." He yawned and headed for the fridge.

"How much did you hear?" his mother asked.

"An awards ceremony, making me a hero so people won't be afraid of me." He emerged with cold pizza and two sodas. "Mr. Kane was right about one thing, I am dangerous. Did I tell you I took out a whole SWAT team with little more than a wave of my hand? If someone could tell me how to turn it off I'd take them up on it in a heartbeat."

Kelsie came over and joined them at the table. Her clothes were rumpled from sleeping in them. He handed her a slice of pizza and a soda.

"So will you do what the mayor wants?" Mom's eyebrows had drawn together and her worry wrinkle was twitching.

"Depends on exactly what he wants. And that business about the president is bullshit."

"Conryu!"

"It is. How much do you want to bet they want me to flush out anyone else that wormed their way into the Department in Central? I can imagine the argument now. 'You've already almost been killed a dozen times, why not be bait one more time? It'll save us all sorts of bother.'"

"You're too young to be so bitter." Mom gave his arm a squeeze. "Maybe it won't be that bad."

"Last time they had a gathering like this I was almost stabbed, so the bar is pretty low."

* * *

Conryu sat in the front while his mother drove and Kelsie rode in the back. Dad wanted nothing to do with the whole affair and went to the dojo this morning instead. If it had been up to Conryu he'd have gone with his father, but that might have been more trouble than it was worth.

He'd offered to let Kelsie sit up front, but she'd insisted she was used to riding in the back. Traffic was light as they made their way to the government plaza. He suspected everyone was still trying to come to terms with what had happened two days ago.

They pulled into the parking lot, but instead of going to the Department of Magic building they headed to the government offices. It made sense that they'd have the ceremony there considering the damage to the Department and the fact that the lobby was still full of injured people.

Jonny hadn't come out of his healing ward. His parents had called Conryu last night to let him know. They'd sounded pretty calm considering.

The parking lot of the government offices was packed, mainly with news vans. An elaborate stage with red-and-blue banners hanging from it had been built off to the right on a stretch of lawn. Cameramen were busy setting up while some poor worker attached the mayoral seal to the podium.

Mom found a parking spot and the three of them climbed out. Conryu stretched and yawned. He wouldn't have minded a little more rest, but the worst of the after effects had passed. Prime flew out beside him and spun around, taking in all the activities. Unless it was an emergency, Prime was under strict instructions not to talk any more than necessary.

They walked to the front doors, trying not to draw any attention. The circus would start soon enough, no sense in rushing things.

"Do you think I can get my cellphone back today? Maria said the cops took it when they came to our apartment." He scratched his head. "Maybe I should threaten not to go through with the ceremony unless they find it for me."

"Don't make trouble, Conryu. Let's just get this over with and go home," his mother said.

"If you play your cards right maybe they'll buy you a new one," Kelsie added.

Conryu did a quickstep and held the door for the ladies. "That's not a bad idea. They always talk about rewards at these things, a new phone is the least the mayor could do after he sicced the cops on me."

Mom went through first followed by Kelsie. He let the door shut and spun around. He hadn't been in this building since he took his driver's test two years ago. Nothing had changed. The floor had the same drab, white-and-black tiles, and the beige walls had faded to dirty white. The only thing missing was the bored woman that sat in the little kiosk and gave visitors directions to their department of choice. It looked like they'd shut the place down for today's carnival.

"Connie, Conryu!" Mr. Kane came around the corner from the elevators. "I'm glad you decided to come. Ms. Kincade, good to see you too."

"So how many hoops do I need to jump through before I can leave?" Conryu asked.

Mr. Kane winced. "It would be nice if you at least pretended to care about receiving the key to the city."

"I'll do my best. I'd be in a better mood if the cops would return my phone. It's probably sitting in an evidence locker somewhere, the battery getting lower all the time."

"That shouldn't be a problem. Now let's go. We need to get you two properly dressed and then there's the interview."

"What interview? No one said anything about an interview."

Mr. Kane couldn't look him in the eye. "It's not a big deal. Just a few questions from Kat Gabel."

* * *

"Are you kidding me?" Conryu raised his arms, sending the billowing black sleeves of the robe they told him to put on waving around. It had nonsense runes embroidered in silver thread on the cuffs and hem, a high collar, and gold buttons. It looked like a comic book version of a wizard's robe. "You want me to wear this ridiculous getup on national television?"

The slender, blond production assistant that presented him with the god awful thing shrank back. They were alone in a small, empty office that now served as a dressing room.

"Isn't that the sort of formal robe you guys wear?"

"No. I've never seen anyone wear anything like this outside of a low-budget movie." He pulled the robe off and handed it to her. "She can interview me in my regular clothes or we can skip the whole thing."

"Kat's not going to like this." The girl peeked at him from behind the robe.

"That's the best news I've heard all day." He maneuvered around the girl, grabbed the door, and yanked it open.

He stepped into the hall and blew out a sigh. Kelsie was in a different dressing room two doors up. Did they have her trying on something equally stupid or was this Kat's way of getting back at him for not doing an interview with her earlier? If it was the latter he was going to fry her cameras and microphone the moment he stepped into the interview room. Let's see her conduct her precious interview then.

He sensed Prime's annoyance coming from the room behind him. The blond girl had taken one look at his scholomantic and insisted he stay out of sight until after. Conryu opened the door and Prime flew out.

"If this is how they treat their heroes I'd hate to find out how they treat their villains," Prime said.

"I hear you, pal. It's only half a day here and another day in Central, then everything gets back to normal. Or at least what passes for normal in my life these days. If you'd told me last fall I'd be anxious to return to the academy I'd have said you were nuts. Now..."

The door to Kelsie's dressing room opened and she emerged wearing an outfit made up of thin black silk and gold chains. The outfit exposed both her legs to the hip, her flat stomach, and both arms. It was hot, but what on earth had they said to Kelsie to convince her to put on such a ridiculous outfit in the first place?

She spotted him standing there, looking at her, and Kelsie's face turned bright red. Conryu raised an eyebrow. "What's with the harem girl outfit?"

"They said it would look good with your robe. Um, where is your robe?"

"I informed the nervous young woman I wasn't wearing the gaudy thing and that if she didn't like it they could do the interview without me."

"And that worked?" She put her hands behind her back which

pushed her boobs out tight against the material. She realized it at once and clasped her hands in the front.

Conryu looked down at his jeans and boots then back at Kelsie. "Looks like it."

"What if Kat has a fit? In my experience she likes things just so when she does a sit-down interview."

"You can't even begin to imagine how little I care what Kat thinks."

Kelsie frowned and marched back into the dressing room. Five minutes later she reemerged wearing the red dress she'd arrived in. "Better?"

"There wasn't anything wrong with the other one, I'm just not sure it was appropriate for national tv."

Their conversation came to an end when the door between the dressing rooms opened and Kat emerged wearing, he noted, a nice, professional blue suit. She looked them over and scowled. "Where are your costumes?"

"Hopefully on their way to the incinerator," Conryu said.

Kat rubbed her face. "Look, don't you know the news has to have an element of the dramatic if you want people to pay attention? We're trying to turn you two into something larger than life here. Think of it like being superheroes. Those are your costumes."

"Those are a variation on clown suits. I looked like a fool and Kelsie looked like someone dragged her out of A Thousand and One Nights. I'm through arguing. We can either do this as is or not at all."

Kat pursed her lips. "I was told you'd be cooperative. And what's that ugly book doing out of the conference room?"

Prime bared his fangs and Conryu was dearly tempted to tell him to bite her face off. "So you don't want to do the interview after all? That's fine."

He turned to leave and Kelsie hurried to join him. "This is an excellent bluff," she whispered.

"I'm not bluffing."

"Wait! Fine. You can wear your street clothes if you promise to answer all my questions."

"No deal." He kept walking. "I'll answer what I want or nothing at all."

He had almost reached the elevator when she said, "Okay."

Conryu winked at Kelsie and turned around. They rejoined Kat by the interview room door. "How long is this interview supposed to be anyway?" he asked.

"As long as it takes for me to ask all my questions. We'll edit it before it goes on the air tonight. Have a seat on the couch."

They went in and found Joe the cameraman fiddling with his tripod and pretending he hadn't been listening to the argument out in the hall.

"How's the leg?" Conryu sat on the left side of the couch so he'd be closest to the door.

"All healed up. I never got a chance to thank you for saving my life."

"No problem, though I'll admit sometimes I wish I'd let the snake eat Kat."

Joe's laugh drew a quick glare from Kat which shut him up. Kelsie sat beside him and Joe adjusted his camera.

"Is that any way for a couple to sit?" Kat motioned with her hands. "Snuggle up closer. Conryu, put your arm around her."

"We're not dating. Kelsie's my friend and if you suggest otherwise my actual girlfriend is likely to get pissed."

Kat stared at him for a moment as if trying to decide if he was serious. "I was told you were dating. My whole angle for this interview is you two as the new power couple in wizard circles. I mean the heir to the Kincade fortune and the only male wizard, how perfect is that?"

"Do I detect my mother's hand in this?" Kelsie asked.

"No, I swear. My information came from a source in the Department."

"If this is the same source that said I'd wear that stupid robe, you're going to have to find a better one."

"Ready when you are, Kat," Joe said.

She held her head in her hands. "I need a minute. All my questions are apparently based on horse shit."

* * *

Conryu and Kelsie left the pleasantly short interview and headed downstairs where they were supposed to wait for the ceremony to begin. It was a little strange walking through the empty hallways. He assumed all the workers were busy helping put the finishing touches on the platform.

"Who do you suppose told her we were dating?" Conryu had been thinking about it ever since Kat told them and he couldn't come up with anyone.

"If Kat's source is in the Department I'd bet my grandmother had something to do with it. What I can't figure out is why she'd bother. It's not like starting a rumor will turn it into reality."

"Why would she care in the first place?"

Kelsie shrugged and looked away from him. He frowned. She knew something, but apparently wasn't willing to share. He wouldn't push her. If she wanted to tell him eventually, fine, if not, well, that was her business.

"If it's any consolation, Master, I don't understand most of the things you mortals do."

"That makes two of us, Prime. It's not a good sign when demons start making more sense than people."

They reached the lobby and found a large group gathered. Conryu didn't know most of them, but he spotted Maria right away. She was standing with her parents looking out the doors and tapping her toe. She had on his favorite black dress and the silver jewelry she favored.

"Maria."

Her toe stopped and she spun around. "Where have you been?"

"Upstairs getting interviewed by my stalker. How's Jonny?"

"Still healing. My ward hasn't broken yet so he still has a ways to go. Mercia really drained a lot of his life force. He was very lucky to survive."

"I should have been quicker with that spell. Damn it!"

She took his hands. "It's not your fault. You did the best you could and I'm sure Jonny knows that."

Conryu pulled her into his arms and kissed her. "Thanks."

Over the top of her head he spotted Terra watching them with a strange twist to her lips. He couldn't read the expression, but it was one he'd never seen on her before. He put Terra's odd look out of his mind. Seeing her reminded him that he still had questions.

He sighed and released Maria. "Excuse me a minute."

Conryu caught Terra's gaze, and nodded off to the side.

She started moving away from the group and Conryu joined her. "So where'd you end up sticking Mercia?"

"She's in a temporary cell at the police station up the road. We put a spell canceller on so if she wakes up she won't be able to cast. She's going to be transported to the Lonely Rock at the end of the week."

"About the time we return from Central?"

"Just about then." Terra grinned. "When did you figure out we had problems in Central as well?"

"About the time I learned the succubus came from there."

Terra nodded. "Just to be safe let's discuss it when there are fewer people about."

"Alright, just one more question. Am I the bait or the distraction?"

"Distraction."

Well, that was better than being bait.

* * *

Conryu sat beside Kelsie on the over-decorated platform and listened to the mayor ramble on about what a close call it was and how they all had to pull together now, and blah, blah, blah. He leaned over and whispered, "You notice he didn't mention getting controlled by a demon and ordering the police to arrest an innocent man."

Kelsie swatted his shoulder, probably something she'd picked up from Maria, and held a finger to her lips. He sighed. He doubted any of the cameras were pointed his way at the moment, and certainly the microphones were unlikely to pick up his quiet comment. God, even being bait would be better than listening to this idiot for five more minutes.

"It is my pleasure to introduce the person most directly responsible for our victory two nights ago. Conryu Koda. Conryu, come up here and say a few words."

There was a smattering of cheers when he stood and walked over to the mayor like they'd told him. He shook the proffered clammy hand and restrained a grimace of distaste.

"Just stick to the script," the mayor said before taking his seat directly behind the podium.

He stepped up to the microphone and looked out over the faces and cameras staring at him. An overwhelming urge to turn and run hit him in the gut. He fought it down, squeezing the sides of the podium until his knuckles turned white.

They'd left a prewritten speech for him. He glanced at the paper. It opened with him thanking the mayor for his brave leadership and became stupider from there. No mention was made of all the efforts his friends had made or that Jonny had almost died.

He couldn't read it, not if he wanted to be able to look at himself in the mirror in the morning. "Thank you for the warm welcome. I'm sure one of the mayor's fine speechwriters worked really hard to get this ready for me, so I want to apologize in advance for ignoring it." That drew a nervous laugh from the crowd.

"Anyway, you've all heard a lot about what I did and how Kelsie helped me, and she did, I couldn't have succeeded without her. What you haven't heard about is all the other people I couldn't have succeeded without. Most of them are right here in the front row. First and foremost is Terra Pain and Clair Tines, they're the Department wizards assigned to this city. The two of them, along with Detective Lin Chang have worked for a year on this case. Without them I wouldn't have had a clue what to do, so give them a round of applause, they certainly earned it."

The crowd seemed a little confused, but obliged him by clapping. Terra looked like she wanted to strangle him and Clair's cheeks had turned bright red. Conryu didn't know where Sarge was, but hoped he was equally embarrassed.

"Next comes the three most important people in my life after my parents: Mr. and Mrs. Kane, along with their daughter Maria. Mr. Kane is the Department chief and he's worked every bit as hard as his subordinates. Mrs. Kane singlehandedly held off the shadow beasts from one of the pillars; if not for her many more people would have died. And of course Maria, who worked herself to exhaustion healing people injured in the chaos. The three of them are family to me and I wouldn't have been able to do any of the things I did without their support."

The cheers came unprompted this time. The mayor's chair creaked as he started to rise. Conryu had no intention of going anywhere until he finished. They wanted him to give a speech and he meant to finish it.

"Last, but not least, I need to mention someone who couldn't be with us today. My best friend Jonny Salazar was nearly killed by the lunatic that caused all this mess. Jonny's going to be okay, but he hasn't woken up yet. If you'd send him your well wishes I'm sure his family would appreciate it. Thank you."

Conryu turned, nodded to the mayor, and marched off the

stage. Kelsie jumped up and hurried to catch him. "I think they call what you just did, muddying the narrative."

"I call it telling the truth. If they didn't want to hear it, they should have had someone else speak."

12

CENTRAL SPY

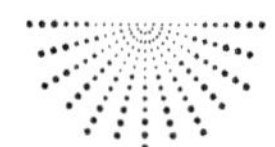

Conryu looked out the window as the scenery whizzed by. It was getting late. The plan was to travel through the night and arrive first thing in the morning. When he left the academy he hadn't intended to be on his way back to Central so soon.

He and Kelsie sat alone in a luxury cabin, Maria having not received an invitation to this get-together. Everything was leather, hardwood, and silver, including a little tray with snacks. He thought the private carriage they insisted he use when he went to school was nice, but this was over the top. It said something that Kelsie hadn't even batted an eye when they boarded three hours after his speech. At least they'd given them a chance to pack a change of clothes.

Terra and Clair were riding separately in the hopes that they wouldn't be noticed. Judging by the amount of press that had seen Conryu and Kelsie off they'd gotten their wish. He doubted a single person noted the two women getting on board with the other passengers. He'd hardly recognized Terra when she showed up in street clothes instead of her usual gray robe.

He'd tried to pry more information about their plan from the two women, but he hadn't gotten much beyond the fact that they couldn't tell him in case he ran into the spy at headquarters. Conryu figured they were still annoyed he mentioned them at the ceremony.

"Penny for your thoughts," Kelsie said when the silence had stretched for an uncomfortable length.

"Just wondering what sort of craziness we'll be drawn into this time. What do you think your grandmother will have to say?"

She grimaced. "I'm not looking forward to finding out. Disobedience isn't well received in my family."

"From what I can tell nothing is well received in your family. Maybe they'll send some more thugs to grab you. I wouldn't mind an old-fashioned fistfight after all the magic."

"I doubt it. There'll be more press waiting when we arrive and we're traveling in the presidential limo as a sign of gratitude. Mom wouldn't want to make a scene with so many people watching."

Conryu settled deeper into the buttery leather. "Probably just as well. You should try and sleep. I'm beat."

He pushed the recliner back and closed his eyes. Prime would keep a lookout so he wasn't worried on that score.

The ringing of the cheap flip phone he'd been using woke him some time later. He blinked the sleep from his eyes and dug it out of his pocket. The little readout on the front said midnight. What did she want this late at night? Maria was the only one who had this number.

"Yeah?"

"Jonny woke up and he's fine. A little weak and a lot hungry, but otherwise fully recovered."

A weight lifted off his chest. "That's awesome. Tell him I'll see him in a day or two. And thanks for calling."

"I knew you'd want to know right away. How are you and Kelsie doing?" She didn't even sound jealous which amazed him.

Conryu glanced at the softly snoring Kelsie, a little drool

pooled under her cheek. "We're good. Happy to be bored for a few hours. I'm afraid it won't last."

"I fear that too. Be careful."

"I'm always careful."

"Says the guy that walked into two portals to the netherworld. I mean it, Conryu."

"I know. I love you."

She was silent for a heartbeat. "Love you too."

He hung up and grinned. Jonny was awake and okay. That was the best news imaginable.

* * *

The train stopped in the Central City station just as the sun was rising. The dazzling sunrise reflected from thousands of windows was breathtaking. He'd lost track of the fact that there were beautiful things in the world amidst all the madness. It was nice to get a reminder once in a while.

Kelsie groaned and rubbed her eyes. She'd slept the whole way. Conryu wished he could say the same. After Maria's call he'd mostly tossed and turned. His joy at knowing Jonny was awake and well made up for it. He felt like he could fly without magic.

"I dreamed the phone rang last night," Kelsie said.

"It did." He told her about Jonny. "His parents must be so relieved. He's an only child, same as me."

She smiled and attempted to fix her hair with her fingers. "Me too. I'm going to wash up."

Kelsie went to the small bathroom and closed the door, leaving him alone. They'd be getting off soon so he wouldn't have time to clean up. Luckily his short hair didn't need much attention. A shower would be great though.

Fifteen minutes later they were standing on the platform along with all the other passengers. A quick scan of the area revealed a man in black holding a sign with his last name on it. Conryu pointed him out and he and Kelsie strolled over. He'd kept Prime in his bag so as not to draw too much attention. It appeared to be too early for the press to be up.

"Conryu Koda?" the man in black asked.

"Yup."

"You look taller on tv."

He shrugged, not certain how to respond to that. "So where are we headed?"

"The director has arranged a hotel room where you can prepare for the meeting with the president which is scheduled for ten o'clock."

"Great." Conryu gestured toward the exit. "Lead on."

They made their way through the crowd and out the door. Waiting at the end of a flight of steps was a black limo with the Alliance flag—ten stars set in a circle on a blue rectangle—on the side. The driver held the door for them and he and Kelsie piled into the back along with their small bags. The door shut and a minute later they were off.

Conryu was too nervous to care about the city outside the tinted windows. Was four hours going to be enough time for Terra and Clair to track down the spy? He hoped so, but it seemed pretty iffy. They'd spent most of a year trying to find Mercia and had come up empty.

"You seem a bit tense," Kelsie said.

Conryu realized he'd sunk his fingers an inch into the leather-covered armrest. "Sorry. We're so close to the end of this and I'm afraid something's going to go wrong."

"That's understandable, since nothing's gone especially right since I met you. Try to bear in mind that you already saved a whole city. Surely you can handle a press conference and shaking hands with the president."

He hadn't told Kelsie the real purpose of their visit and he wasn't sure if anyone else had. Either way, he didn't plan on discussing it in an unsecured location with a guy he didn't know an arm's length away. They passed the rest of the trip in silence and ten minutes later the car stopped in front of a thirty-story bronze-faced hotel called The Luxury Arms. He'd never heard of it, but that didn't mean anything.

Kelsie had a bright smile as they climbed out of the car. Conryu grabbed both bags without thinking about it. Hers didn't weigh enough to say so thanks to the magic.

The driver slammed the door. "I'll be back to pick you up at nine thirty. Please be waiting in the lobby."

When he'd gone they started for the revolving door. "Do you know this place?" he asked.

"I've never been here, but my family owns it. I think Mom meets her boyfriends here when she's in the mood."

"Well, it's a nice place for it."

They pushed through the door and entered a lobby done up in polished brass and warm hardwoods. A collection of leather chairs sat in a clump to one side. A pair of men sat reading newspapers and drinking coffee. On the opposite side was the check-in desk.

Kelsie walked over like she owned the place, which was appropriate. Conryu followed, feeling a good deal more out of his element. It took only a moment when they told the brunette behind the desk their names to get a key and head up to the president's suite.

"Is that gold?" Conryu asked when they reached the suite door. It had designs inlaid in the shiny yellow metal.

"Yeah, this room is ten thousand dollars a night after all. The guests expect the best." Kelsie unlocked the door and pushed it open.

Sitting on the bed waiting for them was Malice Kincade.

* * *

Terra hadn't gotten used to working without her gray robes. How long had it been since she went anywhere in slacks and a blouse? Too long, if she was honest with herself. She flexed the fingers of her right hand. The gauntlet was back in storage and she found she missed its reassuring presence. That and her magic was so much weaker without it. Just as well she didn't get used to it. Magical artifacts risked becoming a crutch if you came to depend on them too much.

Out of the corner of her eye Terra noticed Conryu and Kelsie leaving the station. She'd never admit it, but she wished they could have brought him along on this job. Conryu had proven himself both reliable and powerful. Especially powerful. When he donned the Reaper's Cloak and walked through her wall of fire like it was nothing her heart had skipped a beat. Those flames had been nearly two thousand degrees. Not to mention what entering a nether portal would do to a normal person.

Clair gave her a shake. "Time's wasting. Where are we meeting her?"

"A coffee shack two blocks north." Terra hitched her carryall up higher on her shoulder. It shouldn't take more than a minute or two to walk it.

The worst of the crowd had cleared so they had no trouble making their way down the steps and up the sidewalk. Cars clogged the road, horns honked, and several people shouted obscenities. Terra hated Central, everyone was so rude. It was like they thought living in the capital gave them the right to be jerks. With any luck she and Clair wouldn't be here more than a day.

They had no trouble finding the coffee shack. Sitting at a small table out front, sipping coffee and nibbling a croissant was a young woman in a bright red dress, holding a large leather purse on her lap. She fit the description they'd received perfectly. Terra's instructions were to make contact, collect the artifact, and say nothing about their mission.

She walked right up to the girl in red. "Evelin?"

The girl put down her snack and looked up. "Yes. Terra?"

"That's right. You have something for me?"

Evelin dug a package wrapped in plain brown paper out of her bag and handed it over. "Dean Blane never said what I was carrying."

The unspoken question lay between them, but Terra just accepted the item and nodded. "Thanks."

Evelin shrugged. "I guess I don't need to know. Good luck with whatever."

Terra tucked the item into her carryall, nodded again, and set out down the street. They needed to find a quiet place to perform the ritual.

"Do you know a good place?" Clair asked. She'd been quiet during their meeting with the courier, which was unlike her.

"No, I haven't been to Central since I joined the Department, right after graduation. Do you? You grew up here after all."

"I think there's a park up the street aways. If it's the one I remember there's a bandstand and a thick clump of spruce. Either spot would offer a little privacy."

"Sounds perfect. How do you know about it?" She glanced at Clair whose cheeks were a little flushed.

"My boyfriend and I used to make out in the bandstand when we were in high school."

"I didn't know you had a boyfriend." Clair had never spoken much about her life outside the Department and Terra was just as happy with things staying that way, but for some reason this mission felt less official than their work back in Sentinel City.

"He dumped me after I passed the test. Didn't want to date a wizard I guess. Made me a little wary of men in general."

Terra understood that. It was hard to find a man that understood the pressures of being a Department wizard, always on call, working long hours, hunting down dangerous wizards. When she had a free moment Terra allowed herself to imagine a relationship with Lin, but she never did anything about it. Maybe when this business was finished. She wasn't getting any younger after all.

"Here we are."

She'd been so wrapped up in her thoughts Terra hadn't even noticed the neatly trimmed park that appeared in front of them. It was a nice spot, not overly large, with a fountain in the center. She spotted the green-and-white bandstand not far from the fountain. It was way too exposed. If anyone passing by noticed their casting and called it in they'd draw attention better avoided. The thick stand of spruce near the northeast corner looked ideal.

"Let's use the trees."

Clair led the way. As they approached she muttered a spell and the branches swayed out of their way. The sun hardly reached them in the center of the grove. If they'd wanted to use dark magic it would have been an ideal spot.

When the branches were back in place and obscuring them from view Terra pulled out the parcel and unwrapped it revealing a battered and bent, formerly white mask. She handed it to Clair and pulled out the black mask they'd seized from the still-unaware Mercia.

It hadn't taken Terra more than an hour to figure out the mask was a type of communication device. Once she knew that she'd called the school and discovered they'd dug a second one out of the sorority building's rubble. With the two items in their possession it should be a simple matter to track down the spy.

When they'd gotten as comfortable as possible under the circumstances Terra asked, "Ready?"

Clair nodded and they began to chant.

* * *

"Grandmother?" Kelsie couldn't have been more surprised. She'd hoped for some time alone with Conryu, not that she expected anything to happen, but a girl could dream. "Why are you here?"

Her grandmother's expression pinched even tighter. "We need to talk before your meeting with the president. There are certain protocols and we've prepared a short speech for Conryu."

She glanced at Conryu who'd put the bags on the second bed. He didn't seem especially surprised or put out to find someone waiting in their room.

"It would be nice," her grandmother continued, "if he stuck to it."

Conryu grinned. Kelsie couldn't believe he had the audacity. "If it's more nonsense like they wanted me to read yesterday, don't get your hopes up."

The only sign of Grandmother's displeasure was a slight deepening of the wrinkles around her eyes. "Don't worry, it's only a few paragraphs thanking the president for the medal and how honored you are to receive it."

"That's fine, I guess. You two probably want to catch up. I'm going to hit the shower." He strode off through a side door and closed it behind him.

Kelsie stared for a moment, wishing she had the guts to do something like that. When she turned back her grandmother was scowling even fiercer than usual.

"What a troublesome young man. Why couldn't someone more tractable have been born with his power?"

Kelsie knew she didn't actually want an answer. "So there must be something more important than discussing protocol that brought you out here."

"I had hoped that by coming myself I'd impress upon him the importance of behaving today." Grandmother cocked her head when the shower turned on. “Have you made any progress getting him into bed?”

Kelsie was struck dumb for a moment. She couldn’t believe her mother had shared the details of her plan with anyone else. And that Grandmother would bring it up with Conryu just yards away, even if he was in the shower, was unbelievable.

“No. As I tried to explain to Mother, he doesn’t like me that way. We’re just friends.”

Grandmother snorted. “I suspect if you’d walked into his bedroom naked, nature would have taken its course. He’s just a man after all. What was the point of you going home with him if you weren’t planning on carrying out your task?”

“Maybe I just wanted a couple weeks away from Mother,” she dared to say.

“Speaking of your mother, she expects the two of you for dinner tonight. Her exact words were that since Conryu was kind enough to host you at his home the least she could do is return the favor.”

Kelsie grimaced. She hated the thought of exposing Conryu to her horrid home life. That said, she wasn’t sure she dared to disobey her mother a second time so soon after the first. If it was just one night it might be okay.

“I’ll be sure to tell him.”

“That’s better.” The water stopped and Grandmother changed subjects. “Have you been briefed on the second reason for your visit?”

“I wasn’t aware there was a second reason.”

Her grandmother gave a short explanation of the hunt for the spy. “We’re hoping his arrival will draw the spy’s attention so we can take her by surprise. Either that or she attempts to murder him and we can catch her in the act. Our hunters are in motion as we speak.”

Conryu emerged from the bathroom wrapped in a fluffy white robe. He shook his head, sending drops of water flying. “The faucets are plated in gold, the shower head too. Did you two have a nice chat?"

"Wonderful." Grandmother went to the door. "I'll see you at the ceremony."

When the door had closed Conryu settled on the bed across from her. "So what's this about getting me into bed?"

Kelsie almost choked. "How could you have heard?"

His bag thrashed around. Conryu unzipped it and Prime flew out. "Isn't spying one of the things a familiar is supposed to be used for?"

She'd forgotten all about the scholomantic. "Did you go off on purpose to find out what we'd talk about?"

"No, I really needed a shower. Though I trust your grandmother about as far as I can throw Cerberus, so a little spying seemed in order. Now stop trying to change the subject."

She sighed. There was no way around it short of telling him it was none of his business which it clearly was. "Mother had the brilliant idea that I should convince you to sleep with me so we could add your genetics to the family bloodline. It's something of a Kincade obsession, constant improvement through selective breeding. Mother selected my father after exhaustive genetic research. Adding the DNA of a male wizard is simply irresistible to her."

"So she ordered you to sleep with me in hopes of getting it." He shook his head, disgust twisting his features. "I know I've said this before, but your family sucks. It'll be interesting to see how dinner goes."

"You mean you'll go?" She couldn't hide the surprise in her voice.

"Sure. It's my fault you're in trouble for disobeying. I'll do the best I can to get you out of it, short of sleeping with you that is."

"Would it be so terrible?"

He shook his head. "No, I'm sure it would be fantastic. Then I think of the look on Maria's face when she found out." He shrugged as if there was nothing more to say.

And there wasn't. She realized that. No matter her silly fantasies, he loved Maria and would never do anything that might hurt her.

Maybe one day she'd find someone that loved her that much.

* * *

Terra's consciousness drifted as she sought the connection between the three masks. She held Mercia's in her hands and across from her Clair held the battered mask recovered from the academy. The link between them was weak despite their proximity. That meant finding one even further away would be that much harder.

She needed to focus. She breathed deep of the sweet scent of the trees then blocked it out. Clair's chanting of the ritual spell faded until she was completely unaware of it. The hard ground under her and the pebble poking her thigh vanished from her perception.

All that existed for her was the magic connecting the masks. She constructed an astral avatar and set it loose from her body. With her consciousness now fully freed from its physical host she turned her attention to the thin trail leading up and away from the clump of trees and into the city.

She brushed it with her invisible hand, willing the energy to glow brighter. Under her coaxing the link grew stronger, strong enough to follow. Her avatar flew along beside the tendril of magic. It took all her skill to keep the flow of energy smooth and unbroken. Time was of the essence, but if she rushed it would require her to return to her body and try again, which would take even longer.

So she was forced to creep along. She lost all awareness of time, her entire being focused on maintaining the trail. Eventually it led her to a tall apartment building. When Terra tried to follow the energy inside she hit an invisible ward and was unable to pass.

That shouldn't have surprised her. Many buildings, certainly all the ones in the better parts of the city, had barriers to prevent supernatural entities from entering. It was a basic security precaution in the capital.

Unable to continue pursuit in her incorporeal form, she flew down and hovered in front of the entrance. She memorized the address and willed her spirit to return to her body.

She blinked and opened her eyes. "I found her, or her mask at any rate. How long was I gone?"

Clair fell silent and checked her watch. Her eyes widened. "It's nine-thirty. Half an hour to the speech."

Terra scrambled to her feet, the stiff muscles in her legs complaining about the rough treatment. "The spy's apartment is halfway across town. This is going to be close."

They left the spruce grove and hurried to the sidewalk. Clair raised her hand and let out a shrill whistle when a cab appeared. The yellow car pulled over and the women got in.

"The Sky Bride complex and step on it," Terra said.

The cabbie squealed his tires when he pulled away from the curb and they raced down the street. They hadn't gone more than a hundred yards when they hit the first red light. Terra glared up at the indifferent street light wishing she knew a spell to control electronics. Not that there wasn't one, she just didn't know it.

The light changed and they were off. They hit three more red lights before reaching midtown. Clair checked her watch. "Fifteen minutes."

"Come on, come on." Terra tapped her finger on the window in rhythm to her racing heart. She did not want to have to rely on plan B which was hoping the spy tried to kill Conryu and thus reveal herself.

With five minutes to spare the cab pulled up in front of the building Terra had visited in her astral state. She threw the cabby a fifty and they raced into the building without waiting for change.

When they entered the lobby a middle-aged man in a uniform sitting behind a desk to their right said, “Can I help you ladies?”

“We’re looking for someone. It’s Department of Magic business.” Terra pulled the raven mask out of her bag.

“Got any ID?” the guard asked. “Cause if you don’t I can’t let you through.”

Terra glared at him. “Winds rage and howl, crush all who stand in my way, Gale Burst!”

A focused gust of wind picked the guard up and slammed him into the wall behind his desk. He slumped to the floor with a groan and didn’t move.

“That may have been rash,” Clair said.

“We’re in a hurry.” Terra reestablished her psychic link with the mask. The moment she did the line of magical energy appeared, thicker and stronger than before. “This way.”

Terra ran to the elevator and hit the button for the top floor. As they rode up she watched the line of energy. When it went horizontal she hit the emergency stop. “This floor.”

Clair muttered a spell and flicked her wrist. The elevator doors slammed open. They were a foot above the floor, but Terra just hopped down. Happily there were no tenants out in the hall to witness the two crazy women leaping from the stopped elevator.

She resumed following the line of magic. It led to a closed door sealed with a light magic ward. A quick analysis revealed that it was cast by a different wizard than the one that did the spirit ward surrounding the building. “This has to be it. Do you want to break the ward?”

“The spy will know we’re coming.”

“Do you have another plan? If you don’t we’re out of time.”

“Okay.” Clair broke the ward and blasted the door off its

hinges.

Terra rushed in to the immaculate apartment. No one attacked them and she didn't sense any other magic. She followed the mask's link to a table beside the bed. In the drawer was an identical mask done in blue feathers.

"I'll call it in," Terra said. "Look for anything with her name on it."

Clair set about searching while Terra dug her phone out. She dialed the Central division's number and after three rings a secretary answered. "Department of Magic, how may I direct your call?"

"I need to speak to Director Kincade immediately, it's an emergency. My name is Terra Pane, ID number six three one one two. She's expecting me."

Faint tapping like on a keyboard was followed by, "I'm sorry, the director isn't in her office and her cell phone is turned off. Would you like her voicemail?"

Leaving a message wouldn't do any good. By the time the director checked it the event would be over. "That's not going to work. I need you to run this to her yourself."

"I'm sorry, Ms. Pane, but we're operating on a skeleton crew right now since everyone has gathered in the briefing room to listen to the president's speech. I can't leave my desk."

Terra wanted to scream. Clair came into the room and handed her a paper with a name on it. "Listen to me. Alyssa Warren is a spy and may attempt to kill Conryu Koda during the address. If you want to accept responsibility for not alerting the director, that's up to you, but I suggest you think hard about it."

The sound of a receiver hitting the desk was followed by silence. She'd done everything she could. Terra hoped it would be enough.

* * *

They called the area where the president intended to give his speech "the briefing room" and it was the only one in the building big enough to hold everyone. Conryu looked out over all the faces staring back at him and wondered if one or more wanted him dead. No one had told him anything about the spy getting captured and judging by the extra tightness in her face, Malice hadn't heard anything either.

In addition to the audience watching, there were two cameras trained on the podium. When the ceremony began they'd broadcast the speeches live all over the world. He dearly hoped that this would be the last time he had to be on tv for a while.

Malice sat beside Kelsie in one of the three chairs set behind the podium facing the room. They were waiting for the president to arrive. Apparently he was behind schedule. When you were president you could run late without worrying about anyone complaining. Must be nice.

He glanced to his right. Prime flew near the ceiling just out of sight. He took a deep breath to calm his racing heart. Whatever was going to happen, he'd be ready to deal with it.

Beside him Kelsie was chewing her lip and twisting a ring on her finger. She'd been horrified when she realized he'd listened to her conversation with Malice and he regretted, at least a little, that he'd spied on them, but he needed to know what was going on around him too. The fact that she hadn't done anything to further her mother's plan made him inclined to keep trusting her.

Music blared and a voice said, "Ladies and Gentlemen, the President of the North American Alliance."

Everyone rose and offered polite applause. A moment later the president entered stage left. He was a fit man with steel-gray hair and dressed in a crisp blue suit. He walked straight up to Conryu and held out his hand. Conryu gave it a firm shake. He met the sharp green eyes without flinching.

The president offered the hint of a smile. "Nice to meet you, young man. Malice tells me I have you to thank for saving one of my cities."

"Me and many others, sir."

He broke into a full smile. "Yes, I caught your speech along with Tom's complaints. I trust you won't feel the need to register your feelings a second time."

"No, sir."

"Excellent." The president clapped him on the back and stepped up to the microphone.

He raised his hands and the room fell silent. "Thank you everyone, please take your seats."

Everyone sat save one woman, a slender wizard wearing a billowing gray robe. He guessed she was in her mid thirties. Her eyes glared at the stage, hard and cold as ice.

The president cocked his head. "Did you want something?"

Conryu got a sick feeling in the pit of his stomach.

"Yes." The wizard raised her hand and something flashed. "Your head."

He tried to cast a protective spell, but he was too slow. A blinding flash scrambled his brain and sent him crashing to the floor along with everyone else in the room save the spy.

Conryu blinked, trying to clear the spots from his eyes. The president lay on the floor a little ways away, twitching.

He sensed Prime getting ready to attack, but sent negative thoughts. The scholomantic wouldn't have a chance against a wizard.

Conryu managed to roll onto his back and found himself staring up into the twisted face of the spy.

"So you can still move a little," she said. "I'd heard the reports of your power, but I assumed they were exaggerated to make the failures of others more palatable. You just lie there. Once I deal with the president, you're next."

She turned away and Conryu racked his brain, trying to force his thoughts into some kind of order. The spy chanted and a shining white blade appeared in her hand.

"No." He gasped the word out.

She turned to look at him, her lip curling in a sneer.

Conryu turned his full will on the spell in his mind. "Shroud of all things ending. Cowl of nightmares born. Dark wrap that looks upon all things' doom, Reaper's Cloak!"

"No!" She shrieked and lunged, thrusting the blade at him.

The bright weapon shattered when it struck the billowing darkness that settled around him.

Conryu scrambled up, reached back, and pulled the cowl into place. When he did the world turned black and white save for little blue flames just above everyone's navel.

"You see their souls," said the cold voice of the Reaper.

The spy chanted and hurled a bolt of lightning at him. He didn't even feel it when the spell fizzled against his protection.

"All their souls are yours for the taking," the voice of Death said.

Conryu found his gaze drawn to the blue glow in the spy's torso. The knowledge of how to snuff it out appeared in his mind. He need only reach out with his mind and speak the Reaper's true name.

It would be so easy. She'd tried to kill him once already. Her friends had tried it on a regular basis. It would be justified self-defense.

A second lightning bolt, stronger than the first, crackled in before fizzling. The spy's arrogant sneer had turned to a tremble of fear.

"Take her," the cold voice said. "Send her to me and I promise I'll give her an eternity of torment. It's no less than she deserves."

It *was* no less than she deserved, but it wasn't for him to decide. The woman, whoever she was, posed no threat to him. He hadn't killed Mercia when she was at his mercy and he wouldn't kill this one either.

Conryu darted in and hit her in the gut with an uppercut. Some magical protection broke when he struck it, but it didn't slow his blow.

The air rushed out of her and she doubled over. He stepped back and delivered an ax kick to the back of her head, dropping her to the floor and knocking her cold.

A quick scan of the room revealed no other threat. He willed the spell to end, but the magic lingered.

"Eventually you will have to use my power, boy. You won't be able to resist forever. If you won't kill for yourself, then you'll do it for someone else. I have all the time in the universe and once you use it the first time, the second becomes oh so easy."

The cloak vanished in a burst of chill black mist. He sighed in relief when the Reaper's presence disappeared. Prime flew over and hovered beside him. "Are you alright, Master?"

"Yeah." Conryu was surprised to find he meant it.

He was surrounded by unconscious, but unharmed, people. It appeared this business was settled and he was free to return to what passed for his normal life. All in all not a bad result.

13
THE END

Conryu stared at the Kincade mansion as the limo pulled up beside the front steps. It was bathed in orange light from the sunset. He'd never imagined visiting a place like this. It was the sort of home you saw on tv, not the sort of place someone like him got invited to for dinner. He had to remind himself that no matter how nice the exterior, the inside was rotten.

After everyone recovered from the spy's surprise attack, the president's security detail had hustled him out of the room and for all Conryu knew out of the building. It probably wasn't going to look good on their resume that their charge had been rescued by a teenager. Well, at least he didn't end up having to give the speech. That was a small consolation.

He'd been forced to hang around the Department building while Malice dealt with the fallout from the failed attack. She'd barked orders and waved people here and there for hours. No one had offered him so much as a bottle of water, much less lunch.

The limo stopped and the driver opened the door for them. Conryu climbed out followed by Kelsie and Malice.

Prime flew up beside him. "This place has impressive protections."

"Indeed." Malice started up the steps. "Every generation adds a new layer to the wards. After all these years I doubt even you could break them."

Conryu raised an eyebrow. "Is that a challenge?"

Malice glanced back. "An observation. Please refrain from attempting to dispel our wards. If by some miracle you should succeed it would be inconvenient for me."

She continued up the steps and Conryu looked at Kelsie and rolled his eyes. She smiled and stifled a laugh. It was good to find her smiling again. She'd been pretty shaken up by the attack.

At the top of the stairs the doors opened of their own accord. An old man in a servant's uniform bowed to Malice. "Welcome home, madam. Lady Kincade is waiting for you in the lounge. Dinner will be served in half an hour."

Malice nodded, barely looking at the servant. Conryu had never dealt with a servant before so he just smiled and followed Malice deeper into the mansion. Art covered the walls, but the paintings were the ugliest he'd ever seen. They looked like nothing but random blobs of color.

After a short hike they came to a room filled with soft leather chairs, a chess board on a hardwood table, and a full bar. The lounge was bigger than his whole apartment.

Seated in one of the chairs was a woman that looked exactly like an older version of Kelsie. She wore a black dress slit to her navel, revealing a stunning amount of cleavage. Kelsie let out a soft gasp and Conryu knew just how she felt. Only the strictest mental discipline had kept him from having that same reaction with each new room they entered. Seeing a woman he knew had to be the same age as his mother if not older in such an outfit stunned him. It helped that she looked about thirty.

Kelsie's mother stood up and smiled, revealing teeth too flawless and white to be natural. Not that his gaze lingered long on her teeth, what with all the jiggling going on down below. There had to be some sort of magic holding her dress up.

"You must be Conryu. Kelsie's told me all about you. My name is Cassandra Kincade and I can't thank you enough for helping my daughter with her studies. I'm sure without you she would have failed long ago." She held out her hand and Conryu gave it a polite shake.

"I don't think you give Kelsie enough credit. She works as hard as anyone and harder than many. She's a good friend and I couldn't have accomplished most of what I have without her."

Kelsie's frown had grown into a bright smile just as he'd hoped it would.

Cassandra shook her head causing yet more jiggling. "You're very generous. Would you like a drink?"

"I'm still underage, but thank you."

"Polite and powerful, what an unusual combination." She walked to the bar, working her hips as she went. What in heaven's name was she playing at? Cassandra poured herself a drink and turned to Malice. "Would you like one, Mother?"

"Make it a double. After today, I need it."

Cassandra filled a tumbler three-quarters of the way up with amber liquid and handed it to Malice, being sure to lean over more than she had to so he could get a good look.

Conryu glanced at Kelsie whose face was bright red. If his mother had acted like that Conryu would have been embarrassed as well.

He couldn't begin to describe his relief when the servant opened the door and announced, "Dinner is served."

* * *

Conryu pushed away from a table long enough to seat sixty and sighed. He'd never eaten a meal—no, make that a feast —like that in his life. Eight courses from salad to a little fruit tart for dessert. Beside him Kelsie had only picked at her food. Eating like this all the time probably made you jaded.

He took a sip of water and fought back a yawn. It had been a long day and he was ready to find out if the beds in this place were as comfortable as he imagined.

"Was the meal to your liking?" Cassandra asked.

"It was delicious, thank you." He kept waiting for the other shoe to drop. From Kelsie's description he wouldn't have thought her mother would be this nice.

"Wonderful. Would you join me in my office? I have a business proposition for you."

Here it comes. Still, he couldn't simply refuse the woman in her own house after she provided him with an outstanding meal. "Alright."

Kelsie tugged his sleeve and gave him a concerned look. He offered a weak smile and shrug. Whatever she wanted, Conryu doubted he'd be interested, but it couldn't hurt to hear her out, for Kelsie's sake if nothing else.

He followed Cassandra out of the dining room. As he walked he felt the gaze of both Malice and Kelsie on his back. Prime flew along beside him, but the scholomantic remained silent. They walked down a long hall decorated like the rest of the house before stopping in front of a closed door.

Cassandra spoke a soft word that he couldn't make out and the door swung open revealing a well-appointed office. She walked across to her desk, turned to face him, and sat on the edge. "I'm not going to mince words with you. I want your genetics added to our bloodline. What's your price?"

"Price?" Though he was pretty sure what she was suggesting Conryu was having trouble fully processing it.

"To impregnate me. I've performed the necessary rituals to ensure my fertility and the survival of any offspring. You'll be in no way responsible for the child or children resulting. When we've agreed on a price I'll draw up a contract stipulating that. It will be necessary for you to remain our guest until pregnancy is confirmed. Even with magical assistance the seed doesn't always take on the first try."

He could only stare as she wrapped up her pitch. And that's what it was, an emotionless transaction. She didn't care about him or her future kid. Improving her bloodline was really all that interested her.

"I'm going to have to pass. Not that I'm not flattered, but I don't think I could do what you want."

"Ten million."

He nearly choked. Ten million to knock her up? That was insane. Not that they couldn't afford it, but still.

"What about Kelsie?"

Her lips turned down in a slight frown. "What about her?"

"I thought she was your heir and that you wanted her to seduce me into—how did you put it, improving your bloodline?"

"She's had half a year. Clearly my daughter isn't up to the task." Cassandra gave a disgusted shake of her head. "She so seldom lives up to my expectations I no longer know why I bother to ask anything of her. Though by attaching herself to you she has improved her status in the world as one of the primary saviors of Sentinel City. That alone will fend off any challenges from within the family. However she's simply too weak to trust with the clan's future."

"Kelsie isn't weak or a failure of any sort. The idea of placing any child, much less my own, in your care, horrifies me." Conryu turned toward the door. "I'll accept your hospitality for tonight and be on my way tomorrow. Hopefully we'll never see each other again."

Master, she's preparing a spell. Prime's voice appeared in his mind.

"Cloak of Darkness!"

Dark magic settled around him an instant before a spell fizzled against it.

He spun. An aura of light magic still surrounded Cassandra's hands. She glared at him. "I will have your power, one way or another."

"That right?" He raised his hand, crossed his fingers, and focused on the magic she'd cast on herself. "Break!"

The black sphere slammed into her chest. Magic crackled and broke apart. Wrinkles appeared on her once-smooth face. Her hair turned gray and her breasts sagged, though they mercifully failed to escape her dress.

She held up her wrinkled hands and stared at them then at him. "What have you done?"

"Not done, undone. I've stripped away all your magic. Stay away from me or I'll bring this house down around your head." He turned on his heel and stalked out.

Prime fell in beside him. "That was close, Master."

"Yeah, thanks for the warning." He let the Cloak of Darkness fade away.

"Protecting you is my job. What will you do now?"

"I'm not sure. Part of me thinks I should leave right now, but it's late and I don't want another fight if I can help it. Do you know any wards that I can use to protect myself if I stay the night?"

"Several, Master, have no fear."

They reached the dining room and found Kelsie pacing and Malice sipping another drink.

"That was fast," the old woman said. "I figured someone your age would have more stamina."

"For the record, I'm not for sale." He turned to Kelsie. "Could you show me to my room? I'm beat."

"Of course." She started for the door.

"Wait." Malice stood up and Conryu prepared himself for a second fight. "How much did you turn down?"

"Ten million. She didn't like that very well and tried using magic on me. Mind control of some sort I believe. She was too slow."

He followed Kelsie out of the room, down a hall, then up a set of stairs. They stopped in front of an open door that led to a large bedroom.

"I'm sorry my mother tried to use you like that. I had no idea she'd go so far." She hugged him.

"It's not your fault. I'm leaving tomorrow. If you want to come back with me you're welcome. This is no place for you, for anybody as far as that goes."

"I will, thank you."

He nodded and went inside the opulent guest room. Before he even thought about sleeping he had to figure out how to ward the room.

* * *

Conryu floated in darkness. He had to be dreaming as he hadn't cast a portal. He tried to orient himself, but there was nothing, no sign of Cerberus either. Yes, it was definitely a dream. When slender arms wrapped themselves around him from behind and warm, soft lips kissed the nape of his neck he spun, ready for a fight.

"Hardly the greeting I expected, Master." The Dark Lady floated a foot away smiling and gorgeous in her black dress.

He relaxed. "Sorry. I expected someone else. How are things in Hell?"

"Better since our contract. No one mocks me now."

"Good. I'm glad to see you. I wasn't sure how to contact you and I wanted to say thanks. Our connection allowed me to successfully dominate a demon and send her back to Hell. I'm sure I couldn't have done it without your extra power."

"Rennet, yes, I know all about that. In fact, she's what brings me here tonight."

Conryu cocked his head. "How so?"

"She contacted me and said the leader of the Le Fay Society wishes to talk to you."

"When?"

"Right now."

"Sounds like a trap." Conryu couldn't imagine what they'd have to talk about in the first place.

"No, Master. She selected this place since you'd be protected by the many wards around Kincade Manor. As long as you don't move beyond the steps you'll be safe. She won't be able to reach you."

"What does she want?"

"I have no idea. Rennet was simply delivering a message." The Dark Lady's lips curled in a cruel smile. "After her failure this is what she's been reduced to. It gives me great pleasure to find her so demeaned."

Conryu nodded absently, his mind rushing along as he considered the implications of this invitation. "What do you think I should do?"

She shrugged. "If there was ever a time to size up your enemy, this is it. It can't do you any harm."

"I guess you're right. Thanks for bringing me the message."

Her expression softened. "My pleasure."

He blinked and sat up in bed. "Prime."

"I heard, Master. I agree with the lady, this is a good chance to see what we're dealing with."

"Right." He slipped out of bed and threw on his clothes.

Now he just had to find his way to the front door without getting lost or running into the crazy people that lived here. He deactivated the dark magic ward he'd set around his bedroom and stepped out into the hall. The house was silent. A hint of moonlight filtered in from somewhere. It wasn't much, but he'd manage.

With Prime flying along at his side Conryu tiptoed through the silent halls, eventually reaching the entry hall. He unlocked the front door and stepped out into the cool night air. Ten feet from the foot of the stairs was a dark figure in a mask.

Conryu marched down and paused on the final step. "You wanted to talk?"

She moved closer revealing the details of her green dragon mask and crimson robe. She looked like a performer at one of the Imperial New Year celebrations. All they were lacking was fireworks.

"I am Lady Dragon, temporary leader of the Society. You have done us a great deal of harm in a year." She had a warm, pleasant voice, totally different than what he'd expected.

He shrugged. "You all tried to kill me more than once. I can hardly be faulted for fighting back."

"True. I admit it never crossed my mind that we'd have such difficulty dealing with an inexperienced wizard. Of course, having never encountered a male wizard before, our ignorance is unsurprising."

"So what happens now?"

"Now? Nothing. But we will see each other again." Lady Dragon chanted and stepped back into a portal.

Conryu turned to Prime. "That wasn't encouraging. I was hoping she'd say 'sorry, let's let bygones be bygones' or 'live and let live,' something like that."

"That's far too optimistic, Master. I fear we've begun a war and the first battle just ended."

Sarcasm was clearly lost on the scholomantic. "At least we won. More or less."

"Indeed. Let us hope the next battle ends equally well."

Conryu sighed and looked out over the dark grounds. A war,

huh? How had it come to this? All he'd ever wanted was a nice, quiet life, work at the bike shop, train with his father, maybe marry Maria someday.

Instead he got secret societies, deranged industrialists, and politicians all wanting to use or end his life. One thing was certain. He wouldn't have to worry about being bored.

AUTHOR NOTE

Dear Reader,

Thanks very much for picking up a copy of this Omnibus Edition. I hope you enjoyed reading about Conryu's adventures. If you did, the adventure continues in Wrath of the Dragon Czar which you can find on it's own or in Aegis of Merlin Omnibus Vol. 2 which should either be out now or will be shortly.

Thanks for reading,

James

ALSO BY JAMES E. WISHER

The Aegis of Merlin:

The Impossible Wizard

The Awakening

The Chimera Jar

The Raven's Shadow

Escape From the Dragon Czar

Wrath of the Dragon Czar

The Four Nations Tournament

Death Incarnate

Aegis of Merlin Omnibus Vol 1.

Aegis of Merlin Omnibus Vol 2.

Soul Force Saga

Disciples of the Horned One Trilogy:

Darkness Rising

Raging Sea and Trembling Earth

Harvest of Souls

Other Fantasy Novels:

Death and Honor Omnibus

The Squire

The Rogue Star Series:

Children of Darkness

Children of the Void

Children of Junk

Rogue Star Omnibus Vol. 1

ABOUT THE AUTHOR

James E. Wisher is a writer of science fiction and Fantasy novels. He's been writing since high school and reading everything he could get his hands on for as long as he can remember.

To learn more:

www.jamesewisher.com
james@jamesewisher.com